I0647132

The Hessian

THE HESSIAN

BY

QUENTIN GRADY

Copyright © 2015 by Quentin R. Grady

All rights reserved. No part of this publication may be reproduced, distributed, or transmitted in any form or by any means, including photocopying, recording, or other electronic or mechanical methods, without the prior written permission of Ghost Eagle Publishing, except in the case of brief quotations embodied in critical reviews and certain other noncommercial uses permitted by copyright law.

ISBN-10: 0-9898366-9-2
ISBN-13: 978-0-9898366-9-2

Dedicated to the Most Important Women in My Life
as I Finish This Book.
Their Smiles, Hugs, and Laughter Remind Me of What Is
Truly Important to Remember.

Heather
Brianna
Shannon
Corrinne

CONTENTS

PREFACE

The Hessian is a work of fiction. This sequel and fourth book of the *Tales of the Ghost Eagle* series takes place in Boston, the wilderness areas of Lake Ontario, and the fortress-port city of Louisbourg on Cape Breton Island. This island in 1756 was called Île Royale by the French. The clashes between France and England, which began in 1754, escalates further with more battles in the wilderness of North America. Then it spreads to invasive and naval actions in the Mediterranean. As the book begins, the main characters are now separated. Philippe and Henri fight the war as part of the forces of New France; Philippe in the west and Henri in the east. Corrinne is in hiding with her twin babies, Marcus and Calypso, plus Anamosa and Mathilde in southern Connecticut, hoping to frustrate the servants of the Hessian colonel, who hunt for her and the *châsse* relentlessly. Charles VanderMeer remains in Boston expecting to draw any threat by the Hessian towards him and away from Corrinne. In short, the lives of every character in the book is threatened, either by war, by the scarring wraith, or a combination of both. Because of distances involved, communication is almost impossible. Letters often take six months to travel to its destination. As a consequence, the characters are isolated from one another.

In 1756, having already fought two major wars and a dozen minor ones in only fifty years, the governments of France and England, their treasuries depleted, desperately want to avoid another long and costly land war in Europe. To avoid this while they skirmished over North America, France and England independently created treaties with the other European land powers, with promises to come to their aid if attacked. But paradoxically, these treaty partners were permitted to remain neutral in any disputes that develop between France and England. This allowed France and England to continue their war on each other while "officially at peace." The other heads of state in Europe watched this violent "war of peace" with growing skepticism and anxiety. All of these nations have their own objectives for the next war, which they feel is inevitable. So they begin positioning armies and making secret treaties to get ready for it. So England or France? Which will blink first and declare war? This is a fascinating time and place in history. It is full of deceptive statesmanship coupled with treaty negotiations of bad faith by every participant.

As the English and French navies begin to seize one another's ships, both countries strengthen trade restrictions. Trade from America can only be done with England and no one else. French colonies and island territories trade only with France. Trade among the American southern and northern colonies is permitted, however. Both England and France issue "letters of marque and reprisal" to independent privateers, essentially licensing piracy as long as it is not piracy of the ships of the licensing country. This lucrative "business" catches on very quickly. Global trade is severely impacted by liberal extension of these rules. It was only natural that somewhere, some country would establish a free trade port where everyone could participate. The Dutch Republic declared Saint Eustatius Island in the Antilles as that place. And all the trading nations, France and England included, came there with the warships of every nation guarding the harbor to make certain everyone behaved and traded freely in peace. The VanderMeer Trading Insurance Company controlled much of this bartering in the port of Oranjestad. It made a lot of money. But this unusual free-for-all trading environment would only last until war was officially declared between France and England. Just another reason why they preferred this "war of peace." But…it is an unnatural condition, as one sovereign described it. You are either at war or not at war.

In North America, both England and France get down to the serious business of war on that continent. French and British regular troops arrive with new commanding leadership. Major-General Louis Joseph, Marquis de Montcalm is the new commander of military forces in New France. In the American colonies, General John Campbell, 4th Earl of Loudoun. Lord Loudoun, is the new commander-in-chief of the English forces in North America. Both men have strengths and weaknesses.

General Montcalm preferred line infantry battles with European tactics. But he quickly adapted and was the better general, though he never truly accepted the wilderness style of fighting. And he did not trust the native warriors, who could not be disciplined, did not follow orders, and did not comply with the "honor of war" philosophy associated with a defeated enemy. The Indians were in the battle to collect a share of the booty and trophies of the most gruesome nature, in the aftermath of a victory. If that meant cooking and eating the dead commander, they expected to be allowed to do this. The same behavior was true of the Indians who fought on the side of the English.

Lord Loudoun arrived in Albany, New York, to find an army and command structure in disarray. The American provincial soldiers numbered three times as many troops as the British redcoats. But those soldiers refused to fight under the command of British officers. And they had a signed contract stating this, which also specified other rules associated with their enlistment. The officers leading them explained their "rights" to Lord Loudoun as agreed to by the colonial legislatures. Lord Loudoun was apoplectic when confronted by this American attitude. This "Lord" came from a privileged society of nobility and then there was "everyone else." Period. He could not conceive of a society that worked any other way. It was the first indication to Loudoun how dangerously independent the American colonies already were. But he had no choice but to agree to allow the provincials to be led by their own officers, and those officers would only take orders from a provincial general, who would take orders from the British commanding general. Either that, or their "contract" was broken, and they were allowed to legally desert. And threatened to do just that. Lord Loudoun also learned the colonies had no intention of billeting the redcoats. In Albany, he felt forced to impose this on the citizenry by force with bayonets. He did not accept having to negotiate with each colonial legislature. Yet he spent most of the time doing just that.

Nevertheless, the end result of this war had profound effects on territorial possessions and boundaries of the Great Powers in Europe, America, and globally, in a manner not seen again until the end of World War I.

This story was written around factual events, locations, native customs, and social values and ethics of the times. Every effort was made to conform to historical events. To that end, numerous historical references were researched. If I found disagreements among the references, I deferred to the collective description of the personalities involved and let that guide the story telling.

One of the surprising things I learned in this period of history was how dominant France was as a "superpower" of its time. From 1754 through 1757, France won most of the battles on land and at sea. The British navy is often praised for its superiority. By the total number of ships that was true. But the French navy was almost undefeated in naval engagement in the early years of this war. The French warship captains were tactically superior.

There is a glossary of names in the back. Plus several maps and illustrations have been made to help the reader better appreciate the story locations, the geography, and some of the battles that were fought. The story unfolds through the eyes and thoughts of the characters, both fictional and real. I trust it provides context to the fateful decisions they made...or didn't make.

The Hessian was fun to write. I hope you enjoy it too.

Book 5, *The Abattis*, is already being written. I plan to take a trip to old Louisbourg on Cape Breton Island, Nova Scotia, this year to do research.

Quentin Grady

Illustrations

The Town of Boston Map. Page, Thomas Hyde, Sir. Map of the Town of Boston. London: Engraved & printed for Wm. Faden, 1777. From Library of Congress, Geography and Map Division. http://lccn.loc.gov/gm71000620 (accessed November 19, 2014).

Acadia 1754 Map. From Wikimedia Commons. https://upload.wikimedia.org/wikipedia/commons/9/93/Acadia_1754.png (accessed December 15, 2015).

The Great Carrying Place, Fort Oswego Battle, Frederick II Attack, Henri's Trails of Île Royale maps and cover illustrations by Yoko Matsuoka. http://www.m-y-designs.com/

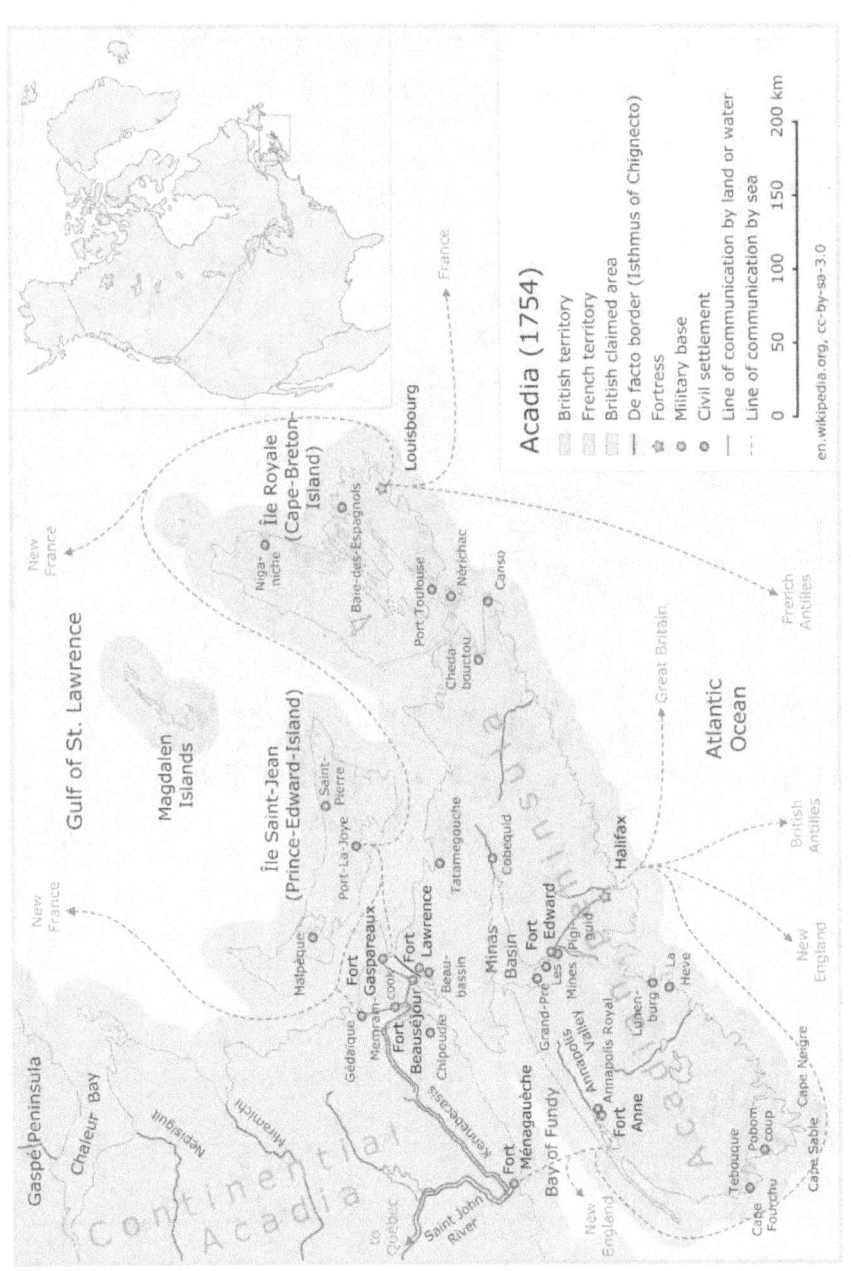

Acadia 1754

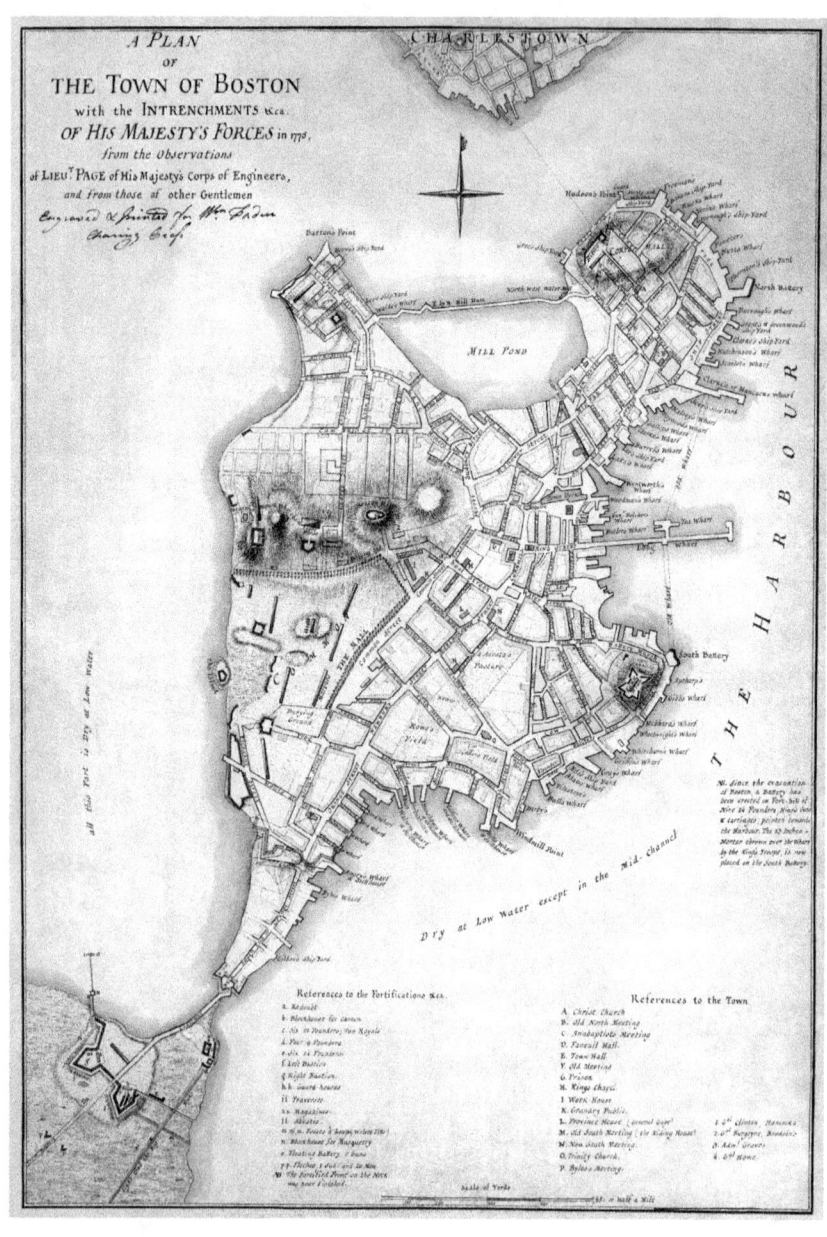

The Town of Boston Map

Ten miles west of Saybrook, Connecticut, the sailors from the Dutch trade ship the *Anamosa* transferred the baggage and the *châsse* in the small harbor launch to the head of a private pier. Their second trip from the ship carried passengers: Corrinne, Mathilde, eight-year-old Anamosa, and the twins, Marcus and Calypso.

Corrinne shivered in the damp, chill wind. She pulled the blanket over five-month-old Calypso's head. Mathilde did the same for Marcus. Anamosa's teeth were chattering.

A property manager awaited their arrival. He was a fifty-three-year-old lawyer from New Haven, who managed the Connecticut properties owned by Thomas Hancock and had acquired the overland coach that would transport them the rest of the way.

"My lady, welcome to Connecticut," he greeted with a polite bow. "We can dispense with names and introductions."

Corrinne nodded curtly. "It's cold, sir. Can we do this fast?"

"Yes, of course." He moved quickly, opened the carriage doors of the coach, and assisted them up the steps.

At Corrinne's direction, the lawyer made sure the canvas-wrapped *châsse* was tied down on the back shelf of the coach and that the personal baggage was strapped to the top and stowed for travel. Then he stood on the step and removed his hat.

"You will find some carriage blankets and pillows in the drawers beneath the seats," he said quietly through the window.

"Yes, I see them. Thank you." She pulled them out and distributed them to Mathilde and Anamosa.

"My lady, here is my card. The coach will take you to the property. I have already seen to the arrangements. The house is clean and very private, as requested. Your servants are there, three local women, all competent at cooking and cleaning. They stand ready to greet you." He handed a slender valise through the window. "This contains a few pages of information about the property's history. A drawing of the town. The stores and the goods they offer are marked. I also included a package of paper and envelopes, some addressed to my office, for correspondence. I plan to return to New Haven from here. Is there anything else I might do for you, or any questions I might answer?"

His tone was genuine and expressed concern. Corrinne knew she would probably not see him again. Her eyes showed her appreciation.

"Thank you. You appear to be a kind and proper gentleman. I...*we* are grateful for this help."

The man gruffly cleared his throat and shifted on his feet.

"The owner of the property would expect me to do no less."

Where she was going was not a very appealing place. The man felt a strong familial responsibility for this woman and her baby children. Her English was precise, and yet foreign-sounding. He could not quite place her accent. He touched his fingers atop her right hand in assurance.

"Um...my lady...my wife, children, and I live in New Haven. It is indeed a coach ride for us, but we are not that far away. And the mail comes to me regularly. If you encounter problems, please write to me. Or send a rider. While the house is safe and adequate, you may find its isolation... well, a little lonely. Your identity is safe with me. So please consider my family your friends."

But Corrinne knew such familiarity could not be allowed. Not if she wanted to remain safely anonymous. Idle talk would lead to gossip, which would eventually catch the ears of the curious. And there were those in search of them, intending to do them harm.

"Your offer is very considerate. I will make sure your employer hears of it. But I expect we will be all right."

"As you say, my lady. It has been my privilege."

With that, he stepped down, bowed his head, and then gestured to the drivers. The overland coach lurched forward down the rutted country road, the next step in Corrinne's journey.

Mustering up an optimistic attitude for the others in the face of their new circumstances and to pass the time during the two-hour carriage ride, Corrinne opened the valise and read aloud the pages describing the house given to her by…

"G. Bernard Conway, Esquire. What a perfect name for a lawyer! Our new home is called *Winter House*." She mused. "An Indian name, perhaps? Winter House sounds a little chilly. Why not Summer House? Or, 'House with Flowers that Smell Good'? But then again, it is not summertime."

"Maybe the name suggests it will be warm in the winter," Mathilde offered.

"Let us hope so."

"How old is it?"

Corrinne read aloud from the house papers: "*Winter House is forty-three years old. It was built by a fisherman to protect his family from the cold of winter; hence its name. Situated near the mouth of the Connecticut River where it empties into the long island water channel of New York, the house was built for defense against the French Acadians who once raided south along the Connecticut River with their Mi'kmaq allies during two previous wars. It is two stories tall with an attic and a stone-walled cellar. Post and beam construction; the main supporting columns, six inches square, four per corner, are made of cured lumber from eight hardwood trees. Hand cut and dressed, their strength is augmented by thick interior joists to hold up the building against storm-driven weather. The outside is overlaid with thick plank siding, the seams and cracks sealed and caulked with resins, more recently with cements, to keep out the wind, rain, and cold. Stone hearths and chimneys are tucked into each corner between the main columns.*"

Corrinne paused. The oddest things would make her ache for Philippe. *Oh, Philippe, my heart, my love, I miss you so.* So much had happened in the last year that it now felt like forever since they were last together. She stopped herself. If she thought too much of Philippe, she would break.

"*The chimneys are installed with multiple drafts, designed to heat the top and bottom floors from the same hearth on the ground floor. The windows were originally shuttered with heavy wood, with vertical loopholes for muskets*…! Loopholes for muskets? Goodness! Was this owned by the provincial militia?"

"Who would want to live in a house like that?" Mathilde wondered.

"Obviously, we do," Corrinne said.

"Maybe its ugliness will be a good thing, *oui*? To discourage visitors."

"Certainly no evening soirées with the Connecticut governor," Corrinne agreed. "But let us talk in English. *Winter House had barred windows at one time.* Barred windows? I imagine that would help convey a charming prison-like quality. *But the threat of Indian attacks so close to the sea ended in 1748. The windows now have panes of glass.*"

"To allow golden morning light to shine in," Mathilde offered.

"Yes, Mathilde! A good way to think about it."

But as they approached the place where they would live for who-knew-how-long, upon seeing its dreary exterior for the first time, Corrinne decided Winter House was aptly named.

The wood planks had been seasoned with pine tar as a natural deterrent to insects. The tar was sticky and had now accumulated layer after layer of fine sand and dust. After forty-three years of weathering, it was now coated in a permanent dark-gray patina, streaked in some places with web-like lines of white mildew.

"Perhaps it is haunted. Maybe we'll see ghosts," Corrinne teased everyone. "That should break up our boredom."

Corrinne would later recall that jest with regret.

Anamosa's nose wrinkled as the carriage traveled the last hundred meters of stagnant wetlands, which surrounded the property.

"It stinks."

"It surely does." Corrinne's brow furrowed, but then she shook her head. "The perfect aroma for such scenic surroundings. But the five of us are going to bring bright light, big smiles, optimism, soap, and hot water with perfumed bathing salts to create a pleasant fragrance on every floor!"

Three servants, in matching gray frocks and dark blue aprons, were waiting on the porch to welcome them. After a short introduction—the servants were a family: a mother and two daughters of seventeen and eighteen years—Corrinne found them acceptable. She did not dispute the contract they'd received from G. Bernard Conway, Esq.

Corrinne took the mother's hands in hers. "Mistress Barton, one more requirement. I prefer to remain anonymous and private during my stay here. Please do not speak our names, who we are, and how we came to be here with anyone. If you can do that for me, there will be financial gratuity for you when my stay is complete. I hope we will get along together like family."

"Yes, madam."

Together, they inspected all the rooms of the house. Then holding a lantern, Corrinne surveyed the cellar. *There*, she thought at finding a proper spot.

When all the personal baggage was unloaded and taken to various rooms, Corrinne gave final instructions. The coach drivers moved the *châsse* down into the cellar and set it down in a far corner. She had them cover it with a larger canvas tarp and encumber the top with heavy stones.

As they turned to leave, the men heard a low growl. Their noses were assaulted by a sudden foul odor. They hastily left the cellar and guessed at the contents all the way back to New Haven.

CHAPTER I
CANADIAN WILDERNESS
FALL 1755
Spirals

The white eagle's weakness was getting worse. Stress had aged the bird's life, an ebbing accelerated by the constant presence of the shaman spirit. The eagle had lived almost fourteen seasons and should still be a strong flyer and hunter for years to come. But the incessant long flights from one place to another had sapped its vitality, that and the eagle's distressing sensation of something clawing, clinging to it, which compelled it to do things against its nature. Things its primitive mind could not comprehend.

The white eagle had been robbed of its joy.

The lands below were covered with trees and hills in every direction. Occasionally, there were open fields filled with crops.

Feeling a lifting updraft, it soared to a higher place in the sky. The eagle's tail feathers adjusted. It began a slanted glide that propelled it forward. If the crosswinds were gentle, little exertion was required. It could do this for a long time, buoyed by the thermal column of air while slowly going down. After falling to a certain point, it would straighten its wings, soar upward, and start the glide over. Repeating this action, the raptor could cover hundreds of miles a day in the same direction, if it had the will to do so, which it did not. This glide had just begun when the warm air rising from the ground suddenly turned cold. A down thrust of colder air followed.

The *ghost* experienced a stabbing pain in the shoulder joint of the raptor's left wing. This spasm had occurred before, but never this strong. The left wing reflexively tucked in to minimize the pain. The eagle slipped into a spiral for several seconds, picking up speed. Then its weakened wings flapped. It leveled, flying straight until it entered another thermal of rising air. The eagle extended its wings more fully. The pain in its shoulder vanished.

It soared upward again. The lifting, sublime sensation of such diving and soaring was usually exhilarating. But no longer. Flying was now painful.

It could die.

The thought was disturbing. The *ghost* had never considered the eagle's mortality. When the eagle's physical cravings became persistent, the *ghost* would withdraw its dominance long enough to allow the animal to fish or hunt and feed itself, to invigorate its vitality, to indulge its natural urges. To do any of these things, the eagle must fly. If it could not fly, the eagle would waste away and die. With the intimate physical connection they shared, the *ghost's* own continuance was in danger too! But not from death. It had passed beyond death. The shaman spirit had a chance to rise toward the light, to embrace the afterlife. Instead, it chose to fight the demon, to dwell in the twilight at the edge of the opaque abyss. If the eagle died, the *ghost* would be absorbed by the black forever, the infinite nothingness.

The *ghost* was confounded. What now?

Return to the breeding grounds, the *ghost* decided. *Let it rest among its own kind.* Allowing the animal to regain its health seemed the best path to follow, for now.

They banked and turned towards the north.

After resting overnight amid the protective branches at the top of a tree and after another full day of flying, they neared a remote valley divided by a river. The river's water source overflowed from a sparkling blue mountain lake that was replenished from higher mountain runoff. The white water rapids rushed and splashed over the rocky cascades. Fish jumped and crowded together in the intermediate whirlpools. Bears waited on the larger boulders to snag a meal with an effortless swipe of their broad, sharp claws.

The valley was filled with old-growth hardwoods and tall pines. The hillsides protruded with rock cliffs and outcrops. Such surroundings provided abundant places for eagles to feed and build their aeries. By instinct they were drawn to this place. They were the largest predators of the skies. They had dark brown feathered bodies, white feathered heads and tails, and long hooked yellow beaks. Most began their lives here. Scores of raptors dwelled along this river and lake at any time. They were visible and they were everywhere.

Skrieee!

The white eagle's call was answered from every direction. At seeing and hearing so many others of its kind, harmonious feelings of sanctuary and contentment swelled within the eagle's spirit. It flew above the rapids following the valley upstream.

The *ghost* eased its dominance as they neared the lake.

The animal's ravenous hunger took over. The lake teemed with fish. The eagle made slow deliberate circles, watching the surface of the water for the telling ripples and darting shadows. Its acute eyesight spotted several prey in the pooling near the marshes. It chose the largest of them. Instinct positioned the eagle's glide so that its silhouette would fall upon the water surface behind it. The prey would have no forewarning. In a practiced, silent drift, it floated down to the surface. At the last possible moment, in one coordinated movement, it arched its wings to pause in flight and lifted its chest. Its body taut, spear-like, it plunged its claws deep into the water. Eight talon points gripped in a clench. The eagle flapped its wings and lifted the heavy wriggling prey. Pangs of hunger supplanted the spasms of pain in its shoulders. It selected a tall branch on which to perch. Its beak tore and ripped. It consumed a pound and a half of flesh in just a few minutes. Then it nestled down in an abandoned aerie to rest.

The *ghost* contemplated the implications of the eagle's weakness. The season of cold and snow was upon them. Prolonged exposure alone could take the eagle's life if it did not have constant food and a place to shelter. The animal must feed and rest to recover its health and maintain strength throughout the cold days. And when the surface of the lake froze, the competition for food would become fierce. The *ghost* would remain subdued until the days grew longer and the air warmed again.

The white eagle was at peace and rested.

But the *ghost* needed no rest. And it was not at peace. It was preoccupied with this new question. What if the eagle dies?

The eagle's strength improved slowly. The *ghost* gave the eagle as much freedom as possible. The *ghost* must be patient. Patience the *ghost* had in abundance.

The *ghost*'s thoughts turned to the demon. In previous violent encounters, it discovered an unexpected advantage. The *ghost* could sense the demon and its servants over long distances. But the demon and its servants could not perceive the *ghost*'s presence until the exact moment when they clashed. By then it was too late. Despite this advantage, the *ghost* was one, and they were many. The eagle was mortal and easily slain by wraith's servants.

The demon had gone back over the great water. It left the servants behind in a relentless hunt for the white woman. She was hiding in safety and unaware of their search. But they were coming.

From a distance, the *ghost* kept careful watch over her.

Another confrontation was inevitable.

*

Atlantic Ocean

Major Wilhelm von Kleinfels leaned against the stern rail of the English merchant frigate. His perceptions suddenly stimulated by the presence of the *châsse*. Over seawater, the *châsse* lost its potency, the strength it drew from being in contact with the land. But the sea crossing had only begun, yet he sensed the *châsse* again… How was this possible? It was too soon. Crossing the sea would take many weeks. He might sense the *châsse* if the two ships passed one another, even at fairly large distances. But this presence he felt was strong. Too strong.

It is resting under land again! But what land? An island?

He reflected on his experience, standing at the very end of Boston's Long Wharf, watching *William's Queen* slowly leave the harbor. He'd watched the trading schooner, carrying the whore queen and the *châsse*, take in its mooring lines and sail away. He remained there, unmoving, concentrating for hours, discerning the *châsse*'s easterly direction until the sensation of its presence was gone. By that time, it was very dark, near the midnight hour. But he had not been overly concerned. He knew the vessel's destination: Amsterdam.

After the departure of *William's Queen*, he'd explained to his merchant contacts and English army liaisons in Boston that it was necessary for him to return to Prussia and confer with his sovereign, and he promised to return again in the spring. With the army's persuasion, he'd found passage on an English trader. It sailed for London three days later. Once in London, he planned to travel over the channel to Amsterdam. He already had dozens of servants in that city. Finding the whore queen would not take much effort. He would locate the *châsse* and possess it. The task would be much less complicated than it had proved to be in Boston.

At least, that was his expectation.

The newspapers said the ship was bound for Amsterdam...

Yet he felt the *châsse* clearly behind him now. So the Hessian faced aft, realizing he was going in the wrong direction. He sorted through the possible explanations.

The announcement in the newspapers about the ship's destination had been a ruse.

The Dutch ship did not go to Amsterdam. It had stayed in American waters and sailed somewhere else. Now four days after *William's Queen* sailed, the *châsse* was resting firmly on the ground somewhere, otherwise he would not sense such a strong presence. But if not in Boston, then where? To the north? To the south? He could not answer that question, not in the middle of an ocean.

The Hessian major speculated whether he might convince the captain to turn this ship around. *Not likely*, he decided. Only when pressured by the English army did the master of this trading frigate agree to provide him transport to London. The enmity of the captain towards him was conspicuous. The man was suspicious of his motives. He avoided the captain and stayed in his cabin most of the time.

Major von Kleinfels would have to endure this long sea journey to London and then travel further to Amsterdam by another means. *William's Queen* was a Dutch trading ship. It would have an agent there. He would find this trading agent, subvert him for information, and design a new plan, one less blunt in approach. One with more finesse than the first. Then arrange a trip back to America.

The whore queen moved the châsse*! She hides it somewhere new. She is convinced hiding it makes her safe. But it does not. Underground, its powers treble. She believes if the seals remain unbroken, she cannot be scarred in her dreams. But she can be scarred in other ways. Her dreams can be disturbed. Once I stand on land, she will know fear. When her fear becomes unbearable, she will flee. She will move the* châsse *from its new place of concealment...and that will be her undoing.*

*

Winter House

The local servants, Jenny Barton and her two daughters, admired Corrinne Gerrard from the day they met her. They could tell she was someone important. The Scottish soldier, Sentry Cheever, who visited every few weeks, addressed her as *my lady*. They wondered why a noblewoman chose to live such a solitary existence. Why were there not more visitors? What had caused the terrible scar on her neck? But it was not their business to ask. Of course, her three children were an absolute delight. The mistress of Winter House was very kind to them, vocally expressed her appreciation, praised their value often, and paid them generously for their services. Jenny Barton and her daughters quickly became enamored with their own good fortune. They were pestered constantly by the town gossips to know more about the beautiful recluse. But they remained loyal and protective of *Lady* Corrinne's privacy, as they had begun to address her.

It did not take long for the loneliness of the house with its isolated location to affect Corrinne's mood. To establish a healthy existence, she created a daily routine to follow, with meals served at a certain time and daily chores for Anamosa to do. They would take an excursion into the village every two weeks to shop, more for the enjoyment of the children. Corrinne was courteous but aloof with the shopkeepers, knowing each trip would generate chatter about her in such a small and predictably boring town. Privacy was essential to their security. Tutoring Anamosa, playing with the twins, and devising simple games for them to master filled the greater part of Corrinne's day, giving her an outlet for the endless love she harbored for them all. Still, she was starved for someone of intellect. Someone with whom she could converse with and share her thoughts and concerns.

Mathilde was still ailing from the sword wound she received in her chest during the attack in Boston. It was healing slowly, but her maidservant was given to harsh fits of coughing. Sometimes coughing up blood. Corrinne offered to have a doctor brought in to see her, but Mathilde refused. To minimize the painful coughing spasms, Mathilde spent much of the day sitting quietly, doing needlework, watching the children play.

The highlight of living there, if one could be found, coincided with visits by Sentry Cheever every few weeks. He created a memorable Christmas for all of them. The Scotsman arrived wearing a white beard and wig, a red sock hat with a tassel over his head, imitating Father Christmas, further dressed in swaths of clothes in green and red, the colors of the holiday. Wearing his eye patch and adorned in such a manner, his imposing body looked awkward and ridiculous…and wonderful. He set down the bag of toys before the fire, wooden rattles, hand-painted dolls, intricate Indian bead necklaces and bracelets for Anamosa, smaller ones for Calypso, and a bulky set of smooth sanded wooden blocks of various sizes, square cubes, rect-angles, and right angle planes. *Marcus will like these*, he assured Corrinne. And to Corrinne's surprise, Marcus immediately started to examine them, attempting to fit each piece in his mouth, before banging them repeatedly on the floor. Mathilde got a warm quilt filled with eiderdown, a shawl, and a fur-lined pair of house slippers. Corrinne got a new shawl and couch quilt too, a letter from Machault, and a new book from Charles VanderMeer. *Dear Charles!* She owed much to this man who had given her the protection of his royal name so that she, a French person of interest, could live in the English city of Boston.

Then with a tiny smile, Sentry pulled the last present from the pack...a three-pound canvas pouch of dark roasted coffee beans from the Antilles along with a grinder.

"Surprise!"

Corrinne clutched the coffee possessively and regarded him with grate-ful eyes.

"Oh, bless you, Sentry Cheever. You dear, dear man."

*

January 28, 1756

It was a cold morning late in January. Corrinne sat up in bed overcome with anxiousness and confusion, breathing heavily as if she'd been grappling with an attacker. As usual, she retained no memory of what she'd dreamt about or what had startled her awake. She rose from her bed, wrapped herself in a heavy woolen shawl, and went immediately to the nursery to check on the sleeping babies before going downstairs. Her temples pounded. This had happened nearly every night since the beginning of the year. What little optimism she had coveted was gone, replaced by a paranoia induced by an overactive imagination she struggled to control.

Corrinne had not entirely recovered from the trauma of the vicious attack in Boston four months earlier. Her neck wound was completely healed. But the long scar on her throat was sensitive to the touch and would often throb for no reason, more strongly on those mornings when her sleep had been disturbed. The assassins in Boston had intended to kill everyone, even her precious babies. Only by the grace of God, the courage of Magistrate Jack

Tasker, and the presence of Sentry Cheever in the household were the plans of the killers foiled. Her dreams after the attack were filled with visions of the beautiful white ghost eagle. Its message was always the same. *You must hide*, the guardian spirit told her repeatedly. *Leave this place and hide.*

And so she did.

Despite the stoutness of Winter House's construction, it was much more vulnerable than her home in Boston. She had no guards. Other than Charles VanderMeer, her dear friend and *faux* husband; Thomas Hancock, her trusted business partner; and Sentry Cheever, no one in Boston knew she was here; presumably. The house was difficult to find, even when you searched for it. Its isolation and remoteness was its security, and also its vulnerability if ever found. But loneliness was the personal price Corrinne paid for this hiding place. However, it now fell to Corrinne to defend everyone if danger should suddenly appear. She had secreted loaded pistols in every room, including two in her library room. She was ready to die to protect the ones she loved. And like every good sentinel Corrinne was constantly on guard.

Shivering in the clinging cold air that sucked away a body's warmth, Corrinne went into the nursery. The flame from the wall lamp was turned low, but there was enough light to see Marcus and Calypso sleeping together. Marcus lay on his stomach with one tiny arm across Calypso's chest. Corrinne wet her index finger and held it near each of the sleeping babies' noses, feeling their breath on the wetness, slow and steady.

"Just like little angels are supposed to sleep," she whispered as she tenderly caressed their silky hair. "Mama loves you."

She pulled the blanket over them and turned to Anamosa sleeping in a bed by the wall. Corrinne stroked Anamosa's hair and checked on her breathing too. Everything was fine.

Corrinne went to the nursery door and took out a pistol stored in a closed box hanging high on the wall. Taking a deep breath, she started towards the stairway. The darkness hung thickly in the air, like cloying curtains. As she walked, it moved around her fluidly. She realized it was only a temporary illusion, caused by a wall lamp burning on a low flame at the bottom of the stairway, offering barely enough light to see the steps. With her appearance, the lamp flame began to gutter. It cast rippling shadows along the floors and walls. Her imagination immediately conjured reasons for the disturbance. None of them were pleasant.

It is nothing, she scolded herself silently. *The wick is turned low. All lamps will flicker when the wick is shortened.* It was a rationale she repeated to herself every single night.

The beginning of this nightly inspection of the house was always the worst part. The nearness of the sea often brought strong whistling winds. The age and draftiness of the old house produced clicks, snaps, creaks, or grunts from the wood, accompanied by unexpected, forceful wisps of cold air. If Corrinne allowed her imagination to gather darkly, as she was wont to do, she would often sense something unseen and feel the gaze of a cruel presence. And interpreting a sudden spurt of draft as an icy breath on the back of her neck, Corrinne would spin and point the pistol—more with anger than fear—at the blackness in some corner. Of course, after a few seconds, she'd realize nothing was there and would feel foolish. Yet the threat was real.

There was an evil *thing* sealed in a wooden chest lined with stone just down in the cellar beneath her feet, hidden beneath a flimsy canvas tarp. It waited with undulating fingers of white vapor, biding its time when it could appear without warning and touch her with the searing points of its long, milky talons. She had endured its malice more than once. Felt its stabbing pain on the back of her neck more than once. Yes, it was real. But for now, it was sealed. The scarring wraith could not physically attack her. Yet it was the cause of her nightmares. She felt certain of that! The primary disciple of this *thing*, the leader of the assassins, was searching for her relentlessly. She must determine a permanent solution to contain the scarring wraith before the leader discovered where she was hiding. The leader need only to break the seals on the *châsse* and everyone she loved would suffer. Given enough time, he might succeed.

"But not today," she whispered grimly towards the guttering lamp to encourage herself not to be afraid.

Taking another deep breath, Corrinne cocked the pistol, gripped the handrail tightly with one hand, held the pistol in front of her with the other and started down the stairs. An overnight snow flurry had brought an icy stillness to the air. The old house was quiet. Even the usual wood creaks on the stairway seemed frozen into silence. Upon reaching the bottom, she turned up the wick in the wall lamp. The brighter light, of course, changed everything.

"You are not a child," she chided herself. She carefully lowered the hammer on the pistol. "You could start a fire in this old house with a pistol!"

With chattering teeth, Corrinne lit fires in two of the hearths on the ground floor corners of the house before retreating into the library, where one of the hearths was located. It was the smallest room and would usually heat the fastest. Shivering in her night dress, she sat down at her writing desk to contemplate the lazy fall of snowflakes in the muted moonlight outside the window. She pulled the heavy shawl tight around her shoulders and tucked the thick couch quilt around her knees. Two pairs of socks covered her feet. She would be alone with her thoughts for a few hours before Mistress Barton and her daughters arrived.

Outside the library window, large snowflakes softened the landscape. They stuck to empty tree branches and covered the shrubbery in large white dollops. A log snapped and popped in the fireplace, while yellow flames roiled around it. She had paid local woodsmen a liberal sum to split and stockpile enough hardwood behind the house beneath sail canvas to last until the summer, if necessary. The fire consumed the wood quickly, the heat pushed outward into the room's cold interior. Her breath puffed vaporously, but it had only been a few minutes. It would take an hour at least for the hearths to get the ground floor warm again.

If Corrinne could keep her disquieting thoughts at bay, the early morning solitude usually produced her best thinking. And she had a lot to think about. She took up Financier Machault's letter, left the desk, and settled into her cushioned chair in front of the fire, extending her feet towards the flames to warm her socks. She turned up the wick on the side table oil lamp for more light to read the letter. She looked at the five pages, as she had every day since receiving the missive.

The first two pages had Machault's distinctive, tight hand writing. The other three pages were pictures of the symbols found carved into the stone walls, floor, and ceiling of the vaulted tomb his agents had found not far from the city of Sankt Goarshausen, on the western bank of the Rhine River, near Castle Kleinfels.

I expected it would take months to locate this ancient sepulcher, if it could be found at all. According to the legends, this tomb was intentionally hidden. It was over a thousand years old, and probably much older, alleged to be somewhere in the mountainous hills near Sankt Goarshausen, a rugged remote area of a hundred square miles or more. Searching for the time-obscured entrance to a tomb seemed pointless. So doubtful was my view of this expedition, I hesitated to invest the money as you directed. To the surprise of my agents, they encountered a local sheepherder who knew exactly of what they spoke. This man had come upon the tomb accidently while searching for some of his lost sheep, or so he claimed. The man led them to the spot but refused to approach the grave because the entrance exuded a very foul odor. This was indeed the lost tomb you were seeking, but we were not the first. It had been reopened and plundered sometime in the last few years. This is, indeed, an extraordinary double coincidence.

Only because of the generous sum I offered for its discovery and inspection did the men I hired dare to venture into the grave. Inside they found skeletal remains of people buried in its walls. But the heavy stones of another wall at the back of the crypt had been broken with levers to reveal a secret vault that was obviously concealed in a way to permanently hide its location. It contained the skeletal remains of several men in rusted, old chain mail armor and carrying broad swords, lying haphazardly on the floor. More ominously, the bones from a newer skeleton lay scattered everywhere. My men claimed these bones still retained some desiccated flesh and were more recent in age than the remains clad in armor.

There was also a sarcophagus with a stone lid, which was broken into pieces. This coffin was filled with a foul-smelling earth. The soil looked stirred, dug up, and turned, as if thoroughly searched. My men did not excavate any further as they had not been paid to do so. I should mention these same men have refused to return, even though I have offered twice their initial payment. However, as you will see on the next few pages, they found three symbols carved repeatedly into the stone slabs of the grave walls, floor, and ceiling, and also inside the lid of the sarcophagus.

I assume these symbols will have significance to you. One of them is easily recognizable, but the other two can be interpreted in several ways. This will require more investigation of a scholarly nature, which I cannot do for you. Perhaps my agent, Wittmann Bootz, in Amsterdam has the necessary competence to organize such an expedition. It should be performed by men credentialed to provide you with the learned conclusions you seek about what was interred there.

Now I move on to issues and events relative to our financial covenant...

To these pages there was also a short note from Charles, saying he had read the letter and Machault's conclusions on the symbols. Furthermore, he'd taken steps to send missives to men he knew in Amsterdam. *Men with avid interest in historical ruins and certainly a tomb like this.* They would be hired and well paid to investigate everything that Machault had located. She should not worry.

The rest of Machault's letter covered financial matters, along with his prediction of a declaration of war between France and England before the summer months arrived. She set that page aside. She did not want to think about war today.

Corrinne laid the three symbol pages side by side on her lap. She pondered their meaning and purpose as she did every day since seeing them the first time.

If I only had more coffee, she mused wistfully. *I'd have divined a solution weeks ago.*

Now, a month after Christmas, the coffee was long gone. Corrinne had consumed it daily. So here she was, back to hot tea again. She liked tea, but it wasn't coffee. Even so, she could use a cup of hot tea just now, except it was too cold to endure the task of getting a fire started in the cuisine hearth to brew it.

"Corrinne?"

Absorbed in her contemplations, she startled and turned in her chair towards the sound of the beautiful little voice. It was Anamosa, shivering in the doorway, with a blanket wrapped around her shoulders.

"Hello, Ana," she greeted with a low voice and inviting smile. Corrinne set the missive and drawings on the side table and held out her arms.

"Come, baby, come sit with me."

Anamosa moved swiftly to tuck herself into Corrinne's warm embrace and lap, nuzzling her cold nose under Corrinne's chin. Corrinne pressed Ana's head to her shoulder and stroked her long black hair. She wrapped the quilt around them both. She felt the icy coldness of Ana's bare feet and pulled them in close to warm them.

"I had a bad dream," Ana said, her voice distressed.

"What about?"

"It was Henri. He was screaming."

Corrinne inhaled sharply at that thought. "No. Don't worry, Ana. It was just a dream. I am sure Henri is all right. Or I would feel it as well. And I didn't. Henri is all right. Close your eyes and go back to sleep for a while."

Corrinne's love for Anamosa, Philippe's adopted child, had grown in this lonely place, on par with her love for Calypso and Marcus. Anamosa had lost everyone in her life. Everyone she knew in the Ottawa village of her birth was either dead or so far away she would never see them again. Her mother, Okeanneh, had been the last to die. There was something magical about the girl. She well understood Henri's fascination with her. Anamosa's very presence was comforting.

Her thoughts drifted. She wondered if Henri had found Philippe as he had set out to do. She marveled at Philippe's boy—no—he was a man now. At fifteen years old, he had seen and been through things…things that hurt her to consider.

Corrinne softly hummed a lullaby from some distant childhood memory. In a few minutes, Anamosa's breathing slowed as sleep overtook her again. As she stroked the girl's hair, Corrinne's fingers touched something hard beneath Anamosa's nightdress. Gently pushing the material aside, she saw Chittaqua's silver talisman. Surrounded by the four sigils of the Great Houses and etched further with enigmatic Indian symbols, the purple jewel at its center captured and reflected the light from the flames in the hearth. Resting her fingers on the jewel evoked a sense of peace, soothing her loneliness. Comforting words abruptly came to mind. *You are not alone in this. You will see.*

Corrinne glanced over at the window. The snow was falling steadily. In the distance, she saw land slope upward to a higher elevated property. She had surveyed that lot. It was five times larger than her existing one, and it overlooked the Connecticut River. It was empty and in foreclosure. Someday, no matter what else occurred, she would have to seal the *châsse* in a permanent tomb and not just behind a wall. It must be someplace deep underground, a vault surrounded on all sides by heavy stone, with no door. It must be created in secret and finished by removing all traces of the tomb's existence as the last step. A remote isolated place, somewhere unlikely for such a thing to exist, where people would not even think to look for it. Like before.

There, perhaps? I will ask Thomas Hancock about this place.

*

Boston Harbor

"Drop anchor!"

Chain rattled out from the trading frigate, the *Anamosa*. The last sails were reefed.

Through his watch glass, Captain Conor Martyn could see the fingers of ice already extending out into the harbor from the shoreline. The water and air were cold and would be getting colder. The *Anamosa* had just returned from Savannah, Georgia, following orders by Commander Rous to forcibly transport fifty-four Acadians, some fourteen families, against their will, from their homes in Nova Scotia to a strange, new American city. Many of the men had sat below shackled to a bulkhead. It had been a miserable, cold, disgusting journey. The French-speaking people had been put off the ship on a Savannah wharf, destitute, exhausted, and bewildered, left in the dubious care of the Georgia governor's agents. And Captain Martyn was certain Commander Rous would order him to do this again as soon as he learned the *Anamosa* had returned.

Nova Scotia's Governor Lawrence and the English army were permanently displacing thousands of Acadians at bayonet point, forcing them to board the waiting ships. They were to be transported throughout the southern colonies, some even further to the Antilles islands, eventually to be replaced by German or Dutch settlers or more acceptable Protestant immigrants, settlers who would be impervious to the endless incitement of rebellious papist priests and therefore proper colonists, expected to be forever loyal to the British crown. It was heartrending to see the suffering faces of these simple peaceful farmers and their families. But the captain of the *Anamosa* followed orders. And his orders were not over yet.

Fortunately, Commander Rous was in Halifax, not Boston.

"Your orders, Captain?" His second-in-command and the bosun looked at him expectantly.

"Divide the men into three sections. Two sections go ashore. A new section to rotate back aboard each day. Bosun, get this ship scrubbed and cleaned. Get the bilges well flushed. I hope to stay here for two weeks if we can. Maybe less, depending on that ice. Lieutenant, get us provisioned with some decent food to eat since we are here. Water, too. Bosun, remind the crew if anyone makes trouble for this ship while ashore and gets us ordered to leave early, they will sorely regret it."

"Aye, sir."

"Lieutenant, I am going to report completion of our mission to naval command in Boston. I will be back tomorrow morning to relieve you. You and I will rotate command at anchor every other day."

"Yes, sir."

*

Captain Conor Martyn was rowed in the ship's harbor launch to the middle of Boston's Long Wharf, where he disembarked. Slinging a large bag of dirty clothes and other personal items across his back, he headed to the apartment he'd rented on Brattle Street just before he'd gone to sea. He'd been gone for almost seven weeks. His rent was overdue. He prayed the landlady had not rented it to anyone else.

"Well, if it isn't Captain Martyn back from the war," the middle-aged woman greeted him after the knock at her door. "You smell like week-old fish."

Conor set his bag down and held his hat respectfully in both hands. "Apologies, Mistress Callahan. I was not aware I would be gone for so long. I will pay you my back rent, of course, and three months in advance this time."

"Oh, really? Perhaps you expected me to save this valuable rental for you, *unpaid*, when I had a line of customers petitioning me for its lease? At a better price, I might add."

Conor's expression sagged. "Please tell me you haven't rented it already."

"I should have. But my husband was a sailor, God rest his soul. Tall and handsome like yourself. Got me with child and went to sea for *six months*, thank you very much. Married me *a year later*, once I confronted him with his new son. Good thing for you he did, or I would not have this

soft spot in my heart right now. And you are going to get that young girl…
what's her name?"

"Molly."

"Yes, Molly. You be getting Molly in a motherly way if you keep rocking
that bed the way you do. It's above my room, you know. I hear everything."

Conor nodded humbly. "Apologies, mistress. I've asked her to marry
me."

"Better hurry. The way the two of you go at it, she'll be showing soon.
What are you going to do with that?" She pointed at the bag.

"Uh, I need to take it to a laundry. Do you know of one?"

"Pay me fifty pence and I'll do it for you. Pay me another fifty pence
and I will heat a tub of hot water for your bath. Molly will thank me, you
can be certain of that."

"Mistress Callahan, you are a saint. You remind me of…"

She smirked. "Just pay me. And the rent too."

Conor took out his purse and counted out four months of rent and an
extra hundred pence before she changed her mind. It was almost all the
money he had. He'd intended to buy Molly a gift. That would have to wait.

"I must report to naval command. I could be there an hour or more
before I come back."

"See if you can get a clean uniform to wear," Mistress Callahan suggested. "Yours is a might crusty."

Conor smiled, reached out unexpectedly, and hugged her tightly, kissing
her cheek. "Thank you, thank you, mistress."

"Peeeuuugh! Go away with you. Your smell is foul!"

"Thank you."

Five hours later, a bathed, clean, and shaven Captain Conor Martyn
arrived at Lord VanderMeer's front walk. The two marine guards saluted and
greeted him warmly from the small guardhouse, which Lord VanderMeer
had constructed to the left of the walk-up, saying it was the least he could
do after his civilian guards had been killed defending him. *And it could
happen again*, he'd warned. Marines were now permanently assigned to
guard Lord VanderMeer's home since the assassins had been disguised as
marines. But as far as the marines were concerned, this guard duty wasn't
bad. The little house contained a standing stove, a round table, and three

chairs. It was small comfort but enough to keep the men dry and warm on cold and rainy Boston nights. Lord VanderMeer also provided them with food and drink from Dianamora's *cuisine*, a feast compared to their usual rations, and permitted them use of a privy he had specially built for them behind the house.

When Conor arrived, it was late in the afternoon, an hour before sunset. The overcast sky thickened the twilight. He knocked gently with the brass rapper. He carried two loaves of freshly baked sweet breads full of nuts and dried plums in one arm, which he had just enough coin left to purchase.

Dianamora answered and her face broke into a bright smile.

Conor quickly put a finger to his lips. "Shhh!" He hugged her and then whispered, "Where is she?"

"She is in the *cuisine*. Lord VanderMeer is in his library."

"Who's there?" Charles asked as he entered the living room, holding an open book in one hand.

Conor bowed his head politely and put a finger to his lips again. Charles smiled and pointed towards the *cuisine*.

A tea pot was hissing just short of a full whistle. Molly was standing over a cutting table, her forehead sweaty from exertion, rolling out some dough to make a pie crust. Her face and the front of her dress were sprinkled with flour dust. Conor quietly set the bread on a chair and came up behind her, slipping his arms around her waist, kissing her neck.

Molly squealed and turned, knocking him in the head with the rolling pin. The pin dropped to the floor with a loud thump.

"Oww!" Conor gripped his head. "Damn, Molly!"

She didn't care. She crushed herself against him, kissing him and moaning with sounds of relief and desire. She was breathless when they broke their embrace.

"Conor! Conor! Oh, I was so worried! The newspapers are always filled with stories about the war and the fighting among the warships."

He kissed her again. "I'm fine, Molly, except for my *head*. Can't you tell?"

She looked down at the obvious bulge beneath her dress. "Conor, I think I am with child," she said in a sobbing whisper. "Please don't leave me!"

The winter crossing of the Atlantic from Boston to London was exhausting and delayed several weeks because of the series of severe storms the English trading frigate encountered, forcing it to take safe harbor in Galway, Ireland. It remained there for over two weeks, weathering storm after storm before the winter seas and skies calmed enough to sail again. But once in London, Major von Kleinfels set to work immediately on the plan he contrived during the long sea voyage. He needed new people, resourceful people. The kind of people who knew how to move about discreetly. His most immediate need would be selecting the servant who could begin a search for the whore queen in America, to find the trail leading to her from Boston.

Within two days of his arrival in London, the major paid a one-month accommodation fee for an unoccupied city mansion. It was the former residence of a deceased parliamentarian, two stories tall with twelve rooms. It was completely furnished, only the dust covers needed to be removed. It included house servants to provide for cooking, cleaning, and one valet and a butler. He declined the offer of overnight servants. The staff was dismissed each day at sunset to return again at sunrise.

On his very first night, alone in the large house, Major Kleinfels lay down on his oversized bed and gripped the pouch fashioned from fine golden threads hanging around his neck. It contained bone shards, the last remaining pieces of the skeleton he'd sifted and exhumed from the sarcophagus in the ancient tomb near Sankt Goarshausen. He closed his eyes and slowed his breathing. In a few minutes, the identity of the Hessian major was displaced. He became captive to a paralyzing trance as the spirit of the *vulnax* took full possession.

The *vulnax* reached outward with its powers of fear and persuasion to invade the dreams of a particular servant across the waters in America. The man resided in the city of Philadelphia, in a section called Germantown. There were four servants living in that city waiting for the Hessian to return or call to them. But he could only control one of them from so far a distance. He picked the strongest and most capable of these laborers, a stonecutter called Ritter Monheit. He was twenty-nine, tall, heavily muscled from his work with stone, black hair and brown eyes. No living relatives. He was not a violent man, unless challenged, which rarely happened because of his brooding, troubled expression. He was a man who preferred to live alone, more so now that he was a servant of the *vulnax*. His strongest quality was his unwavering obedience. His only pleasures were drinking beer and the occasional whore. A simple man with simple needs, who simply wished to serve his master. In his dreams that night, this wish was answered.

Ritter Monheit's bedroom became unusually warm and oppressive. His body trembled as the dream spirit descended.

You will serve me.

In a nightmare, the *vulnax* asserted the services Ritter would perform: He would go to Boston, seek out Lord VanderMeer and keep a discreet watch on the residence. He must learn the location of Lady VanderMeer without arousing suspicions.

Lord VanderMeer communicates with her through someone else. Identify this person. You will know him when you hear his name. Follow this man if ever he leaves the city. Do not interfere or draw attention to yourself. Locate the place where Lady VanderMeer is hiding. Do nothing further. Wait for my arrival. Use the money I left with you.

The next morning, Ritter Monheit awoke early. From under a loose floorboard of his apartment, he extracted a pouch of silver and gold coins, untouched until now. He packed his clothes, armed himself, and bought a horse and saddle. Then he rode north to the city of Boston.

*

Each night, as the Hessian retired to bed, he would calm himself and surrender to the *vulnax*. The spirit would expand its awareness to seek out the *châsse*. It did not know the location of the reliquary, only that it was in contact with the ground…and very close to the whore queen. Near enough that the *vulnax* could use the potency of Lord Vaelblez' relics in the coffin to reach further to interrupt her dreams. The wraith could not scar her, but it could fill her dreams with horrifying images of the deaths of her children. There were many inventive ways to suggest cruelties on ones so young and vulnerable. It never took long to corrupt her rest. Night after night, it ended the same way. She would bolt awake in a panic, overcome with emotions of terror, anguish, and grief, but left with no memories to provide an explanation. The wraith intended to dwell with her further, provoking her imagination, using the night shadows and natural sounds to suggest its presence, so she would be filled with fear in addition to feelings of guilt. The whore queen was strong…but she was alone.

The *vulnax* also discovered it could embrace her memories for a short time as the woman struggled to free her thoughts from the nightmares, to awaken. Briefly the wraith could experience her most recent memories, those moments of time when she was last awake. The images of her current dwelling were unremarkable. But the writing she read on the paper, the search of the Sankt Goarshausen tomb? The description of the symbols!

The whore queen is learning too much!

*

After establishing his household and its routine, Major von Kleinfels set about finding a commercial assistant. He wanted someone familiar with the English army, but further, a person who had American contacts in Boston or New York, preferably both. It took a week, in between meetings with various senior British generals in the Horse Guards palladium to refresh his Hessian credentials, but soon he found someone at a public house frequented by English businessmen in Whitehall.

His name was Carter Trevathan. He was a Cambridge-educated trading merchant and just one of dozens of ambitious London traders hoping to gain contracts to supply the British military for the wars in different parts of the empire. The most lucrative of those conflicts was the new one in the Americas. Carter was a minor partner in a failing London firm and was seeking new employment as much as he was fishing for new connections to the English military elite. Wilhelm von Kleinfels listened to the thirty-two-year-old man boast about established trading partners in New York. Carter had no close family relatives and he was desperate for money. He offered him paid employment and security. Within a day, after consuming several glasses of blood-laced wine, Carter Trevathan became a dedicated servant of the *vulnax*.

*

Wilhelm von Kleinfels had also decided to convert women to his service. He knew where to find them. Marquis de Propei's first of four wives was English. She had two children by him, both daughters. At the time of their mother's death, they were eight and nine years of age. The girls purportedly suffered from terrible delusions, nightmares, and hallucinations. After the mother's demise, the Marquis had them returned to England and committed to Bethlem, a famous hospital for the mentally insane, where doctors were paid to further diagnose incurable madness in both the girls. They'd remained incarcerated there ever since.

Bethlem Royal Hospital was eighty years old, constructed in 1676, relatively new by London standards of 1756. It was designed to be more of an architectural landmark for the city without deference to hospital pragmatism, much less devoted to caring for the unfortunate victims of mental illnesses. Located in the northern part of London in an area known as Moorfields, it was an intimidating structure, the hospital was almost twelve hundred feet long and several stories high, rising to sixty feet in some places.

As the carriage passed along the length of the ostentatious building, Major Kleinfels immediately sensed the presence of both females. They were still alive. These former daughters of the Marquis de Propei were already partially possessed. He planned to complete their servitude today. Padding the palms of those in power with gold and silver, in this case, three Bethlem Governors, solved the necessary requirements for documents, giving permission to visit the facility and to have the women released to him without interference.

He stepped from the ornate carriage in front of the steps leading to the grand façade. Stone pillars bridged the entrance gate, and the archway was capped by two sculptured figures in repose. They were not created to convey artistic beauty and could almost be considered gargoyles. Wearing expressions of acute sadness and pain, names were cut in the stone beneath them: *Melancholia* and *Mania*.

Upon seeing the Bethlem Governors' emblem on the side door of the carriage, an intern from inside the hospital ran down the steps to welcome this important passenger. Von Kleinfels barely acknowledged the man and handed him the papers establishing why he was there.

"I will need a private room to interview these two women together."

"Of course, sir. Follow me, please."

The first floor of the hospital was one long series of patient bed wards interspaced with iron-barred viewing galleries. The bed wards on this floor were kept scrupulously clean. The first floor was used for public tours. People entered at one end of the building and left at the opposite end, with many of the visitors leaving in a state of shock.

They walked by several cage-enclosed galleries full of unsupervised patients. The air was stifling with the foul odors of excrement and vomit. The antics of semi-naked patients, shouting accusations of gibberish and outright shrieks of madness, were only a few paces away. In many places, arms stretched out through the bars into the hallway. A long white line had been painted on the floor.

"Be sure to stay to the right of the white line," the docent encouraged in a bored voice. "The patients in this ward claim to hear voices. Don't let them touch you."

A passing visitor was left with little doubt these poor unfortunate souls needed to be kept at a place like this. Of course, that was the intention of the Bethlem Governors. Visitors completing the regularly scheduled, fee-required guided tours would arrive at the other end of the building to be greeted by several hospital petitioners with cloth-covered baskets requesting extra donations for the ill and infirm. The baskets did not remain empty very long.

Wilhelm von Kleinfels was different. He was escorted to a private room containing a single round table covered with a white cloth. Four cushioned table chairs were arrayed around it; a few more were up against the wall. The room had one tall window, four feet wide and ten feet tall, overlooking the tree-lined greenery of Moorfields, a desultory garden even on a sunny day. Like all the others, this window was barred.

"This will do. Have two bottles of wine, uncorked, and three glasses brought to me as soon as possible. The table must be set before the women are permitted entry."

"As you wish, sir."

They should be in their late twenties by now, von Kleinfels surmised as he gazed out the window.

A few minutes later, a kitchen servant appeared with a tray of two open wine bottles and three glasses. He set them in the center of the table.

"Will there be anything else, sir?"

Kleinfels pulled the loosened corks from the bottles and sniffed each one. He nodded his head and gave the man a silver coin.

"They will suffice. Once the women are in here, I do not want to be disturbed…for any reason," he added with emphasis. "Do this for me and you will earn a piece of gold."

"Yes, sir. I will post myself outside the door. Thank you, sir."

Once he was alone again. He poured himself a glass and two other glasses half full of red wine. He withdrew a small bottle from inside his coat that was full of his blood and poured a generous amount into the two half-full glasses. The remainder was poured into the half-empty wine bottle. Then he sat down to wait.

Only a few minutes elapsed when he heard a respectful knock on the door. He stood.

"Enter."

The intern led two slender women into the room. They were both tall with long black hair worn in a single French braid hanging to the center of their backs. They wore clean, white hospital smocks covering them from neck to floor and white cloth slippers on their feet. They could be twins, except Kleinfels knew they were a year apart in age. Their heads were bowed.

The intern gestured in introduction. "May I present Caroline and Rachel de Propei."

Wilhelm affected a benevolent, friendly expression. "Caroline, Rachel, I am Major Wilhelm von Kleinfels. I am pleased to meet you both."

Slowly, they raised their unremarkable brown eyes to gaze at him. The one called Rachel, the younger one, performed a small curtsy.

He turned to the intern. "Thank you. You may leave them with me." As the intern exited, the major gave his full attention to them. He gestured towards the chairs. "Take a seat, and we will talk about why I am here."

He waited while they sat down before seating himself. Their expressions were cautious.

"First, I would like to toast to your good fortune. Will you join me in a glass of wine?"

The sisters glanced at each another uneasily, and then they slowly reached out for the glasses.

"It is all right." He lifted the glass to his lips and took a healthy swallow. "There. You see. Just a pleasant glass of wine."

Kleinfels exerted his will and they lifted the glasses to their lips. "Drink it all. We do not have much time to talk."

Outside the door, the kitchen servant and the intern waited, speculating in whispers about what might be happening.

"Who is he?"

"A Prussian major. Can't you tell from his accent and arrogant tone?" replied the intern. "According to the Bethlem Governors, he has a need for two house servants while he is in London. He paid to have these two specific patients released, claiming they are related to him."

"Related? Are they?"

"Well, they came to us from France when they were children, so it is possible, I presume, or the Governors would not permit it."

When the women had finished the second glass of wine, Kleinfels gestured for them to stand. They did so immediately.

"Disrobe."

With apathetic expressions, they slipped off their smocks to stand naked in front of him.

"Turn slowly for me."

They were very skinny. He could see their ribs, but there were no signs of mistreatment or any open sores.

"Good. You may dress again and sit."

While they dressed, he shared the last of the blood-laced wine in each of their glasses and poured them almost full from the second bottle.

"Drink these too."

When they finished swallowing the wine, he leaned towards them. The *vulnax* appeared fully in his eyes. The women's gazes did not waver.

"*You will serve me*," he said, his voice deepening, turning command-ing. "You will soon be given new clothes to wear. You will leave this place forever and will accompany me to start a new life. You will find this life satisfying in many ways and not unpleasant. You will obey me in all things.

I will open the door now. Smile and tell them how happy and excited you are to be leaving with me. I am your *uncle*. Do you understand? Say it."

"Yes, uncle," they said in unison.

*

Amsterdam

Accompanied by Carter Trevathan, who now took care of his day-to-day affairs, Wilhelm von Kleinfels brought his two female servants back to Amsterdam. He installed the women in a room at a lavish city apartment he rented with several bedrooms and instructed the women on what he expected. He intended to use them as assassins, of course, but also to collect information.

"You will adopt the persona and appearance of nurses. From now on, your names will be Caroline and Rachel *Bristol*. Say the names back to me."

After instructing Carter Trevathan to protect the women, Kleinfels arranged for them to work in a local English-speaking hospital, caring for people in compassionate ways so they would learn how to act in that role as part of their disguise.

Kleinfels began to frequent the expensive hotels in Amsterdam that were used by foreigners for business meetings. He was looking specifically for a Frenchman. In the restaurants and lounges of the business hotels, there were commercial traders from every nation in Europe and other ports in the world, all seeking a portion of the lucrative Dutch trade, which would operate with neutrality during the war certain to be declared by France and England. Standing amid the business men and Dutch trade ministers at night, he listened discreetly to dozens of conversations where voices grew loud as tongues loosened from too much heavy drinking. In a matter of a few days, he narrowed the candidates down to two men. Not long after, another servant was chosen and subverted with the blood-wine ritual.

The Frenchman's name was Alain Marcoux. He was from Calais, a thirty-five-year-old smuggler with trade associates in New France. He had no family and had formerly served in the French metropolitan army before deserting at the end of the last war. He spoke French, English, Dutch, and German fluently without any noticeable accent. Now he served the *vulnax*.

*

Before another week passed, Wilhelm von Kleinfels finally stood in the Ministry of Trade office in Amsterdam, waiting for the clerk to give him the name of an agent. The clerk paged through the heavy tome of ship registrations and finally came to the recent recording of *William's Queen*. The ship was less than two years old and owned by Lord Charles Vander-Meer, son of the current Duke of Brunswick. That fact alone made the man's brow knit with interest.

"Your name again, sir?"

"Wilhelm von Kleinfels."

"Of House Kleinfels?" the clerk asked, penning notes in another ledger.

"The same."

"And your interest in this ship?"

"I understand it transports goods to Boston."

More notes were made. "Indeed. The local agent's name is Wittmann Bootz, Esquire."

"And his address?"

The clerk regarded him more carefully. "This agent also serves the Duke of Brunswick. I am required by law to make a report with your name and interest in this agent to the Duke's secretary."

"Of course. I understand. I wish to ship goods to the Americas and there are very few Dutch ships registered for that. I learned recently that *William's Queen* was one such ship."

The clerk consulted another registry. "I have four more ships designated with this…qualification."

"Then the names of the agents of those ships will be equally acceptable."

The clerk took his quill and penned the name of two ships along with the name and address of their representatives in Amsterdam. He handed the slip of paper to von Kleinfels.

"These names will be better for you, sir, and I will not have to make a report to the Duke's secretary that might cause you, um, unnecessary inconvenience in the future."

"Very considerate of you, sir. Thank you."

It took von Kleinfels only an hour to locate one of the representatives, who for one silver thaler, was very happy to give him the address of Wittmann Bootz.

He left the representative's office and went back to the café where his two men waited for him. He sat down at the outdoor table. His two servants gazed at him intently waiting for their orders.

"His name is Wittmann Bootz. Here is his address." He handed over the piece of paper. "Learn who he is. Then by tomorrow, abduct him without drawing *any* public attention, and bring him to the apartment, bound and gagged. I will convert him to serve me once he is there."

The next day, Carter and Alain lingered outside Wittmann Bootz' office until the man closed and locked his doors as the day came to a close. As was his custom, Wittmann walked down the street to get something to eat before going home. There were several cafés situated along the canal, but as it was the end of the week, he went to a favorite restaurant to take a meal at a table reserved for seven men, friends of his, who would join him once a week for a meal. One of them was a reporter for the shipping news, one worked at the ministry of trade, and the other five were fellow shipping agents. They immediately began to share news concerning trade, piracy, war, and royal intrigue from all over the world, which they had gleaned from discussions with the captains of the ships they represented. Before the food arrived, the table conducted the traditional toasting of each other for another successful week. This infused good cheer further fueled the laugher and gossip they enjoyed so much. Engrossed in their revelry, they barely noticed the two well-dressed men taking a table nearby.

While learning variations in price for certain commodities and cargoes, which the agents made mental notes to record in their books, during a pause, the Ministry of Trade clerk asked Wittmann if a man named Wilhelm von Kleinfels had come by to see him that day.

"Von Kleinfels? No. I do not recall meeting a man by that name."

The clerk described his brief encounter. The two agents the clerk had named as people who might tell Kleinfels Bootz' office address were also sitting at the table. Neither of them admitted Kleinfels had come by. *Interesting.* The clerk kept that to himself.

"This man, Kleinfels, is a Hessian," the clerk continued. "He was arrogant and demanding. Nothing new there. But he also seemed...menacing, which made me nervous. So I did not give him your address. I gathered he would keep searching for you. Probably just as well he did not find you."

"Well, that is unsettling," Bootz replied in mock horror, enjoying the rapt attention of his friends around the table. "A menacing Prussian searching for me? That is almost a nightmare!"

The men laughed and slapped their hands on the table top.

"Let's toast to his failure," one of the trading agents proposed.

"Yes! To the failure of Wilhelm von Kleinfels!"

The congenial friends drank numerous bottles of wine with their sumptuous meal, enough to get them all a little drunk. There followed vigorous arguments over who should pay what portion of the bill. It was friendly bickering with polite insults about each other's character. But enough coin was soon added to the pile in the middle to cover the bill with a generous gratuity to make certain they would be treated with the same deference by the restaurateur the following week.

Wittmann Bootz was swaying back and forth as he stood at the front door to his city apartment. He never saw the approach of the two men. He only felt a sharp pain on his head and then blackness. When he regained consciousness, he was sitting in a table chair with hemp cords bound around his arms and legs. His mouth had a ball-gag in it. A man sat a step away from him in another table chair, gazing at him intently. He had the cruelest eyes of any person he'd ever met in his life. He looked to his left and right and saw two men in suits standing at his side, also gazing at him with intensity. He recalled seeing them at an adjoining table in the restaurant. His left foot felt very heavy and restrained. He looked down and noticed it was inside a large wooden box of some kind that had a tee-handle mechanism attached.

Wittmann Bootz was now very scared.

"*Goedenavond, Meneer Bootz.* I am Wilhelm von Kleinfels. You have heard of me, yes? Enough, I think, to toast to my failure, yes?"

Wittmann shook his head.

Kleinfels smiled. "No? Ahh!" von Kleinfels pointed down at the box. "I think you need a demonstration. This is a device of persuasion." He reached down and gave the handle a half turn.

Bootz' eyes bulged. He shrieked from the intense pain. Drops of saliva sprayed from around the ball gag. After fifteen seconds, Kleinfels backed off the handle a half turn.

"So now, you see? This device has only one purpose. However, there is no need for such pain."

On the small round table next to Kleinfels was a tall urn full of blood-laced wine. He poured a large glass nearly to its brim.

"I am going to have this uncomfortable gag removed. And you are going to drink this glass of wine. Nod once if you agree. *Goed.*" Kleinfels picked up the glass and took a large swallow. "Very tasty. As you can see, the wine is not poisoned. Your gag will be removed. You will not cry out. And you will drink this entire glass in one swallow. If you do not obey, you will be gagged again, and I will tighten the boot for a long time. Do you understand? Are you ready to proceed?"

Bootz nodded vigorously.

The Dutch trading agent would drink four large glasses of wine from the urn before Kleinfels gestured for the man's bindings and the boot to be removed. Then he moved to within inches of Bootz' placid, unflinching expression.

"Tell me everything you know about the ship called *William's Queen.*"

*

The lifestyle von Kleinfels established for the Bristol sisters was more pleasant than anything the two women had ever experienced. He demanded little in return, except absolute obedience. Over the next few weeks as they received other training, he helped them purchase a complete wardrobe that was expensive in selected materials and design, yet austere and plain as befit their purported profession. He took them to restaurants along with Carter and Alain so they could practice social etiquette forgotten during their time in the asylum.

When they completed a step in their education to his satisfaction, he would immediately introduce them to another venue of training.

He had them reside in a brothel at night for a week and had the head mistress instruct them in the bedroom arts and the purification ablutions to use afterwards to prevent getting with child. But they did not service normal customers. Carter Trevathan and Alain Marcoux would lie with the sisters each night, sometimes in pairs, sometimes all together, practicing every variation of sex the mistress could instruct. The sisters found this activity very compelling. When they expressed the wish this practice continue, he explained.

"You will *never* lie with any man without my permission."

They were introduced to some theater players who taught them costuming, make-up, and the art of disguise in appearance, voice, and mannerisms.

When von Kleinfels was satisfied with their level of knowledge in that area, he took them to a special apothecary in Amsterdam and introduced them to another of his *servants*. This training would take the longest.

"Dr. Osterhout, I present to you Caroline and Rachel Bristol. They have nursing training but require education in the use of medicines, and poisons in particular. They require instruction in the methods for delivering such substances discreetly and the results they should anticipate, including education on appropriate antidotes if available. They will need a means to carry such potions on their person, something easily accessible, simple to use, with devices to administer the substances effectively. Educate them in all these things and fashion a pouch in which they can carry a selection of the substances on themselves inconspicuously."

This instruction took two more weeks. When von Kleinfels thought them ready, he had them change into the disguise of refined courtesans. He sent them into the financial district of Amsterdam to linger in hotel foyers, lobbies, and other places where they would be noticed by men who watch for such women.

"Attract the attention of rich patrons from among the merchant class, bankers, government ministers, preferably older men, someone easily seduced. A foreign visitor would be best. Take him somewhere, a hotel of his choosing perhaps, with an offer of your body for his pleasure. Once there, practice delivering the poisons. Start with one that will make him offer truthful information. Test your ability in learning something about the man he does not want you to know, it matters not what this might be, but it should be something he'd rather keep as a secret. Then use a substance that will paralyze him, but keep him awake and aware. Administer a third potion that will cause serious painful discomfort while he remains in a state of paralysis. Observe his reaction and the levels of discomfort and commit this to your memory. Then administer something lethal. You have all this week to educate yourselves. Do this together if doing so is advantageous. Do this as many times as necessary. And most important…this must be done with caution. You must not be recognized afterwards. Change your dress and disguises frequently. And the man's death should be arranged to appear as if he died of a natural cause or from an accident."

The Bristol sisters used von Kleinfels apartment to venture forth at night to prowl for their prey. Carter Trevathan and Alain Marcoux trailed them at a distance for protection if it ever became necessary, which it never did. Six men would die that week. Four of them were visitors to the city from other countries. When their bodies were found by the police, it appeared most had died of heart attacks preceded by some other affliction. One man's body was covered in red welts and blistering hives. Another had choked to death on his own swollen tongue. Another rolled from his bed after violent convulsions and broke his neck on impact with the floor. One man's face was distorted in a painful grimace. He lay naked on a bed soiled with his own waste, eyes wide open, staring up at the ceiling. After a week of such unusual occurrences, the Amsterdam police wondered if there might be a correlation with these peculiar deaths. But the incidents stopped as abruptly as they began. The investigations revealed nothing out of the ordinary. The rooms showed no other signs of violence. One man was seen in the company of a woman going into his rented room. This was not an unusual sight near the canals and the waterfront busy with a hundred visiting ships. The deaths were soon dismissed as natural.

During the week, the Bristol sisters perfected their methods for assassination. Each morning, as they broke their fast, they shared the efficacy of the different poisons and the best techniques to employ. At the end of the week, their training was done.

They were ready.

Von Kleinfels rewarded them with two days of debauchery with Carter and Alain.

*

Ignoring the sounds of ecstasy coming from one of the apartment bedrooms, Wilhelm von Kleinfels sat in a chair in the early evening, gazing up at the night sky out a window that overlooked the canal. During these last few months, as he trained the Bristol sisters, von Kleinfels remained frustrated concerning his primary goal. *William's Queen* had made no port of call on Amsterdam or on Wittmann Bootz. He wanted to be here when the ship's captain made contact so he could personally coerce the man. But this possibility was diminishing by the day. The season for making a crossing of the seas was well underway. A crossing wasted time. He needed to go back to America…soon.

Wilhelm closed his eyes and gripped the golden threaded pouch hanging around his neck. The hissing sound began immediately. A chill crawled up his back to his neck, and then a further sensation of icy fingers slipped over the top of his head. The *vulnax* surged to dominance.

The powers of the *vulnax* had faded over time as the bones slowly disintegrated inside the millennia-old sarcophagus. Left undisturbed, the desiccated skeleton was decaying into dust. With this particle-by-particle decomposition, the corresponding spirit energy of the *vulnax* would disperse and eventually cease to be. But the tomb had been disturbed and its few remaining bone shards sifted into freedom. Carried in the gold-threaded pouch, the bones were now protected from the ruinous erosions of the earth. Even these few bones were still potent enough to do what the *vulnax* intended. Only the *châsse* stood in the way of the *vulnax*'s return to full manifestation.

Yet even succeeding in the destruction of the *châsse* and the shattering of the seals would not be the end of it. His adversaries still labored with fervor in an alliance to gather the knowledge obscured by the ages. They had resealed the long lost bones of Lord Vaelblez by pronouncing the ritual doom, having gleaned enough from the old writings and legends to learn how to invoke the ancient hex. It was only a few verses from an enigmatic tome, but ritualized in the right order, it was enough.

Or so they thought. They had concluded the sealing would be permanent. It was not.

The major's failed attempt to possess the *châsse* in Boston had revealed to his adversaries this vulnerability. They also became aware of the *servants*. Now they were on guard for another attack.

The *vulnax* pondered this new acuity of his adversaries. There was a danger they might discover the truth on how to make his doom permanent. The whore queen, more than the rest, suspected there was a way. She was determined to find it. She was the high priestess the *vulnax* feared most. She carried the mark of all the seals on her body, as did her children, but as yet had not divined the import of these symbols. The *vulnax* had learned the depth of her wisdom while disturbing her dreams. The danger to him was right in front of her, lying like pieces of a puzzle on a table. She did not see how the pieces fit together but persisted in seeking this knowledge. The attempts to confuse her by invading her dreams, to saturate her conscious thoughts with fear, were only partially successful and only further hardened her resolve.

The new plan was two-fold. Break the seals on the *châsse* and kill *all* the descendants to preempt them from forming another alliance.

Given the mental and physical frailty of human beings, these goals could be accomplished without too much difficulty. But there was another problem. The *vulnax* was defied by something completely unexpected. Something never encountered before. The *vulnax* was being challenged by another of its kind. A shaman spirit that possessed not a human but an animal. And it was helping his adversaries. Inexplicably, this spirit did not seek the light. Instead it had entered the realm of shadows at the edge of the darkness. More vexing was the inability of the *vulnax* to perceive this animal spirit until it attacked. But the spirit's weaknesses were the same as the *vulnax*. It could be defeated, trapped eternally in the animal's body if it died suddenly. His servants would kill the raptor when the opportunity presented itself. But he must not underestimate its power.

This revelation reminded the *vulnax* that Wilhelm von Kleinfels' life was also finite. His presence sapped the human's vitality. The essence of the man's life was being shortened. With this thought, the *vulnax* reluctantly withdrew its dominance, leaving Wilhelm with a throbbing headache.

The Hessian let go of the gold-threaded pouch. He awoke with the pressing demand to travel back to the American lands. He rubbed the temples of his forehead to suppress the pain, stared into the distance, and refocused on his preparations. He had arranged passage for himself, the Bristol sisters, and Carter Trevathan on a ship from London to the city of New York. He would start there, adding the men from Philadelphia to his entourage. He suspected the whore queen was somewhere south of Boston. The *châsse* was hidden, beneath ground, but in contact with the earth. He couldn't see it unless he stood in front of it. But he could sense it, like a bell tolling far away in the darkness. It would be found. With the *vulnax* in dominance this time, Wilhelm von Kleinfels intended to kill her and her vermin offspring.

But before going to the American lands, he would first make a brief visit to Paris with Alain Marcoux. He sent Carter back to London with the Bristol sisters to wait for him there.

*

Boston

It had taken Ritter Monheit almost two weeks to reach Boston over the winter roads. He easily found a place to live and began doing common work in stone cutting and repair to establish his purpose and appearance. Starting near the wharves, he visited the taverns every night and cautiously gained information about Lord VanderMeer, but nothing about Lady VanderMeer, except that she had departed to Amsterdam. Thomas Hancock was a close business associate of the VanderMeers. In his dreams, the night messenger would give Monheit suggestions. *Somehow, Lord VanderMeer is communicating with Lady VanderMeer. Find that person.* The stonemason followed Thomas Hancock for a few weeks, but learned nothing from that. The man had not left the city since he'd been there.

Eventually, Ritter would visit a tavern and started a conversation with a person who was a frequent patron. The man was a drunk and obviously seeking someone to buy him a drink. Ritter had met this type before; such people were not very reliable since they would usually lie or say anything that would procure a drink. But he'd become practiced at detecting the lies. To his surprise, this particular man had real information.

"If you want to know more about Lord VanderMeer, you should ask Sentry Cheever over there." He gestured with a thumb towards a chair in a shadowed corner of the room. "He sometimes acts as Lord VanderMeer's bodyguard."

Bodyguard! Ritter did not react to this comment, but he was instantly alert. He could sense this bodyguard's eyes already watching him carefully. He could not walk out right away, but he must give the drunk something plausible to say about him if he was ever asked any questions. Ritter shifted to another topic.

"Let's have another drink. I am a stonemason and am always looking for work. Usually only the upper class homes, like Lord VanderMeer's, have that kind of need. Do you know of any houses needing that type of stonework?"

They would talk another hour until the drunk was completely sotted. Ritter helped the man out of the tavern and carried him with an arm over his shoulder, taking the man to the flimsy shack he occupied in the slum part of town. Killing him would eliminate any possibility of relating their discussion, but his death would only draw more attention to Ritter. He'd bought enough drinks for the man to knock him out until tomorrow. By then he should have forgotten everything.

As Ritter walked back to his own apartment, he felt certain Sentry Cheever was the likely messenger to Lady VanderMeer. The night messenger would later confirm his suspicion. Ritter Monheit would now concentrate on Sentry Cheever's travels.

The possession of Major Wilhelm von Kleinfels subjugated him to the *vulnax*. The enemies of the *vulnax* were his enemies as a consequence. Their adversaries were dispersed across two continents, Europe and North America. These people were formidable, intelligent, and driven, with the strongest and most dangerous of them on the new continent. Lord and Lady VanderMeer were in the English colonies. Philippe and Henri Gerrard served among the soldiers of New France, moving and shifting locations constantly. Archbishop Nicolet resided in Montréal and Quebec and was influential with its rulers. Pierre Dunemoore was in the wilderness country of the American lakes and great rivers. His personal weapon of choice, the war ax, was one of the seals of the hex.

The *vulnax* was fixated on defeating and killing these descendants of the four Great Houses. But in those less frequent periods when Kleinfels' Hessian personality was dominant, as the head of House Kleinfels, this Hessian officer was preoccupied with serving Frederick II. House Kleinfels was solely dependent on the royal patronage of the Prussian sovereign in maintaining its prestige and rank among its peers, including its on-going financial success. Providing some unique value or performing some extraordinary service that would engender greater support from the king was foremost in the ambitions of the Hessian personality. Major von Kleinfels recognized that the title of "liaison to the English military" could be assigned to someone else by a simple wave of the king's hand. When he had the occasion to consider these things, the major plotted ways to demonstrate more value to his sovereign to enhance the prominence of House Kleinfels.

Unfortunately for House Kleinfels, the *vulnax* dominated the major's consciousness as a cavalry officer dominated his horse. It directed his actions and focused his purpose. Still, as long as the major pursued the primary goals of the *vulnax* persistently, the major discovered he could sometimes manipulate the powers of the wraith to advance the fortunes of House Kleinfels. In particular, using suggestions of fear and arguments of persuasion.

So when it happened during the nightmare intrusions on Lady Vander-Meer's memories that a threat to the *vulnax* was revealed, the same incident also revealed an opportunity the major might use to exploit the Prussian sovereign's contempt and distrust of European royalty…especially of its women.

Frederick II of Prussia, or Fredrick the Great, as he was later characterized, was a skilled military leader. He was twenty-eight when he ascended the Prussian throne in 1740, which some said he celebrated by promptly using his armies to seize the territory of Silesia from the Austrians.

The Prussian king was fluent in several languages, highly educated in military history, was irreligious, scorned political marriage as an instrument of hegemony, possessed a violent temper and admired the writings of Niccolò Machiavelli. He was abrupt, not particularly friendly, dismissive of anyone he considered a fool, and he was acutely aware that the royalty of all the other European powers were contemptuous of him. They detested him and tolerated him at best. They would consistently form alliances against him to steal Prussian lands whenever they could, in his opinion.

"Two can play the same game," Frederick would lecture his generals. "And I am better at it!"

Frederick, some said, would hold lavish feasts and raise a glass to toast his neighbors at Christmas dinner and then would invade them by Eastertime. But he was not concerned about his popularity. He didn't like royal fops anyway. Not a single one of them carried a sword in battle, except as an ornament, as near as he could tell.

Prussia was the strongest nation among a menagerie of German nation-states and territories, most of which were once a duchy or an independent protectorate of The Holy Roman Empire, which was now embodied as the Austrian Empire. Prussia had evolved from the agglomeration of these German regions, territories, and lesser kingdoms acquired through treaties or seized in one of the endless wars Prussia fought, most often with Austria, Russia, and France. Prussia in 1755 was spread across the middle of the most disputed lands of Europe from France to Russia. When any of the European royals looked at the map, they could clearly see the remaining territories that the Prussian king intended to absorb next…if they did not find a way to stop him.

Frederick II intended to unify all the German-speaking nation-states into a single contiguous country with undisputed, defensible boundaries. If he could do it by treaty, so be it. But he preferred the ways of a conqueror. "Leaves little to interpretation by the losing party." And he had no problem using his armies to do it when he saw an opportunity. He would prefer to conquer them all at once. But Prussia just wasn't big enough…not yet. He usually avoided obliterating an opposing army when defeating them, because he intended to incorporate the enemy regiments into his new corps once he won the battle. He made sure this knowledge was widely spread, to make his opposition predisposed to surrender.

Prussia had the most disciplined armies in Europe, but his nation-state was smaller in population compared to France, Austria, and Russia, each of which had populations and corresponding armies ten times in size. It could never stand alone in a war without military alliances. Prussia's greatest diplomatic strength resided in the skilled prowess of the soldiers it could provide as mercenaries to the other great powers as part of an alliance.

The European royalty might despise him, but they all wanted Frederick as an ally in times of war. Frederick knew the Austrians would use the next war they fought to try and regain Silesia back from Prussia, a country he absorbed in 1740. And in 1744, he used that pretense to make an alliance with France, and then he invaded Bohemia as well.

On New Year's Day in 1756, Frederick gathered together his Prussian ambassadors and emissaries to expound on his predictions.

"Beware gentlemen, all of the current alliances and treaties of the last ten years will shortly begin to unravel as a result of the costly military battles between France and England in America and the naval engagements and ship seizures of last year. As many of you are aware, Prussia is already involved with new treaty negotiations. This absurd *war of peace* waged between France and England will infect us all. I have no interest in the American lands, or this war between England and France over who will rule

America's feathered aborigines. But the chess pieces of the royal houses in Europe are moving again. I expect our military alliance with France to lapse. I expect them to align with Austria or Russia because of *me*. I will not wait for their collective attack. Prussia will align more closely with the next winner. This time I predict it will be England."

But the coalition uniting against the forty-four-year-old Prussian king was an unpredictable alliance, one he'd not faced before. All of them women.

Empress Maria Theresa of Austria, thirty-nine, the first female ruler of the House of Habsburg in 1740 and the ruler to lose Silesia to Frederick. She had vowed to take it back and was already creating an alliance with Russia to do just that.

Empress Elizabeth of Russia, forty-seven, who seized her throne in 1741 at the age of thirty-two, using a sword and wearing a metal breastplate. She personally led a regiment of Russian troops. She was ready for a fight and had already deployed a large army of Russian troops on Prussia's eastern border, waiting for the next war to begin, even as she negotiated new treaties of peace. She wanted to expand upon Russia's possession of Poland to include everything east of the Vistula River.

Marquise de Pompadour, or Madame de Pompadour, who at twenty-eight became mistress to Louis XV after only one month of "intimate association." She was a commoner. But she convinced Louie to make her a Marquise so she could attend his court as a royal. And to demonstrate the authority of her new royal station, she used a burgeoning friendship with Empress Maria Theresa of Austria in forming an alliance with France against the Prussian king.

Frederick II considered it a waste of male intellect to communicate with women of any station at any conversational level, let alone three women he was supposed to respect, presumably, as his peers. He could not fathom a venue to conduct diplomacy, or negotiate terms of peace, with women. He found it difficult to accept them as qualified heads of state who abided by traditional protocols.

"Beware again, gentlemen. I expect this shrill trio of shit-stained petticoats will collaborate against me through every channel of diplomacy until the next war is over. It will be a miracle to find a way to end this war civilly while they throw cups at us from across the table. When you talk to one of them, you must presume you are talking to them all. Any communiqués or entreaties from any of them should be regarded as a ruse until you can certify otherwise. And certainly nothing sent by the whore-mistress of the French king should be treated seriously. We need to find a reliable, confidential agency of communication with the French king independent of her. And I do not wish to invade Versailles just to facilitate this conversation."

*

London

Thomas Pelham-Holles, 1st Duke of Newcastle, gazed out his second-story window at the peaceful gardens he enjoyed so much. He should be pleased and comfortable with his diplomatic successes of the past several months, which made continued peace on the European mainland a possibility, in spite of continuous conflict with France in America. Yet the result he worked so hard to fashion now seemed almost too perfect.

"What am I not seeing?" he asked himself.

Diplomacy was all the sixty-three-year-old prime minister of England thought about, every day, all the time. He'd been involved with British statesmanship for decades. So missing something did not seem likely. Overlooking something? Perhaps.

He'd succeeded his brother Henry as Prime Minister of England in 1754 after his brother's death. Prior to that, he was the northern secretary of state over European affairs. It was a career filled with the endless pursuit of alliances and full of intrigue, duplicity, and betrayal; things in which he loved to dabble. But his advancement to Prime Minister was just in time for him to be blamed for the disasters of 1755 in the American colonies by his enemies in Parliament; the most vitriolic of them being Lord Pitt.

A formal war with France appeared inevitable now and the previous decade of treaties would quickly outlive their usefulness. He must start over. Now in early 1756, his attention was once again consumed; first, by defending the diminutive protectorate of Hanover, a land squeezed between the Dutch Republic and Denmark, amidst the northern German states. The House of Hanover had given birth to a line of English kings, all but one of them named George. The latest, George II, the prime minister's current sovereign was adamant, like his father had been, about protecting his family's "homeland."

Therefore, the Duke of Newcastle's firmest objective of English diplomacy was never a secret. The prime minister would take great pains and make great sacrifices to protect Hanover. His inclinations were predictable and gave potential treaty partners gratuitous opportunities to take advantage; which they did.

Hanover, the Duke of Newcastle thought with disgust while gazing at the flowers in his garden. *Hanover is a weed England does not need in its garden. And it is on the wrong side of the channel.*

The Duke of Newcastle feared Frederick II the most and was certain the Prussian sovereign had standing plans of invasion for Hanover. The madman could give the order to invade Hanover on any given day out of sheer boredom.

Frederick II could indeed do that, but this would forever make England his enemy. Something he was reportedly loathe to do. In his ultimate objective of uniting the German states, Hanover was last on the list. But Fredrick appeared happy to keep the Prussian threat obvious by stationing a regiment permanently near the Hanover border.

France was the most likely to invade Hanover, after Prussia, more so now considering the conflict in America. At the end of any war there was always territory trading, and France would invade Hanover and use it in a stronger bargaining position with England at treaty time. So Newcastle planned to surround France with enemies. First, he entreated the Dutch Republic. But the Dutch had lost too much militarily and financially in the previous two wars and had already lost their New Amsterdam colony in America. They had no interest in getting involved with another war. They professed neutrality and expected to reap the profits of cross trading during the conflict.

Next, Newcastle entreated Russia to keep an army on Prussia's eastern border. Frederick would then be too preoccupied by the threat of Russia's invasion of East Prussia to invade Hanover. Empress Elizabeth planned to keep an army on the Prussian border in any case, but George II's ridiculous obsession allowed her, some would claim, to extort England for the money to pay her army. A fee of £100,000 in peacetime each year, and £500,000 if there was a war. Of course, that gambit still would not stop France from invading George II's favorite family "estate."

Next, Newcastle allotted Hanover itself £50,000 annually to increase its standing troops by an additional eight thousand men. This was followed by more money for many other minor German principalities to supply mercenaries to be based in Hanover.

These "subsidy treaties" made Lord Pitt and his followers howl in Parliament. Nevertheless, Parliament voted by a two-to-one margin that providing money for mercenaries was preferable to committing English troops.

Even with all these efforts, Hanover still wasn't safe.

Once again, Hanover became the linchpin in England's treaty alliances. The Duke of Newcastle realized with Austria and Russia's burgeoning alliance discussions with France, to protect Hanover, England would have to cohabit with the devil formally.

The Duke of Newcastle couriered a secret diplomatic démarche to Frederick II in December of 1755, containing the outline of a "convention to observe between our two governments going forward."

As Newcastle gazed out at his gardens, he could almost envision Frederick rubbing his hands together with glee at receiving the missive. And the powerful German king lost no time in beginning negotiations.

Frederick II was aware the *whore-mistress* of the French king was aligning with the *fat-sow* Empress of Austria. The confidential overture from England when it came was immediately accepted and the terms negotiated. The Convention of Westminster pledged mutual defense against aggressors, which ironically now made Hanover a Prussian protectorate. Another clause made Prussia neutral in the expanding war between England and France, though it could still provide mercenaries to England. And Parliament was pleased because they did not have to pay any money to Prussia! But an alliance with Prussia cost England its alliance with Austria.

So the Duke of Newcastle had a new alignment with Prussia, a subsidy treaty with Russia that used its army on the border to *threaten* Prussia not to misbehave and provided Hanover with copious layers of security. The neutrality clauses in all the parallel treaties that would ensue among the great powers as a result allowed England and France to continue their *war of peace* in the meantime, which limited even these hostilities.

The previous hundred years were filled with European wars that had been progressively more expensive to the point of bankruptcy. None of the royal houses wanted another land war in Europe. The new treaties provided reasons to remain neutral or defensive for all the parties involved. At least, until they were ready to act against Prussia, which, predictably, they did in the spring of 1757. Newcastle went down the list of countries, name by name, asking himself what plausible reason could provoke any of them into attacking one another. There were always absurd reasons, of course. But neither England nor France wanted a European war when they had a perfectly available, continental-size battlefield far across the ocean in which to conduct uncivilized slaughter.

This Convention of Westminster also mitigated Lord Pitt's endless oratorical challenges in Parliament to the Duke of Newcastle's statesmanship. The Duke was now being praised for his genius.

"So what have I not anticipated?" Newcastle asked himself again.

*

Berlin

House Kleinfels currently carried the authority of the Prussian sovereign to act as a military liaison to the English military and to American provincial authorities, as it did the year before in Boston. This level of responsibility earned House Kleinfels at least *one* meeting each year with Frederick II. That time had come again.

Given the revelations gleaned by the *vulnax* from Lady VanderMeer's dream memories, Major von Kleinfels was not going to waste this opportunity. He arrived promptly as scheduled with the maps and other documents necessary to support his assessment of the expanding war in America. But the Prussian sovereign had already endured endless presentations by other senior officers of the army, all who gave recommendations of support for England. Most of his officers were focused on the greater danger posed to Prussia by the current continental military positions of the armies of France, Austria, Russia, the neutral Dutch Republic, and Sweden to name just a few. The litany of military opinions by generals and ambassadors had gone on for weeks.

Prussia had no territorial possessions in the American lands. Frederick II was interested in the *war of peace* between France and England in the Americas, seeing as it might affect his current alliance treaty with England. To that point, mercenary requirements were important. Major von Kleinfels spent most of his time discussing the level and disposition of selected regiments.

Frederick II quickly became tired at hearing what he already knew to be true. The conspicuous threat of a land war in Europe required that most of Prussia's best troops be kept in reserve at different places inside Prussia. And that England would have the largest mercenary preferences simply because Prussia would be at war with everyone else.

Near the end of an otherwise boring meeting, Major von Kleinfels unexpectedly suggested a *confidential* military alliance with France was possible, through the means of a regiment of carefully selected mercenaries from several different German regions other than Prussia.

"France has the greatest need. This could prove beneficial."

Frederick blinked. He thought he'd misunderstood.

"Did you say France?"

"Yes, Your Majesty. Mercenaries for France. But not from our Prussian regiments, from other German states. Confidentially supplied by Prussia. Therefore still valuable. Mercenary presence in the Americas on both sides of the fighting could offer a consistent source of strategic information on French military intentions and permit a complementary amount of intelligence to provide the English that would earn Prussia other benefits, perhaps."

The words *confidential military alliance* were being uttered by a mere major. It made the Prussian sovereign skeptical to the point of being offended. He had never liked this Hessian very much, particularly his disturbing gaze. But the role of military liaison had been a perfect assignment for him. And he'd been very effective. Now this? He accentuated each word.

"*Perhaps*? *France*? A *confidential military alliance*? Major, you are a military liaison. It is an uncomplicated channel of coordination, one of many, to communicate with our allies. Am I to conclude the execution of these simple duties has suddenly made you feel *privileged*? Enough to discuss military alliances concerning *France*…with me?"

Wilhelm von Kleinfels was not intimidated.

"My apologies, Your Majesty. It was not my intention to presume without good reason. I feel obligated to reveal a new relationship I have developed recently. He is a person directly connected to the King of France. This man and I share a common interest in military history and certain ancient battle sites. The merits of my idea could not be discussed within normal diplomatic channels. The French are greatly outnumbered by the English in America. I have seen this. They have a great need of mercenaries particularly in Louisbourg and Quebec. The Swiss and Neapolitans they now utilize are inferior compared to what we can provide."

Seeing the king's rapt attention, Major von Kleinfels paused respectfully. "Your Majesty, my suggestion is worthless if I give you offense. This is not my intention."

Frederick II was suddenly very interested. What the major was proposing so far was ridiculous, of course, but it was not boring.

"You may continue, Major."

"Thank you, Your Majesty. The opportunity for a meeting with this French minister is real. But I sense my relationship with this man will quickly diminish with the advent of war. Therefore, I wish to make this opportunity useful to you while the opportunity lasts. At present, I am confident he will see me when I make a request. The more important element of this is to establish a confidential way for Prussia to communicate with France through this man. And perhaps more important strategies beyond mercenaries could be exploited with him, if you so wish."

This last sentence was the salient point Major von Kleinfels expected his sovereign to seize upon. He arranged all of his other arguments before saying these words to support this notion: Here was a way to communicate with the French king without the whore-mistress' interference!

In his limited exposure to the major and the reports by his generals, the Prussian king understood Major Wilhelm von Kleinfels to be perceptive and incredibly persuasive. *He is speaking of a confidential back-channel of communication with the French?* He was observing evidence of that persuasiveness right now.

"So who is this *person*, this *minister* you claim to know?"

"He is the current Naval Minister of France."

The sovereign's skepticism increased. "The Naval Minister of France will receive *you*…in confidence, without introduction?"

"Your Majesty, this relationship developed serendipitously. But I assure you, it is real. I thought it important for you to know of it."

The Prussian sovereign's mood vacillated between annoyance and intense interest.

"You now walk on dangerous ground, Major. Soldiers die for less risky transgressions. So I ask you again. You claim you need *no one else* to provide this introduction?"

"I can do this alone, Your Majesty," Kleinfels asserted quietly. "It would do you no good if I could not act in this manner. I will act as the messenger. The message will be yours. And I can bring a reply from him to you directly…if that is your wish. No one else needs to be involved."

The personal alliances this Hessian had formed with the English military were proving very profitable and strategic. But this was different. This was not just liaison. The French Naval Minister controlled deployments of metropolitan troops and the movement of naval ships of the line.

A direct, confidential relationship from me to this French minister of war? Something not known by the whore-mistress? That would be worth exploring…but is it real?

"No one else, you say?" Frederick pressed. "I will not have any of my ambassadors associated with you. They will deny ever knowing you if they are asked. Truly, your name is unknown to them anyway. Your credentials will be your own. And no one else will know about this. As you observed, it is outside normal diplomatic channels."

"Your grace, I recognize I've risked everything just by telling you this today. But my confidence remains firm."

"Officially, I will deny your credentials if you are ever challenged. And should your overtures cause more serious diplomatic problems…you will be executed as a spy. After a very *painful* interrogation, of course. So, is your enthusiasm for this deceit still the same?"

Major Kleinfels bowed politely. "Your Majesty, I only wish to serve you to the best of my ability. I have no doubt of my success."

Frederick stared hard at the major with unforgiving eyes. The major's gaze did not waver.

"If you do this for me, Major, you will tell no one else of this relationship. For it to have value to me, you will speak only to me. You will assure the French Naval Minister of this strict confidentiality. And he must abide by this too. If he refuses, or betrays us, House Kleinfels will be held responsible and forever in disgrace. And you will suffer accordingly."

"I understand, Your Majesty."

"You do? Very well. So how do you intend to convince the French Naval Minister of the authenticity of your credentials and message?"

"I only ask that I carry a paper certifying me as your military liaison bona fides. One with your signature. And that identity would be the truth in any case. Though it might indeed help to legitimize my arguments, as you point out, if my rank were elevated to above that of a major."

Frederick snorted with amusement. "Oh? So now you presume to be promoted to general as well?"

"No, Your Majesty. A general's rank would draw unwanted attention to me. However, the rank of *colonel* on your staff, acting in a confidential capacity, reporting only to you, *that* would provide me the necessary gravitas…in my opinion."

"Is that all you want? House Kleinfels may never get another audience to speak with me again after today…depending on the success or failure of this enterprise."

"Your Majesty, my only ambition is usefulness to you. I will visit the French Naval Minister alone, accompanied only by my aide, Lieutenant-Colonel Marcoux, who will not be in the meeting. He will later deploy to Rochefort after he confidentially recruits the mercenaries for New France. That recruitment will take a few months' time. But from Paris, I will return immediately to Berlin and make my report to you. Subsequent to the success of this mission, I will travel on to London and then to New York and Boston to continue my liaison duties to the English military and American provincial authorities, much as I did last year."

With the Prussian sovereign's confidential approval, *Colonel* Wilhelm von Kleinfels traveled to Paris incognito, accompanied by his aide Lieutenant-Colonel Alain Marcoux. Once at his hotel, he wrote a missive, sealed it with wax with the Prussian stamp, and had it hand couriered by Alain Marcoux to the office of the French Naval Minister. It was a request for an immediate audience, and that he was on a confidential mission from the Prussian sovereign. He included the single page of credentials, the signature authentication as a military liaison from Frederick II.

A day later, wearing civilian attire, Wilhelm von Kleinfels was escorted before the French Naval Minister: Jean-Baptiste de Machault d'Arnouville.

Their subsequent discussion on providing a German mercenary regiment to New France, independent of Prussia, was productive and successful. The strict requirement of unique confidentiality stipulated that Colonel von Kleinfels was the only person who could carry any messages between the two men.

Upon the colonel's return to Berlin, Frederick II complimented the Hessian officer.

"You have pleased me with this service, Colonel. You are now entrusted with its secrecy and the preservation of its continued value to me. I will leave it to you to decide what that requires. I will call upon you again to speak for me with Monsieur de Machault. Should formal war ever be declared between England and France, you will return to Berlin immediately and report back to me."

*

London

George Montagu-Dunk, 2nd Earl of Halifax, was a forty-year-old English statesman hailing from a long line of English statesmen of considerable family influence. He was named President of the Board of Trade of England in 1748 and set about expanding trade with the American colonies. He considered the colonies of America the crown jewels and key to the future economic strength of the British Empire, although not all his contemporaries agreed with this opinion; many considered India more important. He was highly educated, intelligent, and pressed Parliament for the establishment of Nova Scotia, *New Scotland*, the capital Halifax being named after him, as a counterbalance to the growing naval power threat posed by the French fortress port of Louisbourg on Cape Breton Island. Later, using the troops and naval strength gathered at Halifax, England successfully assaulted Fort Beauséjour and one other French fort in 1755, solidifying English possession of the entire Nova Scotia peninsula. This victory subsequently resulted in the French abandonment of the Acadian lands, as Halifax would later describe the forcible displacement of the Acadian peoples.

Carrying on with this successful strategy, that is, to swallow the French possessions in America "one large mouthful at a time," it came as utter surprise to Halifax that despite the positioning of superior numbers of English and Provincial forces on Lake George—and following the "victory" by William Johnson over these same French forces on Lake George in October of 1755—the result of this overwhelming advantage was an apparent impasse.

"An impasse?! Ridiculous! This strategy has already proven to be sound. The American colonies simply need better organization."

Halifax could no longer accept the repeated complaints by Governor William Shirley, which consisted of blaming everyone else for Shirley's failures and then asking London for more authority, more money, and more troops. Halifax first declared to all the provincial governors that New York would now become the main arsenal and center of commerce and supply for the on-going American war effort with France. From New York, England would build new roads with competent engineering and the sturdiness required for the movement and supplies a modern army needed. They would push westward into the wilderness, ultimately to invest Fort Duquesne. They would further use the major watercourses to push north beyond the Hudson River Valley to Lake Champlain and Montréal, eventually spreading east and west on the Saint Lawrence River.

Halifax recognized even with proper supply logistics and objectives, this would be a fruitless, expensive endeavor without effective military leadership. To that point, Halifax needed someone to provide an assessment he could trust, someone to explain why the current war effort was failing, someone he could trust to speak bluntly without fear of political reprisals. The man he chose was Sir Charles Hardy, a navy rear admiral, and a former childhood friend. Hardy was a brilliant admiral and logistician and had proven his worth many times at investing and holding island territories. Halifax convinced King George II to appoint Sir Charles temporarily as the governor of the New York colony.

Sir Charles Hardy was forty-two when, with stoicism and reluctance, he accepted governorship of the New York province at the encouragement of the Earl of Halifax, his friend and benefactor. But he wasn't happy about it.

"Have you forgotten, my Lord Halifax, I am an *admiral* not a *general*! Governing the Americans? You've told me before, they are all rabble. All they do is riot!"

"Charles, if you please,"—Halifax poured more fine port into the crystal goblet Charles clenched in his right hand—"you are brilliant at seeing the truth of complex situations like this. I need your special skills, my friend. Don't worry about solving the American politics. That is an impossible task for men of refinement like us. This assignment as governor will not be permanent, I promise you. And I will reward you with a nice fat naval squadron of men o' war to command if you do this favor for me."

Unknown to Sir Charles' contemporaries in the colonies, the admiral's primary task was to ascertain and explain to Halifax, and the other military authorities in London, why Fort Oswego on Lake Ontario was in danger and learn the reasons why the French could not be displaced from Crown Point on Lake Champlain.

A royal navy admiral abruptly appointed as governor of New York was a surprise to all of the colonial elite, in particular the elite of Massachusetts.

People began to petition Sir Charles as soon as he arrived. He learned quickly there were as many opinions among the colonials as there were trees. The most vocal came from William Shirley, governor of Massachusetts, who was, by default, the designated second-in-command and commander-in-chief of the English war effort in the colonies after General Braddock's death. Hardy found the man full of bluster and with no knowledge of military logistics. Shirley had the enthusiasm to continue the fight but was incompetent in understanding the challenges of waging a progressive war spread across a continental wilderness.

Once Sir Charles had his aides begin the establishment of an arsenal center in the city of New York, he traveled to Albany to attend a council of war called by General Shirley to discuss military objectives for the 1756 campaign.

Even as Sir Charles traveled to Albany, he began to interview and learn from his experienced escort of wilderness men. Travel in this immense wilderness was mostly by the water courses, he was told. There were foot trails, but few roads, most of which were poorly constructed wagon trails, full of ruts and stumps. Any advance by an army would be disputed every step of the way by the ferocious Indian allies of the French who knew the lands intimately, or the equally formidable Canadians. A marching army must expect ambush at all times, and line and volley tactics were worthless in a forest. Nevertheless, these wilderness men were not shy in opinions and ideas on how to defeat the French. In fact, Sir Charles found their competence so replete, he wondered why he was here at all.

"Have you not explained any of this strategy to General Shirley?"

They rolled their eyes. So Sir Hardy shifted the conversation to the logistical requirements for supply. The rangers had excellent answers to his questions. They told Sir Charles whatever he wanted to know while he scribbled it quickly into his journal.

Sir Charles attended the new council of war in Albany in November of 1755 as just another participant, there to review the objectives and strategies with other interested colonial governors and faux generals. He found the assertions made by most of the attendees regarding the objectives of what could be realistically achieved in 1756 to be absurd. The only person among them who made any sense at all was William Johnson. After reminding everyone he was not a general, the King's Indian Agent advocated selecting just one objective, either Fort Niagara or Fort Carillon, to create a strong line of supply to make victory certain. His suggestions were ridiculed and dismissed as not broad enough.

While other loud, nonsensical arguments spewed from the others, the admiral took out his trusted nautical compass and, using the charts and maps supplied for the meeting, he marked and measured off the distances involved between the various places mentioned by the provincials and scratched with ink and quill in his journal and on the maps themselves, denoting the relative importance of the cities, fort locations, rivers, great lakes, and other bodies of water. Fort Duquesne, Fort Niagara, Fort Oswego, the French forts along the Saint Lawrence, Fort Saint Frédéric at Crown Point, Fort Carillon at Ticonderoga, Montréal, Quebec, Louisbourg, Halifax, Fort Beauséjour, the Acadian Lands, Lake Champlain, Lake George, Boston, New York.

It almost seemed a contest. Every person who spoke ran on at length as if to establish the depth of their knowledge. Meanwhile, Sir Charles measured and made calculations. To his astonishment, even allowing for the crude scale of the surveyed maps, the distances encompassed mountainous and heavily forested terrain with endless water crossings and were spread out as much as 1,200 miles east to west, or 800 miles north to south. General Braddock's defeat at Monongahela had vividly demonstrated the disaster that awaited even the most well equipped army in the remote wilderness. Despite superiority in arms and numbers, an army could get swallowed up by the primitive vastness beyond the end of its line of supply, with no place to retreat.

And yet they still argue about the best way to mount offensive campaigns against four different places at the same time, he thought. *The Roman legions at the apex of their power could not do this in a six-month fighting season. And they had bloody paved roads!*

"Ridiculous," he said to himself in conclusion.

The room became silent. Sir Charles looked up to see all others looking at him.

"Admiral?" William Shirley said, emphasizing the word. "You have an opinion on this *land* operation?"

Sir Charles ignored the clumsy insult and nodded.

"I do."

He rose from his seat and carried the map he had inked, smudged, and scratched with his calculations. There was a much larger map hanging on the wall of the room rendering the disputed lands and territories of the English colonies and New France from Newfoundland, south to Spanish Saint Augustine, west to New Orleans, north to Fort Michilimackinac, and east to Quebec. The scale was immense.

"Gentlemen, what happened last year? General Braddock was soundly defeated by a primitive enemy with weaker numbers deep in the wilderness. General Johnson successfully fought the French to a draw, which forced them to retreat. I know it was claimed to be our victory, but I think we know better. It is just good luck for us that the French forgot to bring their cannon to this battle. Nevertheless, it was a bloody good fight. And well fought. No offense to you, sir."

"None taken, Admiral." William Johnson almost smiled at what he knew to be true. "The only victory England can claim this past year is the subjugation of the Acadian lands and the defeat of the French at Fort Beauséjour and Fort Gaspareaux. Let's examine that victory." He used his compass as a pointer. "This peninsular area is surrounded almost completely by water. We had a provincial city, Boston, ready to support the supply effort. We had dominant naval forces to bring to bear at our discretion, regardless of the threat from Louisbourg, whose naval power played no part in this. Fortress Halifax is—what?—only two hundred miles away. Less than ten days of marching and even less by sea. We had veteran regulars and provincial troops familiar with the lands and terrain, several lines of supply by land or sea. And in the end, the French surrendered with almost no fighting. My compliments to you, Colonel Monckton. But was there ever any doubt in your mind as to the outcome?"

"No, sir."

"Why?"

"I had logistical superiority and the French knew it."

He thrust his compass as a pointer at Colonel Monckton for emphasis.

"Yes! Exactly! Well said, Colonel! *Logistical superiority*, gentlemen. A phrase worth repeating. Fort Beauséjour had a garrison. How many troops were there? Could they hold out against a siege? Is the fighting season long enough? Do they have troops or ships available to come to their aid? What is the quantity of stores necessary to support our march? The ordinance, the provisions, the wagons, the hospitals? By what road and or water courses do we travel? Do we *control* these lines of supply? And if we win…what are the logistic requirements necessary to *hold* what we've won so dearly and *maintain* our garrison through the winter months. If we make our plan based upon gleaning such information, our conclusions will be correct. Then all we need is the proper *leadership*. Questions?"

He paused and looked around.

The room was silent. This admiral was not one to challenge lightly.

"Then I will expound about you further, Colonel Monckton. You were a leader with the military experience determined to do this and who possessed the common sense necessary to evaluate and establish the *logistics* required to win! This is the order of things we should be talking about here today."

Sir Charles walked back around the table and stood behind his chair.

"Gentlemen, the fighting season starts in just a few months. I have not heard any evidence presented thus far on how the colonies will mount *one* offensive…let alone *four*! Look at your map." He pointed. "Set aside the logistical superiority we brought against Fort Beauséjour, which is an example of good planning performed over three years bolstered by an already-built fortress port of Halifax. What did you accomplish in the last fighting season? You built a fort north of this city, Albany, erected in support of maintaining a military position to hold the southernmost shore of Lake George. This fort, William Henry, is intended to provide protection for our larger ambition. It is to be the embarkation fortification to launch forces to lay siege to the forts at Crown Point. Fort William-Henry is sixty miles north of Albany and twelve miles north of the Hudson River. The fort is at a place the French still claim as their own by treaty and formal possession. That is what we accomplished this year. And Fort William-Henry was, and still is, a position easily attacked by the French who have been in command of these lakes and lands for over a century and more.

"And, gentlemen, the French will attack you at Lake George again, right there, at Fort William-Henry. Why? Because they possess the logistical superiority to do so. You surprised them last time with all the troops you brought to bear. I have been fighting the French for twenty-five years. As we English learn, the French learn as well from mistakes. The only defense for your forts at Lake George is the ridiculous vulnerability of Fort Oswego! They will likely decide to invest that one first." He picked up his compass and pointed at the large map again. "The French will be coming for Fort Oswego right now, just as soon as the snow melts. That is what I would do. They can approach that fort by water or land, both of which they control. A war over lands this vast will always be won by logistics. Though it is mere inches on a map, you can only move as far as your supply lines will tolerate. That is a fact. No genius here. So it has been for armies for a thousand years."

"The vulnerability of Fort Oswego is well understood by the people in this room, *Admiral*." William Shirley's abrupt interruption was officious. "I've spent much time there. Despite what you contend, we have supplied and will defend it!"

"Oh? Defend it? Is that so? Good for you, General. But I thought this planning is for attacking...which one is it? Fort Frontenac in 1756, using Fort Oswego as the embarkation point. So I presume that attack is off the table now? And I do not see that you are ready to lay siege to Fort Carillon either, unless you march to command the water and trails surrounding Lake George and parts of Lake Champlain." He looked over at William Johnson. "Your transport boats were sunk in the last battle, is that not correct? So that attack is off the table too? Yes? No? Well maybe you could plan to invest and occupy the lands around Lake George, which would require another fort. And that would indeed be an accomplishment. Of course, the French would certainly attack you even as you build it. But unless you change your focus, an unplanned attack on Fort Carillon or at Crown Point would be reckless. You would be doing the French a favor if you do that."

"Is that all?"

Sir Charles Hardy spun on his heels and faced William Shirley.

"No, Governor, that is not all. If you are determined to defend and maintain Fort Oswego, and based upon all the claims you've made in writing about losing it if England doesn't do more to help you, then I suggest *you* safeguard *your* lines of supply. By my measure, Oswego is three times as far as the forts on Lake George. If I were the French commander opposing you, I would cut those well-known lines of supply running through the heart of French territory this winter and starve the unfortunate garrison stationed at Oswego until they surrender, giving me a victory without firing a shot. The garrison will likely be so weakened by disease that they would become a health threat to the French army when they attack."

General Shirley spoke drolly: "We have a plan, *Admiral*. We've been delivering supplies to Fort Oswego routinely for years, Admiral. Most of us have lived here for a decade or more. I think we, better than you, appreciate the distances involved."

"Well then, Governor Shirley, I will close my opinion on your land operation with this: The concept of leading an army from the front and yelling the word *charge*, while very commendable for the leader, and sometimes can win a battle, usually does not win a war. But I expect with your superior military knowledge you already know that. So I will remain silent now and listen to other opinions."

The admiral took his seat.

No other comments were made on the merits of what they just learned. Instead, the names of several cities and forts were submitted loudly for consideration. Fort Niagara was one of them. The arguing renewed as if Sir Charles' opinion was something they readily understood.

But a few of the men sat quietly embarrassed, staring straight ahead or down at the table. Among them, Sir William Johnson, Lieutenant-Colonel John Bradstreet, and Lieutenant-Colonel Robert Monckton.

*

Later the same day, the admiral penned a letter to Lord Halifax in London, relating his conclusions, providing anecdotal information about the chaos he observed.

> *This situation is leaderless. William Shirley expounds about subjects he knows nothing about. There are plenty of military targets to choose. But the battlefield is as large as all Europe! And very primitive. We need someone with a sound knowledge of logistics who can apply that knowledge to a military strategy.*
>
> *And the good news, you ask?*

Augmented by the provincial troops, we will outnumber the French by four to one. Maybe more. More than enough to win a land war. And there is no opposing army of any size to maneuver against us. The positions of French strength are fixed, very few, and very well known. I can see three lines of advance. If Louisbourg is taken, the supplies from the east are blockaded, the capture of Quebec will follow within two years at most, though maybe less, if this mess is properly managed. Siege and investing Fort Niagara will close the French western supply lines. The other course is Crown Point. But with an army properly supplied and led, Fort Carillon will fall to a siege once it is isolated. Fort Frederick will likely be abandoned outright if Carillon falls. After that, we move straight north towards Montréal.

I will help the man you choose get the logistical problems defined and fixed. Then I hope to drink some more of that fine port you served to me and discuss the angel-winged beauty of a squadron of naval ships of the line.

CHAPTER 4
MONTRÉAL
FEBRUARY 1756
Mending

"**H**enri," Carmen said softly. "Good morning, Henri."

Lying with an arm half over his head, Henri Gerrard groaned his reluctance.

Carmen smiled and stroked his blond hair. "Henri. You should get up now. I am going to work."

Henri extended his arms towards her. Carmen giggled and sat on the edge of the bed. His hands immediately began to search for ways inside her clothes. She smiled and stood up out of reach.

"No. No. Not now. I must go to work."

"Kiss?"

Carmen leaned down and kissed him tenderly. His hands groped her breasts. She giggled and stood again.

"Bring me something for lunch. Come to the shop later."

Henri sat up and rubbed his eyes. "All right."

Carmen left out the apartment side door to make the short walk down the outer stairs to the cobbler shop directly below on the ground floor. Its front door faced the street of Rue Notre-Dame in upper town Montréal.

Henri stood and stretched his arms, back, and legs in the cold air of the room. He immediately began his daily regimen, a series of exercises that proceeded without stopping, as Sentry Cheever had taught him to do. Thirty minutes later, he finished the last set of handstand push-ups and rested, breathing heavily, covered in sweat. After catching his breath, he took up his cutlass and dirk and went into the living room, the second of three rooms in the apartment, the third room being the *cuisine*. He pushed back the couch and chair to make more room and started the cut, parry, chop, and slashing exercises with the two weapons, moving them in a fast pattern until the whirring sound became almost a buzz.

Ten minutes later, he finished with his regimen and retrieved the pot of hot water Carmen had left on the stove in the *cuisine* and carried it into the bedroom to fill the washing basin. Using a sponge, he bathed his naked body with soap and water until he felt clean. He put on the gray and brown trousers and shirt of a common laborer, gray socks, and the shiny, supple black leather boots Carmen had made for him.

In the *cuisine*, he found a plate of food sitting on the warming side of the stove. It was an omelet of meat and cheese, two biscuits, and butter and honey. There was water to drink.

Henri ate slowly trying to remember if he dreamed the night before, but he had not. He felt more rested than usual after a night of dreamless sleep, which was usually the case when he stayed with Carmen.

His worst nightmares occurred at the home of Corrinne's loyal chamberlain, Denis. He and his wife, Mary, had graciously given him shelter and a room to stay in after he returned from the battles on Lac du Saint-Sacrament. He'd awakened screaming almost every night for two weeks, usually from the dreaded visions of Tessier, a man he knew for only an hour before his body was shredded by the grapeshot from English cannons. From one explosion, Tessier had been pinned to a tree by his own bayonet, like a bug in a box. Every blast of the cannon after that ablated pieces of Tessier's body until only the bayonet was left. Henri was hiding for cover behind a tree just a few paces away but directly in front of Tessier. It was impossible to get away without getting killed, impossible not to see each horrible mutilation. In his dreams, Tessier screamed in pain with every shot. Henri was powerless to help him. When the nightmares occurred, Mary would rush to his bedside and hold him, quivering in her arms, until he sobbed away the terrible images.

Henri paid the chamberlain a silver piece for his room and food each week. They were very kind to him. Mary doted on him as if he were her son, stroking his hair, fussing over him whenever she thought he was sick, which he wasn't. The attention felt good. The food was good. The quiet evenings he spent reading books from the chamberlain's small library was a salve to his anguished conscience and his feelings of guilt.

In the third week after his return to Montréal, he began walking the lower town on Rue Saint-Paul, finding simple work with daily wages, moving heavy crates and bales in the warehouses, unloading furs from the trickle of trade wagons or sleds still coming down the Lachine trail. The Dunemoore warehouses were owned by The Grand Company, a monopoly managed by Intendant Bigôt. Lady Corrinne's chief clerk, Paulus Legate, was still there, the only man left from the original dozen company employees. He was always happy to see Henri and would give him work to do. They would take lunch together and converse about news, or reminisce about Pierre Dunemoore's comical anger. Henri did not say much about Philippe and Corrinne, except to say they were living happily and quietly down in the colonies. The winter was harshly cold that year, the snows heavy. There was not much military activity. The clerk expected that would change by late spring when the new army commander was expected to arrive in the first wave of the ships from France.

Henri had met Carmen just after Christmas, when his only pair of winter moccasins had frayed into holes. He was surprised to see a friendly, smiling girl in a cobbler's apron when he entered the shop.

"You are the cobbler?"

"Yes."

Carmen was a twenty-year-old widow with curly brown hair, brown eyes, and an ample figure. Her much older husband had been killed a year earlier by drunken voyageurs as he left his cobbler shop late one night. It was bizarrely tragic. He was only five steps from the front door of the shop to the stairs leading up to the apartment when two voyageurs, after leaving a tavern, suddenly began brawling right in front of the cobbler. Knives were drawn, and, in the darkness, the cobbler was stabbed by accident. He lay there bleeding to death. An hour passed before Carmen came looking for him. It was too late. She never learned who killed him. Fortunately, Carmen had helped her husband in his work and could fashion shoes and boots that were his equal in quality. After his death, she was able to run the shop on her own. But she lived by herself and was lonely.

Henri explained he needed new footwear. Carmen gave him temporary shoes to wear and took measurements of his feet for new and better winter boots. She had very strong hands from her work. The way she moved her fingers and massaged his feet while taking the measurements for the boots felt surprisingly wonderful.

"That feels good," he told her. "I had no idea my feet hurt so much."

Carmen smiled at him. "Sit for a minute, and I will massage them further."

She told him about her dead husband while she massaged his feet and said it would only take two days to create the new boots and what they would cost.

When Henri came back two days later, he slipped on fur-lined boots that fit perfectly, but then she slipped them off soon after to rub his feet. Henri closed his eyes. Carmen saw his face was young, but he had the solemn unhappy look of a person aged prematurely by the experiences of war. Soon she was rubbing his legs and not much longer after that she locked up her shop and took Henri by the hand. He followed her to the apartment upstairs.

Women have ways of mending men that God himself ordained. Reynaud Sager—the bateau man Henri traveled with on the Saint John River the year before—had told him that.

Henri found solace in Carmen's arms beyond just the lovemaking. Respectful of the generosity of Denis and Mary, he stayed with Carmen only a few nights a week. They could see his mood improving steadily and were happy for him. The new relationship went on a few months.

Today was Wednesday. Henri usually had afternoon visits with Archbishop Nicolet on Wednesdays where they would discuss a variety of things, the war, Corrinne and Philippe, Henri's nightmares, the future of New France…and of course, the demon.

After spending a few hours that morning looking unsuccessfully for work on Rue Saint-Paul, Henri drifted down to the market area of the city. There was little in the way of farm produce, a few animals, milk, butter, and cheese, some butchers selling chops and loins, the bakers selling bread with its intoxicating aromas. Henri's mouth watered immediately. He went to those stalls, deciding he would buy a hand-sized block of cheese, a small bottle of wine, a large baguette, and a funnel of puffy sugar biscuits he knew Carmen liked. He carefully placed it all in the canvas food sack he'd brought with him.

"Corporal Gerrard."

Henri spun around, saw who it was, and smiled. He came to attention and saluted Major Péan.

"Sir!"

The major was smartly attired in a clean uniform of the Troupes de la Marine. Over his white and gray uniform with dark blue collar and lapel facings, he now wore a very handsome matching cloak with a fur collar. Standing next to him was Color Sergeant Cabrelle.

"I knew I'd find you in the marketplace one of these days. I see you managed not to starve."

"Yes, sir. I found a place to stay, and I perform daily wage work along Rue Saint-Paul."

"I like your boots," Major Péan observed. "Sturdy and shiny. The cobbler must like you."

"I…I bought them from a street vendor when my moccasins wore out."

"Good. You will soon have use for them. Spring is coming. You know what that means."

"I plan to go overland on the river road to Quebec to see my mother."

Major Péan's friendly expression instantly turned grave. "Don't go to Quebec, Henri. When Intendant Bigôt learns you are there, and he will learn of it, trust me, he will arrest you and jail you in the bastille again. Only this time, there will be no one in Quebec to help you."

Henri frowned. "Then maybe I will pay for my mother to travel up the road to see me."

"You better do that soon. The militia will be called again by the end of the month."

"Why?"

Major Péan snorted. "To go on some muddy, freezing, half-starved, thoroughly disgusting march to fight the English Americans somewhere… maybe Fort Oswego. Who knows? But there is still time for you to become part of the Troupes de la Marine."

Henri recalled Major Péan's extreme dislike of the wilderness. "Because your marines *never* march anywhere?"

"Well, they won't until the new military commander arrives here. That should be in April or May. After that, the war begins anew."

"I'll think about it, Major."

"Don't think too long. Once the militia is called up, you'll be going somewhere. Where's that deadly little cutlass you like to carry?"

Henri's right hand instinctively reached for his sword but clasped at air. He'd forgotten to strap it across his back for the first time since arriving in Montréal. That had never happened before. Knowing it was gone, he felt naked without it. His time with Carmen had made him lower his guard. But he couldn't let them know about her.

"I don't need it," Henri said quickly. "This is Montréal. I have you and the gendarmerie to protect me."

Major Péan laughed. "Protect you? Yes, that's what we do. Well, it's good to see you again, Corporal. The sergeant and I will wait for you in our comfortable barracks."

Color Sergeant Cabrelle slapped Henri on the back in a friendly good-bye as they walked away.

Henri hurried back to the apartment to strap on his sword and dirk and then went down to the cobbler shop. He loved the redolent smell of the shop, the stimulating, healthy aromas of cut leather and polishing ointments. The bell on the door rang as he entered. Carmen was pulling on a long hand-lever that pushed a cording needle though a thick boot sole.

"I brought some food from the market."

"Oh, good." Carmen washed her hands in a basin. "Let's eat it in the apartment."

She locked up the shop.

Later, after they ate, Carmen took Henri to bed for a few hours until they were both well mended.

"Are you going home today?"

"*Oui*, for a day or two. They know where I am, but Mary worries about me anyway."

"Some soldiers came to the store looking for you."

Damn! They already know, Henri thought. "That was Major Péan. I saw him in the market."

"What did they want?" she asked guardedly.

"The militia will be called up by the end of the month."

"You will have to go?"

"Yes. But I don't know where or for how long."

Carmen grew quiet. She had known this day would come again. Henri was years younger than she, that was true. But she did not care what other people thought. He was gentle and kind with her. He made her laugh, unlike most of the men she'd known in her life. Some nights, he called out the name Anamosa in his sleep, so she knew there was another woman in his life. Probably in Quebec, she suspected. She liked Henri. Even if he went with the militia to fight, he would come home to Montréal first when he returned. Carmen hoped to keep him with her for as long as possible. Maybe with enough encouragement, he would forget about this other woman, this *Anamosa*.

"I don't think I will go back to work today," Carmen said suddenly. Her fingers slipped to his groin. She massaged him to hardness. "Let's see how many times we can do this in one afternoon."

Henri wondered at that statement. "You mean this can happen without end?"

Carmen kissed him.

"Well, it can for women. Men, maybe not as much. But with you, there are many ways of encouragement." She began kissing down his chest and stomach...and lower.

*

Fort Johnson

Sir William Johnson read once again the proclamation he'd received from King George II. He had read it almost every day since it was delivered to him. He'd been awarded a baronetcy for life for his military victory at Lake George. He still found it unbelievable that a royal he never met, the King no less, had honored him with a noble rank he had neither expected nor sought. He didn't feel any different, certainly not noble. But now that he had a title, people treated him differently, more respectfully. He certainly liked that. And it came with the astonishing award of five thousand pounds, permanent rank as a colonel in the army with pay, and sole agent supervisor to the Iroquois and the other northern tribes. All of this dischargeable only by the express order of the King himself. He should feel privileged and secure. Yet each day that he surveyed where he lived and the dangers imposed by war, his sense of security did not increase. Still, it was better than not having a baronetcy.

"Sir William Johnson," he said the words softly to himself while sipping tea, sitting in his favorite chair in his library. "I wonder what mother would have thought of me."

It had been an eventful week. The murderous atrocities perpetrated by the Delaware and Shawnee, along with multiple other tribes, including some of the Iroquois, had reached levels of barbarism never seen before, according to the Albany newspapers. When you personally knew, the way Johnson did, the hideous tortures these people could contrive, "barbarism never seen before" was saying a lot. The Delaware were rampaging across Pennsylvania, Maryland, and Virginia killing, scalping, burning, and torturing English settlers in ways so perverse, even the unborn were not spared. It was an elemental part of their nature, Johnson would explain lamely, though he did not understand it himself.

He tried to rationalize it as a primal reaction to the ferocious decimation these peoples suffered from disease alone; nearly seventy-five percent of Indian villages had been destroyed since the arrival of the white man. No one wanted to hear his explanation let alone accept it as a justification for the horrible mutilations. He considered himself a man of history, and there was plenty of history among the European tribes going back a thousand years or more where barbarous behavior was commonplace. Nevertheless, nothing like this had been seen since the discovery of America more than two centuries ago. People all over the colonies were outraged, filled with vitriolic and rancorous sentiments of revenge, seeding emotions he knew would last a long time into the future.

The scathing protests from the governors demanded the King's Indian Agent get the savages to stop. Johnson knew that would not be easy. The English settlements had encroached further and further on Indian lands without obtaining permission. Their anger seethed and was withheld begrudgingly because of the purported dominance of the English military. That reputation of English dominance was gone, smashed by General Braddock's defeat on the Monongahela River at Fort Duquesne. The power now resided with the French. After their victory, the French encouraged the Indians to kill the white man in any manner they chose and take back their lands. They happily complied, hoping to rid their lands of these disease-carrying white vermin forever.

Johnson convened an endless series of councils with representatives from every tribe to convince them it was still in their best interest to ally themselves with the English and cease this raiding. A few of them listened; the great majority did not. The sessions in the roundhouse went on for weeks as usual. At night, they would celebrate, feasting on Johnson's livestock and barrel after barrel of his liquor.

The day before, another contingent of Mohawk arrived. Among them was their half-breed messenger, Peter Blue Jacket. Peter relayed his interesting conversation with Philippe Gerrard at Fort Duquesne, confirming in Sir William's mind that Philippe was indeed the man that had rescued the English lieutenant at Monongahela. But the bigger surprise was a packet of letters Peter had brought to him. *What's this? The Indians are now delivering letters?* He mused. One was addressed to himself. One addressed to a C. Chanaye. And a third addressed to Thomas Hancock. They were heavily sealed with wax all around the edges to protect them from moisture damage. He considered this unexpected correspondence so exciting he kept them securely hidden until a comfortable interlude presented itself, so he could read them in his library, when he would not be bothered by anyone.

Today was that day. He intended to open and read them all regardless of to whom they were addressed, but he started with the one that bore his name.

To my good friend,

I hope this missive finds you in good health. I received word before Christmas about your victory on Lake George, as you now call it. I would say it did not surprise me when I learned the tactics employed. Much as you may have not been surprised to hear about Monongahela. Unfortunately, my effort to restrain the "children" from their reprehensible behavior afterwards was too weak and too late. I managed to protect an English officer, but any of the other wounded were treated cruelly. It has only gotten worse since then, as we feared it would. I also learned of your actions that prevented a certain general from being "eaten." I will try and return that favor if ever the circumstances permit.

Peter Blue Jacket is a spy for the Iroquois as well as their messenger, which you may know already. He has little allegiance to white men. But I have known him for many years. He keeps his word. That quality alone is good enough for me to call him a friend. I never considered using him to deliver missives before, and he does this as a favor to me. I hope this will not cost me too dearly in return for the favor he will surely ask of me one day.

I expect you've learned of my travails with the Oneida. I am uncertain how I managed to survive that, but I took a chance and it worked.

With great respect, I ask your indulgence to deliver the other two letters to Thomas Hancock. I understand you will have to read them both, but please seal them again to protect the writing. The one to C. Chanaye is to my wife. Thomas Hancock does not know of this particular fact, and it is better he does not for her sake. But he will find a way to get the letter delivered. I just wanted to tell her I was alive and to let her know I love her. What else can one say during a war?

I truly hope when this terrible slaughter is over I can share a dinner with you again. Honest conversation seems to be a rare occurrence in retrospect, almost as rare as an eclipse.

Until that time, I will remain your friend,

And humble servant,
Snow Hair

Johnson opened the letter addressed to Hancock and found the writing to be straightforward, just the simple request to deliver the third letter to Lord VanderMeer.

She's probably a servant of Lord VanderMeer, he surmised. Johnson gently tapped the letter to C. Chanaye on his palm. *He gave me permission to open it*, he argued. Still, he decided the words of love by another man to his wife did not need to be inspected by someone of so coarse a nature as himself.

"I am a royal after all," he said pompously, mockingly. "A distinguished man of *honor*."

Johnson took sealing wax and closed the edges of the letter to Hancock as before. He took a larger sheet of precious paper and wrapped it around the two letters, sealing it liberally with wax again. Then addressed the packet to Thomas Hancock. He added that to the mail pouch that would be delivered by rider to Boston today. He could have rider-couriered mail sent out as often as he wanted, one of the few advantages of being a major-general.

CHAPTER 5
ALLEGHENY WILDERNESS
MARCH 1756
Wanderers Far From Home

Philippe Gerrard led his small contingent of *coureurs de bois* marksmen north of the Delaware Indian stronghold of Attiqué, a stockade village situated on the banks of the Allegheny River, forty miles north of Fort Duquesne. When he reached the Cowanshannock Creek tributary, he went east. There had been rumors of English provincials making revenge raids in this area, but Philippe had not seen any evidence of this so far. They traveled up the tributary in three war canoes for a few days until the river narrowed and shallowed. Wanting to avoid tearing holes in the canoes, they pulled them out of the water, hid them among the trees, and started overland.

This was a remote, rugged wilderness of hills and valleys. They did not see much of anything out here, except for a few burnt out farms and cabins. As night fell each day, one of them would climb the nearest hill and gaze around the surrounding landscape for signs of campfires, but there were none. This uneven terrain was disputed between the French and English, like everywhere else. But if anyone ever *owned* this land, it was the Delaware tribe. They had been forced westward by the English settlers for decades, settlers protected by the Iroquois League and reinforced by a trading treaty with the English. But that was before the Battle of Monongahela. After their punishing defeat, the English were considered weak, without any real power. The French were now dominant. Encouraged by Captain Dumas at Fort Duquesne, the Delaware, Shawnee, and many other tribes were killing and massacring English settlers all across the Virginia and Pennsylvania wilderness in whatever manner they chose.

Traveling with Philippe was Chittaqua's son, Chesanin, along with six other men hand-selected from his small troop. He found eight to be the perfect number for these exploratory forays. They were all highly skilled, experienced *coureurs de bois*, two of them of mixed blood. After days of searching but finding nothing important, Philippe decided it was time to turn around. They had not walked a mile in return when they heard the unmistakable sounds of musket fire in the distance further east; it was sounds of battle.

"Let's find out what that is," he told them.

The troop began moving towards the sound. Philippe knew there should be no one else moving about out here…not the French army or *coureurs de bois* anyway. They walked about a mile as the firing became intermittent. The intensity of the fighting was lessening. Someone was winning. When the forest began to thin, Philippe lifted his hand in a silent command. The *coureurs de bois* automatically spread out to Philippe's left and right. They were very close to where the fighting was taking place. The forest abruptly ended. They stayed in the trees.

They were at the edge of a crop field that had been recently plowed. A few short stalks of corn sprouted in the furrows. Philippe pulled a small telescope from his pack. He saw a group of four houses and other out-buildings. Settlers. A small village. Intentionally gathered together in their farming efforts for strength against attack. Two of the smaller houses were burning. The largest was in the center. It had sturdy log walls, slotted with cross-shaped loopholes for muskets instead of windows. They were under attack by the Delaware. And the settlers were losing. A year ago, this type of attack would be unthinkable. But the Delaware had grown more daring the further east they raided when they encountered no opposition. Philippe knew the chief of this Delaware tribe, a man called Handsome Robert by the English. Now this same man had turned against his former ally. He was cruel, merciless, and hated the white settlers.

Philippe spotted some movement in the fields to his right. A boy and a girl were sprinting down the furrows coming directly towards them. The boy was bigger and was carrying a small backpack.

Why are they coming this way? They cannot possibly see us.

Then he saw the two Delaware warriors pursuing them. They would either kill these children outright or take them captive for torture, most likely the latter, such was Handsome Robert's reputation. The chief was proud of his cruelty and would brag to Captain Dumas at Fort Duquesne of the hideous ways he'd tortured captives. Philippe was sick of seeing this slaughter and mutilation everywhere he went.

Not this time, he decided.

"When they come into the trees, take hold of these children. Cover their mouths so they make no noise. These Delaware are dead. No muskets. Use knives or tomahawks."

Philippe's men would obey his orders without question. Minutes later, the two breathless, terrified children rushed into the trees to find themselves immediately wrestled to the ground, their mouths covered by strong hands. They began to squeal.

"Quiet!" Philippe told them harshly in English. They obeyed.

The troop moved quickly, retreating further into the trees, and set their ambush. Philippe looked at Chesanin and hand signaled that he would take the second brave, Chesanin should take the first.

The Delaware braves rushed into the trees following the easy trail of the children. One carried a war club, the other a tomahawk. Philippe and Chesanin lunged from both sides of the trail, slamming tomahawks and skinning knives into the heads and abdomens of the warriors. The kill was quick.

Philippe looked around and pointed at a large tree. "That one," he said.

The *coureurs de bois* lashed the two bodies upright against the trunk. From his pack, Philippe withdrew an Erigh hex sign, the type Chittaqua used to make: a loop of sapling tied in a circle. He scalped the Indians and tied the bloody scalps to the hex along with a white eagle feather, the tip of which was dyed red. He hung it with a broad loop of cord around their heads. He chopped off their hands with his tomahawk to deny them the ability to hunt in the afterlife. It was a warning sign. If the Delaware pursued, they would suffer the same fate. He'd used this hex a few times to good effect in forestalling the savagery. Unfortunately, it was likely to dissuade them for only a week. Their bloodlust was too compelling, the settlers too defenseless, and the plunder too rich to ignore.

The *coureurs de bois* retreated overland back to their war canoes hidden on the riverbank. The two children rode with Chesanin and Philippe in the lead canoe. Philippe learned their names were Joshua and Leah Carlisle and were twelve and thirteen years old. They were scared and crying.

"You will not be harmed," he told them in English. "I will take you to a place where you will be safe."

They proceeded down the river, not stopping when darkness fell, using the moon for what little light they needed to navigate. When they reached the Allegheny, they turned right and proceeded upriver to Fort Machault, a two-day journey of hard paddling.

They stopped to camp and rest for a few hours when the moon set on the second night. From the children, Philippe learned there were thirty-two men, women, and children in the main fighting house of the village. Their father helped them escape through a tunnel beneath the main house and told them to head for the Cowanshannock Creek.

"We were supposed to go upriver," Joshua said. "There are other villages that way, my father said."

Philippe searched their pack and found two, maybe three days' worth of food, a water skin, a few snares, and two wilderness knives.

"You would have died," he told them firmly. "There is no one left alive out there. You're lucky you met me."

"What's going to happen to us?"

"I will take you to Fort Machault. The commandant will decide where you should go next."

"Will he hurt us?" Leah asked.

"No. Of course not. But you cannot wander around out here. The Indians are raiding everywhere."

"What about my father?" Joshua asked.

Philippe did not want to say anything further to disquiet the youths. "Your father knew you would be safer at another place."

"He won't know where we are."

"The French and English trade lists of captive names and their locations all the time. We'll make sure your names are added to the list. So don't worry, he will be told. This is what happens in a war. Now go to sleep. We will be traveling again before sunrise."

The next morning, the three war canoes beached on the bank near Fort Machault. Dozens of *coureurs de bois* and Indians camped around the fort exterior began hailing and welcoming the troop. Philippe knew many of them.

"Stay close to me," he told the children. He gestured for Chesanin to follow him. He told the others they would camp here for a few days. The men were happy to hear this.

The sentries near the commandant's quarters saluted as he approached. "Welcome back, Captain Gerrard. Prisoners?"

Philippe shook his head and marched inside the fort's center keep. More men waved and called to him as they moved toward the commandant's office. Captain Benoit was inside with four other soldiers examining a map. Philippe walked in and waited by the door with Chesanin and the children.

"I will be speaking to him in French," he told the children quietly.

Finally, the four soldiers filed out, nodding and greeting Philippe as they passed.

Captain Jean-Claude Benoit grinned in welcome and eyed the children with curiosity. "A little young to be taken as captives, yes?"

Philippe explained where and how he found them. "There will be a price to pay one day for what these Delaware are doing."

"You say this as if I could do something about it. I trust you don't expect to leave them here?"

"Well..." Philippe hesitated.

"You *cannot* leave them here, Philippe. They have to go with you... somewhere else but not here."

"Where?"

"I don't care where. You rescued them. That's up to you. They just cannot stay here. The spring campaigns are starting."

"To attack where?"

"Fort Oswego, probably. That's the rumor."

"My men and I can be useful for that too. Every scouting patrol I've made out of Fort Duquesne has found nothing but burnt out settler farms and slaughter."

"I will give you some dispatches to carry to Fort Niagara. Captain Pouchot can certainly use your help."

"Then that's where I will go," Philippe said with satisfaction.

Philippe told his men he would be heading to Fort Niagara.

"You can choose to go back downriver to Fort Duquesne. But if I get involved with spring campaigns out of Fort Niagara, I probably won't be coming back down here again this year. If you want to come with me, I welcome your company. But the other men of the troop will stay at Fort Duquesne…you can as well, if that is what you want. Think about it overnight. Chesanin and I will leave by midday tomorrow."

Since half the beds were empty in the officer barracks, Philippe arranged for Chesanin and the two children to bunk near him. When they ate, he explained to them where they were going.

"That's even farther away," Joshua said, alarmed.

"Yes, but it is a fortress with a village inside. It is much safer there than out here in the wilderness. There will be fighting. Don't worry. We will deliver your names to the English army. You father will be happy you are safe, as I would be."

Philippe was trying hard not to feel regret over rescuing the children in the first place.

The next morning, Philippe was pleased to hear all his men had decided to go to Fort Niagara with him.

"We can die just as easily up there," one of them said.

"Besides, the food is better," said another.

"Good. Let's load up and get going."

"*Skriiee!*"

Philippe dropped the mail pouch and pulled the children behind him with one arm. He knew that warning sound and scanned the sky looking for the eagle but did not see it. His men spread out to either side and raised their muskets at the approaching danger.

The scowling face of Handsome Robert along with a dozen other Delaware braves approached Philippe at a fast walk, stopping short by about five paces. It was hard to understand how this heavily tattooed, scarred, toothless, white-haired old man could ever be called *handsome*. But despite his apparent age, the chief was heavily muscled, with a body as healthy as any of his youngest braves.

Handsome Robert threw the Erigh hex sign at Philippe's feet contemptuously and pointed at the boy and girl huddling behind the *coureur de bois*.

"Those belong to me!"

Other marines and militia came streaming out of the fort.

"They are mine," Philippe answered. "I found them."

"You murdered my braves and stole them!"

"They are mine."

Handsome Robert glowered at the growing numbers of French troops gathering around them. He was calculating just how far the French might go to defend Snow Hair. But this insult could not be tolerated.

Just then, a large white eagle glided over the group. Everyone ducked and cowered at the raptor's unexpected appearance, even the French.

A Delaware brave raised his musket to fire on the eagle. Before he could get off a shot, Chesanin slammed the barrel of his musket down on the brave's hands, fouling the aim. The weapon discharged into the ground.

"*Skrieee!*"

The brave pulled out his knife and tomahawk and faced Chesanin, who did the same. They began fighting; metal clashed, grunts of attack filled the air.

Philippe and Handsome Robert recognized any decision they might negotiate was now preempted by this fight. The stand-off would be resolved this way. Like so many other fights, the crowd of men began cheering for their favorites. The idea of Chesanin's death was unthinkable. But even if that happened, Philippe resolved he would not give up the children. He would fire his musket in Handsome Robert's chest and let fate decide who lived in the subsequent explosion of musket fire that was certain to follow.

Chesanin's knife and tomahawk suddenly locked together in a clinch with his opponent. He kicked out with his foot and pushed. The brave was thrown off-balance. As they broke the clinch, Chesanin's knife slashed down into the man's neck.

It was over.

Philippe craned his head and spotted the white eagle perched high at the top of a nearby tree, watching. He no longer doubted its power.

The men on both sides were silent and wary, anticipating more violence would come.

The eagle suddenly left its perch, swooped down, grasped the hex sign off the ground in its talons and flew away.

"Who are you?" Handsome Robert demanded of the victor.

"Chesanin."

"He is Chittaqua's son," Philippe asserted. "It was Chittaqua's hex you defiled."

While the Delaware chief was undaunted by this revelation, his braves became visibly nervous and mumbled to each other.

"This is not over," Handsome Robert spat at Philippe.

Philippe laid his musket on the ground and stepped closer to the Delaware chief. "Then let's finish it today. Right here. Right now."

Handsome Robert began stripping off his clothes to make ready for the fight. Philippe did so too.

A pistol shot split through the air.

"Stop! There will be no more fighting!" Captain Benoit pointed at the Delaware chief. "Take your men and leave this fort."

Handsome Robert gave Philippe another hard look that was unmistakable in its malice and future intentions. Then he gathered up his belongings and retreated to the river and his waiting canoes.

"I see you've made new friends," Captain Benoit said, tucking his pistol away.

"Handsome Robert is no friend of mine."

"Must I remind you that the Delaware are French allies?"

"They are savage murderers."

"Aren't we all? Has there been *any* place you have gone without causing some type of confrontation?"

"You'd rather I give him these children?"

"That's not the point."

"It is the *only* point, Jean Claude. You've not seen what they've done in the east. I have. Handsome Robert *tortures* children! The hideous massacres these Delaware and Shawnee have perpetrated will haunt us all forever. This will never be forgiven or forgotten. And I know you, Captain. You wouldn't give up these children either. I am doing us a favor."

"Ah, this has been a *favor*! For me! What could have made me think otherwise?"

"What would you have me do?"

Captain Benoit regarded his decade-old friend. Each time they met in this warring wilderness, it might be their last.

"Captain Gerrard, you, too, must go…in the other direction!"

*

Fort Oranj
Sint Eustatius, Antilles Islands

Captain Beauregard LaTour rolled over in his bed and gazed languidly out at the beautiful blue sky and the dozens of trade ships anchored in Oranjestad harbor, all visible through the open shutters of his window. A gentle, warm breeze rushed over him.

He'd stayed in this port much longer than he had planned. But he was making net-hauls of money. It was too hard to leave. Even his crew's shares were already more than he personally would make in a normal year. He was almost out of space in his keel chests, and it was only March!

For three months he made cargo runs from the other islands with a skeleton crew, bringing back commodities of coffee, sugar, indigo, and tobacco and many other items to replenish the VanderMeer Trading Insurance Company warehouses. When he found he could not do it fast enough, he hired local schooners and kept them busy.

Oranjestad was the only free trade port in the Antilles Islands. This was now *the* place to do trading. Anything a sea trader wanted could be negotiated here. There was no need to waste valuable sailing time to prowl other islands or ports. Ships of every nationality were here in this harbor. The trading was frenzied.

Vesper Grant, the VanderMeer's trading' agent, was easily becoming the richest man in the islands, and Grant was only taking twenty-five percent of the profits. He begged and Captain LaTour agreed to stay and help manage the cargo transfers and the local schooners. LaTour purchased the construction of seven new cargo barges. They were huge, flat platforms, but they could be loaded at the limited wharf space and dragged out into the harbor and anchored. Out there, they could moor four different ships at a time. The trades could be made faster and they included everything the trading ships could possibly want. In addition to the usual island crops, there were all the things previously considered illegal for trade under penalty of death, such as weapons of every type and size, and even Chinese opium!

War frigates from Spain, Italy, the Dutch Republic, Germany, Portugal, France, and England patrolled the waters outside the harbor, but not to engage in warring disputes. They were there to ensure corsairs and privateers did not interfere with trading ships flying their country's flag.

Captain LaTour had stopped shuttling cargo. He used his crew to manage the barges and assisted Vesper Grant in negotiating prices. He even paid the Fort Oranj commandant for a company of Dutch troops to act as guards and keep peace among the traders.

The commandant was getting rich too; so much so, the commandant gave LaTour an officer's room at the fort, along with servants, which included several different bedmates, the latest of whom slipped her long fingers into his lap, stroking him into hardness for the fourth time since last night.

LaTour groaned. "Odara! You are going to kill me."

She smiled and rolled her lithe body against his. The exquisite pleasure she brought him seemed endless. Odara was so giving, so loving, so apparently loyal.

At heart, LaTour knew it was all a façade, a temporary artifice, the result of the money he provided. Still, he had a lot of money, enough to do this sort of thing for years. And the corruption of the soul that came with it? That was the danger. This gorgeous dark-skinned siren, this island, this seductive peacefulness, was all temporary. It was destroying the continuity of his crew in the most alluring, decadent way.

LaTour groaned loudly as she pulled another shattering orgasm from him, leaving him breathing as if he'd been running hard. Although, he'd simply lain there and let her do all the work, if you could call it work. Odara kissed and licked his lips until he gently made her stop. He rose from the bed and walked over to the window.

The nearby wharves were busy with loading and unloading, as were the ships out in the harbor. *William's Queen* enjoyed a mooring at the pier just below his elevated window in the fort. He saw the deck watch at the end of the brow, talking to an island girl with flowers in her hair.

He's probably never even looked below decks, LaTour thought. In truth, it had been a week since LaTour himself had made such an inspection.

Odara came up behind his back, slid her hands around his waist, and took hold of him. LaTour looked down. To his astonishment, she was exciting him again!

"No! Enough." He backed away and began to dress.

Odara's expression fell.

LaTour felt a pang of regret, but if he said something soothing it would encourage her to start again. He pulled on his boots, grabbed his hat, and left the room. As he walked into the marshalling yard of the fort, soldiers came to attention and saluted him. It was a courtesy he returned with reluctance. The military etiquette assigned to his Dutch naval captaincy made him uncomfortable.

Leaving the gate, he started towards *William's Queen* and noticed a long queue of people waiting outside VanderMeer Trading Insurance Company's offices fronting the main street of the wharf. When the deck watch saw his captain approaching, he quickly left the girl he was talking to and ran back up the brow.

"Let's inspect the cargo holds," LaTour said brusquely as he came aboard. "There better not be anything amiss down below."

Captain LaTour took his time inspecting the lower decks and bilge area. Only the bilge at the stern had problems and was way beyond half full, which meant this deck watch should have seen this before.

"You'll pay the fine for this," he told the man.

"It was like this when I took the watch this morning," the man argued.

"Then the man you relieved will also have a fine levied against him and the two of you will pump it clean, flush it out, and pump it clean again before you go ashore."

LaTour went into his cabin and made a log entry of his inspection and what he found. He went topside next and raised a special pennant to the top of the main mast, which would recall the crew. It would take the rest of the day before they all reported back aboard.

The deck watch saw the pennant. "Is there something wrong, Captain?"

"You will know once everyone is aboard."

Captain LaTour left the ship and went to VanderMeer Trading's offices. He pushed past the line of men waiting to discuss trades and found Vesper Grant and three of his assistants sitting behind four separate, long tables, all busily engaged in negotiating and signing trading orders. A line of five armed Dutch soldiers stood behind the clerks and guarded the large iron chests filled with hard coin and signed documents of trade. A fourth clerk, Vesper's main assistant, roamed among the tables of the junior clerks approving or disproving a particular deal as it was made.

Vesper regarded Captain LaTour with a smile of relief and waved for his main assistant to take his place at the table. The two of them retired to another table further back in the room, away from the noise surrounding the commerce.

Vesper poured two mugs of cool beer for them to drink.

"Thank God for the breeze today or the sweat stink would be overpowering. What have you been up to?"

"I think it's time I sailed," LaTour replied without preamble.

Vesper choked in the middle of a swallow, leaving a streak of foam on his upper lip.

"No! You cannot leave! I'll have no one to manage this clog of ships, barges, and delivery rafts in the harbor. You simply cannot leave!"

"I understand your problem. But I am a ship's captain, a sea trader, not the manager of your warehouses or supervisor of the day laborers."

"I know that. But you are the only one who seems to understand how to manage the harbor business, the anchoring and mooring, the supply schooners. And your crew is all employed managing that effort and doing a splendid job, I might add. You are all making a lot of money, too!"

"I am definitely aware of the money. As to my crew, the quality of their work is a fact I well understand. It is why I am a successful sea trader. But these men are sailors…sailors of *William's Queen* and *William's Queen* needs to sail again."

Vesper Grant looked as if he were in pain.

"All right…do not have a stroke. I will give you one more week of service and help to create a relief capability before I leave. But I want my cargo holds filled with sugar, barrels of molasses, bales of cured tobacco leaf, crates of coffee beans, a portion of that new shipment of spices just arrived from the East Indies, and a small quantity of opium. All at no charge, of course."

Vesper agreed but countered quickly: "Ten days! And today does not count as one of them."

"All right, ten days. But I *will* sail on the first tide of the eleventh day."

To the man, the crew rendezvoused aboard the *Queen* early that evening. Captain LaTour told them of his plan to sail in ten days. To his surprise, they were all anxious to leave as well. He explained they now had the task of finding men to relieve them of their company duties.

One of the crew complained. "We are all working on the barges from sunrise to sunset. "We've no time to locate someone to take our place."

"All right. I will find another way. Go eat."

It was Victorio, not surprisingly, who came up with a simpler solution. "Buy another ship," he suggested quietly, as the crew dispersed to eat.

"Buy a ship? What am I going to do with another ship?"

"Just make sure it is owned by the captain and that it is at least the same size and crew complement as *William's Queen*. Buy out the captain, and hire him and his crew for these jobs for the rest of the season. Make him the promise to load him full of cargo to go home for the winter and return next year to do the same thing again. You know, lie around the Antilles islands, getting fucked every night for free, and get paid at five times the normal rate…would they argue? Hell, you might not even have to buy him out. Maybe just rent his services for the season. The man would make at least twice his normal profit. Why would he turn that down?"

Victorio's logic almost made his own determination to sail again seem foolish.

"As you say. All right…now where do I find a ship like that?"

Victorio smiled at LaTour's doubt and pointed out at the anchorage. "I count at least six vessels out there. Let's take our harbor schooner and visit them tomorrow morning."

On the morrow, LaTour purchased a thirty-two-foot, single-mast schooner to use as a water carrier for his crew. It also transported the men between the barges and the shore. Victorio was made captain, and they named it *Le Chariot de Victorio*.

*

By the second day, Victorio and Captain LaTour had found a captain smart enough to see the advantage of the work LaTour offered. The captain didn't sell his vessel but did agree to hire it out until the end of August, after which he, too, planned to sail home. He was also French, which sealed the agreement as far as LaTour was concerned. The French trading frigate was called *Lyonesse*. Its port of home was La Rochelle. It was half again larger than *William's Queen*, with twice the crew complement. Plenty of men to manage the current activity, with room to grow. The new captain's only suspicion was exactly why Captain LaTour would leave this lucrative opportunity.

"Sounds too good to be true? But I have been here for three months," LaTour answered truthfully, "and I am a man of the sea. My crew needs to go home. I plan to be back in the winter. Probably at the start of the new year."

"Then we will need a third captain to fill in the gap between us," suggested Captain Mistral.

LaTour agreed. "I leave it to you to help Monsieur Grant find someone as honest and loyal as us, *oui*? Someone you trust."

*

One week later, *William's Queen* left Sint Eustatius bound for Amsterdam. Captain LaTour felt a sense of relief as they passed by the war frigates patrolling outside the harbor. The Dutch ship fired a single cannon in salute to his flag as he sped past at fifteen knots of speed. The *Queen* was dressed in full sail.

LaTour had worried he might lose one or two of his crew to the allure of the island. But every man was on board, and they were anxious to get home to Le Havre. He planned to do just what he did last year. Raise the Dutch tri-color ensign to enter Amsterdam and the French blue and gold *fleur-de-lys* to enter Le Havre. The ship was known in both ports and no one ever challenged him.

Victorio studied the charts and followed the course set by LaTour. This time, Captain LaTour would sail north-northeast before turning easterly towards the English Channel. They would traverse an area of the Atlantic where storms from the north could appear quite suddenly as the warmer air from the tropics collided with cold air from the polar region.

"This course will add a week or more to our sailing time," Victorio concluded.

Captain LaTour admired Victorio's analysis. "Yes. It will. So presume you're the captain. You have the choice of encountering a trailing gale or corsairs? Which do you prefer?"

"The Son of the Architect is the Architect for the Son"

Governor General Pierre de Rigaud, Marquis de Vaudreuil-Cavagnial sat in his hard-backed, hard-seated chair behind the elaborate desk in his office inside the Château Vaudreuil in Montréal. He preferred a hard-back chair so he would not succumb to the seduction of a cushion, relax, and lose his focus. This pain in the butt that his portly figure experienced helped remind him that every decision he made in that chair as governor was important. And every decision he made at this point in the history of New France would determine whether it survived as a country or not.

Or so he told himself.

The Vaudreuil mansion-headquarters in Montréal was built fifty years earlier by the king's chief engineer, Gaspard-Joseph Chaussegros de Léry, at the request of Pierre's father, also a marquis, and a previous governor-general of New France. Pierre was born in Quebec City. He had served France and the king in the military and as a civil administrator in New France, most recently as Governor of Louisiana for ten years, before relieving his predecessor, the Marquis Duquesne. He knew the people of his country, the Canadians, the Acadians, the natives, its customs, the culture, and history. He spoke several of the native tongues. The Vaudreuil family had its roots in *New France*, not France. His allegiance lay with New France as far as Pierre was concerned. Although, naturally, he never said anything like that publically.

Pierre stared at the portrait of his father hanging on the wall, with that stern disapproving face he'd seen so often as a boy. And the man was still staring at him. Pierre would be fifty-eight in November, the age his father had become governor. *It was a better place when I left it*, the disapproving face seemed to challenge. *How shall you leave it?* That sudden thought made him pause in the middle of reviewing the military orders he would issue for attacking the English forts on the Mohawk River.

"You never had to fight a war," he whispered at the painting. "How would you have fared with *that*, Papa? And it's a war that I am winning. For now, at least."

Pierre took a deep breath, returned his attention to the plan of attack and finished reading it for the fifth time. There wasn't anything left to correct. He approved it to go forward immediately. It was the type of attack he liked most. Fast-raiding skirmishes that produced as much destruction as possible before withdrawing into the wilderness. So far the English had proven incompetent in defending against such raids. They still plodded forward with large masses of men led by officers hamstrung by European line and volley fire tactics.

These military tactics continued despite the crushing defeat of General Braddock at Monongahela. Of course, New France had lost General von Dieskau after employing similar tactics at the battle of Lac du Saint-Sacrament. Which, as far as Vaudreuil was concerned, only put an exclamation point on the ineffectiveness of waging war in America using lines of battle. Deception, ambush, take no prisoners—these tactics were his personal philosophy on waging war in this wilderness. Raid, skirmish, and plunder, in the style of their Indian allies. So far the western territories of the Virginia and Pennsylvania colonies were overrun and controlled by France, simply by using the Indians as auxiliary troops and condoning their predilection for hideous savagery and torture. He considered it a small price to pay for absolute French domination of the interior wilderness lands south of the lakes. He would wear down the English superiority in numbers with repeated military defeats at high cost. The English Parliament would soon sue France for a new peace treaty. That was his plan. Except for a minor detail: neither country had declared war yet.

"Well, a few more crushing defeats should solve that problem," he mumbled to himself.

The English also liked to wage war based upon the seasons. They liked to stay safe and warm in their *winter quarters*, drinking *French* wine, slowly resupplying to begin campaigns in the spring. His spies reported how the English had been amassing munitions and food stocks at the supply forts on the Mohawk River meant for Fort Oswego. These supplies were destined to support a spring campaign from Fort Oswego to attack Fort Frontenac on Lake Ontario. Since it was winter, they expected the French to simply wait for them while they got ready. That strategy was short-sighted in this wilderness. Governor Vaudreuil was not going to wait. He would take advantage of this. He would attack the English supply forts in the winter. With the supply forts for Fort Oswego destroyed, the English offensive campaigns for 1756 on the great lakes would wither and be over before they even started.

In contrast, Governor General Vaudreuil's offensive campaign objective for 1756 would be to destroy the strategic Fort Oswego on Lake Ontario. When the *next* military commander was sent over from France, intent on fighting the European way, he would give him the supply-starved, weakened position of Fort Oswego to pick like a ripened fruit. But Vaudreuil would make sure to take credit for it.

First, the supply forts. Leading this particular raid, Vaudreuil had selected Lieutenant Gaspard-Joseph Chaussegros de Léry, the son of the King's renowned chief engineer of the same name. He was thirty-two, a superb engineer in his own right, an able artillery officer, and a veteran wilderness officer. Vaudreuil thought it fortunate this man was available. He could not make a better choice.

"How appropriate," he said to his father's portrait, holding aloft the orders in the air. "The son of the architect who worked for you and designed this very mansion will now be my architect for the defeat of the English this year. It's poetic...the son of the architect is the architect for the son! That bodes well!"

*

When Henri Gerrard learned the objective of the militia rally was to raid the wilderness lands along the Mohawk River, he was one of the first to report. The Mohawk River was south of Lake Ontario and surrounded by the Oneida lands. He felt certain they would encounter men of that tribe who would have knowledge of his father, Philippe Gerrard. And the militia would have a greater degree of freedom than the Troupes de la Marine. So he resisted Major Péan's overture to join the Troupes de la Marines.

As it turned out, Major Péan had advanced an argument in writing to the Governor and Lieutenant de Léry that his *vast* experience with the gendarmeries in Montréal and Quebec made him ill-suited for leading troops in the field. That he would better serve New France commanding the city guards in Montréal or Quebec City. Joseph de Léry shook his head when reading the missive. He badly needed experienced wilderness officers and the gendarmerie major seemed to have more experience than anyone else he knew, including himself. By all accounts the major was an excellent officer, a good leader, and fearless in battle. This earned reputation was not mentioned in the major's missive and contrasted sharply with the persistent rumors of his corruption, which, paradoxically, seemed to be promoted by Major Péan himself. He showed Captain Montreuil the written self-assessment and asked his opinion.

"Major Péan proved himself in battle with you and General von Dieskau, did he not?"

Captain Montreuil read the missive and smiled wryly.

"Of course," the former aide to General von Dieskau replied. "The major's remarks are conspicuously modest. This officer was decorated for *valor* at the battle of Lac du Saint-Sacrament. Major Péan is a natural leader. He just doesn't like to lead. He complains all the time, but maintains excellent discipline among his men and personally leads them into battle *from the front*. He will not offer his opinion unless you ask him, yet he is a resourceful tactician. New France needs to utilize him in ways more than just as a policeman. I tried to convince him to join the grenadiers. He actually led them on a successful scouting foray. The grenadiers *praised* the major, believe it or not. When I told him of their praise, you would think I'd insulted him."

Lieutenant de Léry decided the major would participate in the attack on the supply forts, but he would have him lead the Montréal militia. That way he would be subordinate to all of Lieutenant de Léry's metropolitan officers. The police major would be temporarily demoted to lieutenant like before.

When confronted with his orders, Péan frowned and acted offended. In truth, he had expected he would get called up to serve again. So if he must accompany the army anywhere, Major Péan preferred *not* to be in charge.

*

The raiding party rendezvoused west of the Lachine rapids. The small mixed force of approximately fifty regulars, thirty Troupes de la Marines, and the officers to command them all totaled nearly one hundred. This was complemented by one hundred sixty militia called up from Montréal; the militia represented the largest French component of the force. To this was added the native allies, consisting of warriors from several different tribes, who numbered over a hundred. In total, some three hundred and sixty men, an appropriate size for a French raiding party.

Once the various units were mustered and counted, Lieutenant de Léry called his first council of war to establish the order of march. Immediately afterwards, they began boarding the bateaux that would carry them to Fort de La Présentation. This militarized missionary-fort was further west on the Saint Lawrence River, more than halfway to Lake Ontario. From there, they would march south over the arduous wilderness terrain in the harsh conditions of winter to conceal the advance. If not snowing outright, they would endure freezing rain. It was hard to say which type of weather was worse when one plodded wet and frostbitten most of the time. The force would also be entering Iroquois lands, and those six nations were allied to the English. Their raiding party would be in constant danger of ambush.

To Henri's surprise, he saw Major Péan and Sergeant Cabrelle boarding a militia bateau captained by Reynaud Sager and his man Simon. He ran to join his friends.

"Major!"

"Corporal Gerrard? Did you join the Troupes?"

"No, sir. I'm with the militia."

"Well, you are in luck, Corporal. The Governor thinks so highly of me, I've been placed in charge of the militia…again…along with Color Sergeant Cabrelle, of course."

Henri was truly pleased. "That's great news, Major!"

"You think so, Corporal?" the major answered drolly. "Just imagine how pleased I was to hear this."

Reynaud Sager hailed him. "Henri Gerrard! So we sail together again, my friend."

"I know Reynaud Sager and Simon," he explained to the major. "I traveled with them up the Saint John River last year."

Reynaud confirmed this and raved to the dozen militia soldiers he ferried of Henri's courage during that travel. Henri suddenly wished he'd picked another boat. He was uncomfortable with the looks of surprise he received.

"I did nothing special," Henri explained modestly. "Everyone had to fight."

"Nothing special!? He killed nine warriors! Most of them with that deadly cutlass he favors so much."

"Only nine?" Péan grinned. "Impressive. Somehow I do not find that hard to believe at all."

Henri took an oar next to Sergeant Cabrelle. Major Péan sat in the middle of the bench seat, in between them, *to supervise,* he said. The sound of a rally whistle broke the revelry. Forty bateaux pushed off into the river to begin the journey to the next fort. A third of them were loaded with supplies the force of men would carry or pull on heavy sledges across the deep snow. The party would be carrying packs, marching on snowshoes, and pulling the sledges through the wilderness for at least three weeks just to reach The Great Carrying Place, as the overland portage from the Mohawk River to Wood Creek was called.

Once there, they would attack one or more of the three supply forts supporting the more strategic Fort Oswego. The orders were to destroy the stores of gunpowder, food, spike any cannon they found, and burn anything else of value. The supply forts were likely fully garrisoned.

Major Péan lost no time in grousing about the insanity of this expedition.

"If we don't freeze to death, or starve when we run out of food in three weeks, we will have to take the forts by surprise, mind you. Hopefully, they will leave the front gate open, or we will have to hack our way in with axes while they shoot down at us from atop the wall. Won't that be invigorating?" He asserted such criticisms quietly, addressing only Sergeant Cabrelle and Henri. "But wait...maybe we can stand on the shoulders of the grenadiers and shoot over the wall into the fort? Oh, wait again! Probably shouldn't suggest that...or the grenadiers will be standing on our shoulders."

Sergeant Cabrelle glanced at Henri and rolled his eyes. Henri was used to the major's rants and listened quietly. He knew when the time came the major would likely lead the charge himself.

As the monotony of the oaring settled in, Sergeant Cabrelle leaned toward Henri.

"So tell me, Corporal. Did you manage to get...how did you describe it...*mended*? ...while you wintered in Montreal?"

Henri's face reddened, and he nodded curtly.

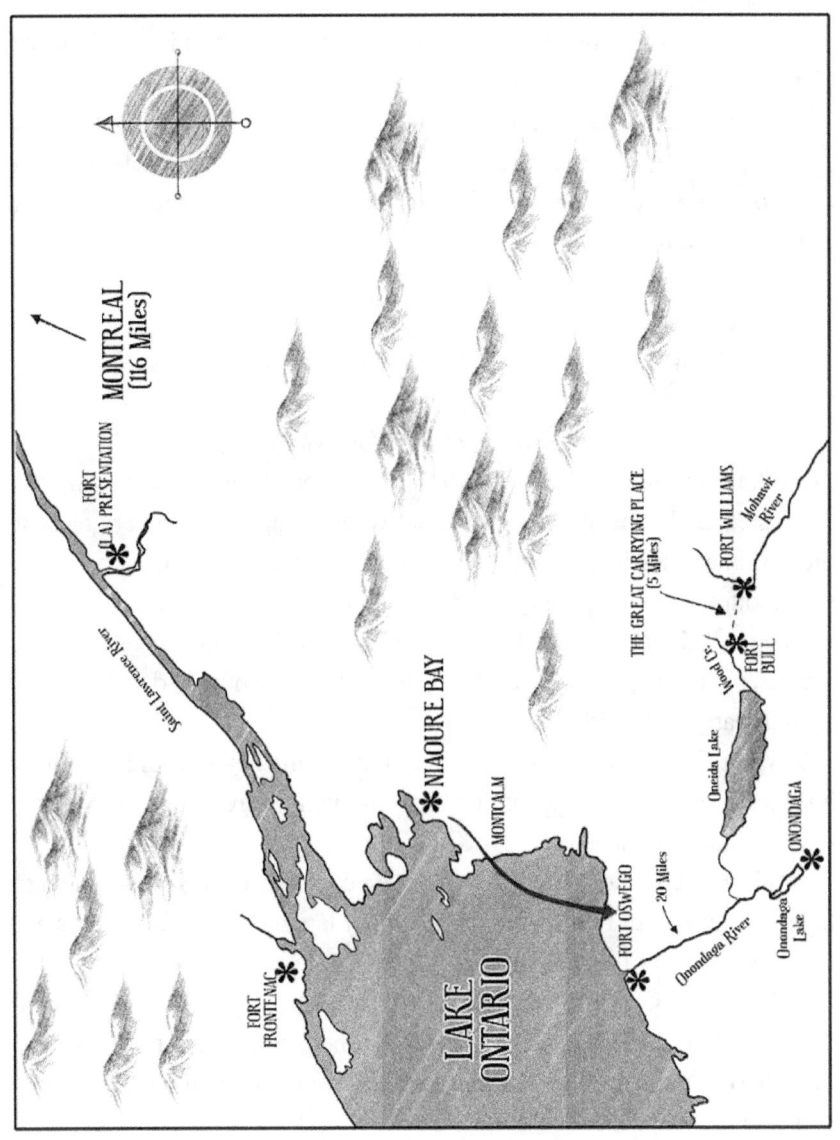

The Great Carrying Place

The sergeant and the major traded surprised looks.

"You did?! What was her name?"

"Carmen."

"You mean that fat little cobbler? The one with the big tits?! Bravo, Henri!"

"Carmen is not fat, Sergeant!"

"Hmm. Corporal Gerrard, I have to ask. Did Mademoiselle Carmen take your penis into her mouth? That is the only way to properly *mend* that organ, you know."

"Major!"

"Ohh...so she *did*!"

"I will not talk about her."

*

Headwaters of the Mohawk River

Like everyone else in the raiding party, Henri Gerrard was cold, wet, exhausted, and hungry. They were nearly out of supplies, but very close to their ultimate destination. Lieutenant de Léry sent out scouting parties to reconnoiter The Great Carrying Place and the two closest English supply forts, Fort William and Fort Bull. They were gone less than half a day when a messenger was sent back to the lieutenant. The scouts had encountered a small party of Oneida.

When Henri heard this rumor, he thought his heart would leap from his chest. He ran to Lieutenant de Léry and volunteered to go with him to talk with these Indians.

"Sir, I lived among the Seneca for a year. And I speak that language fluently along with two others. I know sign language and can understand many of the other Iroquoian tongues."

"Very well, Corporal Gerrard. Join the other translators going with me."

Henri was excited and emotional over the prospect of finally learning the fate of his father, who had reportedly been taken by the Oneida close to a year ago.

Think, Henri. Think. He decided to cautiously approach this topic only *after* Lieutenant de Léry learned the military information he needed. And he should do this privately, he decided further. *No matter the answer, I must not show any emotion*, he told himself. *The Oneida consider it weakness.*

There were six Oneida warriors. Two of them were chiefs. The Oneida did not seem at all disturbed by the presence of a large force of French soldiers, *coureurs de bois*, and allied Indians camping nearby on Oneida lands with the intention of attacking the English forts.

That was a surprise to Lieutenant de Léry. He worried this outward ambivalence could be a ruse. He must presume they intended to warn the English. He invited them to join the camp and stay the night as his guests. The Oneida agreed, interested in finding out as much about French intentions as Lieutenant de Léry was to learn about the garrison and armaments of the forts.

Of the two forts, the Oneida claimed Fort Bull had the greater stocks of food, gun powder, and storehouses of other supplies. Named after its commander, an English officer, the fort was a crowded cluster of internal buildings and storehouses surrounded by a sixteen-foot stockade. Fort Bull was the main supply depot for Fort Oswego. The English had been filling its storehouses and magazines with supplies hauled up from Albany for months. And just then it was completely full. There was a garrison of seven hands of men—seventy. They were only awaiting the spring melt before loading a line of bateaux waiting up on the banks of Wood Creek. And that was soon. They had already started readying some of them. In a few more days, they planned to carry everything to Fort Oswego.

The French had arrived just in time to prevent this. Fort Bull became the obvious target for Lieutenant de Léry's party.

Away from the Oneida, the lieutenant informed his primary subordinates they would approach and attack Fort Bull the next morning. He assigned Lieutenant Péan, as the police major was now ranked, to scout Fort Bull along with another officer from the marines. A third officer was sent to scout Fort William.

The Oneida stayed with the French that night. Henri had listened to the discussions, learning much, but as of yet had no opportunity to discuss his father with the Oneida privately. When the night grew dark and the temperature dropped, most of the Oneida prepared to sleep next to the campfires. Henri sidled politely near one of the chiefs and spoke to him in the tongue of the Erigh, introducing himself.

"I am called Wolf-Bear. I am a warrior of the Erigh people."

Surprised and curious, the Oneida chief stared at Henri for several long seconds before answering him in the Erigh tongue.

"I have not heard the words of the Erigh spoken freely in my lands in many seasons. I am called Skenando, Pine Tree chief of the Oneida Lake clan. You are the second *coureur de bois* I've met with such knowledge. The other was called Snow Hair. Do you know this man?"

Henri found himself unable to speak past the huge lump in his throat. It choked off his words. He took off his sock cap to reveal his long blond hair.

It dawned on Skenando he was talking to a member of Snow Hair's clan. He turned to the other Oneida, pointing at Henri. They all gathered closer to him and made gestures of friendliness. Henri knew he had to say something. He did not know if his father was alive or dead. But after his extraordinary year-long journey, he was about to find out.

"Snow Hair is my father," he managed in an emotion-filled voice barely above a whisper. "I've been searching for him."

Skenando saw the pain in the young brave's face. He nodded with understanding.

"Your father has joined the Pine Tree clan. He is respected as a great warrior."

Skenando told Henri the tale of Snow Hair, how he ran the gauntlet twice without stopping. How he was adopted by Tall Mountain Among Trees.

"I know Tall Mountain Among Trees," Henri blurted, but stopped himself, immediately regretting his rude interruption. "I am sorry, Skenando."

Skenando explained to the others what Henri had just said. They gazed at him.

"How do *you* know Tall Mountain Among Trees?" Skenando asked in a tone of disbelief. He signed this question for the others to understand as well.

"I helped him capture the man who killed his daughter."

He is the one! Skenando blinked with wonder at what he just heard.

"Tall Mountain Among Trees has told us about your bravery."

One of the other Oneida pushed Skenando's shoulder gently, telling him to hurry and tell them too. Once he explained, the Oneida began to have a vigorous discussion among themselves. It was loud enough to draw the attention of Lieutenant de Léry. He walked quickly to the impromptu meet and sat down next to Henri with one of his interpreters. He gave Henri a worried look.

"Corporal, what goes on here?"

While Henri explained to the lieutenant that the Oneida knew his father, Skenando and the interpreter exchanged information regarding what was just said. The interpreter translated it all for the lieutenant. Henri corrected a few minor points.

"We would like to take him with us to our village," Skenando said, speaking once again through the translator.

"Is Snow Hair at your village?" Henri asked before the lieutenant ordered him to stop talking.

Skenando shook his head and spoke through the translator that Snow Hair went to the three rivers' fort to fight the English. A great weight lifted from Henri's soul.

He is alive! He thanked God silently.

"Tell Skenando I am sorry, but Henri Gerrard is one of my soldiers and must stay with me," asserted Lieutenant de Léry. "Corporal, do not say anything else."

"Yes, sir."

Skenando nodded with understanding and stood up. So did everyone else.

"Wolf-Bear, like your father, you are now of the Pine Tree clan," Skenando said in the Erigh tongue, knowing that only Henri understood what was said. The Oneida chief took off a highly ornate necklace of bones and feathers and slipped it over Henri's head. "I will tell Tall Mountain Among Trees he has another son. Knowing it is *you* will bring great joy to him now that he is in his winter days."

Henri knew he must reciprocate, but had nothing to match this honor in value. So he unbelted his expensive skinning knife with the handle of whale ivory and its Mohawk beaded scabbard. He presented them to the chief with both hands.

"Thank you for this honor. Tell Tall Mountain Among Trees I hope to visit my new father someday."

Skenando nodded again, impressed by the respectfulness and wisdom shown by someone so young. But then again, this was the son of Snow Hair.

After Henri took hold of the shoulders of the other Oneida in a greeting of hello and good-bye, Lieutenant de Léry cleared his throat.

"You and I will talk more about this later, Corporal. But for now, rejoin your company."

Henri came to attention and saluted. "Yes, sir."

He walked back to the militia ranks, noticing Major Péan's questioning expression as he left Lieutenant de Léry.

"What have you done now, Corporal?"

*

The next morning, the raiders were on the move well before the sun had risen. The party of Oneida warriors moved south east, to go down the Mohawk River, away from the forts. Nevertheless, Lieutenant de Léry worried about the Oneida, that they might circle back and warn the English of their presence, or worse, that they might ambush his party after the attack for trespassing on the Oneida lands without getting permission first. His main translator assured the lieutenant that the Oneida would do neither and reinforced this opinion by pointing out Corporal Gerrard was the *son* of a high chief of the Oneida tribe.

"They will not attack now, even if they previously planned to do so, which I do not believe was their intention."

The officer grunted skeptically. The coincidence was almost too strange to believe. But he was committed to the attack now in any case.

The lieutenant held his final council of war with his officers. He assigned an officer and a platoon of men to watch Fort Williams in case they decided to send reinforcements once the fighting began. He strongly implored his Indian allies not to make any war cries or other sounds so the attack would be a total surprise.

"The fort has no mounted cannon, but they do have grenades to throw over the walls. There are no firing platforms but the stockade wall has loopholes. There are seventy men in the garrison, half of them regulars. We will fire *into* the fort through the same loopholes. The Oneida claim the gate is open. The garrison is already moving supplies to the bateaux waiting on Wood Creek. My intent is to assault the fort by surprise before they realize the attack has started and have a chance to close the gate."

The lieutenant issued orders to his forces, deploying the companies by platoon, one sent to destroy the supplies, troops, and the bateaux at Wood Creek; another to cover the flanking sides of the fort; others to point their weapons at the top of the stockade. But the majority of the raiding party was to attack through the open gate. After he answered the usual questions on a place to rally after the attack, the lieutenant regarded the faces of his officers and senior men one by one, emphasizing his final words.

"The English do not know we are here. We will surprise them completely. But only if we travel quietly…as you all know how to do. And in your enthusiasm to destroy things, please remember not to destroy all the food! We need some of it to eat!"

The men laughed.

The Troupes, regulars, and militia moved out in full packs. When they were within a half mile, they left their heavier carrying packs on the side of the trail with some men to guard them.

Major Péan told Sergeant Cabrelle to have six of the long axes brought with his men.

"Axes? Why?" Cabrelle asked.

"In case we have to chop our way inside, God forbid."

The raiding party trotted the rest of the way. As they broke free of the trees, Joseph de Léry was elated to see the gate was open. He swung his sword in a circle above his head. "Hurry! Hurry!" he called. It was less than a quarter mile to the gate but they were now in the open.

The French companies began to deploy in directions as ordered. Major Péan was running beside Lieutenant de Léry. Behind him was Sergeant Cabrelle and a select company of militia marksmen, including Corporal Gerrard.

"There!" Péan pointed at some English working on a pile of stores outside the fort.

Though Lieutenant de Léry implored them to be silent, the excited Indians began their ululating war cries to his horrified disappointment. The English soldiers outside the fort dropped what they were doing and ran towards the gate, shouting alarms of the attack.

"Fuck!" Péan exclaimed. He pointed at the English. "Shoot them!"

Firing erupted everywhere. The battle was engaged.

The English managed to get into the fort and closed the gate just as the French reached the wall. Lieutenant de Léry pointed at different loopholes and shouted orders.

"There! There! There!"

Péan barked at Sergeant Cabrelle to begin chopping at the gate's center crossbeam.

Henri Gerrard stood close to the ax men, his musket trained at the top of the stockade wall. If he saw any sign of movement at the top, he was to fire at it. But the wall had no firing steps. He did not see anyone.

Péan and de Léry both could tell the chopping of the heavy log gate was going to take a lot of time, too much time.

"I'll try to find us a ram," Péan shouted to the commander.

"Yes. Good! Hurry!"

Péan ordered eight of the militia to search for a stout log to use as a battering ram. "Go around the stockade walls. They must have a spare timber pile lying somewhere."

The firing was intense in and out of the loopholes. A few of the French raiders had fallen but not as many as Lieutenant de Léry was expecting.

Suddenly, three grenades lofted over the wall to drop on the ground behind the ax men.

Henri Gerrard saw them all. He dropped his musket, picked them up one by one and tossed them back over. Loud explosions occurred inside the gates followed by the sounds of screaming men. Two more grenades came flying over. One of them landed at Lieutenant de Léry's feet. The commander did not see it. Henri pushed the officer out of the way, grabbed the bomb, and tossed it back over the gate again. He looked around for the second one and barely had time to throw it.

It exploded right at the top of the wall.

A piece of shrapnel struck Henri in the left shoulder, knocking him to the ground. Gritting his teeth against the pain, he got back up in time to retrieve and toss back two more grenades.

Lieutenant de Léry admired the young corporal's daring agility, hopping around, and running back and forth, performing the valuable role of throwing the grenades back into the fort.

But the English had caught on. Suddenly, a grenade with a short fuse was thrown over the wall. It exploded right above the men chopping at the gate's crossbeam. Two of them fell dead. Henri took a second piece of shrapnel, this time to his head, grazing the ear that had been injured during the Lac du Saint-Sacrament battle. The hot shrapnel sheared off half of the same ear and lacerated his scalp before it ricocheted off the bone of his skull. Dazed, Henri fell to his knees. He pressed a hand to his bloody ear and scalp. It took several seconds to recover his senses. When he stood again, he was extremely dizzy and moved slower than before. Still, he moved fast enough to toss back the occasional grenade that came his way. Fortunately, many of the other militia were now doing the same thing.

Major Péan's men finally returned with a suitable log to use as a battering ram and started slamming it into the door. In between thrusts, the ax men kept chopping a notch in the wooden gate.

The firing went on interminably for almost an hour. Lieutenant de Léry sensed they were gaining the upper hand as the return fire through the loopholes lessened. He looked around the battlefield. Men were down, but not as many as there might have been after an hour's worth of frontal assault with man-to-man musket and grenade exchanges. Péan was attempting to have a man stand on another's shoulders to gaze over the wall, maybe to fire inside the wall from that elevation. The lieutenant was not certain this was a good idea, but the rugged gate simply would not give way.

Henri Gerrard saw another grenade flop to the ground. He picked it up but instead of tossing it back over, he jammed it into a notch in the gate already cut by the ax men.

When the militia near to the gate saw what Henri had done, they cursed loudly, dropped the ramming log, and ran in different directions. Henri shoved hard on the two nearest men, one standing atop the other's shoulders, eliciting their curses as they fell to the ground, but when the grenade exploded inside the notch with a loud blast, no one was hurt.

The militia returned to the battering ram and assaulted the gate again. This time, on the second heavy thrust, they heard a loud cracking sound from the wood and cheered. The gate's cross log was about to give.

With the next heavy thrust, the gates swung inward. Lieutenant de Léry shouted the King's name, and the bulk of the regulars, the Troupes, *coureurs de bois*, and Indians stormed into Fort Bull with bayonets and tomahawks raised. Inside, the English force was a mix of men, half of whom were redcoat regulars from the 51st Regiment of Foot. The rest were provincial militia in wilderness dress. The redcoats formed a line and fired muskets in a volley. The provincials fired from behind barrels, the corners of buildings, from doorways, or whatever cover they could find. But after just one volley fire from the redcoats, the disciplined lines broke. They were outnumbered almost three to one. The smaller garrison force was going to be overrun. The English fell back into the tight cluster of interior buildings. One of them, the barracks, was stoutly made with logs and had loopholes cut for musket fire. The remaining English rushed inside and barred the door. The fighting continued. The wounded who could not walk or run were left outside the barracks and were quickly assaulted by the Indians.

Amid the intense sounds of musket fire, Henri Gerrard reloaded his weapon. But dizziness was making it difficult to stand and aim. His strength was failing. He slumped against the wide-open gate and slid down to the ground. His head hurt badly and was throbbing with pain. He was too disoriented to join in any more fighting. He observed the Indians attacking the wounded English soldiers. The horrific mutilations were occurring only paces away from where he sat. Scalps were sliced off in a circle with a knife and the hair yanked off. The soldiers screamed in agony, begging for mercy. It did not matter. Other more hideous acts with tomahawks and knives came next: cutting off hands, castrating genitals and shoving them into the screaming man's mouth before he was killed. Henri vomited. One man, a provincial with bleeding musket wounds in both of his legs, crawled desperately towards the gate, obviously trying to escape.

An Indian straightened from his latest butchering. Amid the fog of powder smoke, he spotted the man trying to crawl away. Scowling, the brave strode towards the wounded Englishman, his tomahawk and knife still dripping with blood from his last war prize, his belt tucked full of the slick, bloody scalps he'd already collected.

The wounded man looked behind him and saw his death approaching. He rolled on his back and held up his arms pleading, "No! No! No!"

The Indian sat astride the man's legs and cut open the front of his pants. The screaming man began to thrash. His flailing arms were interfering. The Indian raised the tomahawk to bash him in the side of the head. But before the downward swing began, a musket ball slammed into the Indian's ribs from close range, throwing him sideways. He was dead before he hit the ground. The English provincial looked to his left and saw a wounded French militiaman pushing himself up to his feet.

Henri was reeling, but the horrible sights and sounds of the butchering were too much. He was determined to save this man at least. He staggered to the prostrate man and shouted in English above the noise.

"Give me your hand!"

The astonished Englishman extended his arm. With great effort, Henri dragged the groaning man outside the fort using his musket as a crutch with his free hand. He had just enough strength to drag him about thirty paces past the gate before he stopped. Too exhausted to walk further, even on his own, Henri sat down on the ground next to the soldier.

"When they come out," he labored to say between heavy breaths. "Do not speak in English. Do not talk. Point at your ears. Pretend you cannot hear. Let me do the talking."

The terrified man nodded. With more effort, Henri managed to reload his musket just before the entire French raiding party came boiling out of the fort at a run.

Something's wrong, Henri thought.

Sergeant Cabrelle spotted Henri sitting on the ground, a wounded man next to him. Henri's head and face was covered in blood. Cabrelle and two other militiamen ran toward him. They assumed the other wounded man was militia too, and he was carried by the militiamen across the open field to safety. Cabrelle lifted Henri's arm over his shoulder. Together, they hobbled as fast as they could away from the fort.

Just as they reached the tree line, a series of three huge explosions occurred behind them, all within a few seconds of each other. The combined blasts rocked the air violently. The shock wave was strong enough to flip the sergeant and Henri off their feet.

Henri sat up, dazed, his ears ringing from the pressure of the blast. Sergeant Cabrelle said something to him but he could not hear the words. The sergeant pantomimed that he should stay where he was sitting. Henri nodded feebly. When Henri looked towards Fort Bull, it was…*gone*! What had not been blown into wood splinters was now a pile of rubble burning fiercely. Henri felt around his body to see if he was hurt anywhere else and discovered the shrapnel wound in his left shoulder. When he found it, the pain spiked. Using a boning knife, he carefully cut away the sleeve of his coat and saw a large, angry purple bulge of skin on his shoulder with a chunk of black metal protruding from it. It was not bleeding too badly, the metal acting as a plug. But it sent a shock of pain through him when he grazed it with his fingers. Aching everywhere, he managed to slip his smaller pack off his shoulders, lifting one strap carefully over the shard of metal. He pulled out his water skin and guzzled from it. They he lay back against the pack, using it as a pillow, and in the profound dizzy quiet of his deafness, Corporal Henri Gerrard blacked out.

CHAPTER 7
ONEIDA WILDERNESS
APRIL 1756
Journey to Montréal

It was night when Henri finally opened his eyes again. He was lying by a campfire. His mouth was dry. He sat up and the covers fell away. He was naked from the waist up, except for the talisman pouch around his neck. Shivering with cold, he pulled the blanket back around his shoulders. When he shifted his hips to clear away a rock lodged beneath his ass, he groaned. He hurt everywhere. There was bruising all over his body.

Seven of the Régiment de Guyenne grenadiers sat near him. Hearing Henri's groans, one of them glanced in his direction and grinned.

"Look! Young Corporal Gerrard has risen from the dead! Bonjour, Henri! We thought we'd lost you."

As a group, the grenadiers gathered close to help him drink water and gave him a wonderful-tasting stew to eat. They were telling him so many things at once it was hard to comprehend it all.

"Where are we?" he asked in a groggy voice.

"Going home."

"Did we win?"

Color Sergeant Gosse laughed. "Win? The entire fort was blown to bits. So, yes, I guess we won. But we also managed to blow up most of the food too. So enjoy your stew. We've only enough for two more days."

Henri was ravenously hungry and scooped more into his mouth. He looked at his throbbing, bandaged shoulder. He recalled getting hit by something. He touched his ear. That hurt!

"Owww!"

"Then don't touch it! Half of your ear is gone." The sergeant snapped his fingers by the ear. "Can you hear that?"

"Yes."

"Then you still hear. That's good. You've been out for four days. We carried you on this makeshift litter you're sitting on."

"You carried me? Are others injured?"

"We were lucky. Only three dead and eight wounded, including you. Oh, and the Englishman you saved."

"Englishman?" Henri realized he could not remember much about the attack at all.

"Yes. If not for you, the Indians would have tied him to a spit and eaten him by now."

"I don't remember anything," Henri said. Now he was worried.

Sergeant Gosse sent one of his men to get the surgeon and Péan.

"I don't remember much about the battle," Henri said again. "How bad is my head wound?"

"Well, you're alive. You can talk and see and hear. A minor injury. You got hit by an exploding grenade. There was shrapnel in your shoulder. The surgeon fixed that. More shrapnel cut your scalp. That's been stitched. The surgeon can tell you more, but in my experience, when you get hit in the head with an iron cannon ball, you tend to lose your memory. It could have been worse. You could have blown off your cock!" The other grenadiers laughed. "But it did not break the bone of your skull. So now that you woke up, you won't starve to death. I'm guessing you'll get your memory back again before long."

Besides his hunger, Henri felt uncomfortably itchy and wanted to get clean.

"No! Don't stand up!"

"I need to clean myself."

"Wait until tomorrow. The water is ice fucking cold anyway."

"I don't care. It will be cold tomorrow too. And I cannot rest like this."

"All right. We'll carry you."

Some of the grenadiers lit torches from the fire. Others picked up the litter and carried Henri to a running brook nearby. Gingerly, Henri took off his boots, socks, and pants. They helped him wade into the chilling spring melt water. Henri cleaned off the blood, mud, and other filth caked to his skin. In less than a minute, he was shivering violently from the cold, but at least he could scrub his skin clean with the fine mud and gravel he pulled up by handfuls from the bottom of the stream.

The grenadier sergeant plunged Henri's trousers soiled with excrement repeatedly into the water. "We can dry them by the fire."

"Great," said another soldier. "That should smell good."

"You should know," responded another. "It's like your mother's *parfum*."

Sergeant Gosse threw a blanket over Henri's shoulders. "Stay wrapped in this…not that I have to tell you. Or the water on your skin will suck away all your heat."

Henri pulled on his socks and boots. He insisted on walking back to the fire. He was a little unsteady but wanted to make certain he could walk without too much pain or dizziness. Shivering, his teeth chattering, he hugged his body inside the blanket and sat as close to the flames as he could without catching fire.

Major Péan, Sergeant Cabrelle, and the surgeon appeared.

Péan smiled broadly. "Sergeant Gerrard! Welcome back!"

The surgeon examined Henri's eyes, snapped his fingers near Henri's ears, and looked at the bandaged wounds. "Where do you feel pain?" he asked.

"Everywhere," Henri answered. "But my head and shoulder the most."

"Those wounds will heal."

"I-I don't remember the skirmish."

"That will pass, Sergeant."

"I'm a corporal."

"Uh, no. Not anymore." Major Péan interjected. "You were promoted to a militia sergeant based upon your valor during the battle. Isn't that marvelous? If you'd gotten blown up, you might be an officer now. Something to look forward to next time."

The surgeon stood. "I will leave him in your able hands."

Péan noticed the wet blanket around Henri's shoulders. He frowned and addressed the grenadiers. "Why is he wet?"

Sergeant Gosse snorted and told him.

"You decided to jump into the river!?"

"I stunk. I shit myself."

Péan raised his hands in mock surrender. "I have a lot to tell you, so pay attention. First of all, you can thank the grenadiers for volunteering to take care of you. Since your memory is foggy, I will recount the battle and what you did."

Henri listened with astonishment as the major, Sergeant Cabrelle, Color Sergeant Gosse, and the grenadiers all participated in the retelling. As they talked, certain memories began to return.

"Your gallant act saved the English sergeant, Kenneth Randall, from Albany," Péan said. "He is indeed alive because of you. He said you shot and killed one of our Indian friends, which indeed you did. The bad news? Unfortunately, that Indian was the son of Athanase, the chief. Some of our other Indian allies saw you do this, and they are not pleased. The good news? Lieutenant de Léry has come to admire you. He also claims you saved his life."

"I saved Lieutenant de Léry's life?"

"In between throwing grenades back over the wall," Sergeant Cabrelle added drolly, "and setting explosives to blow the gate. Typical acts of wilderness soldiering by the Montréal militia. A good example for the grenadiers."

The grenadiers snorted derisively at this.

Sergeant Gosse touched Henri lightly on his good shoulder. "Since you did not die, were wounded more than once, and saved you saved your commander's life, we grenadiers feel you now qualify to be a grenadier."

"That, and since you shit your pants in your sleep," Sergeant Cabrelle quickly added. "Also a primary qualification of a grenadier."

Sergeant Gosse continued. "Therefore, we offered to protect you."

Henri looked at the French regulars. "Thank you."

"We stand with you, Henri!"

"The butchery must be stopped!"

Péan listened but did not say anything. Considering what he knew about Governor Vaudreuil's views on Indian savagery, that being one of vigorous encouragement, ordering them to stop would *never* happen. The Indians would never obey such an order anyway.

"Any questions?"

"Do you have my cutlass and pack?"

Péan assessed the wounded youth. "That's your first question? After being unconscious four days and after everything I just told you? You ask if I have your fucking sword?"

Sergeant Cabrelle laughed. "Don't worry, Henri. I have your pack and cutlass."

"Am I in trouble?"

Péan shook his head. "In trouble? Well, that is a better question. But simple reasoning suggests since Lieutenant de Léry promoted you to sergeant and is decorating you for valor…army trouble does not seem to be a problem for you."

"I don't know what else to ask, sir. I remember little of what happened. I now remember dragging the Englishman out of the fort. Then Sergeant Cabrelle helping me. Then there was an explosion. Why was there an explosion?"

Color Sergeant Gosse's expression turned grim. He answered the question in a low voice full of disgust. He explained that one of the Indians purposely shoved the fort commander's wife into the fire hearth inside one of the buildings. When she ran screaming from the coals, her dress and hair in flames, she thrashed around the room in a pain-filled mania and the fire spread. The flames exploded some powder horns hanging on the wall. The fire quickly breached the roof and spread to the nearby buildings housing the powder magazines.

"That's when Lieutenant de Léry told us all to run for our lives, to abandon the fort," Major Péan added. "Good thing, too. I think you recall the ensuing explosion. It destroyed everything, including all the English and anyone else left inside the fort. Plus all of their supplies. Except for the little food we managed to save, some of which was already cooked for us by the fire. And that's almost gone."

"What happens now?"

"Aha! Finally, a good question. So now we are on our way back to Montréal."

"How much longer?"

"We are moving more quickly with no food sledges to drag. We are about half way. But we will head west in the morning towards Lake Ontario. Some *coureurs de bois* were sent ahead to have the bateaux brought down from Fort de La Présentation to Niaouré Bay to give us a ride. We'll load into boats and row our way downriver to Montréal from there."

"So we are done fighting?"

Péan laughed. "Not likely. But we will go home for rest before starting again."

*

The next morning, Henri fully dressed and refused to be carried in the litter by the grenadiers. He shouldered his own seventy-pound pack all day long, despite the pain in his shoulder, head, back, abdomen, arms, legs, hands, and feet. He walked in between the grenadiers who helped him up each time he stumbled. They saw his grimaces with each step and his resolve to endure his burden without complaint. They nodded at one another. *Henri is one of us.*

The march continued across mud, snow, and ice-covered streams in the miserable, dripping rain. The raiding party lines of march crossed and weaved among the trees, ravines, and hills. As they journeyed, Henri could not help but see the menacing glares of Indians and not too few *coureurs de bois* alike. Not all of them, but enough to send him the message his transgression was not going to be forgiven. He'd never seen so much deadly hate leveled at him before, even when he lived among the Seneca as a captive. Yet, alongside the animosity, he also experienced a closer camaraderie with the majority of the militia and soldiers, who vocally supported his actions on saving the English soldier from torture and mutilation. Especially the grenadiers, who waged war in conformance with an unspoken code of principles, almost respectful of the enemy they defeated in their victory, abiding by a marshal chivalry they espoused. They expected no less from their adversaries.

But such compassion and honor was rarely offered in this wilderness.

At the end of that day, Henri had never felt more exhausted, both physically and mentally. He ate whatever food was put in front of him, and a minute afterward, he could not recall what he had eaten.

Henri lay down near the fire to sleep. The skies had cleared to reveal countless stars. A half-moon was low in the sky. He took out the picture of Anamosa's smiling face from his pack. He held it up in the firelight to set that image to his memory before he closed his eyes, hoping it might invoke a dream of walking down a street holding her hand, appreciating her laughter, and the smiles of delight that went with it. But he was so fatigued he did not dream and quickly slipped into a deep slumber.

The mournful howl of a wolf brought him wide awake. It was early morning, not long before sunrise. The moon from the night before had faded and the fire had burnt down to just a few glowing coals. In the dim starlight, he noticed the lumpy shadows of men beneath their blankets around the fire pit.

He listened carefully but heard nothing in the cold, dark stillness. *Maybe I only imagined a wolf's howl...* Then it occurred again. *Roland*, he thought. The beautiful, deep throated cry of a distant wolf all alone in the wilderness brought tears to his eyes. *God, how I miss you, boy.* Unfortunately, he rarely heard that howl. But in the past, like on the Saint John River and at Lac du Saint-Sacrament, it was a warning, portending danger.

Danger?

Henri's senses came fully alert. With his right hand, he carefully and silently pulled his cutlass free from the scabbard on his pack. With his left hand, he pulled the dirk from his belt. He steadied and listened more intently to the sounds of the night.

Think, Henri. Think.

If he was to be attacked, it would come from his blind side. That's what he would do. That meant it would come from behind his head as he was lying down. They would want to attack silently, kill quickly, and then disappear back into the night before the grenadiers came fully awake. The attack would be with a knife or tomahawk, or maybe both. Would it be only one man? Henri decided, no, there would be two of them.

With that last thought, Henri heard a tiny snap on the ground behind him.

Henri's muscles, already tightly drawn, reacted instantly. He rolled left to his knees and turned in one movement, extending the cutlass and dirk up in front of his face in an *X*, which caught the downward slash of a tomahawk. He shoved hard against the tomahawk in time to parry with the sword and stop the slash of a second weapon coming in from his right. He could barely see the shadows of his attackers as he rose to his feet. He began the slashing exercise regimen he practiced every day: up, down, left, and right diagonal slashes. Stepping forward left, then right. If he could not see them clearly they also could not see him.

A man howled in pain. Henri connected with at least one of them.

"Alarm! Alarm!" shouted one of the grenadiers.

The soldiers were on their feet within moments, standing with discipline, their back to one another in a circle, facing outward with their muskets and bayonets at the ready.

"Where away, Henri?" Color Sergeant Gosse shouted.

"In front of me! Two attackers! I think they are retreating!"

Using his foot, one of the grenadiers kicked wood into the fire pit. A shower of sparks ignited the logs and illuminated the area.

Voices sounded from several directions. The entire encampment had been disturbed by the grenadiers' shouts of alarm.

The soldiers lit torches and searched the surrounding trees. A few feet in front of Henri, lying in the snow, was a bloody stump of a hand and arm cleanly cut from just below the elbow. It was still gripping a tomahawk. A blood trail led out to the brook and started again across the stream. Two sets of footprints.

The grenadiers relaxed.

"Fresh meat! Time to break our fast," said one of the soldiers light-heartedly. "Shall we roast this arm?"

The other men responded with sounds of disgust.

Lieutenant de Léry, Major Péan, and other officers and sergeants showed up seconds later to learn what had happened, their weapons drawn and ready to use.

"They've retreated, sir," informed the sergeant. "Two men, attacking with knives and tomahawks."

"Prisoners?"

"Yes, sir." The grenadier picked up the severed arm at the wrist and held it forth to the commander.

The lieutenant winced at the black humor.

Péan noted the blood he saw on Henri's cutlass. He slipped his own sword back into his scabbard. "Sergeant Gerrard. Explain your part in this."

Henri described the attack and the grenadier sergeant added what they had done in response and the direction of the trail they found.

"So they were Indians?"

"Yes, sir," Henri replied. "Two of them."

"And you were asleep when they attacked?"

"No. The howl of a wolf awakened me just before the attack occurred."

"Lucky for you."

"Yes, sir."

Lieutenant de Léry turned to the large crowd of men who had gathered nearby and who were listening to what was being said. More were coming.

"All right. Let's not bunch together! Since we are all awake," the lieutenant announced, "we will break our fast and begin our march. Prepare to break camp!"

His order was echoed to the rest of the raiding party.

The unexpected attack had left Henri feeling bewildered and betrayed. While he did not consider all the Indian allies his friends, he was willing to fight alongside of them, to die for them if necessary. Logically, he understood this attempt to be one of revenge, but it rekindled the sense of being alone in the wilderness again. When the officers left, he dropped to his knees, shaking with adrenaline and breathing heavily.

"Nicely done," complimented Sergeant Gosse. He gripped Henri's shoulder. "Not sure how they got past our guards."

"They were already inside our circle," Henri told the man. "They were part of our camp."

"Impossible."

"No. You heard Major Péan. It was a revenge attack on me. And they will try again and again until they succeed."

The other grenadiers scowled.

"That's not going to fucking happen," one of them stated firmly. "Even if we all stand guard at night. I hate this fucking land."

The bateaux were waiting for the raiding party upon reaching Niaouré Bay on the eastern shoreline of Lake Ontario. Lieutenant de Léry got into the first one along with three of his aides and told Sergeant Gerrard to travel in his boat as well.

"Have the English prisoner placed in the bateau with my grenadier escort. Major Péan, take charge of the men and see them safely to Montréal." He turned to his remaining officers. "Major Péan is in charge now."

Michel Péan frowned. "So now I'm to be a *major* again?"

Lieutenant de Léry smiled. "Just as soon as my bateau is out of sight. Michel, your performance on this campaign has been superb. I will make certain the governor knows of this. Thank you for your leadership when it counted."

They shook hands. Péan spoke quietly, "I would ask you not to boast too much about me to the governor. In truth, I was just following your lead, Lieutenant. My compliments. I don't think anyone could have done this better…not even me," he added with a grin. "Don't let Sergeant Gerrard fall overboard."

The lieutenant glanced at Henri sitting at the back of the bateau, staring off into the distance. "Indeed, I will not. He has several stories to tell me yet, which will provide my entertainment as we go downriver. Do you know much about him?"

"Lieutenant, I know a great deal about him. His father too. But I will let him tell you."

*

Fort Niagara

Philippe Gerrard walked free of the tree-shaded portage road into the open field of fire in front of Fort Niagara. He stopped to stare at how greatly the fortifications had been expanded. The trees were cut back another hundred paces at least, and maybe more. Much farther than a musket shot.

But not out of cannon range, he brooded.

If an English army dug zigzag siege trenches, the extra distance would only give the fort an additional week of time, at best, before the inevitable occurred.

His small scouting party had visited Fort Le Boeuf and Fort Presque Isle on the way to Niagara. He stayed an extra few days at both to rest before pushing on. Fort Niagara was Philippe's goal. This is where he planned to leave the two English children.

"Is this the last fort?" asked Joshua.

"This place is called Fort Niagara. Named after the great falls you saw. That lake you see up ahead is Lake Ontario. You should be safe here."

After leaving Fort Machault, the twelve-year-old-boy had asked Philippe endless questions. A behavior reminiscent of Henri's natural curiosity at that age…a thousand years ago, or so it seemed to the weary *coureur de bois*.

"Will we stay here with you?" Leah's voice was anxious. The question understandable. Unlike her brother, Leah did not speak much. Every day was another day of trauma for her, full of new unknowns and more uncertainty. She felt vulnerable and unprotected, unless she was right next to Philippe. Recognizing this, Philippe often carried her on his shoulders.

Philippe knelt before the apprehensive little girl, hugged her first and then held her gently by the shoulders.

"Leah, I promise, you and Joshua will stay with me until we reach somewhere safe, and we can return you to the English. I'm just not certain how soon that will be. In the meantime, don't worry."

The other *coureur de bois* scouts had walked ahead and were hailing the sentries manning the wall. The guards waved back and rang the arrival bell, which announced to everyone in the fort something or someone new and important was approaching the fort from the Niagara portage.

As Philippe approached the mighty complex of earth and stone bastions and ravelin, he marveled how his former log palisaded home had been transformed into a classical star-shaped, Vauban-style fortress. It was presumably impregnable. That was the plan. Certainly to the Indians. But any Vauban-style fortress could be overcome by a Vauban-style siege, which the English, like the French, were expert at conducting.

"It's big," Joshua remarked with the enthusiasm of a young boy enamored with soldiers and cannons or anything martial in nature.

"And yet it started out no bigger than the cabin in which you were born."

They passed through the gate. Many of the fort's soldiers, missionaries, merchants, and long-time citizens thronged to greet them, always anxious for any type of news from anywhere. Philippe Gerrard was one of their local heroes. He was always big news.

"Oho, Captain Gerrard!"

"Oho, Sergeant Gabriel!"

Philippe felt Leah's hand tighten her grip on his fingers. During their long travel, he had grown fond of this brave young girl…and the boy too. They were now his responsibility, not the army's, not the government of New France's. His. Philippe's conscience sometimes spurred him to hasty action. But he found that he liked it. He liked protecting something innocent and pure from the hideous atrocities committed in this war.

Philippe greeted many familiar faces. Sergeant Gabriel was the first. Theirs was a friendship going back more than ten years.

"You just cannot stay away from home, eh? Just look at our fort now, Philippe! Dozens of cannon and mortar, a battalion of soldiers, even cavalry. It will take a large land army to overcome what we've built here."

And that day is coming, Philippe reflected but did not say.

"I am requesting quarters for all my men, including Chesanin. They need food, beds, and their wages paid, if that is even feasible."

Sergeant-Major Gabriel laughed heartily at this. "Beds are not a problem. Food is not a problem. We were resupplied last week. And I will see they get paid as soon as *I* get paid."

"I thought so," Philippe replied.

"Commandant Pouchot is salivating over your arrival. He is probably staring out his window right now, looking at you, just waiting for you to come and visit. He will give me orders to bring you to see him soon enough. Why don't you wave in his direction? I will make up a story you will come by to see him after you attend to *personal* things."

Philippe waved and smiled in the direction of the castle.

"I am weary, Sergeant. And I have these two young ones to feed and bed down so it may not be until tomorrow."

"I doubt he will wait that long, but I will tell him." Gabriel bowed to the children. "*Bonjour.* What are your names?" They stared blankly at the sergeant. He regarded the boy and girl quizzically. "Do they not talk?"

"Not in French. They are English. I rescued them from Handsome Robert."

The sergeant's eyes widened. "That one is a devil."

"I know. He and I crossed paths."

"What are you going to do with these children?"

"Hopefully, leave them here with Pierre Dunemoore."

The sergeant frowned and shook his head. "Sorry to tell you, but Captain Pouchot has received orders from Governor Vaudreuil that all English captives must be sent to Montréal."

Philippe had heard the same at the smaller forts. He'd hoped this would not be the case.

Sergeant Gabriel saw Philippe's disappointment. "The captives are being assembled there for a prisoner exchange with the English."

"These are children…not soldiers."

"I know. The governor's order explicitly mentioned children would be the most valuable. He expects to get two of our men back for each one of their children. Even if Captain Pouchot agrees with you, he will not disobey that order and let them stay here. It would be too dangerous for them anyway. It is only a matter of time before we are attacked. You know this."

"Don't mention the children to the captain yet. I will bring it up."

"Of course." The sergeant smiled broadly. "It is *good* you've come back, Philippe. It brings hope to the fort to see you here. And you are most famous now for the victory at Fort Duquesne. Your legend grows daily. I've heard it said you personally killed over a hundred redcoats by yourself."

"No, that was Pierre."

"Oh? Pierre claims it was because he aimed the musket for you."

"That's right. He did. And did Juniata have her baby?"

"Oh yes! A baby girl. Last November. Her name is Kateri. Pierre is a proud father. And she is beautiful. Her hair is red!"

Philippe sent his men along with Sergeant Gabriel. Philippe and Chesanin entered the former Dunemoore Company store. Joshua and Leah followed them closely. The store had been empty the last time Philippe was here. Now it was fully stocked.

At seeing her son, Juniata shrieked and ran to Chesanin's outstretched arms.

Claude Guillot, the store clerk beamed. "Philippe!"

"I see the shelves are full again?!"

"Pierre is obviously a better manager than me. Always was. This was all his doing."

Philippe had Joshua and Leah sit at the long trading table and made introductions.

When her tears dried, Juniata hugged Philippe. "Pierre is out at the boat landing. He will be so excited that you are here." She turned and welcomed the children.

Philippe told her their story. Juniata quickly fetched water and wine and a small plate of honey biscuits.

Philippe explained to Leah he was going to find a man named Pierre.

"Pierre speaks English and he will be very happy to meet you. Chesanin will stay with you here. I will not be gone too long."

"I want to go with you," said Joshua. He stood up.

"Me too," said Leah.

Leaving them, even for a few minutes, was not going to be easy. He'd learned not to argue. They would just follow him anyway.

"All right then. Let's go."

He held Leah's hand and walked across the marshalling yard, pointing things out and explained the different parts of the fort.

"Something smells good," said Joshua.

"That's the bakery. Might as well stop there."

Inside, he spotted the portly figure of Madame Herault, the baker's wife, pulling something from the brick oven with the long-handle bread peel. The aromas in the room were heady and mouthwatering. She set the fresh loaves of bread on the wooden counter to cool, turned, and wiped her hands on her apron. She squinted at Philippe.

"My eyes are going bad. Philippe Gerrard? It is you! I thought I heard everyone calling your name."

She came around the counter.

"God, you stink! You must have marched a long time. Who are these little ones?"

"This is Joshua and Leah Carlisle. They do not speak French. They are English. I found them wandering in the wilderness." He told her the story.

Madame Herault cooed words of welcome to them. The children did not understand her French but recognized the motherly warmth in her voice.

"Sit. Yes. There you go. Here, sweetbreads for you both. Good, yes?"

"Can they stay here with you for a while? Until I return?"

"But of course. And you will compensate me for what they eat, *oui*?"

"Of course, Madame," he answered dryly. "Haven't I always?"

"Things are difficult when there is a war. You know this. But they may stay as long as they like and eat as much as they like."

Joshua already had a mouth full of hot buttered bread. Leah's rosy cheeks were dusty with flour. She smiled. They seemed content for the first time since he rescued them: a good sign.

Philippe went out the boat-landing gate and down to the new wharf, recently built to replace the one destroyed by the winter's lake ice. Men surrounded three heavily laden bateaux, unloading various supplies intended for the army. Pierre Dunemoore was using some rare silver coinage to negotiate a third of the cargo be diverted for delivery directly to his store. The voyageurs complained vigorously they would be accused of pilfering if the army did not get all of its cargo.

"Dinnah' lie tah' me, Jacques. Yah' dah' this all the time! Besides, how does the army know how much they are supposed tah' get anyway? Just carry it around the outside o' the fort and bring it in the main gate directly tah' my store. Do tha' first, before yah' bring the rest through the boat landing gate...and...and I'll pay yah' each an extra silver coin."

The voyageurs all smiled.

"So tha' was all I had tah' say?"

"Pierre would have given you more, Jacques."

Pierre spun around at hearing the familiar voice. "Yah' finally made it!" He hugged his partner. "Yah' could no' have come at a better time. I be actually moving furs through the store and selling things again."

"I thought Claude was managing the store for Intendant Bigôt's Grand Company?"

"Claude? Eeeyaaah! Claude could no' organize two wagons in a line on the portage. I pay him rent for the space and a bit o' tax on what I sell, which gives him something tah' report tah' Intendant Bigôt's scribes, and everyone is happy. Is Chesanin with yah'?"

"Yes. And six other men."

"So yah've been assigned here?" he said, his expression hopeful.

"Not exactly."

Philippe explained everything.

The voyageurs started moving the store's supplies around the outside of the fort. Seeing that, Pierre led Philippe through the boat-landing gate while they talked.

"I hope yah' dinnah' plan tah' leave those children with me?"

"Well...why not?"

"Why no'? Because I have a bairn o' my own tah' look after! Kateri. Did yah' see her?"

"No."

"No? Then let's hurry. Yah' are going tah' love her."

They were halfway across the yard when Sergeant Gabriel came running up to them.

"He saw you, Captain Gerrard. I assume that is the mail pouch slung over your shoulder? The commandant requests your report now. Apologies, Pierre."

Philippe came to attention and saluted the commandant.

Commandant Pouchot returned the salute. "Welcome back, Captain. I must confess I will never get used to you saluting me. Ahh, yes!" He rubbed his hands together anxiously. "Give me the bag of mail. I *love* mail. What do you think of my fort now?"

"Impressive. Is it finished?"

"Finished? No. A fort like this is *never* finished. I have eight hundred men here at present. A mix of militia and regulars. And six horses! Almost a cavalry troop! Are you here to join us?"

"No, I am escorting some English children." He told the commandant the story.

"You must already know they cannot stay here. The governor has issued an order..."

"Yes, I know. I will take them to Montréal."

"The voyageurs at the boat landing are going back to Montréal. They can take them for you."

"No. I have to do it. I am responsible for them."

"Well, they will certainly have use for you in Montréal. I just learned we will be attacking Fort Oswego soon. We recently attacked the supply forts at the carrying place."

"I'd not heard that."

"One of the forts was totally destroyed, according to the missive I received. Without proper supplies, Fort Oswego will be starved and isolated. Where did you find the children?"

Philippe told him the story.

"But Handsome Robert and his Delaware are French allies."

"So I am reminded repeatedly. He tortures and murders children. I will kill him the next time we meet."

The commandant shrugged. "This is war. There are brutalities committed by both sides. Not that I blame anyone for killing this particular murderer. But I would be ordered to arrest you if you kill him." What he saw on Philippe's face had him quickly adding, "Don't worry, Captain, I would never do that. But I would rather not be put in that position. So it is better that you go to Montréal."

Later in the afternoon, Philippe sat down with his six men and Chesanin in the forge room of the Dunemoore store and told them what he had learned. Pierre joined them in the room, smoking his pipe.

"I plan to take these children to Montréal. There are some voyageurs already at the fort. They will be leaving again in two days. You can stay here and become part of Fort Niagara's militia. Or go back downriver when you are ready and rejoin the militia at Fort Duquesne, or come with me to Montréal and remain under my command. I will be expanding up to full strength, probably thirty men or a full company, once I report to the army command in Montréal. But I do not know where I will be sent. The English are fighting us on every frontier, so I'm not sure it makes a difference. Before you decide, you should know I will be paying your wages in silver tomorrow from my own pocket, regardless of your decision."

The men looked at one another in surprise. Several began to talk all at once.

"We are truly getting paid? You have just become my favorite captain, Captain."

"I want to go with you to Montréal, so save my wages until we get there, or I will spend or gamble it away here."

"The best whores are in Montréal! Keep my money too!"

Of the six men, five did not want to be paid until they reached Montréal. But all of them announced their decision to go with him on the spot.

Chesanin told Philippe privately after the meeting broke up, he would not be going.

"My mother is here. Kateri is here. Pierre is here. And my father's grave is here. This is my place…these are my lands. I will stay here until this war is settled. And maybe forever after that."

Philippe accepted Chesanin's decision. "This is my home too. But I've come to learn that nothing is forever. My place is with Corrinne and Henri and Anamosa, even if they are in Boston." Philippe turned to Pierre. "What about you? Want to come with me?"

Pierre took the pipe out of his mouth and spit with surprise. "Wha'? Me?! Yah' are daft! Haven't yah' heard? I retired from the army. I have a wife and a new bairn! I've decided tah' go back tah' fur trading. Yah' should thin' aboot' tha' too."

"The war will eventually come here, Pierre."

"I know tha'. So why should I slog my way around the wilderness looking for it? I'll just wait for it here, nice and comfy. I'd rather fight them from behind these gigantic walls with a thousand soldiers at my side."

You'll think differently when the mortar shells rain down on you. But Philippe held his tongue.

They ate a large dinner pilfered from the army supplies of beef at the long table in the store. Pierre, Juniata, Chesanin, Joshua, Leah, and Kateri on Pierre's lap. The six-month-old little girl's head wobbled in every direction, smiling and studying everyone at the table. Philippe was charmed instantly.

"My God, Pierre. Her red hair is amazing to see!"

"Aye, red hair! Just like mine! Now pray God allows her tah' keep it all her life." He rubbed his balding head. "Kateri is a beauty." He smiled at Juniata. "Like her mother."

Joshua and Leah sat to either side of Philippe, being teased in Scots brogue by Pierre the whole meal. It was the first truly happy meal Philippe and Pierre had shared in almost two years.

While they ate, Philippe explained to the children they had to travel further to Montréal, that there would be a prisoner swap with the English from that city.

"We go wherever you go," Joshua stated solemnly.

Leah tightened her hold on Philippe's arm.

Later, Philippe and Pierre sat outside as night descended on the fort. Pierre smoked his pipe, and they talked like they had done so many times in the peaceful days of the past. The war filled each day with uncertainty. Today was no different. This morning, Philippe had finally arrived at Fort Niagara planning to stay, and now he was preparing for an even longer journey.

Pierre emptied his pipe and refilled it. "Two years into this fight, and we are all still here. Tha' bodes well, yes?"

"It should."

Philippe watched the lines and lines of soldiers forming up in the center of the marshalling ground for the evening muster where they would be counted to see if there had been any desertions. They would perform this count again in the morning. Ten lines, eighty men per line, split into two groups of four hundred men.

"But yah' dinnah' think so? Will yah' look at those lads! Those are metropolitan troops. Those regulars *beat* the redcoats in the last war."

"Impressive. Do they buy anything at the store?"

Pierre snorted. "They've no money tah' buy with. They've nah' been paid in…well, I dinnah' know how long."

"Speaking of getting paid. I will see the Jesuits tomorrow and melt down the rest of my silver bars into coins. I'll keep enough to pay my men and Chesanin, and then I'll split the rest with you."

"As yah' see fit, partner. I'll nah' be buying much here either. We mostly trade for everything. How much longer deeyah' thin' this war will go on?"

"Until one of us wins." Philippe shifted his head from side to side to relax the kinks in his neck. "At Fort Duquesne, the scouts and spies tell us the English are amassing thousands of men in Albany, in Acadia, at Fort Cumberland, and all the other colonies for that matter. Since we blew up that supply fort on the Mohawk River, we will seize Fort Oswego before the summer is over. It would make sense to do that. That will delay an English invasion of the lakes and the Saint Lawrence valley for at least another year."

"And yah' thin' the English will make peace after tha'?"

"No. After that, I think the English will bring an army of tens of thousands against us. Only not this year. Maybe next year, but certainly by the year after that. And then…we will lose by the numbers even if they carried only spears and swords."

"When did yah' get so fuckin' cheerful? So how dah' we win?"

"By not standing our ground if it appears we will lose. By running away to fight again. By staying alive. By not losing. The English worship money. Every battle that leaves us undefeated is money they lose. They only made peace the last time because they ran out of money. Not because they lost."

"I thin' we worship money too, yes?"

"You said it yourself. We don't have any money to lose. We have our homes. As long as we can we feed ourselves, we aren't going anywhere. Unless they drive us out of our lands. And the English love land even more than money. Just ask the farmers of Acadia. They carried them away in ships, I'm told. They are all gone by now. You think we will be treated any different? I don't."

Pierre Dunemoore stopped smoking his pipe and frowned at the thought of being driven out of Fort Niagara, with all of its soldiers, all the new cannon and its high walls. It was his home! And Philippe's too!

"Goo' on with yah! Dinnah bring a gloom tah' this conversation." Pierre pointed at the assembled troops with his pipe. "Those lads are nah' goin' anywhere. It'll take a bloody big army tah' lay siege tah' this place. And tha' English will have tah' find it first. They will bloody starve tah' death jist' trying tah' march through this wilderness. And it will be bloody even harder if they lose Fort Oswego, as yah' say!"

"All right. All right." Philippe gently slapped his partner on the back. "You're probably right. The war is just getting to me. *Dinnah*' be angry."

But Philippe knew the English would come here eventually. He'd seen telling maps in Sir William Johnson's library.

*

Philippe and Chesanin decided to visit Chittaqua's grave the next morning. It was the first time Philippe had left Joshua and Leah alone. They were apprehensive, but Pierre coddled them in his accented English. Many of the families in their settlement had been Scottish, so Pierre's accent was familiar and comforting.

Philippe and Chesanin walked out the fort's main gate, across the expanded field of fire to the forest's edge. Going back down the well-worn forest trails was like a walk back through time. Philippe saw a tree he'd marked with his knife, cut with signs as an indicator to Louie Hawkfeeder and Michel Langlois he'd gone that way to search for Michelle and Henri when they were taken captive by the Seneca. That journey would later end in tragedy and success. Michelle and Henri were returned to Fort Niagara. But Louie and Michel had lost their lives in a river battle…after rescuing *him* from the Seneca. Pierre had been wounded too.

"There is a lot of new growth here."

The comment broke Philippe's nostalgic reflections. Chittaqua's burial mound was less than ten paces away and the new trees springing up had already overgrown the area around it.

"It's so hidden now I might have walked right by it. Your father was always happiest when he was surrounded by trees."

Philippe started to climb the mound.

"Should we be doing this? Walking on his grave?"

Philippe nodded. "It's all right, Chesanin. You will make the closest contact with him if you sit down right at the top. Come. You'll see."

As they reached the top and sat down, they were rewarded by remarkable beauty. The mound was fifteen feet tall with a smooth, rounded top. The sky was blue that day and the morning spring sun was warm on their faces. The new trees had only reached about eight to ten feet in height. It created an illusion they were sitting on a small island surrounded for fifty paces in every direction by a sweet smelling growth, a sea-like forest of dew-covered green leaves.

"Just look at this sight. This was the right place. Your father is with us."

And as he said those words, Philippe felt a shiver race up his back.

"Skrieee!"

The white eagle stooped and landed on the crowning branch atop the tallest tree outside the circle of new growth. It stared down at them, unmoving, watchful. Chesanin stood up and started to dance, singing the Erigh song of welcome. Philippe raised his arm in greeting.

"Oho, old friend," he said in a low, reverent voice. His words were muffled by Chesanin's louder singing.

When Chesanin's song was finished, the young man sat again and began talking, telling his father of all the things he'd experienced since he last saw him. Philippe listened, feeling melancholy but pleased that Chesanin felt so joined with his father's spirit.

They stayed on the mound until the bird suddenly took flight, speeding off to the east towards the sun.

"Where does he go?" Chesanin asked with wonder.

"I don't know. But someplace important." Philippe stood and stretched the stiffness from his legs. "Your decision to stay has another benefit. You get to come here as often as you want. Bring Juniata and Kateri with you next time."

Before they started back to the fort, Philippe went down the back slope of the grave and walked south to the perimeter line where the old growth of trees marked the beginning of the broad circle of land that had been cleared to build Chittaqua's mound. He walked along this perimeter until he found a place where there were no trees growing, just wild grasses thick and lush. It was Okeanneh's grave. He had dug it himself years ago. A large stone lay flat in the ground with her name etched into it. He set aside his weapons and lay face down on the grass with his arms outspread.

"*Coutisimah*," he whispered. "Anamosa, she is safe. It has been a year since I have seen her last, but I know she is being well cared for."

A strong breeze rushed over him.

The three supply bateaux pushed away from Fort Niagara's boat landing carrying nine new passengers: Philippe and his six scouts, plus Joshua and Leah. The voyageurs welcomed the extra oarsmen. It would cut the travel time to Lachine in half and allow them to carry better food supplies from their stops at Fort Toronto and Fort Frontenac, making the journey less arduous.

As usual, a crowd of well-wishers congregated on the landing. The signal cannon atop the stone castle even fired a round in farewell to the famed *coureur de bois* captain. Again, Philippe felt an uncomfortable lump in his throat. Every time he left this fort he was not sure he would ever see it again. And this *was* his home…even though his heart was forever with Corrinne.

I hope she has received my letter by now. Maybe I can talk her into living here someday, he mused. Then shook his head and laughed aloud at the ridiculous idea.

Sitting in the same bateau as Philippe, Joshua also manned an oar. With the first oar stroke, he started asking Philippe questions as they traveled north on Lake Ontario. Philippe helped them both practice simple French phrases. At night around the campfires, he taught them some Indian hand signs.

"It's good to learn as many languages as possible. French, for certain, will help you when we reach Montréal. Sign language allows you to speak to Indians anywhere you go. And those people will respect this ability in you."

To Philippe's pleasant surprise, Leah learned the fastest.

CHAPTER 8
CHÂTEAU VAUDREUIL, MONTRÉAL
APRIL 1756
"Then buy a wig!"

It was a beautiful spring day in Montréal. The skies were blue. The sun was shining. It was only April, and New France was celebrating a new victory over the English. As far as Governor General Marquis de Vaudreuil-Cavagnial was concerned, this portended a good year ahead. His strategy against the English was working.

Feeling invigorated, the governor broke his fast in private and again read the revised version of the penned report by Lieutenant Joseph de Léry on this highly successful raid and action at the English supply forts on the Mohawk River. He'd ordered him to create the original as soon as he arrived in Montréal with the news of his victory. It was always important to have something in writing in case there was some blame to assign after such engagements. But the news had been much better than expected. They had destroyed the main supply storehouses and magazines. Fort Bull was obliterated. French casualties were light. English casualties were heavy. All the English forces inside the fort had been killed except one: a wounded provincial sergeant.

That survivor was the only blemish to this great success. One of the militia had killed an Indian ally to prevent the savage from scalping and mutilating a wounded English soldier.

Of what importance is this? was the governor's first reaction.

Vaudreuil told de Léry to expunge any mention of this trivial slaying from his otherwise marvelous report and pen it again. This newer version was more to his liking.

Vaudreuil finished breaking his fast.

But in just a few days, that blemish blossomed into a serious problem.

A war chief from the tribe of the dead warrior came to Montréal to see the governor. Confronting Captain Trieste, the chief *demanded* the governor meet with him.

Demand? Vaudreuil sizzled when hearing this word. Anyone demanding anything would normally wait at least another day or two to gain an audience. But not this man. This was not just any chief. This was Chief Athanase of the Lorette Huron, a tribe that had supported Fort Duquesne when the English were defeated. The Huron were ten thousand strong. They were Vaudreuil's most important tribal ally. Athanase was admitted immediately.

Vaudreuil was respectful and appropriately sympathetic.

"I am aware of the terrible crime committed by one of my soldiers. I promise you, Athanase, I will personally rectify this insult."

"*Insult?*" The Huron chief spoke in French. He repeated the word bitterly, "Insult! The warrior he killed was my son! I demand you give him over to me for justice."

Taken with other escalating events, the *blemish* had turned serious and was now out of control. Vaudreuil soothed Athanase with fervent promises of justice and gifts. Then he sent his aides to bring Lieutenant de Léry to him so he could relate his displeasure with this new trouble.

"I was forced to meet with Athanase. This bone-decorated, odorous primitive demanded...*demanded me!*...demanded that I turn over your militiaman for justice. Can you imagine the kind of justice this savage has in mind for your soldier? You nod? Then consider it a measure of my antipathy by saying if your militiaman had been present in the room, the chief would have left with the man in tow with a noose around his neck!

"As it was, Athanase left with a bateau full of presents and my promise to do something about the offending soldier. Next I learn, as these Indians left the city, there was an armed confrontation outside the walls with my French regulars who disputed the contention any punishment was due. And not just any French regulars, my elite grenadiers from Régiment de Guyenne are defending this militiaman! Thank God the grenadiers possess the discipline not to fire unless they are ordered. I challenged the sergeant in charge of the grenadiers whether or not he was in command of his men. He revealed that you promoted this militiaman to sergeant, and submitted written recognition to decorate him for *valor* in battle! I was stunned. There is no advantage to be gained by commending this man! And you decorated him for shooting one of our Indian allies?! Now he is a hero to the citizens of Montréal. What were you thinking?"

Lieutenant de Léry tried to explain. "Governor, this militiaman saved my life and the lives of several other men during the battle. He was twice injured by grenades while breaking down the main gate of Fort Bull. I felt his singular bravery should be recognized. My entire command agreed with my actions. To answer your question, I was convinced commending him for valor was a good and proper thing to do at the time."

"Based on the problem we have now, we would be better served celebrating his *funeral*! You think that harsh of me to say? The Huron of the mission at Fort de La Présentation sent an additional messenger to me this morning. The Huron have announced their refusal to fight alongside my French regulars in future battles. How am I supposed to fight a war if my Indian allies won't march with my regulars?!"

"Maybe we could offer bribes…"

Vaudreuil's scowl deepened. "*Of course* I bribed the Huron. That always works for a time. Athanase expects bribes as a courtesy for taking the time to honor our privies with his shit. But this time he wants *revenge*! He wants your sergeant."

"Governor, you do not intend to give over Sergeant Gerrard?" Lieutenant de Léry asked, his expression somber.

"You think I lack the conviction to make such a decision, Lieutenant? I assure you, I will not hesitate if I decide it is the only way to resolve this problem."

"Governor, that would cause more serious problems—"

"Stop! Do not presume to lecture me on the obvious, Lieutenant. But considering the import of these unique circumstances, I do not intend to solve this with bribes. It would set a precedent for the Huron to claim similar offenses in the future just to get more bribes! They learn quickly. But this would not work anyway. Athanase is determined to have revenge… or at least *justice*. We could at least argue about that meaning. They must get it, one way or another. And I cannot have them threatening not to fight at our side! We are going to attack Fort Oswego, and our success is totally dependent on their help."

Governor Vaudreuil stood and began to pace.

"Is this sergeant the same militiaman decorated for valor following the battle at Lac du Saint-Sacrament?"

"Yes, sir. Sergeant Henri Gerrard."

"So everyone in the city is hearing the name of Henri Gerrard…again! *Oui?*"

"Yes, sir."

Vaudreuil frowned. He was not going to give up one of his soldiers to torture. *Court-martial him, perhaps. Execute him publicly? Athanase would demand to see it. No, I will not be cowed into that. But if not that, I will need to exile Sergeant Gerrard somewhere before the Huron abduct him. But this cannot appear to the city to be a punishment. And he is militia…a free man…*

Lieutenant de Léry had thought of a solution, though it pained him to suggest it. "What if we offer Athanase the English prisoner instead?"

Vaudreuil regarded Joseph de Léry's genuine chagrin. He liked this unassuming officer. He was impressed by the man's sincere desire to solve this problem. The suggestion was extraordinary for such an honorable man as de Léry.

"A worthy idea, Lieutenant. The Huron would gladly accept the English prisoner and then torture the unfortunate man for days. But in the end, they would still demand the sergeant. But since you mentioned the prisoner, find a way to silence him. He keeps retelling the story of his rescue to anyone who will listen, further enhancing the city's hero worship."

"I will isolate the Englishman in the bastille as soon as I am dismissed. He may not live much longer anyway. Both his legs are rotting from the wounds he received in battle."

"The Englishman is dying?"

"Yes, sir.

The governor paused, staring off into the distance. He suddenly had a new idea. *I am brilliant!* But first he must go to see the wounded Englishman.

"Yes, isolate the Englishman as you suggest. Transfer him to the bastille without delay. And send a message to me when he is there. Treat him well. Have him resting on something comfortable if you please. I intend to puncture this cyst created by your gallant sergeant before the problem gets worse. Come see me again tomorrow morning. And bring Major Péan with you. He should be rested by now. You will be my first meeting."

The next morning, Vaudreuil dusted his hair and rouged his cheeks as was his practice before assenting to see the long line of administrators and petitioners usually waiting to meet with him. He considered himself far more than a governor-general of New France; he was a viceroy, at least! He ruled a kingdom almost larger than Europe. He took his time, fastidious to look the part. Indulging his personal appearance also induced his best thinking because it usually took place in front of a dressing mirror where he could take counsel with his most trusted advisor: *himself.*

With the destruction of Fort Bull, Fort Oswego was next. He entertained no thought of retaining Fort Oswego. His strategy was raid, plunder, destroy, burn, and withdraw. The English would have to mount a long march with an extended supply line through the wilderness to reestablish their presence on Lake Ontario. And he could frustrate any of those attempts with far less resources or expense. With Oswego gone, the local Indians would further align themselves with the French. He might even begin to crack the decades-old English alliance with the Iroquois confederation; certainly, the Oneida appeared friendlier after they observed the destruction of Fort Bull. After ridding Lake Ontario of the pustule called Fort Oswego, which was more of an exhibition of ego by the English—"We, too, are here!"—than a real military threat, he needed only to dominate Lake Champlain and Lake Ontario to maintain control of Canada. Vaudreuil did not have the resources to man all the forts. But the English, too, would have to advance with thousands of troops and enormous resources over a difficult wilderness terrain to dominate and control.

A valet helped him finish dressing. He'd decided to wear his general's uniform today since he was meeting with the military first. It was the most fashionable military dress uniform of the royal court in Versailles and included a ceremonial sword. He turned left and right, gazing at the regal image in the standing mirror.

He gave his appearance an approving nod. "This will do," he told his valet.

Vaudreuil walked down the connecting hallway imperiously, followed by three military aides, all of them ensigns, each of them awaiting orders to perform anything the governor asked them to do.

He had converted one of the three large dining rooms in the Vaudreuil mansion into the official government meeting chamber with a miniature throne for him at the head of the table. But today he would meet with Lieutenant de Léry and Major Péan to discuss the Huron problem. He ordered his staff to arrange for that meeting in a smaller room, the personal office of the Marquis Duquesne, the former governor-general. It contained an ornate desk behind which sat a high-back cushioned chair covered with beautifully embroidered brocade material. In front of the desk were six wooden, armless, cushionless chairs. These were arranged in a line. The walls of the room were adorned with the portraits of the King and Queen. A highly detailed map of New France and its borders covered one entire wall, showing its extraordinary size in contrast to the rest of North America. There were two side credenzas for serving any food or refreshments. That morning there was a bottle of Bordeaux, four glasses, and some berry-filled croissants on the tables. Nothing would be served without Vaudreuil's command.

Captain Trieste waited outside the private entry to the room. When the governor approached, the captain saluted.

"Lieutenant de Léry and Major Péan are in the office. Sergeant Gerrard is waiting outside the other entry."

"Are the documents ready?"

"All the documents we discussed yesterday are on the left side of the desk. I've brought ink and quill and will be standing behind you, with your permission, of course, to address any irregularities at your discretion."

Vaudreuil nodded and the captain opened the door for him. De Léry and Péan stood at attention immediately. Captain Trieste and two of the three aides followed the governor into the room. The third ensign would stand guard outside the door to prevent anyone else from eavesdropping. The two aides stood by the credenzas.

"Good morning, gentlemen. You may sit."

Major Michel Péan glanced at Captain Trieste standing impassively behind the governor's chair. The Corsican police officer was previously one of Péan's direct reports before Péan was forced to leave Montréal to march to Fort Bull at the head of the militia.

You certainly have enjoyed this cat being away, Péan mused.

The major had returned with the remainder of the raiding party only two days earlier. He barely had time to clean himself up and had not been relieved of those command duties yet. He hoped that was one of the topics of this meeting. Once that happened, Major Péan planned to turn Captain Trieste upside down and shake from his pockets all the tax money the captain had embezzled from him while he was gone.

Governor Vaudreuil opened the meeting by making comments as if he and Lieutenant de Léry had not met several times already. The lieutenant found this unusual but decided it was because of Major Péan's presence.

"Lieutenant, I found your formal report to be very encouraging. Your performance was exemplary. Your success will be noted by the King himself. You likely have forestalled the English plans for a campaign on Lake Ontario until next year. Even if they try to recover from the destruction of Fort Bull, I plan to strike Fort Oswego first. I delay that campaign only long enough to refit and resupply our troops and finalize the plan of attack." Vaudreuil abruptly turned to Major Péan. "Major, why are you frowning?"

"Frowning? Governor, I was not aware my expression was a frown. Apologies if it seemed so."

"Accepted. Lieutenant de Léry's missive was most complimentary about your leadership role in this latest foray against our enemies."

Major Péan tilted his head deferentially towards the man sitting to his right. "I assure you, Governor, anything I did only mimicked Lieutenant de Léry's leadership. I say that with the utmost sincerity."

"Still, I find your obsession with commanding the gendarmerie forces in Quebec and Montréal a terrible waste of your obvious military aptitude."

"Thank you, Governor. I have always endeavored to execute my policing duties with the same enthusiasm," he replied, his voice glum. To his surprise, the governor moved to a different topic.

"Major, this situation with Sergeant Gerrard has caused problems with the Huron that cannot be tolerated and must be resolved."

With that comment being directed at him alone, Major Péan sensed that the governor had concluded he was at fault somehow. He decided to say nothing until he understood what was going on.

"Sergeant Gerrard admitted he acted precipitously when he killed the Indian," de Léry offered. "But he does not apologize for his actions."

Péan was thankful for de Léry's unexpected support. Whatever was coming, de Léry was not aware of it either.

Governor Vaudreuil's nose lifted slightly. "The man he killed was the son of Chief Athanase. You do understand, regardless of Sergeant Gerrard's valor in battle, the Huron determination for vengeance will not stop simply because he is back in Montréal." There followed an awkward pause. "Agreed?"

"Of course, Governor. I completely understand your point," de Léry replied quickly.

"Yes, sir," Péan echoed.

"New France cannot abide another incident like this during our attack on Fort Oswego, or at any other time we are facing the enemy. If the Indians decide to torture, kill, or even *eat* those fallen in defeat, you will order your men to turn their heads the other way. Is that clear?"

"Yes, sir," they replied as one.

"The second part of this problem is the repercussions of Sergeant Gerrard's hostile act. His commendation for valor has complicated this. The grenadiers are resolved to defend his actions. This creates a problem on how to satisfy the Huron desire for revenge. At the same time, the solution must not elicit the enmity of my best troops or provoke their unfortunate inclination for reprisal towards the Huron. Do you have any suggestions?"

The governor looked pointedly at Major Péan.

Merde! Péan could see the governor already had a plan. "Governor, I ask your indulgence to let me think about an appropriate solution for one more day. I feel certain I can have something to suggest by tomorrow morning."

"I want to make a decision before this meeting is over. Fortunately for you, I have already devised a course of action. My plan will remain confidential, however." The governor pointed at them both. "One of you, move aside to leave an empty chair." To Captain Trieste, he said, "Bring in Sergeant Gerrard."

As Lieutenant de Léry moved over to his right, he exchanged a look of complete surprise with Major Péan.

Henri Gerrard marched into the office of the governor-general anticipating some honor, possibly a word of personal thanks by the governor. He was surprised to see Major Péan and Lieutenant de Léry in the governor's private office. Péan's expression was inscrutable. Henri was immediately on guard.

Think, Henri. Remember to think before you talk, he reminded himself.

Henri had been in Montreal for four days. He'd learned about this potential meeting three days earlier from Captain Trieste who suggested he wear appropriate clothing.

"Something other than the smelly rags you are wearing now."

With Carmen's help, Henri had a dark gray suit of clothes tailored in a style a city merchant might wear. She cobbled him some new shoes. Early that morning, after he bathed, she cut and combed his hair to hide his mutilated ear, tying any excess back in a tail. She tried to dissuade him from wearing the cutlass over his shoulder and the dirk in his belt. Henri explained he expected to be evaluated as a sergeant, a veteran member of the militia. And the militia carried weapons everywhere they went after being called up.

He noticed neither Lieutenant de Léry nor Major Péan were armed. The governor was, however.

Oh Christ, Henri! Péan thought with alarm as Henri entered. *Why are you wearing that fucking sword?*

Henri walked to the front of the Governor's desk, stopped at stiff attention, and saluted in the manner the grenadiers had instructed.

Good God! He even salutes like a grenadier, the governor thought. "At ease, Sergeant Gerrard. Everyone, sit."

The governor gestured for the wine to be served.

"First, I would like to honor you with a toast for your courage in battle."

The four men raised their glasses. They all took a small sip.

The governor frowned. "It's not aged how I like it, but it is better than drinking tea."

Polite laughter.

"Sergeant, in addition to honoring you, I brought you here to discuss the incident with the Huron warrior you killed at Fort Bull. I understand you saved the life of an enemy soldier by doing this. But in doing so you killed the son of Chief Athanase. He intends to take your life in vengeance. He will abduct you for torture, even here…right off the streets of Montréal."

"Yes, sir," Henri replied. "I am aware of that."

"Good. Does that make you regret your earlier decision?"

"Regret? No, sir. I was dazed by shrapnel to my head at the time and lying against the stockade wall. I saw the Indians mutilate the wounded soldiers lying everywhere. The screams were…were terrible. This particular English soldier had musket wounds in both legs. He was bleeding and struggling to crawl out of the gate to escape. That Indian had just scalped and cut off the genitals of another wounded soldier before jamming them into the man's mouth. He then held his hand over the man's mouth and nose until he choked to death. He saw this other wounded soldier crawling towards the gate. By this point, the man was only a few paces from me. The Indian ran to him, sat down on his wounded legs. His intentions to mutilate were obvious. My dizziness was bad. I could barely aim my musket. But the Indian was close enough. I could not miss. After that, I dragged the wounded man out of the fort."

Major Péan and Lieutenant de Léry were struck by the barely restrained anger in the young sergeant's voice.

Governor Vaudreuil remained unmoved. "A question, Sergeant. Why did you not shoot the English soldier instead? He was your enemy, is that not so?"

Henri paused before making his reply. "The English soldier was wounded, lying helpless on the ground. He carried no weapons. He had become my prisoner. I defended him."

"Who gave you orders to take prisoners?"

Oh, no. Major Péan was no longer looking at the governor. He stared straight ahead.

"Orders? No one. The man was no longer fighting us. It just seemed the right thing to do. Was I mistaken?"

Péan groaned inwardly. He wondered just how far in the western wilderness he could be posted. *Fort Detroit?* Certainly that was a possibility now.

Governor Vaudreuil was amazed at the impertinence of this soldier.

"What's right and wrong in war becomes obscured in decisions of life and death. What is right and wrong is the providence of the observer, who is usually the winner. The loser has no opinion. We French were the winners. The Indian was your ally. You took his life."

"I observed what he was doing to my prisoner was wrong." Henri did not vacillate with his answer.

Major Péan found it hard to imagine how this conversation could get any worse. *Vaudreuil will exile me to Fort Detroit…permanently.*

"I understand you are the son of Captain Philippe Gerrard?"

"Yes, sir."

Vaudreuil picked up a document on his desk. "Are you aware that at one point your father was declared a traitor and a murderer by the King? So asserts this warrant by Intendant Bigôt."

Henri's gaze did not waiver. "I do not agree with what that document states. My father is neither of those things. He is fighting for you, the King, and New France at Fort Duquesne."

This actually can get worse, Péan decided morosely. *I will be posted to a fishing encampment in the north, surrounded by miles of ice.*

"It seems Captain Gerrard has views similar to yours where it concerns English prisoners."

"And I am proud he is my father."

With that comment, Vaudreuil stared hard at Sergeant Gerrard. Part of his new plan was to exile the sergeant to a remote corner of New France. It seemed the best thing to do. Just order him to go. But he was militia. He must first get him to join the Troupes de la Marine.

"And you should be proud of him. Captain Gerrard fights for New France. But I cannot have your notoriety and the threats from our Indian allies jeopardizing our next military campaign. This is more important than a simple militia sergeant. Would you agree?"

Henri answered cautiously. "Yes, sir."

"Good. How old are you?"

Henri realized his birthday, in March, had come and gone. He'd missed it completely. Not that there would have been any kind of celebration, but he was surprised he had not remembered.

"I...I just had a birthday," Henri replied.

"Good," Vaudreuil said. "Then I declare you are sixteen years of age. Please confirm my conclusion."

Henri could not see what difference that made. "Yes, sir."

He spoke over his shoulder to Captain Trieste. "Note that the sergeant's declaration is vouchsafed by Major Péan, an officer of the Troupes. Sergeant Gerrard, I have a proposal for you. I want you to join the Troupes de la Marine, but with the rank of ensign based upon your education, your demonstrated bravery in battle, and the fact you are the son of Captain Philippe Gerrard."

Henri did not respond. There followed another awkward silence.

Vaudreuil watched the sergeant hesitating. "There is no ruse at work here, Sergeant. I think you will find this to be an excellent decision for you. Do you agree with this promotion, Lieutenant?"

Lieutenant de Léry was awestruck by everything Henri had done thus far.

"Sergeant Gerrard saved my life. I have learned through our mutual discourse the sergeant is highly educated. He is an excellent soldier, respected by the militia…well, most of them anyway. And obviously the grenadiers respect his bravery. His commission would be celebrated as a fitting tribute to his valor."

Vaudreuil asked again. "What say you now, Sergeant Gerrard?"

Henri looked at Major Péan.

Péan did not hesitate. "Oh, I agree wholeheartedly with Lieutenant de Léry." *Maybe this will overturn my impending banishment.* "Sergeant, what the governor offers you is a great tribute. It is the right thing for you to do. You have earned this."

Henri took his time before answering.

"Governor, it would be my honor to serve in the Troupes de la Marine. I only hesitate because I am unsure of my ability to lead other men. And I do not see how this will solve the problem I created for you with the Huron."

Vaudreuil brushed away that concern with a wave of his hand. "Worry no longer about that. This document asserts your formal commission as an ensign in the Troupes de la Marine. Sign it."

Major Péan's mind was racing. *Worry no longer? What? Henri is being promoted for this problem? Why?*

Henri took a deep breath. He accepted the ink and quill offered by Captain Trieste and signed the commission.

"Captain Trieste. Have this new commission recorded by an administrator right away."

"Yes, sir."

The governor stood and the three officers also came to attention.

"My congratulations, Ensign Gerrard. Major Péan, Ensign Gerrard will report to you. As his commander, you will lead him in swearing an oath of allegiance to France and the King."

Major Michel Péan knew this oath by heart. He also knew this formality would not be the end of it. The bigger surprise, whatever it was, was still to come. But for the moment, he was proud for Henri. And he was proud to administer the oath.

Henri repeated every word. "Before God, I so swear. Amen."

Major Péan gave him a courtesy salute. "Ensign, as I know the character of your father, I assure you he would be very proud of your decision today."

All the men in the room took turns shaking Henri's hand, including Captain Trieste. Governor Vaudreuil was last.

"Major Péan will take charge of your instruction as a new officer in the Troupes. Major, I assume there is some type of direction for the ensign to read? Perhaps a book of history appreciating the more sordid exploits of the marines when they crawl through the squalid alleys of the city you undoubtedly can share."

"It will be my privilege, Governor."

"Yes…of course it will. Major, I want to see you and Ensign Gerrard here tomorrow morning, same time, for more discussion. I expect the ensign to be properly attired."

"Yes, sir."

Vaudreuil's voice took on an intimidating tone. "This entire proceeding and all of our discussions, including Ensign Gerrard's commission, will remain confidential. I do not want it discussed outside this room with anyone else. You are all officers and that is an order. Is that understood?"

The governor looked at every man directly to receive an answer, including his aides and Captain Trieste.

"Good. Do not forget it. You are dismissed, Major, Ensign. Lieutenant de Léry will remain with me."

Major Péan and Henri saluted and left. They were silent until they stepped out onto the street.

Henri felt struck in the head. "What now, Major?"

"No questions. Let's just get far away from the mansion for now."

Major Péan hurried them to Rue Notre-Dame and the shop of his personal tailor.

"Monsieur, if you please. This man needs a tailored uniform of an ensign in the Troupes de la Marine made before this day ends. Put the expenses on my account. Henri, do what this master tailor tells you to do. After that, while we wait for the uniform to be made, we will talk more about what happened today."

Henri slipped off his coat and pants. The tailor took several measurements and retired to the back of his shop.

"What have I done wrong?" Henri was bewildered.

"You mean in addition to shooting Chief Athanase's son?" Major Péan chuckled. "I am jesting, Henri! Time will soon answer that question for us both. But from what I saw and heard, you spoke from your heart, and you can never be wrong about doing that. Although, too much honesty can sometimes cause problems."

Major Péan did not entirely believe what he just counseled. In fact, just the opposite was true when talking to superiors. But it had sounded good aloud.

"Lying can occasionally be useful too, such as when soliciting the physical affections of a beautiful woman by professing your love for her. You did nothing wrong today. Color-Sergeant Cabrelle will be shocked. From corporal to sergeant to ensign in less than a week. Now, I am going out to find a decent bottle of wine for us to share. And *you* prepare to step into your next role in life."

"Major, did I make a mistake by signing that commission?"

"You are an officer in the army of France now. It was *destiny*. Who knows why? But I am proud to have shared this day with you."

Péan opened the tailor shop door.

"What happens tomorrow?"

"We'll talk in a little while! Have the master tailor lock the door behind me. No visitors until I return!"

Later that afternoon, Henri Gerrard looked at himself in the standing mirror as if staring at a stranger. He was wearing a gray-white coat of fine wool that hung to just above his knees. It was seamed down the back. The coat bottoms' front and back turned out to show the dark blue underside of the wool. The lapels and cuffs were turned back showing similar blue, everything held in place by polished brass buttons. The gaiters rising from his feet to just below his knee were of soft, polished black leather. There was a black leather belt with hanging brass loops on the left for his sword and powder horn when he carried them. The uniform included a standard ammunition bag on a sling to hang over the shoulder. The trousers were a fine wool of dark blue, the leg bottoms tucked inside the gaiters. The shirt was made from fresh, white linen. Three extra shirts and another pair of trousers were included. A cravat of white lace adorned his neck; two more of less pretention were also ordered.

"And now your crown," Major Péan proclaimed. He set the tri-cornered dark blue hat trimmed with gold ribbon on Henri's head. "*Voilà!*"

Henri was speechless at seeing his image. He was also a little drunk from sharing the two bottles of Bordeaux that the major had purchased along with delicious baguettes and a block of cheese.

"This looks…inappropriate for me."

"Nonsense, Henri! If you feel you must, go roll around in some dirt. But not until after we meet with the governor tomorrow."

"Roll in the dirt!?" The tailor protested. "No, Monsieur! *S'il vous plaît!*"

"At ease, master tailor. I was jesting. Your work is magnificent as usual." The major held the sleeve of his coat next to Henri's for comparison. It looked drab. "In fact, make me one just like it."

"What do I do now?" Henri asked dazedly.

"Go home to your cobbler lady friend. But don't be surprised if she drops to her knees and attaches her lips to your crotch."

"Major!"

"I'm just being truthful, Henri. Uniforms can have that effect on women."

"I do not want to discuss Carmen."

"Not even her breasts? Their voluptuousness? All right. All right. Don't scowl. Come. Gather up your wardrobe and we will talk as we walk."

Henri took off the hat and pulled his cutlass scabbard over his shoulder and slipped the dirk on his belt.

"Ensign, do not wear that cutlass over your shoulder tomorrow. It's out of uniform for an officer anyway."

When Henri entered the cobbler's shop, Carmen stopped working and stared at him in awe. She came around the counter, walked up to him, and kissed him deeply.

Major Péan grinned. "Bonjour, Mademoiselle. Don't mind me. Ensign Gerrard was worried you would find him *unhandsome*."

"I did not say—"

"Unhandsome?! I am closing the shop. Let's go upstairs."

"*Voilà!* You see, Henri? I will meet you here tomorrow at sunrise. Be ready! This meeting will be important! *Au revoir.*"

While they had waited for his new uniform, Major Péan had mentioned the transfer of the English prisoner to the bastille. Henri was appalled.

After Carmen's ministrations, Henri donned the less conspicuous clothing of a *coureur de bois* and visited the Montréal bastille to check on the condition of Kenneth Randall. He told the guards who he was and was admitted without trouble.

The jailer opened the dark cell. It was lit by a single candle only. The Englishman was lying atop a cot on a filthy, thin mattress. In the candlelight, Henri could see the fever sweat drenching the soldier's body, giving off a bad smell. The room had a chair and a table with a pitcher of water and a cup. He pulled the chair next to the bed, sat down, and touched the man's arm gently.

The soldier's eyes blinked open. He looked at Henri. "Who are you?"

"It's Henri Gerrard."

"Henry! I'm sorry. I did not recognize your face in this dim light."

"I came to see how you are feeling."

"Not so good. I'm afraid my legs are lost to the rot."

Henri poured a cup of water and helped the man drink.

"Ahhh, yes. That's good. Pour some on my face. Yes, that feels good. Thanks."

"What do the surgeons say?"

"Well…they have no medicines for this. They offered to take both my legs but said the poison has spread so far it may not help. I thought, why go through all the pain of having my legs sawed off if I'm am going to die anyway."

"I'm sorry, Sergeant. I wish I'd made a difference for you."

"But you did, lad. What that Indian would have done to me would have been much worse. And the pain of having your balls cut off? I'd rather die this way. My legs are numb now anyway. Don't worry. I've made my peace with God. Soldiers don't often have that chance."

Henri lowered his eyes. He didn't really know this man, but he liked him already.

"Your governor came to see me today."

"The governor?" Henri asked, puzzled. "Governor Vaudreuil?"

"Yes."

"Why?"

"To talk about you, of course. About what happened. About the war. He is an interesting chap. He told me he was sorry to learn from the surgeons I was going to die."

"I am surprised he came to see you at all. From all I heard, he finds your presence, and the fact I helped you, to be an *inconvenience* for him."

"Yes. He said as much to me."

Henri winced. "He should not have said anything like that to you at all."

The Englishman spoke his next words more thoughtfully. "Your governor had his reasons…I suppose. Hey, I learned they promoted you to sergeant?"

Henri smiled thinly. "Yes. In spite of all the trouble I caused." There was no point in telling him more.

"Well then! Congratulations, Sergeant Gerrard! Since you're here, might I ask a favor of you?"

"Of course."

Kenneth Randall took a locket from his waist pocket. His hands trembled as he opened it and handed it to Henri. There was a picture and a lock of hair inside.

"Her name is Cora. That's a lock of her hair. She is my wife. I know it's probably impossible, but if you survive this madness and can find a way, would you take this to her in Albany for me? I have a farm there. Tell her I love her. I also have a son, James. He is only three. He'll never remember. But maybe you could tell him about me? Make up a story…something heroic?" He chuckled. "If you feel so inclined. He will never see me again. But it is nice for sons to have good memories of their fathers, yes?"

Henri's voice was thick. "I cannot promise you I will survive. But if I do, I will be honored to do this thing for you."

Randall exhaled, relief etched on his exhausted face. "Thank you, Henry. Thank you. You have no idea how relieved that makes me feel. Just the thought they might not ever know what happened to me…" He closed his eyes and patted Henri's hand. "Thank you, Henry. It seems all this talk has made me dizzy. I should sleep now."

The next day, Henri was waiting outside for Major Péan when he walked up to the cobbler's shop.

"Good morning, Ensign. You're looking well-mended."

"Please don't start."

Michel Péan laughed and slapped Henri on the back. "Very well. Let's get to the mansion and find out what other surprises Governor Vaudreuil has for us. We've enough time to visit my favorite brasserie. Good wine. But they serve wonderful flavored teas this time of day, with excellent croissants. We can load up on that and talk about our strategy."

"Strategy?"

"Yes. But not to discuss, until we are sitting, in the brasserie. And your mouth is full of croissants."

Captain Trieste saluted the major and opened the door leading into Governor Vaudreuil's office.

"The governor will be here shortly, Major."

"So, Captain, tell me. What were the collections last month?"

Trieste's eyes shifted towards Henri before he replied. "I'm not sure what you mean, Major. Please close the door behind you." The officer walked across the office and out a side door.

Major Péan scowled. "Captain Trieste just made a mistake. Showing his back to me. He does not usually make mistakes." Péan wondered why the captain felt so bold on this day.

"What?"

"Let's sit. Remember what I said. The governor will likely be giving us orders. And we may not like what we hear. Don't let him see that it bothers you. It will weaken any negotiating room we may have…if there is any left, that is."

"Do you really think it will be bad news?"

The side door opened. They stood at attention as Governor Vaudreuil entered. He eyed Ensign Gerrard's uniform critically as he took a seat behind his desk.

He twirled his fingers. "Turn a circle for me, Ensign. Hmm. Very good tailoring. Is that a nautical cutlass at your waist? The one you wore over your shoulder yesterday?"

"Yes, sir."

"It looks rather…used. You are certainly eligible to wear something of higher quality."

"Uh…Yes, sir. Certainly, Governor. Thank you."

Bravo, Henri. Major Péan thought. *Good start.*

"Sit. This meeting will not last very long. Captain, do you have the orders?"

Merde! Péan thought. *Here it comes!*

Captain Trieste handed the governor two separate documents. Vaudreuil casually inspected them both and signed them.

"The fortress port of Louisbourg exists under the constant threat of a siege by the English. It could come at any time. Nothing new about that. But it is undermanned and needs food and more troops until it can be better reinforced by France. I am sure both of you realize New France cannot afford to lose that port. It is the reason why ships come to Quebec and Montréal. If we lose Louisbourg, we endanger our river access. Therefore, Major Péan, I expect you will conceive something ulterior in this, but I am reassigning you to Governor Drucour's command in Louisbourg. Ensign Gerrard will accompany you. You can also take your personal platoon of strong arms with you. In addition, I have written an order for another hundred Troupes de la Marine to go with you under your command. That is one hundred thirty men in total, a *lot* of our experienced strength here in the west. Use that as a measure of how concerned I am about the future of Louisbourg.

"There is a small fleet of supply ships waiting in Quebec: men-o-war, cargo frigates, and schooners. The river ice has melted sufficiently for you to use bateaux to move these troops from Montréal. There is not enough food to share from Montreal's stores, but I am including a provisioning order for you to give the commissary clerk in Quebec. Questions?"

Major Péan while not surprised by the orders had never conceived *Louisbourg* as a possibility. And Fort Detroit would indeed be worse. But this was a permanent combat assignment. He would be in Louisbourg until any siege was relieved, should one occur, and possibly until this war ended. And that could be years away. *Well…so much for wondering.*

Henri glanced askance at the major, waiting for him to speak first.

"When do we embark?"

Vaudreuil shrugged. "Major, unless you convince me there is good reason for delay, by tomorrow afternoon at the latest. My orders are being delivered to the company commanders as we speak. It also announces your assignment of overall command. As a *real* major this time. The bateaux are ready. It does not take long to load the men. Most of the supplies you will need, ammunition in particular, will be on the transports in Quebec. It is April. If the English do not attempt to lay siege to Louisbourg by August, I do not anticipate they will try this year. By the first of September, that possibility falls by half again. October begins the winter storms. I also anticipate there will be more regular troops arriving at Louisbourg. Ships of the line too. The King values that port almost as much as Quebec, and maybe even more. And he should."

"And if I said I was a coward and scared of dying?" Péan asked with a straight face.

The governor was amused. "Aren't we all, major? And I will tolerate your impudent jest. Out there, confronting the enemy, there are few military leaders in New France like you. And it pains me to say that, considering your other reputation. Governor Drucour needs good officers and men if he has any chance of defending Louisbourg until England and France make peace. Like it or not, you are an excellent war captain. Now I will stop lest I become maudlin. Tears tend to streak my face powder, and it takes me such a long time to get it just right. Ensign Gerrard, questions?"

"How long will we have in Quebec?"

He glanced at Major Péan. "That is up to your commander. Why?"

"My mother lives there."

"Really? I would be honored to meet this woman someday."

The governor stood. The officers followed. Vaudreuil came around his desk and shook the major's hand. "Good luck, Major Péan. I mean that."

"Thank you, sir."

"Ensign, this is two surprises in two days you did not expect, yes? But such is war. Take care of your major. That is an order."

"Yes, sir. I will, sir," Henri said firmly.

"There, you see, Major. No reason to be scared. Ensign Gerrard speaks only the truth, even when he should lie. You have a twice-decorated soldier as your bodyguard. I'm envious."

"Envious? *S'il vous plaît*, maybe you should go in my place. Apologies, my lord. That was a jest."

Governor Vaudreuil met with more petitioners and ministers until the Julien Le Roy standing clocked gonged the hour of twelve.

"That is all for today."

He signaled Captain Trieste to stay behind while the others were ushered from the room. When the chamber doors shut and silence ensued, he spoke again.

"Friday. At noon. In the marshalling yard of the bastille. And I want the grenadiers to perform this duty. Have you invited the appropriate chiefs?"

"Yes, Governor. They will all be here, including Athanase…all of them expecting gifts."

"Of course. Do you foresee any other problems?"

"Only his hair? It's brown."

"His hair!" Vaudreuil waved his hands. "Then buy a *wig*!"

Chapter 9
Saint Lawrence River
April 1756
"Each time she sees you, she will kiss you!"

Carmen cried all night long, even as they made love. There was nothing Henri said that consoled her.

"…it might as well be that mountain land…that land in the mountains… that Switzerland. And I don't even know where that is. You will *never* come back."

It had been an exhausting night. Henri was surprised to learn you could indeed have too much *mending*. He was chafed raw. The expectation of putting out on a river bateau that afternoon at the three o'clock hour filled him with nervous energy. It was still dark out when he carefully rolled out of Carmen's bed. Fortunately, she remained asleep. He went into the small living room area to begin his daily regimen. He tried not to make too much noise, which made the exercises more difficult. He was finishing his last set of twenty handstand push-ups when Carmen appeared at the living room entry. She wore a loom-woven green shawl wrapped around her shoulders. Her eyes were bloodshot from crying.

"I filled the round tub with hot water for you. I will make something to eat while you finish washing and dressing."

His heavy pack was still with Denis and Mary. And he definitely wanted to spend a few hours with them this morning. He sensed he was leaving Montréal permanently. This was a huge good-bye. It would not be easy. At least, he had learned his father was alive.

Maybe I can get a letter sent to Corrinne from Louisbourg…

He washed quickly and dressed in the clothes of a *coureur de bois*. Once he arrived at the chamberlain's house, he planned to mix the clothes of an officer with more durable wilderness wear, as he'd seen other officers do.

Péan had given him several suggestions, one of which had been to save the dress uniform for special occasions.

Henri sat down to eat. Carmen had made omelets but was not eating hers.

"How long will you be there?"

"I'm told not until England and France make peace. And I don't know when that will be, before you ask. But probably not for two more years, at least."

"Will...will you come back here?"

"This was my home until two years ago. I lived in Boston in the English colonies for much of last year. I did not plan to do that. But that's what happened. Again, I don't know, is what I am saying. I am an officer in the marines. The war will dictate where I go now and for how long. When you hear news about Louisbourg, you will be hearing news about me."

"Will you write to me?"

Henri had answered these questions last night, but he remained patient. "If the mail can get through, I promise to try."

Carmen licked her lips nervously and took a deep breath. "Sometimes in your sleep, you call out a name...Anamosa."

Henri laid his hand over Carmen's.

"Anamosa lives in Boston. Her mother and father are dead. She lives with Corrinne de Chanaye as her ward. She has a beautiful smile. She is in love with me. And I love her too. I would hold her hand and take her for long walks. Anamosa is only eight years old. That is the truth."

Carmen looked relieved. Henri decided this was a good time to leave. Everything was by the door: his extra clothes, his folded uniform, his sword and dirk. Before he could pick anything up, Carmen pushed her way into his embrace and kissed him deeply with her tongue, stroking the front of his pants with the palm of her hand.

"There is still time," she said in a husky voice.

For the first time since meeting her, Henri decided this would not be a good thing...for either of them.

"I cannot, Carmen. I must see Denis and Mary, pack, and go down to the boat landing early."

She stroked harder. "Then maybe I can—"

"No, Carmen. Please. This is hard for me, too."

She stopped, her expression one of pain. "I love you, Henri," she said in a voice tinged with desperation.

Henri gazed into her sad brown eyes for a long moment. "I know." He wanted to say more to her but he could not lie. "I will miss you, Carmen." Gently brushing aside her clinging arms, he quickly picked up his things and went out the door.

The few hours he had with Mary and Denis were less stressful. Mary said how proud she was of his advancement to officer. Denis was in awe of his decorations for valor, and most of all, that he saved the life of the English soldier. They both hovered around him while he packed up his clothes and mixed his dress.

"Denis, I am going to try and get a letter to Lady Corrinne. Maybe find a way from Louisbourg to Boston using a foreign ship. If you want, write a short letter I can take with me. Seal it. I won't open it. And I'll send it along with mine if I find a way."

Denis nodded and went into the other room. Mary marveled at this *boy* who was now a grown man in so many ways.

Henri abruptly stopped packing and looked at her with sadness.

"I don't know when I will be back. If ever."

"Don't you say *that,* Henri Gerrard! First of all, you have a destiny. I can see it. And if France loses this war, it will end *here*…in Montréal. Quebec may be the head, but Montréal is the beating heart, the soul, the center, the meeting place. If we fall, Montréal will fall last. I'm not a soldier, but that much I know. And you will come back here with the army, because God intends you to live. And when the war ends, I am sure Lady Corrinne will come back here to visit. This was her home for ten years. She loved it here, too."

Henri solemnly put on the gray waistcoat he would usually wear under his uniform coat. Over that, he wore a dark brown, hooded capote. Next, a gray sash of the same color as the vest around the waist. He wore gaiters over his trouser legs and moccasin boots instead of cobbled shoes. When it came to weaponry, he paused. Péan had suggested what to wear, but he decided not to attach his cutlass on a brass belt hoop. He could draw it faster from over the shoulder scabbard. The dirk he belted, along with a new skinning knife and a boning knife. The new pistol was holstered under his shoulder.

I need to get a war bow, he thought, *and several quivers full of arrows. Maybe in Quebec.*

His backpack was bulging, overloaded with too much. He reopened and transferred many things to a hand bag made of heavy sail canvas. Putting in things that could be afforded if lost or stolen, such as his uniform coat, shirts, and cobbled shoes. But not Anamosa's picture, his money—sixteen pieces of silver left from the three sacks given to him by Corrinne over a year ago, and the bone and feathered necklace Skenando had given him. He took hold of the little pouch of Roland's hair hanging around his neck. The wolf had been Henri's only friend during his Seneca captivity. He checked this pouch often every day.

Henri moved the pack and the canvas bag to the front door and waited. Mary stood in front of him and inspected his uniform, straightening, pulling, smoothing, and patting. He noticed the redness of her eyes. She had a kerchief in one hand. Denis hurried in from the *cuisine* with a small folded envelop. It had a wax seal. Henri turned and knelt.

"At the top of my pack you will find a smaller pouch with paper and some writing things. Put it in there."

When Denis was done, Henri stood and turned. His final act was to don the tri-cornered hat with its gold trim.

With that simple gesture, Mary saw before her an officer in New France's Troupes de la Marine. And such men were dying every day. Mary gasped, a pained sound fell from her lips. Her kerchief and hands rose swiftly to her face. Tears dripped down her cheeks.

Denis abruptly recalled the face of the young boy who had climbed the balcony at Lady Corrinne's townhouse, a place invested by Intendant Bigôt's gendarmeries, just to see Madeleine, a friend from his childhood. His boyish foolishness compelled by the raw allure of a young maiden; he had been all courage and no common sense. But now he saw a man, a soldier of France, a decorated officer. One of many such men. The fate of New France now rested on their collective bravery. He set a hand on Henri's shoulder and squeezed it reassuringly.

"Your father would be proud of you, Henri. So would Lady de Chanaye. Just as Mary and I are certainly proud of you."

Mary kissed both of Henri's cheeks. She looked searchingly in his steady blue eyes, trying to glimpse his future in them. She saw only his innocence.

"God protect you, Henri Gerrard. I will pray for you every day. Come home to us."

Down at the boat-landing gate, three companies of marines had gathered. The area was teeming with voyageurs, carters, and day laborers loading the bateaux. Henri saw Major Péan talking to his officers and sergeants and walked directly to them. Upon seeing the new ensign, the major smiled.

"Gentleman, I am proud to present Ensign Henri Gerrard, recently commissioned in the Troupes."

Color-Sergeant Cabrelle pushed the other sergeants out of his way to be the first sergeant to salute him. Henri returned the salute in the grenadier way, feeling a little awkward.

"I cannot be more proud of you, *sir*," the sergeant said. "And you owe me a silver coin for the honor of your first salute."

Henri laughed. "It's stuffed deep in my pack. But I will get it to you."

Henri shook the hands of his fellow officers: one captain, three lieutenants, and two other ensigns. They all knew him. They were not surprised by Henri's promotion.

"Take off your hat, Ensign."

Major Péan slipped a chain holding a gilded gorget over his head. It was engraved with *fleurs-de-lys* and the insignia of the Troupes de la Marine. It also had his initials and rank engraved in much smaller letters.

"*Voilà*! Now it's official."

Henri saluted. "Thank you, Major."

A bell rang out from a church steeple. They turned. Archbishop André Nicolet solemnly approached the assembled soldiers who knelt at seeing him. He walked among them, offering his blessings. He hesitated a moment longer for Henri, resting a palm on his head, and wished him good luck.

"A well-deserved promotion, Ensign. Here…some gifts for your journey."

The archbishop handed him a book with a cracked and weathered leather cover. Inside, the title page, *Historia Regum Britanniae* by Geoffrey of Monmouth.

"It's written in Latin. It is a collection of histories, fables, poems, and tales of adventure and love. Starts with the end days of Troy, a sequel to the *Iliad*, which I know you like. It has tales of kings and heroes of Gaul and

Britain and their courage fighting the Romans. Some say they are fables, others say truth. Which is why it was one of my favorites when I was your age. It is up to the reader to decide. I think you'll like it."

Henri reverently accepted this treasure. "Thank you, Archbishop."

"Here's a second. This one is centuries' old and one of my favorites. *Ballads of Rome*. It is poetry and history of Rome and the Roman army when it was still a republic…long before there were any Caesars."

"I don't know what to say, Archbishop. Thank you."

"Thank you is enough. And last, the most important book of all."

Henri took the medium-size, leather-covered book in his hands and opened it. "The pages are blank?"

"It's a personal journal, Henri. You should keep a diary now, like all proper officers."

"Archbishop, I am humbled. I should do something in return for you."

"Nonsense. Just come home again and tell me what you thought of all the stories. Corrinne has read *Ballads of Rome*, you know."

"Lady Corrinne?"

"Yes. She has probably read all the books in my library.

The drummers began the beat for assembly.

"It's time, my son." The archbishop hugged the young officer. "*Au revoir*, Ensign Gerrard. May God walk beside you on your journey."

The ranks formed. Major Péan walked over to Henri and pointed at a nearby platoon.

"That one is yours, Ensign. Join it. Sixteen men. Take care of them."

Henri saluted. "Yes, sir."

They watched him walked away.

André Nicolet leveled a cautionary glance at the man beside him. "And you take care of *him*, Major."

"I daresay Henri will probably take care of *me*. But will you not bless me too, Archbishop?" The major fell to his knees, doffed his hat, and bowed his head.

The archbishop hid a smile. *Only Michel Péan would seize the moment to do something like this so publically. Ah, the faith of an agnostic.* He laid a palm on the officer's head, raised his right hand, and pronounced a benediction.

"God loves even the worst of his sinners, Michel Péan. So you can be certain he loves you too. Go with God."

Henri approached his men. The platoon sergeant called them to attention. Henri barely had time to tell them his name before Major Péan called the small battalion to attention. He began speaking about their orders to Fortress Louisbourg, its importance to New France. He did not go on for very long. The men were all veterans. They knew how to follow orders.

At the major's signal, the drummers began to beat the boarding of the bateaux.

"May I take your pack and bag, sir?" a corporal asked.

Henri was surprised. "You may take my bag. I will haul my own pack, Corporal."

"Yes, sir."

At the last minute, Color Sergeant Gosse of the Régiment de Guyenne approached Major Péan and saluted. The grenadier was carrying a large leather dispatch sack over his shoulder.

Péan returned the salute. "Color Sergeant Gosse, to what do I owe such an honor?"

"I'm ordered to go with you, Major. I am entrusted with Governor Vaudreuil's official mail. After I deliver it to Governor Drucour, I expect I will join one of the grenadier regiments already garrisoned in Louisbourg for the duration."

"How fortunate you must feel," Péan jested. "I hear it rains in Louisbourg every single day, except when it snows every single day in the winter. And there is always fog to cheer us up. But I will say it is the good fortune of my marines to have you with us."

The veteran sergeant shrugged with good cheer. "War is war, Major. I go where the fighting takes me, where I am ordered to go. And Louisbourg is closer to France than Quebec. If that city should fall and should I survive, the English will send me back to France. I think there are worse fates. Of course, you are not the grenadiers," he teased. "Your marines are undisciplined. But most of them are better fighters then many of the metropolitan regulars. But do not quote me on that."

Henri took a seat at the back of his bateau near the steersman. His sergeant was up on the bow. As the fleet moved away from shore, bells across Montréal began ringing until they were all chiming farewell. Crowding the riverbanks now were hundreds of people cheering, waving, some ringing hand bells. He scrutinized the faces, feeling certain that Denis, Mary, and probably Carmen would be among them. But the faces were too far away and his telescope was deep inside his backpack.

The outpouring of affection and respect by the people of Montréal was inspiring. Henri knew many of the habitants now, maybe not by name, but he knew the faces of those who would smile and nod good-morning to him, shop keepers and farmers at the market who hailed him like a family member. He was one of their soldiers, going off to protect them and their way of life, to war in a faraway place, to safeguard their future. The majority of them did not know the marines by name either, yet they cherished and honored them with cheers and prayers. Henri felt a tightness expanding in his chest. Leaving this time was achingly poignant. Unintentionally, Montréal had indeed become his home.

Henri casually looked at the faces of the other marines, trying to gauge their emotions, to see if their struggles mirrored his. Their expressions ranged from joy to sadness. It was difficult to glean a common perspective, something to compare with the sudden anxiety he felt.

He reached inside his coat and took hold of the small leather pouch hanging around his neck. It held the white hairs that would drape like feathers from Roland's ear.

I am with friends, he thought. *It will be all right.*

Henri regretted not seeing his father again before this day had come. Where he was going now could result in never seeing this city again. Particularly, if an English siege of Louisbourg was successful. As Sergeant Gosse had said, if they lived through and surrendered, they would be sent to France.

Henri closed his eyes. He thought of Anamosa's smiling face and the affection in her deep blue eyes and he felt immediately calmed.

*

Charleston

Captain Conor Martyn ordered most of the sail on the *Anamosa* reefed before he entered the harbor anchorage in Charleston, South Carolina. Through his telescope, he saw enormous crowds gathered on the wharves and heard the roar of protests from the citizenry who did not want any more Acadian émigrés deposited in their community. There was no way to know just how dangerous this crowd would be. He decided to be safe and anchor further out.

"Drop anchor! Raise the anchor pennant!"

The *Anamosa* carried fourteen Acadian families this time, a total of fifty-nine destitute souls, ranging from infants to aging grandparents. They would be brought up on the main deck after enduring the crowded, cold, fifteen-day journey from Annapolis Royal in Nova Scotia. They made the journey kept below in the aft section of the cannon deck. Half of the men were shackled. Sad and docile as they seemed, they were constantly guarded by three crewmen armed with muskets, sabers, and pistols. This was to forestall any chance of seizure by the Acadians, as this had happened to other ships during such transports. The ship was barely provisioned to feed his crew, let alone all these people. They were almost out of fresh water. Sanitary conditions on the cannon deck were horrendous, made worse by the dozens of buckets overflowing daily with human waste that the guards were forced to haul up to the rocking main deck for disposal over the side. The heavy Atlantic swells produced endless seasickness and vomiting among the unfortunate passengers. The resulting stench was overpowering. But the guards only stood four hours of watch before they rotated. The Acadians remained below the entire trip with only one-hour allotments of deck time for the women and children each day in groups of nine to get fresh air, weather permitting.

Prior to their arrival, Captain Martyn briefly inspected below. He paused several minutes at the forward part of the cannon deck to give his nose time to develop a tolerance to the choking foulness of the air. It was a miracle some type of fever or disease had not swept over them all, his crew included.

He usually made three inspections a day, answering questions as best he could, speaking to them through a woman who spoke English as well as French. He understood French well enough but Acadian French was different. In any case, his spoken French was not very good. One of the families had a pair of daughters, two little girls no older than nine or ten years of age. They had curly brown hair, large brown eyes, and in spite of the noxious, disgusting conditions, they always managed to give him shy smiles when he was near. He often smuggled sweet biscuits to their outstretched hands from his own meals.

"So help me God, I will not make another of these trips," he said in a low voice to Lieutenant Carson, his second-in-command.

A harbor launch accompanied by four other longboats, each rowed by four men, left the city piers and slowly approached them. The primary boat carried Reginald Walters, a man he knew from previous trips. The local government agent was responsible for dispersing the families once they were put ashore. He found the skinny, unpleasant man offensive and abrupt. Through the telescope, he saw a scowl on Walter's face as he was rowed out.

As ordered by Commander Rous, this was Captain Martyn's sixth trip carrying such miserable human cargo since the fall of the French Fort Beauséjour the previous year. And his third trip to Charleston. It was all part of the English plan to cleanse the entire Acadian population from the Nova Scotia lands permanently. In this manner, Governor Lawrence hoped to depopulate anyone given to rebellion in the future as a result of the war. This contention of preventing rebellion was ironic since the Acadian farmers were about as peaceful a people as Captain Martyn had ever met. And the Acadians had already sworn allegiance to the English king ten years earlier. *Rebellion? No*, Conor decided. This was about stealing their land. Governor Lawrence proclaimed the Acadians would be relocated to various other cities and ports in the American colonies in the south. This action was necessary to make room for investing Nova Scotia with English, German, or Dutch settlers, new taxpayers, all of them Protestant, of course.

Reginald Walters climbed the ladder lowered to his boat.

"Good morning to you, Captain Martyn. As you can plainly see, the citizens of Charleston have gathered on the wharves. Some of them are armed. They will not accept any more of these Acadians to be disembarked."

"What?!"

"Don't worry, Captain. I have made other arrangements. We will boat them over there." He pointed at an island close behind them. "That's Coffin Island. Once they are ashore, they will be fed while I will arrange other transport to some other place and at a time when there is less uproar concerning them. But you should tell your superiors that Charleston will not accept any more of these Acadians."

"So what happens to them now?"

The agent gazed at him skeptically. "Do you really care, Captain Martyn? Do you intend to weigh anchor and take them somewhere else if I say something you don't like? Please do so, if you prefer. Raise anchor and leave. The crowd on the pier will cheer for you. No? I didn't think so. And now I will save you the trouble of making any more decisions regarding their future."

Walters did not wait for Captain Martyn's sarcastic reply. He waved and shouted through cupped hands to his men rowing the transports.

"Bring the boats around to the other side."

The captain ordered a second ladder lowered on the opposite side of the ship.

The Acadians came up on deck with expressions of uncertainty and fear. They breathed the cool fresh air of morning. For the shackled men, it was their first time in three weeks. Twice as many guards were armed and ready on the main deck as the men came up and had their shackles removed. It was needless to keep them shackled. There was really nowhere for them to go. The families filed down the side ladder in despondent little groups and boarded the boats. As one filled to capacity it pushed off and then another would tie up for loading. Many of the women were praying aloud when they were not crying.

"A little overcrowded," Reginald Walters observed, "but that should do it. Good day to you, Captain."

The longboats full, the oarsmen began rowing to Coffin Island. Conor had purposely anchored the *Anamosa* far enough away from the Charleston wharves to avoid any type of conflict. As a result, Coffin Island was less than five hundred feet away. The longboats were little more than halfway from the shore of the island when muskets opened fire from the trees along the island beach. The volley was not repeated, but it was enough. Women started screaming. Two of the over-loaded longboats capsized as the rowers and passengers panicked.

"Sweet Jesus! Lower the boat!" Captain Martyn shouted in horror.

He climbed in along with six marines. They rowed quickly towards the sound of muskets, passing the other boats, and rescued a few people from the water along the way. Then with bayonets raised, ready to fire on the perpetrators, Captain Martyn charged into the trees and searched up and down the boggy, mosquito-infested shoreline. They did not find anyone. When they returned to the beach, the Acadians were all ashore. Reginald

Walters was doing his best to calm them. Fires were started. Most of the families were soaked. No one was hurt except for one of the little girls who had drowned under a capsized boat. She was the younger of the two.

Someone had carried her from the water, but she lay facedown on the muddy beach.

"Noooo!" He fell to his knees next to her, doubled over in anguish.

*

Boston

Ten days later, the *Anamosa* arrived in Boston harbor just as the sun was setting. After securing his ship for an extended anchoring in port, Captain Conor Martyn hurried to see Molly. It was near the hour of ten at night before he reached the VanderMeer residence. The marine guards posted out front knew the officer and did not challenge him. Molly rose from her bed to answer the unexpected knock at the door. Her heart pounded, hoping for once it might be him. It was.

"Oh, Conor, Conor!"

She hugged him tightly and hurried him down the servant's hallway.

Dianamora had gotten up too and was smiling, equally happy to see the naval officer. She immediately went to the *cuisine* and retrieved two large pots of hot water, kept warm on the stove, and brought them to the bathing room. Then she left them alone together.

Conor's clothing was foul, mildewed, sweat-stained. Molly helped him undress. When he was naked and kneeling in the tub, she poured water over him. She washed his hair and body with sponges and soap. Now, almost five months pregnant, her usually slim figure had a pronounced bulge. She prattled on about everything that had occurred since he was last in port, which had been two months ago. Conor was exhausted, his mood somber, unsmiling. He nodded and grunted as she talked. But he was not really listening.

The more Molly washed Conor's body, the less she said to him as the sponges glided over the hard soapy muscles of his chest and torso. By the time she finished his legs and worked her way back up to his waist, Conor's expression had eased. She soaped his hardness and gripped his desire. Her own excitement accelerated. Molly gazed into Conor's eyes.

"Conor, I love—"

"*Shhhh.*"

He reached behind her neck and untied the single bow holding up her nightdress. It flopped to the floor, leaving her naked and trembling. He drew her carefully into the tub. They knelt facing one another. He took the soapy sponges from her and washed her body so she could experience how good this had felt to him. He gently rubbed the soap over the bulging stomach and bent to kiss the skin tenderly.

"Hello, little one," he whispered.

Then his hands and the sponge reached that place between her legs. Molly moaned loudly. They lay down in the tub, side by side, hands sliding over their soap-covered bodies, touching and arousing each other to explosions of pleasure, the first of many in a night full of lovemaking.

A shaft of morning sunlight appeared suddenly through a seam in the curtains. Golden dust motes sparkled in the light. Molly Shreve lay naked beside Conor, one leg draped over his waist, covered by only a sheet. Her head was cushioned on his right shoulder, a palm rested over his heart. She was comforted by the strong thumping in his chest.

They were in Mathilde's private room. Molly had hardly slept at all. Not just because of their exquisite lovemaking throughout the night. Conor had said little and seemed troubled. He would not talk about it when she asked, or say much of anything, preferring instead to grip her hips and breasts while she rocked atop his body or squirmed beneath him until they both groaned in ecstasy, only to hold one another tightly until their breathing slowed and they could start again.

Molly was so happy she felt guilty. Even when Conor was not with her, remembering their shameless enjoyment of each other was so delicious, she'd get excited, sometimes touching herself in ways so wanton, she felt surrendered to the sin of lust, over which her Puritan sensibilities admonished her. But she ignored the guilt. Sinful or not, Molly didn't care anymore. Conor was the center of her life. She was willing to do whatever he wanted, whenever he wanted, and most times at her urging. This *lust* could not be a sin in God's eyes, she decided. It was too natural. Each time they made love, they'd learned new ways to please and excite one another. They were one, now and always.

Just before sunrise, Conor finally fell asleep. She listened, comforted by his steady breathing. "I love you," she whispered so as not to awaken him.

The nightmare that made him groan with nonsensical sounds of panic and the word *noooo* until she shook him had passed. Whatever caused the bad dream did not return. Now that morning had come and they could see the nakedness of each other, Molly wanted to make love one more time before they rose from bed for the day. But she also wanted him to sleep. So she remained still and listened to Dian moving about, up and down the hallway, doubtless getting food ready, or cleaning up the pile of odorous clothes they'd left in the bathing room.

Molly decided she would simply rise from bed when Conor wanted to get up. She closed her eyes. *Just to rest them,* she thought. And soothed by his warmth, the giving touch of his muscled strength, the sounds of his strong heartbeat and deep breathing, Molly fell asleep. However long the interlude, just as suddenly, she awakened to find Conor's lips upon her body, moving again on her breasts, then down on her stomach, and eventually to that place between her legs that made her back arch in pleasure.

When they finally got out of bed, they sat together wearing only night robes in the *cuisine*. They sipped tea and ate fresh eggs, bacon, and hot biscuits with mint jelly that Dian had prepared.

"Captain Martyn, your clothes are washed and hanging out in the back. They should dry quickly in the sunlight," Dian told him. "Probably within an hour."

"Thank you," he answered. "And please call me Conor. We are friends."

"But you are my only friend who is also the *captain* of a warship. I like to call you captain. I will do it only once a day from now on."

Dian sipped her tea, taking note of Molly's disheveled hair, which suggested a cause by a very specific occurrence.

Molly noticed her amused stare. "What?"

"Nothing," Dian said, a sly note in her voice as she rose and lifted a full tray of food. "I am taking this up to Lord VanderMeer. He likes to read the paper while breaking his fast in bed. That should keep him occupied another hour at least."

After Dian left them in the *cuisine*, Molly nuzzled Conor's neck and was rewarded with a kiss…but nothing more. Molly was always expecting something would happen to punish her, to end this happiness with Conor.

His reluctance to talk with her only provoked her ridiculous fears this was coming to an end.

"Conor, please…why are you so quiet? Did I do something wrong?"

"*You*? Stop saying that. Of course not." He fell quiet again. "I am pre-occupied. I cannot keep my thoughts straight."

Molly stroked his chin with her fingers to draw his eyes to hers.

"What happened, Conor?"

"All right. I will tell you. But not here. Let's go back to the bedroom."

*

Fort Frontenac
Lake Ontario

The Fort Niagara voyageurs steered the three bateaux ashore closest to the main gates of Fort Frontenac.

Philippe Gerrard gawked at what he saw. The lake fort had been rein-forced with stone works for the cannon emplacements since his last visit. And the garrison forces seemed too robust. At least two full battalions of metropolitan French regulars from the Guyenne and Béarn regiments were milling around, plus companies of Troupes de la Marine and many mili-tiamen. These forces were augmented further by Indian allies from several tribes he recognized and an equal number he'd not seen before. He would later learn the force numbered three thousand in total.

"This army is gathering for the attack on Fort Oswego." He looked specifically at the voyageurs. "Don't get mixed up among these units, or you will be pressed into serving and your bateaux will be commandeered. Just resupply us with food and let's move on before someone notices who we are."

The scouts and voyageurs agreed. They headed as a group to gather stores from the commissary. Philippe remained with the bateaux and the children.

"What is this place?" Joshua asked.

"It's called Fort Frontenac. It is a French supply fort."

Leah's grip on Philippe's arm tightened. "They are looking at me."

Philippe shifted his attention to where she was looking. Several Indians nearby were watching them with interest. He returned their stare in equal measure until they looked away.

"Don't worry. They won't bother us."

He answered their questions about what they saw and repeatedly assured them they were safe. It was almost an hour before the men returned. Each of them carried a heavy sack of supplies. A marine approached Philippe and saluted.

"Captain Gerrard?"

Philippe was surprised at being recognized. He returned the salute.

"Who wants to know?"

The soldier handed him a mail pouch. "The commandant asks that you carry this mail to Montréal with you."

Philippe agreed and the soldier left.

"They've noticed my sash. They know we are in the Troupes," he warned them. "We need to get away from here."

Once back out on the water, they all relaxed a little.

"How much longer to Montréal?"

Philippe had stopped counting how many times a day Joshua asked that question. He answered the boy patiently, "This morning it was eleven days. So it would be ten and a half days now. *C'est compris*?"

*

Montréal

Governor-General Vaudreuil marched briskly into Montréal's Coteau du Fort accompanied by a glittering platoon of guards, officers, and civilian sycophants. He went directly to greet each of the six chiefs who had been invited there to witness the execution. He spoke to Athanase in the Huron tongue and used sign language for the rest. Then he walked to his place of honor, which was a hastily built, small wooden platform covered with plush carpets with a large single chair in its middle.

Vaudreuil would have worn a crown if he thought it might help. He wanted to leave no doubt in the Indians' minds who was in charge of these lands.

Once he took his seat, Vaudreuil made a quick hand signal to Captain Trieste. Other hand signals were passed along. A minute later, ten Régiment de Guyenne grenadiers marched into the fort in a column of twos, preceded by four drummers tapping out a marching beat. The grenadiers were attired in spotless white uniforms and mitre caps and led by an officer with his sword extended in salute to the governor. The officer shouted a command. With military precision, the soldiers rearranged into one long line of ten men facing a long empty wall less than a dozen paces in front of them. The wall face was dotted with countless holes from musket balls.

More hand signals followed. The drummers beat the executioner's march. A side gate on the bastille opened and a blindfolded man tied in an arm chair was carried out into the yard. He was lashed with ropes around his chest, arms, and legs.

The Indians noted the man's blond hair and the *coureur de bois* dress. The chair was placed in front of the wall.

The officer marched forward and read the charges against Henri Gerrard, accusing him of the murder of Athanase's son with a sentence of death pronounced as a result.

"Henri Gerrard, do you understand the charge against you? Nod your acknowledgement."

Though Sergeant Randall's legs were numb, sitting in the chair still caused pain so intense he grit his teeth to keep from crying out in agony. In spite of the pain, he was pleased to offer his life in this way for Henri Gerrard. He even understood the French governor's dilemma regarding the Indians, which the governor described to him when he had come to his cell to make the extraordinary request.

Kenneth Randall had no idea what was being said in French. But when the officer stopped talking, he nodded as he'd been told to do.

The Indians, half of whom understood French, saw the grimacing man nod.

Randall could feel the fever sweat dripping through the sopping blindfold which held the blond wig in place. He was dying. Sergeant Gerrard risked his life for him. At least now his death would have meaning.

Please hurry… he thought.

The drummers' beat elevated to one continuous rapid sound.

The execution officer returned to his detail and gave the orders.

"Ready! Aim! Fire!"

Ten grenadier marksmen shot directly at the seated man's chest, the balls all striking within an inch of his heart. The combined slugs blew a six-inch-wide hole in Kenneth Randall, knocking the chair over backwards. Governor Vaudreuil had spoken to the firing squad as a group only two hours earlier outlining their part in this charade as a way to protect Henri Gerrard. "Since the Englishman is dying of the rot," the governor explained, "he has agreed to solve our little problem. Sergeant Gerrard has been transferred to Louisbourg. You men will do them both an honor."

Knowing this, the Guyenne grenadiers were proud to help.

With the explosion of musket fire, the drums silenced. The grenadiers rearranged into a column of twos and marched out of the citadel. The governor walked over to the Indians to appreciate their attendance. They were nodding, satisfied with this outcome.

"You see," Vaudreuil said to Captain Trieste as the Indians left the fort. "Now everyone is happy. Lessons learned all around. Make certain the Englishman's body is never found."

*

Quebec City

As the Troupes de la Marine rowed down the Saint Lawrence, the river widened. The fingers of ice receded more and more towards the river's edge. By the time they reached the capital city of New France, the ice had disappeared altogether.

Henri saw a dozen major vessels in the harbor. Two of them war frigates. He wondered which of the ships would sail them to Louisbourg.

As soon as the bateaux were anchored into the riverbank of Quebec City, Henri informed his platoon sergeant he would be gone an hour to visit his mother. He slipped the cutlass over his back.

"Corporal, make certain my pack and bags are delivered to the proper ship. Then wait for me on the riverbank."

"Yes, sir."

Henri approached Major Péan and saluted. "I want to see my mother at the Hotel Dieu. Do I have time?"

"Two hours. No more. And maybe less."

"Yes, sir."

Henri hurried to the hospital and found his mother at the back of a soldiers' ward, sitting beside a bed, holding a wounded man's hand.

"Hello, Maman!"

Michelle de Propei turned and stared at this officer until she realized her eyes were not playing tricks. It was Henri! She covered her mouth to muffle her scream of joy and then jumped up to hug him tightly. She repeated his name softly and dragged him out into a hallway and on into an empty room so she could cry and ask questions without disturbing the sleeping wounded. He talked for half an hour, telling her what he learned about Philippe, that he was alive. He explained about the battle at Fort Bull, showed her his wounded ear, which she kissed in a motherly way, what happened with the Englishman, his promotion to ensign.

"I am being deployed to Louisbourg along with three companies of the Troupes. We stopped only long enough to add more supplies and ammunition to the transport ships we will sail. In a few more hours, we will be going downriver again."

"You don't even have time to see your little brother, Crispin?" she lamented. "He is already so big. He is walking and even says a few words now."

"No, Maman. I'm sorry. But I wanted you to know where I will be."

"Oh, Henri, my heart is sick for the dangers you face. But I am also so proud of you. Have you written Corrinne? To tell her everything?"

"I will try when I'm in Louisbourg. You might try as well. I'm not sure how to get any mail through to Boston, although Archbishop Nicolet may know a way."

She followed his glance to the window. "You have to go already?"

"Yes, Maman. We are loading the ships. I am supposed to be there. Can you walk with me down to the river?"

"No. There are too few of us for all the sick and wounded. I am needed here," she said, her voice trailing off. "Oh! Wait! Have you seen Madeleine?"

Henri shook his head. "No. I came to you directly." He wasn't sure that he should see Madeleine.

"Come with me. She is working at another ward."

Michelle took Henri's arm in hers, leading him down the hallway and up a stairway to another ward. As they walked, she told how her days were filled with caring for the wounded men and civilians injured in battle, tortured or maimed by Indians, some suffering the loss of multiple limbs, paralyzed, disfigured forever.

"And these are only those fortunate enough to be brought to Hôtel Dieu. A much greater number have died alone and in great pain somewhere in the wilderness."

"Who are the Sisters?"

"They are the Order of St. Augustine, called the Hospital Sisters. They are good nurses, some of them excellent healers. They manage this hospital and provide care for the sick and wounded."

"You didn't join the order?"

"No. I refused to take vows, though they invited me to do so. I took vows once, I told them. And I've broken them many times since then. Besides, I have Crispin to care for. They evaluated my healing skills to be as good as any doctor. The good Sisters of Saint Augustine feel fortunate to have me. And I can still fulfill my calling to care for the sick."

They came upon the upper ward full of wounded men, most of them recovering from some type of surgery.

"Here we are. This is the ward where Madeleine spends most of her days and often many nights. Wait over here. This room is empty. Try to be quiet. I have to go back. Oh, my baby, I am so glad you came to see me. I've missed you so." Michelle kissed his cheeks. "I will tell Madeleine you are in this room. So don't go anywhere else." She hugged him tightly. "Now smile for me." Michelle searched his face intently, memorizing its new lines and scars.

"I love you. Write to me!"

"Yes, Maman. I promise. I love you too."

Her face drawn with sadness at this too-soon parting, Michelle left the room without looking back.

Henri walked over to the window. He could see the entire harbor from here. A long line of supply rafts were carrying supplies out to the waiting ships.

"Henri?"

He turned. His mouth sagged open. Madeleine looked more beautiful than he remembered. She was dressed in a light blue blouse covered with a white bib overgown and an apron. Her auburn hair was curled up and back in a bun. She wore a large silver cross around her neck. Dried blood and other dark splotches stained the bottom of the apron she was wearing. Henri felt drawn to her luminous brown eyes.

"I thought Michelle was jesting! It is you! *Mon Dieu!*"

Madeleine Louvet was awestruck by how much bigger Henri was since she had seen him last. He looked so striking in his uniform. She walked slowly towards him, uncertain of his reaction to this meeting. Last year they had spent one beautiful night together…But the next day, he had seen a man kiss her and that had enraged him. He surprised her by taking hold of her hands.

"Madeleine…I…I owe you many apologies for how I acted when we were last together. It was unfair of me to judge you…or to doubt you. I …"

Before he said another word, she leaned in and kissed him. When she pulled back, she smiled at his look of surprise.

"That was scandalous of me. But I have missed you so much. Look at you! It's so marvelous. You! An officer of the Troupes!?"

"I don't have much time," he explained. "I've told my mother much of my news. It took a while to do that, which she can share with you."

"Of course. I understand." She smiled. Her tone lowered. "*How much time do you have?*"

Henri reddened and stammered, "I…I wish I had more." He pointed out the window. "They are loading those ships. When they are finished, I will be sailing. I have to get back down to the quay. Can you walk with me?" He looked down at her apron. "Or do you have to go back?"

She looked down at herself. "*Merde*! I kissed you wearing this bloody thing! Why didn't you say something?" She stripped off the soiled apron and threw it on a chair. Slipping her arm in his, she said, "Let's go."

They talked more on the way to the wharves. He told her about the war and the battles. She talked about the horrible wounded men she had nursed, and the rumors of an English blockade. They chatted to one another like the friends they used to be when they met secretly in the sacristy of Saint Ouen's Cathedral in Rouen so many years ago.

Before they got too close to the river, Henri stopped at the end of a street and turned. His face was filled with regret.

"Madeleine, I want to be with you, but it's better if I part from you here."

Madeleine expression fell. She replied in a tiny voice, "I know. I understand."

"Madeleine, there is so much—"

She kissed him then, this time with desperate desire, pressing her hips tightly to his. When Henri finally pulled back from her, he was breathing hard, surprised at how strongly he'd reacted.

"I…I'm sorry," she said. "I cannot control myself with you. And there is so much more to say. And no time."

"I will write to you from Louisbourg. I don't know how often. But as long as there is mail, I am sure the military mail will get here somehow."

He took hold of her hands. They stared longingly into each other's eyes.

"The world is so unfair to us, Henri. Every time we get close to one another, one of us gets taken away."

"Well...not every time," Henri reminded lightly, his lips tugging upward.

"Well...well, I want you to think about that *one time* while you are gone. I want you to remember it. We barely explored each other and I have much more I want to do with you and *to you*," she teased.

"You do? What things?"

"You'll just have to wait," she taunted, "until you come back to find out."

"Oh, I *will* be coming back to you," he said with certainty.

The drummers began their assembly beat down by the wharf.

Henri's shoulders slumped. "I have to go."

Madeleine leaned in close, kissed him hard, and pulled one of his hands up over a breast before the embrace ended.

"Something for you to think about."

Henri stared at his hand to see if it was burned. "I don't want to leave." He started backing away, slowly, and reluctantly. "But I have to." He turned and began walking quickly.

"Henri! Wait!"

He turned. "Yes?"

"I have...I have something I must tell you." Madeleine had her hands pressed together under her chin, as if in prayer. "I've not been with anyone since I was with you. I want you to know that. And I will not be with anyone else while you are gone. *I love you, Henri.* I...I cannot let you leave me without saying that to you. You don't have to say anything back," she added quickly.

Henri was speechless. Strong emotions swept over him. The worst one was *guilt,* as if he was betraying Carmen. *But I'm not betraying Carmen! I do not love Carmen! I love Madeleine!* He walked back quickly and kissed her.

"I love you too," he told her, his hands gripped her shoulders. "I promise to come back. *Au revoir.*"

Madeleine watched him until he was out of sight, savoring his words of love while torrid thoughts swirled in her head. She licked her lips at the new memory of his kisses. This assessment was instantly followed by a more troubling thought. *Henri has obviously been kissing someone in Montréal!*

Henri's thoughts and emotions spun in so many directions it distracted him and he made a wrong turn on his way back to the river. He soon found himself facing a wider intersection of the city streets. The buildings and townhomes in this area were much more refined, built of fine masonry and stone, taller and grander in scale and quality. It suggested the occupants were important or wealthy, or both. Some habitants were crossing in different directions, some walking in pairs of well-dressed men and women. One solitary man nodded at him pleasantly as he passed by. Henri greeted him politely in return and wondered why the man would bother to speak to him at all.

It's the officer's uniform, he thought.

Henri turned right at the next corner, which he felt to be the correct direction towards the river. But he stopped instantly when he spotted Major Péan standing with his back to him, not ten paces away. He was talking to a woman! Her hair was bound upward in golden curls, and she was wearing what must be the most expensive dress Henri had ever seen. It shimmered in the sunlight, a silvery blue and pink brocade trimmed in white ribbons. She carried a matching parasol hooked over one arm. They were holding hands, gazing at one another intently. She was speaking to the major with affection and warmth.

Henri froze. He did not want to intrude on the major. When they suddenly embraced and began kissing, Henri crossed to the other side of the street, walking fast before he was noticed. The road began sloping downhill again. He abruptly came across something else he'd intended to search out: an armament store. Feeling fortunate, he hurried inside. The proprietor greeted him heartily.

"Hello, young sir. How may I help you?"

"I am in a hurry. I need a good war bow and four quivers of arrows. But I did not bring money to pay for them."

"That will not be a problem, sir. You need only sign a document stating what you purchased."

Henri evaluated several bows until he found one made of a richly hued Blackwood. It was highly polished. The grain looked deep. There were no discernible knots. It was perfect.

"This is the one."

After signing the bill of sale, at a rather exorbitant price in his opinion, he ran from the store with his new bow and four quivers of arrows that numbered to nearly one hundred shafts. He arrived back at the river with plenty of time to spare.

"Ensign Gerrard! Over here," his corporal hailed. "Back so soon?" The soldier was standing by his pack and canvas bag.

"Soon?" Henri handed over the bow and quivers. "Keep these dry and with my other things. Why do you say so soon?"

"Oh, the ammunition will be loading for another hour. Our packs and kits will be loaded last, so they are off-loaded first."

"But I heard the drummers' assembly beat."

"Oh, they will do that again. The first time is just a warning."

"Where are the other men?"

"Four of them have already boarded the ship. I have their names." The corporal pointed. "Ours is that one, a trading frigate, *Le Belle Fortune*. But the rest of the platoon went to one of those three taverns over there."

"And you stayed here?"

"Yes, sir. Following your orders."

"Your name, Corporal?"

"Chapelle, sir. Luc Chapelle."

"Good job, Corporal Chapelle. Stay here while I get the men out of those taverns before they are drunk."

Henri walked away quickly.

"Ensign!"

Henri turned to see Major Péan, four drummers, and three sergeants, one of them Color-Sergeant Cabrelle, approaching from another direction.

He worried that the major may have noticed him after all. "Sir." He saluted.

"You do not have to salute *every* time you see me. Just once in the morning and each time I give you a *firm* order to do something throughout the day. To where are you running?"

"To search those taverns over there to find my men. They might be getting drunk."

"Might? They are certainly getting drunk. But play time is over. Now observe. Beat to assembly," he ordered loudly.

The drummers began the familiar beat, calling the men to battle order. Hearing it the second time, the marines now began spilling out of the taverns as if the buildings had caught fire. They were stepping on one another, some of them falling as they all ran to the open area. The sergeants shouted and cursed at them to fall into ranks.

"Wow," Henri said softly.

"Impressive, yes? One of the differences between the Troupes and the militia. The Troupes follow orders. By the way, I was walking back to the river not long ago, just a few streets short of the hospital. And what do you think I see?"

Henri swallowed hard and did not answer.

"There on the other side of the street was Ensign Gerrard…tightly hugging, crotch on crotch, a rather tall, shapely, red-haired woman dressed in blue and white. I thought it very polite of me not to intrude on such an intimate moment. Particularly since she was licking your face. No need to thank me. But who was she? And please do not tell me that was your mother."

"Her name is Madeleine. She is a nurse at the hospital. I knew her when I was last in Quebec, but before that, too, in France."

Michel Péan gaped at him. "*She* was your first? Damn, Henri! She is gorgeous! My first was some kind of fat hairy gypsy back in France. Oh, I have to know more about this."

With great effort, Henri resisted the urge to respond with what he had glimpsed of the major not even an hour ago.

"It is inappropriate to tell you anything about her, Major."

The men had finally formed into four long lines, and the sergeants stopped shouting.

"*Merde*! You will eventually. But that will have to wait. Join the ranks with your men."

Major Péan walked over to his color sergeant in front of the formation of a hundred and thirty-seven men, including one engineer, a doctor, the cooks, and voyageurs.

Color-Sergeant Cabrelle shouted in a commanding voice. "Battalion…
attention!"

Up and down the ranks came the sounds of boots snapping together.
Henri found he liked that sound.

Major Péan looked up and down the lines with a scowling face. "All
right! Recreation is over."

Someone puked loudly at the back. The men laughed.

"And that is why! The ammunition and supplies are almost loaded. The
quartermaster over there has your ship assignments. Check with him if you
don't know your duties. I want you all aboard within the hour. I have left
orders with the city gendarmerie commander that any man who does not
sail with us will spend the next *year* inside the Quebec City bastille praying
for his own death. I used to run the bastille, and I can tell you that is no jest.
Color-Sergeant Cabrelle, take charge of the men."

Two hours later, the fleet of three cargo ships preceded by a war frigate
escort was moving downriver in a line. Every member of the Troupes was
aboard one ship or another. The next two nights they anchored in the river
to sleep. The morning of the third day they sailed free of the mouth and
changed course south-southeast to head for the Strait of Canceau between
Île Royale and Nova Scotia.

When night fell a day later, signal beacon fires were ignited along the
strait. The beacons were relayed up the Atlantic coast side of Île Royale
towards the fortress city. A small, fast schooner had been sent ahead to alert
the port of Louisbourg the Quebec supply fleet was coming. When they
exited the strait on the Atlantic side, they turned north. Three French war
frigates from Louisbourg rendezvoused to escort them safely the rest of the
way. The waves became larger.

Henri could not resist his inclination any longer and asked the cargo
frigate captain if he could spend a few hours on the helm after explaining
his former seamanship and experience.

The captain was cautious but indulged the French officer. Prudently,
he stood right next to the man. But within a few minutes he could see the
natural ability of this officer and relaxed. Soon they began to chat about
the places they had sailed to and on what ships.

A sudden frothy swell threw spray up over the starboard bow. It rushed down the deck on the wind and drenched his face. Henri smiled at the cold salty taste and instantly thought of the *Falcon Queen*.

"The sea loves you, lad," Captain LaTour had told him long ago. "No matter how long you stay on land, each time she sees you, she will kiss you, and you will know I am right."

CHAPTER 10
THE ENGLISH CHANNEL
MAY 1756
Nightmares and Dreams

The Dutch trading ship *William's Queen* was passed by no less than seven warships in the channel, all of them heavy frigates, four of them English, two French, and one Dutch, as it sailed east-northeast towards a new line of latitude, eighty miles north of Ouessant Island.

Captain LaTour raised the Dutch Republic colors when he saw the first man-o-war and did not take them down after that. He'd not seen this level of warship inspection activity in over ten years. *Not since the last war*, he recalled, which made him wonder if the new war had been declared. As far as he knew, the Dutch were neutral. He hoped it stayed that way, as each new war between France and England was always worse than the one before.

"Something's happened," said Victorio after the Dutch man-o-war passed them.

"Yes, but what? The French and English warships clearly saw one another, yet they did not engage."

"They must be close to declaring. After all that's happened? How can they claim they are not fighting a war?"

"We'll hear something in Amsterdam. But if war is starting, we will not be sailing into Le Havre. We could get trapped in that harbor by the English...or seized by the French navy for that matter. If the crew wants to visit their families, I will stay at anchor in Amsterdam an extra month. They can travel overland or by coastal schooner. As soon as I know our situation, I will give them dates. Pass that word around."

Victorio dressed in his sea soldier uniform to go to the Amsterdam trading district to see Wittmann Bootz. Wearing his favorite plumed hat, Captain LaTour met him on the main deck. They left the bosun in charge of the ship at anchor. The speculation about war on the waterfront was

175

feverish. Just the few conversations they overheard confirmed that England and France could declare at any time. Victorio purchased one of the daily trade newspapers. It announced as much with its front page story.

Victorio could speak Dutch, but he read the language haltingly. "'The English island...of Minorca...in the Balearic Islands...has fallen to French... invasion. The English fleet...defending the island...was defeated.'"

"One of them is certain to declare after that," the captain replied grimly.

When they reached Wittmann Bootz' offices, they found six clerks busily making ledger entries with three traders waiting. But the senior clerk long ago had been told to watch for the captain of *William's Queen*. He knew the man by the plumed hat he wore, even though he'd not seen him in almost nine months.

The senior clerk rose from his slanting desk and came out from behind the counter to greet them.

"Captain LaTour. I am so very pleased to see you again. Meneer Bootz has asked about your ship nearly every day for the last three months."

"Really? Why?"

The clerk shrugged. "He hopes to see you again, I presume. Probably has a missive for you. Let's get your ship to the dock and unloaded. Do you have your cargo manifest?"

LaTour handed it over.

The clerk liked what he saw and nodded. "Very good. This is a rich load from the Antilles. With war expected to be declared at any time, most of your cargo has tripled in value in less than a week."

"Good!" LaTour replied brightly. "Then my profits will be adjusted in step with those new prices?"

"Of course. I will have a pilot sent to your ship to guide you to the dock. Will you wait for him out there, or do you have other business elsewhere?"

"I will wait for him out there. So I'm to be unloaded today?"

"We will try. But we will certainly have it finished before midday tomorrow. And you can collect your shares immediately afterwards, right here as usual."

"Any knowledge of where I sail next?"

"This early in the year, usually it's back to the Antilles. But with war expected to be declared, I don't know. I wasn't working here during the last war. Meneer Bootz can answer that question. But the larger trading ships, like yours, will not be able to sail the channel unescorted much longer. There will be privateers. Too many traders are seized no matter what flag they are flying."

A few hours later, Captain LaTour gathered the crew on deck and told them what he had learned and their options.

"We will not make a port call at Le Havre. It's too dangerous. I will pay you what you are due, and you can travel there on your own. I would not go overland, but it is up to you. Or, you might hire a coastal schooner as a group. Hug the shoreline and sail into Le Havre. And hire them to bring you back. We will pilot to a dock this afternoon and begin unloading. Starting tomorrow, I will need six men to act as an anchor watch at double the normal wage while the *Queen* rests at anchor."

William's Queen began unloading its valuable cargo from the Antilles Islands by mid-morning the next day. While they were unloading cargo, some crewmen followed LaTour's advice and hired a small schooner to make the three-day coastal journey to Le Havre.

Dragging the extra harbor launch behind them, they took the *Queen* back out into the harbor and dropped anchor. Seven men volunteered to stay aboard while at anchor and rotate the three man watch every other day.

"You will have until the twelfth of June to get back aboard. And you all know my normal practice. I will start looking for your replacements tomorrow. If you don't come back, I will not wait for you. There are plenty of seamen in this port. I will not pay you until the morning…not until my ledger profits are balanced and the ship gets paid by the trading agent. If you want to get paid, stay aboard the *Queen* tonight."

Captain LaTour and Victorio were back at Wittmann Bootz' office by the noon hour. The VanderMeer company agent had been waiting impatiently for them and rose from his desk the moment he saw the captain enter.

LaTour was taken aback by the physical appearance of the man he had seen only a year earlier. Bootz had lost an enormous amount of weight. His usual fastidious style of dress had degenerated to that of someone who spent most of his time on the streets. His clothes showed stains of every kind. He was bent, haggard, and carried a look of exhaustion.

"I've been waiting for you to arrive," Bootz said, his tone an uncharacteristic mix of anger, aggression, and resentment.

"Bonjour to you too, Meneer Bootz. Are you sick?"

Bootz straightened. "No. You must be here for your share of the profits?"

"I am."

"Come to my office."

They followed the trading agent, along with the senior clerk, who looked embarrassed and uncomfortable. Bootz fumbled on the floor behind his desk and hefted four heavy pouches full of coins one at time and dropped them with a thud on the desktop. Three of the four belonged to the VanderMeers and Thomas Hancock. The other to the ship. He turned a ledger sheet around so Captain LaTour could see both the accounting and the total amount. The total on the paper appeared correct, but there should be much more than four bags of silver; twice as much, at least.

"That amount of profit in only four bags?"

"It's in gold ducats."

"Gold?"

Captain LaTour and Victorio opened each bag to inspect the contents. They were full of gold ounces.

"Again you surprise me, Meneer Bootz. This is more than fair. But I will need a guard to escort me back to my ship."

"Of course. Of course." Bootz gestured to his senior clerk. "Bring four guards."

*

On an English privateer carrying mercenaries and other passengers to the New York colony and city, William von Kleinfels suddenly became aware that Wittmann Bootz was talking with Captain LaTour. They were less than a day from entering the port. At this distance and over water, his ability to influence Bootz' words would be impossible without intense concentration. He went below to his private cabin and threw the bolt on the door. Lying down in the bunk, the Hessian closed his eyes and gripped the fine golden purse around his neck carrying the *wraith*'s bones. His breathing slowed, and his body stilled completely. The trance became death-like as the spirit of the *vulnax* surged to take full possession of Kleinfels' consciousness, temporarily displacing the man's identity.

*

The senior clerk left the room to find the guards.

Wittmann Bootz jerked forward in his chair and gazed at the captain intently.

"I would like to know where you sailed this time." Bootz' tone had become guttural.

Captain LaTour felt unnerved. The man's eyelids were half-closed, veiled. The eyes had a blackish color. The pupils seemed like vertical slits, not round, and were yellowish in color.

The veteran captain quickly glanced at Victorio to gauge if he had noticed the same.

The first mate, too, looked shocked.

"Answer me," the trading agent demanded.

Captain LaTour thought the question none of the man's business. *But…*

"You appear unwell to me, Meneer Bootz. I will not waste your time."

LaTour gave the agent a brief history of his travels leaving out many details, explaining his delay in returning was due to the extra months in Sint Eustatius.

"But given the expectation of war declarations at any time, I don't think the open trading in Oranjestad will be tolerated much longer," LaTour added.

"And you sailed to Boston to see Lord and Lady VanderMeer?"

With so many other more important questions of trade to speak about, Bootz' question was telling. Every expression and question was out of character for this man.

"They are the owners of my ship. I see them on every voyage."

"And they are both alive and well in Boston?"

Several seconds of awkward silence elapsed before LaTour replied.

"They are both alive and well."

"In Boston?"

"Meneer Bootz, why do you continue to ask questions regarding Lord and Lady VanderMeer?"

"War is being declared! I need to know where they are! *Both* of them!"

"In Boston."

"*Liar!*"

Victorio glanced at his captain quickly. Captain LaTour's face was red with anger. His hand gripped his sword's handle.

"I have been told by other captains, *English* ones, recent of Boston," Bootz continued, "that Lady VanderMeer left Boston on *your* ship last October bound for Amsterdam, which we both know did not happen. The Duke of Brunswick, among other people, is interested to know what has happened to Lady VanderMeer and the two infants she had with her. I am being harassed by agents of the Duke concerning this. And by now they know your ship has finally anchored. So answer my question."

At that moment, the senior clerk returned with the four private guards. He sensed the tension in the room and wisely did not speak. The clerk had also brought two larger leather pouches with shoulder straps.

Captain LaTour stood. With Victorio's help, he deposited two bags of gold in each of the leather pouches. He faced the agent again.

"Meneer Bootz. I will be happy to answer any of the questions you posed to legitimate agents of the Duke. But not to you. I will wait for those agents out on my ship."

Wittmann Bootz' expression twisted, looking increasingly gargoyle-like.

Captain LaTour hurried from the office with Victorio and the guards. Neither of them spoke as they fast walked to the waterfront piers. When they got to the rented harbor launch, LaTour saw *William's Queen*'s usual launch tied alongside it.

"What is that doing here?" he asked the man tending to the boats, a man who worked for Wittmann Bootz.

The man shrugged. "Three members of your crew rowed it ashore. They said to tell you they would be back tomorrow morning."

LaTour and Victorio traded frowns. "We'll take both launches out to the ship."

"Do you still need me?"

LaTour dug into one pocket and pulled out a silver coin. "Wait here until the end of the day. If we don't come back, we will not need you until the morning."

"Yes, sir. Thank you, sir."

They tied the second launch behind the first. The two seamen talked as they rowed.

"I thought I was imagining things," LaTour said. "Did you see his eyes?"

"At least we got paid."

LaTour grimaced. "We are sailing, Victorio. Just as soon as we can make ready for sea."

"Where are we going?"

"I don't know yet. But I want you to find a place on the waterfront to sleep tonight. Not a hovel. Someplace safe and clean. Don't drink. Don't go out anywhere. Stay out of sight until the morning. Start watching for our missing crewmen at sunrise. When you bring them back to the ship, we are leaving."

"How long do I wait after sunrise?"

"They know to be aboard in the morning. Hopefully they stayed together. But if someone is missing, I cannot wait for them. You be the judge of this and make the call. I will stand by your assessment."

"What about Wittmann Bootz' men? Or the Duke's agents?"

Captain LaTour looked sideways at his first mate. "Meneer Bootz is not working for the Duke or even Lord VanderMeer any longer. I think he is working for the people trying to kill Lady Corrinne…or something much worse. Bootz' eyes will haunt my sleep tonight."

"You think it has to do with the *châsse*?"

"You saw his face, his eyes. We need to leave this port now."

Wittmann Bootz questioned the guards when they returned and learned Captain LaTour and his soldier had gone back out to the ship. But that three of his crewmen had come ashore in the interim.

"Search the waterfront. Find them. Bind and gag them. And take them here." He gave the mercenaries an address. "Then come get me."

*

Montréal

Philippe Gerrard tried to count the number of times he'd portaged around the Lachine rapids west of Montréal by recalling events that occurred during those trips. He stopped when he reached nineteen, only because Joshua asked about a bear he'd spotted once on the other side of the Saint Lawrence River. *Henri had asked about that bear once upon a time.* It broke his concentration. This was followed instantly by a second question.

"How much longer now?"

Philippe shook his head. "About another week."

"A week!? This morning you said by tomorrow!"

Philippe tousled the boy's hair. "I was jesting. No more river. We are walking the rest of the way. This is a well-traveled road. We will be in Montréal before nightfall."

"Before nightfall?!" This voice of surprise came from one of his scouts.

"Maybe *sooner* if we all stop talking and walk faster!"

The road was crowded with voyageurs and marching troops. Only a few traders and farmers headed towards the city. Militiamen were moving west. Philippe found this journey from Fort Niagara much more wearying than before. *Age*, he decided. And the fact his body was a scarred sack full of mended bone and muscle at any spot he could touch. But his mention of the journey's end made the pace increase.

Four hours later, by mid-afternoon, he came around a familiar bend and saw the long line of warehouses on the right. Nothing was built on the left of the road at this point. The land on that side was damp as it tended to collect and hold water. A few of the split log buildings he saw were new. Some showed signs of scorching as if there had been a fire.

The warehouse road ended and turned sharply to the right for the length of one building, then split sharply left and straight. Now there were buildings on both sides of the road. He went straight. These were the last structures before the two roads ended near small bridges spanning a stream that emptied into the broader river and anchorage. On the other side of those bridges was the troop road circling the formidable walls of Montréal. There were guards walking the top of the walls. Cannons protruded every ten paces.

The buildings on his right were tall and occupied the prime location on this short stretch of land; these were The Dunemoore Company headquarters. The buildings faced the road on the front and the river anchorage at the back. Three of them were two stories tall, to allow the furs and other trade goods to be piled high towards the roof. The last one contained warehouse space on the first floor, a company office on the second, and a comfortable apartment on the third floor; Corrinne de Chanaye's apartment.

Or used to be, Philippe reflected nostalgically.

Across the road from the headquarters was the Palais de Voyageur, a hotel Corrinne had financed to be built specifically for the fur traders. It was one that offered a hospitable place to stay, with good food, a tavern, better beds, and a bath house, for those who could afford it. Philippe planned to put up his scouts at this hotel with his own money instead of the flea-infested city barracks.

Suddenly, he had a better idea. "Wait here," he told them.

Philippe entered the front door to the warehouse with Joshua and Leah in tow. He was surprised to find the large warehouse only half-full. The accounting office had been moved from the second floor to the ground floor. And where five clerks once sat, there was now only one man. Philippe recognized him at least; Paulus Legate, the senior clerk.

Legate set aside a ledger and squinted with puzzlement at the visitor who entered through the front door with two children at his side.

"May I help you, Monsieur?"

"*Bonjour*, Paulus."

The voice was familiar. The clerk stood, still squinting, and walked cautiously towards the visitors.

"Have me met, Monsieur?"

"Many, many times, and usually about this time of year."

The voice might be familiar, but the man was tall, gaunt, heavily bearded, and wore the sash of an officer in the Troupes de la Marine. But when he took off his hat, Paulus saw the unmistakable blond hair that was not covered by dirt.

"My God! Monsieur Gerrard? Is it truly you?"

Philippe bowed generously. "The one and only."

The clerk was overjoyed. He hugged his former employer, expressed his happiness, voicing questions so fast, Philippe did not have time to answer one before the next was asked.

"This is Joshua and Leah Carlisle. They are English. I found them in the wilderness. I've been teaching them French, but speak slowly to them."

Paulus knelt before Leah.

"*Bonjour*, Leah."

She stepped forward tentatively, glanced at Philippe who nodded. Then she carefully kissed the clerk on both cheeks.

"*Mon Dieu*," Paulus exclaimed. "I am so honored. Come in all of you. Oh, this is so exciting. I want to hear everything!"

Philippe held up a hand. "And I want to tell you, but first I need to find a place to quarter my six scouts waiting outside. They also need to clean up from the road."

Paulus brightened and held his arms wide. "*Voilà*! There are twelve beds at the back of the warehouse behind the supply stacks. I usually rent them. There is also a hearth-stove. Plenty of wood. Two empty tubs. They can go out the back door and haul water in from the river. Heat it on the stove. No food, but they can eat at the Palais de Voyageur or bring something back from the city."

"How much?"

Paulus laughed. "For you there is no charge! Usually the people who stay here are sent by Intendant Bigôt, who has his seconds collect the money in advance…who knows how much. But that is mostly in the summer. The beds stay empty this time of year. In either case, I don't have to account for the costs."

Philippe went to the door and waved his men into the warehouse. The clerk led them directly to the back and showed them the sleeping area. There was a long table. Lots of chairs. There were six lamps, which he lit to provide light.

"There is the back door to the river." He pointed. "You can see the crossbar. There are the buckets to collect your water. Large pots on the stove for heating. Dump the dirty water out back. I can get someone to wash your clothes if you like. You are all welcome here."

This is perfect, Philippe thought. He looked at the scouts. It was better than they could hope and certainly better than any of the city barracks. They nodded vigorously and thanked the clerk.

"I am going inside the walls to find a place for the children," Philippe told the scouts.

When they reached the front again, he said to the clerk, "I was hoping to come back and use that wonderful bathtub in Corrinne's apartment…"

Paulus nodded. "The third floor is still completely furnished, only draped in dust covers. The bed is made, and by the time you get back I will have the tub filled with hot water with more heating."

Philippe moved to give him two silver pieces.

"No, no! There will be none of that. Your fee is the promise to tell me everything that has happened since you left. I will have some hot food arranged at the Palais de Voyageur as well when you get back."

Leah gripped Philippe's hand tightly, staring shyly at the sentries, as they entered the river-side gate of the city. The lower town street, Rue Saint-Paul, was busy with craftsmen and traders. This street was lined with the shops of tradesmen. There was hammering, pounding, sawing, chopping, and other familiar noises of production. He looked east on Rue Saint-Paul. Nothing much had changed as far as he could see, except he noticed more sentries than usual high on Montréal's walls.

Straight ahead on the west end of Montréal was the city marketplace. The aromas of cooking food wafting on the air currents made their mouths water.

"Let's get something to eat."

Half the stalls of the farmers' market were empty. Unusual for a late spring day. Philippe took them to a pastry stand and bought some powdered cake with berries. It cost ten times as much as he remembered. He purchased an extra two full cakes to take to Corrinne's former chamberlain and his wife. Philippe and the children sat at an outdoor table and ate the cake, watching the people. Philippe pointed out who some of them were.

"Those are goat farmers. See all the rounds of cheese in their stall. That man is a tailor. His stand is full of clothes to buy. That's a butcher, of course. Mostly wild meats, deer, some beef. Fishing stalls, something new and fresh every day or smoked to store for winter. Next, you can see the cooking stands. Then comes the people who make and sell metal ware, pots, pans, ladles, big spoons, and the like. The blacksmith sells plow heads, tools, axes, saws. A few of them also make swords and knives. Of course, you see the fur traders, cured furs, much of it beaver, some fox, some ermine, some wolf and bear. That stall in the corner over there sells bows, arrows, knives, maybe some muskets. Those two men in the long robes by the cooking stands are called Récollets. They are friars…priests who work with the poor. The cups they hold out to people are for alms. Some of them are good healers too. That church behind them over there is where they live."

"Those are Indians!" Leah said cautiously.

Philippe saw a group of six, four of them women, moving among the various stands and stalls. They were dressed colorfully; the men carried knives, tomahawks, and muskets.

"Yes, they are. They are called Huron. They come to shop and trade like everyone else. They like to wear their best clothing when they come to the city. The dresses the women wear take almost a year to make and are decorated with beads, feathers, and shells, all of it collected in the wilderness and sewn by hand."

Philippe saw a look of fear on the girl's face.

"Not all of the Indians are bad, Leah. Many of them took care of me when I was hurt." *Since they couldn't kill me.*

"Some are bad," she replied in a voice burdened with gruesome memories.

He rubbed the back of her neck gently. "Yes, Leah, some of them are bad. Some white men are bad as well. There are bad people everywhere in the world. But not these Indians."

On their way through the maze of streets and alleys of the city's western section, called the *rue ménagerie* by the people who lived there, Philippe happened to see his reflection in the glass of a shop window and realized just how disheveled and dirty he looked. He needed his hair cut and beard trimmed. Fortunately, the beard hid the star-shaped heavy scarring on his right cheek, and he decided to keep the beard from now on.

At the door to the chamberlain's house, he knocked and stepped back into the street. A woman appeared and looked suspiciously from him to the children and back to him.

He took off his hat. "*Bonjour*, Mary."

Her hand went to her throat. "Oh, my God! Philippe Gerrard! What? How?"

"We've just arrived."

Mary let them in right away and directed them into the *cuisine* to sit in some chairs. She put on a pot of tea. He quickly made introductions, explained where he'd come from, how he came to have the two children, and why he was in Montréal.

"Then you already know about Henri?"

Philippe froze. "Henri? What about Henri?"

"You missed him by only a week."

"Missed him! Henri was here? In Montréal?!"

"*Oui*, Philippe! He has been here since last summer!"

"Last summer! He is supposed to be in Boston!"

"Henri thought you were killed by the Oneida Indians. He came back here to search for you. But then he was called up with the militia. He was in battle at Lac du Saint-Sacrament and again at the English supply forts on the Mohawk River."

"What?" Philippe asked sharply. He could not believe what he was hearing.

Mary nodded. "Yes. He was decorated *twice* for valor…"

"Where is he now?"

"He joined the Troupes de la Marine. His battalion was sent to Louisbourg last week."

"The Troupes…? *Louisbourg*!"

Every sentence she uttered brought a bigger surprise. Philippe suddenly felt old…and tired.

Mary touched his arm sympathetically. "I am sorry you did not know, Philippe."

Philippe massaged his face with his hands.

"What's wrong?" asked Joshua in a nervous voice.

"Nothing." Philippe turned, noting their worried faces, and said more softly, "Nothing is wrong. Mary was just giving me news about my son, Henri."

If he has not heard about Henri, he may not know about Corrinne and the twins. Mary decided not to tell him anything else to give him time to absorb this news about Henri. In simple words of English she spoke gently to the children.

"*Vous* hungry?"

"*Oui*," said Joshua.

Leah nodded.

"They can understand a little French but not much. I will get them a book of translation. They will be part of a prisoner trade with the English. I brought them here to turn them over to…well, I don't know who that is. But in the meantime, I need to have them stay with someone while I figure this out. You and Denis were my first choice…but I know it is a lot to ask of you. So I will not be offended if you say no. I can probably find someone else."

Mary stroked Leah's hair and spoke soothingly to her, "How could I not want someone as lovely as *you* to stay with me? Of course, I will do this."

"Thank you. They have been at my side every day for the last few months…since their rescue. It's not been easy for them."

Philippe turned his attention to Joshua and Leah and switched to English. "For the time being, Mary and Denis will give you a place to sleep. They are very dear friends of mine. You are inside the city and completely safe. But you both need to be strong for me now."

"You promised…" Joshua reminded cautiously.

"I did. And I will not break that promise. But I must find out how this trade will take place…where….when…and by whom. Things like that. You will still see me every day. I promise."

Leaving Leah and Joshua with Mary was much more difficult than Philippe imagined it would be. His promise to see them cared for hung around his neck like a heavy stone. One he could easily remove if he chose to do so. But he didn't. He decided to go back to check on them again after he cleaned up and ate something, just to demonstrate he was telling them the truth.

By the time he got back to the warehouse, Paulus had filled the tub in Corrinne's apartment with hot water. The senior clerk had paid four cleaning women from the Palais de Voyageur to help him. As usual, it took three tubs of water for Philippe to get himself clean. Fortunately for him, one of the women was a barber. She cut his hair and trimmed his beard. Like any good barber, she was full of city gossip. Philippe learned the people of Montréal were expecting a famine. Too many farmers had been called up to the militia. The enemy army movements seemed to be happening everywhere. Tribes loyal to the English were raiding homesteads in the wilderness. A new military commander from Paris was expected at any time. Governor-General Vaudreuil lived and acted like a king. The Royal Intendant had monopolized all the trade and commerce, forcing everyone to buy through the Grand Company at oppressive prices. Fur trade had fallen to a trickle. Ships were not getting through from Quebec unless escorted by the navy.

After the women left the room, he took off the bathing robe and examined himself naked in Corrinne's full-length mirror. As before, the man he saw was a complete stranger compared to the last reflection he recalled. He was too lean. The muscles looked wasted. Scars crisscrossed his torso, arms, and legs from every direction, shocking evidence of the brutality he'd suffered running the Oneida gauntlets. The beard helped his face, giving it a fuller look. It covered his scarred right cheek, but the vertical scars were still visible. His forehead was permanently creased from frowning and worry. His hands were rough and thick with calluses. His left leg was forever bowed from the improper healing of the break below the knee two years earlier.

At least I'm not gray, he thought. *The enemy wants my scalp. And they are never going to get it.*

After soaping and rinsing it multiple times, Philippe's blond hair, now cut and combed, shined with a healthy cleanliness, free of lice and the fine sands from countless muddy rivers and streams. He had scratched his head so often when it was dirty, festers occurred. In many places, the scalp was now tender with open sores after the scabs were washed away. One of the women said the skin would heal now that it was clean, but he would have to rinse it carefully every day for a week.

"But do it gently. Don't wash away the new scabs," she warned.

He lay down naked in Corrinne's bed and groaned with relief. It was like lying on a luxurious cloud. The pillows still held the delicate scent of her perfume. He plunged his face into them and breathed the heavenly fragrance. But he didn't dare close his eyes and dwell on her seductive memory too long lest he fall asleep. Instead, he groaned and pulled himself upright.

Thinking ahead, Paulus Legate had gathered fresh clothing for Philippe to wear: the vest and pants of an officer in the Troupes, small clothes, clean shirts, socks, even a decent pair of leather boots. There was a sash matching the color of the vest as well. The one he usually wore was part of the pile awaiting washing, along with every other item of clothing he'd carried in his pack. The overcoat was a dark brown cut of supple leather with some Indian beadwork; nothing ostentatious. It would cover his skinning and boning knives attached to the new belt. Paulus had even found him an officer's saber as well. And a weathered tri-cornered hat.

Fully attired, he actually *looked* like an officer of the naval marines. Philippe was surprised. He felt like an imposter. Except he wasn't.

"I *am* a marine," he told his reflection firmly. "There, I can say it."

Philippe took his large sack of coin from his pack and went downstairs. The four middle-aged women were waiting for him to reappear. They clapped their hands in appreciation, touched his clothing, and patted his arms and back, smiling and complimenting the way he looked.

"You've certainly lost that feral shit smell of a *coureur de bois*," the oldest one said. "I might even take you to my bed now, if you ask me nicely."

Though she was the oldest, she was definitely not matronly like the others. On the contrary, she was attractive, even with the strands of white hair he saw among the brown. There was still mischief in her eyes. Philippe liked her immediately.

"I'm sorely tempted," Philippe answered. "But alas, Mademoiselle, I am married."

"So you say." She pretended a frown. "Does she live in Montréal?"

"No."

"He is married to Lady de Chanaye," Paulus interjected quickly before this conversation went further.

"Lady de Chanaye? Well…" She stood on her tiptoes and kissed Philippe's cheek. "Just in case you change your mind, I will send my husband away to stay with his sister. Make sure you tell him where I live, Paulus," she said over her shoulder with a flirty smile as the women went back upstairs to finish cleaning up his room.

"Catherine is jesting, of course," Paulus said nervously. "Just ignore her. She has a good heart. A dinner awaits us at the Palais de Voyageur."

Philippe dropped a heavy sack of coin on a nearby table. "I need to count wages for my scouts. I need six leather pouches."

"I can help with that."

After paying his scouts as promised, Philippe gave all the rest of his silver to Paulus for safekeeping, but kept a small pouch for himself. Paulus opened a hidden door on the warehouse floor and placed Philippe's remaining money in a safe cemented in rock.

"Let's eat," the clerk announced. "I promise to pause between questions just long enough to permit you time to chew."

An hour later, it was dark. Philippe made the excuse of having to check on Joshua and Leah as his reason for leaving, which was true. The clerk said he would stay in the warehouse office that night.

"To let you all in when you're drunk," he explained. The clerk himself was already drunk.

To his surprise, hungry as he was, Philippe could not eat all the food the Palais offered in the meal. His stomach had shrunk from weeks of small rations and strenuous travel. He was light headed after only a single glass of wine. He did not want to walk around the city with the drunken militia carousing at night. They brawled without much reason. Just being alone was risky enough.

Though it was dark, he found the chamberlain's house without trouble. The chamberlain was as happy to see Philippe as Mary was. In the time he was gone, Mary had managed to bathe Leah, plus wash and comb the girl's hair into a long braid decorated with ivory combs. Joshua had just finished his bath. Denis had borrowed clean clothes for the boy from neighbors.

The children gawked as Philippe entered the house. He was equally surprised with them.

He knelt before Leah. "Look at how beautiful you are," he told her. "Your clothes. Your hair!"

Leah rewarded him with a blushing smile, the first since the rescue.

"And Joshua! You look years older. Like a young woodsman."

"Do you have time to eat?" Mary asked.

Philippe had eaten only an hour earlier, but he knew it was important to be together. "Yes, of course."

Mary had spoken to Denis, and they both agreed it was better not to mention Corrinne and the babies on this first night. They would keep the attention on the two English children. It was a simple dinner, a fish stew with vegetables, bread, cheese, wine. Philippe picked at it. They discussed the city. Joshua's curiosity-fueled questions returned in full strength. Philippe assumed the role of translator to allow Mary and Denis to bond with the boy.

After dinner, they sat around the fire in the small living room. Leah crawled onto Philippe's lap and went to sleep in his arms. She was like Anamosa in many ways. Just holding her provoked strong feelings of protectiveness.

Joshua asked more questions. They answered him patiently. It was not long before the boy began yawning. Mary went into the small bedroom and pulled back the blankets. She had shortened a gown for Leah to wear.

"I'll be back tomorrow," he told Denis and Mary after the children were in bed. "I will see Archbishop Nicolet in the morning, learn what goes on in the city, ask about the war and the prisoner exchange. He can probably tell me more about Henri."

Denis was certain the archbishop knew about Corrinne and the babies, as Henri would have told him. He decided it would be much better for Philippe to hear it from André Nicolet.

"You look so exhausted, Philippe." Mary hugged him, holding tight for several seconds. "It's good to have you back with us again."

Philippe hurried back to the apartment to lie down, this time to stay underneath the sheets in Corrinne's bed. With the window ajar, the room was cooled by the breeze coming from the river. He felt every ache of his bone-deep bruises as he stretched out his body and legs beneath the covers. The energy that had driven him here now turned its full attention to thinking only of Corrinne, his love for her, his longing for her. Surrounded by such relaxing comfort, he imagined being in her arms. He pulled a pillow close to his cheek, rested his head, and gazed at the glow of the hearth. The flames were hypnotic. Within minutes, he was deep asleep and joined with her in a dream.

CHAPTER 11
SAYBROOK, CONNECTICUT
MAY 17, 1756
One Day in May

The *ghost* was pleased at the renewed strength of the white eagle as the warmer days grew longer. The winter-long rest had indeed revitalized the bird. And the extended time in subdued reflection seemed equally restorative for the quality of the *ghost*'s conclusions. The rest was good for the eagle and good for the *ghost*; a lesson it would not forget in the future. The eagle had endured a long flight when the *ghost* came to the aid of Snow Hair. But the *ghost* learned the white eagle would remain strong as long as it remained subdued for longer interludes after such flights. It rested for several days. This was followed by another flight to the grave mound where the human bones of the *ghost* were buried.

While at the grave mound, the *ghost* unexpectedly sensed a servant of the demon. It focused and perceived that the servant was close to the white woman. There would be no rest. A longer flight was now required. The longest one of all.

They flew until dark, rested all night, and started again at first light. So far, the eagle seemed strong. They were gliding down the warm thermals, going south to the place where the white woman dwelled. It could clearly sense the servant now. It was getting closer to her, but the demon itself was much further away to the south and inexplicably moving in the opposite direction. The white woman had no idea danger was approaching her again. The *ghost* would find a way to warn her. But it must be careful in these more populated lands. The hunters who lived here would not hesitate to fire on the white eagle. The rarest of the great raptors was considered a valuable prize. And sudden death for the eagle meant ghastly entrapment for the *ghost* in the black abyss…forever!

That mid-winter conclusion was not an answer the *ghost* was seeking, but it did bring an intense focus to its concentration on other questions for which he sought answers.

*

Sentry Cheever arrived from Boston with arrangements for Corrinne to rendezvous with Charles VanderMeer. Tomorrow morning they would ferry across the Connecticut River to an estate house on the east side of the river in the farming community of Lyme. The house was maintained by people who lived nearby and were in the occasional employ of Thomas Hancock, the owner. Sentry had already escorted Lord VanderMeer to the house where the lord now awaited Corrinne's arrival. The Dutchman was anxious to see her again, as well as the babies and Anamosa.

After months of the dreary, lonely winter days and nights, Corrinne was overjoyed at making the short trip to the other side of the river. They planned to stay only three days at the estate house. So far, their efforts to hide her identity and past history from the locals were successful. Too long an absence from Winter House, or too long a visit there, might draw unwanted attention. They had created another fiction as well. Charles was *Charles Jamison,* a shipping merchant from New Bedford as validated by a letter of introduction from Thomas Hancock to the maintenance servants. These people had been notified of Charles' approaching arrival a month earlier. They had the house prepared with rooms made up for several guests, as per instructions.

In addition to the visiting arrangements, Sentry also brought chocolate and toy gifts for Anamosa and Calypso and Marcus. While the children giddily enjoyed the gifts, Sentry announced he'd also brought a present for Corrinne.

"How thoughtful of you, Sentry! What have you brought me?"

Sentry glanced at Mathilde. "Mathilde, you may want to watch the children for a bit," he told her. "My lady, it may be better for yah' to receive this present in your library…in private."

Corrinne made a face. "So serious, Mr. Cheever? What could be so important? Very well. A present is a present. And I do love presents too."

Corrinne went into the library.

"I'm ready. Surprise me."

Sentry reached inside his coat and withdrew a letter completely sealed around the edges in wax. It had never been opened and had blotchy dirt and rust-colored stains on the outside from months and months of journey. It was addressed to C. Chanaye.

Corrinne's eyes widened, knowing immediately who the letter was from. She inhaled sharply. Tears formed in the corners of her eyes as she reached out with trembling hands. Sentry handed it to her. Corrinne slowly hugged the letter to her heart and bowed her head, rocking gently back forth, as if holding a small child. She repeated Philippe's name in a whisper over and over again.

Sentry cleared his throat. "I will wait in the other room, my lady."

Corrinne did not hear him leave. She wept with relief, with love, with happiness.

Mathilde glanced at Sentry as he closed the library door and posted himself outside. Seeing the emotional expression on his face, Mathilde became alarmed and moved to push by him, but he held out a hand.

"No, if you please, Mathilde. Leave her be."

"What's wrong? What's happened?" she demanded.

"I gave her a letter from Mr. Gerrard. She needs some time alone."

Mathilde inhaled deeply and tears welled in her eyes. "Oh, thank God." She knelt down on the floor where she stood, clasped her hands, and began a prayer of thanks.

With Corrinne weeping in the library and Mathilde weeping and now kneeling, Sentry shifted on his feet, confused as to what to do. Finally, he knelt by Mathilde and bowed his head.

When the welcomed shock had passed, Corrinne rose from the chair. Holding the letter against her heart with one hand, she retrieved a letter opener from her desk and a linen napkin from the side table to daub her wet eyes. Sitting down again, she smoothed the delicate missive on her lap and carefully peeled away the wax with her fingernails. Then with even more care, she prodded the edges of the delicate paper sheets with the letter opener until they separated without damage. There were six pages. Much of the ink and writing had bled or was smudged from constant dampness. But she could still read every single word. To her surprise, it was written in English.

My dearest love,

I hesitate as I begin this letter as so much has happened. What do I tell you first? What's most important? You may have heard rumors. But first, be assured I am alive and whole, no doubt because seeing you in my dreams each night makes me determined to come back to you. However, I cannot predict when that will be. This war will consume the lands in ways the French, the English, and the tribal peoples involved have ever conceived. Some of the changes may be good, but I fear most will not.

I wonder about you often, worry about you every day, and worry about Henri and Anamosa. I know I should be there for all of you. But had I stayed, there is no doubt I would have been arrested, or worse, endangered you with my presence. I live in the war now. Every day. With its dangers and horrors and death. It is all I know.

But I have found my old partner again! You will be as surprised as I was to learn that he is married! Yes! No longer an ill-tempered bachelor. And there is more—his new wife is Juniata, who I think you know. They both appear to be very happy. And more still. Juniata is with child and will probably give birth by the time you receive this. He went north to our former home at the fort, where Juniata lives now. He says to tell you hello and that he misses you.

Corrinne pressed the pages gently to her heart again. "I miss you too, Pierre," she whispered with sad fondness. *Pierre Dunemoore, a father?* It was hard to see him in that role. An uncle, perhaps. But now the hope of seeing Pierre, Juniata, and their baby someday was added to the long list of reasons to survive this war.

You should tell Henri that Chesanin is a member of the scouts I lead. He is very tall now, like his father. And like his father, he is a quiet man of few words, but fearless when there is fighting to be done.

And now I should stop, and let you talk to me. But that is not possible. C., I ache for you. I long for your arms, your touch, and your kiss. The thought of holding you is so healing to me I only dare do this as I am falling to sleep. Because then, in the privacy of my dreamy imagination, I am running my fingers over the smooth skin of your body. I submit to my euphoria so completely I often disturb anyone sleeping nearby. Unfortunately, the men shake me awake because I am making too much noise. They claim I moan too loudly as I sleep and presume my wounds are bothering me, hence their worry. Of course, this act of compassion always happens at exactly the most inopportune time in my dreams of you. Imagine my disappointment. I cannot tell them the truth that just the thought of my wife lying naked with me excites me to rapture in my sleep. The danger here is never far away to allow myself such wonderful indulgences.

    Nevertheless, I think of you every night. And on the nights of a full moon, whenever possible, I sit somewhere alone and gaze up at its brightness. I imagine it is you and dwell on the memory of your face, your smile. I whisper words of love to the moon and encourage my eyes to play tricks, to let me see the moon whisper back with an echo of your voice. I hunger to hold you naked in my arms, to touch you...

There followed a page and a half of vivid description of what Philippe would do with her and to her if she were there. All of it based on memories they could both recall, which made the words vivid. She knew that was his intention. Her breathing quickened and she licked her lips as she read through the page, sometimes closing her eyes to recall each explicit image from her memory.

    ...But this is only what I can imagine. What else can I do?

    The man I give this letter to start its journey to your hand is the most unlikely of messengers. He is more my enemy than a friend, and yet I trust him with this favor more than anyone else, simply because he gave me his word. This delicate, very perishable object, could melt away forever in water, turn to ash in fire, or be carried to oblivion on a sudden gust of winter wind.

    If this precious missive, safeguarded by the hands of many strangers, is nevertheless spirited to you, then I say it is proof my promise to return to your arms was not made in vain and that there is a greater power at work for us. Together, we can do anything, yes? We have a destiny, yes? Those are your words.

I kiss the single letter of my signature. And after I seal this with wax, I will press it to my heart and trust you will do that first when you receive it. And if the wax seal holds and you press the missive to your heart? Then my love and touch comes to you unbroken. If so, draw meaning from it. Make a wish. Because it will come true.

All My Love,

P.

It now seemed more than coincidence that her dreams the night before were more explicit than usual. They were in bed again in the warehouse apartment in Montréal, inducing explosions of pleasure in one another. One had been so strong that she'd awakened breathing heavily, disappointed to learn it was just a dream. She'd tried to force herself back to sleep, but the sun was up. At least the sweet reverie displaced the fearful nightmares she might otherwise have had. And no headache that morning!

She marveled further at the letter. *This took months to reach my hand, and it is unopened. A miracle. If such a miracle can happen*, she decided, *then today even wishes are possible.*

The ink of the *P* was smudged. In the blotchiness, Corrinne imagined the outline of his lips.

"I wish Philippe to meet Marcus and Calypso as soon as possible," she whispered.

She carefully kissed the *P* and pressed the missive to her heart again.

"I must find a way to answer this."

*

On January 16, 1756, Britain signed the Convention of Westminster with Prussia. This new convention, negotiated in secret, pledged neither Britain nor Prussia would invade or distress the other. Prussia was to remain neutral relative to the disputes between England and France. Britain would not aid Austria, a current treaty partner, in any renewed conflict to regain Silesia from Prussia, as long as Prussia agreed to protect Hanover from France.

Austria, however, was determined to regain Silesia, and when Empress Maria Theresa learned about this secret convention, she now turned to Madame de Pompadour, looking to France to be their ally against Prussia. But any action would first take several months of negotiation.

At the end of January 1756, the Duke of Newcastle was boasting he had *negotiated* more time to focus his attention on restoring the financial health of the crown. This was welcome news, as England's coffers were severely depleted from fighting a series of multi-year wars on the continent over the last fifty years, each new one steadily growing worse and more expensive.

Prussia had a defensive treaty with France, thus it was disingenuous for Prussia to align with the English in secret. Or for England to throw over Austria, their former ally. But the Convention of Westminster would protect Hanover from invasion and no money subsidies were required for Prussia.

The Duke of Newcastle detested managing the money of the crown. He detested dialogue with the base-born bankers who snobbishly insisted on higher interest rates. He'd rather work on foreign policy, where diplomacy, intrigue, and conspiracy could be used to advance British global aspirations. True, the *American* problem was beginning to be a drain, but that could be managed without a European land war; at least, he thought it could and planned as if that would be the case.

*

Amsterdam

It was early evening when Wittmann Bootz' hired mercenaries found and brought the three crewmen to von Kleinfels' apartment. Two of the men were left tightly bound and gagged in the bedroom. The third was ball-gagged and lashed to the same chair Bootz had endured months earlier.

On the other side of the ocean, Colonel von Kleinfels was lying in a hotel bed in the port city of New York. His identity and consciousness fully seized by the *vulnax*. In this death-like trance, the *vulnax* now had the strength to see and hear through Wittmann Bootz' eyes and ears.

The first seaman's eyes widened with terror as one of the hired men slipped the tee-handle *boot* over his foot. Another man sat down in a chair in front of him, so close, their knees almost touched. But it was the scowling face and eyes that provoked the most fear. The almond-shaped eyes were enormous vertical slits of pale yellow. They fixed on him predatorily, like an insect, ready to strike. A grotesque tongue flicked out and wet the lips. The visage was paralyzing.

The *vulnax* relished the fear he saw in the sailor's eyes. "You have questions, yes?"

The voice the seaman heard was low, guttural. The seaman nodded quickly, presuming this was the desired answer.

"No. *You* do not have questions. I have questions. *You* have only answers. But first, a demonstration of the device on your foot."

Bootz gave the handle a full clock-wise turn.

The seaman convulsed up and down in the chair, his eyes bulging, mucous spewing from his nose. Saliva sprayed around the edges of the gag driven by a rapid series of choked howls.

Bootz back turned the handle. The seaman gasped with relief.

"So you see? It is a simple instrument of pain. That was one turn of the handle. Imagine how two turns would feel. Now I will remove the ball gag, so you may speak. If you cry out, *the boot*," he warned. "I will ask you questions and you will give me truthful answers. If you lie to me, *the boot*." He leaned closer to the seaman until his eyes were only a flicker away. "And I will know if you are lying to me."

Bootz gestured to one of his men who removed the gag.

"Give him some water to drink."

The seaman gulped down the goblet of water.

"You are a crewman of *William's Queen*?"

"Yes." The answer came quickly.

Bootz asked what his job was aboard the ship and the jobs of the other two crewmen. He asked when the ship had left Boston. The answers only validated what he already knew. But more importantly, it validated the man's intention to speak the truth.

"What is the name of the island?"

"It is called Apthorp's Island."

"Who is Apthorp?"

"A…a trader in Boston. A man of wealth, some have said. But I do not know that for certain."

"And the name of the other ship?"

"The *Anamosa*. It is a trading frigate."

Bootz asked many questions about that ship. Among them, the captain's name and where it was bound. He learned it was going to Philadelphia to be outfitted with cannon. That Lady VanderMeer, her maid, her children, and all their baggage was transferred aboard, including the *châsse*.

"Where were they taken?"

"They were to be off-loaded to a waiting cargo launch in waters some-where to the south of Boston, reached after two days of sailing. The captain did not name the place to us, never mentioned it to us since then. I am not sure he knew. Some of us thought it was the long island near New York. But we did not really care. We are smugglers as well as traders. Keeping such things secret is the nature of our business. It is better we do not know. And that is the truth! I swear it!"

"What else?"

"Nothing else that I recall. But ask me more questions." The sailor was desperate to please. "From there we sailed for the Antilles. Stayed in Sint Eustatius almost four months, then sailed here."

"Where are you sailing next?"

"Captain LaTour has not told us yet. But the rumor is back to the Antilles."

"You are lying!"

"No, Monsieur! No! I am not lying!"

Bootz reached down and took hold of the handle. "Where are you sailing next?"

The crewman thought wildly for a better answer. "Uhhhh…most of the crew has family in Le Havre. We normally stop there for a month. But then we will sail to the Antilles Islands again. I am almost certain that is the truth! Please…please! Do not hurt me again!"

Le Havre, Bootz thought. *He may go there.* He was satisfied he gained as much as possible out of this man. He gestured for the boot to be removed and the ball gag to be put back in place.

"Take him to the other room and bring me the next man."

Bootz learned little more from the other two men. Except that Captain Martyn of the *Anamosa* had a mistress in Boston, but they did not know her name. And that it was Captain LaTour's intention to sail that morning, most likely to Le Havre, but maybe not.

"Kill them all," Bootz told the hired men. "Strangle them. Hang them together in a noose down on the wharves near the boat landing where they will be seen."

He paid in gold. Within an hour, the hired killers would do as he directed.

As the spirit of the *vulnax* withdrew from Bootz' body, the trading agent collapsed on one of the beds. He slept until almost noon the next day. He awoke feeling sluggish and with a dry mouth, heaving sickness, and a throbbing headache. He could not clearly recall what had occurred the night before. But he remembered the sights and sounds of men screaming in pain.

*

Amsterdam Wharf Hotel

Victorio had left the window curtains wide open in his third-floor hotel room. This was purposeful. The window faced east. When the first glimmer of morning light hit his eyes, he awoke and dressed quickly. He wanted to be at the boat landing down on the wharves as the sun came up, hopefully to greet the three crewmen, presuming they showed up early.

He went to where he'd left the *Queen*'s harbor launch and found the man assigned by Bootz to provide transport to and from the ship, waiting for him with a deep frown on his face.

"My boat is missing," the man said immediately.

"It's out at my ship. I can take you to it. I'd hoped to see my three crewmen. They should be here by now." Victorio glanced down the street where a small crowd had gathered by another pier. "What goes on there?"

"Someone said bodies were found," the man answered. "The harbor marines plan to drag them up on the street."

"What? How many bodies?"

"I don't know."

With a sick feeling, Victorio walked towards the crowd followed by Bootz' man. He approached cautiously and sidled his way closer.

"Oh, fuck," he whispered under his breath

It was them. Their heads and necks were purple, eyes bulging, tongues extended, the bodies swollen grotesquely. They had been hung in one common noose, like bulbs of spoiled garlic from a *cuisine* hook but exuding a stench far, far worse. The bruised skin of their throats also showed rope ligature marks, signs of strangulation. The left foot of each corpse was ballooned, colored like a wet loaf of moldy green bread, with a two-inch round hole bored into the top of the foot arch.

Victorio had seen such signs of torture before. *This is bad*, he thought.

With a final heave on the line by the four marines, the slimy bodies were dragged up on the wharf.

As more people gathered to gawk, a soldier shouted, "Does anyone know these men?"

"That's them, isn't it," Bootz' boatman asked quietly. "Your crewmen?"

"No. It's not," Victorio refuted firmly. He started back towards his launch. "I will take you out to my ship so you can retrieve your boat. I need to report to the captain they did not show up this morning. I will come back later to wait for my crewmen."

*

After Bootz' boatman rowed away from the *Queen*, Victorio followed Captain LaTour down to his cabin. He told him what he'd seen and learned.

"They were tortured, Captain. With some kind of Spanish boot device. Strangled with garrotes, taken to the pier, and hung in a common noose."

The captain listened with a grim face. As Victorio finished, LaTour stared out at the deck and pondered the import of it all.

"Even if they were robbed and killed for their money, they might be left in an alley somewhere with their throats cut. I wouldn't like it, but I could accept that explanation. But this? Tortured and left hanging together? No need to do that except to send a message. No. This is something sinister. What could provoke this type of brutality, with the intention of having us see the results?"

"The same people who attacked Lord and Lady VanderMeer in Boston? Lord VanderMeer claimed there were other houses in Germany and Amsterdam seeking his death."

"Possibly. But after seeing Wittmann Bootz. The way he looked. The way he spoke to us. The things he said. I believe this was his doing somehow. But why torture our *crewmen*?"

"Information?"

"We are traders of the sea, Victorio. What knowledge could these simple men possess that Wittmann Bootz would act so savagely to learn?"

But LaTour knew the answer to this question. Victorio confirmed it.

"The *châsse*."

"Yes…the people that crave that evil reliquary. Meneer Bootz has been corrupted to join them. We saw it in his eyes and manner. What black wickedness did they employ to subvert that polite gentleman?" The captain shook his head slowly. "They must know we transferred Lady VanderMeer and that coffin to the *Anamosa*. Our crewmen could confirm that much. And I must assume that they learned the *Anamosa* was bound for Philadelphia. One of the crewmen, at least, would know that too."

"But why hang them on the pier? Why display this at all?"

"It was for us to see, to learn about. That our crew would speculate fearfully amongst themselves as to the reasons for the tortured deaths of their shipmates. To remember such speculation. They intend to capture more of the crew…if they cannot capture you or me first."

"So what do we do?"

"We don't let them! Our business here is over…probably forever. I don't plan to come back here again. We've been paid." He paused to consider what else was necessary. "I think it's better not to speak of what you saw today with any of the crew. Just say the men simply did not come back. That you left a message with the boatman to tell them they should make their way to Le Havre. Tell the crew…with war being declared…you were advised by our trading agent to leave the anchorage. We are leaving. Prepare to raise anchor and set our sails. I will decide where we are going before the day is over. For now, we will sail into the channel and go west."

Victorio left the cabin to so inform the crew.

A few minutes later, Captain LaTour heard the sounds of activity begin on the main deck. He went to his navigation table and perused various charts, plotting courses, measuring distances, estimating time to various points of navigation.

This war may begin before we transit the narrow channel between Calais and Dover. The men-o-war of both countries will fire on any ship that does not fly their flags. Hell, the batteries on the shore will probably fire on us anyway. And they will board all the trading ships no matter what flag they fly. That's what happened last time.

LaTour began to mutter while he did the calculations

"Full sail. No cargo. Assume fourteen knots on average. Travel dark at night. Pray the weather gauge works in our favor. Two…two and a half days to get clear of the channel all the way to Brest. With no stopping. If a warship engages…do I run or not? Even if the winds are with me, do I run? What if there is a squadron of warships in chase?"

The thought of running the English Channel between two warring navies suddenly seemed fraught with so many deadly outcomes he hesitated.

Stay here, maybe? Anchor somewhere else? But for how long? Will the threat of war be any less by tomorrow? No. If the war has started, the opportunity to sail freely will decrease with each passing day.

LaTour heard the metallic rattle-clank of chain links as the anchor windlass was being turned. It was as if the *Queen* had made the decision for him. It spurred his thoughts.

"We leave now! While we still can!"

*

Montréal

Philippe awoke early. His dreams of Corrinne had never been stronger. He sponged his face and body clean in the basin, dressed quickly, slipped the dispatch pouch over his shoulder, and went downstairs to the offices. Paulus Legate was already awake at the slant desk, writing numbers in the ledgers.

"Good morning, Philippe. Sleep well?"

"Better than I have in a year. I want to stay in this apartment while I'm in Montréal. I will pay—"

"Stop! Nonsense! I told you. The money never comes to me anyway. Stay as long as you like."

Philippe pulled five silver pieces from his pouch. "Well, here's something for the cleaning women at least. Maybe they can clean the bunks and wash my men's clothes as well? Let me know if you need more. I am going into the city to see Archbishop Nicolet and then probably to army headquarters. Joshua and Leah are staying at the house of Corrinne's former chamberlain, Denis, and his wife Mary. You know them? Good. Keep that to yourself. I am going to tell them to bring the children here…to you…in case any problems arise and they cannot find me. You must be able to hide them…will that be all right with you?"

"Of course. I will make arrangements. If it comes to that, they will be fine."

"Thank you, Paulus. I will not forget this charity." Philippe hesitated as he looked toward the back of the warehouse. "I don't have answers for them yet. Tell my men I will come to them this afternoon after I visit headquarters."

"As you wish."

Philippe headed into the city through the river-landing gate, returning the salute of the sentries. Salutes made him uncomfortable. His years as a *coureur de bois* inclined him to anonymity.

Montréal was flanked by two long streets, Rue Notre-Dame on the upper town, and Rue Saint-Paul on the river side. He walked by the west market towards Rue Notre-Dame on the upper town. The mouthwatering aromas of baked goods and cooking meat pulled him immediately into the stands. He broke his fast with hot bread and butter, spitted meat, hot tea, and sugar-powdered biscuits. It all cost ten times more than he could ever remember paying, another ominous sign of the gathering famine, but he did not complain.

Half an hour later, he walked up the broader street of Rue Notre-Dame. It was lined with shops and stores, many with residences on the upper floors. He passed the door leading up to the artist's loft Charles VanderMeer used to occupy. The street was alive with carts and wagons, goods being moved by farmers and merchants, but the majority of the walkers were the armed militia and the Troupes, going in every direction it seemed, by twos and threes. The saluting he endured quickly became tedious. He was pleased to reach the Terrain des Jésuites and knocked on the door. A black-robed man answered and waited for Philippe to speak.

"*Bonjour*, Father. I am here to see Archbishop Nicolet. I am Captain Philippe Gerrard."

"Is he expecting you?"

"No, but I am certain he will want to see me."

The Jesuit priest stood aside and gestured towards a chair in the vestibule. "*S'il vous plait*, you may wait here, Captain."

A sergeant of the Montréal gendarmerie was walking west on Rue Notre-Dame when he saluted a leather-coated officer of the marines as they passed one another. The officer wore the clothes of a captain and possessed the hardened look of a veteran. The sergeant knew most of the officers in the marines, at least by name or reputation, but he did not recognize this man. *He must have come from the western wilderness,* he thought. Any person meeting him could not overlook that thick blond beard. Someone must know this man. He followed the officer at a distance and saw him enter the Jesuit compound. Now *that* was unusual…and could be profitable for him.

The sergeant went to the building across from the governor's palace. He nodded to the two gendarmes standing guard at the front door and went upstairs to Intendant Bigôt's offices. He stopped before the hallway desk outside the intendant's door. The gendarmerie corporal who temporarily acted as the intendant's secretary stood to greet him.

"Is he in? I've something important to tell him."

"I will ask if he will see you." Seconds later, the corporal returned. "You may go in."

The sergeant entered and stopped before the Intendant's desk and waited patiently at attention.

François Bigôt had only arrived in Montréal from Quebec two weeks earlier. The notoriously corrupt official hated Montréal and always had. It provided none of the regal comforts he'd created for himself at his estate of Beaumanoir in the Saint Charles River valley north of Quebec City. It also provoked his worst memories and reminded him of his greatest failures. It was here that Corrinne de Chanaye and her woodsman obtained the documents from his office that would be used by Archbishop Nicolet and the Marquis Duquesne to have him recalled to France at the end of 1754 on charges of fraud.

Previous to that, the Royal Intendant of New France had established the Grand Company of Traders, essentially a monopoly of all imports and exports in New France. Subsequent decrees issued by Bigôt in the name of the King made certain all commercial activity in New France now passed through this company and the hands of his associates. He controlled the prices and availability of every type of good or commodity. The profits for the Grand Company were enormous. To safeguard any interference with his decisions, the intendant had shrewdly allied with members of the Second Estate in Versailles, as persons of nobility by lineage or given by the King were referred to as a class. These people received dividend shares and profits in the company as his partners. Thus, they were all vested in ensuring François Bigôt remained the chief administrator in charge of collecting taxes, financial matters, food and grain distribution, and administration of all trade in New France.

There were still exceptions to this monopoly, most notable was *Les Négociants Dunemoore*; the Dunemoore Company. But he managed to crush it out of existence by the end of 1754, although not before Corrinne de Chanaye had collected embarrassing papers from his secret desk compartment, which had led to his recall.

But now, with the advent of war, the flow of money derived from the fraud had become too lucrative and too constant to all the allied partners to allow replacement of François Bigôt. The charges were dropped and Bigôt was returned to his former post in early summer of 1755. Governor General Pierre de Rigaud, Marquis de Vaudreuil-Cavagnial was now in power. The governor had already been recorded as a full partner in the Grand Company. They supported one another publicly, though rarely met alone in private.

With the spring campaigns of 1756 already in progress, Intendant Bigôt was required to remain near the governor at all times, to be available for Marquis de Vaudreuil's summons.

Intendant Bigôt hated Montréal, always had.

Bigôt sighed with annoyance at the sergeant's presence as he looked up from some documents he was reading.

The Intendant had a distinctive moustache, curled on both ends, which would wiggle like a tortured mouse when he talked. "Sergeant Deforge? What is so important for you to interrupt my morning?"

The sergeant explained what he saw and where the officer went.

"But I don't recognize him."

"So you profess to know *all* the officers in the Troupes?"

"No, sir. But I do not recall seeing him before, not in Montréal or Quebec. He wears a mixed dress of uniform and a leather coat with Indian beadwork. He presents the appearance of a veteran. I would not bring it to your attention except that he knocked on the door of the Jesuit compound and was admitted as if they knew him."

Bigôt's lips spread in an unnerving smile. "Maybe he confesses his sins?"

"Possibly, sir, but doubtful. He just arrived in Montréal. He was carrying what looked like a dispatch pouch over his shoulder. The man has a heavy blond beard and very light hair that cannot be missed. Even though I've never met him, I would have heard of a senior officer in the Troupes with this distinction. I presumed you might know someone resembling him. He is heavily armed and walks with the purpose of someone you do not want to confront."

It couldn't be? François Bigôt slowly straightened in his chair. *Could it?* "You say a blond beard? Are you certain?"

"It cannot be missed, sir. It is the first thing you notice before the skinning knife strapped to his belt...and a sword...and a shoulder pistol."

Intendant Bigôt was aware that Philippe Gerrard had been fighting with the marines at Fort Duquesne. Intriguing as that was, would the *coureur de bois* be foolish enough to return to Montréal? *Maybe he heard about his son being jailed in the bastille last year? And if it's him, he would definitely go to see Archbishop Nicolet.*

"Very well, Sergeant. There could be a reward in this information for you. Follow him. Find out where he goes, where he stays, and who he sees. Learn everything you can about him and report back to me tomorrow."

After the sergeant left, Bigôt rose from his desk and stared out at Governor Vaudreuil's mansion broodingly. All the memories of the painful humiliations he'd suffered at the hands of this particular *coureur de bois* and the man's whore, Lady de Chanaye, came rushing back to him. The torture, his disgrace, his embarrassment, the financial loss. Bigôt's attempt to take revenge on the son, Henri Gerrard, had been frustrated by the governor. Now the son was an officer in the Troupes at Louisbourg, out of reach.

If it is you, Philippe Gerrard, I owe you a lot of pain. And I will see you suffer before you die.

Inside the Terrain des Jésuites, a man with a familiar face walked towards Philippe.

"Thanks be to God and what must be a battalion of guardian angels looking after you, Philippe Gerrard." Father Tinian, the archbishop's secretary, hugged the officer and patted his back. "My God, it is good to see you! The archbishop will be so happy. He is saying Mass right now. Come. Let's wait for him in his offices."

When Philippe entered the pair of rooms on the second floor, he could see that not much had changed at all. Father Tinian's desk and the waiting chairs and benches were all in the same places. As he glanced through the open doorway to the bishop's office, he saw it was still surrounded by floor-to-ceiling bookshelves filled with books of every size, shape, and age. In addition to the ornate desk, he saw the two familiar reading chairs with a table between them next to the six-foot-tall window that permitted plenty of sunlight, a good place for reading.

"So take a seat there. I will prepare some hot tea and bring back a full plate of confectionaries, the kind the archbishop always chastises me about… if only to ease his guilt before he gobbles them down. Then, I will consume your time to glean as much as I can before he demands your full attention."

"Father, do you happen to have a book of English to French translation I can borrow for a time? I have some friends of mine who need one."

"Of course. I will give you one to keep before you leave the office today."

Father Tinian left for the *cuisine*.

Philippe ran his hand over the spines and covers of André Nicolet's fascinating collection of books while he waited for Father Tinian's return. Hundreds of them, from ancient tales and mythologies, to books of science and mathematics, to the philosophers and poets.

He has read every one of these, Philippe thought admiringly. *And Corrinne has probably read half of them.*

When Father Tinian returned, they sat down together in the archbishop's office. He asked about Corrinne's well-being.

"Healthy and well, I hope. But I've not seen her for a year and a half and have received no letters. She should still be in Boston where I left her."

With that simple report, Father Tinian scrutinized the captain. He seemed completely unaware of Corrinne's pregnancy. He decided he would leave that matter to the archbishop.

"Lady Corrinne was the only person to visit me at Hotel Dieu when I was sick with a terrible fever," Father Tinian said as they sipped tea. "She actually forced me to go to the hospital, which probably saved my life. She said if I didn't go, she would tell the bishop I had grabbed her breast. And then she took my hand and placed it on her breast…*so it would be true*! She extorted me. Then when she visited me at the hospital, she wiped my brow with cold, wet cloths. It felt so marvelous. It was like being touched by an angel. She gave me the will to live. Or I might not be here."

Philippe smiled at the priest's story. "Lady Corrinne is an angel. God knows she's kept me alive."

"Before she left, she asked me to take care of the archbishop. That she would try to write him and he should try to write her."

Talking about Corrinne depressed Philippe. He missed her too much. He changed the topic.

"Yesterday, I learned for the first time that my son Henri arrived here last summer. And that he joined the Troupes and was deployed to Louisbourg."

Father Tinian put down his cup. "Yes. All of that's true. I am sorry you did not know. Henri has grown to be..."

They heard the sound of steps on the stairs. Father Tinian moved quickly to the outer office.

"Eminence, you have a special visitor in your office."

"Special?" he challenged his secretary. André Nicolet stopped in his office doorway to gape in shock at the bearded officer standing before him.

"Philippe?"

Philippe dropped to one knee and bowed his head. "Eminence."

The archbishop pulled Philippe to his feet and hugged him tightly. "Good God, look at you! I mean, you look healthy, but thin. A little beaten... well, maybe a lot beaten...and scarred too! Did you fight the English by yourself at Fort Duquesne? Well, sit! I want to know everything! Father Tinian, may we—"

"It's on the table, Eminence."

"Stay with us, Father, and listen," the archbishop encouraged.

Father Tinian stood by the door. For the first hour, Philippe did most of the talking, disclosing the entire adventure of getting to Boston after stopping in Halifax and eventually starting a company and getting a place to live in Boston.

"In January last year, I was advised the local magistrate suspected me as a spy. So I left. Went north through Albany. Got captured by the Oneida. Was forced to run their gauntlet...twice. That's where I got most of this." He gestured at his face and body. "Somehow I survived. And because I did, they made me a member of the tribe. A few months later, after I could walk again, they helped me get back to Fort Niagara. I traveled further to Fort Duquesne. I've been there ever since, leading a troop of scouts until I came up here. And I think you know what happened at Fort Duquesne and since."

At this pause, Father Tinian sensed a shift toward personal matters and excused himself.

Philippe continued. "I only heard about Henri yesterday."

"What do you know?"

Philippe told him.

"Be proud of him, Philippe. The governor commissioned him as an ensign in the marines."

"Why commission him?"

"To honor him for his valor. But there's more to this story."

The archbishop began with Henri's surprise arrival in Quebec the year before. His sudden incarceration in the bastille. *Bigôt.* The governor's decision to add the men in the bastille to the militia. Henri's part in the battle of Lac du Saint-Sacrament. His decoration for valor. The battle at the English supply forts. Henri's second decoration for valor. The incident of saving an English soldier's life by killing an Indian fighting as their ally.

"The dead Indian was the son of Athanase. The Huron was determined to kill Henri. The grenadiers vowed to defend him. Governor Vaudreuil did not want this to escalate. He needs the Indians. The governor thought it best to transfer him to keep him alive. But Henri had to join the Troupes first so he could order him to Louisbourg. Within a few days, the governor ordered a hundred and thirty Troupes moved to the defense of Louisbourg until more regulars arrive from France. Ensign Henri Gerrard commands a platoon."

Philippe was silent, distressed that Henri was now a full participant in this brutal, deadly war, a war he realized would go on for several more years. And Louisbourg would be a prime objective for the English. *Probably before Quebec.*

"I took him to Boston to spare him from this."

"God had other plans. Have you no more to tell me, Philippe?"

"About what?"

"About Corrinne."

"Corrinne?" Philippe straightened with concern. "What about Corrinne?"

The archbishop held up a palm. "Be at peace, my son. Nothing bad, but you should brace yourself." The bishop leaned forward. "Henri told us Corrinne was with child when he left Boston."

Philippe jumped to his feet. "What—! With child! You mean she is going to have a baby?"

"That is the usual implication, except she has probably given birth by now. You've been gone a long time. The birth would have occurred last summer."

It was another in a series of stunning revelations. "Last summer!"

"Henri claimed the doctors thought it would likely occur by July. Henri had left long before July. So he was not certain when it happened."

"Is she all right?"

"Corrinne is young, healthy, and strong. I presume so, but I don't know. There has been no communication. We are trying, but with the war…"

"Corrinne had a baby…" he repeated, his face pale.

"Well, actually, Henri said the Boston doctors told her to expect twins." Philippe gaped. "Twins!?"

"Henri plans to send letters to Boston from Louisbourg on a foreign ship. Or maybe using a chain of fishing vessels."

"Twins…" Philippe still could not believe this. "I…I should have been there for her. I would have stayed had I…"

A flood of memories assaulted him. The look on Corrinne's face. The things she said while they embraced outside the house the night he left.

"She knew."

"What?"

"Corrinne knew she was pregnant before I left. She almost told me as much as I was leaving. But she didn't. Because she knew I would stay. So she didn't tell me. I should have been there."

Father Tinian knocked and opened the door. "Apologies, Eminence. Father Eric has come to see you."

Nicolet thought this the perfect interruption.

"Philippe, don't act so glum. You are a new father! Possibly of *twins*! By the most beautiful, most intelligent woman I have ever known. One who loves you more than her life. Now, let me introduce my younger brother, Eric, recently arrived from Paris." He gestured to Father Tinian.

A Jesuit priest entered the office. The man genuflected and kissed Nicolet's upheld ring.

"Captain Gerrard, Father Eric Nicolet, my younger brother. Eric, Captain Gerrard is one of our brave officers in the marines and a good friend of mine."

Still in a daze, Philippe shook hands. Philippe vaguely noted how much they looked alike. Eric could be the bishop's *twin*, except he was thirty years younger.

"My pleasure, Father."

"The pleasure is mine, Captain. Actually, I've heard much about you and would hope to speak with you more. Perhaps another time?"

"I am at your service, Father."

There was more André Nicolet wanted to inform Philippe about regarding the military politics that would bubble over soon, so he'd be better prepared for the coming storm.

"Are you planning to report to the army today?"

"I was. But my mind is now…on other matters…I'll report tomorrow. The army doesn't know I am here anyway. And I wish further counsel from you before I report. There is another topic to discuss. Also important, but it can wait."

"Perfect. Tomorrow morning then? Same time?"

"Yes, thank you, Eminence."

Father Tinian handed him the French to English book of translation as he exited the office.

As Philippe left the Jesuit mission, he squinted at the bright sunlight. It was a warm, beautiful day in May. He decided to go back to the chamberlain's house. He expected the army would give him multiple things to do as soon as he reported his presence. He was not prepared for any more surprises that day.

He shook his head again. "Twins!"

Sergeant Deforge had only been with the Intendant Bigôt for twenty minutes. When he came back out to the street, he decided to take a chance that the marine captain was still inside the Terrain des Jésuites. He leaned against a building to wait on the other side of Rue Notre-Dame. There were plenty of people walking around the nearby buildings. He should not be noticed. After an hour had passed, he was going to leave when the tall blond-haired officer appeared, coming out the Jesuit compound's main doorway.

He was in there for almost two hours, Sergeant Deforge noted.

This was a wilderness fighter, he reminded himself. He would be alert for someone following him. Deforge waited until the marine captain was at least one street ahead of him before shadowing him on the Rue Notre-Dame. If possible, he wanted to do this without help from any of his men and keep the reward money all for himself.

Near the market area, the officer turned into the short streets of the *rue ménagerie*. It would be easy to lose track of him in there, so Deforge quickly closed the gap between them. He came around one corner at a fast walk just in time to see the marine enter a building. An older woman answered the door. There was really no place to linger on this street without being obvious. He saw an outdoor café a block further beyond the doorway. He would be in plain sight, but his presence there would be plausible.

While he sat at a table to wait, he tried to learn what he could about the people who lived around there.

"Are there any rooms I could rent in this area," he asked the waiter. "Any of the buildings on that side of the street over there? Do you know anyone who might want a tenant?" And with that question, he casually inquired about who lived behind a particular doorway.

Deforge ordered some biscuits and tea while he waited and asked for a paper to read. Before another hour passed, the captain appeared again and started walking directly towards him. The sergeant sipped his tea and studied the trading news intently until the man passed him by. The officer walked towards the market area but went left at the corner. Deforge paid the café owner and followed after him.

CHAPTER 12
LONDON, PARIS, BERLIN, VIENNA
MAY 1756
Waging War Peacefully

The First Treaty of Versailles between France and Austria was a disturbing development. But the Duke of Newcastle had not lost hope. The Westminster Convention and Versailles Treaty specified that the treaty partners only had to come to the defense of France or England if they were ever attacked by a country other than England or France respectively. England was never going to attack Austria because that would provoke a full-scale land war in Europe. England had no reason to do that. Likewise, France was never going to attack Prussia or Hanover for the same reason. It had its hands full contending with England.

Thus, with Prussia and Austria on the sidelines, France decided it could conduct war with England *peacefully*, as long as the clash of arms did not expand onto the European mainland. Since England was invading French possessions in America, France decided to invade some of England's possessions in the Mediterranean. This was a far more important region than the Americas and would be hotly contested in a real war.

The French selected the island of Minorca.

"Why Minorca?" The French Minister of War René Louis de Voyer de Paulmy d'Argenson was not certain of this new military venture, even after the arguments were presented to him. "The fighting will be too close to the mainland. It could spill over to southern France or even to Gibraltar. This would defeat the purpose of the Treaty of Versailles."

But the decision had been approved.

D'Argenson imagined the Versailles royals sitting around a gilded table, drinking wine from crystal goblets, tossing out reasons, and King Louie nodding in approval, agreeing with their every word.

They would argue the island is small. *Good.* Its single fort would fall quickly. *Better.* Minorca has no treaty neighbors. *Even better.* No treaty convention would be violated. *You said that already.* War will come again someday, so why give England the time to reinforce it? *Valid point.* More strategically, once captured, France could offer to return Minorca to Spain as a gift! *Yes! A gift to our good friends!* The Spanish already covet this island. *They do?!* The Spanish considered it stolen from them, forced and forfeited by the terms of peace at the end of the last war. *You're right! This did indeed happen. We were the ones that did it. We must make amends! To our good friends!* In this manner, we could induce Spain, our good friends, and the other great sea power to join our alliance treaty! *Against England! Bringing another fleet of ships greater than our own!*

All of this without declaring war! It seemed very clever. And audacious.

In theory, d'Argenson thought.

Within two weeks of signing the Treaty of Versailles, France landed its forces on the island of Minorca and besieged the British garrison at St. Philip's Castle.

*

Seizing one another's ships, displacing one another's colonists, the repeated clash of armies in the wilderness of the American colonies, far, far away, across an ocean, with accompanying compelling, horrible anecdotes about the painted, tattooed aboriginal warriors, who tended to torture and eat their enemy prisoners—yes, all of that might be tolerated.

But the capture of British Minorca by France?

Minorca! That idyllic island with beautiful beaches that existed in the Mediterranean Sea, the collective royal backyard of the Great Powers. Employ enough imagination, the royal houses could almost glimpse the English flag being lowered and the French flag being raised.

The Duke of Newcastle was fatalistic as he faced the round table of his supporters in Parliament to explain what England intended to do.

I say, it is a bit hard to ignore. This loss of an island territory! And the defeat of an English fleet so close to home! It makes dinner conversation with the King quite tedious.

Such an outrage could not be tolerated.

The Duke of Newcastle's plan had been to isolate France and make them unable to be the first to declare war, thus precluding an expensive land war in Europe. This had worked.

France did not declare war first.

England did.

Given at Our Court of Kensington, the Seventeenth Day of May, 1756
In the Twenty ninth Year of Our Reign
God Save the King

So it was decreed just above the place for signature. Thomas Pelham-Holles, 1st Duke of Newcastle, prime minister of England, signed the declaration of war against France with reluctance. Copies of the declaration, accompanied with orders to the commanders of the British army and navy, were now expedited by his military aides to King George II, to White Hall, Parliament, and ships waiting in the anchorage. He would allow the newspapers to collect the story from someone else. No reason to spur their inevitable criticism.

After two years of conflict, "None too soon," would be the universal reaction from England's military elite. The British navy was pleased too. At least now they would not have to return the hundred French trading vessels they had seized as prizes over the last two years.

Before a month elapsed, on June 9, 1756, France reciprocated with its own declaration of war against England. After reading the French declaration, the duke rose from his desk and walked again to his favorite window overlooking the spacious and beautiful gardens to gaze and sulk. All his designs, treaties, pacts, and agreements with the other European powers over the last six months were intended to prevent war. France was now encircled by enemies.

Well, by England and Prussia anyway. And Hanover too, he sighed. *So here we stand. England and France formally at war!*

He took consolation from news abroad. The Great Powers on the continent had taken a deep breath...and nothing happened. The Conventions of Westminster and Versailles essentially provided for this. The war declarations seemed only to legitimize the *war of peace* between England and France that had been transpiring for two years.

As the Duke of Newcastle looked out upon his garden, he thought what an extremely odd circumstance this was. England was at war with France, yet with unspoken words, both countries held their fire. They intended to not fight within mainland Europe. *Oddly, these conventions still work.* But for how long?

The combatants were ready. All the guns were loaded and cocked. The treaties were all in place. But who would be mad enough to fire the first shot?

Newcastle speculated. *Prussia would have to do it. No one else will. Not this year.*

The only thing that would knock over this house of treaty cards would be for Frederick II to attack Austria, alone, by itself, because England certainly had no plans to do this. But Newcastle and all the other royals of Europe knew Frederick could not. Because if he did, then Austria could attack Prussia with all its forces to recover Silesia, and they would quickly be backed by Russia and France. Prussia barely had enough military forces to fight just one of the treaty partners, let alone all three of them. Prussia would lose possibly everything. Even if England came to its aid, which England would be loathe to do.

No. Frederick won't attack. There is no reason to attack. It would be madness...Will he attack?

The Duke of Newcastle knew what all the great powers of Europe feared true: You cannot trust the Prussians.

Prussia was now dangerously isolated and truly surrounded by enemies. All of them led by women! And Frederick II was a suspicious and vindictive sovereign.

*

New York

Colonel von Kleinfels awoke abruptly from a deep trance and gasped for air. His arms and legs moved slowly, laboriously. But he was aware of everything learned from the seamen on *William's Queen*.

Philadelphia, he concluded. *So be it. We have more people there.*

He was extraordinarily tired. With great effort, he stood and unlocked the door to his room. Opening it a few inches, he gripped the top to support himself and shouted, "Carter! Attend me!"

Carter Trevathan presented himself at the colonel's door.

"Yes?"

"We need to leave. Make arrangements for an overland coach to take the four of us to Philadelphia."

*

Connecticut River

Ferry Crossing

When Ritter Monheit learned Lord VanderMeer had traveled out of Boston in an overland coach escorted by Sentry Cheever, he set out in pursuit. He was two days behind them. But he estimated they would stop to rest at least once somewhere. There were several overland coaches moving about in the southern towns of Boston's countryside. It took him most of a day to determine the description of the proper coach and the road leaving the city on which it traveled. So it happened that Ritter Monheit had been riding continuously for almost three days as he reached the ferry crossing on the Connecticut River. The ferrymen remembered the overland coach matching the one Ritter described, crossing the river heading west earlier in the day. He was finally catching up to them! He paid the fee for the crossing but had to wait while the ferrymen collected more fares, loading more people to have a profitable crossing. Ritter reached the town center of Saybrook in the late afternoon as the sun was beginning the final hour of its descent. Making friendly conversation at the roadside farm stands on the western outskirts of the town, he was able to learn no overland coach had been seen that day going west.

Are they resting here? he brooded. *Or maybe they went north on this side of the river?*

He found both of the inns catering to carriage travelers but did not see an overland coach at either place. He was exhausted from three days of riding and needed sleep. *They are sleeping somewhere near here, too.* It would be dark soon. He would eat and get some rest. Start a fresh search again in the morning. He picked the inn closest to the main road. It also had a horse stable.

He had only slept an hour when the night messenger visited his dreams.

What have you learned? the *vulnax* demanded.

Monheit reported he was still following the coach, which was heading west. He was now in a town called Saybrook in the Connecticut colony.

Most of the towns were small farms or coastal fishing villages. The road he was traveling would eventually lead to New York. But the next city of any size was New Haven.

When the spirit withdrew from him, Ritter slept as if in a coma. After two days and one night of hard riding, the night messenger's visit left him drained of his remaining energy. He'd intended to get up at sunrise but did not awaken until mid-morning the next day.

*

Old Saybrook, Connecticut

After Sentry Cheever's arrival the day before, excitement began to build. They had planned for this short outing for over six weeks. Now the day had come. Corrinne was so thrilled about going somewhere, *anywhere*, she wanted to start early.

She planned to be absent for only three to four days but gave instructions to Jenny Barton and her two daughters as if they would be gone for two weeks, giving the servants reason to believe they were heading to New Bedford, part of the fiction she wanted to perpetuate. She had the final discussion with Mistress Barton when the time to depart was upon them. They were in the library. Corrinne was at her desk.

"Most importantly, do not tell anyone where we have gone. And do not speculate."

"But who might ask?" Other than Mr. Cheever, the servants had not seen any other visitors.

"Probably no one. So you need not worry. But do not say anything if someone happens by who is lost, perhaps. And please…certainly none of the Saybrook gossips. I know these precautions seem excessive, Jenny, but my privacy is vital. We have a house full of small children. And we are all women. I do not want to give the impression we are vulnerable."

"Yes, my lady. I understand."

Sentry loaded the baggage aboard the overland coach that could hold six people. It was pulled by a team of four horses. Sentry's individual mount was tied to the rear to trail from behind. He would ride up top beside the driver. The plush carriage had brought Charles VanderMeer down from Boston. Sentry had left him at the estate house in Lyme and ferried the carriage over the Connecticut River to pick up Lady Corrinne, the children, and Mathilde. It could comfortably carry all of them. There was plenty of room. They were ready. He went to get Corrinne from the library.

"The baggage is loaded, my lady."

Corrinne turned in her desk chair. Sentry was standing in the doorway, smiling, wearing his tartan eye-patch, and politely holding his tri-cornered hat with its purple Scottish thistle, which she had presented to him last year.

"We just need to load the passengers and be on our way."

"Thank you, Sentry. I will be out momentarily."

Corrinne looked at Mistress Barton once more, thinking. All the arrangements for their absence had been made a week ago. Jenny Barton and her daughters, hired to help Mathilde, were very fond of Lady Corrinne.

"Don't worry about a thing, my lady," Mistress Barton encouraged. "Now go…enjoy your holiday."

"Yes. You are right. I worry too much. I will enjoy my holiday. Thank you, Jenny."

Corrinne stood and glanced around the office convinced she was forgetting something. She had read Philippe's letter countless times since the day before, savoring every word, imagining the strokes of the quill, the room he was in, the expression on his face as he thought of her. The dream it provoked the previous night induced a surging pleasure that was so strong it brought her wide awake and gasping for breath. She thought about leaving the letter behind before they made their excursion that morning to protect it from any accidental damage.

And if the house catches fire? The idea of losing Philippe's letter made her inhale sharply. *No, I should read it every night before I go to sleep*, she thought. *At the very least my favorite page*. She brightened. *Oh yes, I must take this with me!*

She placed the letter inside a thick leather valise at the bottom of a bag. She also took the diagrams of the three tomb symbols and all of her deductive notes about the *vulnax* and the *châsse*, and Machault's letter, all of it intended to support the discussions she planned to have with Charles.

Corrinne looked around the library.

"What am I forgetting?" she murmured. "Oh! The telescope!"

From a closet she retrieved the beloved watch glass Captain LaTour had given her so many years ago. There would probably be vessels sailing on the river. It would be fun for the children to watch them looking through the glass.

She gathered up the large carry bags containing cloth diapers and other things for the babies, who were almost not babies anymore; they were growing so quickly. Corrinne went outside and handed these to the coachman who loaded them beneath the seats inside the carriage, making them easily accessible during the journey.

Sentry was lying on the grass, laughing, allowing Marcus to climb all over him. Anamosa was walking with Calypso picking colorful flowers from the wild grasses and vines around the house. The toddler already had several white honeysuckle blossoms in her light blonde hair. Calypso and Marcus were obviously twins, except Marcus' curly hair had slightly darker reddish undertones. "He is a strawberry blond," the housekeeper once told her. "That's what we call hair that color. It means his blood runs hot. He will likely become a warrior when he is grown…so claim the old legends."

"How wonderful," Corrinne responded drolly. "What else could a mother hope for?" The sarcasm was lost on the servant.

The twins were eleven months old now and walking—fast! They had been walking for two months, to everyone's surprise, and skipped the crawling months. Calypso was also saying several simple words: *mama, marc, oooh,* and *no.* Marcus' language consisted of loud, brave yells, interspaced with proud smiles and raised arms. Or equally loud growls in play, as he tried to scare his sister, who tended only to stare affably at him in response. They were both affectionate to each other. Hugs were common, as was sleeping in each other's arms. And they could exhibit guileless, bright smiles that brought instant joy to those lucky persons fortunate to be the focus of their attention.

After months and months of disciplined exercise and Mathilde's careful food choices, Corrinne's body had slowly returned to its former shape and weight. Her pregnancy didn't seem so bad in hindsight now that she'd recovered. "Marcus and Calypso have been worth every discomfort I suffered," she had confided to Mathilde, and in the next breath told her, "Just be sure to obtain enough Apiaceae powder to last me a lifetime!"

Corrinne was long overdue for a journey, any kind of a journey, even a short one. She looked forward to the few days of visiting with Charles.

The day was bright and sunny. The warm breezes coming over the lands carried little spinning parasols of dandelion seeds.

Corrinne knelt and held her arms open. "Marcus! Calypso!"

They ran to her with excitement, jealously sharing her hugs and kisses. She picked them both up and went to the carriage, handing first one then the other to Mathilde already seated inside. She turned and hugged Anamosa who had grown a foot taller, almost to her shoulder over the last year, and helped her into the carriage house as well.

"Where are we going?"

"Just on the other side of the river, Ana. Someplace where more *surprises* wait for you," she promised.

Sentry closed the door behind her. "Everyone ready? Good. Here we go." He climbed up next to the driver.

With a gentle snap of the whip and a few *heeyahs* the horses started away. Mistress Barton and her daughters were standing in the yard waving. The carriage rocked comfortably. Corrinne gripped Marcus tightly around the waist while he gazed excitedly out the carriage window, yelling and pointing at anything that caught his eye. Anamosa held onto Calypso who was similarly affected but not as vigorous in her exclamations.

They reached the ferry landing in less than an hour. Sentry jumped down and grabbed the harness of the lead horses to walk them slowly across the ramp to board the long flat raft. Four ferrymen took up positions on the raft's downriver side and used long poles to push and guide it against the current towards the other embankment a thousand feet away. On the other side of the river, a horse walked in circles around a windlass with a heavy tow line attached to the raft, which pulled the ferry across. Another horse and two men paid out the line from the opposing windlass behind the ferry. Theirs was a long work day that would start at sunrise and end at sunset for as long as people lined up to pay the ferrying fee for the crossing.

Once on the other side and the raft was secured to the mooring cleats, Sentry led the carriage horses by the harness bits and the coach moved across the portable ramp. He paid the ferrymen a gratuity and went on his way. They traveled east for a short time and turned south on a river road. They crossed several bridges. The coachman took his time at Sentry's direction to permit the passengers to appreciate the surrounding homes and farms. There were wetlands to the right of the river road, reedy marshes full of a variety of cranes, ducks, and gulls flying overhead with other water fowl. On the left, they occasionally saw cattle and horses grazing. The trees and plants were past their spring blooming. The land was alive with fresh greens and a multitude of colors from different wild flowers. Bees dipped and buzzed around the blossoms in droves.

After an hour of slow travel, they arrived at the estate house. It was white with black shutters and three stories tall, including the attic. It was a hundred feet across on the front and sixty feet in depth, suggesting the rooms would be large. Chimneys stood on all four corners and another at the very back in the middle. The crown of the house had a decorative iron-fenced widow's walk along the full length of the roof from chimney to chimney. The grounds were covered by short wild grasses and a variety of bushes and shrubs. Corrinne also saw a livery stable and a barn in the back. The approach ended in a horseshoe circle around an island of trimmed shrubbery.

It's beautiful, peaceful, Corrinne thought. The river was visible from the rear of the house. The grounds were not overgrown and obviously kept up. She could not ask for a more appealing place to visit after living in a dank box over the winter months.

But the biggest surprise came last. Waiting at the portico were several people. The maintenance servants, a beaming Charles VanderMeer, plus Molly Shreve and Dianamora, who were barely containing their excitement.

Corrinne glanced up at Sentry and saw his mischievous smile.

"Surprise," he mouthed silently.

For the next quarter hour there was a non-stop babble of happy, laughing voices as the women and Charles became reacquainted and fussed over Marcus, Calypso, and Anamosa. When Corrinne hugged Molly, she felt a prominent bulge at the maid's waist. She glanced down quickly to confirm what she suspected as they separated. *A baby.* But Corrinne decided to make no mention of it, though Dianamora must know. This was not something easily kept secret. Not among women. *Whenever Molly is ready, I will listen.*

The servants and coachman moved the baggage inside before it was sorted into the rooms, which Molly had already assigned. Delicious smells wafted through the house. Dianamora was cooking and had already stocked the *cuisine* with food.

After a short interlude to become familiar with the rooms and layout of the house, Molly announced that an early lunch was being served in the backyard. It was presented on a long table, shaded by two large umbrellas. There were other cushioned wicker chairs in sets of twos and threes around the yard. The view of the river and the marshy wetlands another hundred feet away was grand. The wild life abounded. It was spectacular. Their lunch was filled with remember-the-time stories and laughter.

A perfect day, Corrinne thought.

*

When the bright sunlight beamed through the window and hit his eyes, Ritter Monheit dragged himself from bed. While he dressed and collected items for his saddle bags, he staggered around. He sat in a torpor for nearly an hour in the restaurant of the inn, picking at his food listlessly. Finally, when he could assemble enough words together to make a sentence, he paid the fee for his room and stabling the horse.

"Long journey ahead of you yet?" the friendly proprietor asked, seeing exhaustion in the man's eyes.

"Could be," Ritter replied in a non-committal voice. "Do you get many overland coach visits here?"

"No. People like yourself, mostly. Heading to New Haven or New York or the other way to Boston, New Bedford, or Rhode Island. A few carriages. And the cargo wagon trade. Them the most."

"I saw an extravagant overland coach yesterday." Ritter probed. "It passed by me. Seemed in a hurry. It beat me to the ferry. Forced me to wait an hour for the next one. Just made me curious where it might be going. Someplace important, I expect. Probably New York, like you said."

"Saw a large coach this morning," the man offered. "But it was going east, heading towards the ferry. A big carriage house on it too. Four horses."

"Really? Do you think it came from New Haven?"

"No. Too early in the day for the New Haven coaches to pass through. My guess is that it started out from one of the large coastal homes south of the town."

"You have a lot of those homes?"

"Oh, maybe six to eight of them."

*

The *ghost* flew down the center of the great river to stay clear of the more populated shore lands. It could sense the demon's servant moving around on one side, and the white woman *not* moving on the other side. They were directly across from one another.

The white eagle glided to the left towards the white woman. It landed at the top of a tall tree behind a house. It would sit on this perch to see what happened next and keep a careful watch on the servant across the river.

The eagle was much stronger now after months of winter rest. But after this long flight the *ghost* sensed the ebbing begin once more. The raptor's strength would not last the warm season. As the animal grew weaker so would the *ghost*. The question on what to do must be answered before then. The white eagle sensed the weakening too and struggled constantly to resist the unnatural dominance of the *ghost*. By force of will, the shaman remained dominant. But he had to calm the terrified creature continuously, soothing its fears, blinding it to reality, much as if he'd placed a hood over the head.

*

Lyme

When the babies were laid down in their cradles for a nap, Corrinne and Charles finally had time to sit and talk by themselves in the backyard wicker chairs. Corrinne carried out her hand bag filled with notes and the watch glass. Charles had brought several books, a ledger, and a sheath filled with correspondence.

"Tell me about Boston," Corrinne asked quickly before they lapsed into something more serious.

Charles took a deep breath and began. He talked about the war, the rumors of what would come next, of Thomas and Lydia Hancock, the insurance business, his renewed interest in making jewelry and painting.

"Those interests have taken over the back room in the office. It's a gallery of sorts now, filled with some minor paintings, easels, shelves of paint pots, and a tooling bench for my jewelsmith skills. I even set up a small forge to heat metals. I stay there most of the time during the day. It is a very relaxing diversion for me. Fortunately, I do not get many visitors, maybe one or two a day to talk politics or what I might hear from the trade ships. Magistrate Tasker visits at least once a month. He's friendly enough, but I think he is worried about my safety. Asks questions about anyone I might randomly see passing by the house for the first time. It's good to know I have friends like Thomas, Sentry, and Jack Tasker watching over me. But when I was left alone, I managed to craft some things in my *atelier* that you will find...quite interesting, I think."

Corrinne perked up, curious. "So tell me. Like what?"

"When you come back to Boston, I will show you. We'll leave it as a surprise."

"*Mon Dieu*, Charles! Then why did you tell me? You know I cannot tolerate secrets like that."

Charles smiled, satisfied. "There is the fiery Corrinne I know. Finally, we get to talk. I've missed all of you," he said. "But you the most. How are *you* doing?"

Corrinne stared out at the peaceful river.

"I don't sleep very well. The house is haunted by the ghosts of my imagination, real or otherwise. I get up in the middle of the night, or I should say nearly every night. Cannot go back to sleep. Walk around with a cocked pistol in one hand and a lamp in the other, checking all the dark corners. There's no one for me to talk to...not really. Unless you consider baby gibberish conversation, though I love speaking to them. I have no idea what I am saying. But they seem to make sense of my invented babble. I just repeat back what they say to me. Their smiles are the salvation of my sanity. Anamosa too. She is a beautiful little angel. I help with her studies, which helps me too. She learns so quickly! She's reading now by herself and is growing so fast! She dotes on the babies, Calypso especially. Mathilde, I worry about constantly. She is still very weak. Stays in bed a lot. Her chest wound does not seem to be healing very well. Sometimes she coughs up blood. I offered to get her a doctor, but she refuses. Says it would compromise our privacy. She's right, but I would do it for her anyway if she'd let me. This existence is not an existence. I think the initial danger has passed. I feel it's time to think about what's next."

"You could always return...the house in Boston is enormous when it is not full of people."

"And I miss being there," Corrinne replied. "Winter House across the river is little more than a large box full of small stuffy rooms. But it accomplished what we planned. I am anonymous there, and my privacy is respected. But thank God for Sentry's visits." Corrinne turned and looked around. "This house has a beautiful view. How often does Thomas Hancock use it?"

"This house, like the other one, were both collateral on the same loan of money. Hancock provided the loan that defaulted. He owns them both. He told me he has been here twice in three years. Usually just as a stopover for his travel going to and from New York."

Corrinne picked up the telescope and scanned the opposite bank of the river. "Amazing. I can see the top of Winter House from here." She handed him the glass. "Right there. That rise of land hides all of it but the roof. That rise of land, by the way, is the property I wrote you about."

Charles handed her back the glass. "You'd consider staying here?"

"As opposed to going back to Boston? Unless something changes, whoever is the leader of the assassins, I am certain he is searching for me… trying to find the *châsse*. At least, here it won't be easy to find me. But even as I say this…how do I know? I've thought about how he would do it. It would take time, but somehow I feel the *châsse* itself will draw him to me…eventually. It's childish of me to say, but I think he is the one who provokes my nightmares."

Charles patted a small canvas sack of books that sat next to his chair.

"Then let's talk about this. My scholarly contacts shipped these old books to me on ancient legends and history, including one written by the church concerning Lord Vaelblez. I've read them all and taken notes. I'll leave the books with you to read."

"What do they say?"

"A *lot*," VanderMeer replied. "But what I learned only created more questions. And I struggled to sort through the conflicting tales and stories to draw sensible conclusions. Mostly because I am a person of both faith and of science, like yourself. And I wonder…will the answers to this *thing* come from faith or science?"

Corrinne frowned at the conjecture.

"Neither. Both. Does it matter? The archbishop did not like what it portended either, but now we know better," Corrinne argued. "We sealed this thing…this *vulnax wraith*. Sealing it *works*. Just like it did before. Who cares why? This is a fact. No faith or scientific proof is necessary. "

"Then what worries us both so much?" Charles posed, though he already knew the answer.

"What do I worry about? That the seal will be broken somehow. That the thing will get out. That it will torment us all to our deaths. And now my children are in danger."

"Exactly. Something very old and very evil was buried under a mountain in Germany, hidden inside a vault of stone. What we did does not feel very permanent, does it? The *châsse* is more akin to a carriage we use to take the relics from one place to the next. And it is vulnerable every step of the way. So I think we…"

Corrinne had already settled on the conclusion.

"I know. We need to create a permanent vault. Place the *châsse* in a secure tomb. Somewhere secret. All right. Presume we do that. We do it in a way that makes it extremely hard to find. Is it over? No. The people who found the old tomb the first time, found it by accident. They stumbled upon it. They were not looking for it. The people searching for the *châsse* now, are doing it purposely. Why? Who or what drives that behavior? We are still missing something."

Corrinne's brows drew together.

Charles lifted the bag of books again. "Well, we have our experience. Now we have books full of history, legends, and the meaning of runes. I don't know which of the assertions in them to believe and which to discount. There is much disparity in the legends and history, a lot of interpretation and disagreement. But between the two of us, we will solve this puzzle."

From the house, Dian and Molly approached. Molly carried a small, round, wooden table and Dian a tray with wine, glasses, and sweet biscuits.

"I am so happy to pour wine for you again, my lady," Molly effused as she poured each of them a glass.

"*Merci*. And how is Captain Martyn?"

Molly blushed and she stammered. "Conor…that is, Captain Martyn is very well. He is at sea a lot, but when he comes to Boston, we are…we spend time together…and he is very gentle…I mean, he is *kind* to me."

"Of course he is." Corrinne smiled and ended Molly's awkward discomfort. "Are the babies still asleep?"

"Calypso is asleep. But Marcus is up. Sentry is playing with him. He brought Marcus a present. A box of hand-painted little tin soldiers."

"Little tin soldiers? Of course he did," Corrinne said dryly.

When Dian and Molly left them, Charles leaned forward.

"Molly and Conor were married, privately, in our house in April, when he was in port. She asked me not to tell you."

"Why? Because Molly is pregnant?"

"Presumably. They did not offer me that as the reason, however. Just that they were in love and it was time. You and I are not supposed to know she is pregnant. I think they do not want to trouble you."

"Trouble me? Why would it trouble me? And the bulge in her stomach is a little too prominent to miss."

"I pretend not see it."

"Well, you are a man. They expect you wouldn't notice. The only thing men look at where women are concerned is...well, you know."

Corrinne rested back in the chair and took a full swallow of wine. It was a Bordeaux and her favorite. A strong breeze rattled the leaves in the surrounding trees. She closed her eyes, enjoying the taste of the wine and the music of the trees.

"Such a beautiful day," she said.

Charles decided to leave the subject of the *châsse* behind for now.

"Sentry gave you the letter? It was from Philippe, yes?"

Corrinne's face softened further. "Oh yes. He did. It was from Philippe. The letter was...was simply wonderful."

She told him what Philippe wrote, and about Pierre, omitting the intimate passages.

"The letter was not dated. It was written in English, oddly enough. He did not mention Henri. I'm assuming it was written before Christmas, because he did not mention snow or the cold. So he probably wrote it in the fall months around the same time I came down here. The man who first carried it was '*more enemy than friend*,' Philippe described. But he trusted the man. I assume he was an Indian...and someone who knew William Johnson. The letter came from him, yes? There seemed to be no other path."

Charles marveled at how quickly she'd deduced the date and origin from what was not written in the letter.

"An Indian messenger delivered it to *Sir* William Johnson...he's been knighted...then to Thomas Hancock and then to me. Then Sentry, of course."

"So this Indian protected and never opened the letter. He carried it on his person for months. That is simply extraordinary! And Sir William did not break the wax seal either, even though he is an English general. Philippe is French, the enemy, but he did not open the letter when he had every right and many would even say the *duty* to do so. Also extraordinary. They must have become close friends. I like this William Johnson even though I have not met him." After a moment, Corrinne added, "I want to write to Philippe."

"Well, it's easy to send a missive to Sir William, but where is Philippe now? Maybe we should send something to Archbishop Nicolet and include a separate missive for Philippe, one for Henri and one for Michelle too?"

"How?"

"By water. It's the safest way. Though not without obstacles. Sentry knows the fishing captain that took Henri on his journey last year. Maybe he can work out a path with that captain through the French fishermen."

*

Ritter Monheit asked about the location of estate homes from the roadside farming stands at the western edge of town.

"What's your interest?" asked the farmer suspiciously.

Ritter pulled three sheets of folded paper from his pocket which he'd prepared for questions like these. It was a heavily wax-sealed missive, concealing white pages. On the outside was penned a name: *Lady Corrinne*.

"I've ridden up here from New York. I have a missive addressed to a Lady Corrinne. No last name. All I know is that she lives somewhere in Saybrook…and that she's supposed to be wealthy. The proprietor of the inn suggested she may be residing in one of the larger homesteads."

"Wealthy you say? Well…I've not heard of a Lady Corrinne. But the largest homes are located south of here along the coast. Many of them farms. A few estates. The roads leading to them tend to wander through the woods. And some of them are guarded, so ride slow, don't act suspicious when you approach. Holler out in plain sight and stand back from the door so they can see you."

"I will remember that. Don't want to get shot delivering love mail, eh?"

They laughed together.

Ritter paid the farmer for three large green apples with a generous gratuity.

The farmer looked at the few pence and the conspicuous silver coin. "You paid me too much."

"The silver is for the information. I am really tired of searching for this woman."

The farmer now felt obligated to tell the cordial stranger even more, as Ritter planned.

"Those houses are spread out. It could take you all day or even longer. Go down that road over there"—he pointed—"and you'll come to the coastal road soon enough. It's hard to miss because it is at the end of that one. Go left at that junction and watch for the entryways on your right. They resemble less used wagon roads. There are salt marshes to either side of the approach for some of those houses. Quicksand, too! So go slow and don't leave the wagon path."

"It's a beautiful day. I don't mind going slow. I have these juicy apples you sold me to enjoy, eh?"

Ritter easily found the coastal road, went left, and came to the first way in after about a quarter mile. He decided to search eastward back towards the river from there, going down each way in, one after the other. He checked that his pistols were loaded and primed. This home would be the furthest away from the Connecticut River, he estimated.

He chewed another apple as he plodded along. There were wetlands like the farmer said. He saw water fowl, cranes, storks, and ducks. Screeching gulls glided overhead. In about half an hour, a tree-shaded house loomed straight ahead. He approached it slowly and dismounted a dozen paces from the front door. Holding the reins of the horse in one hand, he took off his hat and shouted out.

"Hello, the house!"

An older woman appeared at the door, holding a musket. The face was not friendly. There were two children behind her, both of them boys.

"What do you want?" she asked tersely.

"Good morning, Madam. My name is Ritter Smith. I am from New York." He held up the missive. "I was hired to deliver this letter to a Lady Corrinne of Saybrook. All I know is that she lives around here."

"No one here by that name," said the woman in a tone slightly less curt. She shut the door.

There should only be a young girl and babies. No boys.

"Thank you, Madam," he called. "Sorry to bother you. I will be on my way."

The next two houses were much the same story. The first, grandparents with a married son. The second, a fishing boat captain. That house was closest to the shoreline and had a pier extending outward with a boat tied up on the pier. The third house was empty. He found an unlocked door and went inside. No signs of any occupancy for a long, long time. The fourth house had two baying hounds that came charging at him, growling, until the musket-toting male owner called them back. Ritter explained his purpose.

"You've got the wrong house." Another unfriendly voice.

Ritter wiped sweat from his brow and feigned weariness. "I'm beginning to think I have the wrong *Saybrook*. This person would have come up here late last year. Do you know of anyone like that?"

"You said Lady Corrinne?"

"Yes, sir."

"And who are you again?"

"Ritter Smith, sir. I am a mail courier from New York."

"What's in the letter?"

He shrugged and then held it up. "I don't get paid for the delivery if the wax seal is broken. I can see you're cautious about strangers. I understand. I would be too. I don't mind visiting all the houses. It's what I do. Sorry to bother you, sir. I will be on my way."

When Ritter mounted his horse, the owner's suspicion relaxed and he offered more.

"I've not heard of any Lady Corrinne. But a woman did move into Winter House in the fall of last year. That's what it's called locally. The house is close to the river. Don't know who she is. Go back to the coastal road, go right. Skip the next three approaches. I know those folks, all farmers. Go all the way east to the river. It's at the end of the last way in just before the road turns north."

"Much appreciated, sir." Ritter touched his hat as he turned and started back toward the main road at a slow gait.

*

Calypso awoke crying. Corrinne returned to the house to feed them both before bringing them out into the garden to play in the sunlight. A few minutes after she went in, Sentry Cheever came outside to gaze at the river. He was carrying a pistol in his belt and his cutlass in a scabbard over a shoulder.

Charles VanderMeer's eyes widened. "Are you expecting trouble?"

"No, m'lord." Sentry smiled. He disarmed and placed the weapons up in the low branches of a nearby elm tree. "This place is unknown to me. Where you, Lady Corrinne, and the bairns are concerned, I do not take chances. She intends to bring them out in this large garden to play."

"Come sit with me."

Sentry pulled over another of the wicker chairs. "Thank you, m'lord."

"Would you care for some wine?"

"Thank you, no. It's just a habit of mine, to take no drink while I am… on watch…meaning no offense."

"None taken. It's been a tough winter for us all, but for Lady Corrinne most of all. The letter from Philippe you brought her could not have come at a better time. Your visits have meant a lot to her…and to Anamosa and the babies."

Sentry smiled. "Aye, those bairns! They've captured my heart. They stare for the longest time, making me wonder if I did something wrong. Then they smile and I want to ask them what I just did to make them smile."

"I know what you mean. But if I may change the subject, I want to discuss another matter while we have a chance to talk privately. Corrinne and I want to send letters back to Philippe, Henri, and Michelle. We were thinking of sending a sealed packet to Archbishop Nicolet in Quebec City. He is a friend of ours and will see the letters delivered further. But getting a packet to him is the challenge. Do you think it's still possible to use the fisherman Henri used for his travel last year? Maybe through a connection with the French fisherman he knows?"

"That captain's name is Jackson Fletcher. He was a mate of mine when I was in the marines. I will ask him for you, but from the stories I've been told, the English navy is now intercepting every French vessel larger than a skiff, including the fishing boats. If you pay enough money, someone will agree to try, but I doubt the letters will get delivered. They will probably just pocket the money."

Charles frowned, disappointed.

"You could try a foreign ship, if one visits Boston or New York," Sentry continued. "Sometimes they will deliver mail if the price is right. But it would likely cross over to Spain or the Dutch Republic before it comes back…*if* it comes back at all. Unless it is formally couriered by someone, often mail just disappears. To that point, you could hire a courier to carry it. Not sure where to find one, but they are around. But that will cost you huge fees for the crossings and large fees for the courier. All the fees due up front. Even then, there's no guarantee the mail will get through."

"Expense is not a problem. What about the French fortress-port at Louisbourg? If we can get a packet delivered there, I feel certain it will go the rest of the way."

Sentry nodded. "That might be the best possibility. It's also the most dangerous. In addition to being intercepted along the way, the courier will have to get by the English patrol squadrons outside the port to deliver the packet. The fishermen won't try. If they are caught going in *or out* of that port, the English will assume they are spies and just hang them from one of the yards without any questions. What about overland?"

"We don't know where Philippe is. The risks are even greater for a courier to traverse the Indian lands and the areas of fighting."

Sentry raised his brow. "Maybe Captain Martyn might try?"

"I cannot ask him to do this."

"Or Captain LaTour will visit you again?"

"I thought of that first. But his ship would be seized just sailing *near* that port. Still, he used to be a smuggler. He still is, for that matter. If anyone can do it, he can. But with the war, I'm not sure he will want to try. Then again, Lady Corrinne can be very persuasive with him. He would probably do it for her. Except he'll have to visit us first, and who knows when that will be?"

*

Ritter Monheit arrived at the box-like two-story house. This one looked abandoned. It was dark gray, ugly in appearance, and heavily weathered. He got down from his horse and doffed his hat.

"Hello, the house!"

For a few minutes, nothing happened. Then the front door opened a foot and a woman's face appeared. She was an older matron. Her hair was streaked with white. He saw a big dragoon pistol hanging from her right hand. It looked almost too heavy for her to lift, let alone aim. She was frowning.

"Apologies, Madam. My name is Ritter Smith. I am a courier from New York. I have a wax-sealed missive addressed to Lady Corrinne? No last name." He held it up for her to see. "I was told she lives in Saybrook in a coastal home, but I don't know where. I've been searching most this morning until a neighbor directed me to this house. They said not to disturb her privacy, but I don't get paid unless she accepts the letter as she is the one who must pay me."

"She is not here."

Ritter's heart pounded. "I can come back later today, if you like."

"She won't be back for several days."

But she is coming back, Ritter thought. "Very well, Madam. I will get a room at one of the inns and wait until she returns. I will come back when it is more convenient. Just send someone to fetch me. Is that acceptable?"

She responded with a brusque nod. He could see she wanted him to leave.

"Will you be sure to tell her I was here? Ritter Smith. That I am a paid courier?"

"Yes."

"Thank you, Madam. One more indulgence, if you please. I was told the Connecticut River is nearby. Do you mind if I go up that rise and take a look at it before I leave?"

"Don't linger here. I am not alone. We all have weapons."

Ritter held up both hands. "Oh, no, Madam, truly. I mean you no harm. Just a quick look at the river and I will be on my way."

She shut the door.

Ritter saw her shadow peeking out at him from behind the curtained windows. He decided the next time he came, it would be by water. So he wanted to make sure there was a place for a small boat to beach and find a good landmark visible to a boat on the river to guide the landing.

The *ghost* watched the three children walking around the yard below the tree. The two small ones had the sealing symbols on the back of their necks, just like their mother. And the older girl wore the talisman around her neck. This offered some protection against the demon, but it would not protect them from being physically attacked by the demon's servant who was now standing at the top of a rise of land across the river.

The big man sitting with the children had a pistol. The *ghost* had to be careful the eagle was not hurt by a weapon.

The backyard of the house in Lyme had become festive. Corrinne took her chair again next to Charles. Sentry remained seated in the one he pulled over. The sun was high in the sky. The large trees provided plenty of shade over the tables and chairs. All the women came out along with Anamosa, Calypso, and Marcus. Anamosa catered to Calypso. Marcus toddled after them as they ventured further toward the back of the yard, twenty paces away beyond where Corrinne was sitting. They played in a broad patch of wild grass in the bright sunlight; some wild flowers were sprouting. Molly stayed close, just a few steps behind Marcus. Mathilde and Dian took seats at the long table set with food and drink.

Every one of the adults was watching the children. So when Marcus halted and dropped to his hands and knees to stare intently at something in the grass, the adults rose from their seats, alarmed.

"Marcus!? What are you doing?" Corrinne called with concern.

Marcus' right hand slapped down on something before anyone had a chance to react. A small lizard-like creature jumped straight up in the air and skittered quickly into deeper vegetation.

Molly shrieked and snatched Marcus from the ground, examining his hand for signs of bites. She carried him to Corrinne who inspected his hand carefully.

"I am so sorry, my lady! It was just a tiny green newt," Molly continued apologetically. "I did not see it. It blended too well. Harmless, I think. They only eat bugs. It ran off into the taller weeds."

"No harm done," Corrinne said nervously. "Marcus! You almost made my heart stop!"

Marcus was squirming strongly to get down from Corrinne's lap.

"All right, all right! There. Go to your sister."

Charles laughed lightly.

"Does he remind you of anyone?" Corrinne said with annoyance.

Molly followed Marcus more closely now, carefully scanning the ground in front of him now, as Marcus was doing. They reached Anamosa who was holding Calypso by the hand. Marcus took Anamosa's other hand.

After a few moments of quiet, Corrinne noticed all three children had stopped moving. They were looking upward, staring at something high in the trees.

"Molly! What are they looking at?" Corrinne was already up and moving swiftly in their direction. Charles followed too.

"Oh, my God!" Molly said it almost as a shout when she saw it.

Sentry grabbed his pistol and cutlass from the elm tree and ran to them.

Corrinne gathered both children into her arms as she looked up. At the At the very top of a large oak, perched on a branch, she saw a white eagle…a big one. "*Mon Dieu*," Corrinne said in a softer voice.

The eagle was staring down at them. The children did not seem frightened at all.

Sentry reached Corrinne's side and cocked the weapon.

"No! Sentry, don't!"

"That's a raptor, m'lady. A predator! It's big enough to stoop and grab one of the bairns!"

"It won't, Sentry," she replied in a firm voice. "I've seen it before, many times. It brings good luck to us."

Sentry looked baffled but lowered his weapon.

"I don't believe it," Charles whispered, awestruck. "How would it even find us?"

The eagle's head shifted perceptibly, its eyes locking on Corrinne's. Then the eagle's head turned fully to its left. Corrinne followed the eagle's gaze. It was looking across the river at the rise of land near Winter House. There was a man standing atop the rise. He seemed to be looking at them!

"Oh, no!" Corrinne reacted instantly and moved quickly with the children back into the shade and shadow of the trees, hoping the sunlight was blinding the watcher's eyes.

"Take them back into the house," she told Molly handing them both over to her.

Mathilde and Dian followed Molly.

"What's wrong?" Sentry asked.

"Who is that?" Charles demanded.

Corrinne rushed to the wicker chairs and took up the watch glass. She peered through it. She had not seen this man before. He was big, with dark hair, and was holding up his hat to block the sunlight and looking around the area with interest, but not directly at them.

"He hasn't spotted us yet."

"Who is he?" Sentry asked.

"Look!" She handed him the watch glass. "There. Standing on the rise."

Sentry recognized him as soon as he looked through the glass. "Bloody hell. I've seen him before, back in Boston. Caught him staring at me a few times from a distance, almost like he knew me. Didn't think much of it. He must have followed the carriage down here somehow."

"They've found me, Charles." Corrinne's face was washed of color. "I need to leave right away."

"What? And go where?"

"Back to Boston! We are too vulnerable here. In Boston, we have friends. We know they are coming for us. We can take steps this time to protect ourselves."

"Is he one of the attackers from before?" Sentry asked and handed the watch glass to Charles.

"You killed all our attackers," Corrinne said. "But maybe he's one of those who left the city early. The magistrate, Jack Tasker, claimed there were others who left Boston. But whatever his identity, he is certainly looking for me now."

"Well, I know his face. I'm going back to Winter House. I'll find out what he's done and what he planned to do. If he is a danger to you, I will take care of it."

"I am going with you," Corrinne said firmly.

"Don't be ridiculous!" Charles managed in a stunned voice.

Sentry gaped at her. "No, my lady! I dinnah' thin' tha's a good idea! This man will likely be a seasoned killer."

"*I'm going*! Listen to me, both of you. We need to leave here! Today! This very afternoon! Molly, Dian, and Mathilde need to load the overland carriage. I am going back to Winter House to retrieve the *châsse* and a few other items. I will pay off the servants, tell them to close up the house today and not come back to it and that I am going on to New Bedford. There is a wagon in the small barn. We'll take a pair of the carriage horses with us to harness to that wagon."

"And if you suddenly encounter this other man?" Charles posed with barely restrained anger, fuming, thinking her actions foolish to the extreme.

"Then Sentry will kill him...or *I* will!" Corrinne answered hotly.

Sentry touched her shoulder and spoke gently. "I will be doin' any killin' tha's necessary today. Understood?"

"That is fine by me. I would rather our location die with him before he tells anyone else. It might give us a few days, maybe a week. I will ride one of the servant's horses."

Charles was thin-lipped. "You should let Sentry do this alone."

Corrinne spun around. For the first time since he'd met Corrinne, Charles felt frightened at the coldness in her glare.

"They intended to kill my babies! If I can arrange to make this man die slowly and painfully, I will do it."

*

It took almost three hours to wait and transit the river by ferry and ride to Winter House. Sentry and Corrinne each had a carriage horse tethered to the saddle of the mount they rode. When the house came into view, Sentry raised his hand to stop. Corrinne checked that her double-barreled pistol was ready. She also carried a blade on her belt.

Sentry handed over the reins of his carriage horse to her. He was heavily armed with a musket, two marine pistols, a knife in his belt, and the cutlass over his shoulder.

He spoke to her firmly. "Wait here until I see if it's safe for you to approach the house. If you hear pistol fire, promise me you will leave the carriage horses, turn around, and ride like hell to the village magistrate."

Corrinne stared at him stonily.

"Promise me, my lady! I will not allow you to go any further until you do."

"I promise," Corrinne muttered. *To ride to your support immediately if I hear shots*, she added silently.

Sentry sensed she was not going to listen to him. He exhaled audibly, turned, and went forward at a slow gait to the house. He pulled a pistol and disappeared around the back to search the rise of land. The wait was maddening for Corrinne, but five minutes later Sentry reappeared and waved her forward.

"He's not here," he told her when she rode to him. "And Jenny is all right."

Mistress Barton was waiting by the door.

"I sent my daughters home for a few days, my lady," she said fretfully. "I hope I did nothing wrong."

Corrinne got down from her horse and gave over the reins to Sentry. "Don't worry, Jenny, you did nothing wrong. I'm just glad you are safe. Now tell us all about the man who came to the door this morning."

The servant related what happened. Corrine had only a few questions.

"Did he say where he planned to stay?"

"No, my lady."

"I dinnah' think it wise to go searching for him," Sentry cautioned. "Let's use the time to get our business here completed."

"I agree. Take the horses to the barn and harness them to the wagon. I'll start gathering up things inside."

"You're leaving?"

"Yes, Jenny. Help me to gather up my things and I will explain everything."

Corrinne told her a fiction that Anamosa had taken ill and that they must return to New Bedford to a doctor who understood her malady. It was enough to gain Mistress Barton's urgent cooperation. Together, they stacked clothing and other personal items outside to be loaded on the wagon. The library was the most difficult move, with over a hundred books to pack. Once she and Sentry got the wagon loaded and lashed with room to spare at the back, she led him down to the cellar and pointed at the tarp in the corner.

"It's right there. Try not to jostle it too much. It won't do to disturb that coffin."

The rancid odor was almost overpowering as Corrinne and Sentry wrestled the reliquary up the stairway and out onto the wagon. The low growls it emitted made Mistress Barton cross herself repeatedly. The housekeeper had no idea such an ominous thing had been down in the cellar this entire time.

"What is that thing?"

"Nothing for you to worry about." Corrinne handed the lady a small leather sack with a mix of gold and silver coins. She pressed the sack into the woman's hands.

"There's no need to clean up this house today. Just put out the fires and leave. Keep the remaining food if you like. Don't come back here for at least two weeks. Don't speak with anyone about what happened here today. Not even to your daughters. Will you promise to do that for me?"

"I promise, my lady."

"Good." Corrinne hugged her before continuing. "You were wonderful, Jenny. Your daughters were wonderful. I won't forget this. I will be in New Bedford, but keep that to yourself as well. The owner of this house will hear good things about you."

Mistress Barton looked nervously at the reliquary lashed tightly in the back of the wagon.

"Will you be safe, my lady?"

"Don't worry about me. There is nothing for you to worry about," Corrinne assured her. Then continued in a tone of warning. "But it is best for you never to mention what you saw here today...to anyone. Promise me."

"I promise, my lady." The woman made the sign of the cross.

Corrinne crossed herself to show solidarity.

"Good." She kissed the servant's cheeks. "Now, put out the fires and go home, Mistress Barton. Kiss your daughters for me."

As soon as Corrinne was seated next to him, Sentry snapped the reins and the wagon lurched forward. They moved at a fast pace heading to the coastal road.

Their quick pace filled Corrinne with a strong sense of relief, almost approaching joy. She was finished with this exile. Done. She had thought fleeing Boston would ensure her safety, but that had not been so. She would take control over her life again. And she would fight to protect the ones she loved. It was her nature to fight rather than hide, to act instead of react.

Next to Corrinne, Sentry's military vigilance guided his thinking. *Where there's one, there could be two.* He concentrated on driving the horses but glanced back down the road often, checking to see if anyone followed. He wanted to get across the river as quickly as possible, to put the great watercourse between them and the adversary lurking somewhere in town. Lady Corrinne was right. They needed to move with haste, to get as far away as they could while daylight lasted.

Corrinne touched Sentry's arm.

"My lady?"

"I am in your debt, Sentry. It was a miracle you picked this day. We were at Winter House only *this morning*! If you had not come yesterday...if we had waited but a day more...I fear something terrible may have happened."

"My lady, your luck seems predestined. But"—he gestured at the sky—"I think you have a guardian angel watching over you. I've never seen anything like that in my life. I am not even sure what to make of it."

Corrinne stared up at the white eagle circling above them. She smiled warmly.

"You have certainly earned the right to know the whole story about this…wondrous creature…though *creature* sounds disrespectful of its nature. I've only hesitated telling you sooner because the truth will sound fanciful and superstitious. The eagle is a good spirit, I can tell you that. I only wish Henri or Philippe were here to help me explain. They know so much more about its history than I do. But it all concerns the *châsse*. This reliquary has an occult history and is very dangerous. It will spur your skepticism when you hear the story. But I tell you truthfully, I have seen things that challenge all my beliefs. Terrible things. Good things. And wonderful things. But it's better to wait until we are back in Boston, settled and secure, and have time to talk of such matters."

Sentry cast a suspicious glance toward the back of the wagon. "Well, I smelled the foulness. I heard the growls. You'll have no argument from me, m'lady. We've enough to worry about right now."

Corrinne fell silent, pondering what was to come. The assassins were certain to try again. But she would be ready for them this time.

The demon intends to break apart the châsse. *Shatter the seals. Possess the relics. Take the bones. That's really all he needs to do. We must make that impossible.*

A n overland coach company plying the road from New York to Philadelphia was contracted to make this trip. Colonel von Kleinfels paid
extra money to travel without rest, stopping only long enough to change
the team of horses and the drivers. They covered the ninety-mile journey in
two days, arriving in Germantown at noon on the second day. He engaged
rooms for everyone at the same inn as the year before. Caroline and Rachel
Bristol immediately retired.

"You wait here at the tables. Some other men will be joining us."

"And when they arrive?" Carter asked. "What will they do?"

He ignored the question. "Just keep them together until they are all
here. Then come get me. I will be in my room."

Carter Trevathan was weary from the long coach ride but settled at one
table and ordered something to eat and drink.

The colonel followed the desk clerk who carried his baggage. He paid the
man a tip and did not undress before lying upon the bed and falling to sleep.

Four hours later, a knock at the colonel's door brought him instantly
awake. It was Carter Trevathan.

"There are four men downstairs. They claim no one else will be coming."

Wilhelm splashed water on his face and followed Trevathan to the
dining room. The servants were waiting attentively. He remembered them
all, but just to be sure, he waved over the waiter.

"A bottle of wine and six glasses."

When the bottle arrived, von Kleinfels poured himself a glass and then
took a small bottle of his blood from a coat pocket. It was half full. He had
to remember to refill it. He discreetly poured the blood into the open wine

bottle, covered the spout with his thumb, and shook it before pouring it out into the other five glasses.

"A toast to our reunion."

After they swallowed it all, the *vulnax* appeared in the colonel's eyes.

"*You will serve me.* In the morning, come back to this inn and be ready to travel to Philadelphia and further north." He took a small sack of coins from his pocket and dropped it on the table with a clinking thump. "Mister Trevathan will distribute money to you. Take only what you need to settle any local matters. Bring horses and weapons. You will not be coming back here for a long time. Until tomorrow then."

The *vulnax* withdrew its dominance so the colonel could rest.

Even after his earlier short respite, von Kleinfels was lethargic. But he took off his clothes and went back to bed, secure in the knowledge he now had enough men to do what he wanted. Sleep came quickly, but only for a few hours before the *vulnax* reached out to Ritter Monheit.

I found the house here in Saybrook. But the servants claim she will be absent for a few days. She is expected to return by the end of the week.

Von Kleinfel's eyes opened wide. *Stay there. Do not approach her until I arrive. I am coming.*

Everyone rested through the night. It was necessary. Even after the overnight rest, the colonel was still tired the next morning. But he had the long coach ride ahead as well.

Carter Trevathan took charge of the arrangements with the overland coach company to return them to New York right away. Then he hired a new coach to take them on to Saybrook and possibly further. The four new servants would follow on horseback.

The colonel pushed them to make progress. They traveled at first light and did not stop to rest until long after dusk. But they rested each night. The servants needed the rest if they were to be effective in Saybrook. Even with aggressive travel, it took five days until the town of Saybrook was reached just before sunset. The coach stopped at the same inn where Ritter Monheit was staying.

Ritter Monheit was waiting outside as the passengers stepped off the coach. He was surprised to see the two women, but saved his questions.

"As you requested, Colonel, three private rooms are reserved and a bunkroom for the outriders. The stable master will care for the horses and house the drivers."

The colonel nodded once and permitted everyone except for Ritter Monheit to proceed about their business. He went into the dining room with Ritter to a table already set with food and drink. Kleinfels took a long swallow of wine and chewed on a piece of bread.

"Tell me everything that happened from the time you arrived in this town."

Ritter talked quietly while the colonel ate and asked the occasional question. He thought the man looked drained and hardly seemed to be listening. He would learn otherwise.

"I've been waiting here at the inn ever since I've visited the house. But no one has come to ask about me. But I have learned the name of the housekeeper, a Jenny Barton."

"The whore queen is gone from here and has taken the *châsse* with her."

"She has gone? Gone where?"

"While we rest, learn the name of the local agent for this...*winter house*. Tomorrow, I will have the Bristol sisters learn where she has gone."

"The Bristol...who?"

"The women! Do as I say. I must sleep now until morning."

The next morning, Caroline and Rachel Bristol called on the home of Mistress Jenny Barton. They were dressed in simple gray dresses of fine cotton with a similar colored short cape over their shoulders. A woman answered the door and regarded them with surprise. She noticed a one-horse carriage outside.

"May I help you?"

"Good morning. We are sorry to bother you. My name is Caroline Bristol and this is my sister, Rachel. We are nurses from New York looking for work in this area. But for now, just a house to rent for two weeks while we seek employment. The proprietor at the inn where we are staying gave us your name and said you may know of a vacancy."

The woman looked at their smiling faces. "Two weeks you say?"

"Yes. We are looking for a place near the sea, perhaps. We both love the sea. Reminds us of our home in Portsmouth, England. We thought we'd like New York, but the city was too crowded and the streets were surprisingly hazardous. Someone suggested we look in Boston, but when we reached Saybrook, we thought, why go on to Boston? This little town is pretty enough. Surely it needs nurses too?"

"Apologies for my sister, Mistress," Rachel said. "She tends to babble a lot."

"No apology necessary," the woman said with a smile. "I'm given to babbling too. There is a house I know about. But it will not be available for another week. Will you be seeking servants as well?"

"Oh, yes," Caroline replied quickly.

"There are three of us. I have two daughters, but they are working at another estate today."

"I'm sorry. We need only one person. Actually, just someone to cook for us. We are good nurses but terrible cooks. Once, I—"

"Oh, stop your prattle, Caroline. Mistress Barton does need to hear about your terrible cooking."

Jenny Barton laughed. "It's all right. I don't mind. But the one house I know about won't be ready for another week, as I said."

"Well, can we visit it for a short time today? If we like it, we will simply stay at the inn until it is ready. Presuming we are successful in finding employment, we may need a house even longer. But it will work out, I think. It may take us a few days to find work anyway. Isn't that so, Caroline?"

"Now who is babbling, Rachel? Mistress Barton, we will pay you a silver ounce to escort us on a visit today. And you can ride with us in our carriage."

Mistress Barton's lips pursed in thought. It had only been a week. Lady Corrinne had said to stay away for two weeks. *But they will not be staying, just looking…And it is an ounce of silver.*

"How long will it take you to look?"

"Oh…I'm certain no more than an hour," Caroline assured her. "And here, a Scottish silver ounce for your time." She fished the silver piece out of her purse and handed it to the woman. "You may have it now. Does that sound fair? If it's not convenient, perhaps there is someone else you know…?"

The housekeeper tested the coin with her teeth, and then slipped the ounce into a deep pocket on her dress. "And we will all ride together in your carriage?"

"Yes, of course."

"Well then, let's go."

The ride took about twenty minutes. After the carriage turned off the main road and continued down toward the house, Colonel von Kleinfels and Ritter Monheit came out of the trees where they'd been waiting on horseback. They would follow but stop just short of the open marshy section and watch the front door to the house for a signal to approach the rest of the way.

"Oh, what a beautiful day," Caroline remarked when they reached the front of the house. "We have a small basket of food and drink. I propose we share it! Is there a place outside to sit?"

"There are table and chairs out in the back." Mistress Barton was starting to like these handsome, friendly sisters. "You can also see the view of the river from there."

Rachel clapped her hands lightly. "Oh, that would be perfect."

Once at the table with the food arranged, Caroline buttered a sugar biscuit for the housekeeper and filled her cup from a bottle of local cider.

"This cider is from one of your farm stands," Caroline confided.

Between bits of biscuit, Mistress Barton nodded approvingly. "Our cider is indeed the best. You should try some."

"I will. Can I go over to that rise and see the river?"

"Of course."

"I will stay here," said Rachel.

When Caroline reached the rise and saw the expanse of the Connecticut River, she looked back. Rachel was already waving at her.

"She drank the full cup," Rachel said as Caroline reached the table.

Caroline had seen this docile, dazed look before. "You get her into the house. I will signal the colonel."

Wilhelm sat down in a chair knee to knee with the docile Jenny Barton.

"Did Lady Corrinne live here?" he asked right away.

"Yes."

"Where is she now?"

The housekeeper squinted as if in pain. "She went…she went to New Bedford with the Scottish soldier."

"And her children?"

"They were already across the river."

The colonel learned what he wanted to know but continued to question her for another hour until he was satisfied she had nothing of value left to say. The house was owned by Thomas Hancock who lived in Boston. They had taken the *châsse* on the back of a wagon with them. She thought it evil, that it smelled and growled. Said they might be going to see a man named Charles Jamison in New Bedford.

"That's enough," the colonel said. "Move her to the couch and give her something quick and deadly. Something that leaves no trace."

Caroline and Rachel helped the pliable woman to the couch and had her lie down. She did what they said without complaint. From an oblong leather pouch, Rachel took out a vial of clear liquid. It was sealed with a cork that was inlaid with a long slender stem of glass. When the cork was withdrawn, some of the liquid would coat the glass.

"Open your mouth," Rachel told the woman.

Jenny's mouth sagged open. Rachel touched the glass stem to Jenny's tongue and allowed two drops to fall from its tip.

"Now swallow."

Mistress Barton gulped, inhaled sharply, and then stiffened almost immediately as the paralysis took hold. Seconds later, her heart stopped. Life was draining from the woman's body even before Rachel replaced the cork in the vial.

"What the hell is that?" Ritter asked in amazement.

"*Aqua tofana*," Rachel replied. She calmly retrieved the Scottish silver ounce from the woman's dress pocket. "It is a poison of the Borgias."

Wilhelm entered the room. "Enough! Search the house to see if there is anything left of informational value to us. Tell me if you find something. Do not disturb anything. We are not here to steal."

Later in the day, upon reaching the river ferry, Ritter inquired from the operator if he'd seen a large overland coach passing recently. He described the carriage.

"Yeah," the operator replied. "Seen one like you say a week ago. A wagon full of boxes. Same driver."

"Did the driver have a Scottish accent?"

"Yeah." The man folded his arms and went silent.

Ritter flipped him a piece of silver. "Where was he going?"

"He claimed they were bound for New Bedford."

The next day, Jenny Barton's body was found by her daughters after they went searching for her. Why she went to Winter House or how she got there was a mystery. The local doctor was called. He was unable to determine her cause of death. And because her eyes were wide open, her face peaceful, no signs of struggle or discoloration to her skin, he diagnosed her death as an unexpected stroke.

"Unfortunately, it happens."

*

Boston, Massachusetts

They had lost two days in Providence when Marcus and Calypso came down with fevers. Hot ones! They called in the best of the local doctors, who assured them it would likely pass in a few days.

"Children this young tend to fever very hot. Then *poof*, they are cool again and no worse for it. We don't know why. But we think this happens when they are exposed to a local malady. It can happen several times at their age. Always good to call a doctor, if there is one around, just to be sure."

The next day, the twins' temperature was normal again, just as the doctor predicted. They wasted no time in leaving. Corrinne decided to ride in one carriage along with Mathilde, Anamosa, and the twins in case the malady was something from the Lyme house so as not to spread it to the others.

The two carriages from Providence entered the city gate at the Boston neck with no challenge by the guards, who recognized Sentry Cheever driving the first carriage.

"Just Lord VanderMeer and the other women behind me," he explained to the lieutenant. They had yet to decide whether to officially announce Lady VanderMeer's return to Boston from her supposed stay in the continent.

"You travel with you own harem now, Color Sergeant?"

"Ahh, Lieutenant. If only tha' were true. But they are Lord VanderMeer's household servants."

The carriages were waved forward. As they reached Marlborough Street, Corrinne saw the familiar home she had come to love so much. It brought tears of relief to her eyes. It wasn't Quebec or Montréal, but it had been home to her for a year.

"Look, Marcus. Look, Calypso! We're home again!"

The coaches turned into the expanded carriage drive Charles had constructed in the spring. The marine guards ran over to the coach and spoke with Lord VanderMeer before they allowed them to go further. Lord VanderMeer had the driver continue around to the large landscaped carriage roundabout he'd constructed in the backyard of the house. The outbuilding had been moved to the far side of the property. A new vaulted carriage house and stable had been built beyond the roundabout. The entire back of the house had been modified with a newer more pleasing façade.

Corrinne gazed out the window to appreciate the changes. She saw a large portico with stone steps and polished brass railings and an overhanging roof with an awning that extended another six feet. A person could now get out of a carriage even in the rain and hardly catch a drop.

Getting out first, Molly and Dian hastened up the steps to the back door to make sure nothing was in the way. Charles sent his carriage around again so it would end up behind Corrinne's to allow her to enter the house before him. The entryway was changed as well. An addition was added to the back wall of the house as part of the portico. It added a wider hallway that first went right, then left in a dog-leg, so that one need not go through the *cuisine* to enter the main hall leading to the front of the house. This also hid the mud room behind a door at the back of the *cuisine*.

Corrinne held Marcus and Calypso in her arms and stopped at the top of the short riser steps, another feature Charles added to the portico for the convenience of the guests.

"You have been very busy, Lord VanderMeer," she remarked with admiration.

"Gracious of you to notice, Lady VanderMeer. Welcome home to all of you. And I agree with your decision to come home whole-heartedly. Proceed inside while Sentry and I pay the drivers and take care of our…baggage."

Two hours later, Dianamora was almost finished preparing a meal. Mathilde was resting in her beautiful bed, sleeping better than she had in a year. Molly sat in the front living room watching Marcus and Calypso play with their toys, wondering how soon Conor would return home to her again.

Anamosa was in her room arranging all her new dolls along a window sill and on her bed pillows. She took out the talisman and kissed it and said a prayer for Henri as she did every day. Sentry Cheever had returned to his job in the tavern.

And Corrinne de Chanaye prayed a rosary of thanks to God. Then she took a soothing, languid soak in the perfumed salts of her bathing tub while her thoughts turned to the assassins, who she knew would soon follow in pursuit.

"Just hurry along, as I know you will. A surprise awaits you this time," she promised in a whisper. A surprise? The sudden notion made her sit up in the tub.

He was unaware that we saw him...that we know who he is! How can we use this?

*

Narragansett, Rhode Island Province

The overland coach stopped to rest for the night in the town of Narragansett. The colonel wanted to continue but darkness was upon them, the animals were spent, and if that was not enough, the ferry had stopped. It would not carry anything across the Jamestown channels until morning. They got rooms at a hotel near the ferry, which also had a large bunkhouse attached to the stables. Carter Trevathan took care of these arrangements. Everyone welcomed the respite of uninterrupted sleep.

Physically spent, the colonel lay down on his bed fully clothed. The *vulnax* surge to dominance forced him to get up again only an hour later. He stumbled downstairs and outside, heading straight for the large rocks at the edge of the water. The *vulnax* sensed the *châsse* in contact with the land again. It was underground. But he sensed it was *not* east, towards New Bedford. It was north, towards Boston.

New Bedford was a ruse. The whore queen knew I was coming. How would she know? The white eagle?

The vulnax withdrew its dominance and allowed the human to return to bed.

*

The next morning, Colonel von Kleinfels gathered Carter Trevathan, Ritter Monheit, and the Bristol sisters together in a private dining salon of the hotel to break their fast. They ate small amounts of food and drink, but not enough to interrupt their rapt attention to the colonel. With a tired face, he looked at them individually as he talked.

"I am changing plans. The *châsse* is underground again in Boston. I will take the outriders with me on horseback, cross the bay on the ferry, and continue my travel to New Bedford. Caroline, you and Rachel take the coach to Boston. Find an apartment together and get work in a hospital.

"Carter and Ritter will follow the coach on horseback. Enter the Boston gate separately and find accommodations separately. You do not know one another. Ritter, find work as a stone cutter when you get to Boston. Do not stay at the same inn as before. Find someplace new where you will draw no attention. Do not go near the bodyguard and stay away from the VanderMeer residence. Carter, you are a man of business seeking Boston trade contacts to associate with your contacts in New York. Find a place to stay equal to your status. After a few days, have someone introduce you to Thomas Hancock. Represent yourself as a trading associate from New York, but do not mention the VanderMeers at any time. If he asks if you know them, feign ignorance. I am interested to see what he might suggest to you about the Dutchman.

"You must all beware of a certain magistrate by the name of Jack Tasker. He is still looking for those who attacked the VanderMeer residence last year. You should anticipate that anyone arriving to Boston subsequent to Lady VanderMeer's current return will be scrutinized by him, in person. He will ask you questions. He is very probing. Have your stories we practiced ready to present to him and anyone else who may press you for information on how you came to be in Boston at this particular time. If the magistrate approaches any of you, be very circumspect. This man is intelligent, extremely suspicious, and dangerous to all of you. Await my arrival. Once I am there and have a routine established, we will meet again somewhere in the city."

Carter Trevathan was the only one with the courage to ask, "Why are you going to New Bedford?"

"I will arrange for ship travel from New Bedford to Boston for the rest of us. We will sell the horses and sail separately. I will enter the harbor in a Hessian uniform and resume my military liaison with the English army as I did last year. A state of war now exists between England and France. I will have much to discuss with the military authorities that validates my identity and purpose. If you encounter me by chance in Boston, I must remain a complete stranger to you. Do not even look in my direction if you see me."

"And the coachman?" Caroline asked. "He knows all of us, including you."

The colonel nodded. "Find a way to kill him in Boston. Do it discreetly and quickly before the magistrate questions him. And without drawing attention to yourselves."

*

North of Boston

From high in the sky, the *ghost* had watched the woman enter the water city with her children. She would be safer there. She was aware the demon and its servants were in pursuit. The men around her would be watchful to protect her.

The white eagle's weakness had returned. Not as bad as before, at least not yet. But the *ghost* sensed this problem would only worsen. They continued flying north.

We will return to the valley, the *ghost* decided.

From now on, the *ghost* would fly long distances only if the eagle was fully rested. And it would return immediately after such journeys to the breeding place. This would constrain the *ghost*'s efforts to defeat the demon. It was not something the *ghost* wanted to do, but there was no choice.

When night approached, the *ghost* withdrew its dominance to allow the eagle to hunt and find a place to sleep. This time it stooped on a rabbit, killing it instantly. It flew up a nearby cliff, perched, and devoured the meat. Then it floated down to a river. Amid some rocks in the shallows near a bank, the eagle cleaned its feathers, talons, and beak to rid them of residue blood and gristle from the rabbit. With its bath complete, the eagle flew to the top of the tallest tree it could see and found a secure place to perch for the night.

The next day, the *ghost* remained subdued and allowed the eagle to find its own way to the valley. The path the bird chose was not straight and it was not fast. It meandered back and forth across the sky and landscape, hunting when it was hungry, resting when it was weary, but generally moving in the right direction. This would add several days to a one-day journey, but there was no hurry. Already the *ghost* felt the raptor's strength returning. So it did not interfere.

Then something occurred the *ghost* never anticipated.

There was one more day of flying to reach the valley when the raptor banked sharply to the left and began a predatory glide as if attacking. But they were too high! The *ghost* readied to dominate the eagle, thinking it might somehow be impaired. In the distance, the *ghost* saw a distinctive spot moving against the blueness of the sky. The eagle was gliding to attack another flying creature, it would seem. But as they neared, the *ghost* saw it was another eagle, one with white feathers! They were coming down on it from above. The white eagle had positioned its glide to put the sun at its back. They were going to collide with great force. In the last moment, the other creature reacted to the attack and rolled, extending its talons.

A frenzied series of sharp loops and turns followed, with constant screeching from the two adversaries. They were no longer flying. The pair of eagles continued clashing and falling at the same time, amid feints, twists, arched wings, temporary pauses in full flight, and talons clicking between them. Even if the *ghost* exerted all its dominance, it was not certain what would happen. So it remained subdued but concerned as the ground dipped and rushed beneath them.

With each pass, the *ghost* saw that the other bird was not completely white. Its chest and belly was speckled with dark brown feathers but was much larger, as much as half again larger in size. The struggle was mismatched. Yet for all the close clashing, neither of the animals seemed injured.

The fall was steady. They were dropping into a forested valley between some foothills. If they fell below the hilltops, the *ghost* intended to exert its dominance to stop the conflict. Once more, the raptors collided and locked their talons in a strong grip. Now they began spinning end over end. It was too late for the *ghost* to force a break from this feverish clench even if it tried.

The talons of both eagles pulled with great strength. *It is female!* The white eagle physically joined with the other bird. For a few moments, the *ghost* perceived a burst of mixed colors and light accompanied by a short, powerful surge of pleasure it never thought possible to feel again. It was the most wondrous, rushing, numbing sensation it ever experienced. But it was brief.

One moment the *ghost* was looking directly into the eyes of the female eagle, and in the next moment it was looking into the eyes of the white eagle. The talons relaxed, the female arched her wings to separate, extended them to pull out of the free fall dive. It steadied in flight only a few meters above the ground. The female was lucky. The speed of the fall was great. Just as the white eagle rotated to fly it slammed into the dry bottom of the rock-strewn valley. The bones of its left wing shattered. Its neck broke. The body bounced once, flopped over on the rocks, and lay still.

The white eagle was dead.

CHAPTER 14
MONTRÉAL
JUNE 1756
"Then do your duty!"

Philippe Gerrard stayed with Mary, Joshua, and Leah for the rest of the day. His thoughts were vacillating after the recent revelations about Henri, Corrinne, and her twins. Mary saw how troubled he was but did not pry. She suggested they go to the market while they waited, hoping to improve his mood.

They went as a group and she bought some things to eat. They sat at one of the empty tables provided nearby for the market visitors. This helped to expend some time in a pleasant way. For most of it, Philippe remained preoccupied. Although not rude, his conversation and answers to Joshua's questions were abrupt.

"Philippe, I will take the children for a walk around the city and show them some things. Then we will go back home. You intended to visit army headquarters today, *oui*?"

"Yes. Yes, Mary. *Merci*."

Philippe began walking to the Dunemoore Company warehouse, now the Grand Company warehouse. Just outside the river gate he sensed someone followed. He stopped to fiddle with his moccasin laces and from the corner of his eye saw the uniform of a sergeant of the Troupes. Over the right shoulder draped the red signet cord of the gendarmerie. He'd seen the man before, sitting at a table at the café across from the chamberlain's home in the *rue menagerie*. *One of Intendant Bigôt's men!* And that meant trouble. It also meant the man had seen Mary and the children.

Philippe walked into the warehouse and found Paulus Legate. After greetings, he explained his suspicions.

"I need to arrange another place for the children to stay if it becomes necessary…if Bigôt arrests me. If that happens, he might attempt to arrest

Denis and Mary too. I will not allow that. And I will not allow him to get his hands on these children. They will have to stay with someone else or…or I will take them from the city. Only then I will have problems with the army."

The clerk did not hesitate. "Don't worry, Philippe. I know many people who will be glad to help you. Let me see what I can do."

"I cannot delay my report to the army any longer. Maybe they can help in some way."

Philippe left the warehouse and saw no sign of the sergeant. He entered the river gate and turned right. The headquarters and main barracks of the army were at the other end of the city. He walked at a fast pace up Rue Saint-Paul, returning frequent salutes as he went. He passed the shops of the artists and tradesmen. Work on the city's defenses along the top of the wall proceeded with an ambitious design of stone-reinforced cannon emplacements. Once at the headquarters, he was received by a major in the Troupes he'd never met before.

"Welcome home, Captain Gerrard. I'd heard you arrived."

"You did?"

"Yesterday, the river-gate sentries reported a captain of the Troupes from the west with blond hair and beard entered the city. I deduced it was you. You carry dispatches from the forts, yes?"

"Yes, sir."

"Don't leave them here. The governor demands all dispatches to be delivered to him first, accompanied by the courier. He is at the mansion. I'm sure he will want to talk with you anyway. Your orders will come from him."

If this major deduced this, Bigôt already knows I am here.

Philippe entered the governor's extravagant mansion. He gazed around at the gilded lamps and chandeliers, thick carpeting, brocade curtains, and other finery. With all the paintings and portraits and expensive furnishings, it was like entering a city palace in France. He checked his feet for mud. *Too late.* He was saluted by an ensign and two guards posted by the foyer and escorted to an office on the first floor. There was another captain of the Troupes standing behind a desk, shuffling through papers. The man regarded him with surprise.

"Captain Gerrard?"

"Yes. And you are?"

"Captain Marcel Trieste, at your service. I am first aide and secretary to Governor Vaudreuil."

They shook hands.

"Governor Vaudreuil will be most anxious to converse with you, Captain. You carry dispatches, yes? Even better. I will take those to him. The governor is meeting with important visitors so it could be a wait. But he will definitely want to talk with you. Please, make yourself comfortable." He pointed at some chairs and the credenza nearby. "There is brandy available."

Captain Trieste gathered up maps and documents from his desktop and then paused on an afterthought. He pulled another rolled document from a drawer before hurrying out of the office.

Philippe sat for a time but grew restless. He stood and poured himself a small dram of brandy and went over to a window. He took a few sips. It was biting and the resulting warmth in his throat and chest felt foreign. He put down the porcelain cup. He could see the second-floor offices of Intendant Bigôt directly across the plaza in front of the mansion. He stared at the windows but saw no movements inside.

I must get the governor on my side. He can stop Bigôt if he chooses. Or maybe Archbishop Nicolet could provide the children with shelter?

That seemed an even better idea. So good, in fact, he left the office of Captain Trieste and the governor's mansion and walked to the Terrain des Jésuites.

It will take the governor time to read all the dispatches anyway, Philippe told himself.

Governor Vaudreuil was in full argument with his new adversary. They were in the main chambers of government. Vaudreuil sat at the head of the long table. Attending him on the right were Captain Montreuil, former aide to General von Dieskau but now his military adjutant. And Captain Rigaud de Vaudreuil, a ten-year veteran war captain of the Troupes, who also happened to be his brother. Captain Trieste had been sent from the meeting that was already past its second hour, to locate the lists of troop dispositions among the French forts of New France.

To the governor's left sat Major-General Louis Joseph, Marquis de Montcalm-Gozon de Saint-Véran, forty-four years old, the replacement for the captured General Ludwig von Dieskau. Montcalm had been in the

French army since the age of fifteen and had risen steadily through the ranks. He was a natural leader and fearless in battle, having suffered five saber cuts, including two in the head in the last war. He'd been captured and later exchanged, promoted to colonel and engaged in battle once again but was wounded by a musket ball. The treaty at the end of the last war gave him a chance to rest. He was a Brigadier-General by then and had been noticed by the French Minister of War d'Argenson who had an eye for talent and influence with the king. Montcalm was appointed by King Louis XV to replace General von Dieskau and promoted to Major-General and commander-in-chief of the French army in New France.

Sitting next to Montcalm was Brigadier General François de Lévis, his second-in-command, and Colonel François-Charles de Bourlamaque, his third.

All three of these French officers were veteran, professional soldiers and some of France's finest military tacticians and strategists.

Governor-General Vaudreuil did not like any of them; he did not need them. The feeling was mutual, as reflected in the grim, unfriendly expressions around the table. This relationship would be strained even if they had grown up as boyhood friends. The chain of command was split by politics. Governor Vaudreuil reported to the Minister of Marine, Jean-Baptiste de Machault d'Arnouville. The Troupes de la Marine of New France were under his command along with the civilian militias.

General Montcalm and his subordinates reported to the Minister of War, Marc-Pierre de Voyer de Paulmy, Comte d'Argenson. All the French metropolitan troops, the regulars, grenadiers, artillerymen and engineers, were under his command. And just recently, the King delivered a personal directive to Governor Vaudreuil that in terms of command in battle, Montcalm's authority would further extend to the Troupes de la Marine, the militia, and any of the Indian allies.

General Montcalm was aware of the King's recent directive but wisely did not press the governor on this issue. It was not necessary. Effectively, this directive meant General Montcalm had control of the dispositions of the troops employed in war. But Governor-General Vaudreuil was in charge of the strategy and the targets.

When Captain Trieste returned, Vaudreuil tilted his head and received Trieste's whispered report on the arrival of Captain Gerrard. He saw the two satchels of missives from the western forts.

"Did you bring the troop dispositions?"

"Yes, sir." Trieste placed the documents in front of the governor.

"General Montcalm, to summarize what I have already explained, the English Fort Oswego is ready to fall. Since I destroyed its line of supply three months ago, the garrison is starving and sick. This condition has been certified by my spies. Since then, I've been conducting more raids on their supply lines." He looked at the troop documents. "Yes…here it is. As I said, I have deployed three thousand men, supplies, and the bateaux to carry them, at Fort Frontenac specifically for this attack. They will soon start for Niaouré Bay. The English fort should fall without much of a fight. When it falls, any English claims to territorial possession on the Great Lakes will disappear forever. They will no longer have a presence on Lake Ontario and will no longer have any lines of supply for invasion and siege to recover the fort. Furthermore, as I intend to raise and destroy Oswego, there won't be any fort to recover! With Fort Niagara's dominating position, augmented by Fort Frontenac, we do not need another fort on Lake Ontario. So my army lacks only a commander to lead our forces from Fort Frontenac. This attack needs to go forth immediately. In light of your heralded reputation, I must presume you are up to the task. In the meantime, Captain Rigaud de Vaudreuil will sail up river and take command at Niaouré Bay. Though he is my brother, he is also a veteran of the fighting in this wilderness and speaks many of the Indian languages. The Canadians trust him, and I have complete confidence in him. As I have in you, of course."

General Montcalm thought carefully before he responded.

"Governor, I know our relationship has not begun in friendship or trust. However, do not doubt that my intentions to defeat the English invasion of French territory will be any less vigorous and aggressive than your own. I hope we can start any discussion on future strategy with the presumption of a common objective: the utter defeat of the English Americans. I will indeed take your leave, but not for Niaouré Bay. I will first inspect the forts on Lake Champlain because they are near and since it is the enemy's overt intention to attack them. I see this water route as the most dangerous threat to Montréal. I would like to be sure we have a sound defensive posture at these forts before leading an attack on the Onondaga River forts in the west."

"Very well." Governor Vaudreuil nodded. "Captain de Vaudreuil can conduct further raids on the English supply lines while he waits for you at Niaouré Bay. Now, let's discuss the troop dispositions at New France's other forts and the future targets. Please accept this information as my strategy for the future conduct of the war. But we will discuss it again at the end of every new victory to assess its effectiveness and make changes to the strategy if necessary. Is that acceptable to you?"

"Of course."

The governor stood and went over to the large map of North America covering the wall. He began pointing and…lecturing.

The meeting would last for two more hours.

Archbishop Nicolet was pleased to see Captain Gerrard. Upon seeing the captain's grave expression, he had Father Tinian cancel his other appointments.

Philippe told the story about his rescue of the English children. He related his new concern that Intendant Bigôt would try to arrest him or worse, abduct and incarcerate the children.

"I left the mail pouches with a Captain Trieste. The governor was engaged in a long meeting. I planned to discuss this with him. But I wanted your counsel."

"First of all, do not worry about the children. Bring them here to the Terrain des Jésuites and I will make them our wards. I can educate them too. We have a school here of sorts with about a dozen students. Mostly private tutoring. And all of my fellow Jesuits speak English. I think they will be well served. Or they may stay with Denis and Mary and come here each day for tutoring, if they are more comfortable with that. Or bring them all here together and I will work out arrangements with Denis and Mary to use our grounds as a sanctuary should that ever be necessary."

"Thank you, Eminence."

"Now, let's talk about your new military commander, who is meeting with Governor Vaudreuil at the moment. His name is Major-General Louis Joseph, Marquis de Montcalm. He is a veteran metropolitan officer with great battle success in Europe. But he is not familiar with wilderness fighting. He is smart and adapts quickly. I like him. I think you will like him. I anticipate the governor will *not* like him and that is where you will have to be careful."

Archbishop Nicolet explained and answered questions for half an hour.

"General Montcalm will need someone he can trust to help him make the right decisions. Governor Vaudreuil will likely ask you to be his advocate to the general. You will have to find a way to do this for the sake of New France. As always, getting information to me will only help everyone else. My relationship with the governor tends to be…shall I say, advisory. More so since he discovered how much Marquis Duquesne trusted my counsel."

Philippe looked relieved. "I can do that."

André spoke his next words carefully. "Not to alarm you, but you should not delay in bringing Denis, Mary, and the children to meet with me, *today*, as soon as you can. The army here in Montréal will march in two days to rendezvous at Niaouré Bay with forces from Fort Frontenac for the attack on Fort Oswego, and I expect you will be marching with General Montcalm."

Philippe stood. "Then I will do that now, before I return to the governor's mansion, as I don't know how long I will be there."

Philippe left the Jesuit terrain and trotted down Rue Notre-Dame to the chamberlain's house. He sent Mary to bring Denis home. While she was gone, he sat with Joshua and Leah and explained what he learned, that he would be going away tomorrow and that they would meet with Archbishop Nicolet as soon as Denis came home.

"But you promised," Joshua said.

Philippe hugged Leah who was already tearful. "Don't worry."

"You…you promised."

"Listen to me. I *will* keep my promise. But I must go away for a while and you can stay with Denis and Mary. Bishop Nicolet will be your new friend and teacher. That's all. These people will protect you with their lives, just like I have. You have to be strong for me, Joshua. Can you do that? Leah, you are like a daughter. Joshua, you could be my son. But I have to go away for a while."

"For how long?"

The door opened and Denis rushed in.

"Mary explained. We should go now, *oui*?"

Philippe nodded. He took Leah by the hand. After leaving the house, they went up another block above Rue Notre-Dame to use the road paralleling the north wall so they would not be seen from the main streets. They walked it to the back gate of the Terrain des Jésuites.

Philippe stopped at the gate before pulling the bell cord. "See, that was just a short walk. And this is the best way to come here whenever the need arises. Then you pull this cord. Here. You do it, Joshua."

They heard a bell ring inside. A smiling, black-robed Jesuit opened the door and welcomed them in English.

"Archbishop Nicolet is expecting you."

After an hour of introduction and questions in English, Philippe knew he must leave.

"I will meet you at the chamberlain's house later."

"Wake us up, even if we are asleep," pleaded Joshua.

"You can be certain of that." He kissed Leah on both cheeks. "And I want a kiss of good luck from you."

Wearing a slight frown, her tiny arms slipped around his neck as she kissed his cheek.

*

Philippe arrived back at the mansion and was sitting in Captain Trieste's office for no longer than ten minutes when the officer came rushing in.

"Good, you are still here. I worried you might leave. Why are you sweating?"

"The brandy did not sit well with me." He pointed at the cup. "I've been in the wilderness for too long."

"The governor just finished a long meeting with General Montcalm. Once we see the general leave the mansion, we will go up to the governor's office."

"But I want to meet the general too."

"Well, the governor wants to meet with you *first*. You will be given command of a company of marine scouts and will be deploying within two days. A word of advice, Captain. The meeting between the governor and General Montcalm was not very pleasant. The governor is in a poor mood. Try not to be insulted by what he says."

Philippe was amused. "Compared to what I've experienced, I do not take verbal insults personally."

A short time later, Philippe was escorted up the stairs to the private office once used by the Marquis Duquesne. The governor and Philippe both knew of each other, but had yet to meet.

Philippe came to attention, saluted, and introduced himself.

Vaudreuil came around to shake hands with the *coureur de bois* officer.

"Well, well. Another day, another Gerrard. I am most pleased to finally meet you, Captain. I think you know Captain Montreuil. Have you met my brother, Rigaud?"

"Not formally. I've heard good things about you, Captain," Philippe lied. He'd heard nothing good about this man, except that he was the governor's brother and should be treated with respect.

They shook hands.

"Likewise, Captain Gerrard. I look forward to sharing stories with you on the way to Oswego."

Vaudreuil interjected. "Yes, yes, all good. Please, sit. Captain Trieste, have refreshments brought to us."

"Governor, I brought two satchels of dispatches with me and gave them to Captain Trieste."

"Yes, I know. They are safe. But neither of us have time to discuss those dispatches. I must say, you are as rugged looking as people have described. Your facial scars seem excessive."

Philippe was surprised by this frank comment. "I earned every one of them. Is my scarring good or bad?"

"And impertinent, too!"

"Apologies, Governor. I do not mean to be impertinent. I've traveled constantly for almost two months, beginning with a scouting patrol from Fort Duquesne. I am tired and ill-tempered from the journey. That is no excuse, sir, just a reason. Military etiquette was never my personal strength. But I will give you honest assessments and opinions even if I think you will not like what I have to say."

Vaudreuil leaned forward in his chair. Rigaud was nodding with appreciation.

"Absolutely refreshing, Captain. And I think my brother agrees. My position tends to encourage sycophants to gather around me like nectar compels bees. Your honest opinion will be welcome. As long as you understand, in spite of what you tell me, you will obey my orders even if you don't like them."

"Yes, sir. I've been obeying bad orders for a long time…not to say your orders will be bad, of course."

Vaudreuil was surprised again. "I can see we are going to enjoy this candid conversation. You wear that uniform and fight so France can win this war, *oui*?"

"Yes, sir."

"Good. Let's remember we are on the same side and want the same thing."

The side door opened and Captain Trieste returned leading two servants with trays of food and drink. He had them set places for five on a nearby round table.

As the table was set, Vaudreuil related the results of his meeting with General Montcalm. "My brother can fill you in on the other details."

Once the servants were finished and exited the room, Captain Trieste waited for a pause in the conversation before speaking. "Governor, I've set five places. Shall I stay?"

"Yes, I want you to stay, Captain. Let's all move to the table and have some wine. Captain Gerrard, if you will indulge me, please tell me a little of your history, a lot of your experience at Fort Duquesne, and the reason for your journey to Montréal."

Philippe did as requested with brevity.

The day before, Intendant Bigôt had ranted to the governor about this *coureur de bois*…

"He is a traitor, dangerous, and independent! He is a killer! You cannot trust him."

The governor responded that New France currently had a need for such men.

Governor Vaudreuil was surprised to learn the captain had no stomach for the Indians' savagery.

"After all your time living here, you find the Indians' butchery on the frontier intolerable? You must be very familiar with their predilection."

"Yes, I've seen it often enough. The tribes do it to one another with no less viciousness. But Handsome Robert of the Delaware is paid a double bounty by Captain Dumas at Fort Duquesne if the scalps he brings are those of American *children*. I find French endorsement of that behavior abominable."

"And so you bring the two American children to Montréal to protect them? Commendable. But the actions of our allies will continue to be rewarded for such activities. The Americans must suffer consequences for invading French territory. We do not possess the troops to safeguard our borders. Since American trespass includes the lands of our allies, they have reason to defend them too. I will indeed encourage them to do this for me. And it is my decision to make. I've already had this conversation with General Montcalm. I will not repeat it here. Rigaud can represent my position at length. But let's talk about you.

"Your *coureurs de bois* scouts will be expanded to a full company, if you have not been told already. The Americans have men they call rangers, reputed to be your equals, though I find that hard to believe. The special nature of your knowledge and skill in fighting in the wilderness coupled with your relationship with the tribes will make your advice valuable to the general. He is smart enough to recognize and use this. I want you to become a trusted advisor to General Montcalm and his seconds. He will ignore any suggestions made by Rigaud, no matter how tactically superior they might be. So I will look to you to be supportive and convincing. Conversely, I need to know how General Montcalm thinks, how he makes decisions, and, most importantly, his longer term perspective on strategy. I want to know this before he presents them to me. Accordingly, we will establish routine messengers between us."

"So I am to be a spy?"

Vaudreuil shrugged. "If you prefer. Label it what you want. You are not naïve, Captain Gerrard. The fate of New France is at stake in the decisions we make. The Marquis de Montcalm will never be candid with me. He is an elitist royal. He considers the Troupes de la Marine and our militia to be buffoons...and all Canadians unsophisticated. I am a Lieutenant-General of the army, his senior. I am also a marquis. But I was born here. I am Canadian *first*. He knows this, and therefore he will never trust me. He will not tell Rigaud for the same reasons, but based upon your...*reputation*? I believe he will tell you. And I want you to tell me. And where possible, I want you to sway him to the correct military decisions, which I anticipate will not be too different than my own."

Philippe understood. "Governor, I will try to do what you ask, but it is not my nature to be deceitful to my commanders. I would not be very convincing. As I said, I offer my honest opinion, even if I think you will not like it. I will not be any good as a spy."

"Perhaps. But as I am your ultimate commander, you will follow my orders. And it is your persuasive candor I will rely upon to influence the Marquis de Montcalm. If he convinces you of a strategy, and you think he is right. Tell me. If I disagree, I will not hold you responsible. You may be surprised how often you and I will agree. There's no need for you to be deceitful. Just *withhold* endorsing opinions that are averse to mine."

At that, Captain Trieste slid a document in front of the governor.

"Oh, yes." He lifted the edge of the document so Philippe could see his name in writing. "This document was issued by Intendant Bigôt almost two years ago. It is a royal warrant accusing you as a traitor and a murderer…" He flipped the page and smiled. "And several other crimes…there seems to be a list! *Piracy*? A *coureur de bois* pirate?"

Philippe grit his teeth and narrowed his eyes. "They are all *lies*. It is all contrived. Intendant Bigôt is corrupt to the point of being treasonous by his own actions."

Ah, the wilderness man has a weakness, thought Vaudreuil. *Bigôt.*

"Indeed? The intendant came to me yesterday morning to inform me you had returned to Montréal three days ago and had secreted American children in the city, despite my standing orders to have them turned over to the army for prisoner exchange."

Philippe's anger was now on full display. "The intendant would incarcerate them in the bastille just to provoke me. It would be unwise for the intendant to do that."

Impressive and dangerous, the governor thought.

"The intendant is following my orders, Captain," he replied tersely. "And you should remember that I hold his tether."

Philippe's stare grew hard, cold. Captain Rigaud de Vaudreuil instinctively placed a hand on the hilt of his sword. The governor's tone softened.

"Come, come, Captain. I can see your anger and distress. Be at ease. I have already ordered the intendant not to apprehend these children…and that he is not to disturb any arrangements you have made regarding their care. Nor are the gendarmes to harass or intimidate them in any way."

The bastard will keep them hostage to control me, Philippe thought, but he calmed himself.

"They lost everyone they knew to Handsome Robert. I only wish to see them safely delivered to whatever relatives they have left...when the opportunity comes."

"As do I, Captain," the governor said in an attempt to placate. "However, that could take *years*, I am afraid. Nevertheless, I have formally withdrawn the warrant for your arrest. It will be recorded today. Captain Trieste?"

"Yes, sir. I have already delivered these orders to the administrators to record."

"Good! There. You see. That problem is solved too. Of course, this is a royal warrant, which usually requires approval by the king. But this is a time of war and my powers are those of a viceroy. Our King has far greater things to worry about. You are a valuable officer and a war captain in the marines of New France. I take care of men like you because of the great danger we face...*together*."

"Yes, sir."

"As you are deploying soon, I expect you have some preparations to make with your new company of marine scouts and the scouts you brought with you from Fort Duquesne. Report to my brother for the time being until General Montcalm gives you new orders. My messengers will contact you at some time in the future. Send your reply to me in writing."

So you will have my insubordination to Montcalm written in my own hand, Philippe noted.

The room became silent as the governor waited to see what Captain Gerrard would say next. Philippe wanted to ask about Henri, but he'd already been threatened twice. *Keep Henri clear of this.*

"Questions, Captain?"

Philippe stood. "No, sir."

Vaudreuil's chin was in the air, his shoulders back, as he looked down his nose at the captain. "Then do your duty, Captain Gerrard. You are dismissed."

After the door had clicked shut and the wilderness man's footsteps diminished down the hall, Governor Vaudreuil began issuing new orders:

"Rigaud, take your Canadians and go directly to Fort Frontenac. Take command of the Guyenne, Béarn, and La Sarre regiments, and the marines and Indians we have there in support and bring them all to Niaouré Bay.

Captain de Villiers with his militiamen and Indians are still raiding the supply lines to the south of Oswego along the Onondaga River to disrupt any attempts being made by the English to resupply the lake forts. By now de Villiers should have some victories to report. If he does, do not bother to inform General Montcalm. Tell me and I will inform him. I want to do the reporting of this to d'Argenson and Machault. And I do not want Montcalm to interfere with my latest troop movements. Let him inspect Fort Carillon and Fort Saint Frédéric as he planned. Captain Gerrard's scout company should guard Montcalm wherever he goes and provide protection and advice, of course. Make certain you give him that order. But tell him it is from me. Then proceed with your mission to Fort Frontenac without delay."

*

General Montcalm did not travel very far from Montréal before he signaled his fleet of bateaux to beach at La Prairie on the southern side of the Saint Lawrence River. Once there, he called an unanticipated council of war with his officers.

"Captain de Vaudreuil, you will continue upriver with the Canadians and militia to oversee the establishment of a stockade fort to store supplies at Niaouré Bay in support of the final advance on Fort Oswego. Once that stockade is secured, reconnoiter Fort Oswego and its environs in a manner that does not provide forewarning to the enemy that our attack is imminent."

Captain de Vaudreuil acknowledged that order but did not mention the superseding orders given to him by his brother, the governor.

"The rest of us will march to join the Royal Roussillon regiment at Carillon and inspect our defensive positions on Lake Champlain. Captain Gerrard's scout company from the Troupes de la Marines and the militia will come with me. General de Lévis and Colonel Bourlamaque will act as my second- and third-in-command for this inspection. Captain de Bougainville has remained in Montréal to provide liaison services to Governor Vaudreuil for me."

The council ended and the officers carried out their individual orders.

Philippe Gerrard was surprised to hear his name mentioned so prominently in the general's first orders of march. *Probably not a coincidence,* he thought. He was hoping for an introduction to the general. This would provide an opportunity. The full scout company of Troupes de la Marine he commanded was composed of fifty-six officers and men, three subordinate lieutenants, two ensigns, and two cadets. He'd added his scouts from Fort Duquesne to this group and could not be more pleased of the prowess and capability of these men. Even though his command was only three days old, he had already spoken to many of them individually and collectively to answer questions. It helped that he was known to them and had a reputation from the battle on the Monongahela River.

"My primary objective is to advise General Montcalm on the best way to win our battles here in the wilderness. As scouts, you will never fight in a line. You will fight in a manner that brings gloom to the hearts of our enemies. During this march, I hope to learn more of your opinions and benefit from your experience."

It was not much of an introduction before they were all loaded into bateaux, but he saw cautious approval in their faces. These men had heard such talk before. They were men of action and would measure their captain by his actions. He would do the same with them.

While his company was part of the Troupes de la Marine, their uniforms were folded and carried at the bottom of their packs. The officers wore the blue sashes and carried sabers as indication of their rank. But his men had deep wilderness experience, including the officers, and they dressed like it. Most of them were former *coureurs de bois,* scouts, or voyageurs. A third of them were of mixed blood. The majority had been involved all their lives with the fur trade at some level. Among his men were people expert in the wilderness trails, lakes, and rivers in the lands from Fort Duquesne east to Philadelphia and New York and north to Acadia. A handful of them had even traveled to the mountain ranges beyond the western grasslands. Every native language could be spoken by someone. They all knew Indian hand signs. They were practiced in ambush equal in skill to any of the tribal warriors. No matter where Philippe was sent, he was confident someone among them had experience in the area. They would never be lost.

Within two days of leaving La Prairie, the scout company was using a total of ten six-man war canoes on the Richelieu River heading south. The men, paddling in unison, sped down the river to scout the area ahead of General Montcalm, including both sides of the lake. They would do this five canoes to each side, breaking off to search certain areas before catching up with the others. It was methodical and thorough. A series of musket shots would provide a signal if there was a problem, that is, if it was a problem that could not be handled with their bows.

General Montcalm followed in more traditional bateaux that were lightly loaded, each one manned with six experienced oarsmen. They were no more than half a day behind the scouts.

The army traveled thirty miles or more a day. They planned to reach Fort Carillon by the afternoon of the fourth day. General Montcalm wanted to see this fort first and visit with Fort Saint Frédéric on the way back.

Once they reached the place called Ticonderoga by the natives, Philippe sent two scout canoes across the lake's eastern side to climb the heights opposite to the construction of Fort Carillon. What signs of the enemy could they find? He sent two more to the south side of the fort to scout La Chute River and the cascade with the same mission. They were to beach and climb the heights above Fort Carillon to the southwest and the various trails of approach and report what they found.

The rest of the scout canoes beached at Fort Carillon's bateaux landing, which was guarded by regular troops from the regiment garrisoned there. The men spread out and across the lands surrounding the peninsula area, looking for signs of any enemy spies. Philippe sought out Lieutenant Michel-Alain Chartier de Lotbinière, the chief engineer in charge of its construction. He saluted and alerted him of General Montcalm's arrival.

"He is accompanied by Brigadier General François de Lévis."

The officer paled at the news.

"It's only been a year! The fort is nowhere near completion!"

"General Montcalm plans to inspect it for himself and will probably offer you aid. He will not stay very long."

The lieutenant gave immediate orders to prepare quarters and food for the general and the visiting troops and to his assistants on gathering the drawings and plans together for a briefing.

Across Lake Champlain, atop the heights and amid the trees, Captain Robert Rogers lay out of sight, spying through his glass. He noted all the new French regulars arriving at Fort Carillon. He traveled with a contingent of eighteen elite *rangers* and warrior allies who were spread out further south in the eastern forests along the Wood Creek water course leading up to Lake Champlain. Rogers also noticed the furtive movements of the *bushloper* scouts, as he referred to the *coureurs de bois*. They beached war canoes on his side of the lake and slipped into the forest. The *bushlopers* would definitely come up to the heights. They might pick up his trail. He withdrew with his two companions. He needed to report these new troop movements of the French back to Albany.

General Montcalm was astonished by the majesty and beauty of the lands of New France. The raw, unblemished work of the Creator loomed large everywhere he gazed. And not the least was the stunning green forests and shimmering blue waters that was Lake Champlain and its adjoining rivers.

This land is vast and hardly occupied, he wrote in his journal. *I am told there are even greater wonders to behold in the west, and that it would take several months of travel to reach the other ocean. Yet we still find reason to war over these small places.*

As they passed down the lake by the point of land dominated by Fort Saint Frédéric, he was not impressed by what he saw. It was made of stone, but the fort was not well-sighted for defense of the point, he decided. It had bastions but lacked the more defensible star shape. It had a four-story stone tower with cannons at every level. To the tribal peoples, it must be a daunting structure to observe. But when compared to the structures of the military engineering genius Marquis de Vauban, the impressive stone tower was no more than a well-elevated target for siege cannon. One that would collapse in on itself upon receiving the first volley of cannon balls.

It is good for defense against raiding parties and the natives, but useless if the English come against it in force, he thought.

"I can see your frown is as large as mine," said General de Lévis.

"Our defense of this water course will undoubtedly rest with the defensive works of Fort Carillon. Let's trust we are creating a proper fortress there."

When they reached Fort Carillon, they were greeted by Lieutenant Lotbinière. The commandant and engineer-architect had prepared a tour to present what had been accomplished so far, explain the intention of the fort's full design, and the schedule for completion.

General Montcalm did not let his expression display his abject disappointment with what he saw. If Fort Saint Frédéric would not withstand a siege by cannon, this fort was not ready to withstand a bayonet charge by a redcoat regiment. Much of the stone framework, the outline of the fort, could be seen. The four bastions were built. But the multiple passages into the works were not yet defensible. The work crews seemed too few, and the supplies to support the work were not visible.

"I will need you to stay here and take command of this for me," he said quietly to General de Lévis.

After what they saw at Fort Saint Frédéric, his second-in-command could plainly see the imminent threat to Montréal that the incomplete status of this fortification represented. Montcalm called for a council of war among the officers as soon as the men were refreshed from travel and had been fed. They listened to the commandant's explanation on why the work was progressing so slowly. After a few questions about why the materials and stone masons necessary for the work were being delayed, Montcalm understood by the architect's evasive answers the reason for his embarrassment.

Corruption.

Philippe had taken the time to survey the entire perimeter of the fort. He thought it not sighted correctly, according to what he'd read in Vauban's work on the subject. There was a large area of forest south of the fort before the land met with the lake. Enemy boats could go down the La Chute River and make a landing beneath the cover of the heights. Once the trees were cleared, they would have to build a defensive work down there or it would become a convenient landing place for the enemy. But what concerned Philippe more was the report by his scouts that the hill he saw a mile to the southwest was indeed a perfect place to position a battery of siege artillery. And the hill on the opposite side of the lake offered the same opportunity, and it was only a half mile away. Another fort was needed over there to prevent the enemy from building a second artillery position.

Philippe would wait until he received the reports from all of his scouts before he would make his own forays into the forests. *Tomorrow*, he decided.

General Montcalm stayed at Fort Carillon for several days, conducting a broad inspection of the lands surrounding the promontory. He noticed with unease the small mountain heights a mile to the southwest. He knew the danger that could come from an artillery battery in that position. Scout-Captain Gerrard had further confirmed the mountain had ample level land at the top to construct such a battery. *We must either build a battery or defend the heights so one could not be built*, the general thought. He would decide that later. For now, they needed to clear a wide field of fire completely around the fort and construct outer breastworks. *Defend out there*, he thought. *Use the fort as the citadel to fall back upon.*

Each day, Montcalm gave orders for improving the outer defenses. Together with Lieutenant Lotbinière and General de Lévis, they designed the form of the breastworks, made it *U* shaped, at the farthest edge of the promontory just before the ground descended, creating an incline the attackers would have to climb. The shape of the defense also shortened the distances to send men from one part to the other to reinforce. It permitted the redeployment of the defenders in a manner that gave them maximum flexibility against the enemy attacking with much greater numbers.

"Which the English will undoubtedly bring against us."

Three days after arriving at Fort Carillon, Philippe Gerrard and fourteen of his scouts were spread out and carefully following a trail south on the lands of Lake Champlain's eastern side. The men who made this trail left footprints in the ground that were not of Indian origin, yet their movements were those of expert woodsmen. He followed the difficult trail for half a day when they came to a place where canoes had been hidden. The men had escaped down the narrowing slender arm of Lake Champlain that ran parallel to Lake George. This water course would narrow even further and eventually turn into shallow wetlands of marshes and unnamed tributaries. More importantly, this was Iroquois territory. There was no sense following these enemy scouts further. Philippe turned back.

"Were they rangers?" one of his *coureur de bois* asked.

Philippe nodded. "Yes. We will meet them in this wilderness. They will be the ones we fight."

Two days later, Montcalm announced his departure at the morning officer's call.

"Tomorrow morning," Montcalm confirmed. "General de Lévis will remain here in command. Engineer Lotbinière, create a list of what else you need and I will see that you get it. Every soldier and able-bodied man must work to get this fortification completed. We can still be attacked this season."

Though so far, the English had given no indication of leaving their forts.

The next morning at sunrise, Philippe sent his scouts ahead to search both sides of the lake to cover the general's withdrawal up Lake Champlain. Montcalm stopped at Fort Saint Frédéric and spent two nights there, conferring with the commandant and inspecting the defenses. Manned by the Troupes and militia, he gave orders on how to improve the defenses against attack. But the deciding battle, when it came, would take place at Fort Carillon. If it fell, Fort Saint Frédéric and Crown Point would not be defensible for very long.

General Montcalm had a dozen officers of the fort join him for a dinner on the second night. He wanted to hear their opinions. They were optimistic, generally because Montcalm was here with them now. They claimed they were spied upon almost daily. There were frequent skirmishes. Scalps taken by both sides. To Montcalm's ears, these were just small squalls before the greater storm.

Montcalm announced they would proceed to the Saint Lawrence River at first light. As the officers spread out to sleep, he asked Philippe to stay behind and talk with him. What Montcalm knew about Captain Gerrard came from the man's reputation. The rumors alleged good and bad things about this officer, depending on who did the speaking. He noticed the more hostile accusations tended to come from people in the government of New France and the most virulent of those came from Intendant François Bigôt. The more favorable characterizations were attributed by people fighting in the war, and they gave Captain Gerrard extraordinary praise. Few people who knew the *coureur de bois* officer had no opinion. They were either of one view or the other. Which meant to the veteran French general, only one of these views was correct. The majority praised him. And since Governor Vaudreuil pressed the captain into joining Montcalm's staff without first being introduced, the general was curious.

But Montcalm had another motive. He was anxious to gain a counselor, someone with a Canadian view, and someone who he could trust to tell him the truth. It was obvious he could not trust the governor's brother, Rigaud de Vaudreuil. Based on what the captain had said at dinner, his instincts told him Philippe Gerrard might be that person.

"Captain, I am pleased to get to know you. Let me start by saying your reputation is mixed. You are described to me either as a villain or a hero.

But if you are to follow my orders, I need to know the truth of this. What say you?"

"General, when you ask me for an opinion, I will always tell you what I think to be the truth. I will give you my opinion even if I think you will disagree."

"Well, that certainly starts our conversation from a place of honesty. Tell me your story."

It took about thirty minutes for Philippe to finish. Most of Montcalm's questions regarded the Monongahela battle and its aftermath. *What had Philippe learned scouting the American wilderness? What about the reliability of the natives? What did he think the English would do? Where would did he think they would attack New France next?*

"They amassed troops under Sir William Johnson last year to attack Lac du Saint-Sacrament to capture Fort Saint Frédéric. The battle with General von Dieskau upset that plan. I've heard rumors they have amassed six thousand or more troops at the south shore of Lake George, which they now call it. Prisoners captured said new English commanders are arriving from England. They may or may not be here yet. But they plan again to attack up Lake George again this season. They may only be waiting for the new commanders to arrive."

"So do you think we should not attack Fort Oswego?"

"Attacking Fort Oswego may still be the right thing to do. It is the only English presence in our territory. If we destroy it, they will never be able to rebuild it. The loss of the Oswego forts will disrupt all their plans to move troops up Lake George. If you will permit, your inspection of Fort Saint Frédéric and Fort Carillon can be used to spread a false rumor among the natives; a rumor that claims we intend to attack the English fort built on the south shore of the lake this season. This might also stop all of their attack plans…and cause them to instead make defensive decisions."

Montcalm digested this opinion. When he spoke again, he changed the subject.

"As I travel through New France, the faces I see of the people have the look of starvation."

"Most of our farmers have been called up to the militia. The English have destroyed the Acadian farmlands in the east and exiled its people. So at least half of our crops have been lost…and possibly more. Montréal is the center of our grain supply. But if the farmers are used as militia, we cannot produce the harvest we need. The famine will only worsen."

"Governor Vaudreuil seems to be unaffected by this."

"I know that he cares about the loss of Louisbourg more than Acadia. He sent three companies of marines there in the spring to aid Governor Drucour. My son was among them."

Montcalm was surprised. "You have a son in the marines?"

"Yes, sir. Ensign Henri Gerrard. But I only learned this about him in the last week."

"How would you not know this?"

"That is a long story, General, and a personal one."

"Perhaps you can tell me at another time. Let me ask you this. Will the governor and I ever trust one another?"

"I do not know. I can tell you Governor Vaudreuil cares deeply about New France and winning this war against the English. So you both have that in common."

"That brings me to the most important question of all. Do you believe we can win?"

"If a peace is ever declared and New France still exists, then we have not lost. That is winning for us, I think. The English-Americans are the invaders. They want to conquer us. They have taken Acadia and are exiling all of its people. At war's end, we will not be getting it back."

"The English returned Louisbourg to France at the end of the last war."

"Not this time. They will siege Louisbourg again and keep it. The Americans did it before. They already know how to do it. We may declare a truce with the English. But the Americans will not observe it for long. They lay claim to this land. The fighting will begin again. I lived among them in Boston. I've heard the tone in their voices and the resolve in their words. They number over a million people. The Americans will never stop. They are pushing west."

"Should we defend Fort Duquesne?"

Philippe hesitated with his answer. "The English learned from their mistakes. Scouts claim they are building a new road straight west from Philadelphia. One that can carry heavy cannon. That will take well into next year, maybe even longer. But if they set up an artillery battery across the Monongahela River from Fort Duquesne, they will obliterate that fort without having troops attack directly. So at some point it will make better sense to save our garrison and withdraw…in my opinion, sir."

Montcalm had studied the land holdings of New France on the beautifully detailed, large maps hanging on the wall at Governor Vaudreuil's mansion. The territory was enormous when viewed this way. It was one thing to boast that France had territory in North America larger than Europe. But defending something this large required money and troop commitments fifty times beyond what France was capable. *Or England for that matter.* Montcalm was already envisioning new territorial boundaries he cautiously would not voice to anyone. *At some point, when we stop fighting, we must preserve the continuance of New France, even if our territory is smaller. Give the English what they want,* he thought. *Defend the lands north of the lakes and the Saint Lawrence River as the natural border in the north. Defend Montréal and Quebec City at all costs. Defend Lake Champlain. Accede to their claim of Lake George, as a concession if they demand it.*

"And Fort Niagara?"

Philippe frowned. "General, Fort Niagara is my home. I've lived there for ten years. I have watched Captain François Pouchot slowly refashion the original fort into a Vauban-style fortress."

Montcalm's brows lifted. "So you have studied Vauban?"

"I have read the marquis' book. Enough to know that neither Fort Niagara nor Fort Carillon will withstand a siege conducted using the method outlined in that book."

"So then? Fort Niagara?"

"If the English are determined and bring enough men and artillery… Fort Niagara is worth defending. It is the gateway to the west and all of our fur trade. We must bring troops to raise any siege started there."

Montcalm nodded. "All right, Captain, assume I agree with you. But if the English ever reach Fort Niagara with the men and siege artillery as you suggest, which is a place much farther to the west of Fort Oswego, this would suggest England will have logistical control of all the territory to the south by then."

Philippe did not reply. The answer was obvious.

Montcalm went further. "Other than Fort Duquesne, New France has no military presence in the lands south of Lake Champlain, or east of Fort

Duquesne. The governor argues our Indian allies hold these lands for us so long as we give them bribes. Do you agree with this?"

The moment of truth had arrived. Philippe took a breath, fortifying his resolve.

"General, with due respect, I hesitate to give you an answer opposed to what Governor Vaudreuil claims. And I expect he will one day ask me to tell him what *you* think. But to your question, encouraging the tribes to act with more barbarity against the Americans beyond their traditional inclinations is madness. I have seen this new level of barbarity with my own eyes. The Americans will *never* forgive this. If it were us, I do not think we would forgive it either."

"So, Captain, will you tell the governor you advised me thusly if you are asked?"

"General, I will claim we never discussed this. I will claim you do not seem to trust me."

Montcalm grinned. "Good. That is the same claim I shall make about you to my subordinates. But in private we can speak candidly, yes?"

Philippe nodded with great respect. "I would like that, General."

"Now, Captain…as in every war, you must realize that the English will not stop fighting until the cost in men becomes too dear and the cost in money nearly bankrupts them. France is much the same way. Therefore, how does France make this American war cost more in men and money for the English? And at a greater pace, so France does not sue for peace first?"

The question was unexpected. Philippe blinked. He had never thought about this.

"Perhaps…we should invade them?"

Before General Montcalm broke camp to leave Fort Saint Frédéric the next morning, a courier arrived with a missive from Governor Vaudreuil, asking General Montcalm to return to Montréal. The governor added that Captain Coulon de Villiers had been dispatched two months ago to harass the supply lines on the Onondaga River. A large clash had occurred. The English had suffered heavy losses and valuable intelligence was collected from the prisoners returned to Montréal.

*

Captain Louis Antoine de Bougainville, was General Montcalm's aide-de-camp. He was twenty-seven, highly educated, and had written and published two books on Integral Calculus. In England before the outbreak of the latest war, he had so impressed his English colleagues, he was elected a member of the British Royal Society. But he also desired a career in the military, was loyal to the French king, and thought serving in New France as Montcalm's aide-de-camp, when it was offered, might also allow him the opportunity to write a journal on the war.

Montcalm had left him as a liaison to the governor in Montréal, which Bougainville found unchallenging. It left his journal filled more with rumor than actual experience. But then Montcalm returned from Fort Carillon and gave the governor a summary on the conditions of the forts on Lake Champlain. Together, they further impressed upon Intendant Bigôt of the great need to supply more food and building supplies to General de Lévis.

In mid-June, he had a new entry for his journal:

> Today I leave with the Marquis de Montcalm bound for Niaouré Bay. I am excited that my boring days in Montréal have ended. I expect my journal entries will now overflow with new experiences and descriptions. And I have met a man named Captain Philippe Gerrard. He commands the marine company of coureurs de bois scouts. He is full of amazing stories and other information. I go to him constantly with my questions. We are becoming great friends.

CHAPTER 15
LOUISBOURG, ÎLE-ROYALE
JUNE 1756
Water Cities

Île-Royale and Île Saint-Jean were the last of the diminishing territorial lands still held by the French in the Gulf of Saint Lawrence now that all of Acadia had truly fallen to the English by the end of 1755. This left no doubt to the governments in Versailles and Quebec that Louisbourg on Île-Royale would be next, which would be disastrous.

The French had occupied this deep water port more or less for fifty years. It provided safe haven for the multi-cultural fishermen of the Grand Banks and the ships traveling to and from Europe to America or further south to the West Indies, regardless of their flags in times of peace. Louisbourg harbor was a convenient place to anchor for a visit before or after a crossing. It was a coveted strategic port in the Atlantic, though never considered as a location for retirement; it was too cold and too wet.

The island was roughly eighty miles wide, east to west, and a hundred and twenty miles long, northeast to southwest. Striated by large salt water lakes across its entire length on the northeast-southwest axis and hundreds of smaller fresh water lakes dotted the rest of the lands. Marshes and bogs were frequent. Farming was difficult. The lands surrounding Louisbourg itself were hilly and forested. The adjoining coastlines were rocky with cliffs and stony beaches. The weather was hardly ever good. If not cold and rainy, there was an abundance of fog. The heavy swells driven towards the island by far away storms in the North Atlantic arrived unpredictably. Large waves would appear without warning to crash against the rocky shore. This made military landings in longboats problematic and dangerous.

Despite this hazard, during the last war the American provincial troops from New England had taken Louisbourg in 1745, at the cost of hundreds of American lives. They suffered more deaths in subsequent years among the garrison men left holding the fortress to retain the harbor. Men were lost to disease, exposure, and starvation up until the war ended in 1748. Then, to the outraged surprise and bitter disappointment of the American colonies, the island and fortress was returned to the French with the signing of the Treaty of Aix-la-Chapelle in 1748. The English gave Louisbourg back to the French in trade for the enormous land territory of Madras in India, which the French had captured in 1746 during the war. Madras was considered the jeweled key possession of the England's East India Company.

The French navy, its fishermen, and citizens surged back into this treasured strategic possession of New France. Louisbourg's natural, deep water anchorage could accommodate only a small fleet, but a fleet large enough to protect the bay of Saint Lawrence and its river. It also threatened the American colonies. This time, the French made plans to refortify its possession with more troops and guns and rebuilt the battlements.

In 1748, peace returned, and with it, commerce. Ships from every seafaring nation in the world would visit Louisbourg to conduct trade in the safety of its harbor; the English and the Americans included. The island grew stronger than before the war of 1740. The local citizens relied on fishing. Neutral, commercial trading between foreign ships transpired cross-deck almost like a free port. Smuggling flourished. To protect Louisbourg from siege, another city and fort was established in a bay on Cape Dauphin of Île-Royale on the inland lakes. It was called Port Dauphin. This provided a place for troops to land and travel overland in case of a naval blockade on Louisbourg. In a similar manner, Port-Toulouse, a city and fort, was established on the southern shores of the island near the Strait of Canceau. Both of these ports were easily reached by boat over Bras d'Or, as the largest of the striated saltwater lakes was called.

Louisbourg itself was shaped like a large hand, the index finger and thumb were lands curved towards one another around the deep water harbor, leaving a defensible entrance. That channel was clogged half way with small rocky islands and a few tidal reefs. The spaces in between these random rocks and reefs was not navigable to the larger sailings ships with deep drafts, or so it was presumed. But the largest of the islands existed halfway across the entrance. From that point, the channel it guarded was deep and wide enough for ship passage. This island was fortified with stout heavy cannon, henceforth referred to as the island battery. Across the remaining channel from the battery, at the top of a hill, stood a lighthouse marking the harbor entrance. It was also fortified with cannon.

With French warships in the harbor, the English navy could not enter to attack the fortress. And Louisbourg was almost never without French warships at anchor.

The French knew that any siege would come from the south, on the landward side, miles south of Louisbourg at a variety of places in Gabarus Bay along a line of beaches running west for eight miles. The heavy swells and unpredictable waves of this rocky coastline would make these landings very difficult; not to forget the usual miserable weather. But all the invaders had to do was somehow get a foothold on shore. The rest was outlined in Marquis de Vauban's book on siege warfare.

Ten years earlier in 1745, American forces from New England at the behest of Governor William Shirley of Massachusetts, proved Louisbourg could indeed be captured, even by provincial "amateurs." The French vowed never to let that happen again.

*

It was Sunday. The only day of the week the French did not work the shoreline battlements of Gabarus Bay. On the elevated lands in an area of heavy forests west of the bay and south of the French fortress-port of Louisbourg, Ensign Henri Gerrard stepped carefully and silently through the trees, heading towards one of the isolated sandy beaches. He'd left his cavalry mount uphill, tied to a tree a quarter of a mile behind him. He'd been blazing scout and dispatch trails for Governor Drucour for use in case any of the main roads were seized by an English invasion. In a place on the upper lands, the trees at one spot thinned all the way to the shoreline. By chance, Henri spotted what looked like a small fishing boat, beached, turned upside down, and covered with leafy branches. If he'd not been looking right at it, he would not have seen it.

English scouts? They were expected.

He saw no sign of anyone moving about, but they could be anywhere. The Americans were usually expert woodsmen. Or this boat could be owned by their tribal allies. He'd left his horse tied to the tree and moved with stealth towards the shoreline. He also left his musket with the horse, prefer-ring to use his war bow. As he got closer, he would stop more often, stoop, watch, wait, and listen. Henri speculated about their scouting plans. That they would want to get closer to the fort, maybe to count the ships in the harbor, watch, and make note of any posted sentinels, any marching patrols, or new cannon batteries. Also to measure and inventory the extent of the new defensive battlements the French were building around Gabarus Bay, the site of the last invasion of Louisbourg. That invasion had been successful. So it was anticipated the English would make landings at the same place again when the time came. There were now dozens of new fortified positions. Henri's hands were blistered and bloody from all the digging, chopping, hammering, and shoveling he had undergone with all the other Louisbourg soldiers. Even the junior officers worked. And the work was never done. Every day, it seemed, someone would have a new idea to construct. That's why Henri volunteered to blaze these dispatch trails for the Governor. For no other reason but to allow his hands to mend.

No one works on Sunday. They must know that, he thought.

He stayed among the trees. When he reached the treeless area near the beach, he took out his small telescope. With disciplined movements, he scanned the shore. He searched everywhere, left and right, in front and in back of him but did not see anything unusual. Beside the camouflaged boat, there were drag marks in the sand behind the boat. They were short of the water, but the seas were out.

They landed at high tide, he decided. *That was six or seven hours ago. They have been at this scout for a while. I would certainly not want to stay here much longer than that. Too many chances of being seen.*

"By someone like me," Henri whispered softly to himself and smiled.

Henri decided to pick up their trail leading inland from the boat, but he did not want to go out in the open to find it. So he sidled left, moving along the tree line amid the trees, moving back towards the fort. At some point, when the enemy scouts entered the trees, they would leave a trail. And just as he thought this, he saw it. Moccasin prints in the sand of two men and boots from a third. Their trail led towards the fort as he suspected it would. Two men he might handle. But three?

Wait until they come back? No. I need to find them.

Henri followed the trail moving much faster now. He also needed to find a place for an ambush. He notched an arrow in his blackwood bow. That plus a pistol under his arm, the cutlass over his back, and the dirk and skinning knife on his waist made him formidable one on one. But three of them? Only the bow gave him distance. At medium range, it was better than the musket; at least he thought so. And faster.

He was looking for a narrowing in the path they'd chosen. He found it soon enough. The trail came dangerously close to a shallow cliff face above the rocks and waves below. A drop of about twenty feet. High enough to kill you if you fell. The trail was now two paces wide. The edge was softened and eroded by rain and gravely in spots. It could be used if you were careful to stay as far away from the edge as possible. The slope of the land rose steeply from here. The roots of some trees were exposed where the rain eroded the earth. In another spot, a tree had fallen over the cliff leaving a raw gaping hole in the dirt where it stood before.

Henri cautiously stomped his foot close to the edge. A foot-square clump of mud-softened earth fell away.

They've used this trail before, he thought. *Otherwise, why come this way for any other reason. It's too dangerous.*

But looking upslope, he knew. It could not be seen from a sentry trail that ran parallel to this one thirty paces further up the slope. Henri had walked that other trail dozens of times. Anyone using this one would be out of sight except to someone in a passing boat on the water. But fishing boats would not come this close to the rocks very often, if ever. They didn't have to.

This narrow section ended in another hundred paces and the walkers would be forced to step back up into the trees. Sure enough, he saw the foot marks of the scouts where they stepped up. His footprints were now visible on the trail and good scouts would spot them instantly. Henri was vulnerable, but he could not stop. He climbed up and watched for where the trail turned. And it did, going right back through the woods towards the fort, well short of the sentry trail.

This is the spot, he decided. He would just back off into the trees several steps and wait. Just as abruptly, he changed his mind. This was not what he would do if he were one of the three scouts. As this trail could not be seen, the scouts would also be blind to the sentry trail. If they were discovered and chased, they could get trapped.

They'll come by both trails.

Henri went further up until he found the sentry trail in another twenty paces. He stepped out and chanced a quick look up and down that trail. He did not see anyone. When he turned to go back towards the hidden trail, he spotted a notch cut in a tree at the head of the improvised path. It was a new cut. And it wasn't big. One would only see it if one were looking for it. Anyone who used the sentry trail would be moving fast. They'd reached this spot sooner, see the mark, and go down the slope. They would rendezvous with the others before they stepped out on the cliff again.

So someone will be concentrating to see the notch mark on that tree as they trot along the sentry trail, he thought.

Henri set his ambush position on the opposite side of the wider sentry trail, across from the notch-marked tree. He had cover from anyone coming up the trail by sitting at the side of a tree, but none from the other side. Of course, if no one came this way, he'd miss them all. But the sun would be setting before too long. And the tides would change. They would have to return and soon. He stayed alert and waited patiently.

It seemed an hour passed while he waited. To keep his mind busy, he came up with other plans but kept his eyes on the sentry trail for signs of movement.

Maybe I should run back to the fort and raise the guard? But I might run right into them. Get my horse? No, too much noise. If it gets close to dark...maybe run back down the sentry trail, then down to the beach and cut a hole in the bottom of the boat. Shit! I should have done that already! Maybe I should do that now...?

Henri heard a sudden clinking sound. It was a recognizable noise. Metal on metal. He'd heard something like this when he was captive at the Seneca village years ago. He'd been sitting in a forest, among the roots of a large tree, in the shadows, not moving when it occurred. Enemy warriors had been scouting the Seneca village before an attack. They walked right in front of him on the other side of a creek, only several steps away. He did not move a muscle. They were trying to be quiet. Not to make any noise. But they were too close to him for the sound to be missed.

Like now.

Without moving his head, Henri scanned his surroundings but did not see anyone on the trail. He remained frozen in the shadows of the trees, hoping the sound would happen again.

It did.

His eyes shifted instantly towards the source. Someone was lying near the notched tree on the ground directly on the other side of the trail. There was movement. He pulled on his bow. Arrows passed in flight across the trail simultaneously. Henri was hit. The arrowhead pierced the top of his left shoulder from the side, penetrated beneath his clavicle, and on through the flesh until the point was stopped by the bone near his neck. The pain was worse than anything he'd experienced before. He started to scream and brought the sleeve of his right arm to his mouth to stifle the yells. He struggled to his feet, pulled out his cutlass, and staggered towards the other man. His right leg was numb. He dragged it along behind him.

When he reached the shooter, he found the man still alive, thrashing around on the ground trying to draw another arrow. But his wound made it difficult. Henri's arrow entered through the man's mouth and part of it stuck out the back of the neck. He was a Malecite warrior.

Henri didn't hesitate, but his injury made him slash clumsily with the cutlass before cutting into the warrior's neck, finishing him. It would not be long before the others came running down the sentry trail. He retrieved his bow and stumbled down the sentry trail until he came to that spot where the trees thinned. He saw the boat.

You will not get away, he promised.

Grimacing, breathing heavily, using his bow as a hand cane, grunting with each step, with shockwaves of pain, he went down the hill and over to the boat. He used his cutlass to stab, cut, and twist several large holes down the length of the boat to make it unusable. He was feeling lightheaded. Blood dripped constantly from the wound on his shoulder.

Get to the horse.

Going back up the slope to where he'd left the cavalry mount tied to a tree was double the pain of going down. But he knew he would die if he did not get back to the fortress, and he could barely walk. The horse was the only way. That was if the enemy scouts didn't find and kill him first.

It was a hundred paces uphill. With the pain it seemed a mile. Reaching the horse, the simple task to climb up onto the saddle appeared impossible. His left arm had numbed and became useless. His right leg crippled. He didn't have the strength to pull himself up. So he turned the horse around and walked down the trail he'd recently blazed until he found a high spot on the adjoining slope.

"Steady boy! Steady!"

He looped the bow over his neck. That hurt too! Tying the reins around his right wrist, he prayed the animal would not bolt with fear or he would get dragged. He carefully stepped up the three-foot rise of land, gripping dirt, roots, branches, anything he could find, and when high enough, he swung his numb right leg like a heavy sack of rocks over the saddle.

The horse lurched sideways. Henri's face contorted with pain. He yelled and almost fainted. Tears streamed down his face. But he managed to hold onto the saddle.

"Easy boy! Whoa! Please! Whoa!"

The animal stopped at hearing Henri's voice.

"Good boy. Good boy." He patted the horse's neck.

Henri panted heavily. It was almost dark. He wiped the sweat and tears from his eyes and gently urged the horse to move down the blazed trail. The rocking motion made the arrow saw back and forth beneath his clavicle. It felt like his shoulder was being cut from his body. Henri ripped free a piece of his shirt and stuffed it into his mouth to muffle the groans of pain. Mucous shot out of his nose until none was left. He kept going and soon he saw one of the lamps of the fortress. He was terribly thirsty but could not think where he'd left the water skin. Fortunately, the horse was sure-footed and adjusted its step for the uneven trail.

Don't close your eyes. If you can see the lamp, you are still alive, he thought.

He squinted and focused on the lamp. The plodding seemed endless but he finally reached the bridge before the Dauphin gate at the fortress' west end. There was no moon. Thick clouds and a pitch-black night. He was challenged by the sentries to identify himself. Henri's body shivered with violence from the cold. He answered with loud gibberish, the sentries would later claim. The horse plodded forward without stopping. Once inside the gate, guards surrounded him with bayonets and took hold of the bridle.

Henri slid off the saddle and let go of the reins just as he passed out.

*

Boston

"I still do not think this is a good idea, Corrinne," Charles groused. "It's too public."

"But necessary. We've been here for ten days. The reporters are bribing our sentries just to knock at the front door. The speculation about us in the newspapers is becoming ridiculous. It's time for the VanderMeers to greet our many friends, who I want to influence to be our new city guard."

"We will be vulnerable."

"Perhaps. But no one expects us at Trinity Church today. And we have four marine guards and Color Sergeant Cheever with us.

"Are you certain you want to stand in one of those interminable receiving lines, like Rector Hooper does at the end of a service? There will be hundreds of people. And holding Marcus or Calypso? They will be squirming like eels."

"Eels! Don't describe them like that! They are my little angels!"

Two identical coaches came to the back portico of the VanderMeer residence. Lord VanderMeer, Anamosa, and Sentry Cheever, along with Thomas and Lydia Hancock would ride in the first. In the second, Lady VanderMeer, Mathilde, Molly, and the twins.

Trinity Church was still filling up with the usual Sunday congregation when the two conspicuous coaches stopped in the street before the stairs. When the people observed who stepped out, expressions of joyful surprise swelled from the small crowd along with a few shouts of approval and light applause. The rumors in the newspapers were now confirmed. Leading the procession was Color Sergeant Cheever. Lord and Lady VanderMeer came next. Corrinne carried Marcus, whose head swiveled in every direction smiling and waving at all the new faces. Charles carried Calypso who smiled and waved her fingers with a more gentle vigor. To either side of the VanderMeers, a marine guard politely held back the crowd of well-wishers. Mathilde and Anamosa were arm in arm with the other two marines. Anamosa was dressed in a beautiful blue dress, her long black hair braided up in a bun, adorned with small white flowers and ribbons. She glanced up and smiled frequently at the red-coated officer who had taken her arm so formally. He glanced down and smiled at her too.

There was a pew reserved for them in the front row on the right.

As soon as the VanderMeers were seated, the rest of the seats in the church filled in quickly. The Sunday service proceeded as usual. The rector, William Hooper, stood in his elevated pulpit. He would lead the congregation in a service beginning with prayers, next a sermon, and a culminating summary in a special prayer. At some point in the service, at the discretion of the rector, the congregation would rise to their feet to chant and on special occasions to sing a specified psalm or canticle. This was a new practice adopted to strengthen the feeling of unity and fellowship among the congregation. It was becoming a favorite part of the service. The rector was thinking of expanding it to offer more song.

When the middle of the service was reached, the time came time for the rector to give his Sunday sermon. Seeing the smiling faces of his flock, William Hooper acknowledged the presence of their famous church members and then talked soberly of the declared war between England and France. He lamented the extensive loss of life anticipated for both countries.

"Many of our family, friends, and fellow Americans have lost their lives in battles, even before this war was declared. Those of you present when the last war began in 1740 experienced heartbreak at the loss of so many loved ones. Regretfully, this one portends to be much worse. More tragic news is certain to come to Boston before this conflict will be over. The armies are assembling, fleets are sailing to confront one another. I fear our colony, Connecticut, New York, Pennsylvania, New Jersey, New Hampshire, Rhode Island, and Vermont will suffer the brunt of the fighting. But on this beautiful Sunday morning, the guns are silent. So as we still embrace this blessed peace, today we celebrate the happy homecoming of Lady VanderMeer. I have granted a special request by Lady Corrinne VanderMeer who asked that she be allowed to address the congregation today. Lady VanderMeer," the minister invited. He gestured down at a step below the pulpit at the front of the main aisle.

"What?" Charles muttered as Corrinne stood and stepped around him into the aisle. She'd not told him about this.

Anamosa gently took hold of Marcus to restrain the urge to follow his mother. She was the only other person he would obey without complaint. They rubbed noses.

Corrinne saw a blue piece of carpet set atop the first step, placed there intentionally for her to stand upon and would prevent slipping. The step would also elevate her enough to be seen at the back of the church.

"Mama!" Marcus shouted loudly.

The congregation laughed.

"Yes, Marcus. Mama is right here." She smiled. "Marcus just learned that new word last week. As is the nature of most men, Marcus already enjoys that I come running every time he calls."

They laughed again.

Corrinne looked over the audience and was surprised at just how many faces she recognized. Not all by name, of course, but they were still people she had greeted politely in their stores, or in passing during walks around Boston's streets. She knew these people, their smiles, some of them now gently waving a hand, others with their hands clasped beneath their chins, their eyes wide open and luminous. To see so many people overjoyed at seeing her again had an unexpected and powerful effect.

Corrinne's eyes filled and tears slipped down her cheeks. This was not part of her plan. She wiped the tears from her eyes and took a deep breath.

"My goodness. You are such wonderful people," she began in a voice hushed by her strong emotion. "I am overwhelmed by the expressions of friendship and affection I see in your faces. I am so blessed to be back among you."

"God bless you, Lady VanderMeer," a female voice called out from somewhere among the congregation. This was followed by a multitude of *Amens*.

Corrinne wiped her eyes again and took another deep breath.

"My children and I have been in Boston for ten days now, as many of you are aware. We came back to the city by another way, hoping to draw as little attention to us as possible. I've remained reclusive for good reason. Forgive me again, it is not possible to see all of you individually. So I asked Rector Hooper for this indulgence. The attack on us last fall was completely unexpected, vicious in its intent, and traumatic in its outcome."

Corrinne paused and unbuttoned the high collar of her dress to permit the scarlet ten-inch scar on her neck to be seen. Gasps rose from the congregation. Corrinne waited a moment and then buttoned up the collar again.

"I do not mean to be so dramatic, but I thought you should see this scar to understand why I fled the city so quickly. This wound was meant to be fatal. And it should have been. These killers stabbed my dear, dear maidservant, Mathilde, sitting just there holding Calypso. She was stabbed in the chest with a rapier. She only lived because of the doctors of Boston and God's grace. Lord VanderMeer, too, was injured and lay unconscious for days afterwards. But God brought him back to me as well. The assassins killed all the guards we had posted outside, invaded our home, and intended to kill us all. To kill Anamosa and my baby children as they slept in their beds! Only by God's grace did we survive." She paused a few seconds, bowed her head, and crossed herself. "We were saved by the grace of God, and the courage of our city magistrate, Jack Tasker, who was seriously wounded defending us. Saved by the grace of God and the astonishing bravery of Color Sergeant Sentry Cheever, who by mere happenstance, was a guest in our household that evening." She paused to point, acknowledge, and smile at him. "Bolstered by the grace of God, those two brave men, outnumbered by professional assassins, defended us. They are the reason why my family is alive today. And only by the grace of God it was a miracle our wounds were not fatal. Yet even after the assassins were defeated, the threat still existed. We learned there were more of them in the city. So Lord VanderMeer arranged for me and the children to leave Boston, though our wounds were barely healed. He decided to stay, hoping to constrain their enmity to him alone.

"I want to thank so many of you who sent us flowers, letters, and missives full of extraordinary words of love and blessing. In my life, I confess, I have never seen such an outpouring by so many people before. Among these words of sympathy, some said that an attack on one of us is an attack on all of us. Such powerful, courageous words from people who barely knew me. People of Boston who hail from every walk of life, yet here in Boston, in this special place created by you and your forebears, here people speak with the same voice. I am *humbled* to be so fortunate to live among you. I can never thank you enough for the kindness you showed when I was bedridden, my husband in a coma, feeling despondent and alone and praying to God for his protection. And He sent all your letters to me. Truly something wonderful happens here. Your unity of spirit and congregation one day will be the envy of the world."

Hearing Lady VanderMeer's heartfelt words, many in the audience were equally moved. Corrinne swallowed hard and spoke with resolve.

"A few months ago, I was advised that hiding, no matter where, would pose an even greater danger to my children, more so now that war has been declared. Such is the malice that continues to thrive among the old cultures and hatreds across the ocean. I concluded that if we must defend ourselves, I would rather be in Boston, a place that had become my *home*...even before I left it. So I've come home again to Boston. And come what may, I hope to stay in Boston. But I felt compelled to warn you the threat to my family will certainly follow us. And I worry our presence may endanger you as well. I wish it were not so, but in good conscience I thought I should tell you."

"*Mama!*"

Gentle laughter followed Marcus' outburst.

"Yes, Marcus. I hear you. But most of all, I wanted to thank the people of Trinity Church. Charles and I are honored you have accepted us into your congregation and into your hearts. We will be forever grateful. Thank you."

The congregation was silent, broken only by sniffling. Charles suspected there would have been applause if it were not considered indecorous.

Corrinne took careful steps back to her seat. Marcus crawled out of Anamosa's arms into Corrinne's. A tearful Lydia Hancock reached forward with a hand and touched Corrinne's shoulder.

The rector stepped to the front of his elevated pulpit.

"May God's blessings be upon Lord and Lady VanderMeer and their family. And I speak for the congregation that we are equally honored by your gracious words and very pleased you sit among us. And in that spirit," he spoke in a lighter voice to the greater audience, "I think this calls for a special psalm. Let us rise to our feet and sing Psalm twenty-seven."

The Lord is My Light and My Salvation...

Leaving the church pew and walking to the coaches would take almost half an hour as the people gently pressed to either side to wish them well. As many that touched Corrinne, she touched them back, kissing the cheeks of a few, caressing the heads of any children who approached. After a few minutes, Marcus found all this unwanted attention bewildering. He rested his head on Corrinne's shoulder next to her neck and regarded all the strange faces cautiously. Calypso remained attentive in Charles' arms but returned only those certain smiles she found appealing. Even Anamosa was touched and appreciated, many women telling her how beautiful she looked. Sentry Cheever, too, received back pats and nods from the men.

The VanderMeers were glad when the coaches eventually pulled up to the back of the house.

During the ride, Marcus had fallen asleep in Corrinne's arms. She carried him straight up the stairs, undressed him, and placed him in bed, smoothing back a few stray curls on his head. Charles carried in Calypso right behind them. She was still awake but yawning. Corrinne slipped off Calypso's shoes and dress before lying her beside Marcus. The little girl reached out to touch her brother's face and closed her eyes.

Corrinne returned downstairs and gave each of the marine guards a silver ounce of gratuity in appreciation of their services. This was beyond their pay, but she knew with a large silver coin and a light kiss to their cheeks, each of these men would gladly give their life to protect her.

Before Sentry left, she took his hands in hers and gazed up into his eyes. "They were there."

Sentry frowned. "Who was there?"

"The assassins."

He was aghast. "You mean in the church?"

"No. Somewhere among the crowds outside." Corrinne's brow furrowed. "Somehow, I can sense their eyes upon me even now. I'm not sure why. Probably because of the nightmares I had in Saybrook. I could feel a presence in Winter House. They were there as we left. But I think the city will help to keep watch for them too."

"If you mean the man at Winter House," Sentry said, "I've nah' seen him anywhere. And I look for him every day."

"Even so, there was more than one. And we will not know the faces of the others until they strike. That is the problem."

*

Carter Trevathan had learned long ago the benefit of frequenting those places where newspaper reporters liked to meet at night and gossip. Buy them a few drinks and they would tell you anything you wanted to know and more, such as the VanderMeers' intention to attend Trinity Church on Sunday. "The rector, William Hooper, was bragging about it to everyone."

Standing on separate corners, their presence hidden amid the crowds of onlookers across the street from the church's main doors, Carter Trevathan and Ritter Monheit had watched the VanderMeers leave Trinity Church.

At an appointed time, they rendezvoused at that same tavern frequented by the newsmen down near the waterfront by the port's administration offices. Ships were the best news source from abroad. Even on a Sunday evening, where only certain people were admitted through doors that were supposedly closed for business, money supplied to an outstretched hand made the difference. It was busy inside and it was noisy. Sitting at a table

in the corner, they sipped beer while Ritter went over the identity of each
of the people seen in the VanderMeer party leaving the church.

"And the big, red-coated sergeant?"

Ritter nodded. "Color Sergeant Cheever. I have to stay clear of that man.
He knows my face on sight, I think. And he is dangerous. He will kill you
in an instant if he perceives you as a threat to the VanderMeers."

Carter looked at the list of names he'd made for Colonel von Kleinfels.
They expected him to arrive back in the city the next day.

"All right. The colonel wants to do this slowly. I'll go over the list with
the Bristol sisters."

"That still does not get us inside the house." Ritter pointed out.

"If we do this right, there will be no one inside the house left alive to
stop us when the time comes."

*

North of Boston

The female eagle dropped straight to the ground when the *ghost* first
surged to dominance. Fortunately, they were only a few meters in the air.
She was not injured, but she screeched, hopping around, making wild, frantic
movements, as if trying to throw off something that landed on her back. The
ghost carefully took control of her wings. She fell forward on her belly still
screeching in terror. As her head twisted back and forth, in the wild swings
of her vision the *ghost* saw predators appear. Two coyotes were loping over
the boulders of the valley moving towards the white eagle's dead body.

The *ghost's* reaction was intense. *They are not going to desecrate him!*
It pressed its will upon the female. The screeching stopped. The raptor stood
and turned. The coyotes were almost upon the white eagle's body. It made
one heavy flap of the wings and a bounding leap. The female flew at the
coyotes, screeching, her deadly talons extended.

The animals retreated immediately, though not very far. They sat on
their haunches and waited.

It took more concentration than usual. The *ghost* eventually managed
to dominate the female, enough to take hold and lift the white eagle's body
from the valley floor. It started flying towards the south. The white eagle
was half the weight of the female. The bird labored to maintain flight and
still hold onto the body. The *ghost* spotted a rock ledge on a hill and headed
to it. It set down the white eagle first and then landed several paces away.

The *ghost* sat there for a long time, easing its dominance a little at a time, allowing more of the female's consciousness to surface, but staying watchful lest her panic get out of control. When her terror subsided, it eased its dominance further. It would surge, then ease, again and again. From its human memory arose the image of riding an unbroken horse for the first time when the shaman stayed among the tribes in the grassy lands. He had been a young shaman at the time. And it seemed to the *ghost* that horses were much more predictable in temperament than eagles.

It would take the rest of the day to gain enough discipline to get the female to fly off with the white eagle held again in its talons. Again they flew straight south, crossing the lower hills and a few valleys until the heavy burden became too great. They landed high in the branches of a hardwood tree. The white eagle lay draped across two thick boughs near the trunk. They flew again and the *ghost* marked the location of the tree. He allowed the female's hunger to take control. She flew directly to the nearest river, glided down the center with the current, and caught a large fish in the shallows near the bank with the first strike. The *ghost* forced the raptor to return to the same tree before it consumed its meal, which took only a few minutes. Then, without much coaxing, the female perched close to the trunk and rested.

The *ghost* was in a quandary. Certainly the youthful vigor of this female showed no sign of weakness. The *ghost* must improve its ability to surge in dominance with less aggressiveness. But the willfulness of this female was so strong it was difficult to dominate with anything less. The instinctive impulses driving the female eagle's actions seemed to change *constantly…* unlike the other raptor. And what should be done with the body of the white eagle? The idea of it being eaten by scavengers, as natural as that was, seemed too disrespectful an end for such a valiant creature. It had shared its existence with the shaman for many, many seasons.

It should be honored before it is buried, the *ghost* thought. *But how can this be done?*

The *ghost* realized it had avoided an eternity in the black abyss by only a few moments. A few moments' difference and it would now be trapped in the dead body of the white eagle. It avoided this end only because it joined in coupling with the female. The *ghost* never intended to dominate this new being. But the talons locked and the *ghost* was physically drawn into this marvelous creature. Overwhelmed by the glorious sensation that followed, the female's eagle spirit was too compelling. The *ghost* had been immersed in her wonder, like a raindrop in a waterfall.

All because the white eagle had suddenly turned to intercept her.

And she was white feathered too. A rare coloring for its kind. The white eagle had crossed paths with not just another, rare, white-feathered eagle, but a female as well. Their joining had been extraordinary. Two rare creatures meet by chance and mate amid the infinite sky they occupied. When such occurrences had happened in the *ghost*'s human life, it was never a coincidence.

Neither was this! So why? What does this portend?

The *ghost*'s concentration deepened. The answer revealed so suddenly seemed too simple. The *ghost* knew how to defeat the demon.

CHAPTER 16
LA ROCHELLE, FRANCE
JUNE 1756
"What scares you, Captain LaTour?"

Warships of the English navy were patrolling the English Channel and the seas northwest of Brest, seeking engagements or prizes. Several hailed Captain LaTour's ship, challenging his flag. However, between the captain and Victorio using speaking trumpets, they satisfied the suspicious questions of the English. They were just another Dutch trading ship heading south towards the horn of Africa. But an English privateer with a *lettre de marque* challenged, grappled, and tied alongside. They made an armed boarding. When they found the holds empty of any cargo, they left disappointed.

"This will happen again, and we may not be so lucky next time. Even if we pass France unscathed, the pirates along the coasts of Spain and Portugal loom ahead of us. Dutch flag or not, we need to get into a port," LaTour announced. "And stay there awhile."

They passed Port Louis at Lorient next. LaTour had been there before. It was too prison-like for his smuggling roots, an impregnable fortress-citadel guarding the Baie de Locmalo and other surrounding waters, which were bristling with French warships. He continued further south down the coast. The port city of La Rochelle was at the center of France's western coast. The waters outside the port of La Rochelle seemed hardly patrolled at all. He took a chance on this harbor, though the French navy might seize him just as impulsively as the English. And there were French warships at the naval base just hours away in the harbor at Rochefort further south.

But once inside the defensive walls of La Rochelle's harbor, LaTour became more at ease. He quickly made arrangements at the local yard for his ship to be hauled up out of the water on a shipway, impulsively deciding to have the hull cleaned and resealed. It gave him a commercial reason to be in the port. As soon as he was up on the shipway, *William's Queen* was visited by the harbor master who made a perfunctory belowdecks inspection. The naval officer took down information about Captain LaTour, the registry of the ship, and his intended business in La Rochelle. But to LaTour's surprise, the harbor master simply wished him good day and little else occurred. On the first day the *Queen* was out of the water, Captain LaTour also sent a missive by a paid courier to Jean-Baptiste de Machault in Paris explaining his current situation, what had happened in Amsterdam, and his future sailing intentions, petitioning his advice. That done, he focused his attention on repairing the ship.

The next morning, the real work began on the hull. Amid the sounds of hammers and chisels, LaTour spoke to his crew, who were anxious to go ashore.

"The *Queen* will put to sea again by the twentieth of July," LaTour told the crew. "That gives you a month to go home and visit your families and return. I think you will agree your share of profits from this sail have been rich. I expect our next sail to be the same. So do not be late coming back. As I have said many times before, I cannot guarantee I will wait for you. And any of you who come back early can assist in the repairs at double the normal wage."

All the crew but four men took their full shares and found the means to travel back home, wherever that was. The four crewmen who stayed behind earning double wages helped to oversee the repairs by the yard laborers. He paid for all their rooms in the city and Victorio helped establish the daily routine.

The hull of the *Queen* was foul with barnacle growth, more than LaTour expected, due to the extended stay in the sweaty warm waters of Sint Eustatius. But after two weeks in La Rochelle's navy yards, the hull emerged clean, caulked, seasoned, and sealed against worms. It looked almost new again. He was so satisfied he decided to extend the repair contract with the yard to include a long list of other work on the main and interior decks as well. This included an astringent purification and caulking of the bilges.

"And three new bilge pumps of improved quality! They have double the dewatering capacity!"

"That's a lot of money," Victorio remarked when seeing the tally figures from the shipwrights.

LaTour shrugged. "Might as well make the *Queen* as fit for sea as possible," he replied in a voice well-pleased with his decision. "My lady Queen deserves this care. And I'm not sure when the opportunity will come again. Besides, we have the money for it. The payment for this comes out of the owner's share." He grinned at his cleverness.

As shipwrights worked on the starboard hull, a naval courier approached the captain.

The French naval officer, an ensign, saluted Captain LaTour.

"My compliments to you, Captain. I bring you dispatches. One of them needs your official reply. I await the answer at your pleasure."

The officer stepped away to give the captain some privacy.

And I will have your answer now! LaTour guessed at the unspoken words.

Victorio looked over LaTour's shoulder.

"Two missives from Financier Machault. We'll look at those later." He broke the wax seal on the envelope titled from the Ministère de la Marine and read the single page aloud to Victorio. "'To the captain of *William's Queen*. You are ordered to appear before Admiral Dubois de la Motte at the Admiralty Court in Rochefort on June...'" He was incredulous. "Tomorrow morning, Victorio! That's all it says. It doesn't say why or for what purpose. That doesn't bode well."

"It doesn't necessarily bode ill either. I mean if we were in trouble, the marines would already be here, yes?"

"The naval anchorage at Rochefort is twenty miles south of La Rochelle. I will need to leave right away in order to appear by tomorrow morning."

"Should I go with you?"

"No," he answered quietly. "You should stay here and make certain no one gets into the keel chests." LaTour waved over the naval ensign and addressed him. "I will report to Admiral de la Motte as requested. Can you offer me transportation?"

"Yes, Captain. If you wish, you can travel in my carriage to Rochefort."

"And accommodations in Rocheport?"

"Yes, Captain. There are officer quarters already reserved for you."

LaTour made as if impressed and looked at Victorio.

"Officer quarters! If they have assigned me quarters, I should stay for as long as possible."

"I will make certain the repairs continue as planned. Two of us will live aboard ship until you return."

Captain LaTour told the ensign the name of his La Rochelle hotel, and that he would clean himself for travel and meet him there. The ensign went back over the brow to the wall surrounding the shipway.

"You'll have to wait to hear what Financier Machault has to say until I get back."

Victorio's expression suddenly turned perplexed. "Why would missives from Financier Machault be delivered by a naval courier from Rochefort?"

"You're right! I don't know." Captain LaTour was equally bewildered.

"Do you know this Admiral de la Motte?"

"Only by reputation. He is old French navy. Won most of his battles. Very tough. But if I am to be arrested, or the ship seized, it would have already happened, as you surmised. No need to show me any courtesies. And they are giving me officer quarters in Rochefort? That is respectful! Even a compliment, yes? And we are still a Dutch ship."

Too complimentary. Victorio did not like it. "What could they want with you or the *Queen*?"

"Well, France is at war. It must have to do with that."

Victorio nodded and spoke somberly. "France is at war. And we are in a French port."

"Well, that's obvious!" LaTour's frown deepened. "I am trying to find some good fortune in this summons. You do understand as my second-in-command all your replies are supposed to remain *optimistic*…when you are not busy praising my brilliance as your captain."

"Captain, I simply meant to imply we are protected from the English navy, at least, while we are in this port."

"But not from the French navy." LaTour mulled Victorio's unspoken words.

Victorio noticed the captain's sad frown and remembered his captain had a penchant for black humor.

"Take heart, Captain. In fact, they have probably forgotten our smuggling reputation by now."

"God's balls, Victorio!" LaTour rubbed his neck. "Don't remind me of that. That's not funny!"

The ensign had little to say to Captain LaTour during the ride to Rochefort, except to drone on about his wine-soaked upbringing in the vineyards of Bordeaux. LaTour asked about the admiral. The ensign praised Admiral de la Motte as one of France's greatest warriors. Otherwise, the ride proceeded in silence, while LaTour pondered the significance of a mounted escort of two marines.

An escort of honor, he imagined Victorio saying. But he didn't think so.

A few miles short of the Rochefort city walls, the carriage turned to the right, taking a road heading west towards the river.

"We are not going into the city?"

"No, Captain. We are going to Fort de la Pointe. The admiral moved his headquarters to this citadel at the mouth of Le Charente River when war with England was declared. He spends most of his time there. You will see the warships at anchor."

It was still light outside when the carriage pulled into the fort. It stopped in front of a stone barracks purposely built beneath the reinforced stone battlements, according to the ensign.

"This one contains the officer quarters."

Captain LaTour stepped off the coach and looked around the fort interior. It could be used as a prison in his estimation. The thick stone walls were twenty feet tall and well-guarded. There were at least thirty visible cannon emplacements, eighteen and twenty-four pounders, all pointing seaward. When he saw the permanent gallows in one corner of the marshalling yard, he swallowed hard.

French sailors collected LaTour's few bags and went through the iron doorway of the stone barracks.

"Just follow them, Captain, if you please." The ensign gestured. "You will find your room somewhat Spartan but comfortable. A meal will be brought to your room in an hour. You will be eating alone. There will be a knock on your door in the morning at sunrise to awaken you. An hour after that, you will break your fast with the admiral's aide, Captain Trémoille. The Admiralty Court will sit at ten. Everything will be explained to you then. Before you ask, I have no knowledge of what is to be discussed. I apologize for any distress this causes you, sir. But it could just be a formality about your arrival at La Rochelle. Any questions?"

The first sympathetic words he has spoken to me, LaTour thought.

"No questions, Ensign. Thank you for your escort. I trust you will also accompany me back to my ship in La Rochelle?"

The ensign smiled pleasantly. "I hope that is so, Captain LaTour." Then he saluted and gestured at the doorway.

The room was a ten-by-ten-foot square. Adequate. LaTour found his bags waiting atop a bed in the room, which was no bigger than his personal bunk aboard ship. The bedding was clean. A chamber pot in the corner. A wash basin. Soap and towels. Two lamps instead of one. *A good sign,* he told himself. One lamp was on the table. The copper lamp on the wall had collected the green patina of verdigris. There was also a small mirror on the wall so the officer-occupant could inspect his uniform appearance. No windows. A table large enough for a dinner tray, and an arm chair. The room was cool but dank. The air was still and not fresh, but did not smell rancid. He saw a hook on the door for hanging clothes. He carefully tried the door and found it unlocked. He looked up and down the passageway and saw only the ends and the wall at the crossing passageways fifty feet either way. No sign of any guards. *Also good.*

LaTour settled into the wooden arm chair and withdrew Financier Machault's two missives from his jacket pocket. He turned up the wick on the lamp. One missive was addressed to him. The other to Lady VanderMeer. He broke the wax seal on the one addressed to him.

> *My dear friend, Captain LaTour,*
> *Please forgive this surprise upon receipt of my missive. I received your letter and read with great concern the circumstances related to the deaths of the crewmen and your experience with Wittmann Bootz in Amsterdam. I assure you this behavior is so out of character for this polite gentleman, I will investigate his rudeness immediately. But I agree there is no reason for your return to Amsterdam until I can arrange more agreeable agency for Lady VanderMeer.*
> *It was fortuitous that you selected La Rochelle to conduct repairs on your ship. This permitted me to intercede on your behalf with Admiral Dubois de la Motte in Rochefort who is an old friend of mine. Be certain you would have been boarded by the French navy and your ship seized regardless of its Dutch registry. The English have already*

seized hundreds of French fishing and trade ships. Our country is in desperate need of such vessels. I have informed the admiral of your exemplary seamanship and other "skills" and suggested he use such skills in the interest of France as opposed to removing you from command for a French naval officer.

"Remove me from command!" His heart was pounding in his chest. He felt nauseous. This was a horror! Worse than he thought it would be.

> *I do not know what the admiral intends to tell you when you meet with him. But I have contacts at the admiralty who will keep me informed of the proceedings and the results. Be assured I will come personally to your aid if anything untoward happens to you. But I do not expect that type of outcome. Please remember France is at war, and your allegiance must be with France and the King above all else. It would serve you well to represent this to the admiral at the appropriate time. You will never meet a man more dedicated to the King and France than Admiral Dubois de la Motte.*
>
> *I am not familiar with the procedures of an Admiralty Court to give you advice other than be cooperative and be truthful about your past. It is likely the admiral knows more about you than you realize. And he values honor and integrity in a man above all else.*
>
> *Do not open the missive to Lady VanderMeer. I give it to you early in case you are unexpectedly dispatched by the admiral to perform some other service. No matter what comes in the future, you must find a way to deliver this missive to Lady VanderMeer by your own hand.*
>
> *Yet now, as I read back over my words, I have decided to make arrangements to travel to see you in La Rochelle without delay. Until then, I expect fate to smile favorably on you.*
>
> *I welcome you home, Captain.*
> *And I remain your humble friend and servant,*
> *Jean-Baptiste de Machault d'Arnouville*

That evening, Captain LaTour hardly touched his food or got any sleep in his cell-like room. It was so quiet he could hear the blood pulsing through his head. Twice, he got up and dressed to make a nervous escape. The second time he even went down to the iron doorway and opened it with a creak to look out into the empty marshalling grounds of the fort. The night sky was full of stars. He could not perceive any activity anywhere in the fort, almost as if it were deserted, except he knew otherwise. The outer gate was not open. He would have to go over the wall.

And then where would you go, Beauregard?

He returned to the room and lay back down in the bed, lying awake, speculating what might happen the next morning. In spite of his fear, he finally did fall asleep. The next thing he knew there was a sudden knock on his door. He lurched awake. It was black. The wall lamp had gone out. He got up and staggered around the small room with his hands extended, feeling down the wall until he found the door and opened it.

A marine corporal carrying a lantern saluted. "Good morning, Captain. It is sunrise, sir."

"Uh...*merci*. Can you light my lamp?"

The marine lit the table lamp and left. The one on the wall was out of oil. He filled the wash basin and began to clean himself. He wanted to shave but had forgotten to bring his razor. He rinsed out his mouth several times and had remembered to bring some cloves, which he chewed. He hung his uniform-like jacket and pants on the door hook and picked away any stray threads and lint before donning them again. He took out the extra clean shirt he'd brought with him. He smoothed the feather in the hat he wore, wondered if he should remove it altogether, then decided he didn't care. He liked the plume. It signified who he was.

When he stepped out into the passageway he was surprised to find the marine corporal waiting patiently for him several paces down the hall.

"This way, Captain."

He followed the man to another building that emitted the aromas of hot food. There were several simple tables. At one of them, two officers were quietly breaking their fast. The marine pointed at another table on the far side of the room where a single officer waited sipping a mug of tea.

"That is Captain Trémoille." The marine pointed.

LaTour approached the table and took off his hat. The naval officer stood and smiled in greeting.

"Captain LaTour?" They shook hands. "I am Captain Pierre Trémoille, aide to Admiral de la Motte. A pleasure to meet a man of your reputation."

LaTour swallowed hard again, but remembered to return the smile. "*Bonjour*, Captain. Um, my reputation?"

"*Oui, oui*. Please sit."

The officer waved at a steward who brought over two plates full of omelets, cheeses, vegetables, biscuits with butter, and more tea.

"You have a reputation of being a very competent seaman, who is not above doing dangerous work. By that I mean smuggling."

LaTour swallowed a mouthful of omelet quickly. "Is that why I am here?"

The officer nodded in agreement. "Yes…but that is not the only reason. The admiral is aware that your ship is undergoing repairs in La Rochelle. He is also aware you fly a Dutch flag. And that you entered the harbor without invitation by France."

LaTour explained quickly. "An English privateer boarded me northwest of Brest. Since war was declared, I presumed there would be other pirates prowling the seas all the way down the coast, even off Spain and Portugal. I hope to stay in port a few months until the pirate frenzy has lessened. Brest and Port Saint Louis were…busy with warships. And I needed maintenance performed on my ship. La Rochelle has commercial yards. And I carry the correct papers for my ship. It is owned by a Dutch trading company. I've brought them with me."

LaTour noticed the French officer continued to feed himself with good appetite as if this discourse was something he heard every day.

"But you are French, yes? So is your crew, I presume?"

"Yes, we are all French. But the ship is owned by VanderMeer Trading Insurance Company. They purchased my ship in Quebec in 1754. Governor Duquesne of New France witnessed and approved the sale. Since then I have made two crossings full of commodities, mostly from the Antilles, and delivered them to Amsterdam. I just came from there."

"To where are you bound?"

LaTour had not expected this question. "I assume back to the Antilles, but I am waiting for my sailing orders from the company."

"How do they know you are in La Rochelle? You came to this port by accident, *non*?"

"What you say is true, Captain. As soon as I arrived, I sent a missive by courier to my agent in the company and asked for my sailing orders."

That was not exactly true, but LaTour was now boxed in by his own words.

Captain Trémoille regarded him quizzically. "And who would that be?"

"The agent?"

The officer nodded.

LaTour exhaled with quiet resignation. He had no choice but to tell him the truth.

"Financier Jean-Baptiste de Machault d'Arnouville."

The officer stopped eating. "Financier Machault?" he asked skeptically. "The former Controller General of the French government? The current Naval Minister? This man is your *agent*?"

"Naval Minister?" Captain LaTour was stunned by the revelation of Machault's new importance. This officer was astute at seizing on ambiguities. He must be careful and tell the truth as he knew it to be.

"Yes, Captain. I knew Financier Machault as a man of finance. I am completely unaware of his other titles. He consults to the owner of Vander-Meer Trading. I was supposed to contact him when I came back to France."

"But you went to Amsterdam?"

"Yes, to unload my cargo. Which I did. But most of my crew comes from Le Havre or places close to it. I was going to stop in that port for several weeks to allow my crew time to see their families and await my new sailing instructions there. But then I worried my ship might be seized because of the war."

Captain Trémoille looked away from the table in thought.

Suddenly unsure when he would ever get another meal, LaTour used the pause to push more biscuits into his mouth. He swallowed the food and washed it down with tea.

"Captain Trémoille, *s'il vous plaît*. I am greatly concerned about the reason for my appearance here today. More so now from the questions you've asked. Can you tell me why I have been ordered to appear?"

"Of course. France is at war. We have need of ships." The officer's tone was pragmatic. "You are a French captain of a ship flying a Dutch flag and have just sailed into a French harbor in a time of war. That by itself would permit France, by law, to seize your ship. But you carry no cargo and do not appear to be involved in any smuggling. Which official records in Le Havre clearly document is often your business. And there was this instance of leaving Le Havre while under cannon fire, transporting a man wanted for murder and high treason?"

"I do not deny being fired upon. But I was not aware I was harboring a man wanted for high treason."

Captain Trémoille waved this away. "You could have returned to port, yes?"

"Captain, no disrespect, but once the harbor cannons start firing at a ship, they usually do not stop until they sink it. It does not happen that often thus the cannoneers enjoy it too much to do otherwise. It is better to sail away and hope they have forgotten about it after you've been gone a year or more."

"And if they do not forget?"

"Well, the port of Le Havre has never challenged me about the… incident…up until now. Most of my crew have family in that port. I am considered a…*citizen*…of Le Havre, if you will."

"And sometimes silver or gold trade hands, yes?"

"I have heard it said such is the cost of doing business. That is the truth, Captain. I swear it."

"Oh, strange as it might seem, Captain, I believe you. I am just trying to decide how much of what you told me should I validate to Admiral de la Motte. You see, this is the purpose of my meeting with you this morning. To ask you these questions, so the Admiralty Court does not have to waste time doing this."

LaTour's nerves were reaching a breaking point. "So what is to happen to me today?"

"Well, you are not being charged with anything…*yet*. But it is important you tell the truth today. I will report to Admiral de la Motte my personal discussions with you. He is aware of your present circumstance. You will stand in front of the Admiralty Court when called and answer their questions. It would be good to remember that you can say *too much*. If you say too much, it tends to sound invented, yes? I will be there and I know the truth. Well, at least the truth I believe from you. The court may look to me to certify your answers. I will, but only if I feel comfortable doing so. At the end of the inquiry, I expect Admiral de la Motte will give you new orders."

"New orders?!"

The officer was amused. "Yes, Captain LaTour. New orders. So you are not surprised and exclaim something disrespectful you might regret, you and your ship will now take orders from *France*. France is at war. You are French. Your ship is French, despite its new owners. That is all I am going to say for now. Admiral Dubois de la Motte is the finest naval officer I know. He is strict but fair. He abhors dishonesty and he does not tolerate fools. Be proud of who you are, Captain LaTour. Shameful men tend to be liars too. Speak truthfully as you've done with me. Take heed, you will have to mention your relationship with Financier Machault. That question is certain to be asked."

"He is coming here," LaTour interjected.

"Who is? Financier Machault? The Naval Minister is coming here?"

"Yes. He sent me a missive indicating he is coming to see me…though probably in La Rochelle. I don't know when. But soon. I have the missive with me."

Captain Trémoille nodded. With that revelation he stood. "What you said is enough, I think."

LaTour stood as well. "So what am I to do now?"

Captain Trémoille gestured towards the marine corporal waiting across the room by the door.

"The corporal will escort you back to your room. And he will knock at your door and bring you to the court at the appointed time."

"Should I be worried?"

"Do not posture as a guilty man. Just be respectful. And answer, 'yes, sir' when you are addressed or given any orders. The admiral will respect you more for that. And in truth, you will not have any other choice."

"Yes, sir."

"Yes. Like that. Very good."

*

Admiralty Court
Fort de la Pointe

Captain LaTour was led to a large stone room, square, eighty feet to a side. It was never intended to be used as an administrative court and had been converted from one of the fort's ammunition magazines. The stone walls were fifteen feet thick, with no windows, but in the middle of each wall were thick double doors, ten feet wide, made of iron. The doors LaTour used to enter the room were wide open. A series of wooden benches arranged in two sections of six rows were provided for the attendees. LaTour was directed by one of the guards to take a seat on the front bench.

In the front of the room was a long table covered in a pristine white cloth. The flags of France, *fleur de lys*, were draped across the front of the table. Three chairs were evenly spaced along its back. A large one, high backed and ornate in design, was in the middle. To LaTour's left and right were side tables. At the one on the right sat three scribes wearing square-like black hats with matching black robes. They all had ink pots and quills laid before them along with liberal stacks of paper within reach.

The table on the left also had a white cloth and less ostentatious chairs for two people. As LaTour wondered about who would sit there, Captain Trémoille marched into the room accompanied by another officer. They took seats at the left side table. They were carrying books and other loose documents overlapping the bindings. Captain Trémoille nodded respectfully towards LaTour, who glanced behind him as five other people entered to sit on the other benches. Three of them naval officers and two civilians dressed in fine attire. LaTour recognized none of them.

Am I the only one to be questioned?

LaTour was sitting alone on the front right bench. A small leather valise lay at his side. It carried the ship's documents, presuming he would be asked. There was a perceptible draft of cool air moving in through the open back doors, which was welcome as the room would be stuffy without it. The air moved up and out six iron window-like vents propped open at the top of a ceiling slightly vaulted to induce the flow of air to rise, taking any heat with it.

Standing lamps lined the walls to create plenty of light. Spaced evenly amid these lamps were a dozen marines, standing at attention and carrying bayonet muskets. A singular man, dressed in some type of ceremonial naval attire, stood at the top of the left side table. He was the court steward. He carried a six-foot polished wooden staff with a brass foot and a circular brass head with an emblem LaTour did not recognize.

The room was quiet and somber except for the sounds of people breathing. No one was smiling, including the glum-faced Captain LaTour, who abruptly felt very alone and fatalistic. Despite being a smuggler, he was a mostly honest trader. He did not see himself as a criminal. *Lots of people smuggle*, he thought indignantly. Yes, there were risks, but he didn't steal or murder. He took care of his crew, cherished his ship, and always respected the power of the sea. Never in his most colorful daydreams or musings did he ever expect to see himself sitting where he sat today.

I am not that important a person! Surely they would not go to all this trouble if I were only to be hung.

Just then, the doors behind the long table were swung open by the guards. The court steward clanged his staff twice on the stone floor.

"Attention! The Admiralty Court is now in session!"

Everyone in the room stood.

"Vice-Admiral Emmanuel-Auguste de Cahideuc, Comte Dubois de la Motte, commanding."

The admiral's uniform was immaculate and covered with large, jeweled medallions, braids of rank, epaulets, a gold sash, and other decorations. The admiral was seventy-three years old when he walked into the court chambers that morning, accompanied by his two senior naval commanders. He was of medium height, slender, white haired, and had a hawkish-looking face with piercing blue eyes. He did not smile. He had joined the navy as a young midshipman almost sixty years earlier. He had been awarded a knighthood of the Order of Saint Louis almost forty years ago. He'd won many, many sea battles as a captain of a warship and as the admiral of a fleet. He was highly esteemed by his English adversaries. He loved France, revered his King, but hated the parasitic nobility. He prayed every day, petitioning God to allow him to die at sea, in battle, by cannon fire, fighting the enemies of France.

Admiral de la Motte sat in the high-back chair. He inhaled deeply.

"Get on with it," he ordered in a terse, commanding voice.

"Captain Beauregard LaTour of the Dutch trading ship *William's Queen*," Captain Trémoille declared loudly, "come forward, sir, and address the court."

As instructed, LaTour stepped forward and took off his hat, wondering immediately if he should have done that. He was about to say something in greeting when Captain Trémoille spoke.

"Captain LaTour entered La Rochelle harbor nineteen days ago without invitation or license. His vessel, *William's Queen*, sails under the Dutch Republic flag. The ship is now undergoing repairs." Captain Trémoille walked down the long table and left a copy of his written report before each of the officers. The admiral stared at LaTour, ignoring the document.

"I present you with a summary of the briefing I made to you earlier. Captain LaTour is a known smuggler with warrants outstanding in France and New France."

"What say you about these charges, Captain LaTour?"

Honesty and integrity, Captain Trémoille had told him.

"Yes, Admiral. I am a smuggler, but not all the time. Most of the time I am a simple trader."

"How fast is your ship, Captain?"

The question was unexpected. LaTour stammered his answer. "Uh... when the hull is clean, the *Queen* will do eighteen knots in a good wind with no cargo. With cargo, she can average fifteen knots, maybe sixteen. Fully sailed."

"The *Queen*?"

"That's her name, the *Falcon Queen*."

"The registry says *William's Queen*."

"The Dutch owners changed the name when they purchased it."

The admiral pondered these words. "After William? The son of Queen Anne?"

"Yes, sir."

The admiral nodded thoughtfully. "I prefer the *Falcon Queen* too. It sounds more...seaworthy."

LaTour felt a glimmer of hope. "I agree, Admiral."

The admiral lifted his copy of the papers and shook them in the air.

"I am told by these papers and several officers you might be the best smuggler France has produced in the last twenty years. Do you agree with that assessment?"

LaTour felt as if he were sailing at eighteen knots into uncharted shoals.

"I am honored to be considered the best at something that is seaworthy."

"That is not what I asked you, Captain."

LaTour took a fortifying breath. "I have that level of skill, Admiral. Though I am less certain I stand out in everyone's opinion."

The admiral squinted at him. "Help me, did you just say *yes*?"

"Yes, sir."

"Good. Are you an honest man?"

"Yes, sir. I think so."

"Good. Have you smuggled goods into Louisbourg harbor?"

LaTour thought he now understood the nature of this conversation.

"Yes, sir. Six, maybe seven times."

"Day or night?"

"In the daylight under cover of fog. At night, a darkened ship, if there's enough moonlight."

"By what channel?"

"At high tide, between Salmon Rock and the island battery."

The admiral gazed at LaTour skeptically. "I've never heard of a ship of your size managing to sail between Salmon Rock and the island battery. The channel there is not deep enough."

"Um, apologies, Admiral. Was that a question?"

"*Mon Dieu*! Yes!"

"Admiral, you may not have heard of that before today, because before today I have never boasted how I did it."

The admiral nodded. "Very well. So how did you do it the first time?"

"It was not intentional. I made a mistake in my navigation. And I was just lucky, it would seem. But I made a note of it in my logs. That channel is only thirty feet wide, if that wide. It was deep enough for my draft. But if the seas are heavy, you dare not do it at all."

"Have you engaged warships?"

"No, sir. I usually out run them. I've engaged corsairs twice."

"And?"

"The first time I was beating to windward. I maneuvered to come about and cross their bow so the weather gauge would give me a speed advantage. Used musket fire to keep them out of their sails until it was too late to overtake me."

"And the second time?"

"Off the Azores. Dropped my colors, turned to let him come close. But this time I had three swivel cannon, the kind you lift and hoist to fire. Kept those hidden until just before they grappled. Fired twice, the second time we aimed at their rudder as I came around their stern. Then the wind and our speed, with God's grace, permitted our escape."

"And your butcher's bill?"

"One man dead. Three wounded."

"How long have you been a captain?"

"Fifteen years, maybe sixteen."

"What scares you?"

LaTour paused at that question.

"Storms, Admiral," LaTour said gravely and truthfully. "Storms."

"France is at war. I need ships with captains."

LaTour said nothing.

"Do you have anything to say?"

"Yes, sir?"

"What?"

"Uh, yes, sir. I volunteer…sir?"

"Good. Captain Beauregard LaTour, before God and this court you have formally accepted a commission in the French Navy for the duration of this war. Any and all previous charges levied against you and your ship are to be expunged. Make a record of that," he ordered the scribes.

The admiral waited until the scribes finished making notes of what he ordered. Then he gestured with one hand for them to put down their quills. He took up the copy of Captain Trémoille's report and flipped through a few pages. He looked up at LaTour and then hesitated when he noticed the audience still in attendance.

"The court is adjourned. The observers are dismissed. Not you, Captain LaTour."

Admiral de la Motte signaled the marines to usher out the audience. When they returned he asked the marine sergeant, "Are they out of the building?"

"Yes, sir," replied the sergeant.

"Very well. Continue to rest your quills," he told the scribes. "Captain LaTour, I am strangely compelled by the charges in the warrant delivered to the naval magistrate in Le Havre from the Royal Intendant of New France, François Bigôt. Are you aware of this warrant? Do you know the Royal Intendant?"

LaTour swallowed hard, reminding himself to be careful.

"I know the Royal Intendant, but I was not aware of this particular warrant. To be honest with you, Admiral, there are probably other warrants he's issued against me."

Out of the corner of his eye, LaTour noticed Captain Trémoille's small smile and his nod of approval.

"Why have you not been arrested?"

"I evaded capture at sea, and when I was in New France, someone usually intervened for me."

"Someone important, I presume. And in Le Havre?"

LaTour's heart was pounding. "When I am pressed in Le Havre, I usually pay the fine levied on my ship."

"The fine?"

LaTour nodded nervously. "That is what they call it, Admiral."

"But you knew otherwise, yes?"

"Admiral, I know that once I gave them the money they wanted, my men were allowed to go ashore and see their families."

The admiral grunted. He looked at the warrant again.

"This warrant from François Bigôt"—he waved the papers in his hand—"demands your immediate arrest should you return to Le Havre. It was fortunate you came to La Rochelle instead. Now, I have the warrant. Impressive that the Royal Intendant, with so many more important matters facing New France, not to mention the war, names you so specifically. The Royal Intendant charges you with numerous crimes, which, after our discussion here today, I am finding rather difficult to believe. Did you really try to assassinate the Royal Intendant of New France…" He paused to read the document. "…with an Iroquois hunting bow?"

"Assassinate the intendant?! Me? No, sir!"

"Meaning someone else did?"

Much as he did not want to, LaTour decided to tell the story. He spoke with reluctance.

"Admiral, my ship was purchased by the VanderMeer Trading Insurance Company in Quebec City in the fall of 1754. Coincidental to the day of that transaction, a wedding was performed on my main deck in the afternoon by Archbishop Nicolet."

"The Jesuit Intendant of New France performed a wedding on board your ship?"

"Yes, he was a friend of the bride and groom."

"Who are…?"

Captain LaTour spent the next few minutes explaining what happened, being careful to leave out certain names and incriminating facts about Corrinne de Chanaye and Philippe Gerrard. The admiral and the other officers listened, finding themselves thoroughly entertained.

"…when suddenly, the intendant fired his pistol at the bride, but his aim was fouled when the major struck the barrel of the pistol with his sword just before it discharged. The ball struck the groom in the head instead. It was almost fatal. The ship owner, Lord Charles VanderMeer, protested to the governor. Governor-General Duquesne sent a letter of apology for the incident. I should probably mention Lord VanderMeer happens to be the son of the Duke of Brunswick."

The admiral raised a hand. "Stop! You say the owner of your vessel is the son of the Duke of Brunswick. And by that I mean Duke Louis Ernest, Captain-General of the Netherland armies?"

"Yes, Admiral. He can attest to the truth of this story," LaTour added helpfully.

"We will not be bothering the Duke of Brunswick," the admiral answered drolly.

"Well…but Governor Duquesne is back in France, yes? He can also attest to my truthfulness."

Captain Trémoille sunk further into his seat, fervently hoping Captain LaTour would simply stop talking.

The admiral replied tersely, "The Marquis Duquesne is indeed here in France, but we will not be bothering him *either*. And it will do you well, Captain LaTour, *never* to mention these associations again!"

"Apologies, Admiral. I was just trying to help."

"Where is this owner? This Lord VanderMeer?"

"He resides in the Boston colony in America. VanderMeer Trading Insurance Company is managed from there."

The admiral was dumbfounded. *The son of the Duke of Brunswick lives in Boston. And this captain has access to that port.* The admiral stared at Captain LaTour, contemplating possibilities. *Jean-Baptiste Machault was right. This captain may be useful to France in extraordinary ways.* He signaled to the scribes to pick up their quills.

"Captain LaTour, you will retain the rank of a ship captain in the French navy with fifteen years' seniority, with pay and privileges associated with this rank. You will report to me directly. How soon will the repairs to your ship be complete?"

"Another six weeks, maybe less."

"Captain LaTour, you are ordered to finish repairs to the *Falcon Queen* as soon as possible. Return to Fort de la Point to see me three weeks from today for further orders."

"Return to see you in three weeks. Aye, aye, sir."

"Very good, Captain. You are dismissed."

*

The feeling was like one Captain LaTour would have after surviving a powerful storm. He'd been very lucky. Yet he did not know whether he should remain happy or worry as he climbed into the naval carriage with the ensign. The smiling young officer now saluted him as his senior. As the coach lurched forward and left the fort, the ensign was suddenly talkative.

"Captain, I know a tailor in La Rochelle who will make you a handsome uniform. Admiral de la Motte will expect you to wear one next time he sees you."

LaTour replied with less enthusiasm.

LaTour looked out a window as the coach moved forward. He contemplated his new status in life and grumbled under his breath.

England will kill me now for being the enemy.

The Dutch Republic will hang me for being a spy.

France will chop off my head if I disobey orders.

And the authorities in Boston will hang me for…well, for being the enemy or for spying…but probably for smuggling!

"Did you say something to me, Captain?" the ensign asked, hearing the captain mutter. "I could not hear you over the sound of the horses."

He leaned toward the young officer. "I said…*God's balls!*"

CHAPTER 17
BOSTON
JUNE 1756
A List of Names

Colonel Wilhelm von Kleinfels was standing at the rail of the New Bedford fishing vessel, his baggage resting on the deck at his side. The schooner navigated among the ships in the Boston anchorage and neared the working piers.

The captain of the schooner approached the colonel and touched a hand to his cap in a greeting of respect.

"Morning, Colonel. We will tie up to those fishing wharves just ahead to unload my catch. You can disembark there. Sorry to do this to you. The foul smell of that place may linger in your nose for the rest of the day."

"I assure you, Captain, I have smelled much worse on a battlefield. You have brought me to Boston in two days, as you promised." He handed the man another gold coin. "Can one of your crew carry my bags until I hail a carriage? I will pay him, of course."

"No payment necessary, Colonel. It will be our privilege."

Von Kleinfels left the fishing wharf and hailed a carriage to take him down Fish Street to the commercial area near Faneuil Hall. There were several small hotels with restaurants near there. He selected one of the more expensive ones, contracted a room for a week, refreshed himself, and went to the port authority buildings where the English army headquarters were housed. He entered the building and was greeted warmly by many of his contacts from the previous year. He acknowledged the congratulations he received on his promotion to colonel. Kleinfels replied with short but polite answers to their questions. His mind was preoccupied with the new information regarding the whore queen. He planned to meet with Carter Trevathan later in the day.

"This way, Colonel," invited a lieutenant.

320

At this unexpected interruption, Kleinfels hesitated.

"What did you say?"

"This way, sir. Colonel Webb wants to see you."

Colonel Webb? Kleinfels followed the officer. *Who is that?*

Colonel Daniel Webb was a thirty-six-year-old career army officer. He'd arrived in America as third-in-command behind Major General James Ambercrombie, who was second-in-command to General John Campbell, 4th Earl of Loudoun, the new commander-in-chief of the English forces in North America. Lord Loudoun's arrival was delayed by the North Atlantic storms. He would not arrive for another month.

Nevertheless, General Ambercrombie was already on his way to Albany to relieve Governor Shirley as commander-in-chief of the army ahead of the earl's arrival. Colonel Webb expected to accompany Ambercrombie and was impatient to do so. He was temporarily tasked with finding the Hessian colonel to establish contact with the Prussian liaison, England's ally in the declared war with France. They needed German mercenaries, particularly in North America.

Colonel Webb had been waiting a week in Boston for Colonel von Kleinfels to appear. No one seemed to know where he was. This was irritating since Webb had arrived in New York a week *after* Colonel Kleinfels' purported arrival. He'd learned that the Hessian's final destination was Boston so he had come here. Webb's intense annoyance with having to wait for the Hessian was reflected in his greeting.

Von Kleinfels saluted his scowling superior.

"Where have you been hiding? I have been waiting a week to meet with you!"

Kleinfels had dealt with pompous English officers before. "I took ill, sir. But I am here now. How can I be of service?"

"This is for you," Webb replied tersely. He handed Kleinfels a sealed packet of mail. "Your mail from Prussia. It came on my ship from England. I am most pleased to act your personal mail courier." Webb's tone was anything but pleased.

Kleinfels accepted the packet with complete surprise. It was wax sealed with the stamp of the Prussian king, Frederick II.

"Read it at your leisure. I will suggest its content. You may presume it states that England requests a regiment of soldiers from your king to be supplied to America before the fighting season is over. Since you are the Prussian liaison in America, I anticipate it will fall to you to facilitate this and to manage the difficulties associated with supplying a regiment of your soldiers to America now that war is formally declared. Since it is June, you will need to return to Prussia, find a regiment, and get them aboard an English ship for transport. Maybe we will see them by October, yes?"

"If this missive from my sovereign validates what you've told me, I will first need to find transport back."

"Oh! Is that your only problem? Luck has followed you, Colonel. There is an English frigate at anchor in the harbor, which will be carrying our mail along with passengers back to London. It is waiting only for *you* to step aboard before it weighs anchor. I encourage you to do this by tomorrow at the latest! I will order the captain to wait for you and expect your arrival."

Expecting the Hessian would do as he ordered, Colonel Webb left Boston that afternoon to be with General Ambercrombie in Albany.

Von Kleinfels went back to his hotel and read the missive from his sovereign. It was a single page. *Prussia is at war. Return to my service at once.* Nothing about supplying mercenaries. With Webb gone, he discarded all thoughts concerning English desires. He would eventually have to return to Prussia, but he had no intention of getting aboard an English frigate the next day.

He changed into civilian clothes before he met with Carter Trevathan at a hotel restaurant. They ate a light dinner together.

"Where are the other men?"

"One of them is a day laborer at the fishing piers. Two are working cargo on the Long Wharf. And the other is cobbling boots for a shop with a contract to supply the provincial army. They live in shacks near the distilleries and can respond to your orders within an hour. Caroline and Rachel are nurses at the Marine Society Hospital on Sudbury Street. It is new, not very large, and caters to the merchant class. They overhear much of the gossip of the city. They are already held in high esteem. And Ritter Monheit is doing work as a stonecutter, staying well clear of the VanderMeer residence. He suspects he would be recognized."

Kleinfels looked at the list of names. "All these people were at the church?"

"Yes. That appears to be most of them except for, maybe, a few servants at the house. We will find that out. Rachel is learning where the marine guards tend to gather when off duty. She will befriend one or more of them to gain information."

Kleinfels rubbed his temples absentmindedly. The endless cycle of headaches that resulted in visiting the servants' dreams had become almost debilitating. The Hessian was further plagued with constant exhaustion. He could fall asleep simply by closing his eyes while sitting in this chair. He needed more rest. Since everyone was now in Boston, Kleinfels decided to use Carter as his go-between.

"We will proceed slowly. When we finally enter the house, this time we must be unopposed. Find some type of commercial work, but nothing that commits you to anyone else. Start your own company. I care not what you do, just have a reason for living here. You will be my main point of contact and direct the actions of the others." He studied the list and pointed at a name. "That one. Tell Caroline to start with this one. Tell her today. I want this done as soon as possible. But she must do this publically and discreetly. The death must appear natural. She is not to be noticed. We will observe how the household reacts. See what weaknesses this exposes.

"Have one of the men stop working and find a room to rent near the main house. He must watch it and learn where they go, when they go out among the populace. Learn their routines."

Three days later, a laborer came to the Marine Society hospital with a blood-soaked bandage on his forearm complaining the bandage covered a deep gash that needed stitching. The doctor in charge of the new hospital did not want to foster a reputation that this hospital was for just anyone in the city, unless, of course, they had money. Clearly this common laborer was not from that class of people. He refused the man any service.

"Go and see the penny surgeon at the Long Wharf. He will stitch you up."

The penny surgeon was a seventy-two-year-old retired seaman. He was formerly a shipboard sail maker and learned the precise stitching of his former trade could earn him money by treating cuts and other wounds. While the tiny shop he occupied near the Long Wharf was not very sanitary, his stitches were excellent and, most importantly, he was cheap, charging a penny per stitch.

Caroline Bristol recognized the laborer immediately. She found Rachel and told her she was going out for a few hours. In her handbag, Caroline carried a very expensive, specially crafted, needle-like knife. The handle was a plunger. In the hollow tip was a substance that would induce convulsions and death. It was mixed in water. The tip of the knife was clogged by a tiny amount of wax, but not enough to stop the force of the plunger that would inject the substance into flesh.

Caroline rendezvoused with the wharf laborer at a prearranged corner. His name was Felix. He had removed the fake bloody bandage on his arm.

"She is walking around the flower stands right now."

"You will need to provide a distraction for me."

Felix nodded. "When we near, nod when you're ready, and I will cause something to happen on the opposite side of the street."

"We should not be seen walking together. Lead me to her. I will follow you from behind."

It was Wednesday. Down at Dock Square at the head of the Long Wharf, from April through September, Wednesday was the day that farmers, citizens, or anyone with a flower pot in bloom, could offer their flowers for sale. As usual, Dock Square was alive with people of every class and a variety of flowers of every color, many of them wildflowers. Everyone liked flowers and the square resounded with laughter and the calls of flowers for sale, mixed with the competing calls of the usual food purveyors who appeared at any public gathering. Some bouquets were offered at a tabletop, some cradled in the arms of the sellers, who were mostly women and girls of every age, many of whom wore their blossoms in their hair.

Mathilde was bending over a table, choosing various types of flowers to mix in a bouquet to be used to adorn the dinner table later that day.

Caroline Bristol nodded at Felix who stepped in front of a passing carriage on the other side of the street and yanked hard on the bridle of the horse. Felix kept walking. The horse reacted with a loud neigh and lurched sideways pushing into one of the flower stands, knocking it over while the driver struggled with the reins to get the frightened animal back under control. Screams of surprise rent the air, drawing people's attention.

Mathilde and the flower vendors turned towards the commotion. In one movement, Caroline slammed the needle through Mathilde's summer dress into the back of the woman's left thigh, depressed the plunger at the same time, and withdrew it as she walked away.

Mathilde's scream of surprise was hardly louder than those from others in the flower market reacting to the panicked horse.

"What...?" She gasped in agony.

Mathilde grabbed at the terrible burning pain expanding in her left leg. A few seconds later, overcome by a spreading numbness, she fell to her knees before collapsing further on her back. Her eyes rolled white. Her mouth foamed. Her hands and feet twitched spasmodically. Her back arched in stiff, convulsive movements. Several people gathered, not knowing what to do. In less than a minute, her heart stopped.

Mathilde was dead.

The three doctors who hurried to the VanderMeer house subsequent to the incident examined the body. One of them was Dr. Gordon Angove. They agreed on two potential but very different causes of death. They believed it was a sudden stroke brought on by the poor health and advanced age of the woman, or from severe convulsive paroxysms induced by exposure to foreign flora or a stinging pestilence indigent to the blossoms on display at Dock Square that morning. The second conclusion might better explain the swollen glands and abnormal skin discoloration. Mathilde's face was mottled purple as was much of her skin. The doctors were pressed by two ranking members of Boston's General Court who had come by immediately to offer their condolences and support to Lord VanderMeer. Upon seeing the shocking condition of the body on the dining room table and listening to the conclusions of the physicians, the politicians reacted with quiet but strong language.

"Christ, gentlemen. She looks like she died of the plague! *Convulsive paroxysms* sounds too evil. A stroke? Better. People who witnessed the death are ready to corroborate that story anyway. No need to disrupt future commercial trade on the square. And certainly no need to create undue panic among the population of Boston by using words suggesting some virulent disease!"

The doctors agreed with the common sense of the city leaders. The diagnosis of a stroke was the simplest and most appropriate explanation. As soon as the casket was brought into the house, they helped moved the corpse inside and closed the lid. They recommended to the VanderMeers it remain closed because of the body's appearance.

Mathilde now lay inside a dark walnut-wood casket with polished brass handles. The interior was cushioned with cotton wadding covered in pure white silk. It was the best Molly could find and buy on such short notice.

Sentry Cheever arrived to help. He brought in two of the marine guards from outside. Once the doctors were finished, the dining table was covered with a dark blue velvet draping. The casket was set on top. All the other credenzas and serving furniture were removed temporarily from the dining room. Ten rows of chairs, eight chairs per row, divided in the middle, four to a side, many of them offered by neighbors, were arranged before the flower-draped casket. Four funeral candles in brass stands were delivered by Trinity Church. Two large vases of seasonal wildflowers were sent by the city leaders. The front living room was rearranged for food and drink, to be used as a reception area.

But no visitors would be permitted until Corrinne was ready, and she would not be ready for the remainder of that day.

Corrinne, orphaned as a young child, Mathilde was the only mother she had ever known. They had been together so long, Corrinne could not imagine her world without this gentle, loving, wonderful woman who'd cared for her during the worst of Corrinne's trials in New France. She was overcome with grief and sat on a chair next to her oldest friend, head bowed and resting against the brass side rail of the casket. She ached for Philippe's comforting presence more than ever. She discouraged the sympathies of anyone who tried to console her. It was too much trouble to acknowledge them.

After an hour, Dian brought in a cool pitcher of water filled with slices of lemons. She filled one glass.

"My lady," she whispered and touched Corrinne's shoulder gently. "I've brought you some water should you need it. I've also wet a cloth on the tray you can use to wipe your neck. It might give you comfort."

Corrinne looked up. Her face was puffy. The cook's eyes also were red and swollen from crying. She touched a hand to Dian's.

"*Merci*. Tell the others I prefer to be left alone."

But a short time later, Molly brought Marcus and Calypso to her. Corrinne saw their happy faces and smiles. She took them gently into her arms and hugged them tightly. The babies' tiny hands touched her cheeks and hair. Every touch brought healing to Corrinne's injured spirit.

Molly sat in a chair nearby, her eyes dripping with tears, waiting until Lady Corrinne asked for the children to be taken from her.

Dianamora returned and knelt next to Corrinne's chair. She prayed in the language of the islands, a mix of French, Spanish, English, and old African dialects. She chanted prayers for the dead. Prayers to protect the soul from the devil. Prayers for the angels to come forth. Prayers to ward away any evil spirits that were certain to gather and try to take possession before the soul ascended into the heavens. Her gentle, accented voice rose and fell as her body swayed back and forth, sometimes with her hands extended towards the casket.

Corrinne was drained from the utter shock of it all. Just a few hours earlier, it was a normal morning before Mathilde's body was delivered to the house by wagon and carried into the house by the guards. Strangers in business suits crowded into the foyer and explained that people tried to help when Mathilde suddenly collapsed among the flower stands on Dock Square. "The convulsions were too strong and then…then she just stopped breathing." Then came the doctors. Corrinne was numb with disbelief. She accepted Dr. Angove's explanation without argument. A stroke? That seemed too easy, and strange, logic told her. But dead was dead. She was too disconsolate to question the *why* of it just now.

Dianamora, however, was convinced Mathilde had been murdered. Her island instincts sensed the work of something evil. *She was cursed or poisoned*, she whispered to Sentry Cheever. Sentry was of the same opinion. "A stroke does not cause the skin to turn purple. Not like that. And never so soon." But they agreed for now neither of them would voice their opinion. There would be time for that later.

Finally, Corrinne gestured to Molly the children should be taken up to bed. They had fallen asleep in her arms anyway. Once they were gone, she took a long swallow of water from the goblet of water Dian had set out and used the wet cloth on the back of her neck. It felt good, just as Dian predicted.

"My lady?"

She turned. Sentry Cheever stood there with his hat in his hands, his face anguished. The man had Philippe's strength. Impulsively, she stretched her arms to him.

"Oh, Sentry."

He knelt quickly and embraced her. She sobbed strongly on his shoulder. When the surge of sadness passed, she sniffed aloud and wiped her eyes again.

"Did you want something?"

"Yes, m'lady. I dinnah want to bother you, but Deputy Magistrate Jack Tasker is on the porch. He *begs* you allow him an audience."

"Oh, God! Why, Sentry?! Can't he come tomorrow like everyone else?"

"My lady…the magistrate does not think Mistress Mathilde's death was a stroke. He suspects *villainy*."

Corrinne caught her breath. "What!" Deep inside her mind and heart, tiny coals of anger began to glow. She'd not even considered that possibility. *Stupid! Stupid! Stupid!* She sat up straight.

Sentry saw her expression tighten.

"My lady…I agree with him."

"Bring the magistrate to me. But no one else, only him!"

Charles VanderMeer caught sight of Jack Tasker entering the house and came out from the *cuisine* where he waited for Dian to prepare Corrinne some tea. He followed the magistrate.

"Deputy, why are you here?"

"I asked him to come in, Charles."

Tasker was holding his hat.

"My Lord VanderMeer. Lady VanderMeer. My deepest sympathies for your loss. But time is of the essence in these matters. I have something to relate to you that you may find disturbing. May I speak candidly?"

They all looked at Corrinne.

"Of course you can."

"Very well. I've interviewed several people who were present on Dock Square when Mistress Mathilde collapsed. I've also talked with the doctors standing outside. Based on what they have told me, there is a real possibility your maidservant's death was not from natural causes."

"Meaning what?"

"I think she was poisoned. The doctors claim they saw a small puncture wound on the back of her left thigh. They all felt it was benign and unrelated to the stroke. They presumed she'd fallen on a sharp stone, considering the heaviness of her collapse reported by all of the witnesses. I did not mention the possibility of poison to the doctors. If someone killed Mistress Mathilde, it is better they assume we suspect something. And I do not want my suspicions getting into the papers. Not yet, anyway."

"Poison?" Corrinne was simmering. "Why poison?"

"Another person was poisoned about three weeks ago. A carriage driver from New York was found dead at the western stables shortly after he arrived in Boston. I was called and saw him within two hours of his death. His skin was mottled and purple. He had choked to death on his own tongue, which had swollen so large it protruded from his mouth. The stable master found him. But no one knew how many people this driver carried on that coach. I am still trying to find out who was on it. But when I heard what happened today and learned what the doctors saw, it could no longer be a coincidence."

"What do you want to do?" Charles asked.

Jack Tasker looked uncomfortable. "Well…it might appear disrespectful…but…"

"You want to examine her," Corrinne stated flatly. "Just say it."

"Certainly not!" Charles protested.

"No, Charles. If Deputy Tasker is right, I want to know the truth. How do you want to do this?"

"My lady, Sergeant Cheever is no stranger to death either. I propose you step to the back of the room. And the sergeant and I will open the casket, and, as respectfully as possible, turn the body over and look at the wound on her left thigh…if you will permit me."

"I will look too, Deputy Tasker."

The only person unhappy with Corrinne's sudden determination was Charles. He moved to the back of the room, having decided not to look.

The lid was opened. The odor was already corrupt. Corrinne put a kerchief to her nose. Charles backed up two more steps. But Sentry and Jack Tasker immediately lifted the shoulders and feet and turned the body over. The rigor of the body made it seem like turning a heavy tree limb. The magistrate pulled up the dress. The discoloration of the skin was the same as on the carriage driver. But he had found no sign of a puncture wound on that man's body. And considering the grotesquely swollen tongue, he assumed a poison was administered directly into the mouth.

With Lady VanderMeer looking over his shoulder, the magistrate pulled the dress all the way to her waist. The puncture wound was visible just beneath the left buttock. Web-like black lines spread in all directions from the wound as if some toxin or venom had gotten under the skin. He took out a small wooden drafting scale and measured the lesion.

Tasker nodded grimly. "That measures four to six inches of invasion in every direction. I think if she lived longer the effect would have spread even further. As it was, the body reacts to poison by increased breathing and blood flow. People appear flush. There are large blood vessels in that part of the leg. If the toxin entered one of those, it would be carried everywhere and fast. Hence the extensive skin discoloration. I have a book in my office on poisons. I will try to identify this one. I'm assuming the knife used to make the puncture was a thin spike of some kind, probably coated with the toxin. The kind assassins use."

Assassins, Corrinne thought. *That word again.*

Tasker pulled down the dress. Carefully, they turned the body over, crossed the arms over the chest, and shut the lid. Charles went over to the windows and opened them to let in the outdoor air.

"My lady, I am deeply sorry you saw this," Tasker said sincerely.

"No, Deputy Tasker. It was necessary for us to see this, to understand what we are facing…again. I invite you to stay longer. Let's go into the library and discuss this further. I want to know everything you can tell me. Many people are expected to visit this house tomorrow to offer condolences to us. Why not assassins too? I want to prepare for that."

*

In a special edition of the Boston newspaper for Wednesday was a notice of Mathilde's sudden death while visiting the flower stands on Dock Square.

```
Formal services will be held, tomorrow,
Thursday morning at nine o'clock at the Van-
derMeer residence. Close friends and associates
of the VanderMeers are welcome to attend, as
room permits. General walk-through visitation
```

```
to the VanderMeer residence is permitted from
one to four in the afternoon.
```

Somberly dressed people filed in through the foyer to take a chair for the service, Deputy Magistrate Jack Tasker greeted them in the foyer. A rumor was intentionally spread among the visitors, to the few given to gossip and callous enough to ask about Mathilde's relation to the family, that the maidservant was actually Lady VanderMeer's *mother*. Also, that there was now a suspicion her death might be the result of villainy. Magistrate Tasker had changed his mind about this after the previous day's discussion with Corrinne. She thought this might inspire speculation among the people present on Dock Square, bringing them forward. And perchance provoke comments or questions among the visitors that would otherwise seem too inquisitive or direct.

A registry book was filled with the names of every visitor, no matter their station. Two of Thomas Hancock's scribes were hired for the day for this purpose. A second registry book for personal comments was left open on a table in the front living room for those people invited to visit further.

A round table to the side of the front door was covered with a large, expensive lace doily. In the center was a silver bowl reserved for visiting cards of the people and families familiar with the practice. Magistrate Tasker and Lord VanderMeer had decided it was another good way of recording who came by. By the end of the week, every person in Boston who considered themselves *important* would ask a local printer to have some cards made up. Thomas Hancock's personal printer would advertise the stock and preparation. He would also collect examples of the new cards as they were made.

Corrinne and Charles stood at the back of the room, where the rows of chairs began, to greet the people who came. Sentry Cheever stood in his uniform on her left. Arranged in a crossed sheath hidden from view over his back were two long, pointed dirks. They collectively didn't expect anyone to be so bold, but...

"The assassins tried in public before. Who can say for certain they won't try in public again?" Sentry had argued.

A small dais had been placed by the casket. At precisely nine o'clock, Rector William Hooper stepped to the dais and looked over the room. All eighty seats were filled, the majority of them with women. Another dozen people stood in the foyer, all of them men. Since he also heard the rumor that Mathilde might be Lady VanderMeer's mother, Reverend Hooper recited scripture about the sanctity of motherhood. They sang two military songs of grief that were well known. Several people who knew Mathilde spoke about her. Corrinne and Charles, of course, then Molly and Lydia Hancock, their favorite seamstress Mary Beth, and the flower vendor from Dock Square. The ceremony took an hour. At the end of the service, Rector Hooper announced that Mathilde would be interred in the Granary Burial Ground at ten o'clock. The audience did not move until the reverend formally announced the service was over. Many of them moved to the reception room.

In the afternoon, a long line of curious people began to file into the house. Most of the chairs were now stacked close together in the middle of the room to encourage the line to move to the left once in the front room, pass by the casket, and down the room on the right and back out the front door. For the next three hours, Corrinne greeted them, thanking the people who came by, making sure they said their names loud enough so the scribes could record. A step behind her to the right was Sentry Cheever who examined the faces and hands of each person as they neared Corrinne. Jack Tasker was to her left a few steps behind, but close enough to see each person's face and overhear what they said. A few of these visitors were invited by Corrinne to step over to the front room for refreshments. Charles VanderMeer was in that room with two of the marine guards, overseeing the other registry book.

Two hundred sixty-two people were listed as visitors that day to offer condolences for a woman most had never met in their life, but out of respect and admiration for the VanderMeers.

Later, when the list of visitors was reviewed, seventeen of them were considered interesting enough by Magistrate Tasker to warrant his personal follow-up.

Corrinne read over the list of names several times, trying to envision who they were, trying to recall a face. But none of them were familiar to her.

One of you will die painfully for this, she promised silently.

*

The female eagle labored to fly high above the city so as not to tempt the guns of any hunters. She carried the body of the white eagle in her talons.

The *ghost* spotted the dwelling of the white woman and glided down to a landing atop a smaller structure behind the big one. The female stepped away from the white eagle.

The *ghost* perceived the demon and its servants in every direction. Two of the servants were moving towards the white woman. The body of the white eagle was left atop the smaller structure and the female took flight again. It wasn't long before they began circling above a small crowd of people huddled around a hole in the ground.

The Granary Burial Ground was one of Boston's best cemeteries, usually reserved for persons of the upper class. Corrinne had a tombstone created and inscribed with Mathilde's name, *Mathilde de Chanaye*, and the date of her death. Thomas Hancock had used his influence to make these hurried arrangements. Some of the wealthy residents in the city fumed this privilege should not be extended to a relatively unknown person of foreign birth, particularly one that was obviously *French*. As a compromise, Hancock offered an accommodation from Corrinne, that if the VanderMeers ever moved from the city, Mathilde's casket would be disinterred and taken with them. This satisfied the dissenters.

There were only a few dozen people invited to attend the burial, most of them out of respect and friendship to the VanderMeers.

Six of the attendees at the cemetery were not intentionally invited. The funeral goers paid them little heed. Most of them were newspaper people.

Carter Trevathan was standing with another man on Tremont Street, in sight of the funeral congregation but far enough away not to be overheard. Carter did a quick count of the VanderMeers.

"All right, they are all here." He turned around to face the street and thrust with his chin so Felix would look where he was looking. "See that fence line? Get to it and you'll see the loose board. You cannot miss it. You have the torch?"

Felix opened his coat to show him the three-foot-long unlit torch with paper and rags on one end.

"Go in through the hole in the fence. Go in the back door. Break it down if you have to. There should be no one inside. Go into the *cuisine*. Light the torch from the hearth. And set as much of the house on fire as you can. Don't go upstairs. Stay on the ground floor. Then retreat out the hole again. Do *not* go out the front of the house. The marine guards are there. You probably have an hour to do this at most. So do it as fast as you can. Come back out the same way through the fence. Walk! Don't run. And go all the way down to the docks. I will find you later. Now go!"

Carter made his way across the grass at a deliberate, casual pace to mingle with the crowd in time to hear Rector Hooper's benediction and other prayers.

Felix found the loose board on the back of the fence. He slipped through easily and leaned the board against the fence to cover the hole again. Sprinting across the yard to the back door, he tried it and found it unlocked. He stepped through quietly and listened for sounds of movements. Hearing only quiet, he moved to the door he imagined led to the *cuisine*. It, too, was unlocked but led to a mud room. There was a third door four paces further. It was open. He could see the hearth stove. The next room was definitely the *cuisine*. This was almost too easy.

He passed another door partially ajar to his left and stepped up into the *cuisine*. He stopped again and listened. No other sounds. He went straight to the hearth, took out his torch, and removed the iron lid on the stove. Suddenly, he felt a terrible pain in his back.

He turned around to see a scowling woman. She was holding a bloody knife. She hissed some words in a strange language. The island woman shoved the long kitchen blade into him again, into the front of his chest, directly into the heart. The sharp pain hurt Felix for only an instant before he collapsed dead on the floor.

*

Almost half an hour had gone by. The burial ceremony was just about over. People were tossing handfuls of earth into the grave. Carter kept glancing at Tremont Street to watch for smoke or catch a glimpse of Felix returning from his mission. But he saw neither. *Something's gone wrong,* he thought.

The services ended. People began exiting the cemetery. Carter moved along with the small crowd walking just a little faster and took streets leading to the plaza area around Faneuil Hall. It would be crowded on a Friday. Colonel von Kleinfels was waiting for him on the street near his hotel. Setting the house on fire was the colonel's idea. "The house is like a fort. Let's use the interval of the burial services. We'll drive them out and return at night to go through the ashes and get the *châsse*."

Carter saw the colonel as planned, but the Hessian officer was standing before an English naval officer, an English army officer, and several enlisted men, a mix of seamen and army redcoats. They were arguing, arms gesturing vigorously. Carter stopped well short of that confrontation to watch the dispute. Other civilians began looking on with curiosity.

"*Skrieee!*"

The scream of the large eagle made everyone's heads turn upwards. Those standing in the vicinity were shocked to see the huge predator swoop past the colonel's head, knocking off his hat and inflicting a small laceration in the scalp before it flew up, away, and out of sight.

Voices of surprise and amazement burst from every direction.

"Did you see that?!"

"That was a fucking…"

"A bloody eagle, that's what! A white one, too. Never seen a white one before. Have you?"

"No," Carter replied.

But Carter was not paying attention to what the man said. He was gazing with a different type of shocked amazement at the body of the colonel lying motionless on the ground surrounded by military officers and men. As the Faneuil crowd moved towards this new scene, Carter moved with it and got close enough to hear what was said.

"Who is that?" asked a man who was already scribbling notes on a piece of paper.

"Stand back. I'm a doctor," another man said.

"Right! Great!" the naval captain of the frigate at anchor spoke in disgust. "Well, I am not holding up my sail any longer. Do you know where Colonel von Kleinfels is staying?"

The army major volunteered he did.

"Then take your men to his room and pack up his belongings and load them on a boat at the pier I will have waiting for you. I've a doctor on my ship. My men will carry him on a litter and take him aboard. Is it a stroke?"

The doctor looked up from the Hessian. "I presume it is. He is responding to my questions in whispers. That is a good sign. But I think his right
arm and leg are paralyzed. And he has a cut on his head."

"All the better," the captain said. "Find me a litter," he ordered his
seamen who instantly adopted expressions of confusion. "Don't look at me
like that...I don't care, just...just anything I can use to carry him out to the
ship." He looked at the shocked face of the kneeling physician. "Don't worry.
We'll take care of him at sea. And we have even better doctors in London."

The Hessian colonel suddenly made a loud groan and fell still. His
eyes closed.

The doctor felt the colonel's pulse. It was fast and strong. "This is very
odd."

"What? Another stroke?"

"I don't know. But he appears to be unconscious."

"Good. The less trouble the better."

The seamen returned with a flat table they had commandeered from a
nearby restaurant.

"That will do. Break off the legs. Are you the owner of the restaurant?"
he asked an angry man who had followed the table. "Yes? Here's a silver
piece for taking one of your tables. More?! You bloody pirate. Two more
then. Now be off with you."

Carter Trevathan leaned back against the outside wall of Faneuil Hall,
completely at a loss what to do. He closed his eyes and still sensed his
unconscious connection to the colonel, but it was different now, as if he
were in a room with another man who was fast asleep.

"Well, he will wake up again," he grumbled to himself. "That's for certain. And he will be in a very foul mood, one that will give us all headaches
we will remember for a long time."

His thoughts turned back to Felix. *Something has happened to him.* He
knew where the laborer lived. Once he witnessed the colonel being lowered
into a boat and rowed towards an English warship, he went to linger near
Felix's hovel. But the man never came. Next, he went to the busy public
restaurant they would sometimes frequent to mix in among the people and
noise. But Felix was not there either. However, he found Caroline and

Rachel Bristol waiting for him near his own apartment. He gestured they should follow him into one of the large farmer markets until they found a place noisy enough to stand together and talk.

"I don't feel him anymore," Caroline said straightaway.

"Neither do I," confirmed Rachel.

"He's suffered a stroke." Carter explained what he saw at Faneuil Hall. "But I definitely sense him still. I think he will wake up again."

"So what do we do?" Caroline pressed with impatience.

"Just go about your business, as you do every day and be patient. Like I am going to do. When the colonel contacts us again, I am sure we will all know it."

"Are we in danger?"

"None that I am aware. Except something must have happened to Felix."

"What happened?"

"I don't know yet. Look, just go on being the good nurses you know how to be."

"It is not that easy. I feel trapped in a cave with no way out. Can you invent an ailment to come by the Marine Society hospital on Monday and talk to us?"

"Yes. But only after I get to the other men and tell them what's happened."

*

Returning from the funeral, Molly went around the hallway and upstairs to put Marcus and Calypso to bed.

Everyone else crowded into the *cuisine* and stood in shock. From Dian, they heard the tearful, astonishing story of how a man came to be lying dead in his own blood on the *cuisine* floor.

"He came through the back doors carrying an unlit torch. I think he intended to set the house on fire. I was terrified. So I stabbed him. Please... please don't hate me!"

Corrinne hugged Dianamora right away. "No, no, Dian. No. We don't hate you. You did the right thing. We are all so glad you are safe. Aren't we?" she said to Charles, Sentry, Magistrate Tasker, Anamosa, and the two guards who were gathered there.

They all quickly assured Dian that she had done the right thing.

"Magistrate," Charles said. "What do we do?"

"You are an artist, yes?"

"Um...yes..."

"Can you make a sketch of this man's face? Something I can carry around with me."

Charles nodded with understanding. "Of course." He left the room.

The magistrate told the guards not to speak of this to anyone. "We don't want the people behind this to know what has happened. And can one of you go to the magistrate's office and have them bring back our wagon? So I can dispose of this body. Don't tell them why, just that I sent for the wagon right away."

The corporal and private left the room.

"It would be better if the rest of you waited somewhere else."

Corrinne took Dianamora into the library with Sentry and Anamosa.

"Stay here while we get this mess cleaned up. No, Dian, you stay here with Sentry. You've been through enough today."

Charles came in with his sketch pad. Jack Tasker opened the man's eyes until Charles had captured the likeness and then propped up the head with towels. Charles made four sketches in less than ten minutes. He tore off the entire sheet and rolled it up for the deputy.

"Now what?" Corrinne asked.

"I will take the body away to the mortuary and examine the man and his clothes for anything else of use. He will be buried in the pauper's cemetery."

"I cannot believe they tried to burn down our house," Charles said.

"And that means they have been watching you carefully," Tasker replied. "They believed everyone was at the Granary cemetery. Dian was lucky she was in the spice room when he entered or this might have ended very tragically. She is a brave woman. But this man has been staying somewhere out of sight and close by. I can use the sketch to learn where that was and see where that leads me next. Unfortunately, I think the marines will now have to post guards in your backyard too. You probably have only a day at most before the rumors of this appear in the papers. I am sorry. People care about you. They are interested to hear about you. In the meantime, I will do my job."

"Oh, my God!" Molly had entered the *cuisine* and her hands were covering her mouth.

"We will talk later, Molly. Go to the library and sit with Dian and Sentry." Corrinne sat down in a chair. "What about the list of names?"

Tasker nodded. "Someone on that list will be his accomplice, someone who learned enough about the house to give directions to this intruder, whoever he was. I will learn his name too."

"But he was not the leader," Corrinne said firmly. She unconsciously touched the scar on the top of her right hand. "I shook the hand of every single man who came here yesterday. I would have known the leader instantly."

They heard the sounds of a wagon pulling up to the back of the house.

"That will be my men. We will clean this up for you…at least take away the majority of the bloody rags so Miss Dian does not have to do it. It will not take us long. Why don't you join your family in the other room, my lady? We will finish this nasty business."

"They will attack us again." Corrinne stared at the stove fatalistically. Her hands rushed to her face, which had broken into an anguished expression. "I almost left my babies home this morning. If the house had caught fire…!"

Customarily, not an emotional man, Tasker was moved. He took Lady VanderMeer's hands in his.

"My lady, they have left me too many clues now. I will find them all and stop them before they ever bother you again. You have my word."

*

Monday, June 21
Boston

The *ghost* flew north again, deep into the wilderness where the eagle could wander, feed, and rest without interference. For two days, the female existed freely as her spirit was intended. The *ghost* admired this raptor's strength, its hunting prowess, and its joy, comprehending more than ever how corrupting his presence was to the purity of this beautiful life. But she was still young.

The *ghost* was determined to help the white woman understand how to defeat the demon. Because only she could do what was necessary.

As the sunrise blazed with yellow-orange-red colors above the horizon on the morning of the third day, the *ghost* gently surged to dominance again. They flew south into the great city and found the large dwelling. The body of the white eagle still lay atop the smaller structure where the *ghost* had left it days earlier. They lifted it into the air and dropped the body on the ground near the large garden area of the yard. The eagle returned to the small structure. It perched and waited.

*

Corrinne and Charles sat in the library reading the last three days of newspapers they'd neglected because of Mathilde's death. The papers had articles about the long lines of sympathizers, the burial at Granary cemetery, and the rumor of a bizarre intrusion into the VanderMeer home, though details on what or why this happened were limited. The newspapers were only a few pages long. All of them had continuing stories about Mathilde's death and the suspicions it was not natural.

Reading each new story made Corrinne wince with grief. She put the papers aside and sipped her coffee. She could hear Sentry's deep voice behind the door to the *cuisine* as he talked with Dian. He had stayed at the house every day since Mathilde's death and most nights too after coming from his job, to comfort Dianamora. They heard the back doors open as the two of them went out into the yard.

"It's good that Sentry is here for Dian," she commented idly.

Charles handed Corrinne one of the Friday papers.

"Did you see this story on the shipping news page? It's on the bottom-right column."

Prussian Officer Attacked by a Large Eagle at Faneuil Hall

Colonel Wilhelm von Kleinfels, Prussian military liaison to the army, while standing in discussion with English naval and army officers near Faneuil Hall, was suddenly attacked by a large eagle. No explanation was given for the bizarre attack by the creature, reported to be completely covered in white feathers. The colonel was evidently so surprised he suffered a stroke and collapsed. He was still alive and was transferred to a navy frigate at anchor in the harbor but bound for London. The army claimed

```
it was the Prussian officer's intention to go
aboard that ship that day anyway. The captain
of the frigate said the officer would receive
the best medical care while on board, but due
to the war, it was important for this man to
return to Prussia as he was recently given a
summons to return by Frederick II, the Prussian
sovereign.
```

Corrinne's mouth sagged open with surprise. "A white eagle?! This Prussian officer! He is the leader! We need to tell the magistrate—"

Their discourse was interrupted by a woman's scream out in the yard. Corrinne and Charles hurried through the *cuisine*, the mud room, and out into the yard to find Sentry holding Dian protectively in his arms. A basket of vegetables lay overturned at their feet. Atop the carriage house perched a very large white eagle, except this one had a chest speckled with brown feathers.

"Look there," Sentry added loudly. He was pointing at the body of another white-feathered eagle lying on the grass further back in the yard at the edge of the garden.

"Oh, no," said Corrinne.

She walked over to the body and knelt beside it. With a sense of dread, she touched its head gently. It was obviously dead.

"Oh, no," she repeated tenderly. "No…no."

Before she could say or do anything else, the eagle atop of the carriage house suddenly took flight. It circled above them several times before calling loudly.

"*Skrieee!*"

Then it flew away, leaving everyone speechless to comprehend the import of what just occurred before their eyes.

Charles was still carrying a newspaper in one hand and his spectacles in the other. He noticed Sentry's expression of disbelief. *I must have looked like that the first time*, he thought.

"Don't worry, Sentry. Remember, you saw the white eagle down at the house in Lyme. It warned us of danger. I have seen many things like this over the last two years."

"Forgive me for saying this, your lordship. But that eagle now lies *dead* in your garden…How many of these bloody creatures are there?"

CHAPTER 18
LOUISBOURG, ÎLE-ROYALE
JULY 1756
Le Héros

The two remaining enemy scouts were never caught. Three *coureurs de bois* of Henri's platoon eventually tracked the scouts overland, down to Port-Toulouse, and learned the spies had stolen a boat and escaped back across the Strait of Canceau to Nova Scotia.

Back in the Louisbourg fortress, a surgeon attended to the wound in Henri's shoulder. It was a painful operation. Henri was sitting up, his chest, arms, and legs belted tightly to a chair. The surgeon sliced open six inches at the top of Henri's left shoulder, beginning the incision near the neck. He took a pointed metal probe from his roll of surgical instruments and inserted it through the incision amid the bone and muscles. He twisted and turned the tip until he located the arrowhead.

"Aha! There it is!"

The men of Henri's platoon held tightly to his convulsing body, weighing it down to keep him from moving too much. Henri's screams were muffled by the leather scabbard he was biting tightly.

The surgeon took up another instrument that resembled a miniature prying bar intended for lifting broken ribs. He inserted that into the wound next to the probe and, using both, guided and pressed the arrowhead back and forth, forcing it up through the intervening muscle tissue.

"This way the edge of the arrowhead will slice cleanly through the muscle in line with the tendons," he explained logically to the horrified onlookers, who were watching and holding up lanterns for light, "thus allowing the muscle to heal with more strength and less scarring."

At some point, Henri's head slumped forward. He'd fainted from the pain.

The arrowhead, still attached to the shaft, abruptly popped above the muscle.

"*Voila!*"

The surgeon was very pleased with himself. He clipped the bloody flint arrowhead from the shaft and removed it. He washed the blood clean and examined the edges to be sure no infectious shards of flint had broken off and were still in the wound. Fortunately, he got it all. Then he yanked on the feathered end, which slipped the shaft backwards through the tunneled wound. It came out without resistance.

"There, you see. This technique on arrow wounds causes the least amount of pain."

"*He passed out from the fucking pain,*" one of the soldiers reminded him angrily.

"Yes. Well…he was lucky. The pain would have been much worse had he remained awake. This method also causes the least amount of damage to the muscle, presuming the nerves have not been cut. This was really… yes…it was quite a remarkable wound. A half inch in almost any direction and the ensign would be dead. I am surprised this officer chose to ride his horse, considering the way the edge of the arrowhead sawed away at the clavicle bone from the rocking motion. This is one for my journal."

"When will he wake up?"

"Hard to say," the surgeon replied. He started on the stitching. "Just as well that he's fainted. He won't feel this stitching either. And he needs the sleep…obviously."

Henri was up and out of bed within three days of the operation. He ignored suggestions by Major Péan to stay in bed and rest. As soon as he could walk all the way down the quay wall and back without passing out, he volunteered to do work, any type of work that contributed to the defenses of Louisbourg. By the end of the first week, Henri argued he had a good right arm and could use it to chop or saw wood to help build fortifications.

Governor Augustin de Drucour observed this wounded officer doing heavy manual labor without complaint. Citizens of Louisbourg noticed too and protested. Feeling guilty, the governor assigned him back to surveying duties.

Henri made numerous entries in his personal journal during this time, taking long overland rides on his horse to scout longer trails and marked them up on a map of Île-Royale given to him by Governor Drucour. He drove a wagon to carry out food to the Royal Battery on the west side of the harbor. He rode all the way around the harbor and climbed up to the lighthouse just to view the harbor and its defenses from another angle. The fortifications at the lighthouse were light, with just a few cannon. And the island battery was vulnerable from this position. He told the governor of this vulnerability when he returned, but the man already knew this. It made him wonder why they were spending so much time creating new fortifications in Gabarus Bay and neglecting the existing fortifications in and around the harbor. Those defensive fortifications on Gabarus Bay were well made, but they could never extend far enough to stop the English from making a landing and marching overland to begin a siege. And they did not have the troops in large enough numbers to man all the fortifications even after they were built.

"All the English have to do," a grenadier colonel remarked drolly, "is establish one spot on this beach that they can reinforce with more troops. Then no matter where they land, if they do this, our entire line will be flanked. The line will collapse, and we will have to fall back to the fortress. Our losses during such a retreat could be great."

Henri looked out over Gabarus Bay from a hill and could see the weakness in his mind just as the colonel described it. On horseback, he blazed a new trail higher on the hills, one that the troops could use when they had to retreat to the fortress, to prevent them from being cut off.

Henri also marked that on the governor's map, which was now becoming very valuable to Drucour. So much so, the governor directed Henri to survey farther along the crude road overland to Port Dauphin at the island's northern cape. Henri canoed across Mira Lake and walked north. He inspected the maintenance of the bridges, such as he was able to do, and usefulness of the ferry crossings. After visiting the small garrison and resupplying himself, he made an arduous four-day journey south to Port-Toulouse. He fished to feed himself or set snares, which rarely caught any animals. He repeatedly tried to use his bow, but his left arm simply would not withstand the full strength of his draw on the bow by his right arm. All the while, he made careful annotations on the governor's map, marking the locations of any

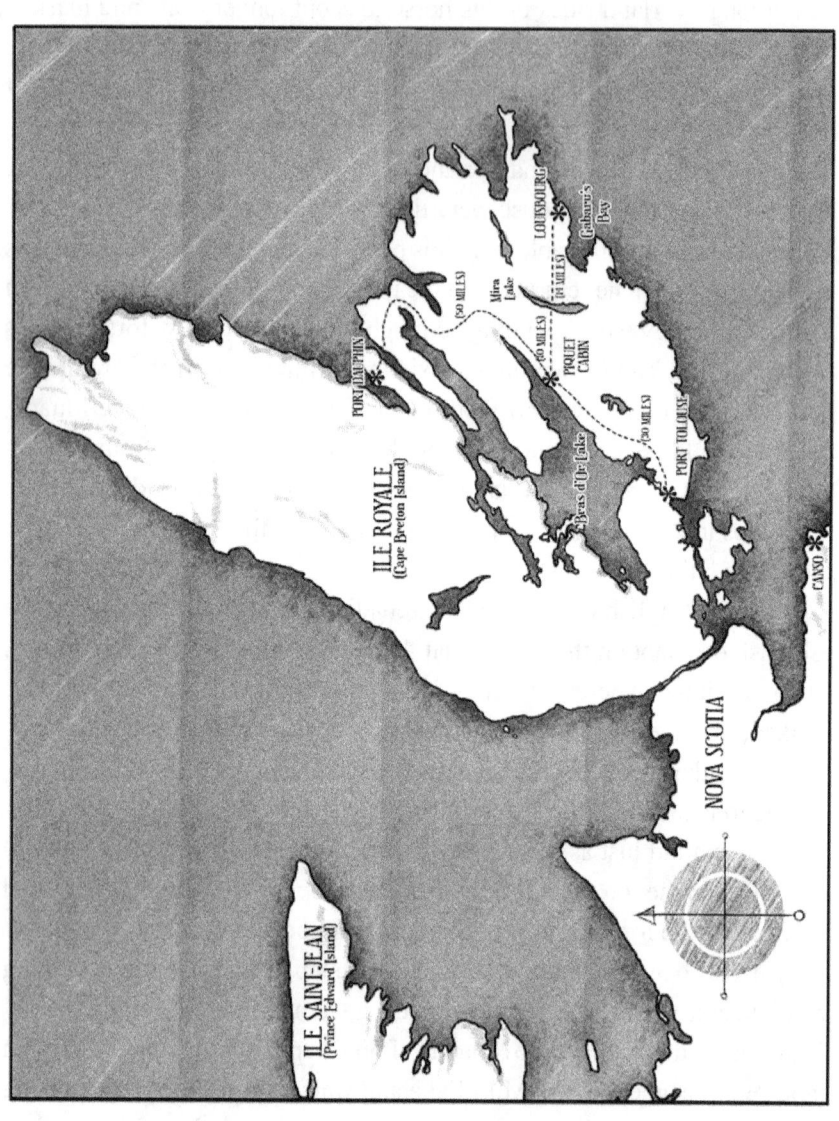

Henri's Trails of Île Royale

Indian settlements or the solitary fishermen piquet houses, particularly the ones on Bras d'Or Lake.

He stayed at Port-Toulouse for two days and nights and learned the area. He asked for a particular fisherman, Beau Sarchet, to deliver a sealed missive from Governor Drucour. But he was told the man and his boat had been lost in a storm. So he made contact with other local fisherman who agreed to be available for transporting a few passengers or taking mail to Quebec City. He restocked his pack with food for his travel back up the lake. This time, he followed the shore as closely as possible, counting his previous blaze marks in an attempt to identify the distance he traveled. He wanted to stop at a mid-point and go east to Mira Lake and establish a crossing point where he'd hidden a canoe weeks earlier. He finally selected a spot he estimated was midway, plus or minus half a mile. To his surprise, he found someone living there.

As he stepped out of the fog, he saw an overturned, roundish boat near the beach, covered in seal skins. Henri met an old Inuit couple, Pauloosie and his wife Yakone. He held up his right hand in greeting. The Inuit couple returned the gesture. They looked very old to Henri; too old to be living alone out here in the deep wilderness and cold. He learned they originally came from far up north. That they had grandchildren who had children too. Their hair was pure white. However, they seemed healthy, happy, and were very friendly. Fortunately, they knew a common sign language and it did not take long for them to communicate with the young white man, who had so suddenly showed up at their house.

They invited him inside the dwelling. It was five paces wide and long, a perfect square of vertical logs chinked with a mix of clay and sand. A vaulted roof of tree limbs, covered in overlapping stitched seal skins in a way that made any moisture roll off the outside. This roof was further covered in grassy sod. They had created a small rock hearth and chimney in one corner. It did not take much of a fire to heat the inside to a sweat. The floor was like a small hill, no more than a bulge, but enough to resist moisture from collecting. It was also covered in overlapped, stitched seal skins. There was a bed to one side made of furs and a few articles of woven cloth. They had a small wooden table, the legs cut short since there were no chairs. Other furs and skins were folded neatly into piles. The walls were adorned with nets, fishing baskets, snow shoes, bone tools, a musket with powder horn, several fishing poles, all sorts of knives and spears, and a bow with arrows. Henri would learn their food and water was collected daily and was abundant enough for their needs. Henri was the first white man to visit their home in almost a year, so their first questions to him were understandable. Pauloosie signed to him as they sat together near the warm hearth, under the golden, smokeless light of the whale oil lamps.

"*What are you doing out here? Are you lost?*"

"*No. I am scouting. I come from...from the large white man's camp.*" He signed and pointed to what he thought was east.

"Ah, ah!" Pauloosie responded and nodded with a clear understanding. Henri asked. "*Why are you here?*"

"*My grandson went to the warmer fishing waters to fish with the white men, to learn from them. That was two summers ago. He never came back. Our tradition requires the family to send hunters to find him. But we said it is for the oldest hunters to search for the youngest. We are old hunters. We have lived our lives. And we love our grandson. If we die searching for him in these waters we will walk with our grandson in death. And he will not be alone.*"

Yakone chimed in, babbling something at Henri. Then she smiled and patted his head.

"*What did she say?*" he signed.

"*She says it is a good sign you have found us. Our grandson sent you to us. She says our grandson was young and brave, like you, and often listened to the calls of his dreams, like you.*"

"*How long will you look for him?*"

Yakone answered in their tongue.

Pauloosie nodded. "*Until we find his spirit.*"

Yakone laughed and signed. "*My husband is our shaman. Our bodies mean nothing to him. Only the spirits they carry have meaning, he claims.*"

Pauloosie said something that sounded like a protest.

Yakone cackled. "*He said, Yakone's body had meaning to me when I was young.*"

Yakone signed back at Pauloosie. "*Only one part of my younger body interested you.*"

They both laughed and hugged one another. Pauloosie pointed at the small pouch around Henri's neck. Henri opened the top of the pouch without removing it and showed Pauloosie the white hairs.

"*They belong to a wolf,*" Henri signed. "*He was my friend. And he died saving me from a bear.*"

Seeing Henri's pained expression, Yakone touched her cheeks and then she touched his. Henri felt great warmth and comfort in her touch.

Pauloosie tapped Henri on the shoulder and motioned to follow him outside. It was getting very dark. The auroras were visible, the green growing brighter in the deepening twilight, flowing curtains, whipping and twisting. Pauloosie led Henri into the water of the lake, just deep enough to cover the toes of his boots. He pointed at a star and whispered its name in his tongue.

"Polaris," Henri said. Then Henri pointed at a star. "Sirius."

Pauloosie nodded and smiled and called it by a different name. Back and forth, they traded names of the stars.

Henri pointed and said, "Moon."

Pauloosie had a lot to say about the moon. He pointed at a star low on the horizon.

Henri did not know the name of that star. This seemed to make Pauloosie happy.

Pauloosie started singing loudly, gesturing with his arms.

Henri heard slow clapping behind him. Yakone had come outside. She started humming in different but repetitive tones.

Pauloosie tapped Henri's shoulder and pointed at the auroras. As he looked on, the green auroras twisted into the face of a wolf.

Henri gasped at the image and called out, "Roland!"

But it roiled back into curtain shapes as quickly as it came to be.

The couple stopped singing and clapping. Each held Henri's arm in support as he breathed heavily. Then they led him back inside the piquet. When they were seated, Pauloosie explained.

"*I asked our grandson if he would bring us your wolf spirit. Only a spirit can lead another spirit over the water. That he did this was a very great sign. Now we know our grandson's spirit is very near to us. We have found him! This makes us very happy. And now the wolf spirit who guards you knows where you are. This makes the wolf happy and you are happy.*"

"*Will I see him again?*"

"*Yes. When you have need to see him. He knows where you are.*"

Yakone began to prepare a meal. As a pan heated on the small hearth, she stopped for a few seconds to tie a bright red ribbon in her hair, which she took from a seal-skin pouch filled with ornamental things hanging from the wall.

Dressing for dinner, Henri thought. He signed how attractive she looked.

She poked Pauloosie and signed. "*He called me pretty! Now you must tell me too. Or I will sleep with him.*"

Pauloosie made as if he were thinking about this.

"Eyaah!" She poked him even harder.

They both laughed and hugged.

Yakone made grilled salt-cod in a pan. It became obvious to Henri he was an honored guest as she used the best of their foods, including their meager supply of dried peas mixed with water to begin a soup. Henri dug into his pack and gave her half the loaf of bread he'd brought with him from Port-Toulouse, along with over half the supply of dried beans he still had in a pouch. She babbled happily over these offerings and began to add bits of dried meat to the mix. Henri allowed her to pinch at the tiny sack of precious pepper he carried. He had a small bottle of brandy in his pack, but thought he'd wait to see if that was the right thing to do. Strong drink, though always accepted with a smile, usually did not sit well with the natives. And these people were old.

The meal was remarkably good, the cod was fried in a melted blubber of some kind, the thick soup of water, peas, beans, meat, and a mashed tuber root tasted *wonderful*. Henri had no better word for it. And when he asked for more, it was a high compliment to Yakone. She babbled in good words, nodded happily, and patted the side of his face and the top of his head with her hand.

After they ate, the room grew warm from the fire and the warmth of their bodies. Pauloosie propped open the door, the width of a hand, with a rock. It was dark and the cooler air rushed in to mix with the heat going up the chimney creating a natural draft.

They signed and talked for hours afterwards. They were very aware of the anger that existed between the warring white tribes. "*The Inuit are a very old people,*" Pauloosie explained. "*We no longer fight. Living is hard enough.*"

When Henri slipped off his coat to sleep, Yakone noticed him favoring his wounded left shoulder. She moved to his side, unbuttoned his shirt, and pulled it open to stare at the stitched incision on the top and the puncture on the side. The wounds appeared red and inflamed from the strap of his pack.

Yakone muttered her disapproval. She pulled over a small box of potions and herbs. She popped things in her mouth and chewed it into a paste and then spread the goo over the incision and puncture, further covering it with what looked like dried sea moss before carefully closing the shirt again. Henri didn't dare refuse her care. Besides, he found he enjoyed the way she mothered him.

"Yakone, you are quite possibly the only nice person I know on this entire island," he said sincerely in French.

Detecting the gracious tone of his words, she nodded and babbled back at him. Then she gestured to him to lie down on the small bed of furs she quickly arranged. She pulled the furs up to his chin and caressed the side of his face and hummed some kind of song.

Before they dimmed the lamps, she said something else to him. *Sweet dreams, young boy.*

The piquet home was small but surprisingly comfortable. And it felt safe, as if he rested among family. Outside, the wind whistled and some rain pelted the side of the house. The pitter-patter noise of the drops were like music. He was asleep in minutes.

The next morning, he rose and went outside to relieve himself. The fog was very thick, but the sun was up in the east. *Just head towards the blur*, he reminded himself.

Yakone fed him again in the morning. He searched through his pack and found the metal needle with the large eyelet for stitching skins. He had carried it with him since Boston. It was precious, but he felt he could get another at Louisbourg. He gave this to Yakone, who almost came to tears when receiving the valuable gift. He gave Pauloosie his long, sharp boning knife and scabbard.

As he stood and shouldered his pack to leave, the two Inuit hugged him tightly as if he were their grandchild. He was surprised at how fond he'd become of them in so short a time. Their saddened expressions were difficult to see. He bowed and rubbed his nose beneath their chins then started on his way. Every time he looked back, they were holding hands and still waving at him. In a few minutes, the fog closed in behind him. He planned to march east towards the yellowish blur in the sky for the two days it would take to reach Mira Lake again. Once there, he located the canoe he'd left hidden on its west bank. He went directly across and marked a tree as the sight for a bateaux hangar.

*

Louisbourg

Henri returned from his long journey and sat down with Governor Drucour to give him a full report of everywhere he went and what he'd seen. The governor had many questions. When it came to recounting his visit at Port-Toulouse, Henri returned the missive he was supposed to deliver to a fisherman named Beau Sarchet.

"The other fishermen said Beau Sarchet and his boat were lost in a storm," Henri said, his face downcast.

The governor reacted with pained concern and disappointment at seeing the missive.

"I did not want to open it or give it to anyone else. But I can go back there tomorrow, Governor," Henri assured. "It would only take me a week, maybe less, and I don't mind."

Governor Drucour shook his head sadly. "You did the right thing, Ensign. This missive was intended for Monsieur Sarchet and no one else." Then he said decisively, "What I want to do now is have you present what you have learned about Île Royale to the other officers."

After Henri received his shoulder wound, he carried his left arm in a sling for two weeks before starting his surveying duties. Now eight weeks later, Governor Drucour asked him to show the other officers the map he'd created. Henri had resumed his daily exercise regimen only a week ago. The pain in his shoulder when he did a handstand had been excruciating, but it was also getting better.

The governor and the other fortress officers looked down at the table as Ensign Gerrard rolled out the map he'd been using to mark another new trail he had just finished blazing. Henri placed smooth, heavy stones at the map corners, wincing each time he overextended his left arm.

"After two months of scouting trails, I think the best alternate to either Port Dauphin or Port-Toulouse is straight ahead to the west, about twelve to thirteen miles. I will take final compass readings next time I survey it, but west is the simplest direction to remember. It's not an easy trail. It is hilly, and there are a few bogs to get around. But it's well marked with notches in the trees about fifteen feet high. It can be walked in a day by men determined to do it. Or by noon the second day, even if they are exhausted.

"The masons are finishing a hangar they created to hold four bateaux. It will be made of common stone with roofs covered in wood, further protected by sod all around. Simple doors made of wood too. The floors will be poured with mortar, slanted five degrees and elevated a foot above the ground so the water will not collect inside. They will be hard to see, but just look for the bulge in the ground. Each bateau will carry ten. But Mira Lake is not that wide and we could ferry fifty people across using just two of the bateaux in less than an hour. By the end of this week, the hangar work will be complete. We will deliver the bateaux next week and let nature cover up all our work. That does not mean you cannot use the other roads going to the northwest, but if they are blocked by the enemy, this route will work too. Questions?"

The grenadier colonel frowned. "And we made this, why?"

Because I was ordered to do this. Henri glanced at the governor before answering.

"To use during a siege. It provides an alternate path for sending dispatches, or for bringing reinforcements from either of the other two ports, or it could be used for scouting, or to sally forth with forays to the north and south. Mira Lake poses a long barrier to get around…unless you want to swim across. It's about a thousand feet wide at this crossing. Any other questions?"

"What is on the other side of the lake?"

"More of the same terrain. From the other side of the lake it is another ten to twelve miles walking west to reach Bras d'Or Lake. Then another thirty miles south-southwest on Bras d'Or to Port-Toulouse. And maybe forty miles north to Port Dauphin, depending if you boat or walk. But you would probably have to find a boat to seize, unless we position one on Bras d'Or Lake. If you walk north or south, there are several well-marked trails to follow encompassed with all the hazards associated with that type of travel from both man and animal."

Governor Drucour admired the confidence of the young marine officer.

"Thank you, Ensign. This work is just another part of our preparations for invasion by the English. If there is siege encirclement, we will also need to have several ways to send and receive messages from Quebec. Now to the next topic."

Henri rolled up his map while Drucour continued.

"I expect all of you rejoiced at the welcome arrival of Commodore Beaussier de Lisle's squadron of four warships, which successfully confronted the English blockade to enter our harbor, bringing us supplies, plus mail and dispatches from France. He plans to stay here until he lifts the blockade. He intends to sally forth on his flag ship-of-the-line *Le Héros* to engage the English. *Le Héros* normally carries seventy-four guns but was reduced to forty-six guns to transport the Marquis General de Montcalm and his regiments to Quebec. So I have authorized him to borrow some of our cannon temporarily to rearm his ship for engagement with the English blockade. Accordingly, he is looking for volunteers from the garrison to go with him and man those cannon."

"I volunteer," Henri blurted before anyone else. "I'll go!"

Governor Drucour laughed lightly. "Of course you will, Ensign. All right, gentlemen, that's one volunteer. The commodore will need two hundred more."

Nearly the entire garrison volunteered. Within an hour, all the volunteers were selected and they helped winch over twenty cannon to *Le Héros* for the volunteers to man. It was a mix of just about everyone, grenadiers, metropolitan troops, marines, and militia, selected as long as they had some type of sea experience. Many of them lied for the chance.

Henri saluted Commodore de Lisle and reported his experience as soon as he boarded.

The commodore liked the young officer's enthusiasm immediately.

"Good to know, Ensign. But I have plenty of officers who can pilot. However, I will give you command of four cannon teams. Do you have any experience with that?"

"I have fired a few artillery pieces and have been under fire several times, Commodore. But before I fire one for you, I will become an expert."

Henri held up a book he retrieved from the governor's library on firing shipboard cannon.

The commodore looked at the cover, amused. "Your motivation is commendable. But you'll need to know much more than what is in that book." He turned and shouted out across the main deck. "Gunnery Bosun Kerbenard!"

A man ran to the commodore and saluted. "Sir."

"Bosun, this is Ensign Henri Gerrard. He will command four teams of the volunteers and their cannon. He needs instruction to make him an expert. You have the rest of the day to do this, Bosun. And Ensign Gerrard has agreed to pay you, uh, how much were you going to pay the bosun again?"

Henri swallowed. "Three ounces of silver?"

The bosun grinned, his eyes twinkling. "Ahhh, yes. Let's go below."

The next five days were some of the best Henri had ever experienced. *Le Héros* sailed forth to confront the English, without the support of the sixty-four gun ship-of-the-line *L'Illustre* or the two escort frigates, which the commodore ordered to remain in port. Henri was to learn firsthand that Commodore de Lisle was one of France's finest captains. The *Le Héros* engaged the stronger English squadron of two ships-of-the-line and two supporting frigates. Signaling between the English ships with flags and pennants to coordinate movements created tactical delays. The solitary French warship tactic of maneuverability was more agile. While none of the single pass engagements were decisive, the English ships received the greater damage from the French cannon.

Henri got very little sleep due to his excitement. His face, along with other exposed skin, was blackened with gunpowder soot. Cannon broadsides made the loudest sounds he'd ever experienced; so loud that his ears were ringing for hours afterward. Each night, he prayed he would not go deaf. Each day, his four gun crews reloaded with greater speed, now at twice a minute. He adapted his point of fire to the angle and sway of the ship, and the delay associated with the fuse of each gun. Their accuracy improved dramatically.

On the night of day four, he was invited to eat at the commodore's table and found a way to clean himself up. At least he thought so. But he had brought no other uniform to wear and the other shipboard officers were dressed in their finest to dine with the captain. When Henri entered the captain's quarters and saw how unprepared his appearance was compared to the others. He turned to leave and bumped into the commodore coming from the other direction.

"Ensign? Where are you going so quickly?"

"I beg your pardon, Commodore, but I think my appearance is too foul to take a seat at your table."

"Nonsense, Ensign…Gerrard, is it not? You are a cannoneer! They are not known for their body cologne, only for their accuracy. Get in there. My officers will be toasting your aroma. You'll see."

The dinner was almost a party with the commodore telling stories that had them laughing half of the time. Henri was seated almost at the very end of the table and learned he was the only volunteer officer invited that night. There just wasn't room enough. But the other more senior volunteer officers had preceded him on the previous nights in accordance to their rank.

While the dessert pastry and brandy was being served, the commodore reviewed the two engagements of that day. One of the English ships-of-the-line had already broken off engagement to limp back to Halifax; its cumulative damage after three days of cannon fire had become too great to repair at sea.

"The other English line ship is not in much better shape, though we also have not gone unscathed. I think they hope we will leave the fight first, so they can claim victory. They are wrong. We probably can make several passes tomorrow. And as long as the English want to stay and fight, I say we give it to them!"

The officers cheered.

The commodore sought out Henri's face at the end of the table.

"Ah! There you are! The soot makes your face hard to see. Ensign Gerrard?"

"Yes, sir."

"I am pleased to report, Gunnery Bosun Kerbernard claims all of your cannon shots found targets today."

The other officers smiled and offered him congratulations. "To Ensign Gerrard!"

They drank. A lot! Henri would later write in his journal. *It does not take much to get them to make toasts.*

"So tell us what you think?"

Think? "I think this is the greatest experience of my life."

The commodore's eyebrows waggled above his rosy face. "Indeed? This was your peak experience, you say? Of your life? You mean this is better than laying your head upon the perfumed, creamy breasts of a beautiful woman?"

The officers laughed and slapped the table-top.

The feeling of fraternity warmed Henri. They were all alike.

Henri slept well that night, augmented by several glasses of brandy he'd consumed. But his sleep was interrupted by the tolling sound of four clangs of the ship's bell. He did the mental calculation. It was the morning hour of six. He rolled out of his hammock and dressed. He stopped at the mess table to slice the end off a loaf of hard brown bread to chew upon and then climbed up the ladders to the main deck. It was foggy and wet but he could see the blurry orb of the sun rise. The sunrise near Louisbourg was usually blurry.

That's east, he mused. He trembled with a shiver from a gust of cold air. Looking at the bow compared to the sun meant they were sailing north-north-east. From the set of the sails, he knew the wind was out of the north. *They will be turning soon,* he guessed when the sun rose higher. *And* Le Héros *will come about to gain the weather gauge. Run all day with the wind until they engage the English, or turn more towards the west and return to Louisbourg.*

Henri walked aft until he stood near the rail just in front of the bulkhead wall below the massive bridge deck and helm. Having this bulkhead at his back gave him some shelter from the wind. He watched more than a dozen sailors moving about, tending busily to the yard arms and lines. There were a multitude of shell hits from previous days' cannon duels. Loads of deadly grapeshot had raked the main deck, ripping chunks of wood from the masts and rails, gouging holes in the deck. Men had been killed. Others wounded. The sails were littered with holes; most small and a few very large and those were taken down. Three sailmakers were sitting in a row slowly pulling the long pieces of canvas across their laps, quietly stitching and patching the holes.

Henri ate more bread, but now his mouth was dry. He soaked the bread from the sea mist dew atop the rail. It tasted cold and salty, but it was food.

"Is that you, Ensign Gerrard?"

Henri turned and looked up towards the bridge. It was the commodore! "Yes, sir."

"What are you doing down there? Come up to the bridge."

Henri climbed the ladder. In addition to the commodore, there were three other officers on the bridge, all of them looking through watch glasses in different directions, scanning for signs of the English. The rocking motion was more pronounced on the higher bridge deck. Henri's sea legs adjusted to the motion.

"Where is your coat? Are you not cold?"

"I am, sir. I only came up long enough to see our course and where we're going."

The commodore turned and told the attending steward to get the ensign a mug of black coffee. Then he turned back.

"And in this foggy morning you figured that out?"

"No, sir, I only guessed at it. Later I hoped to see if I was right."

"Tell me now. I will tell you if you were right."

"Uh...would that be impertinent, sir?"

"Nonsense. Assume it is an order. Tell me."

Henri did.

The commodore grinned. "Not bad. But the English are nowhere near us. They are just cruising back and forth across the Louisbourg harbor entrance, waiting for us to return. That's all Commodore Holmes knows how to do. He is no doubt following orders too, but he's never been very creative. This gives us the advantage of attack. We will come around on the perfect course when we near the entrance and attack for another go at their windward side. Probably in about three hours. I trust the fog will be completely gone by then. Ah! Look. Good. There's your coffee. That should warm you up. It will make your teeth stop chattering anyway. What have you learned about our enemy?"

Henri took several welcome sips and swallowed the wonderful heat before he replied.

"Not very much, sir, except for what I can see out a cannon port. Our turns seemed tighter, with much more precision than the English. Their cannon don't always broadside together. They miss many shots."

"Good eye, Ensign. You must always try to come at the enemy with the wind behind you and to *their* windward side. That way the enemy ship leans away from you in the wind. Because of that, their cannon tend to fire high into our spars and rigging. Plays hell with us nevertheless. Of course, the same thing means we lean towards them. This makes our shots fire low. But if our cannoneers compensate the roll and anticipate the delay in the fuse, they will fire true. And because of that, we do far more damage, straight into their sides. But it takes constant practice and very careful aiming by the gun captains, as you have learned. Anything else?"

"They seemed to turn away from us too quickly."

"They do. That's to gain more wind to get away. Problem with that, nobody wins. What else?"

"Their two frigates seem more daring. Of course, they turn quicker too."

"A frigate rarely attacks a ship-of-the-line. We have two to three times as many cannon. They are not in our class. Sometimes they manage a lucky shot. But most of the time they just get in the way and risk being blown into splinters."

"I noticed the one called *Jamaica* always tries to cross our stern when we turn, but we are usually turning too fast and often in the frigate's direction, so they do not get a chance. But they get pretty close. They tried it three times that I've counted so far. Even got off a few shots. Captain LaTour…a captain I sailed with before…said a stern crossing is a maneuver made to fire on the other ship's rudder, to damage it."

"And he is right, your former captain. You say the *Jamaica* did this?"

"Yes, sir. Three times that I saw."

"Then I predict that brash young English captain will try again today. But even if we are crippled, a frigate should never engage a line ship's cannon. But if he can damage our rudder, he will give the advantage of maneuver to the ships-of-the-line. Spineless tactic, in my opinion, yet very smart if you are trying to win a battle on a frigate as part of a fleet. Foolish for that captain to get so close to us by himself when it's not required. We'll prepare a lesson for him."

At mid-morning, before the engagement, Commodore de Lisle gathered his officers and all the cannon deck gun captains on the bridge and explained the tactics he would employ that day. He knew the remaining seventy-gun English ship-of-the-line was sorely damaged from the previous engagements. Several of its cannon were disabled. Many of its yards were broken. The holes in its sails spilled wind, affecting the speed. Only so much heavy damage could be repaired during the dark of night.

"One more solid broadside from us, concentrated at its mast and rigging will force it to turn and run while their sails hold any air. If they do not withdraw and become slowed in the water, we will broadside them into surrender. I expect the escort frigates to cross our bow and fire to delay our pursuit. However, Ensign Gerrard tells me the frigate *Jamaica* has tried to cross and fire on our stern three times. If it does this again today, this is what I plan to do…"

When the English ships came into sight, they were hull-down, sailing south-southeast on a course away from the *Le Héros*. Both escort frigates were sailing to the starboard side of the English ship-of-the-line. Fully sailed, *Le Héros* closed the intervening distance quickly. Shots from the low caliber bow and stern cannon of the two ships-of-the-line caused minor damage to one another as the distance shortened.

"Get out of the sail!" the commodore shouted through his speaking trumpet to the crewmen in the rigging.

The French seamen dropped straight down the dangling lines to lie flat on the main deck. The line ships traded full broadsides, damaging the deck, sail, and rigging on both ships.

After the broadside, down below, Gunnery Bosun Kerbenard tapped Ensign Gerrard on the shoulder and shouted into his ear above the noise of reloading, "Get up to the bridge, Ensign! Commodore's orders! I will command your cannon!"

Henri did not have time to ask why. He ran to the aft ladders and scrambled up to the bridge as he was told.

"Take the starboard wheel," the commodore ordered the ensign.

There were two helm wheels side-by-side on the bridge deck. To maneuver the heavy ship with any precision, it needed two rudders.

Henri took the starboard wheel. The sailor he relieved repeated the last order given to him.

"Steady as she goes!"

He also pointed to the compass and course and the rudder angle indicator. His orders were to allow the marine officer to do this alone. But the experienced helmsman stood a step behind Henri's right shoulder watching carefully…just in case.

Henri immediately felt the heaviness of the rudder and the sea through the helm. He glanced at the port helmsman. He tried to match his moves to the other man's. He knew both rudders must work together.

The damaged English ship-of-the-line turned to the left to capture more wind and flee. The escorts also came left with intentions to cut across the bow of *Le Héros* and fire cannon to interfere, as the commodore had predicted. Except one of the escorts kept coming farther to the left, intending to go down the French warship's right side to make a stern crossing. It was HMS *Jamaica*. The other English escort, HMS *Hornet*, fired cannon at *Le Héros'* bow, expecting the French to turn away from it to the left.

But instead *Le Héros* did something different.

"Right full rudder," the commodore ordered.

Sailors scrambled back into the rigging to make frantic adjustments to the sails as the big ship turned towards the *Jamaica*. The escort easily matched the French warship's turn. It could outrun the slower ship-of-the-line. Through his watch glass, the commodore could see the opposing captain's expression of shock when he saw the line ship coming around to attack.

"That's right, Captain! You can turn faster! But you cannot outrun my guns!" The commodore shouted.

Down below, Gunnery Bosun Kerbenard fired the four cannon one at a time, personally controlling their aim. After the four direct hits, the splintered main mast of HMS *Jamaica* toppled into the sea. Its sister escort was now too far away to assist. It was still cruising with the English flagship. Both were hull-down and moving away.

"Raise the truce pennant," the commodore ordered. It was a signal for a parley.

The frigate's mainmast lay half into the water with all of its sail. The affect was the same as a sea anchor. The frigate could no longer move. As

Le Héros finished its turn and slowly ran alongside the heavily damaged frigate, the gun ports of all three starboard cannon decks slammed open. Glancing quickly, Henri thought he was about to see the smaller ship disintegrate before his eyes.

Commodore de Lisle picked up his speaking trumpet and hailed the opposing captain. His English was accented but as clear as any English Henri could speak.

"That was a foolish maneuver, Captain!"

The English captain was about to strike his colors to save his crew when he saw the French commodore was not going to fire on him. He lifted his trumpet. "My apologies, Commodore!" Then he came to attention and saluted his enemy.

"Left full rudder," the commodore ordered.

Le Héros came all the way back around to the left while the sailors in the rigging readjusted the sails again. It sailed directly for the harbor entrance. The English battle squadron, such as it was, continued sailing for Halifax. HMS *Jamaica* chopped loose its damaged mainmast and eventually followed its flagship. This latest blockade of Louisbourg harbor had come to an end.

Six *Le Héros* crewmen had lost their lives and twelve were wounded during the five days of engagement.

Late in the afternoon, as the Louisbourg cannon were being winched back ashore, Henri approached the brow to leave *Le Héros*. He saw the commodore up on the bridge and decided to thank him.

"Request permission to come on the bridge," he shouted.

Commodore de Lisle waved him up. "Granted."

"I wanted to thank you, Commodore. This has been...*amazing* for me."

"Good. Any more questions before you leave?"

"Yes, sir. Just one. I wondered why we did not sink the frigate, or take it as a prize."

The commodore frowned. "If you were to duel with a boy half your size using that nasty cutlass of yours, would you kill him?"

Henri shook his head with embarrassment. "No, sir."

"There, just so. If this were a battle between two fleets, I would have destroyed the frigate without hesitation. With fleets it is a battle of attrition. Whichever side sinks the most ships wins."

"Yes, sir. I apologize for the question."

"Nonsense! You handled the wheel with expertise today, Ensign. And your cannon too! You are missing your true calling. You are not a soldier. You are a man of the sea. You should come with me. I am certain Governor Drucour would not mind giving you up. Not after I lifted the blockade of his fortress. *Oui?*"

Henri's heart sank, saddened at the thought of saying no. But that is what he did.

"Commodore, I am honored you would ask me. And I *want* to go with you...but I cannot leave my men. I am responsible for them. They depend upon me."

The disappointed commodore knew better than to cajole this dedicated young officer. He spoke respectfully to him.

"I am certain you would be greatly missed by your men, Ensign Gerrard. I admire your call to duty. But I also expect this war to last a long time. If you change your mind, send a missive to my ship to request your transfer. And I will make it so."

Weeks later, in the middle of August, Henri would watch with regret as *Le Héros* and the rest of the French battle squadron sailed from Louisbourg harbor bound for France. Governor Drucour would publically read aloud Commodore de Lisle's commendation to the garrison volunteers for their brave performance in action against the stronger English battle squadron.

"Commodore de Lisle makes special mention of Ensign Henri Gerrard, who manned the battle helm of *Le Héros* during the final action."

Six weeks later, Jean-Baptiste de Machault d'Arnouville, the Naval Minister of France would read Commodore de Lisle's report that the blockade of Louisbourg was lifted. He saw a familiar name mentioned. *Ensign Henri Gerrard!* If he had known the whereabouts of this young officer earlier, he would have sent the ensign a letter in a ship he recently dispatched to Louisbourg, but now at the end of September his chance to do that had passed.

*

The North Atlantic

Colonel Wilhelm von Kleinfels could barely stand up, though he tried every day. He forced himself to eat and struggled even to chew. He tried not to talk since he could only manage whispers.

During the crossing, the wraith twice surged to dominance in the colonel as he slept. The first time, he visited Alain Marcoux.

Alain explained to the night visitor that the regiment of mercenaries he recruited for use by the French had been abruptly incorporated into Frederick II's land army, when it rapidly mobilized following the war declaration, adding that the Prussian sovereign had ordered Alain to begin recruitment of another regiment. Alain was using the same people who recruited the initial group of men. With the advent of war, the few professional soldiers left in the lesser German states looked to join with the highest bidder for their services. Alain made certain the money he offered was twice the amount of any other bidder, but even so, trained mercenaries were now becoming a rarity. It would take until spring to raise the numbers to make a new regiment.

The colonel is on his way back to Prussia, Alain was told by the night visitor. *Find a way to gain transport to Quebec.* Alain was not told why.

So Alain traveled in civilian attire to Paris to inform the French Naval Minister of this delay via a couriered confidential missive. He offered to be of further service in New France in the interim. In a return missive, the Naval Minister demanded that Alain meet with him, in person, in Rochefort, and to bring his baggage.

Carter Trevathan was visited next. Carter explained the failure to set the whore queen's house on fire and the death of the servant called Felix. The night visitor gave him the name of the next person on the list to poison.

A different poison should be used. Not like the other, Carter was told.

Each time the wraith dominated the colonel, the man was weaker afterwards, dangerously so after the second time. So the wraith resisted any more attempts until the colonel recovered his full strength, which might not be until long after the crossing. The debilitating weakness of the colonel could not be ignored. Over water, if the colonel should expire, the body would be weighted down and thrown overboard. That was a disturbing possibility. The wraith contemplated whether it was time to possess a new host. It would not be easy to arrange and would take time, even when the colonel gained back his strength. And such a thing would be impossible whilst over water. Water was a vastness devoid of human life. But over water, the wraith was also not constrained by the sealing hex of the *châsse*. The wraith wondered if it might visit the dreams of these sailors. It was a tantalizing possibility. They were close enough. Surge into dominance and take but a small sip of their vitality? Leave only a small scar? But even that minor strain on the weakened colonel could be dangerous.

The *vulnax* decided to wait. It was used to waiting. It could wait forever if even a piece of bone from the host survived.

*

Rochefort

Before meeting with Admiral de la Motte, Alain Marcoux met with the Naval Minister who demanded to know the whereabouts of Colonel von Kleinfels. Machault needed to communicate directly with the Prussian sovereign and only the colonel could do that. Alain volunteered that the colonel was on his way back to Prussia from America by now but did not know when he would arrive.

"The colonel will surely communicate with you just as soon as he sets foot on land."

Machault thought about this. The Hessian would probably land in London first. By then it might be too late to alter the Prussian sovereign's war plan. But the Naval Minister also had personal reasons to communicate with people in New France outside the prying eyes and influence of Governor Vaudreuil and Intendant Bigôt. He decided to have Admiral de la Motte add this man and destination to Captain LaTour's orders.

"You can perform another service for me in the meantime. You will deliver a dispatch pouch to the governor of New France. You will tell Governor Vaudreuil you are a courier from me and explain what you are planning to do for him regarding the mercenaries. He may have messages to bring back to me. Collect those. But I have another dispatch packet I need couriered that cannot be disclosed to the governor or anyone else. It must not be opened by anyone except the recipient. I will use your services as a measure of trust between Colonel von Kleinfels and me."

Alain Marcoux bowed. "It would be my privilege to be of service, my Lord Minister."

"Good!" Machault handed over the small packet containing two letters. The packet was sealed and addressed to a Father Tinian, Terrain des Jésuites.

"This priest will be easy to find in Quebec. Do not fail me in this regard, Monsieur Marcoux," Machault added gravely. "Father Tinian will surely give you sealed messages for me in return. Wait for them and bring them back to me."

"As you command. But I must first find a means to get to Quebec. It is late in the crossing season."

Machault smiled. "Fortune smiles on you, Monsieur. I have the perfect accommodation for you. Dangerous but fast."

*

Captain LaTour entered Admiral de la Motte's offices at the Fort de la Pointe headquarters, the citadel at the mouth of Le Charente River in Rochefort. He wore his new tailored naval uniform as a ship captain in the French Navy. He came to attention and saluted.

"Reporting as ordered, Admiral."

The admiral assessed the former smuggler with a critical eye.

"I see you've groomed yourself, undoubtedly bathed…and shaved too. I must say, Captain, you wear that French naval uniform very comfortably. Is your ship ready for sea?"

"Yes, sir. The hull and deck repairs are complete. Our patched sail is being replaced with new ones as we speak. We have taken on food stores. And we are loading the cargo you sent to us."

"But you need to know where you are sailing to, *oui*?"

"That would be helpful, sir."

The admiral handed the captain his written orders. "These are confidential orders for no other eyes but your own. Read them carefully, Captain. You are sailing into danger."

Captain LaTour read his orders with a combination of surprise and dread. He was ordered to deliver the loaded cargo to fortress Louisbourg. Collect dispatches as available from Governor Drucour. Sail to Quebec City and deliver a special passenger, *to be named*, to see Governor Vaudreuil. Collect dispatches as available. Sail to Boston under the flag of the Dutch Republic and deliver sealed dispatches to Lord VanderMeer. Set sail for Louisbourg and embark such passengers as may be directed by Governor

Drucour consistent with available space aboard the ship. Then return directly to Rochefort to report completion of this mission.

LaTour saw at least a half dozen opportunities to get his neck stretched by a rope.

"God's balls," he mumbled to himself. *I gave up Odara's bed for this?*

"Captain? Did you say something?"

"I said, *God protect me*, Admiral."

The admiral frowned. "Yes, I am sure he will. Now come to attention and salute your Naval Minister."

LaTour turned to see Officer Trémoille escort Jean-Baptiste de Machault d'Arnouville into the admiral's office. Machault was accompanied by another man. LaTour smiled, came to attention, and saluted.

"Monsieur Machault! I am so pleased to see you again."

They embraced as friends.

"Captain LaTour! Destiny provides us with unexpected surprises and coincidences, does it not? Allow me to introduce a special passenger you will carry. This is Monsieur Alain Marcoux. He performs a special service for me. He will hand deliver the dispatch pouch to Governor Vaudreuil. You are to take him to Quebec City and personally escort him to Governor Vaudreuil. Then you may leave him there. That is all you need to know."

After shaking hands, Alain Marcoux was excused from the office, leaving the admiral, Captain LaTour, and the Naval Minister to sit and have an in-depth discussion of the objectives of Captain LaTour's mission, which were part trade, part smuggling, part intelligence, and all together dangerous. Admiral de la Motte explained this was not a combat mission. That he should evade the enemy. Captain LaTour agreed this was good counsel since his vessel was not armed with any cannon. Machault explained the confidential dispatches he carried must not fall into enemy hands.

"You are a smuggler, so you possess a means to safeguard these missives, yes?"

LaTour confirmed that he did.

"Questions?"

"My crew normally gets paid a share of the profits from a voyage. I do not see an opportunity for profit in anything I will be doing."

"You are a French naval officer!" the admiral responded sharply. "You do not sail for profit!"

The Naval Minister was more sympathetic. "Captain, deliver your confidential messages to Boston to the people addressed and someone there will give you funds to pay your crew…I cannot be more specific than that."

The admiral pointed at the two large sealed sacks of dispatches on a nearby table.

"Those are for you, Captain. One is for Governor Drucour, the other for Governor Vaudreuil."

Naval Minister Machault handed the captain a smaller sealed valise. "This one is for Lord VanderMeer in Boston."

Admiral de la Motte gave the captain one more roll of official documents.

"You can show these credentials to any French warship that chooses to challenge you. It certifies under my signature you are a French officer on a mission for me. Of course, if you are challenged and show these to the English, they will hang you instead. Better that you wear your Dutch hat in the event you meet the English. But I suspect you know that."

"You do not have to warn me, Admiral."

Alain Marcoux waited in another room for Captain LaTour. He had come to Rochefort with his baggage as directed by the Naval Minister. Now he understood why. He would travel with the captain back to La Rochelle and take passage on *William's Queen* to Quebec City. Except for delivering dispatches to Governor Vaudreuil and the confidential courier, he would perform for the French Naval Minister. That was all Alain knew to do. He presumed the night visitor would provide him more purpose. But not until the colonel landed in England. He had no choice about this except to wait once he got to Quebec.

*

The Eastern Atlantic

As always, to Captain LaTour's pleasant surprise, every single man in his crew had returned in time to sail with him again. He decided not to tell them where he was going just yet. He showed Alain Marcoux the cabin that would be his home for the next six weeks. Then he ordered the anchor raised and set sail.

William's Queen sailed due west from La Rochelle. LaTour wanted to cross the coastal shipping routes running north and south as soon as possible to avoid being challenged. He saw plenty of merchant ships for the first two days, but only one war frigate, and that one was French. But English cruisers patrolled these waters too, and corsairs, and privateers carrying *lettres de marque*, giving captains sanction from King Louis to board and seize ships as prizes. He worried about them the most. They were French, but these men operated like pirates. They would approach in a friendly fashion, one French ship to another, but then would seize his cargo if they thought it had value and sink the vessel if given the chance. Corsairs were more deadly, but openly more honest in their intentions compared to privateers.

Speed was the *Queen*'s best advantage for now. Her new sails gleamed. The hull was clean and smooth, but his forward speed of advance to the west was reduced as strong shifting winds forced the ship to tack back and forth at different angles to make headway against the pounding seas. LaTour spent much time on the helm to pilot. He was the best man for it anyway.

On the second day, Victorio spotted another sail on the horizon, tapped the captain on the shoulder, and pointed. LaTour gave over the helm to a regular crewman. He took up his glass and together they watched the vessel's approach. It was a large cargo vessel, fully sailed, coming from the east. He saw a second sail to the left of the cargo vessel. A warship flying the *fleur de lys*.

"She has an escort," LaTour said. "They won't bother us, I think. But we'll not cross their bows." He took back the helm and came left to a more west-southwesterly heading that would keep them well clear of the warship before giving back the helm to the regular watch. He looked at Victorio.

"Stay on this course a while. Come back to a northwest course after we are well past them. I'm going below to eat something and chart out courses. I will be at the long table. Ring the bell if you need me."

The captain went down to his cabin and gathered up his ocean charts, compass, and dividers. He went to the long table in the mess room amid the passenger cabins. He told the steward what he wanted to eat and spread out his maps. It was mid-summer, but he already sensed the winds moving more northward, earlier than usual. *Maybe my fortune changes, too*, he thought glumly. This was the most dangerous voyage he'd ever taken. He wanted to be done with it as quickly as possible.

"Good morning, Captain."

LaTour looked up. It was Monsieur Alain Marcoux. LaTour nodded curtly in greeting and went back to his chart as the man took a seat at the other end of the long table and told the steward what he wanted. The captain did not trust this man. There was something familiar about the pitiless gaze of those brown eyes.

"I am sorry to disturb you, Captain," Marcoux said loudly.

The man's interruption was intentional. LaTour stopped measuring distances and regarded the passenger.

"Monsieur, we have weeks of travel ahead of us, so let me be candid with you. You already know we are sometimes a smuggling ship. As such we are not a very *talkative* group of seamen. I have told my crewmen your name, that they should treat you with courtesy, but not to answer any question about who we are, what we do, or our history. If you show too curious an attitude, they will not answer you, but they will tell me, and you and I will have an unfriendly conversation. So if you have any questions, ask me, and me alone, *s'il vous plait.*"

The steward came in at that moment and put a square, footed, tin plate in the slots before the passenger. It had eggs, sausages, vegetables, bread, and butter. LaTour gestured to the steward to hold back his own food.

"And enjoy the fresh food, Monsieur. It will only last another week."

Alain Marcoux put a piece of sausage in his mouth and chewed with relish.

"Mmm, yes. Very tasty. Captain LaTour, I do not want an adverse relationship to exist between us. As you say, we have a long cruise ahead of us. I, too, have smuggling in my past, an undistinguished history. I was not very good at it. But I was also a soldier in Marshal de Saxe's army. I was wounded in the head and left for dead at the Battle of Fontenoy. Indeed, the army listed me as dead. So I decided to change my name and occupation. Fate has brought me here, ten years later, to sail aboard your ship. I will be a respectful passenger for you, but I will not be a monk. I will come up on deck and breathe fresh air. I will probably ask your crew questions about sailing, or the weather, or where we are, and, of course, I will probably ask you most often…'How much longer?' like an impatient child."

The passenger's eyes narrowed.

"But I am *not a child*, and I will not tolerate unfriendly conversation from anyone. Like you, I have a mission of government to complete in Quebec. And that is my business. So, captain…how much longer?"

Captain LaTour noted the menace in the man's words. He'd been measuring distances on the chart and made a quick decision.

"And I will not tolerate threats of any kind to my captaincy. Out here on the seas, I am king. Just so we understand one another, *oui*? Monsieur Marcoux, I have great respect for Admiral de la Motte and the Naval Minister. You do something important for them, no doubt. You will be pleased to hear I plan to travel Quebec City first. The winds are against me just now, but that will change. I expect the weather to stay fair this time of year. But in this part of the ocean, storms can arise at any time. If the winds become more favorable, I will have you in Quebec five weeks from today, maybe sooner. And it is in my interest to get you there as soon as I can. Like you, I have several important missions of government to complete. You are but one part of it."

Alain Marcoux took another mouthful before replying.

"Your food is good, Captain. You know, I have the strangest feeling we have met before. Do I seem familiar to you?"

I was thinking the same thing, LaTour did not say. It was, indeed, an odd feeling.

"Your face is not familiar to me, Monsieur. I am not good with names, but my smuggler's memory is excellent with faces. We have never met."

"Well then, thank you for the information. I will finish breaking my fast in silence and leave you to contemplate your charts...*and your stars*."

CHAPTER 19
LAKE ONTARIO
JULY 1756
In Hoc Signo Vincunt

A hundred and fifty miles east of the French fortress of Fort Niagara
was the only English possession on Lake Ontario. It was called Fort
Oswego. Located at the mouth of the Onondaga River, later called the
Oswego River, it was a collection of three forts. The original Fort Oswego
began as a simple log palisade trading post in 1722 and was situated on
the western bank of the river mouth. Five years later, a machicolated stone
blockhouse was built at the center of the palisade, ostensibly to offer better
protection to the garrison, much like a citadel. Built of local stone and clay,
as time passed, the clay mortar dried out and would fall away in the presence
of any significant vibration of the ground near the base of the structure,
or a shockwave created by, for instance, a cannon fired anywhere near it.

By 1755, to further protect this fragile fort, a breastwork of logs and
earth was built on the landward side, west of the blockhouse. To the east of
the block house there was no defense except the river. A quarter of a mile to
the south of Fort Oswego on a low hill near the river, another log redoubt
was built to protect Oswego's vulnerability from a southern approach. On a
small hill to the west, a log stockade was erected to deny these heights from
enemy cannon, should the enemy ever come to this place. It was officially
named Fort George. The soldiers referred to it as Fort Rascal. This fort
was built without any loopholes to fire muskets through, or any ramparts
to stand upon to fire over the top of the walls. Thus, the tactic to employ
when attacked was to throw open the gates so the defenders could see the
attackers in order to shoot at them. The tactic unfortunately mitigated the
defensive integrity of the log walls.

On the eastern bank of the river across from Fort Oswego, the land rose
up fifty feet. At a distance of five hundred yards, a more defensible third

fort was erected. It was a more modern five-pointed star-shaped design, intended to defend the vulnerable eastern face of old Fort Oswego, which lay open to the river. Its name was Fort Ontario. It was built entirely of logs cut smooth on two sides and fitted together tightly all around; some would later say its workmen must have been cabinet makers. The joints were tight, the walls were tall, with positions of defense built using carpentry squares. But its main flaw was that it was entirely made of wood, not stone. Against musket fire, it was adequate. Against a twelve-pound cannon ball or anything larger, the walls would burst into splinters. Typical siege cannon used twenty-pound iron balls...*or larger*.

Fort Oswego was legitimately part of the New York province's western territory. A series of New York governors never really showed much interest in it; it was too far from Albany. But Governor William Shirley of Massachusetts was obsessed with maintaining Fort Oswego on Lake Ontario. As each defect in the original fort's design was pointed out by military engineers, his solution was to build more breastworks, horn works, and earthworks. Eventually, the outlying stockades were hastily erected to compensate further. When the newer Fort Ontario's fatal flaw was presented to the governor, the next solution was to build a navy on Lake Ontario to counter the navy the French were also building at Fort Frontenac across the lake. He sent shipwrights from Boston to do this work. Following the death of General Braddock at Fort Duquesne, William Shirley became the new commander-in-chief of armies in North America. Invested with these powers, he stationed two regiments of troops at Fort Oswego to defend it all. A battalion of the 50th Foot would defend the old Fort Oswego forts. A battalion of the 51st Foot manned the newer Fort Ontario. Added to this were several provincial companies of New Jersey Blues.

Now fully garrisoned, *General* William Shirley had to deal with the requirement of creating adequate barracks for these men, provisioning them with food and ammunition, and establishing a line of supply that would deliver replacements, food stores, and ammunition on a routine basis. For this task, he assigned Colonel John Bradstreet who possessed a commanding presence as a leader and an extraordinary flair for logistical organization. It was a good thing Shirley had such a man to rely upon, because the task of resupply was no simple endeavor.

But first Shirley had to convince the legislatures of eight different colonial provinces to contribute money to buy the necessary provisions and to build the needed wagons and flat-bottom *battoe*-boats to carry the supplies. Then somebody would have to build staging points along the route, essentially more forts of the wooden stockade variety. It was one hundred and fifty miles from New York City to Albany, but the Hudson River was navigable by sail for the transport of goods. From Albany, the journey got decidedly more difficult. Over land from Albany to the Mohawk River was eighteen miles of wagon road. There followed a journey further west on the Mohawk River for eighty miles until that river turned north. Facing them now was a five-mile portage, the Great Carrying Place, also called the Oneida Carry. At this point, the battoe were unloaded. The goods were put on wagons pulled by horses. Of course, the horses first had to be purchased and stabled there permanently. Wagons were built, some of them large enough to carry a large battoe-boat, if necessary. To be protected, a large staging fort called Fort William was built at the beginning of the Oneida Carry. At the other end of the portage, a second staging fort was built. It would be the last fort before the final push to Fort Oswego. It was called Fort Bull. It was the weakest link in this weak chain of supply. The French exploited this in a deadly fashion.

At the end of the carry, the wagons were unloaded. The food, provisions, and munitions were either stored at Fort Bull or loaded on hundreds of battoe sitting on the bank of the next water course, called Wood Creek. Seven miles down Wood Creek, the battoe entered Oneida Lake, followed by a twenty-mile crossing of Oneida Lake. The outflow from Oneida Lake to the Onondaga River descended four hundred feet over a fifteen-mile water course, including a twenty-foot waterfall near the end that required another mile-long portaging of the battoe-boats overland. All of the portages along this route from Albany required horses, wagons, and extra men to assist in the laborious task of unloading, dragging, and reloading as required. The final twenty miles down the Onondaga River to Lake Ontario traversed a place of river islands at the midway point known for constant ambushes by French militia or their tribal allies, sometimes both.

In total, from Albany to Lake Ontario and Fort Oswego was a journey of a hundred and eighty arduous miles with danger at every turn of the river and portages involved.

General Shirley had left the Oswego forts in October 1755 with every confidence in what he believed to be a well-fortified and well-defended position with two full battalions of Foot. He traveled back to Albany to chair a mid-December council of war, as commander-in-chief, to plan the military campaigns of 1756. In that meeting, he received with bile a blistering assessment of Fort Oswego's vulnerability from the governor of New York and former admiral of the British Navy, Sir Charles Hardy.

Shirley dismissed the assessment as Hardy's own ignorance of what had already been accomplished at Oswego.

"We have a plan, *Admiral*. We've been delivering supplies to Fort Oswego routinely for years. Most of us have lived here for a decade or more. I think we, better than you, appreciate the distances involved."

*

From November of 1755 to February 1756, winter came to the lake and river wilderness that surrounded Fort Oswego. The water courses of the one hundred and eighty mile supply line had begun to freeze over by the time of the war council in Albany. The food provisions at Fort Oswego had begun to run out. Worse, while many preparations were made for the defense of the Oswego forts, very little preparation was made for the garrisoning and survival of the men who would live there. Minimal barracks. Bark-covered hovels for dwellings. No floors. Sleeping quarters invaded by snow and chill winds. If the soldiers did not freeze to death, their weakness from lack of food made them all susceptible to deadly diseases. Scurvy, dysentery, and the bloody fluxes that had plagued soldiers since armies first marched.

The commanding officer, Lt. Colonel James Francis Mercer, sent messages to Albany complaining about the perilous conditions, pleading for more food, supplies, and reinforcements. At the worst of the winter, he actually held a council of war among his own officers and considered abandoning the forts before everyone starved to death. He was a fifty-three-year-old Scot, a veteran officer in the English army. He'd fought in Flanders in 1745 and was part of the garrison at Louisbourg when it was captured the first time. In the end, Mercer's conscience would not allow him to do it. He would not give up the fort to the French without a fight. They would stay.

Lt. Colonel John Bradstreet was forty-two. He'd been in the English army almost twenty years. He was a brilliant strategist in the area of logistics and a charismatic leader men would follow into dangerous situations. He also heard Sir Charles Hardy's prophetic words that confrontational day in December 1755. But he already knew the truth of Hardy's argument. And he'd seen Colonel Mercer's messages for help.

With assistance from Sir William Johnson, he was already moving supplies down the Mohawk River in that direction, though because of winter, it proceeded in a very slow fashion, a few miles at a time. When the battoe-men reached Fort Williams, they would stock pile and go back for more. Fort Williams would move the provisions overland with great difficulty to Fort Bull. But there it stopped. Wood Creek was frozen solid. They tried moving it by sledges to Oneida Lake, but the lake's ice thickness was unpredictable. Those few who tried to go forward were never seen or heard from again. But Bradstreet had personally recruited his thousand-strong professional corps of battoe-men. They were experienced and dedicated. They continued to persevere, moving supplies forward a little at a time. Eventually, they began rolling barrels down the frozen Onondaga River and pulling other supplies piled on sledges by hand. Some relief got through. And by March 1756, Fort Bull began loading battoe on Wood Creek in anticipation of the ice thaw and snow melt which had begun.

Then the French struck and destroyed Fort Bull.

When word of this came to John Bradstreet, he knew the need at Oswego by now was more than desperate. He personally took charge of the next group of battoe. Reinforcement troops from other companies in the 50th and 51st Foot regiments were sent ahead, up the Mohawk River ahead of him. Another Fort Bull had been quickly rebuilt by the time he reached it. Even so, more battoe were needed for the ones destroyed by the French. It was not until the middle of May in 1756 that Bradstreet's three hundred boats finally reached the Oswego forts. The condition of the men was dire and shocking. More than half of the garrison had already died of disease, lack of food, or both. Most of the rest were so sick they could barely stand guard. And more were dying every day. The food was most welcome.

Colonel Bradstreet recognized they needed more of everything and a lot of it, if they were going to defend this fort…forget any thought of attacking Fort Frontenac. He returned to Albany as fast as possible to organize another, much larger shipment of provisions and ammunition. General Shirley was now alarmed by what he heard and sent more reinforcements to the garrison at Fort Oswego. Those soldiers, Colonel Bradstreet, and more supplies had started back upriver to Fort Oswego just before the new English officers sent to relieve General Shirley of his command arrived in Albany.

The new English commander-in-chief was General John Campbell, 4th Earl of Loudoun, or Lord Loudon, as he was referred to by everyone. But Lord Loudoun's ocean crossing had been delayed by storms. General Ambercrombie, Loudon's second-in-command, relieved General Shirley and sent him back to New York City to await Lord Loudoun's arrival. But other than that, Ambercrombie was indecisive on what orders to give the large army he now commanded, which included three thousand British redcoats in Albany and another seven thousand American provincials, encamped at Fort William-Henry, presumably prepared to strike out against the French at Fort Carillon or Crown Point.

Complicating these matters was the sudden refusal of the American senior officers to serve in subordinate rank and position to the redcoat English officers. This was followed by a vote of the provincial soldiers, who threatened to desert if they were forced to serve under English commanders!

General Ambercrombie had never seen anything like this in his entire career. He was stunned at this level of insubordination and could not conceive a solution. Having been apprised of the severe supply problems debilitating the supply line to Fort Oswego, he decided to have his redcoat regulars guard the supply route between Albany and Fort Edward and Fort William-Henry on Lake George. He decided further to await Lord Loudoun's arrival, to allow him to direct any new combat actions undertaken.

Colonel Bradstreet reached Fort Oswego with more supplies and men on July 3rd. Not much had improved from his visit in May, but the new replacements for the 50th and 51st Foot, along with another company of provincials from New Jersey, permitted the Oswego forts to establish a military posture again. Bradstreet, Colonel Mercer, and Captain James MacKellar, the military engineer, held a small council on the situation. MacKellar summarized in detail all of the defects in the current forts that would render the works indefensible if the French decided to mount a large attack, which was a constant threat, even though the garrison had fresh reinforcements.

"Collectively, the defensive positions of these fortifications are untenable," Captain MacKellar said with regret, knowing the opinion would not be popular. "If the enemy brings siege cannon, there are as many directions to attack these fortifications successfully as there are points on a compass."

But John Bradstreet thought this statement only confirmed what his eyes could plainly see already. He ordered his battoe-men to man their oars and start returning back down the Onondaga River. At the midway point of river islands, Captain Coulon de Villiers' raiding party of militia and Indians attacked the departing supply boats.

In the ensuing back and forth battles that continued all day long among the islands, Bradstreet lost seventy of his men, and the French, he believed, lost an equal number. But it was a draw, and the battoe-men proceeded south up the river. Two French prisoners had been captured, who disclosed that a much larger French force, purportedly several thousand, was now advancing on Fort Oswego. They planned to attack before summer was over. Alarmed by what he'd learned both from Captain MacKellar and from the French prisoners, John Bradstreet proceeded ahead of his battoe-men as fast as he could travel to warn Albany of the imminent danger to Fort Oswego. He arrived on July 12th, providing his eyewitness account as to the deaths and sickness experienced by the garrison over the winter, the alarming report of the defective fortifications by engineer Captain MacKellar, and the testimony of the French prisoners he captured in the river battle, stating that an attack by a French army would occur by the end of summer.

Much as he preferred to wait for Lord Loudon, General Ambercrombie decided he must act on this. On July 16th, he ordered Colonel Webb to go to the relief of Fort Oswego at the command of the 44th Foot regiment. But now the rumors, faulty intelligence, command disputes, and logistical muddle had taken hold. An Indian horde was attacking from the north! Not true. The French were moving south from Ticonderoga. Not true. Any excuse would do; the purported lack of money, not enough wagons and worst of all, no sense of urgency, despite Colonel Bradstreet's continuous appeals to do *something*! It would continue for two more weeks.

Lord Loudon arrived in Albany on July 29th. The officious Scot's acerbic disposition, even on a good day, was confronted by a command in disarray. The American provincial officers' refusal to subordinate their rank and take orders from English officers bordered on treason. *Bordered? It is treason!* The rampant rumors of enemy movement were in continual conflict. Was it Oswego or Ticonderoga? All of this was compounded by the absence of any real British leadership or direction for over a month. The situation could not be more acute.

Lord Loudon focused on the most important problem in his estimation... *the insubordination of the provincial troops.*

Colonel Webb and the 44th Foot regiment would not begin its march to relieve Fort Oswego until August 12th.

*

August 10th
Lake Ontario
One mile east of Fort Oswego

The Marquis de Montcalm completed the final push of his forces from Niaouré Bay and came ashore on Lake Ontario just after sunset as planned. They were little more than one mile to the east of Fort Oswego. And still his forces were undetected! He could not believe they encountered no patrols or scouts previous to this. He would be landing two divisions, thirteen hundred highly trained French metropolitan regulars from the Béarn, La Sarre, and Guyenne regiments, plus fifteen hundred Troupes de la Marine and militiamen. This first division brought most of the highly trained regular troops with some defensive cannon and entrenchment tools.

The advanced reconnoitering by his engineer, Captain Descombles, was also successful without being detected. Unfortunately, Descombles, upon his return, had taken off his coat amid the summer heat, exposing the red vest he wore beneath it. He was shot by accident by an Indian ally who mistook him for an English redcoat.

Fortunately, before his death, the engineer had inked Montcalm a report with sketched pictures. It described an arrangement of English defensive works that were seriously flawed. When firmly ashore, Montcalm ordered Ensign Desandrouins, the assistant engineer, to mark out the first siege parallel just short of two hundred yards from Fort Ontario and ordered Colonel Bourlamaque to supervise this construction effort.

"Make certain they are very quiet," he cautioned.

The French soldiers would work all night digging the trenches.

Days earlier, captured deserters from Oswego gladly spoke about the ineffective defenses of the main fort that consisted of simple musket loopholes. Fort George to the west was overcrowded with a mass of sick men. The half-square log redoubt to the south was little better. Rampant disease plagued the remaining garrison in the main fort and they could barely stand up.

The French asked the deserters about the heavier defenses of the forts. What type of weapons do they employ on the walls?

"Weapons?! Frim the dep creviss of the arse, we kin spout a foul strim that bursts intah a fire by tichin it witha a spark!" One had claimed angrily. "We nah food all winter! We et boiled barks!"

The coarse accent of the soldiers was difficult to interpret even by those officers learned of the English language. *A crevasse de arhs*é *de shooting fire? Oui et bouillant barques*? Fearing the English planned to use some type of weapon carried on their bateaux similar to *Greek fire*, a flaming mix of naphtha and pine resin, the French consulted their books of translation. They were perplexed, even when they understood what the man had actually said.

Nevertheless, General Montcalm cautioned himself against over confidence. He'd seen overconfidence create disasters during battles. His biggest potential problem was the Indians, the over two hundred Indians who had joined his forces randomly from every part of New France, representing several different tribes, all of them anxious for prisoners, trophies, and plunder. He did not trust the Indians who barely tolerated any military discipline before a battle and were completely uncontrollable after a victory. Once a battle had been won, they tended to commit hideous acts of savagery: scalping, torturing, allegedly cannibalism, though he'd not personally seen evidence of this yet. He would not use them at all except for the insistence of Governor Vaudreuil who overruled his protests.

Montcalm expected his second division of men and the heavier artillery to arrive the next day. Sitting inside his tent beneath a thick canvas covering the light of his candle lamp, he was finishing a letter to his beloved wife when a sentinel outside the tent whispered an apology for interrupting the general.

"Yes," he replied in a whisper.

"Captain Gerrard wishes to see you, sir."

The Marquis extinguished his lamp and set aside the canvas cover. "Let him approach."

Philippe pulled back the tent door and stepped inside the darkened interior.

"I'm right here," the general said. "There is a chair directly across from me. Take a seat there."

Philippe reached out with his right hand until he found the arm of the chair and took a seat. There was just enough moonlight seeping through the tent seams to make out the general's shadow. They spoke in whispers.

"Apologies for interrupting, General. I want to leave now for the morning scout of the perimeter. The moonlight is bright enough for me to start. I know these lands. I can be in position on their southern perimeter by sunrise. I will be able to learn more about their patrols and hope to intercept and take more prisoners. I wanted you to be aware I was leaving early. I will be back before noon."

"Very well, Captain."

"Thank you, sir. Good night."

But there was another reason why Philippe was leaving early. Rigaud de Vaudreuil had arrived that afternoon having marched overland from Niaouré Bay. The majority of the militia and the Indians were only half a day behind him. Rigaud had learned that the main attack may begin as soon as the next day. He also learned Captain Gerrard was ordered to perform a scout by Montcalm. Rigaud de Vaudreuil pressed the general that he be permitted to accompany the morning scout. Montcalm did not care either way.

Captain Bougainville was aware this could pose problems for his new friend and told him.

"I suspect Rigaud plans to surprise you in the morning."

Philippe knew this would be something Rigaud would write about to the governor to claim credit for any part of Montcalm's success. Philippe would not permit this.

"Thank you, Antoine."

"Philippe, you must take me on one of these scouts one day, so I might learn more about it for my journal."

Philippe shook the man's hand. "And so it shall be. You are invited to go on the next one the general commands me to do…if he allows you to go, of course."

Philippe had selected twenty of the scouts he trusted most and told them not to talk with anyone what he planned to do. *Just be ready*. As soon as he returned from speaking with Montcalm, they left quietly. They used the light of the moon to move through the forests. Philippe had crossed these lands many times, the latest after he departed the Oneida village to go to Fort Niagara, over a year earlier. He planned to reach the Onondaga River islands south of Oswego and scout both sides of the river carefully, going north until they reached Oswego's southern perimeter. His orders were to intercept and capture any patrols or deserters, take counts of men and artillery or any new defensive works that they could see, to observe and record any type of defensive activity, then withdraw to the east and go back around to the French encampment.

They used well-known trails. This was dangerous but they moved quietly, single-file, without making a sound and reached the islands after three hours. Philippe was surprised they did not encounter a patrol anywhere. Once at the river, he took half the men and went across to the western bank. They spread out and moved forward in a line for the next two hours. Just before sunrise, one of the scouts to his far left gave a raven call. The other scouts gathered to the man. He had come across a camp. It was several months old. The fire pit was full of dead leaves and other forest debris blown in by the wind. There were eight bodies lying around it in a circle. Mostly skeletons, dressed with ragged pieces of uniforms. English redcoats. Philippe recognized the epaulets of a lieutenant on one of them. Small animals had been eating at them. Some of the bones were scattered. But the uniforms showed no signs of musket balls or arrows. No real signs of any struggle.

"Deserters," concluded one of the scouts.

"They must have frozen to death," said another.

Philippe agreed with both assessments. He searched the pockets of the officer and found only a locket. Inside was a small painting of a woman with black hair. He kept the locket. There was nothing else.

"Let's keep going."

In less than an hour, they reached the southern tree line and lay down in a line among the bushes to study the fortification. A hundred yards further were the logs of the southern half stockade; a simple redoubt.

Philippe took out the small telescope he'd brought with him from Montréal. There was no movement along these earthworks.

Taking half his men around in the trees to the west, he studied the larger stockade called Fort George. Using his telescope, he carefully searched the walls. No guards on the ramparts. No sentries on the outside patrolling the perimeter either. In fact, the sun was rising and he saw no activity associated with anyone stirring, or breaking their fasts. Further east, along the wall of Fort Oswego proper, he did see some men walking those ramparts, but only three. *And why no noise?*

"This is way too quiet," he said to the man on his right, a sergeant. He handed him the scope.

An hour went by with little change. They went back around the way they came, withdrew back up the river a quarter mile before they crossed to the other side. His other scouts had seen no movement either.

*

As the sun's first rays glimmered over the horizon, Montcalm's second division began arriving with the remainder of his troops and the heavy siege artillery. The forward entrenchment of the camp was finished and shored up by multiple bundles of sticks, the *fascines* they'd created and brought with them. Added to this were the two-foot-tall, woven baskets made of sapling branches that were filled with dirt from the digging. Called *gabions*, they were easily placed when empty, and when filled with dirt, these offered versatile and strong defense against enemy fire.

With the new morning breaking, engineer Ensign Desandrouins began constructing a road inlaid with logs. This was to support rolling up the heavy siege artillery from the shoreline, through the encampment, and up to the edge of the trees. When night came again, the cannons would be moved under cover of darkness into an elevated battery position he'd created behind the new trench dug the previous night parallel to Fort Ontario's walls.

*

The English morning patrol from Fort Ontario had paddled east in a canoe, intending to go half a day searching for any sign of the French before returning. The man was alone, one of just a few soldiers who still had the strength to endure a day of continuous paddling. A mile down the shore, he back-paddled to a stop, stunned at the sight of a massive army of French regulars, some of them muscling artillery pieces forward. The scout hesitated for a few moments making some counts when muskets balls began whizzing by him. He turned and paddled furiously back to Fort Ontario. By the time he reached the walls, the alarm bell had already been rung. Musket fire was being traded in both directions.

*

"We are less than a mile away from them," Philippe said with disbelief. "It is daylight. And they still have no idea we are here."

Just as he uttered those words, the sounds of sporadic musket fire occurred to the north.

"Well, someone is awake now," the sergeant said.

The scouts began running back up the trails towards the main encampment. The rate of musket fire increased as the men in Fort Ontario engaged with the French troops firing from the trees bordering the field of fire. Most of the shots from the fort went wild. Many fell short because of the distance. But inside all the Oswego forts, the drummers were beating to arms.

*

Colonel James Mercer strapped on his sword and ran to the boat landing to be ferried across the river. On the other side, he tramped the zigzag path leading up the five-story eastern river bank. It was a path he once ran with ease. But he was weak from lack of food. He'd lost almost fifty pounds over the winter along with several of his teeth.

He entered through Fort Ontario's rear gate, walked swiftly across the marshalling grounds now teeming with the 51st Foot soldiers stumbling into ranks. Panting heavily, he ran up the wooden stairs to the ramparts above the main gate. The lieutenant on watch gave over his telescope.

"The French are here, sir," the officer said with a slight tremor in his voice.

In the bright morning sunlight, Mercer saw the line of gabions in the distance marking the main entrenchment of the French camp without the use of the scope.

"Do you think so, Lieutenant?"

But what worried him more was the second parallel trench that had somehow been completed overnight! It was also supported by fascines and gabions! And that one was much closer! Dangerously so!

"Did none of your posted sentries hear *any of that* being built?" he shouted at the watch officer.

Obviously, the answer was *no*. But burning with fever, the officer just stood with his mouth open, unsure what to say. More redcoats had run up the stairs to man the eastern ramparts. The firing increased steadily after that.

Through the scope, Mercer spotted the barrel of a very large artillery piece being moved into position at the edge of the trees a mile away.

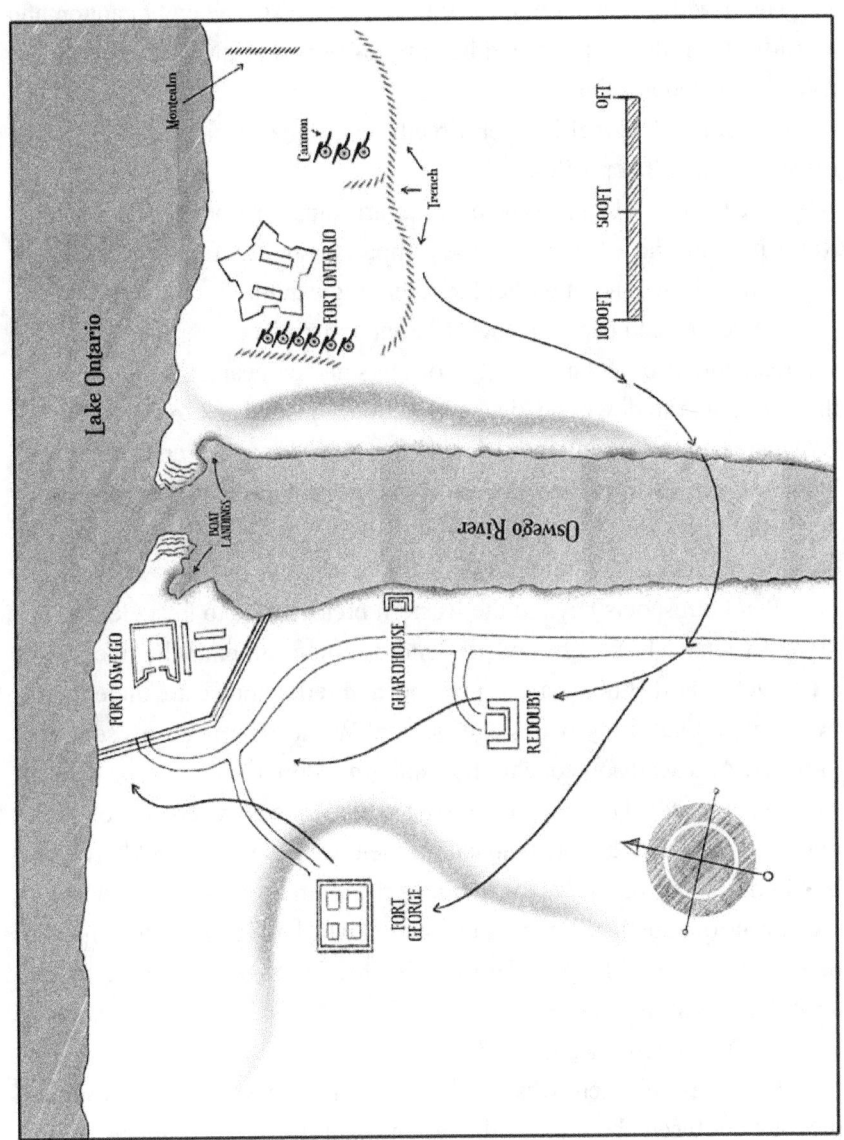

Fort Oswego Battle

"Good Christ! Where is our artillery?"

The dazed lieutenant pointed towards the west. The eight cannon and a mortar from this rampart had been repositioned to provide cover to the river-facing side of Fort Oswego.

Of course, Colonel Mercer already knew that because he'd ordered them moved to that position.

"The battle has begun, Lieutenant! Start using your brains and initiative. Reposition all the artillery to these ramparts and start returning fire. Aim for the trenches…and in particular at that big cannon!"

Mercer handed back the telescope and ran down the rampart stairs. He shouted similar orders at the other officers and sergeants. He left through the rear gate, ran down the zigzag slope and ferried back to Fort Oswego. Exhausted from running, once inside the fort he stopped and rested with his hands on his trembling knees. Mercer was pleased to see the men of the 50th Foot were already manning the defenses there. He found his second-in-command, Lt. Colonel John Littlehales.

"Send out scouts beyond the western breastworks to Fort George and learn if we have been surrounded! Send two men south, up the river! They are to get to Fort Bull as fast as possible and tell them we are under attack by a large French army with siege cannon! We need more troops sent to us in relief! And send someone to the southern redoubt…"

Mercer suddenly could not think what to tell the New Jersey provincials manning the redoubt; more than half of them were seriously sick! Over two hundred sick lay all around the inside of the main Fort Oswego, along with the dozens of equally scrawny, sick women who had insisted on being with these men, even to the point of their deaths. But this was not the time to consider any of the sick.

"Tell the redoubt what, sir?"

"Um…just tell them what we know so far. In case they are so addled, they are confused about all the bloody musket fire! That a French army is attacking us from the east! That the redoubt should stand ready to defend itself!"

Mercer went back down to the boat landing to speak with the captain of his small *navy*, which consisted of one armed sloop and four schooners. The schooners were used to catch fish to eat when they were not making armed patrols of the lake. They were better at fishing.

"Captain Broadly! Take your sloop and any of the schooners with cannon to the east. Bombard and harass the French encampment as much as possible. Aim for their cannon."

Captain Broadley sailed forth on just the sloop, HMS *Oswego*; the armament of the schooners was simply too feeble. He sailed east and fired one broadside from his light cannon at the French. The French responded with their heavy twelve-pound field artillery, which blew holes in *Oswego*'s sails and damaged its rigging. Captain Broadley was seriously outgunned. He withdrew out of range of the French cannon. Uncertain how to engage them effectively, he spent the entire remainder of the battle sailing in circles on the lake north of the main fort, avoiding the occasional volley of cannon fire the French sent in his direction as a reminder. From that point on he became a spectator.

*

Philippe Gerrard found Montcalm at the center of the main entrenchment looking through his telescope. The general was puzzled why they had received no cannon fire from this fort.

"Yes, Captain?"

"I encountered no patrols and no deserters, sir. There was no one moving about near that southern redoubt. At the western fort, there was no one manning the walls. Like they were all asleep until the musket firing started. Even then the reaction seemed muted."

"Very good, Captain."

While the skirmishing with muskets continued, Montcalm called his officers together and announced his new plan.

"Captain de Vaudreuil, take your militia and the Indians, go south from here to the disputed islands on the Onondaga River. Sweep north on both sides of the river from there until you reach the southern perimeter of the fort. Stop in the trees. Cover the southern redoubt. Send men to the west to cover that stockade fort. Hold those positions until tomorrow morning. We will advance and position the siege cannon tonight under cover of darkness. With the sunrise, our cannon fire will be your signal to attack."

Captain Vaudreuil was elated. Fort George in the west was full of sick men only; he'd learned this from the deserters. He planned to storm the fort's defenses with the first cannon shot the next morning. Then the investment of Fort Oswego would be credited to him. He glared at Philippe as he left the war council. He had expected Montcalm's order for encirclement and had word passed to the scout company marines that Captain Gerrard was in disfavor with the governor. They were encouraged to join with the main body of the militiamen. He hoped to have all the men in the scouts follow him from now on.

Vaudreuil proudly announced the new objective and left the main camp without delay to lead his seven hundred men to encircle the forts.

Seventeen men from the scout company, including three lieutenants, approached Philippe saying they would like to join with the other marines. He had been waiting to see which among the scouts would suddenly show an allegiance to Captain de Vaudreuil's arrogance. He was glad they finally made this choice. Philippe wished them good luck and dismissed them without further comment. None of the men who were on the midnight scout with him had elected to join Vaudreuil. Philippe was pleased he'd selected the right men. His company now numbered thirty, but he knew they were men he could trust.

Once the council of war ended, General Montcalm gestured Philippe aside.

"Captain, I will have other uses for you now that we are engaged. Remain near me today."

Philippe was glad for that order. He wanted nothing to do with Vaudreuil. As far as he could tell, and it was Captain Bougainville's opinion as well, Rigaud de Vaudreuil overtly gave himself credit for any military action or venture that had a positive outcome and would lay the blame for any type of adversity at the feet of General Montcalm. Rigaud was sending routine missives with a courier, at least one per day, to the governor saying as much. Except that Montcalm's new liaison in Montréal saw these missives too. He would courier a missive back to Captain Bougainville, who would then brief the general on Captain de Vaudreuil's duplicity. Montcalm was disgusted about this insubordination but accepted it as something he must endure. It was the governor's brother after all. Winning the war was more important.

None of the governor's couriers had ever approached Philippe directly to ask for his signed missive. This gave him a plausible reason to explain why he'd never sent anything in writing. But Philippe was unaware that Rigaud de Vaudreuil intended to discredit him. When the courier from the governor came to collect the reports, Rigaud would tell the man to report back to the governor that Captain Gerrard had not prepared any reports. When Governor Vaudreuil heard this for the third time, he decided the marine officer needed a lesson in obedience.

*

The musket fire was eventually joined by light cannon fire from Fort Ontario for the rest of the afternoon. By late afternoon, Vaudreuil's militia was in position and opened fire with muskets from the western and southern perimeters. But even with this increased rate of fire, few casualties were experienced by either side.

Colonel Mercer, however, knew the French would move up their large cannon under cover of night to the elevated battery they had created behind the parallel trench. He also knew such cannon would obliterate the wooden walls of this fort. So as the afternoon grew late, he decided that it was senseless to lose this garrison of soldiers to the overwhelming strength of the French cannon. Mercer ordered the 51st Foot garrison to evacuate across the river as expeditiously as possible.

"Spike the cannon. Drown the excess munitions and powder in the well." It took the 51st Foot less than an hour to retreat.

It suddenly seemed to Montcalm that the rate of fire from Fort Ontario had diminished greatly. He ordered a cease fire. In the distance, the general could still hear the musket fire in the south. But the open field of fire before Ontario's walls were quiet. Suspecting a trick, he waited for another half hour, then rewarded an Indian brave with brandy to go the wall and investigate.

The warrior scurried across the open field carefully watching the top of the watch for movement. When he reached the walls of the fort, he placed an ear to the wood and listened. Hearing no noises, he climbed up the wall, glanced over the rampart, and saw the inside was empty. He climbed over the top. The fort had been abandoned. He stood and waved to the French commander. Then went down and opened the main gates.

Montcalm ordered the Guyenne regiment forward to invest the fort. They captured it without firing another shot. The engineer was ordered to expand the entrenchment road to the fort's front gate for the heavy cannon. Two hundred men would pick up shovels for that. They would have it finished in a few hours before the sun set. Montcalm and his officers climbed the western ramparts of Fort Ontario and peered through their scopes at the fortifications of the main fort. The general ordered his artillery officer to build a new fortification raised outside the western wall but close to the slope where a line of cannon could be placed ready to fire on Fort Oswego's vulnerable side and have it done by the next morning. They would work through the night to accomplish this.

Philippe Gerrard felt the impending sense of victory spreading among the French troops. He felt it himself. The fact that Fort Ontario was abandoned so unexpectedly only punctuated the desperation of the English position. When he gazed through his telescope at the utter vulnerability of the older Fort Oswego across the river, he did not see they had any better chance over there. True, the river was a barrier to be crossed. But there was no need for such actions by Montcalm's army. The artillery position of twenty-pound siege cannon would be on the elevated ground above the opposing fortress. With the barrels of the heavy cannon pointed directly inside the interior of the fort, the mortars too, there was no need for troops to charge. They would simply pound away at Fort Oswego until it surrendered.

He looked at the southern redoubt and Fort George in the west and saw no sign of Vaudreuil's militia or Indians. But there were continuous puffs of musket smoke coming from the tree line.

Colonel Mercer knew his position was not the best, but he was not going to surrender. At seeing and hearing their commander's resolve, many of the veterans of the 50th and 51st regiments were equally motivated. The 51st Foot were very thankful that Mercer ordered the retreat to Fort Oswego. In addition, Mercer directed the detachment of Royal Artillery officers and men to take charge and create an artillery position that would be ready to duel with the French as soon as possible. All the moveable cannon at Fort Oswego was repositioned to the river side of the fort. Those that could not be moved were turned around in their current position to fire on Fort Ontario. New defensive works of pork casks, gabions, and other barrels of supplies were hastily erected to protect the new gun positions.

When dawn broke, Mercer could see the line of French cannon that were emplaced overnight on the heights. He counted only nine of them. He had more than that, some of them equal in caliber. And at this range, the strength of the English position was a match.

"By God, I am proud of you men," the commander shouted. "Now give them hell."

The English cannon opened fire. The accuracy of the British gunners proved true. The defensive works of the French began to erupt with hits.

Presuming the English cannon fire signal to be their own, the frightening screams of the Indians to the south and west roared as they left the trees to start approaching the half-redoubt and Fort George. The collective hideous screams were dispiriting even to the defenders of Fort Oswego. Two of Oswego's heavy mortars had been pre-sighted on the field of fire before the western walls of Fort George. Another three mortars were similarly sighted before the fields of fire of the southern redoubt. All the mortars fired, killing and scattering the Indians' advance, but it did not stop them.

Another volley of cannon fire by the English batteries at Oswego created more damage to the barbette earthworks of the French.

The French fired back and the shock and power of the heavier caliber twenty-pound balls created geysers of dirt and debris everywhere in Fort Oswego no matter where they hit.

The English fire proceeded in response. If they did not have the heavier balls, their accuracy was better. They gave better than they got.

The artillery duel continued.

Montcalm was not too concerned, but could tell this English commander was going to fight in spite of his perilous position. The withdrawal from Fort Ontario had been made without being observed and without any losses. That meant this commander had created alternatives in advance and likely had more to execute

What would I do? The general contemplated.

Montcalm immediately ordered the Béarn regiment to move south of the forts and across the river in support of the militia. He expected Fort Oswego would not withstand this artillery barrage for very long, and the English commander might attempt to break out in an escape upriver as a last resort. More importantly, he wanted regular troops in place to stop any English forces that might be heading to the fort's relief. With an afterthought that a potential surrender might soon come, he gave the commander of the Béarn regiment one additional order.

"Move quickly to protect the English in that western fort, Fort George, from the Indians if a surrender comes to us."

As the first three hours of morning progressed, the fighting carried on despite the superior firing position of the French battery. The wheels of some of the French cannon were sinking in the mud, disrupting their aim even as new pieces were being rolled into position. Ironically, many of the cannons the French were using happened to be ones captured from the English after General Braddock's defeat at Monongahela a year earlier.

Colonel Mercer was pleased to see they were holding their own. But clearly his position was seriously deficient from any point of view. The possible outcomes coursed through his mind. His second-in-command, Lt. Colonel Littlehales, was already rattled at the prospect of losing. But so were a lot of the men. He told his second to organize a plan for a fighting withdrawal up the Onondaga River. Mercer knew it was improbable he could do that. His forces were already plagued with wounded and sick. He would not leave them. But it gave Littlehales something to contribute and the officer was good at planning such tactics. Of course, a miracle was still possible…a relief force might arrive at the quick step upon hearing the sound of cannon. They may have run out of food several times over the last year, but Fort Oswego did have an excess of ammunition and powder. Maybe the French would run out of ammunition before he did?

Unlikely. But the idea made Mercer smile momentarily. *At least fighting is better than starving.*

"There is reason to smile?" the engineer, Patrick MacKellar, asked in a bleak tone of voice.

Seeing the man's terrified expression, Mercer gripped Mackellar's shoulder.

"Steady, man! We have more ammunition than they do! I was just thinking of the French general's surprise when I hold up a flag of truce, cross the river to explain our martial superiority, and ask if he is ready to surrender."

The gallows humor did not work. The engineer stared at him with disbelief. Mercer shook his head.

"I am jesting!"

Colonel Mercer thought it very positive, though unexpected, that his artillery seemed to be winning this duel. For now, anyway. The fort's interior mortars abruptly belched two more balls towards the field of fire before Fort George. The height of the explosions of dirt created by those larger balls was...*Simply glorious*, he thought.

"I see French regular troops crossing the river to the south," one of his captains shouted, pointing.

"Indeed?"

Mercer climbed a pork barrel on the forward battlements to look southward with his scope to observe the reported troop movements. Then he turned his scope toward Fort Ontario and the French cannon line.

At that very moment, a twenty-pound ball struck him directly in the chest. Colonel Mercer's body exploded in a red mist of gore in every direction.

The dramatic obliteration of their commanding officer into tiny pieces had an immediate and deleterious effect on all the troops. Colonel Mercer was the heart and soul of their morale. None of the other officers was looked to for command leadership. Most of them were sick anyway.

A dispirited Colonel Littlehales stepped up and called a council of war inside the stone castle. He saw their anguished expressions. He explained his hastily drafted plan to withdraw upriver.

"We will have to fight every step of the way and must first break through the lines of the French and their Indians allies." In the quiet gloom of the room, the constant, terrible howls of the approaching Indians could be heard in the distance.

"But if we are to do this, we have to do it now. While we still have the strength. While there is a chance. This is our only fighting option. The artillery duel may be a draw for now. But as demonstrated, the French have the high ground. More cannon will be brought into that position. The barrage will continue until the walls and this stone citadel are utterly destroyed. So again...if we are to withdraw under fire, we must start this now."

There was a pause of several seconds.

"And the wounded?" someone asked.

"If we are to succeed, they must remain behind, given to the mercy of the French."

Grumbles of disapproval arose.

"Yes. I hear you. That is my feeling exactly. So the alternatives are to face this barrage until we are all killed or too wounded to even wave a white flag. Or, I will cross the river under a truce and ask for terms while we live and can still protect our wounded. What say you?

*

Just before noon, a white flag was raised on Fort Oswego's flagpole.

"At last," Montcalm said in a soft voice. "Cease fire!" The general had already given Captain Bougainville the written terms of surrender, expecting this to happen today. "Captain de Bougainville, proceed to the riverbank and wait for the English to cross. Captain Gerrard, accompany him as escort."

Philippe carried the white flag of truce and he and Bougainville descended the zigzag path to the river bank. On the other side, they saw two British redcoat officers get into a boat with four oarsmen, which began a row towards them. In the distance, the howls of the Indians had not diminished.

"This is certainly a scene to describe in your journal, Captain."

Antoine de Bougainville glanced at his friend. "To my surprise, my feelings are not those of victory but empathy for this defeated enemy. After all this time? All this death and misery? I suppose this means I am at heart just a mathematician. I am not intended to be a general, I think."

"General Montcalm's terms show compassion. I think it is an essential quality for a commander."

The English boat pushed up on the bank. The redcoat officers, a colonel, and a captain, stepped out, walked up to them, and saluted. They saluted back.

Colonel Littlehales did not waste time. His tone was angry and exhausted.

"I come for terms. Do you offer any terms?"

Bougainville replied in perfect English. "Cease all hostilities and surrender. Your men will lie down their arms and become prisoners of war. But you may keep your baggage. We will transport all of you to Montréal to await prisoner exchange."

"And my sick and wounded?"

"We will provide care for your sick and wounded as well as we are able."

Colonel Littlehales presented his sword. "Then I surrender Fort Oswego to you, sir. I have ordered my men to cease fire..." He looked over his shoulder at Fort George where the firing continued. "I expect they will, too, when the Indians are not a threat."

"On behalf of General Louis de Montcalm, I accept your surrender, Colonel. You may keep your sword."

Colonel Littlehales thought he should say something more, but there was nothing more to be said.

Suddenly, there was a great howl from the Indians in the south. Upon finally noticing the white flag raised at Fort Oswego, the soldiers in the southern redoubt had started retreating to Fort Oswego, many of them supported on a shoulder or carried upon stretchers. The men at the western Fort George streamed out their rear gates, also heading for the main fortress.

The majority of the Indians were now charging across the open ground in pursuit. Many of them even ran past the retreating men and headed towards the main fort; the bigger prize.

"Send more boats across to us," Philippe urged the English officers. "We will come over and stop them!"

Colonel Littlehales got into his boat. He was already gesturing and shouting to the other boatmen to cross the river.

Bougainville climbed back up the trail. Philippe waved at his scout company to join him on the bank. Montcalm sent two companies of grenadiers down to the river. One company to defend the gates of Fort Oswego, the second one to cover the men retreating from Fort George. Behind them was the entire La Sarre regiment intended to invest Fort Oswego.

The first six English boats rowed across, one man each. A mix of grenadiers and scouts piled into them. They rowed themselves to the other side of the river and ran inside the fort.

The Indians poured into the outer forts, howling, screaming, swinging tomahawks, and stabbing with knives. They killed maniacally.

More than a hundred wounded and sick from Fort George and the southern redoubt pushed inside the gates of Fort Oswego to escape howling killers. The English foot soldiers formed a line inside the gate as the Indians boiled inside. They fired a volley. Some of the warriors fell, absorbing the majority of the musket balls, but more charged through from behind them. The foot soldiers had no time to reload and were pushed back by the onslaught. Seven months of starvation and sickness had taken an extreme toll on their health. Firing muskets at the enemy from the ramparts and loopholes was one thing. Fighting at close quarters hand-to-hand was quite another. They simply lacked the strength to stand up to the ferocious attack by the healthier and physically stronger warriors. And if they were forced to the ground, the deadly tomahawks would fall.

Fortunately, before too much time had passed, the French crossed the river and ran into the fort. They moved to the front gate. Captain Gerrard shouted orders to the bayonet-wielding grenadiers who formed a *U*-shaped line of defense surrounding Fort Oswego's front gate. It was a tense stand-off where the warriors and the French eyed one another with menace.

"Hold your fire! Bayonets only! Step forward!" Captain Gerrard ordered, pointing with his sword.

The highly disciplined grenadiers understood exactly what Captain Gerrard wanted to do. Standing in the center of the line, Philippe led the French troops as they slowly prodded the braves at bayonet point and forced the warriors to retreat back out the main gate. They followed them out of the gate and reversed the U to create a place for the sick and wounded English defenders still huddled against the outer walls to crawl behind them or be carried by others into the fort and to safety.

The chiefs confronted Philippe directly, gesturing at him with their weapons, accusing him of depriving them of their just rewards.

He understood what they were claiming, but Philippe did not reply. There was nothing to say. He was not going to let them mutilate the prisoners.

Dozens of wounded and sick were scalped and killed before the French had restored control. The carnage was worse among the sick and wounded left behind at Fort George until soldiers from the Béarn regiment arrived and put an end to it. Anyone left in the southern redoubt was already dead.

To the surprise of the French as well as the English troops, General Montcalm and his personal bodyguard of grenadiers suddenly marched through Oswego's interior. The marquis was appalled by what he saw. He pushed his way out through the main gate to the front of the *U*. Standing next to Captain Gerrard, the general expressed his fury at the Indian chiefs who had disobeyed his orders. They, of course, did not care what the French general thought. They complained bitterly about his denial of their plun-der, scalps, prisoners, and trophies, which had been promised to them by Governor Vaudreuil for their support.

Many of the thronging warriors became more agitated at seeing the anger and emotion of their chiefs. They started taunting the grenadiers.

"Hold your fire," Philippe repeated loudly, sensing the danger.

The disciplined veteran grenadiers understood the captain's intent. Use the points of the bayonets to hold them at bay.

"We need to give them something," Philippe quickly advised his commander.

Reluctantly, Montcalm nodded and offered each of the chiefs five thousand livres worth of gifts of their choice.

"But only if the English soldiers reach Quebec City without further harm," he demanded.

Two of the chiefs understood the immense value of this commitment and explained it to the others.

But the chiefs were skeptical. "And who will give us these gifts?"

"I will," Montcalm answered. "By my hand."

The chiefs were not completely mollified. They wanted plunder now. But they were also not stupid. At best, the collection of plunder after a battle in the chaos of carnage inside a fort was a matter of chance. Not everyone came back with something to demonstrate their bravery. The promise of gifts to all of them from the French commander eliminated this uncertainty. There would not be as many scalps, but most chiefs knew they could depend on Governor Vaudreuil, their great French father in Montréal, to see the promised rewards were fairly given.

Only then did the hideous incidents cease.

The Oswego *citadel* fell to the French attack in just three days. Its loss to England was highly symbolic and devastating. Considered as important as the fall of the island of Minorca just a few months earlier and following so soon after the other loss was politically calamitous. The Duke of Newcastle was blamed. The London elite were unaware what an indefensible pesthole Fort Oswego had been, but they knew its name and knew it to be the only outpost of British power on the great fresh water lakes of North America; like Minorca represented in the Mediterranean Sea.

The collection of forts at the mouth of the Onondaga River had existed since 1722. For thirty-four years it stood as an obstacle to French domination. In truth, it was never really an obstacle. It was more of an annoyance to the French fur trade, which flowed around it like a river would a small rock. But the real threat it posed was a place to establish an English navy on Lake Ontario, as Governor William Shirley had so earnestly tried to do.

The deaths at Fort Oswego attributed to starvation and exposure over the winter months estimated to twelve hundred men. The English deaths from the French attack on Fort Oswego were less than two hundred. French casualties sustained in the attack were less than fifty.

*

Montcalm assigned Colonel Bourlamaque as commander of the forts. The English soldiers, civilians, sick, and wounded were evacuated across the Onondaga River and held under guard at Fort Ontario for their own protection. When the majority of French troops crossed with the prisoners, the Indians swarmed and plundered Fort Oswego's storehouses of ammunition, food, and rum. Colonel Bourlamaque brought over more regular troops to stop the Indians and forced them to leave at musket point. Over the next few weeks, the greater part of the French army and its prisoners were transported by bateaux back across the lake and downriver to Montréal. Colonel Bourlamaque stayed behind and supervised the demolition of the forts, blowing up fortifications when necessary, but setting fire to them all in the end.

The English dead were buried in a mass grave. The French left a sign in Latin to mark the spot.

In hoc signo vincunt
Manibus date lilia plenis

At this place we conquer. Leave lilies.

*

August 19, 1756
Fort Williams
The Oneida Carry

Colonel Daniel Webb led the 44th Foot regiment to the Great Carrying Place. He was not pleased with his new assignment. Fort Oswego was reputed to be the worst possible duty in all of England's global possessions. It was certainly not a place to gain fame and promotion if attacked. And since the French were purported to be attacking already, he was not anxious to get there and become the senior man blamed for its fall. Nevertheless, he proceeded towards the destination steadily. He paused at Fort Williams for a day of rest while the baggage of the 44th Foot was unloaded from the river battoe and reloaded onto wagons for overland transport to Fort Bull.

Upon reaching Fort Bull, the wagons were being unloaded and reloaded onto the hundreds of battoe waiting on Wood Creek. Amidst that heavy labor, the colonel was abruptly confronted by the two breathless scouts he'd sent ahead of him days earlier to Fort Oswego, to announce his pending arrival.

"It's gone," came the terrified report of the first scout. "All of it gone! Burned to the ground!" he exclaimed between pants.

"What?! Calm yourself!" Webb heard the grumbles of surprise rising from the gathering throng of troops. "All right. All right. Quiet! At ease! All of you! Go on." He pointed at the scouts. "Tell me what you saw."

And they did. All three Oswego forts were destroyed. Not one stone was left piled on another stone. It was abandoned. What was left was a large pile of smoking wood. There was a mass grave where the dead were buried. They gave him a piece of paper.

"They left a sign…written with these words. But neither of us read French."

"It is written in Latin, not French."

Webb was educated in Latin as a school boy. The interpretation was awkward but he kept it to himself.

The scout spoke again. "And the French army is coming again…in this direction…now! Thousands of them!"

The colonel frowned with disbelief. "You saw this?!"

"Yes, sir. I saw hundreds of boats on the lake loaded with more troops coming ashore!"

Colonel Webb was a veteran of war. But he harbored a breath-gulping fear in his heart from nightmares of being captured by these vicious, tattooed savages. He'd heard the endless graphic stories of torture. He'd seen them carry the disgusting bloody scalps at their waists and the gruesome necklaces of noses and ears they'd wear around their necks. He heard the tales of the slow, agonizing deaths by fire, of men having their genitals roasted over a fire pit. Of course, so had all the soldiers of the 44th Foot. Panic took flame and started to spread. Webb did little to stop it.

His first order was to the ax men. He sent them back down Wood Creek for a few miles, ordering them to fell trees across the creek to obstruct passage. That creek had only been cleared last May from the natural fall of trees during the winter at great cost in heavy labor and time by Colonel Bradstreet's battoe-men.

The ax men obeyed the order enthusiastically. After all, thousands of Indians were approaching at the head of six thousand French soldiers!

Webb's second order was to reverse the baggage flow.

"Reload the wagons for transport back to Fort Williams."

Fort Bull was emptied of any useful stores. As they left, they threw torches into the buildings. For the second time in less than five months, Fort Bull was set aflame. But this time it burned along with hundreds of battoe on the banks of Wood Creek.

At Fort Williams, the panic continued. The garrison of soldiers and civilians alike were assailed and terrified by the embellished rumors.

"Fort Oswego has been massacred! The garrison is dead! All the survivors are being tortured! Some of them spitted alive and eaten. Eight thousand French are approaching! And almost as many Indians! They will be coming down the Mohawk!"

Webb gave his next order as soon as he arrived.

"Unload the wagons directly onto the battoe for the Mohawk River. We are leaving immediately."

The only discipline still remaining was by a few redcoat officers who did their best to remove the more precious stores from Fort Williams, mostly coffee, sugar, but *all* of the rum.

The portage wagons were set afire. The horse teams were shot in the head.

Then Fort Williams itself was set ablaze.

As Colonel Webb and his men retreated down the Mohawk River, the magazines at the fort finally exploded, destroying whatever was not burning, including a dozen siege cannon slated for use at Fort Niagara.

If the English had any thought of returning to the mouth of the Onondaga River on Lake Ontario, Colonel Daniel Webb had just reversed thirty years of progress in only two days.

It was hot and humid late in August when word reached Boston that the entire English garrison at Fort Oswego was either killed or captured by French forces commanded by the Marquis de Montcalm. Lord and Lady VanderMeer read all the Boston newspapers avidly, trading them back and forth while they sipped a mug of cold mint tea that Dian had stored in jugs in the cooler temperatures of the cellar.

Corrinne prayed she would see Philippe's or Henri's name mentioned in the columns somewhere. At least one of them should have been involved with this. There were lurid stories of the Indians scalping and torturing the wounded or sick soldiers. The fort had surrendered after only three days of siege.

"They surrendered in three days?!" Charles said with disbelief. "All those forts have been destroyed! Unbelievable! What happened?"

Corrinne set aside the newspapers and sighed wearily. With no mention of Philippe or Henri, she'd lost interest. She no longer cared who won or lost this war. She just wanted it to be over so Philippe could come home to her yearning arms. Sipping tea, she looked idly towards the front window and saw Magistrate Jack Tasker coming up the front walk wearing that frayed checkered vest he fancied so much.

"Oh, good." She set aside the tea and almost jumped from her chair. "Mr. Tasker is here."

Molly answered the door and brought him to the library.

Corrinne hid her frown at seeing the same food stains on the magistrate's vest from the previous week. *Part of his eccentric charm.* She kissed both his cheeks in welcome, lingering just an instant more than proper on each cheek. Long ago, Corrinne sensed he liked this and now did it on purpose.

"Mint tea?"

"Um…coffee…? You have spoiled me with that drink, my lady. I don't care if it is hot outside. I find I think more clearly after drinking it."

She smiled. "So do I."

Dian brought it to him right away.

Corrinne unconsciously rubbed her hands together. "So…what is your news today?"

Tasker put the list of names on the card table in front of them. All but five of the seventeen names had been crossed off.

"Three of these people I have been unable to find…yet. That is very disturbing to me. But I will find them. Of the other two, I've located them both and will be talking with one of them tomorrow….that one…" He pointed at the name. "Carter Trevathan. He is a merchant trader from New York City and new to Boston."

Charles looked surprised. "I know this man."

"You do?" Corrinne asked.

"You do?" Tasker said only a moment later.

"Yes, though not very well. Thomas Hancock introduced him to me down at his business square at Faneuil Hall about three weeks ago. Mr. Trevathan came in by happenstance to talk with Hancock. He seemed a good acquaintance, young, just starting his own company, hoping to gain some military contracts in association with Hancock's company. The man knew a lot of the import-export merchants in the New York City markets. Friendly enough. We talked a while about the war. He knew some of the senior military in White Hall. He did not stay very long."

Tasker's mind seized on just a few words. *…came in by happenstance…*

"Good. That little encounter will help me break into conversation with him tomorrow."

There was a knock at the front door. Molly answered it and came into the library.

"Corporal Thomas said Mr. Hughes is waiting at the curb for you, my lord."

"Thank you, Molly."

Tasker leaned forward in his chair and looked out the window.

"May I ask how you came to know Mervyn Hughes?"

"You know him too?" Charles asked.

"You could say that. I've jailed him a few times."

"What?" Corrinne rose from her seat to take a closer look through the window at the man in question.

"Don't be too concerned. I know him quite well. What does he do for you?"

"I hired him to be my bodyguard. I hope that wasn't a mistake," Charles replied.

"Why was he jailed?" Corrinne asked tersely.

"He is a Welshman. He fought in an English Foot regiment in the last war against the French. Was wounded in the leg. That's why he limps so badly. Was discharged. Came to Boston in '48 looking for work and a new life. Hard to find work when you are uneducated and appear to be crippled. But loyalty is one of his qualities. He is good with his fists is the other. They have immense value in combination. He's worked for some of the warehouse companies on the docks. A lot of fighting among those concerns. I jailed him for murder once. But there were no witnesses. None that remained alive. He was released. He keeps to himself. And is actually polite for a hired ruffian. How did you come by him?"

Corrinne answered. "After Mathilde's death, I wanted Charles guarded at all times when he left the house. Thomas Hancock recommended this man to us. I truly hope he wasn't wrong about this. Mr. Hughes seems to be dependable. He does not drink. He's is polite, as you say. He is never late and looks after Lord VanderMeer from door to door. Am I right, Charles?"

Charles nodded. "Yes. He sits in my outer office all day. He hopes to improve himself and mostly reads books. I find that an intriguing quality in a man of his age and history. He's also developed a taste for my coffee, which I do not begrudge him. Occasionally, he asks me the meaning of some of the words in the books. Lingers about me as he is supposed to do when I am out, but not intrusively. In the single instance where another citizen accidentally bumped into me on the street and became confrontational, Mr. Hughes grabbed him by the arm and collar and convinced him, rather professionally, to move on. If he was going to hurt me, he's had many opportunities to do that before now. Oh…and Sentry Cheever knows the man. They seem to respect one another. Oddly enough."

"All right," Tasker responded and rose from his chair. "Apologies. I did not mean to alarm you. I will return to tell you about my discussion with Mr. Trevathan. And I will chat with Mr. Hughes for a few minutes as I leave."

Mervyn Hughes tipped his hat at seeing the checkered-vested man approach.

"And a very good morning to you, Magistrate Tasker."

Tasker nodded. "Mervyn. I see you are keeping better company of late."

"If you please...sir. Do not pollute this relationship. I like these people. This is a good job. And I am good at this, as you well know."

"Don't worry, Mervyn. I have already endorsed you."

Mervyn Hughes looked visibly relieved.

"But I like these people too...*a lot*! I took a sword in my stomach for them, as you well know. And I expect you to do the same for them too, if needed."

"No need to worry about that, Magistrate. I will do this job for the rest of my life if they will allow me. They do not treat me like scum...like some others."

"Good. You should remember there are several people in this city who are looking for the opportunity to kill them. These killers are smart, clever, and move about like citizens. One of them tried to burn this house down during the funeral. His name was Felix. He came from out of town, and people who knew him said he had a German accent. You should remember I am searching for that man's associates. Maybe you can help me?"

Mervyn nodded vigorously. "Yes. I can. I'm glad you asked me."

"Be *subtle* about how you do this...clever, you hear me? No strong arming. No rough questioning. If you see or hear something you find suspicious, bring it to me. Let me follow up on it. That will keep you out of trouble."

*

Mervyn Hughes escorted Lord VanderMeer back home near the hour of eight that night. He'd thought all day long about everything the magistrate had told him. He already knew people were trying to harm the Vander-Meers. And he would defend them with his life if it ever came to that. But he had not known these people might have German accents. He knew a lot of people on the docks and others who had such accents. He was excited with the idea he might be able to help, to do something important for these generous people who'd been so kind to him.

He stopped at a bakery and purchased a few loaves of "old bread," still warm, to take to the apartment. His own apartment! To have enough steady pay for a one-room apartment was a luxury to Mervyn. It was more money than he would ever make cracking skulls down on the docks. And now that he was learning to read competently, the possibility loomed he might actually have a future after all. Lord VanderMeer even gave him paper, quill, and ink each day. He was learning to write the letters of the alphabet. He could now print his name. Reading and writing would open up the world to him, Mervyn decided. Lord VanderMeer said he would also teach him numbers at another time. Lord VanderMeer knew so much about so many things; he often sat and listened to the man talk for hours.

He got to his street and climbed the single flight of stairs in the alleyway leading up to the door of his apartment atop a dressmaker's shop. The room had a slatted bed. He had to buy two mattresses to make it thick enough to not feel the slats. A small table with two chairs. Three hooks on the door for clothes. His own chamber pot. A sink for water with a bucket underneath for a drain. One shelf above it for dishes. Two sets of those with knives, forks, and spoons. One glass. One fry pan. One stew pan. A square stove with a pipe to the roof. He bought his own wood. Water, he had to bring up from the well out back in a wooden bucket. He bought a second bucket to have on hand. It was horrendously painful work. He winced on every step as the bones in his right knee popped and cracked loudly. They moved bone on bone. He took them one step at a time. The army doctors claimed the connecting bones and tendons around the knee were hopelessly damaged by the musket ball wound. He could stand and walk stiff-legged well enough. According to the doctors, the pain he felt as the bones *clicked* on one another would only get worse as he got older. Older? He might never get older, he'd replied. Older was years away.

At the top of the stairs, Mervyn put the key in the lock, bowed his head, and said a silent prayer she would be inside. He opened the door and smiled warmly.

"The most beautiful woman I've ever seen."

Rachel Bristol came in swift steps to hug and kiss him.

"You are so late tonight, Mervyn. It is not proper to keep your lady waiting like this."

Your lady? He liked the sound of that.

"His lordship was painting again. Sometimes he loses track of time. He likes to paint. He is very good. But I cannot interrupt him when he paints. Look here," he said, unwrapping the newspaper. "I brought home some bread. It's still warm, soft, and smells good."

Rachel kissed him again, this time slipping her tongue into his mouth.

"We should eat quickly and begin our *dessert*," she said, running her hands down his chest. "I have brought a small crock of beef and vegetable stew. You have brought bread to go with it. I have some fresh cider. The table is set. Put out all the candles except the one in the corner. This will leave the room dim…and mysterious. The night air is cool. I left a window open. I say we eat naked."

"Naked? You mean without any clothes?"

"That is the usual implication of the word. Unless you are too shy, of course."

"No. I mean *yes* to naked," he answered softly. "What other possible answer could there be to that question?"

He started to undress. She kept her gaze on him and very slowly took off her clothes in rhythm with him. In the dim golden glow of the candlelight, her porcelain-white skin gleamed like an angel.

"You are…*beautiful* is not good enough to describe you. But I am learning new words every day. I plan to write you a poem. You'll see."

Rachel stepped forward and pressed her body against his, rocking her hips against his hardness. She licked his lips.

"What you said is good enough for me. Sit at the table."

Mervyn had met Rachel Bristol only three weeks earlier at a farmer's market. Rachel had backed into him by accident. *Like out of a wonderful dream*, he thought later. She'd dropped some apples she was carrying. He helped to pick them up and she smiled. They touched hands. "Thank you," she said. "Would you like to share some cider with me?" He would learn Rachel loved to eat anything made from apples.

On that eventful day, Mervyn had just started his new job with Lord VanderMeer. And it was only the day after he moved into his apartment. Now, he had met a beautiful young nurse by accident. His whole future had turned for the better. He did not know why. She brought so much more to him. He was thirty-one years old with no family. The very next morning, he vowed to learn to read and write. He was not going to waste this turn in fortune.

Within two days, they spent their first night together. She was even more wondrous in bed. Mervyn had another key made and gave it to Rachel so she could let herself in whenever she wanted. Rachel did not come over every night, mostly every other night. But when she did, the nights of pleasure in bed were unlike anything he had ever known...or could hope for. She was passionate, inventive, would try or do anything he wanted, which for him wasn't much more than one position. He apologized to her. He was just an uneducated ex-soldier from Wales. He did not have much experience in the ways of the bedroom. *You know enough*, she replied. She suggested everything from then on anyway.

They sat down to eat. She had kept the stew warm on the small iron stove. It tasted wonderful. All her cooking tasted wonderful. He spooned and gulped down the first bowl in less than thirty seconds along with mouthfuls of bread, anxious to get to bed.

"Slow down, Mervyn! Eat slower. You need to learn to do things much more slowly. You must learn to enjoy it more."

He frowned, ashamed. "You're right. I'm sorry. I must improve my table manners. You deserve to be treated like the lady you are. I should try to deserve you. You certainly deserve better than me."

He noticed a fleeting wince cross her face.

"Did I say something wrong?"

"Nooo!" Her smile returned. "Never speak ill of yourself. You are a *good man*, Mervyn. I knew it the moment I met you. And try to remember I am sitting here naked."

"Oh, I have not forgotten that! And what a magnificent sight you are," he said softly. He ladled more stew into his bowl. "Now...I will watch you carefully and eat slowly," he assured.

Rachel's eyes stayed on his. He saw the very delicate, slow way she put food in her mouth, and the way her tongue moved as she licked the spoon. He attempted to match her movements.

"Good. No matter what I do, keep eating very slowly or I will *stop*."

"Stop what?"

Rachel smiled. Her bare foot under the table slipped into his lap. Her foot was cold and he inhaled sharply. She started massaging him with her toes, something new she had never done before. He reacted with an erection he didn't think possible. All the while she was taking small spoonfuls of stew and watching him with a little smile of satisfaction.

Mervyn impulsively reached across the table and took her hand.

"Rachel, I love you. I know we've only just met. And I am not a cultured or wealthy man by any means, though I hope to be some day. I am just scared this will all end. And I will not blame you if it does. So I want you to know, before this ends, that *I love you*…more than…than anyone else in my life."

Rachel had stopped smiling.

"Did I…say something wrong?"

"No, Mervyn. What you said was beautiful." She brightened. "And I think it's time we go to bed. You remember what I taught you to do to me with your mouth the last time? How much I liked it?"

His voice was thick with the memory. "Oh, yes."

She took him by the hand and led him to the edge of the bed.

"Lie on your back. I will lie atop your face so you can do that again to me, very slowly and gently with your lips and tongue. And since I will be facing the other way, I will do the same thing to you with my mouth. And if we do this just right, we will both have pleasures at the same time. Would you like that?"

"Oh, yes."

*

At Carter Trevathan's request, Caroline and Rachel Bristol met with him at a restaurant near the Marine Society Hospital.

"I must meet with Magistrate Tasker at Faneuil Hall at four o'clock today. I am uncertain why he suddenly wants to talk with me. But I want Lord VanderMeer killed tomorrow as we planned." He looked at Rachel. "I assume you have a plan perfected."

"I do," Rachel answered in an emotionless voice and with a placid expression. She did not explain further.

"It must not lead back to you," he warned.

"It will not."

"And what of Colonel von Kleinfels?" Caroline interjected. "Have you dreamed of him? Because neither Rachel nor I have dreamed of him."

"He is still recovering from his stroke. The strain of his recovery is not easy. So he is visiting only me...for now."

"And what of Alain Marcoux?"

"He does not speak to me of Alain...and I do not ask."

The food was served to them. They stopped talking while the plates and food were arranged.

Carter had leased a small commerce square in Faneuil Hall where he had begun a trading business as the colonel suggested. He'd started trading in cotton, buying it wholesale at a premium price right on the docks to guarantee his supply. He sold the ginned bales to a weaving mill in western Massachusetts. He guaranteed the price he would pay up front to the weavers for the finished bolts of cloth. He shipped the bales of cotton to them and received the pure white bolts of white cloth back using the same cargo conveyors, once again for a premium but fixed price. To his surprise, he actually made a small profit in the first month.

But all of this was possible only by using the sacks of silver and gold coins the colonel had given him. With it, he bought the cotton at a premium above the other bids. He made advance payments to the shippers and accountants at ten percent above the normal wages for their estimated work to ensure they attended to his needs first. Then he garnered the retail buyers and direct customers in Boston for the finished goods. It was a very costly way to do business compared to the competitors. But he did not have to borrow any money. So he did not owe any money and lost no money to high interest payments inflated further by the war. Avoiding interest and using no middle men created his profit. It almost seemed too easy. Take away the fat bags of coins and it would be impossible. But for now, until the colonel returned, he planned to find other avenues to make even more money. He fervently hoped the colonel did *not* get better, not quickly anyway. He hoped that monster stayed in Europe. This new life was very tolerable without the usual morning exhaustion and the constant headaches.

"What will the magistrate ask you?" Caroline asked as soon as the food was on the table and the waiter left.

He sipped some of the soup first. "As I said, I do not know."

Rachel ate her food with good appetite and listened carefully. She did not miss much.

Caroline picked at her food. "Well, you are too secretive, Carter. We should always know what you know. In case something happens to you."

"And just what would happen to me?" Carter demanded.

Caroline chewed a small bite and did not answer right away.

Carter found Caroline argumentative and demanding most of the time. It was tedious to have even the simplest discussion with her. But long ago in Amsterdam he found her to be extraordinary in bed; better than Rachel. More fortunately, Caroline had bedroom needs equal to his own. She came to his bed at least every other night without argument. Silently, they took an intense interest in finding comfort in each other's arms in a variety of ways. Carter sometimes felt sorry for poor, quiet Rachel, as she always slept alone. But he did not dare take Rachel to his bed. Of the two sisters, Caroline was the more pitiless killer. She liked it too much. And her eyes carried a wild gleam. He wasn't sure what Caroline would do if she ever got angry with him. And he did not want to find out. These women used the most adverse poisons, some of them torturous as well as deadly.

Caroline finished chewing.

"Well? Go on. What would happen to me?" he asked in a whisper.

"I don't know," Caroline replied, her voice rising. "That is the problem. What if the magistrate arrests you? And we can no longer meet? Then what do we do? The colonel does not visit us. And you know everything."

"Lower your voice, Caroline. If the magistrate was going to arrest me, he would not make an appointment to meet with me in the middle of Faneuil Hall. For all I know, he may want to ask me why I went to the VanderMeer funeral. But I have a good reason for that. I am trying to gain business with that man. And that's the truth."

Caroline pushed food about her plate.

"I thought you went there to burn down his house," Rachel remarked casually.

"That too!" He crossed his arms. "But the funeral gave me a reason for being nearby. Is there anything about *your* plan I should know?" he asked pointedly to change the topic.

"It is better you do not know," Rachel replied politely. "Your expressions betray you. I can tell when you are lying, Carter." Rachel smiled at him warmly.

Carter felt a chill and swallowed more soup. Caroline was more wanton. Rachel, however, was the smarter of the two and no less deadly.

I should make her a closer ally. Maybe I should take Rachel to bed... Carter mused. He noticed Caroline glaring at him. *No! Bad idea!*

*

Rachel went to Mervyn's apartment again that night. She had told him she would come two nights in a row.

"As soon as the sun goes down," she promised.

Mervyn was there, waiting for her. He had bought a bottle of red wine, a fully baked coquelet chicken, warm bread, with a small butter crock, fresh squash and beans, sea salt and pepper corns with a grinder.

He let her in and proudly displayed the waiting meal, gesturing with one hand.

"*Voilà*! Your meal awaits, *Mademoiselle*."

"*Oui? Merci beau coup, mon amour.*"

Mervyn looked embarrassed. "*Voilà* and *mademoiselle* are the only French words I know."

Rachel kissed him tenderly and deeply. "Then I will teach you some other words of French. The ones they only use in bed...but *after* we eat this sumptuous dinner. What a surprise! And did you bring coffee too?"

"Yes, yes. I have a small sack of some of Lord VanderMeer's finest coffee on the window sill near the stove. I have become a glutton for it. But he does not seem to mind. I make it for him every morning. Do you want some now?"

Rachel pretended to think on this. "No, let's eat first. We can sip some coffee later. Afterwards. After we lay in bed and touch each other the way we like most, yes? I cannot stay the night tonight. But I can stay until the midnight hour. We should use all that time."

Mervyn swallowed. *Touching each other the way we like most. What does that mean?* He liked every way she touched him. He had printed a poem that day to give her as a surprise. It was in his coat pocket. But right then he decided to wait. Maybe she would do something new! Something to add to the poem.

"But I should still eat slowly?" he asked to be certain.

Rachel laughed lightly. "Oh, yes, Mervyn. Eating delicious food slowly to savor its flavor is always important."

He pulled out a chair for her. Poured her wine. At seeing his awkwardness, she cut the chicken and served the food. While they ate, she asked him questions on his childhood in Wales. Why he joined the army. About his family. He asked her similar questions but she always steered the conversation back to him. She complimented him on the food. When they were full, she took him by the hand and led him the few steps to bed.

Rachel had him stand still beside it while she undressed him. She took off her clothing a piece at a time with each of his, until they were both naked. Then she took a pillow from the bed and placed it on the floor in front of him. She knelt down on it and took hold of his hardness.

"The pleasure for you will be better if you remain standing as I do this," she explained.

Mervyn learned how true that was, until a shock of pain went through his injured knee as his legs buckled in weakness from a withering orgasm that went on and on. She caught him in her arms and helped him lie upon the bed. She straddled him across the thighs and gently massaged with her hands until he was hard again.

She bent over and kissed his lips. "Now, you just stay very still and let me do everything," she whispered.

Moving up his body, she lifted her hips and slowly lowered onto him with a deep sigh.

Mervyn reached up and took hold of her breasts, touching them the way she liked, the way she had taught him. Rachel's hips undulated back and forth. She slowly drew out the pleasure for as long as possible; achingly so. And when the time came, they were together.

"I love you," he groaned in the middle of it.

Afterwards, she wore his shirt more for warmth than for modesty and sat at the table. Mervyn wore his pants, definitely for modesty, and made the coffee. In the candlelight's glow, the scarring on his stomach, back, and torso was much more conspicuous.

"You have many scars. The pain must have been excruciating."

He shrugged. "Soldiers sometimes fight with bayonets. The officers use swords. They slash with both weapons as well as thrust. I learned to turn quickly to avoid the thrusts. I got cut a lot but I lived."

Mervyn's scars were visible. Rachel's were not.

"Now, here! A cup of Lord VanderMeer's excellent coffee that he gets special from the islands." The aromatic liquid was hot and steamy. "Here's a little cream." He tasted the cream to make sure it had not curdled. "Mmm. Still good. Now the sugar."

"Wait," Rachel said. She rose and withdrew a small leather pouch from her uniform pocket. She sat back down and opened the pouch. "This is the very special brown sugar I told you about. It has some kind of spice ingredient added to it. But it is much better than the white." She wet her finger and dipped it into the pouch until some of the sugar stuck to it. "Here. Taste it."

Mervyn sucked on her finger. It did have a spicy, sweet taste.

"Tastes like *you*," he said huskily, proud of himself, thinking it a clever thing for him to say.

Rachel pretended shock. "Mervyn!" She dipped her finger again and tasted it too. "Mmm! It is good. Yes? I've not tried it in coffee yet."

They each used two small spoonfuls and stirred.

"Now let's taste it together."

Mervyn was surprised how good it was. "It's has a mellow taste, like chocolate, but different somehow."

"Yes," Rachel said. "The lady at the market who sold it to me is from the islands too. She would not tell me which island or why it tastes so good. But this sugar is very expensive. Hard to get, she claims. Anyway, you can share this with your lordship tomorrow morning and impress him. But promise me you won't tell him where you got it."

"Certainly. I promise. Oh, I have a surprise too." He went to the shelf above the stove. A dish there was covered with a towel. He set it on the table along with two smaller dishes and removed the towel like a magician.

"*Voilà!*" It was a pie. "Apple," he said proudly. "With cinnamon sprinkled on it. Baked especially for you."

He cut them both a piece.

Rachel was gazing at him with great affection. "You are a good man, Mervyn."

They ate the pie and finished the coffee. It was delicious. Rachel was quiet while they ate the pie. As soon as she finished the plate, she got up, deep in thought, and dressed to leave. Still quiet she went to the door.

"Rachel, wait! Is something wrong? Did you not like the pie?"

She turned to him. "Of course I liked it. I'm just sad because I am so lucky."

"Now that does not make any sense!" He hugged her. "I am *happy*… because I am the one who is so lucky!"

"Yes. You are right. I misspoke. I am happy too," she said. "Oh, before I forget." She went back to the table and took up the brown sugar pouch and carefully swapped it with another one she had in her pocket. "This one has a prettier bow. Promise me you will share it with him?"

"I will. In the morning. I promise. But if I do, you must let me introduce him to you."

"Maybe. We'll see. But only if he tries the sugar. So we have something to talk about when I meet him, yes?"

He stared at her with wonder. "You always know the right thing to do."

He hugged her again. They kissed for a long time.

Mervyn stared into her large brown eyes. "I love you, Rachel."

She looked away at this and did not reply. Without saying anything further, she went out the door and down the stairs. She stopped, turned, and waved to him before disappearing into the fog of the Boston night.

"I love you too," Rachel said to herself as she walked down the street.

*

Mervyn accompanied Lord VanderMeer to the office, arriving in the carriage at half past the hour of nine. As soon as they were inside, Lord VanderMeer took his three newspapers to his studio in the back, waiting for Mervyn to prepare the coffee as he usually did.

Lord VanderMeer was commenting about the war, which Mervyn listened to half-heartedly, concentrating more on making the coffee.

The coffee brewed perfectly. Mervyn liked that Lord VanderMeer preferred the large nautical mugs used by sailors. He filled each with hot coffee, added cream, and set the mugs on the serving tray before he untied the ribbon on the pouch of brown sugar. He added two spoonfuls to each. Stirred. He stuck a finger in his cup and tasted the flavor. It was not quite as sweet as the night before. *Must be the larger mug*, he decided. So he added a third spoonful to each. Stirred, then took a large swallow from his to see if the flavor improved. It did. He carefully carried the tray to Lord VanderMeer.

"A serving tray, Mervyn? What is this?"

"A surprise, my lord. I think you will enjoy the taste of the coffee today. I was given a new pouch of sugar from the islands—"

Mervyn Hughes abruptly stopped talking.

Charles set aside his paper. The bodyguard's mouth opened and shut but no words came out.

"Mervyn? What's wrong?"

Mervyn's hands clasped his throat. The tray and cups crashed to the floor and shattered. His eyes grew large with terror. Mervyn fell to his knees and made a loud grating, inhaling sound before he collapsed forward, lacerating his nose and forehead on heavy shards of broken mug. Blood spurted from the wounds but stopped seconds later when his heart muscles seized in paralysis.

Charles VanderMeer was stupefied. He snatched a pistol from a desk drawer and cocked it. He rose and went over to the body. Mervyn's face, neck, and hands were swollen. The body twitched a little.

Poison!

Still carrying the pistol, he ran out the front door and grabbed a boy he knew who was playing on the street.

"Billy, do you know where to find Magistrate Tasker?"

"Yes, your lordship."

Charles handed him a silver piece. "Find him and bring him here and I will give you another piece of silver. Tell him I said to hurry."

Jack Tasker came with two of his men and on his corpse wagon when he heard Lord VanderMeer was carrying a pistol. He examined the bodyguard carefully. He looked at the man's open-eyed expression, the grimace of pain, the extreme swollen appearance of the skin. He bent over and carefully smelled the open mouth. There was a sickly sweetness to the odor there. He shook his head with regret.

"It was poison. I don't know what kind, but if it happened as fast as you described, it might be known. Tie off that sugar pouch and bring it with us," he told one of his deputies. "Get the canvas and bring some towels. We'll take him to the Marine Society Hospital," he told Lord VanderMeer. "The doctors there are the most educated."

"I'm going with you."

"As you wish. But if they decide to perform any dissections, it will not be pleasant."

"That poison was meant for me," Charles stated grimly. "I want to know all about it."

They pulled up at the back of the hospital only a few city blocks away. A doctor came out the back door waving his arms in a gesture to stop. He was followed by two nurses. One of whom was Rachel Bristol.

"What are you doing, Magistrate? You cannot bring one of your murder victims here. Dead is dead. Take it down to the hospital by the docks."

"I need your educated opinion, Doctor. This man was poisoned. I want to know by what kind. You can examine him inside the wagon if you like. But you will indulge me this courtesy." His tone indicated *or else*.

Frowning, the doctor climbed up and threw back the canvas flaps. "How did he come by these deep lacerations?"

"From his collapse. On shards of pottery. There was not much bleeding."

"Only a little bleeding? From cuts this deep into arteries of the face and lower scalp?"

Charles held firm. "It was as I said."

Grunting, the doctor took a scalpel and cut the seams of the clothes to examine more of the skin. As the coat fell back, a piece of paper fell from a pocket. Tasker picked it up with two fingers, read it, and held it up to Lord VanderMeer, who was holding a kerchief to his nose to mute the smell of shit.

"A poem?" Charles said in surprise to the magistrate. "That's Mr. Hughes' printing. I recognize it. He was teaching himself to write."

"Then a woman's involved," Tasker said with certainty. "Poison is a woman's weapon. Did he have a lady friend or talk about one?"

"No. He did mention he just received that brown sugar from someone. Said it came from the islands."

Still holding it with two fingers, Tasker dropped the paper outside the wagon and wiped his fingers vigorously on his pants.

"That's not good enough, Magistrate," the doctor warned. "You need to cleanse your hands. All of you will need to cleanse your hands. I have bottles of alkali solution inside." He turned to the nurses. "Bring out some bottles for them to use."

"What kind of poison would act so fast?" Tasker asked.

"Lots of them," the doctor said impatiently. "Drink some lye and find out." He dropped the canvas back over the corpse, deciding he was finished with this examination. "The hives, prolific swelling all over the body, the tongue and throat especially. Something that would choke him immediately. But if, as *you* assert, there was not much bleeding from those head wounds, this suggests the heart stopped quite suddenly. Paralysis, or a seizure. Maybe it was a toxin in the coffee?"

"I drink that coffee every day," Lord VanderMeer protested.

"So then something from this sugar." He spread open the pouch carefully. Took a very brief smell. "But that's not brown sugar. It is white sugar soaked in something...your poison most likely."

Rachel brought out three quart-size bottles full of a yellowish liquid. They stepped down from the wagon.

"Take these." He handed them two bottles. "And someone needs to pay for them."

VanderMeer handed him a silver ounce.

The doctor had the nurse pour the liquid over his hands as he rubbed to cleanse them. "This body needs to be cremated or burned in a pit. Poison can linger for a long time."

"Do you have a notion as to the kind of poison?" Tasker asked him again in a voice as terse as the doctor's.

"All right...well, the use of sugar is clever. The sweetness would disguise any taste of bitterness. Fruit seeds are intensely bitter. Only poisonous if eaten in large amounts, and I am talking about a lot of them. It's not likely people would do that naturally. But if the seeds are crushed and boiled until the water almost evaporates, the remaining liquid is thick, a highly concentrated gravy, potent, and potentially poisonous...according to some apothecaries," he added. "This has been written up in a few journals. But this is not a conclusion derived from human experiments. Well, at least not by men of science. The medical texts I've seen on this are more akin to Wiccan tales, lore collected from the history of a darker age."

"What kind of fruits?"

The doctor shrugged and gestured with his hands. "All kinds, cherry pits, apricots, almonds, apples. Or it could be castor beans."

"How would you do it," Tasker pressed.

"*Me*? I would not do it at all!"

"And if I held a knife to your throat?"

The doctor scowled. "You are not going to let this go, are you? You are wasting my time, Magistrate, and my goodwill."

"I need your best educated answer, Doctor. It would be a shame for your customers to learn someone in your care died of poison," Tasker said calmly but unflinchingly.

"You wouldn't dare…" The doctor exhaled with aggravation. "All right…this body's adverse reaction was powerful. The poison worked fast in many respects. If I were to use seeds, I'd use several different fruits, because I don't know what I am doing and I'd be unsure which one to use. There are some plants in the Spanish Americas said to be used by the natives for arrow poisons that allegedly causes instant paralysis. There are snake venoms." He paused and thought more carefully. "Maybe it is a concoction of several of these…if the person was a student of the killing methods of the Borgias. But, again, I studied *medicine* in Paris for seven years to learn *to cure*, not to kill."

"I understand that, Doctor, which is why I am talking to you. Please continue."

"Like I postulated, maybe use a mix of several types of seed and plant poisons, each one specific to cause a particular physical reaction. Perhaps hot liquids, to create a vapor to inhale. I am just guessing, but that is my best diagnosis I can give you." He looked at Charles VanderMeer and spoke as politely as his impatience allowed. "My lord, I hope he was not a close friend. With respect, Magistrate, I have other patients waiting for me inside. I do not want to practice medicine in an alley. I would much appreciate it if you would take this wagon somewhere else."

With a curt nod to the magistrate, the doctor took his leave.

Jack Tasker poured the bottle to cleanse Lord VanderMeer's hands with the solution.

"I will do my own hands with my men after we dispose of the body. I learned enough from the doctor to help me. Fruit seeds and plants. I don't need to know the exact poison. This was done by a professional assassin, one who knew poisons. Probably the same person who poisoned Mathilde. And she is still among us."

"So you are convinced the killer is a woman?"

"That poem tells me she is a woman. Mervyn Hughes fancied women. But few of them fancied him, if you don't count the whores. He was a ruffian, but a soldier too. He did not deserve to die like this. Mervyn fell in love with a woman who used him to try and kill *you*. And this cold bitch wanted Mervyn to die at the same time. I suspect he tasted some of the coffee before giving it to you, probably to make certain there was enough sugar in it. And died within a minute of doing it. That's my conjecture. Otherwise I would be looking at your corpse too."

Jack Tasker and his men pulled away in the wagon.

And she is still among us. The magistrate's words hung in his thoughts. Charles decided to walk and breathe the morning air to cleanse the stench from his nose. He took the half-empty bottle of alkali solution with him. He would use some of it to scrub and mop up the spilled coffee and blood from the floor of his office—*just pretend it is splotches of paint*—then cleanse his hands with the remaining solution afterwards.

Like the doctor, he did not want to display evidence someone had been murdered in his place of business. There would be rumors, of course, but he could discount those, maybe say the bodyguard got sick from eating spoiled food. He felt selfish with this fiction. Because the real truth was his bodyguard did something unwittingly noble.

He died protecting me.

*

After the magistrate and Lord VanderMeer were gone, Rachel slipped out the back door of the hospital when she was not needed for a few minutes. She retrieved the slip of paper lying in the dirt.

> *You hold my gaze and I feel strength*
> *You take my hand and I feel warmth*
> *You touch my body and I feel joy*
> *With you I know comfort*
> *With you I know love*
> *You are my love*
> *You are my life*

The rush of pain and guilt was instant. Rachel gasped for breath, overcome by the result of the terrible thing she had done. She hugged her stomach and vomited by the side of the building. It took her some time before the emotional trauma subsided and her breathing steadied.

"What are you doing out here?" Caroline asked, standing at the back door. "Are you ill?"

Rachel straightened, wiped her tears, and faced her sister with a calm face.

"Just a moment of nausea. A sulfurous odor. One of the eggs you cooked us this morning was putrid."

"I ate the same eggs. I am not sick," Caroline said defensively.

Look in a mirror, Rachel thought silently and pushed past her sister.

*

Montréal

The portaging began around the Lachine rapids. The sick and wounded English soldiers were loaded into wagons. Once on the other side, they would be reloaded into more bateaux to be conveyed further downriver to Quebec City. Once there, transport ships would take the prisoners to a neutral place in the Saint Lawrence bay, where a corresponding number of French troops could be traded. Some of them would go back to England and the others to seaports in the American provinces.

At General Montcalm's order, Captain Gerrard walked alongside Colonel John Littlehales to see to the officer's personal needs as such needs arose. The English commander was depressed and morose about the defeat and his surrender, understandably.

"After all that sacrifice, death, and suffering. We could barely hold up our muskets to return your fire. I will be blamed for it all," he groused to his enemy. The colonel was pleased Captain Gerrard could speak English. "They will never consider the poor conditions of defense or the lack of food for six months in the middle of the winter. They will only remember that I surrendered."

"The fort's defenses collapsed faster than we could move our cannon. You were defending a fortification that was simply not defensible. And your senior commanders know it."

"They will still blame me."

"Probably. Victory or defeat, those privileges follow the commander, yes? But unless a force had come to your relief, even a Vauban-style fortress would fall to siege in five weeks or less." He reached into his pocket and handed the English officer the locket. "Here, before I forget."

"What's this?"

"Something I found during a scout upriver." He told him about finding the skeletons around a camp fire. "It appears they froze to death. I found this locket in the coat of a lieutenant."

Colonel Littlehales scrubbed a hand over his face. "Lieutenant Culver. In February we sent him with a squad of grenadiers to try and reach Fort Bull to bring us back food. We wondered what happened to him. This must be his wife. She is in New York. I will try to find her and return it. How far did he get?"

"Half way," Philippe lied without being more specific. "Even if he froze, he died bravely. That's the story you should tell her...or something more heroic. For the benefit of his family and children, if he had any."

"You're right. I am surprised Culver made it that far. They were all pretty sick when they volunteered."

Whistles sounded ahead of them.

"That's the next group of bateaux. You will get some bread and other food to eat before you board for Quebec City. Our grenadiers will guard your troops for the remainder of the river journey for your protection."

"Aren't you going to Quebec?"

"No, Colonel. I am going to Montréal."

"Then this is where we part ways, I presume. I am thankful you came to the fort as fast as you did, Captain. The Indians would have left none of us alive...or worse."

"They are hard to control by either side."

"I wish we'd met under different circumstances. I hope to see you again someday, Captain Gerrard...after this nasty business is over, of course."

They shook hands. Philippe saluted the senior officer.

Captain Gerrard beached his bateau at Montréal's western boat landing. He brought the six scouts from Fort Duquesne with him, telling the rest to use the boat landing on the other side of the city and report to the barracks. They made plans to rendezvous at a tavern later in the afternoon.

The city bells were already ringing in celebration and welcome as the bateaux arrived. He went directly to the Grand Company warehouse and was greeted by Paulus Legate.

"We've all heard of your great victory, Captain! Surely this means a peace treaty with the English?"

Philippe didn't think so.

"We can always hope. Can I quarter my six scouts here?"

"Yes, of course."

Once the scouts were in the back, Philippe asked to retrieve some of his money.

Legates handed him a small sack of coins from the underground safe. "Where do you go now?"

"To find out how the English children are doing and then to army headquarters. I am certain I will be leaving again for somewhere. But I will come back to see you in any case." He noticed Paulus had adopted a strange expression. "What's wrong?"

"The children…were moved somewhere. I don't know where."

Philippe's anger surged. "*By whom?*"

"I swear, I don't know! No one saw it happen. They disappeared a few weeks after you left. The chamberlain and his wife are gone too. Maybe the archbishop knows?"

Without saying more, Philippe left and walked determinedly through the riverside gate, ignoring the salutes of the guards. He went straight to the chamberlain's house in the *rue menagerie* and knocked on the door. No answer. He knocked on a neighbor's door. A woman answered guardedly at seeing the bearded, weathered face of the marine officer.

Philippe removed his hat. "Excuse me, Madame. I am Captain Philippe Gerrard."

She opened the door wide. He asked about the chamberlain. She knew only that they had left suddenly.

"Over a month ago. They left quietly. In the middle of the night. No commotion or noise. To where, no one knows. It was a few days before anyone on the street even knew they were gone."

Philippe tried the chamberlain's door again, was about to break it down, but changed his mind and went to the Terrain des Jésuites instead. He was admitted, told to wait, and Father Tinian came down to get him. The monsignor was smiling. Philippe was not.

"Where are they?"

Father Tinian put a finger to his lips and motioned for Philippe to follow. When they were in the privacy of the archbishop's office, he spoke.

"I don't know where they are, Captain. The archbishop has a letter for you but wants to give it to you himself. I've sent someone for him. We learned that the gendarmerie were going to arrest them. We went to warn the chamberlain, but they were already gone. The gendarmerie did not find them either. That much I do know."

They heard footsteps. The archbishop came into the office and embraced the marine officer.

"Welcome home, Captain."

Father Tinian explained what was said so far.

"And still, no one knows where they are." The archbishop opened his desk and withdrew a letter. "Here, this is for you. I've already read it. Forgive me."

It was from the chamberlain.

> *I leave this at the Terrain des Jésuites in Archbishop Nicolet's care. I learned two hours ago from a friend that gendarmes will be dispatched to arrest Mary and me tomorrow. The children will be taken from us. We cannot let that happen. I know a safe place and will go there now. I will not say where that is. This letter could be intercepted. Know they are safe. I will send the archbishop another message when I learn you are back in Montréal. You might write a letter to the children and leave it with the archbishop to deliver back to us. They are very nervous. Do not worry. We are taking good care of them. I must leave now.*

"Nothing since?"

"No. But with your return, another letter might come suddenly."

"The gendarmerie," Philippe seethed. "The governor promised Intendant Bigôt would not bother them."

"It was Governor Vaudreuil who issued the order for the gendarmes to apprehend them, not the intendant," the archbishop replied. "I have learned that much. So calm yourself, Captain. This is a time for thinking, not for reacting. Let me start by saying this matter is too minor a problem to occupy the governor's attention in the middle of war. What is his reason?"

There followed a long discussion about the governor's solicitation of Philippe to supply and report on General Montcalm's military views on fighting the war. Montcalm's future plans and strategies. The confidential couriers that never seemed able to locate Captain Gerrard, and his easy avoidance of them the few times they tried. In the midst of the Jesuit intendant's probing questions, Philippe indicated that Rigaud de Vaudreuil may have played a part in this as well.

"The governor threatens these children because he knows I am attached to them. He also has the royal warrant for treason issued by Intendant Bigôt. He claims he dismissed that warrant. But I am not deluded. He can reverse that decision too if it suits him. So he has me by both ears. The governor wants me to assert that his brother Rigaud is responsible for the success of this last campaign. He wants my assessment in writing. I have not done that. I cannot do that. General Montcalm is a very good commander. The best I've seen. The metropolitan troops trust him. The marines trust him. Most of the militia respect him. I trust him. The governor does not."

"This is not a matter of Montcalm not having the governor's trust." Muscles tensed and worked in Archbishop Nicolet's jaw. "This fool of a governor intends to discredit his commanding-general simply to aggrandize himself at a time when we need all of Montcalm's military expertise. New France sways at the brink of its existence! With the fall of Fort Oswego, the governor has convinced himself New France is going to survive! He ignores our desperation. The famine has only started. We are just about out of food with winter upon us. With the loss of Fort Oswego, the Americans will now focus all their attention on Fort Carillon. They have thousands of redcoats and provincial militia amassed at their forts south of the Lake Champlain."

"Eminence, I do not think the English will attack Fort Carillon in winter. General Montcalm admitted this opinion to me after Oswego fell. We have earned a year's respite by destroying Fort Oswego."

"A year? Six months, I would contend. Maybe until March. But certainly when the snows melt next spring. They are poised to attack nowhere else. They will come for Fort Carillon next."

Archbishop Nicolet was as smart as any general Philippe had ever met.

"General Montcalm will reinforce Fort Carillon with more troops, including my scout company. He will order me there in a week. I will start scouting the American forts. But I would like to confirm these English children are safe…"

"No, Philippe. For now, you must accept they are safe. Your appearance would endanger them. Someone would follow you. My advice to you, Captain, is not to inquire any more about the children or even talk about them. Avoid Intendant Bigôt. Let the governor come to you. You have a reason for your lack of correspondence. The couriers never approached you. If the governor asks about the children, profess you just found out they have disappeared. Say you have no idea where they are, but you are searching for them. Which is the truth. From now on, use my office for communications with the chamberlain. Be satisfied they are hiding in safety wherever they are."

Philippe pulled out his sack of coin. "Let me give you money for them."

Archbishop Nicolet held up a staying hand. "Let me worry about that, Captain. You worry about writing them a letter, yes? You should do that before you leave my office today. And be at peace about this! They are safe. Now, can you do something for your archbishop? I do not have a relationship with General Montcalm but I want to create one over the winter months. I want to earn the general's trust. I want to help this man. So mention my name to him. Encourage him to seek my counsel."

Philippe decided writing letters to the chamberlain and Mary and to Joshua and Leah was the best he could do. He felt fortunate to have a friend like Archbishop Nicolet. The archbishop was right. And the Jesuit's wise counsel had always served him well.

All that would change in another week.

CHAPTER 21
QUEBEC CITY
LATE AUGUST 1756
"The Line Is One of Blood!"

Captain LaTour maneuvered his ship into the river anchorage in Quebec and found a place to anchor amid dozens of other ships, many of them warships. He'd created two name plaques for the ship, the *Falcon Queen* and *William's Queen*. Either of the plaques could be slotted into place, depending on what his charade would be on any given day. Today, it was the *Falcon Queen*. But he was part of the French navy now and wore his captain's uniform. The crew gazed at his formal wear with interest. Each time they saw it, they were unsure how to posture themselves. They gathered before the bridge deck.

"Stop gawking at me!" LaTour shouted at them. "Beneath this pretty suit of clothes, I am still your captain. For this port, we are again the *Falcon Queen*. We are a French navy transport ship. We carry cargo from La Rochelle. That's all you need to know."

"Can we go ashore?" one of the crewmen asked.

"Of course. This is Quebec City! But Victorio will assign two watches. Half of you will be aboard the ship at all times. I expect to stay here several days. Don't get into any trouble. Do not boast or tell any tales about where we have been other than the islands. And don't go too far from the wharves. We may have to leave without much warning. Lower the harbor launch, port side." He turned to Victorio. "You will be in charge until I return."

Alain Marcoux stepped on deck from the bridge house with his two bags. "Good morning, Captain. *Ahhh*! So this is Quebec City. It's more beautiful than what has been described to me. You are familiar with it?"

"I am. Enough to deliver you to Governor Vaudreuil. After that, you are on your own."

"Fair enough."

LaTour pointed. "When the ladder is dropped to the harbor launch, go down, and get seated. I will be along shortly."

Captain LaTour went below to his cabin with Victorio. He gathered up his credentials given him by Admiral de la Motte.

"All right. If something happens to me—"

"What would happen to you?" Victorio demanded.

"Nothing, most likely. I am just being cautious. If something happens that prevents me from returning to the ship…use your own judgment… but if you have to leave, finish this mission. Go to Louisbourg next, then Boston, back to Louisbourg, then to Rochefort."

Victorio's frown deepened. "I will find that very difficult to do without you. Wait…let me change *difficult* to *impossible!*"

"I know. That's why I plan to come back."

"Take a crewman with you to act as a messenger to me…in case there is something I need to know.

LaTour nodded. "Good idea. I'll take Pierrik. You don't need a steward anyway."

The captain ordered his steward to grab a sack of clothes and come with him. The twenty-eight-year-old sailor was elated to be going ashore with his captain.

The harbor launch came to rest with a thump against the foul stairway leading up the side of the stone wharf. Captain LaTour carried up one small bag and the satchel of dispatches over his shoulder. He had decided not to give the dispatches to Monsieur Marcoux to carry until they were within fifty paces of Governor Vaudreuil to be certain they were delivered.

"Where are we going?" an excited voice asked.

"Pierrik, enjoy your travel with me, but try to be quiet unless I ask you something."

"Yes, Captain."

"Monsieur Marcoux, the governor's palace is up there." LaTour pointed towards the heights. "I will get us a carriage."

They arrived a half hour later and entered the gilded front doorway guarded by uniformed soldiers who saluted him. Captain LaTour gingerly saluted them back. He went over to the receiving desk and showed his credentials to the ensign.

"I am Captain Beauregard LaTour of the *Falcon Queen*. I have just arrived from France. This is Monsieur Alain Marcoux. We are here to deliver dispatches to Governor Vaudreuil."

The ensign rose and saluted. "I am sorry, Captain. The governor is in Montréal and left orders that any dispatch satchels arriving from France are to be hand-carried to him immediately. We have a comfortable coach already waiting at the stables at your disposal. There are multiple relay stations set up on the river road to Montréal with fresh horse teams at each station. You may also receive food and refreshments at each station. You will travel day and night and sleep in the coach. You will have an armed cavalry escort of two men. The journey should take only two days. No other delays will be tolerated in your delivery."

"You have that little speech memorized, do you?" Captain LaTour stared at the ensign in disbelief. "After five weeks at sea, I am not allowed even a day's rest?"

"It is because of the war, sir."

God's balls! Captain LaTour frowned. "Very well. Bring the coach around to us." He turned to the sailor. "Pierrik, short journey for you. Go back to the *Queen* and tell Victorio I've been ordered to take a coach to Montréal. When the dispatches are delivered, I will return the same way. But I will be gone for a week at least."

"I should go with you," Pierrik argued. "You may need something."

"Go back to the ship, and tell Victorio what I said."

The sailor left with a sad face.

"Anything to eat in the coach?"

The ensign looked regretful. "Bread, cheese, and bad-tasting wine… oh, and water. Our very best army rations."

LaTour groused to the ensign he was going to use the privy, at least, before the long ride began.

Only minutes passed until the ornate coach with a team of four horses pulled up in front of the governor's palace. When Captain LaTour came out the front door of the palace, Alain Marcoux was already inside the coach. The drivers approached the captain for his baggage. LaTour gave them only one, keeping the dispatches with him.

"The wine is really not that bad," Alain remarked as LaTour took a seat across from him in the carriage house.

The seats were wide enough to seat three people comfortably. Which was good, LaTour thought. He could lie down to sleep when he was ready. There were also blankets and pillows beneath the seats.

"Do you want to share a glass of wine with me?"

"No, Monsieur. The coach will not stop again until we reach the first relay station."

"Then if I feel discomfort, I will piss out a window."

"*S'il vous plaît*, Monsieur Marcoux. Do not do that!"

"I am jesting, Captain."

*

Boston

Hard as he tried, Jack Tasker was unable to identify the woman.

"A woman was seen entering and leaving the apartment where Mervyn Hughes lived. But her head and face were always covered by a hood. And she approached and walked away on different streets each time. She is a professional assassin," he summarized to them two days after the incident.

Corrinne fumed as she paced back and forth across the dining room with arms wrapped around her chest. Her instinct was to fight back, to strike back more acutely, to kill someone, but the poisoner was a phantom. And she was frustrated.

Corrinne replied bitterly, "So she is still among us."

Tasker understood her angst.

"Yes, my lady. I have started to investigate women who came to Boston just after you did. There have been hundreds of them, unfortunately. I don't have all their names. I am focusing on those with German names or accents as a possible connection to the arsonist."

Corrinne was deducing possibilities with what information she possessed. "This woman has skills with poisons, which she brought with her. What else can she do with that skill? She also has to live somewhere and eat. So she both lives alone and has money. Or she lives with someone who supports her."

"All good points," Tasker agreed. "I will use them in my search. On the list of names from the funeral I've made more progress. The three men I could not identify turned out to be Portuguese fishermen. They all serve on the same boat, which is at sea just now. They've lived in Boston for several years. Two of them have families whom I visited. They all expressed great sorrow for you and admire your charitable works. So I do not think they are suspects at present. But I will interview these fishermen when they get back, of course. The fourth man died a week ago. He lived in Boston a long time. He was a drunkard and his body was found lying dead in his hovel. He was known to pilfer when he could, so I assume he came to the funeral to see if there was something he might steal inside your house."

The last name was Carter Trevathan. There was still a question mark after the name on the paper.

"I had a long conversation with Carter Trevathan. His arrival in Boston coincides almost exactly with your return. But this man appears consumed with his new business of cotton imports and cloth manufacturing. Spent half an hour educating me with enthusiasm on how he made a profit in his first month. Seems he brought money with him from New York to invest. Claims he is using family funds. So why not do this in New York? Why come to Boston? Better opportunities and less competition in Boston, he claims. But I've not heard others say that before, so he remains on the list for now. I will confront him again about this poisoning in the next few days. See if he flinches. I should add that Mr. Trevathan lives alone."

He paused.

"Is that all?"

"Yes, my lady. But I will not stop searching."

"Then let us not keep you," she said brusquely.

Tasker bowed and turned to leave.

"Wait!" Corrinne stepped over to the magistrate, hugged him, and kissed both of his cheeks. "I apologize for being so rude. You deserve my praise not my resentment. You are a friend to Lord VanderMeer and to me as well. We both value that friendship."

"Thank you, my lady. You do not have to apologize to me. I understand your anger and frustration. Just know that my own is always ten times greater. And searching out these enemies? That is all I do. I will find something to connect these people."

"I know you will." She hugged him again and he left.

Corrinne sat down in the library and exhaled. "So what do we do now?"

As Charles listened to Jack Tasker's summaries and observed Corrinne's distress, he pondered a longer view on their adversities. He had several ideas. Some of these actions he could do without Corrinne's help. But that brilliant mind of hers, he decided, badly needed something to do.

"A question," he said. "What if Colonel von Kleinfels walked through our front door right now? What would we do?"

"What? Are you jesting? Kill him! Without hesitation!"

"And then what?"

"*Then what?* Charles, I am too frayed for this game. Just tell me what you are thinking."

"I don't think we should wait for the next attack. That is not to say we shouldn't take precautions to protect ourselves. But we have an advantage. Let's look further ahead. Presume the colonel is dead. What are our plans for the body?"

"To entomb him and seal it with a hex, as before."

"All right, where?"

Corrinne told him about the rise of land in the lot next to Winter House. "Hancock owns this. We buy it from him. Winter House, too. And we dig a deep grave at the center of the rise, say twenty feet deep. Line the bottom and sides with thick granite like a shaft. In goes the dead colonel and the *châsse*. We seal it with the hex and more stone. That is what I am thinking."

"Why there?"

"Why not there? If we own the properties, this place gives us the privacy we need to construct it in secret. We do this in a way that does not draw undue attention and in a way that will not make the tomb easy to find. Eliminate any physical trace on the surface. Like the tomb in Germany."

"All right then. I will make arrangements to buy the properties from Thomas Hancock. *You* draft plans for constructing the tomb."

Corrinne was surprised. "You mean now?"

"Yes. That's my point. Why wait? This is something that needs to be done. It is not going to happen overnight. And we cannot give this planning to someone else to do. Presuming we prevail against this…*thing*, which we will. I want to dispose its carcass from our lives as soon as it is dead, as quickly as possible. So let's not wait."

There was a pause before Corrinne answered.

"I agree with you. It should be me suggesting this," Corrinne replied in a wistful tone. "It shows you how preoccupied I've become."

"Maybe. But it also shows what an inspiration you have been to me. You are enduring in the face of any uncertainty."

Corrinne was barely listening. Charles could see her mind already at work.

"I have several ideas how to do this," she said. "Oh! *Enduring!* No one has ever said that to me. Thank you. Now, in the meantime we must hire another bodyguard."

Charles shook his head. "No! I will not put another man in danger for me."

"They get *paid* for such work!"

"They get paid to protect me from physical harm. Not to act like some... royal food taster! I will not allow a person to willingly be *poisoned* for me. Ever again! This will haunt me for the rest of my life."

He stared at the floor, his shoulders hunched.

Corrinne knelt beside him and lifted his chin with one hand. She kissed him lightly on the lips.

"Charles, you may not be my real husband, but I care deeply about you. I love you. Not like Philippe, but I love you no less. You must allow me to arrange protection for you, before I start following you around with a pistol. So do this for me. Or do it for the children. If anything happens to you, what would become of us? I would have to go back into hiding somewhere. Should I start making those plans too?"

Charles looked into her eyes. They were deep green with emotion. *They just draw you in*, he thought.

He exhaled, resigned. "Has anyone, or any man, I should say, *ever* said no to you?"

Corrinne looked askance, as if pondering this question. "I do not recall... that any of them...ever did. So, with this sincere and startling revelation from the very depths of my soul...you must *not* be the first. It would be... it would be bad luck. And you would get *hives* for the rest of your life."

"Hives?!"

Charles barked out an astonished laugh.

She smiled. Then her expression abruptly sagged into anguish. She started sobbing.

"First Mathilde and now you. I don't want to lose you too!"

Charles held her in his arms and gently rubbed her back as if she were a little girl. He had never seen her cry before; not like this. Her body trembled from the deepness of her sobs.

"Don't cry, Corrinne," he murmured into her hair. "Don't cry. It will be all right. We will get through this. I promise. And I will allow myself to be guarded, as you insist."

Her head resting on his shoulder, she sniffed several times. They started talking again as he held her.

"I was thinking we could have Dian prepare all your food and have it delivered to you under guard."

"No. Too complicated. I will simply break my fast with an ample meal in the morning, and again at night. I will take a basket with me to work, otherwise, no meals for me during the day. The guards can escort me to work and come back later to escort me home. My office doors will remain locked and barred all day."

"And what about your business?"

"Business? No one except Thomas Hancock and Jack Tasker have come by to talk with me about business all summer long. The war has changed everything. The trading ships need no insurance. They are all in a feeding frenzy hauling smuggled goods at high profit. You do not declare your intention to smuggle goods in order to arrange its insurance. In fact, I think VanderMeer Trading Insurance Company should publish its final set of books for the commonwealth of Massachusetts to audit and tax. We should end the business formally by year's end."

"And do what after that?"

"I don't know. Maybe change the name of the company and become an investor? Buy shares in Thomas Hancock's company? Or invest in one of the other Boston companies. Maybe you should ask Thomas and Lydia to dinner and we can discuss it."

"Yes..." she said softly. "An investor..."

Charles could already see the brilliant, beautiful wheels turning behind Corrinne's far away gaze.

Corrinne stood, then bent and kissed his forehead. "I will see if they can come tonight." She left the room. Within a minute, Charles heard the front door open and shut.

Charles had already made plans that would occupy his complete attention in his studio office over the next few weeks. Artistic plans. Ones concerning stone and metal and jewels; his favorite pastimes. Now that he decided what he was going to do, he could not wait to get started. But this unplanned conversation about the company's future compelled Charles to evaluate this other aspect to his life. The business of trade would change dramatically because of the war.

He pulled the cord on the bell and asked Dian to bring him coffee, which she shortly brought to him on a tray. She poured. He mixed in cream and sugar and sipped.

"Wonderful. Thank you." He took a large swallow, rested his head back on the leather chair, and closed his eyes.

The Dutch Republic will remain neutral, he thought, *and reap uncountable millions in trading profits by that decision.*

But could the VanderMeers remain in Boston? Or should they even try? Surrounded by unseen assassins just waiting to strike again. *And a female assassin? The suspects are getting hard to count.* And if they must leave…to where would they go? If not Europe…maybe to New York or Philadelphia? But would they be any safer there? He really needed his father's counsel…and consent, considering the royal implications of being the Duke of Brunswick-Wolfenbüttel's firstborn.

What if this prince died or that king or some important mistress, or the head of some lesser German state? Lordship of the ancient Duchy of Brunswick was forever contested by other German families. Charles VanderMeer, the first heir to the Duke of Brunswick was an unpredictable and greatly envied personage. He could abdicate, of course. He wanted to abdicate, but the Duke had said no. Not yet. But now a great war had started. *The Duke must have a plan?*

Charles visualized all the royal houses of the middle kingdoms plotting moves on the gaming table, gauging opportunities to eliminate rivals like him by, well, by his assassination. *Get in line,* he thought morbidly. Charles was certain the Duke of Brunswick was using Charles' existence as heir of the duchy to gain something for the family. Charles never wanted any of this, but now it affected Calypso and Marcus. These children, though not truly his, carried his name. Even if he abdicated, they were not safe. They would automatically become next in line!

Charles had asserted he would abdicate willingly to Major-General Hollenberg of the Dutch Republic, when the senior officer visited Boston the previous year, at the behest of the duke.

"If I abdicate, so do my unborn children."

"No, your lordship, they do not I'm afraid." General Hollenberg emphasized. "Unless they can say so themselves the abdication of your children is not your decision, or Lady VanderMeer's. The line is one of *blood*. Only the King can mandate otherwise. William VI will not come to majority for another ten years. The matter could remain unresolved until then. I am not saying that will happen. His mother, Queen Anne, is now regent. You can never know what she might do. You should be aware of all the *possible* implications."

Charles reflected on the general's ominous words and the menacing suggestion that Marcus and Calypso were in great danger too. And likely worse danger *if* he abdicated. And if this struggle among the middle kingdoms came to America, the uncertainty of living in Boston would only become more uncertain.

"I should write him a letter," he whispered aloud to himself. "Except how do I mail it in confidence? If only the Duke would communicate with me."

Charles' wish would soon be granted.

*

Europe

August 29, 1756

Frederick II found it astonishing, with war between France and England officially declared for three months, there were still no land battles in Europe. England had lost Minorca to France. This loss was followed by more bad news. England had lost a major fortress city-base in America called Fort Oswego. A place the English had ruled for more than thirty years.

And it had fallen to the French in three days, after the capitulation and capture of its entire garrison. Three days!

Pathetic. Contemptible. Cowardly. How else could this be described?

England was demonstrating weakness. Battles were easy to understand. The strong survived. The army that attacks first most often wins. Prussia could not tolerate weakness for very long. Not where they were positioned.

The King of England, George II, wanted to preserve his birthright to rule the Electorate of Hanover in Germany. George II cared more about maintaining his sovereignty over Hanover than he did the Americas; some would say even more. This was ridiculous, in Frederick's view. *Hanover is German! Its people are German!* England also did not have the troops to defend this territory if ever challenged. Nor did England have the money to hire enough mercenaries to do it for them. But Prussia was an ally and by treaty Prussia would protect Hanover. Which was fine with Frederick. He would defend it. He considered Hanover his territory anyway. He planned to make it part of Prussia at some point. Maybe not with this war. Maybe in the next war.

But now it was the end of August, three months after England had declared war, and his Prussian impatience had peaked. The three women had plotted against him. He already knew their intentions to attack him early next year. They were positioning troops in various spots, great distances apart from one another, to force Prussia to spread its army so they could attack him from three different directions at once, with an overwhelming numbers of troops.

Of course, this plan depended on Prussia simply waiting for them to attack. *Women!* Frederick II thought. *Delusional and foolish.*

Frederick had been slowly marching south towards Silesia with an army of one hundred thousand men. Dozens of spies riddled the ranks of his army. Most, he knew about. But he did not care. He permitted them to learn about his military intentions, that was, to go into Silesia to defend it. None of what he said in any of his war councils was true. He'd kept his real intentions to himself alone. He did indeed worry about Russia positioning more troops on Prussia's eastern borders. But Russia was poor and dependent on annual subsidies of one hundred thousand English pounds. *To defend against me! England's ally!* But Prussia did not protest. Not yet. Austria was moving artillery up to the Bohemian border. *For defensive purposes*, the fat-sow empress had communicated to him through an ambassador. *Obviously, it is her best ruse. She must have thought about it for six months before she acted.* He almost communicated back she was an *idiot*…except it might dissuade her from further acts of ignorance. If Frederick continued his army's march directly into Silesia as the Austrians and Russians expected he was doing, they had an opportunity to trap him in a pincer. That was their plan if winter didn't come first.

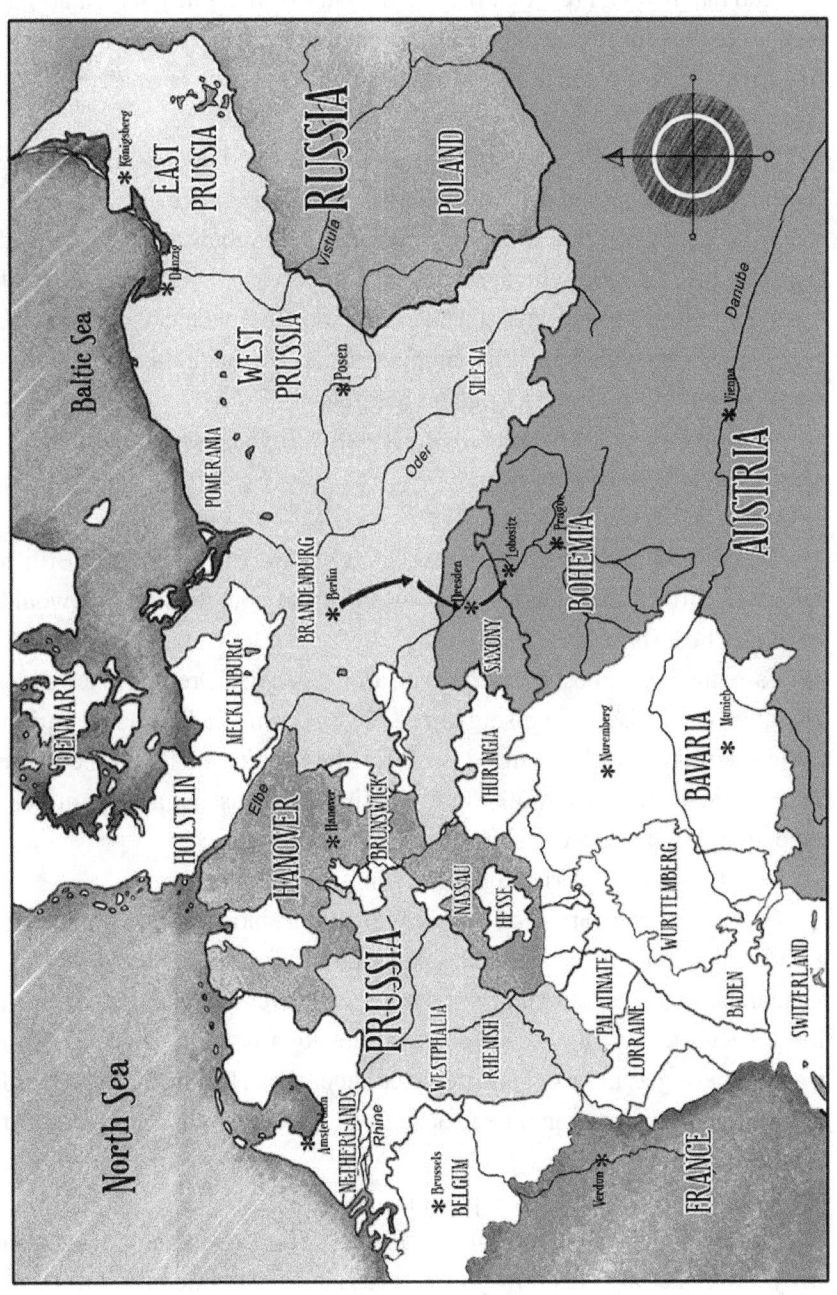

Frederick II Attack

And that is what Frederick II wanted them to think. Each of their armies was larger than his. So he planned to defeat them one at a time. He planned all along to take advantage of the naïve smugness of the empresses.

On August 29, Frederick called an unscheduled council of war. He laid out his maps, pointed at the objective, *Dresden,* and gave orders to his generals. With great precision, they maneuvered to the west and marched fast. The Prussian army invaded the state of Saxony, another territory of Austria. Frederick had always considered Saxony just another *German* state, hence it was destined be a Prussian possession. He made this uncontested invasion without informing England beforehand.

As Prussia's primary and only treaty ally, England protested this outrageous lack of consultation.

"Why did you not tell us first?!"

"*Why?*" the Prussian sovereign exclaimed calmly to the infuriated British delegate, as if it were obvious. "Because if I told you, the invasion would no longer be a *surprise!*"

Essentially unopposed, the Prussian army occupied Dresden in ten days. The utterly surprised and disorganized Saxony army had retreated until it could establish a well-organized, well-fortified position on the Elbe River near Pirna. There they waited, anticipating the Prussian army's attack, expecting to pulverize it with cannon.

Good choice, Frederick thought. *Now stay there.*

Leaving three quarters of his army to hold a static position of defense without attacking the entrenched Saxony army, Frederick bypassed Pirna. He marched south another thirty-five miles with twenty-eight thousand men and invaded Bohemia, too. He engaged the equally unprepared Austrian army gathering at Lobositz and defeated them too. Then he turned around and returned to Saxony in time to accept the surrender of its entire army at Pirna on October 14.

All in just two weeks of expert maneuvers.

Frederick II added the well-trained corps of Saxony infantry to his own army since Saxony was now part of Prussia. He intentionally left them unbruised by any real battle. All part of his plan. This increased his army by fifty percent.

Frederick then requested England, through its military delegate to, *one*, revoke its £500,000 annual subsidy to Russia and give it now to Prussia because, *two*, Austria would be asked to replace it and, *three*, Austria had just lost an army at Lobositz and could not afford to subsidize the Russians and, *four*, Austria would then petition France to subsidize Russia but, *five*, France's war funds were already so depleted, this would not be possible to do this year...and France may never be able to do it.

By attacking so late in the fighting season, even if France wanted to come to Austria's aid, it was too close to winter to start this campaign. Which France would later use as an excuse. The Great Powers would all have to wait until the spring of 1757. Except in addition to Silesia, now Saxony belonged to Prussia.

Russia had no money and the Austrian army had to rebuild.

All part of Frederick's plan.

"As the French would say...*Voilà!*"

*

Albany

September 1

Lieutenant General John Campbell, 4th Earl of Loudon, was a fifty-year-old Scot with a penchant for rigorous military discipline and organization. He was an experienced army officer and respected as a very able military administrator. He was purposely selected by Lord Halifax, the Duke of Cumberland, and the War Department to bring organization and order to the war effort in America and to be the new commander-in-chief of colonial forces reputed to be seriously deficient in leadership, discipline, and organization.

During his two-month journey from England, he was educated by staff members traveling with him on the status of the war against the French. He reviewed the Battle of Monongahela, the Battle of Lake George, and the Nova Scotia campaign resulting in the capture of Fort Beauséjour, with the ensuing deportation of the Acadian population, which was still in progress. He read a variety of letters written by various provincial governors to the War Department and members of Parliament, including many from William Shirley of Massachusetts, Sir William Johnson, the royal Indian agent, and the more recent scathing assessment of the army's capability and reasons for these conclusions by the governor of New York, Sir Charles Hardy. Other documents explained the lack of cooperation among the provinces, the competition among the appointed governors, fueling dissension in American politics. But one aspect he seized upon was the reported and flagrant insubordination of the provincial army to English command. He intended to resolve this disgraceful insolence. It would receive his immediate focus and attention.

The new commander-in-chief brought six thousand more regular troops with him, some of England's best, including regiments of the 35th Foot, the 42nd Foot and the renowned Black Watch of Scotland. A new regiment of four battalions to be called the Royal Americans was to be raised largely among the German immigrants in Pennsylvania, because...*The Germans have better marshal instincts and discipline, you see.*

In addition to Lord Loudoun's unquestioned military powers, the commissions granted by Parliament gave him the broadest and most comprehensive civil authority in the history of Britain's imperial governance. He was almost the viceroy of America within the limits of the law. He was authorized to issue orders to the provincial governors and legislatures, although the War Department and Parliament left it up to Lord Loudoun to find a way to get these obstinate legislative bodies to do what he might order. And they appointed him Governor of Virginia to give him standing among the American peerage.

Lord Loudoun marched into Albany feeling confident and well prepared to assume his duties.

He was in for a surprise.

The disorder he found among the chain of command was the worst he had ever seen in his career. General Ambercrombie seemed baffled on what to do. This disorder became undeniable when General Winslow's six thousand provincials started its movement up Lake George to attack the French forts on Crown Point. This advance was occurring in the face of new reports of the imminent capitulation of Fort Oswego.

Lord Loudoun immediately dispatched Colonel Webb in command of the 44th Foot to resupply and reinforce Fort Oswego. And he recalled General Winslow back to Albany to discuss his insubordination.

Lord Loudoun found out there were *two* armies in America. There was the army of British regulars. And there was the provincial army.

The soldiers of the provincial army were drawn from the colonies of their residence. They were recruited to serve usually for a year but explicitly under the command of officers also recruited from their colony. The officers of the provincial army assumed their positions of rank and responsibility with an understanding they would *not* be subordinate to British officers. The soldiers' recalcitrance had developed over the years after former provincial soldiers, serving under the command of the British army, became subject to the harsh disciplines with routine floggings and occasional hangings dispensed by British officers. They were not going to subject themselves to that again. The provincial *officers* did not want to lose rank to the English officers; the provincial officers' commissions were issued by colonial governments that were not formally recognized by the English army. Hence, the integration with the regulars would demote provincial colonels to a rank beneath the most junior captain in the regulars. They would not allow that again.

Such command problems were observed by General John Winslow most recently in the Nova Scotia campaign. He was born in America but served as a regular officer in the 40th Foot since 1740. Because of that experience, he understood the contractual necessity the American recruits demanded at every level to remain separate and equal to the English command. In this new war against the French, American senior officers agreed to take orders from an English commander-in-chief, but the provincial troops would *not* be integrated into one command structure. General Winslow was appointed commander-in-chief of all the provincial regiments, by the provincial governments of New England, including New York, under this strict proviso, which he agreed to by contract.

Lord Loudoun was enraged this irregular army had moved forward independent of British command against the French. He demanded General Winslow explain why provincials should not be joined with the regular troops.

General Winslow appreciated Lord Loudoun's anger and indignation.

"My lord general, the provincial soldiers were recruited from their colonies with the understanding they would serve under the command of colony officers. If we try to enforce an integration, you will be faced with mass desertions by the soldiers who will cite this action is a violation of the terms by which they serve."

"They would desert?!" Lord Loudoun was apoplectic. "This is unacceptable!" His face was red and the veins stood out on his neck. "This is all Shirley's doing!"

But Winslow stood firm because there really wasn't any other choice. He knew his men.

"Sir, if I may suggest—"

"No! You may not suggest!"

Lord Loudoun's anger had peaked. He was panting like an overworked cavalry horse. He had never seen such raw insubordination, but he was completely perplexed as to what to do about it. *Am I to use force of arms against them?*

"I thought the *French* were England's only enemies in this land," he accused.

Words of warning came to Winslow's mind. *Steady! Remain calm.*

"Your lordship, I stand ready to obey your commands. My officers are ready to act in unison with His Majesty's troops in accordance with and under the terms and conditions by which they serve. They will obey your commands."

Lord Loudoun had only heard about this insolence in anecdotes from other serving officers. The *American arrogance*, they called it. Their rejection of crown authority, resorting to claims about *their rights and privileges* that *they* had bestowed upon themselves. To experience it firsthand was both disconcerting and *alarming*. Even if Lord Loudoun found a resolution to this, which he knew he must do, it would not solve the underlying defiance that insisted on this nonsensical independence.

But he had a war to fight. Loudoun decided he must rebuild the command authority starting from the top down. With his hands clasped behind his back, Loudoun spun on his heels and faced the colonial officer, looking down his nose at him. His eyes were filled with passion.

"General Winslow, you and each of your officers will sign a formal written document, swearing to your submission to the king's authority. That is an *order*. *And I warn you to think carefully about repercussions for any refusal.* Before you ask, the document will be drafted for you to sign. It will be simple to understand, straightforward, and consistent with what you have asserted. In return, I will agree to allow your command to march without integration with regular troops, or under the command of regular officers. But you *will* follow my orders."

General Winslow knew better than to challenge this. To do so was borderline treason.

He came to attention and saluted. "Yes, sir!"

After Winslow's departure, Lord Loudoun began writing the first of many reports to the Duke of Cumberland, Lord Halifax, and White Hall, explaining the American insubordination was caused by William Shirley's complicity to outrageous contractual terms of service. In view of the siege of Fort Oswego and the on-going campaign against the French, he would have the colonial officers sign a declaration of loyalty to the king and swear an oath of submission to the king's authority.

Yet in this short exchange with General Winslow, the assertions were so plainly said and so extraordinary in meaning, Loudoun realized this was not the end of this story. The truth was not that simple. Neither was it singularly William Shirley's fault, even though the Massachusetts governor had agreed to such recruitment *contracts*. Shirley was slated to be blamed for all of this in any event. Someone must be blamed and there was no one else to choose. Even as Loudoun listed the steps he would take to resolve the impasse in command structure, it occurred to him there were more profound reasons to explain the brazen disrespect of army command authority and the confrontation to his higher social class. But Lord Loudoun left that out of this report because as a man of his nobility, rank, position, and life experiences, he was unable to relate to this classless American society. So he could not envision how to build a bridge to it. The best he could do was petition to White Hall, the Duke of Cumberland, and Lord Halifax, that Parliament pass laws for a new model of colonial government. This was needed to suppress what was a burgeoning sense by these provincial legislatures that they could establish their own rights without Parliament's approval.

This, however, was only the start of Lord Loudoun's challenges. Having applied a temporary bandage, in his opinion, to the *rights and privileges* of the provincial army, his next most pressing issue was how to provide winter quarters for his eight thousand redcoat regulars. Most of them were currently living in warm-weather tents, which would not protect them from the harsh winters of North America. He was astounded at the widespread lack of concern by colonial legislatures and local governments when he confronted them with this problem and insisted they provide barracks or quartering for these men.

Loudon voiced his frustration to an admiral aboard a ship-of-the-line anchored in New York harbor.

"The king's soldiers are here to fight the French for you, I told them. They reacted with indifference, almost with a shrug. Then they cited the English Bill of Rights of 1689 against quartering of a standing army without the explicit consent of Parliament!"

Lord Loudoun learned that William Shirley had been faced with the same problem. His solution was to pay the market rate for room and boarding of his soldiers, a *temporary* solution at best. Shirley petitioned the local legislatures to build permanent barracks. Unfortunately, the provincial government felt no pressing need to make it easier for the English redcoats to be quartered among them in official barracks, or worse, in their private homes. But as long as Shirley paid the rent, a public housing arrangement could be accommodated. This quickly depleted the war funds allocated by the crown.

A civilian advisor suggested Lord Loudoun might create a sense of cooperation by enlisting the support of respected colonial politicians, like Benjamin Franklin, who had convinced the populace of Pennsylvania to supply wagons for General Braddock's army. But Lord Loudoun considered that level of appeal beneath his station. He should not have to request cooperation. They should just do as he told them.

Instead Loudoun threatened that quartering would be provided by force of arms, if necessary, if the local legislatures did not present him with a solution. Albany capitulated to that threat immediately, with thousands of redcoats on its doorstep, but it did not have enough room for all the troops. The other legislatures balked and reacted to that display of force. The building of barracks commenced down the Hudson into New York and Philadelphia. Public quarters were found but in the end some of the redcoats were quartered and boarded in private homes. The Americans were not happy about how this was handled. They would *not* forget Lord Loudoun's high-handedness.

The quartering problems were pressing and severe enough to bring a halt to British offensive operations for 1756. September was already passing. The fighting season would be over soon. Loudoun would place battalions of redcoats into Fort William-Henry and Fort Edward to secure those vital forts. He foresaw the winter would be filled with skirmishing among militias, rangers, *coureurs de bois*, and their respective Indian allies. It would be vicious, constant, and deadly to the men involved. Regular troops would be reserved for larger battles.

Logistical supply was the third problem on the list and the most important for sustained operations. In this area, Lord Loudoun excelled. He ordered that supply and provisioning of the army be performed by British contractors who would establish American partners in the provinces to fulfill these needs. It would prove to be very expensive, but it would work.

Wagons and boats were built specifically for the army to use in conducting campaigns over the long distances in the North American wilderness. Warehouses for storing all the supplies would be erected inside forts, if necessary, to protect them. Military roads would be built, the kind that could easily carry the weight of heavy siege cannon. Transport ships were contracted to support transport of troops and invasion by sea for Louisbourg and on the Saint Lawrence River against Quebec City and Montréal.

It was not very glamorous work for the officers more used to marshalling long lines of infantry to the sounds of drums and bagpipes. But the effect of this logistical organization, as predicted by Sir Charles Hardy, would soon bring an overwhelming strength of arms by English and American forces against the French.

CHAPTER 22
MONTRÉAL
SEPTEMBER 1756
The Châsse Pain

It was the second night of travel on the rutted, overused river road between Quebec City and Montréal. The substantial metal spring bands suspending the coach's undercarriage were meant to mitigate bumps and depressions in the roads at a much slower pace. The military transport proceeded at a speed just short of a gallop. The spring bands could not counterbalance anything. Instead, the speed created a new problem of a constant swaying and rocking. With the leather covers pulled down and corded tightly over the windows to prevent dust, stones, clods of dirt, and horse manure from flying into one's face, the passengers could not see outside to compensate for the motion. It was nauseating even for a veteran sailor like Captain LaTour. In the dark of night any restful sleep was almost impossible, except at the brief interludes of about an hour while the team of horses was changed at each of the relay stations.

There the passengers would get out, stagger around to regain their sense of balance, quickly urinate, no time for anything else, and get back into the coach to lie down to sleep before the ride started again.

Captain LaTour and Alain Marcoux were long past attempts at polite conversation, which had not been likely anyway. They preferred to ride in silence and obtain whatever rest was possible. It happened that fifteen miles short of Montréal, as the coach pulled out of the last relay station and the two men were both deep asleep from exhaustion, Alain Marcoux's dreams were interrupted by the *vulnax*.

Alain had not been visited by the night messenger in over two months. But the *vulnax*'s ability to induce fear and absolute obedience in its servants had not lost any of its potency.

Where are you?

The ethereal discussion went on for almost ten minutes, a very long time by the measure of these occurrences. Once the *vulnax* had absorbed everything that Alain had to offer, it gave him commands to follow in Montréal.

At the exact same time, the speeding coach encountered a fairly long depression in the road that was beyond the length of the horse's stride. It was dark and hard to see. The horses stumbled into it and jumped to recover. The coach pitched forward with the sharp reduction in speed. LaTour's sleeping body rolled off his seat. The coach then rocked backwards just as strongly as the team recovered. The result was that Alain Marcoux was thrown into the arms of Captain LaTour who was already struggling to sit up on the floor between the seats.

The night messenger was now staring directly into the other man's face. In the darkness of the coach's interior, yellowish spots of light loomed only inches away from the captain.

"Captain LaTour!"

For an instant, LaTour was almost paralyzed with fear. The voice had the same tone and menace as Wittmann Bootz' voice had. The stench was overpowering.

LaTour shoved hard against the other man's body and reeled in panic. He grabbed the handle of the door to stand. It opened, and he was flung from the speeding coach, hitting the ground with an *oof* and rolled. The larger rear wheels almost ran over his feet. The alert cavalryman managed to pull hard on the reins before he trampled the man.

The coach drivers brought the team to a halt. The escort riders came to the dazed figure of the captain who got to his knees. One of the coachmen lit a torch and ran back.

"Captain, are you hurt?" A dismounted cavalry officer took hold of his hand to help him stand.

LaTour moved slowly and felt his body. To his surprise, he'd broken no bones nor had he sprained anything. But he did have bruises! A lot of them!

I was lucky.

"I'm...I'm all right. I was thrown from my seat for some reason. I gripped the door handle by mistake to stand up," he offered quickly. "I won't be doing that again!"

The actual reason was too bizarre and embarrassing to describe. He decided it was not real. And seeing Alain Marcoux's concerned expression in the torchlight helped LaTour convince himself it had, indeed, been just a bad dream. Probably brought on by his exhaustion and the sudden upheaval of the carriage house.

"How soon will we be in Montréal?"

"Two and a half, maybe three hours," answered the coachman.

"How many hours to sunrise?"

"Maybe six."

"Let's slow it down."

It was still dark when they came to the city's eastern gate. There were four sentries and a sergeant on guard. After a short inspection, they were waved in and the coach went directly to the hotel nearest to the governor's mansion. A gendarme was working beside the hotel clerk. His job was to make a record of the names of anyone who came into the city for the first time.

Intendant Bigôt, LaTour frowned in disgust. The last time he saw the man, the intendant tried to kill Lady de Chanaye and ended up shooting Philippe Gerrard in the head. He almost gave the wrong name to avoid this creature, who would certainly send soldiers to search him out at seeing his name.

They learned Governor Vaudreuil would start seeing people at the hour of nine. But if dispatches came, he would accept those interruptions at any time.

Alain Marcoux was almost bent over from the painful headache he was enduring.

"I say we sleep for three hours, then go see the governor."

The man nodded weakly in agreement. They were escorted to their rooms to be awakened in three hours.

Captain LaTour awoke when he heard the knock at the door. He asked for more bathing water. He stood in front of the mirror and vigorously washed his face with soap and cold water to wake up. Then he used a straight razor to trim his short beard. Another knock at the door, and the steward brought in a small bathing tub with lukewarm water. It was round, three feet in diameter, and only two feet deep. It was enough to wash himself.

Before he left his room he'd picked his teeth clean, chewed cloves, rinsed them again, and spit into the chamber pot. He carefully removed any stray lint from his uniform. He used a towel to buff his boots. Fully dressed, he stood in front of the mirror wearing his saber, inspected his appearance, and practiced a salute.

Good enough, he thought.

With the dispatches over his shoulder, he went down to the small dining room to wait for Monsieur Marcoux.

"You woke him, did you not?"

The concierge assistant assured him Monsieur Marcoux was awakened an hour ago.

"Knock again and see if he needs anything."

LaTour spent time drinking tea and talked with the head concierge about the latest news of the city. Among the things he heard was the arrival of a general, le Marquis de Montcalm, the new army commander, and the fall of Fort Oswego.

"But food is short. Some feel we will have famine this winter."

"Famine? In Montréal?"

Alain Marcoux showed up at that moment with a pained expression on his face, still looking exhausted.

LaTour almost felt sorry for the man…except he did not like him.

"Do you want something to eat?"

Marcoux nodded.

LaTour signaled for food and drink.

"May I ask a favor of you?" Marcoux said unexpectedly.

"Depends on what it is," LaTour replied.

"I do not know how long I will be with the governor today. But when I am done with him, I hope to return and go straight back to bed."

Marcoux wrestled a thick envelop from his pocket. It was wax sealed and addressed to Father Tinian.

"Do you know this man?"

How the hell did he get that missive? "I've heard the name," LaTour answered evasively.

"I don't know what this contains, but Naval Minister Machault wanted me to deliver this to Father Tinian. He thinks the priest may have a reply to send back to him. Asked me to wait for it. I don't mind, but I don't know if I will be going back any time soon. And who knows what the governor might direct me to do. I thought it would be easier for you to return any reply to the Naval Minister…since you will probably be going back to France long before me. If this is inconvenient, I am certain I will find another way."

It might be good to see Father Tinian, he thought. *He might have news about Philippe.*

"All right." Captain LaTour accepted the missive. "I will do this favor for you. Maybe you can do a favor for me someday?"

"I hope that is true, Captain." His words held a note of regret, as if he did not think it was possible.

LaTour found that puzzling. This man seemed a different person from the rude passenger he knew from the crossing. He wanted to ask about his business with Governor Vaudreuil, but decided the less he knew, the less he would have to deny knowing when Intendant Bigôt confronted him, as the little maggot surely would. And with that thought he decided to find out how soon a coach would be returning to Quebec City. The concierge indicated one would leave at the noon hour unless there were no passengers and another late in the day with or without passengers.

They ate mostly in silence. LaTour mentioned what he'd learned about the fall of Fort Oswego.

"That English fort had stood for more than thirty years, and we invested it in three days. Hard to imagine, *oui*?"

Marcoux smiled weakly in acknowledgement and nodded but did not reply. He seemed very preoccupied.

Don't ask him anything, LaTour warned himself.

*

"Governor Vaudreuil will see you immediately," the ensign said. "I will take you to Captain Trieste."

"Here's the bag." Captain LaTour handed over the satchel. "Just remember to say you received this pouch directly from the Naval Minister and Admiral de la Motte."

Alain Marcoux slipped the dispatch bag over his shoulder.

"Thank you, Captain. Good luck."

LaTour watched him walk away with mixed feelings.

No, he thought. *I still don't like you.*

LaTour walked quickly from the governor's mansion and headed to the back door of the Terrain des Jésuites and rang the bell. A priest answered.

"Good morning. How may I help you?"

"I am Captain LaTour of the *Falcon Queen*. To see Father Tinian."

In less than a minute, Father Tinian came to the door, breathless from running. They embraced.

"Come, come. The archbishop will be jubilant to see you again."

Once inside the inner offices, a scene similar to Father Tinian's greeting repeated itself.

"Your history first," the archbishop said, taking a seat again behind his desk.

Captain LaTour handed over the missive from Jean-Baptiste de Machault to Father Tinian.

"This was to be delivered by my passenger I carried on my crossing, Monsieur Alain Marcoux, but he is with Governor Vaudreuil and decided not to delay its delivery. He claimed it may need a reply, so I can carry that back to France with me if you like."

Father Tinian handed it unopened to the archbishop. "It's for him anyway."

Nicolet broke the seals and scanned the eleven pages, then set it aside.

"I will read this later. Father Tinian, stay with us and listen. Please continue, Captain."

"Well, you remember Philippe was shot in the head by Intendant Bigôt. Philippe recovered. But if that was not bad enough, we were forced into Port Halifax. Driven to it by a storm."

That is where LaTour's story began. He finished an hour later, indicating where he delivered Corrinne, Mathilde, and the children after the attack on them in Boston.

"I gave her over to Captain Martyn of the *Anamosa*, on Apthorp's Island, off Boston's coast. He was taking her somewhere south, someplace secret, to prevent any more attempts on her life. Not certain where that was, but I am guessing either the long island or southern Connecticut. That's the last time I saw them. I went to the Antilles islands after that. Back to Amsterdam in May to sell my cargo. Got forced into entering La Rochelle in June to escape the privateers after war was declared. Admiral de la Motte commandeered my ship in July, in the name of the king. Commissioned me, obviously!

Fate works in strange ways. Actually, he has me *smuggling* for France. I carry two flags now and two ship names…there's probably a dozen ways I can be hung." He gestured outward with both hands. "But I get to wear this pretty uniform as a captain in the French navy. Who would have guessed?"

André Nicolet's expression was still stricken with the revelation that Corrinne had her throat slashed in a murder attempt. Hearing she survived was some solace.

"I am distraught for Lady de Chanaye…that these…*people*…hunt her still."

"She is Lady VanderMeer now," LaTour said. "Part of the charade she assumed to live in Boston. Have you heard from Philippe and Henri?"

"Yes. Both alive and well."

The archbishop told the story of how Henri came to Quebec and his two decorations for valor.

"Now he is an ensign in the marines, deployed to Louisbourg along with Major Péan."

"Louisbourg! That is where I sail next! Then to Boston. Then back to Louisbourg before crossing to Rochefort."

Archbishop Nicolet brightened. "We can send and receive letters! To Henri and Corrinne! Oh, this is very good news! And I do need to reply to the Naval Minister. I will have Father Tinian bring the missives to your hotel."

LaTour hid his dismay. He would miss the noon coach.

"Of course! But what of Philippe?"

"Captain Gerrard is here in Montréal! They will know his whereabouts at army headquarters! And he can tell you all about his adventures…which is a chilling tale, indeed. Father Tinian, see if you can find Captain Gerrard." He turned back to LaTour. "I do not think it wise for you to tell him Corrinne was attacked. If you do that, he will desert New France and try to find her…and likely lose his life trying. You saw her babies. End your story with something happy. Philippe will be going to Fort Carillon for the winter. He will want to send a letter to Corrinne. Maybe Lord VanderMeer in Boston can get it to her, wherever she is hiding, *oui*?"

*

Captain LaTour returned to the hotel. Father Tinian would find Philippe. It would be easier if he stayed in one spot. Standing away from the intendant's gendarme spy, he told the head concierge he would remain another night.

"Does Montréal have a paper with written news?"

"No," the head concierge replied. "But this hotel creates a paper of information each week."

From behind the high counter, he pulled out a four-page handwritten copy made with quill and ink.

"This one is two days old. We only make four of these. It's only for our guests. Please return it to me when you are finished."

"Of course, of course. This is wonderful!"

LaTour had his personal bag delivered back to his room and took a chair in the atrium.

The paper talked about the war, ship arrivals and departures, the rumors, the prices of food, the price of furs and other commodities, lists of men killed or wounded, announcements by the various religious congregations, and personal letters from the citizens of Montréal looking for loved ones, making requests, selling things. It even had a few jests. Some of the humor was dark.

> *An Indian comes into a Montréal tailor shop and hands the propri-etor a stringer with twenty-two bloody human scalps. "Can you sew a coat out of these for me?" "Depends," the tailor replies. He counts the scalps. "I will need four more to do that. And they must all be English scalps!" He insists sternly. The Indian nodded with understanding. He left the shop and returned fifteen minutes later with four fresh scalps dripping with gore. "All of them are English," the Indian assured him.*

LaTour laughed out loud just as a tall, smiling marine officer stood in front of him blocking his light. He jumped up from his chair and hugged Philippe Gerrard. LaTour nudged and pointed at the gendarme. They decided it would be better to sit in an outdoor café to talk. Philippe knew of one on Rue Saint-Paul in lower town. They spent the rest of the day talking about old times and new. The captain heard about Philippe's capture by the Oneida. The battles at Fort Duquesne and Fort Oswego. Philippe heard more about Corrinne, Anamosa, the twins, Marcus and Calypso, the house in Boston, the captain's journeys and adventures, the corsairs off the Azores, how he came to be in the French navy.

"So tell me, Captain, is there any country in the world that does not have an excuse to hang you?"

LaTour's hand rubbed his throat. "That is not funny, Philippe! If I raise the wrong flag or mismatch the name plaques, for instance in Louisbourg or Boston, they will hang me on the wharf!"

Philippe sat up straight with surprise. "Louisbourg and Boston! I can send letters to her! Henri too!"

"You can. But I am leaving tomorrow. I will need them sealed with wax before then."

"Then I will take your leave, Captain LaTour, and get to writing. I would take dinner with you tonight, but my general asks that I eat with him."

"Do not worry. I plan to go to sleep if we are done talking. Just come by and see me with your letters."

In the early afternoon, Father Tinian came to the hotel to deliver the archbishop's letters. One for Corrinne and one for Henri. Both of them were thick.

"The archbishop is still writing the one to the naval minister. He will send it in the next pouch. One goes out about every other day."

They talked a few more minutes and said good bye. Before another hour was gone, Father Tinian would be dead.

LaTour was restless, but he did not want to walk around Montréal lest he get stopped by the gendarmes. So he went to his room and climbed into bed. It was still daylight.

*

The knock on Captain LaTour's hotel room door came at night. He stumbled in the dark, raised the wick on the lantern, and opened the door. Two gendarmes waited in the hallway: a very big sergeant and an ensign.

"Captain LaTour?"

He nodded. "Yes."

"Get dressed please, Captain. You are to come with us to see Intendant Bigôt."

"Why?! Am I under arrest for something?"

"I don't know, Captain."

"Then fuck you!"

He moved to shut the door. The sergeant slammed it back open with his fist.

"If you refuse to come with us peacefully, I am authorized to arrest you, Captain," said the ensign. "And after talking with the intendant, you will spend the rest of the night in the bastille. Your choice."

Fifteen minutes later, wearing his uniform, Captain LaTour stood before the desk of the Intendant of New France.

"Captain LaTour, how nice of you to visit us. And a *captain* in the French navy, no less. Are they aware you are a smuggler wanted on a variety of warrants?"

"Admiral de la Motte read the charges aloud to me...and said they were ridiculous. Then he commissioned me as a captain," LaTour responded, irritation plain on his face. "I am performing a special courier mission for him. What is this all about?"

"Courier mission? To where?"

"I have been ordered by Admiral de la Motte not to reveal that information."

"What have you done in Montréal?"

"I delivered the dispatch pouch to Governor Vaudreuil as I was ordered to do."

"Is that all?"

"Yes." He decided not to mention visiting with Archbishop Nicolet.

"But you spent the rest of the day sitting in a café, talking with Captain Gerrard."

"Yes. That was not official. He is my friend, and you know that."

"And what else do you plan to do while you are here?"

"Nothing. In the morning, I return to Quebec."

"Where is Lady de Chanaye?"

"I have no idea. Maybe you should ask Captain Gerrard? I am sure he would have much more to say to you."

"So you have friends in high places back in France? Well, so do I, Captain LaTour. Let's find out which of us has friends of more importance, shall we?"

The intendant gestured to the guards.

"Let him go."

*

The next morning, Alain Marcoux saw Captain LaTour waiting in the atrium.

"*Bonjour*, Captain. You are leaving today?"

"Yes. On the afternoon coach."

"You must first see Captain Trieste. He has dispatches for Louisbourg. I told him I would tell you."

"Very well. And you?"

"I am meeting with the governor most of the day. I go there now. If I do not see you again, then fair sailing. *Adieu*."

As Alain walked out the front of the hotel, he met a marine captain coming in. The man looked very familiar.

"Excuse me, I am Alain Marcoux. Have we met before? You look familiar to me."

Philippe thought the man looked familiar too.

"I have been in the west of New France for over ten years. So unless you were doing fur trading, it is not likely. Good day to you."

Without saying more, Philippe went by the man and into the hotel. He could feel the stranger's hard stare as he entered the hotel doors.

"What did he say?" LaTour asked.

Philippe shrugged. "Said I looked familiar."

"He told me that too. I actually thought he looked familiar as well. Did you know him?"

"No. Let's eat. Here are my letters. Two for Corrinne. One for Henri."

*

Alain Marcoux took a short walk before he went back to see Captain Trieste. He slowly circled the Terrain des Jésuites. He saw the back door had a bell pull. It was a private entrance. He returned to the governor's palace and waited most of the morning. Shortly before noon, he was called to the governor's conference room where all the large maps were hanging on the wall.

The first hour was spent answering more questions from the governor and captains Trieste and Montreuil about the war in Europe. Alain told them what he knew and what he thought might happen. The governor regarded him with skepticism.

"And you are a Prussian?"

"No, I am from Alsace-Lorraine."

"Aren't you supposed to be my enemy?"

"I could be your enemy." Marcoux smiled and allowed in a more practical voice, "That is, if someone paid me to be your enemy. But that is the essence of why I am here. As I told you yesterday, I can bring you a regiment of German mercenaries to fight for New France against the English, or anyone else you might choose. Not all of the other German states are aligned with Prussia. Some are aligned with Austria. Others are aligned to the highest bidder, yes? So my employer has offered your Naval Minister a regiment of mercenaries, which he has commissioned me to recruit. But Frederick II is already hiring as many as he can find. There are many left who do not have a fondness for the Prussians. And they know their worth. The Naval Minister has offered to pay for them. He will send this regiment to Louisbourg or send them to you. He directed me to come here and answer any questions you may have for me. He will send them to Louisbourg in the spring if you do not want them. But this was all explained in the missive to you in the dispatch pouch. Have you read this?"

"Yes. The missive was there. Otherwise Monsieur Marcoux, I would have turned you over to some very vicious Indians allies and paid them to prolong your misery before you died."

"Then I am *very* pleased the mail was properly sorted."

The governor and the captains smiled.

"Well," the governor said with reservation, "even after reading the missive, I find this very unusual. But if the Naval Minister makes this offer, it is my duty to explore how we might use such a regiment. I would like you to sit with grenadier Captain Montreuil, my adjutant, and have a robust discussion on the capabilities of these men and the different ways they might be deployed."

"As you wish, Governor."

The captains stood and Alain Marcoux stood with them. He bowed politely and followed Captain Montreuil down to another office on the ground floor of the mansion.

"Captain Montreuil, do you mind if I take a short walk? My stomach has been queasy ever since the coach ride from Quebec City. A little fresh air would help rejuvenate my thinking, *s'il vous plait.*"

"Of course. I will be right here when you are ready to start."

"I will not be long."

Alain Marcoux went to the back door of the Terrain des Jésuites. He pulled on the bell cord. A priest appeared at the door.

"Hello, my name is Vincent Trestle." He pulled out a wax-sealed missive addressed to Archbishop Nicolet. "I have a confidential missive that requires I hand deliver this to the archbishop. May I be escorted to him?"

"I am Father Xavier. I can escort you to his secretary, Father Tinian."

Alain followed the priest, memorizing the interior arrangement of hallways while he was escorted. He saw no one else as he was taken up a private stairway to a landing before a single doorway.

"Do you mind waiting here for me to escort me out? I should be a few minutes at most."

Father Xavier decided he could watch the back door from the landing. "Of course, sir."

The priest opened the door and Father Tinian looked up from his desk.

"A confidential courier for Archbishop Nicolet."

"Of course. Come in, Monsieur...?"

Alain heard the landing door close behind him. "Vincent Trestle." He pulled out the wax-sealed envelope. "I am required to hand this to the archbishop."

"Of course." Father Tinian knocked once on the archbishop's office door. "Eminence, a courier is here to hand deliver a missive."

Archbishop Nicolet did not look up from what he was reading but gestured with a wave the man should enter. Father Tinian stepped aside, allowed the man to pass, and closed the door.

Nicolet held up one finger. He wanted to finish the last paragraph, but asked, "And where have you come from, Monsieur?"

"*Hell*," a voice answered softly.

The archbishop looked up in time to see the point of a rapier pass into his chest. He felt a terrible pain and pitched forward atop his desk, dead.

Alain cleaned the blade on the bishop's shoulder. Then he opened the door to the outer office.

"Father Tinian, his Eminence has fainted for some reason!"

"What?" Father Tinian rushed into the office. He reached over the desk to touch the man's face when he felt a terrible pain in his back. He looked down to see six inches of a sword blade coming out of his chest. He collapsed but was caught in Alain Marcoux's arms and gently laid on the floor out of the doorway.

Alain cleaned his blade again and rested it by the door inside of the office. He left the office door ajar and went to the door leading to the landing and opened it.

"Father Tinian needs you!" he called with urgency. "I think something is wrong with the archbishop."

Alarmed, the priest rushed into the office and gasped twice. The first time over what he saw. The second time in response to the rapier thrust through his back and into his heart.

Alain Marcoux cleaned his blade thoroughly. He took the key from the landing office door and locked it behind him as he left. He put the key in his pocket and went down the stairway, retracing his steps to the back entrance. He went outside and looked carefully left and right. He saw no one. He went left down the street along the wall and left again on the next street, walking down and across Rue Notre-Dame, heading to lower town. He turned left again on Rue Saint-Paul. He approached the governor's palace slowly from the riverside direction and made a point to ask the ensign at the reception desk a question.

"I went for a walk down Rue Saint-Paul a little ways. What is on the far end of that street?"

"Oh, the marketplace, sir."

"Good for finding food to eat?"

"Well, usually it is," the ensign replied. "But since the war started, food is becoming scarce, I'm afraid."

"Oh, I was going to bring something back for Captain Montreuil."

"We have plenty of food here, sir. What would you like?"

"Thank you, Ensign, but based on what you just said, I will check with the captain first."

Alain Marcoux and Captain Montreuil met for much of the afternoon, discussing the skills of the mercenaries. They learned a lot about each other.

Alain invented most of his background. Later the adjutant walked Marcoux back to the hotel.

"So I will tell the Naval Minister I will continue to recruit this regiment, but that the governor will reply sometime soon about his needs for these men."

Captain Montreuil smiled. "It is not over yet, Monsieur. You will still need to meet with the governor sometime tomorrow to close this discussion. He will have more questions. Come by early in the morning."

"I will stay a week if you think it will help. Maybe I should learn more about Montréal."

When Alain Marcoux made it back to his room, he was so exhausted he fell into bed without undressing. Within minutes he was asleep. The night messenger visited him before another hour had passed.

Philippe Gerrard had to sit down. He gently rubbed the throbbing pain in his left leg, which had appeared so suddenly and was centered on the terrible scar from three years earlier. The pain had been much worse than this the last time this happened. But it was still bad enough that he would walk with a limp. And he knew this meant something related to the *châsse*. *But what?*

Pierre Dunemoore doubled over with a pain in his stomach. He'd been napping in his bed at Fort Niagara when the terrible cramp occurred. He got up and walked around. It did not help. He could tell it was not going to get better. He'd experienced this before.

It was that pain, he thought suddenly. *The* châsse *pain...Something has happened.*

Charles VanderMeer was sketching designs in his office when a sudden weakness came to his hands. He knew immediately what it was and stopped work. He put on his coat and went to the street door. His numb fingers could barely move the handle or turn the key. He walked swiftly to the house and waved at the guards before he fumbled with the handle on the front door. He found Corrinne lying back in her chair in the library. Dian had placed a hot cloth around her neck and a cold cloth on her forehead.

"Thank God you're all right. You feel it too?"

"Yes, my hands are too weak to do anything."

"I fear something has happened to Philippe or Pierre or Archbishop Nicolet."

*

Captain LaTour was refused passage on the noon coach. They would not take even one passenger. He went back to his hotel to wait. He asked the concierge if he had a book he could read. He received one of poetry. *Well*, he thought with a frown. *At least it will help me fall asleep.*

And it did. In the comfortable hotel bed, he slept soundly. And since he'd left no request with the concierge to be awakened, he did not get up in time to get on the evening coach.

He paid for another night.

*

The lamentations began early the next morning as the dreadful rumor spread that his Eminence, the Archbishop André Nicolet, was dead. Women wailed, many of the townspeople thronged to the churches and prayed. Bells tolled throughout Montréal. The Terrain des Jésuites was overrun with gendarmes searching the grounds, looking for a killer.

His Eminence was killed by a sword! Sitting at his desk! In his own office! His secretary too! And another priest!

Three Jesuits had been ruthlessly murdered, including Archbishop Nicolet. A crime so heinous, Governor Vaudreuil came to the compound right away to see for himself. The three bodies had been moved to a tiny chapel within the compound and laid out on tables. Two Jesuits trained in the healing arts had already examined the bodies.

"Murder, possibly assassination," the eldest of these men, a monsignor, told the governor. "A sword thrust to the heart killed all three. All three bodies were found in the archbishop's office at the hour of six this morning. We started searching for him when he did not appear for Mass. His landing door was locked and had to be broken down to get in. *Rigor mortis* had occurred. We think death occurred sometime yesterday afternoon. No one else was seen, so the murderer was a visitor and was freely admitted at the back door. Father Xavier had been missing since yesterday afternoon as well. So he was killed at the same time. He was positioned to control visitation at the back door. This was someone he knew or someone using credentials to see the archbishop."

"And the reason? Was anything stolen?"

"Nothing of value was taken. And there are items of gold and silver freely visible in the archbishop's office. This person entered, murdered, and left. He did this quickly or he would have been seen."

"Are you telling me someone entered the Terrain de Jésuites in the middle of the afternoon and not a single one of you noticed a stranger walking among you?! How is this possible?"

"Governor, there are less than ten of us here. We all have duties. Mass. Confessions. Visitations with the sick or poor around Montréal. There was only one other priest in the compound. He was in the front, to answer that door. But he did not hear anything. The stairway to the archbishop's office rises up from the back entrance."

"The Jesuit Intendant of New France was murdered for a reason! Start thinking about what that could be. I want an answer for this crime!" Governor Vaudreuil fumed with fury and disgust. "The gendarmes are collecting the names of everyone seen even near this compound yesterday. You should help them too!"

*

Captain LaTour had just sat down to break his fast at the hotel when the bells began to toll. He went out to the street and saw the commotion, people running, dozens of gendarmes were marching towards the Jesuit compound. He went back inside to quickly finish his food.

A man came running into the hotel, claiming loudly to the concierge that Archbishop Nicolet had been murdered! Conversations of shock and surprise broke out among the guests all around him. Captain LaTour slumped in his chair in disbelief. After the initial shock, he went over to the concierge.

"How is this possible?" he demanded. "Have you learned anything else? Who would do such a thing? And to a bishop of the church? Why?"

But the concierge, who was sobbing like many others, was at a loss. He only shook his head.

An anguished Captain LaTour gathered up his bag and walked over to the governor's mansion. He took a chair near the reception desk. No one was there. So he waited. Finally, Captain Trieste came running into the mansion.

"And who are you?"

LaTour stood. "I am Captain LaTour of the *Falcon Queen*. I delivered dispatches here."

"No, I do not recall that," Trieste challenged.

"I carried the dispatches aboard my ship, which awaits me at anchor in Quebec City. My orders were to deliver the dispatches and Monsieur Alain Marcoux to see the governor. I gave the pouch to him when we arrived at the mansion. I came here this morning to retrieve any dispatches that might be going back to Louisbourg and France."

"Where else have you been?"

"Um, I had a long discussion with Captain Philippe Gerrard. He is a friend of mine."

"Captain Gerrard is your friend?"

"For almost ten years. My ship carried furs for his company."

Captain Trieste was impatient and indecisive. "Well, stay here. We do have dispatches to go back. But I am preoccupied. You've heard the news?"

LaTour nodded solemnly, the tremor in his voice betrayed his emotion. "I've known the archbishop since I first came to Montréal. He is the most decent man I've ever known. Who would do this? For what possible reason?"

Trieste shook his head. "We don't know. It was an assassination. The wounds were from a rapier or a saber. But I am busy answering questions for the governor. So stay here, if you please. The ensign will return soon."

A few minutes later, the reception ensign appeared.

"Captain LaTour. I am sorry. I am late. But you've heard, yes?"

"This is a terrible, dark day for us all. Montréal has lost a great man."

Alain Marcoux entered the mansion.

"Have a chair, Monsieur. We will all be waiting for a while."

"Did you deliver the missive?" Marcoux asked.

The question hit LaTour like a bolt of lightning. A stream of warnings moved through his mind just as quickly. *Be careful, LaTour. They are looking for anyone who visited the archbishop yesterday. Intendant Bigôt will pounce on you for this.*

"Yes. I delivered it."

"And the reply?"

"I was going to go back this morning to check. But after what has happened…"

The two of them spent the entire morning, mostly in silence, watching officers and civilians going to and from the mansion. The governor finally returned at noon. Alain Marcoux was dismissed and asked to return the next morning. Captain LaTour was invited into Captain Trieste's office. The officer shut his door.

"How much do you know about Monsieur Marcoux?"

"I met him briefly at the harbor fort of Rochefort when I met with Admiral de la Motte and the Naval Minister. He was assigned passage on my ship. As I said, my orders were to deliver the man to Governor Vaudreuil for discussions along with the dispatch pouch. And to bring back any dispatches the governor may want to send back to France. But I travel to Louisbourg first."

"And Monsieur Marcoux?"

"I was told to escort him here. That was all. He was to find his own way back."

"Do you know why he came here?"

"I do not know, Captain. And *please* do not tell me. I'd rather not know."

"We have a pouch of dispatches for France you can take today. A smaller one for Louisbourg."

Trieste sealed the outside of both pouches with several large blots of wax and handed it to him.

"You are permitted to take the evening coach. It will gather you at the hotel."

Captain LaTour accepted the dispatches. Since the coach would pick him up at the hotel he decided to wait there. This was not a day to be wandering around Montréal. The hotel's atrium was crowded, mostly military officers, and all discussion was about the archbishop's murder.

The evening coach gathered him at the hotel. There were no other passengers.

*

The archbishop's body was placed in a brass casket, left open for four days of visitation by the citizens of Montréal at the Notre-Dame-de-Bon-Secours Chapel. Guarded by gendarmes, lines of people streamed past, continuing throughout the day and night, some mourners coming from Quebec City and other nearby towns to pay their respects. Many of them visited several times to say more prayers for their beloved archbishop. Priests of all the congregations, particularly the Jesuits held a *salut*, the benediction services of hymns, litanies, and canticles every night. The interior of the chapel was redolent with the smell of burning incense. On the fifth day, a Requiem Mass was scheduled in the evening. The chapel was not that large, and it was filled with people of high rank, close friends, and family. Captain Gerrard was one of those invited by the Jesuit congregation.

Philippe was devastated by his friend's murder. He was at a loss to explain so senseless a death. It was done with a sword. A saber or a rapier, they claimed. And the murderer killed Father Tinian and another priest. Desperate to find the guilty person, the gendarmerie was now questioning each of the Jesuits themselves, thinking it might have been done by one of their own.

Philippe knelt as long as the pain in his left leg would permit, then he stood up along the side aisle with the other spectators. A Récollets bishop performed the service. Philippe noticed the bishop's brother, Father Eric Nicolet, assisting in the Mass.

Governor Vaudreuil and Intendant Bigôt attended, as well as the Marquis de Montcalm. At the end of the service, the Récollets bishop held up a gold crucifix dangling from heavy wooden rosary beads for the people in the church to see. It was a Norman cross, treasured by the archbishop's family for many centuries. It was old, an object of mystery and legend. André Nicolet had been fascinated by the beauty of the dark purple jewel mounted at the center of the cross. The archbishop had worn it all his life.

"This golden, bejeweled, ancient object has immeasurable value," the Récollets bishop proclaimed to those attending. "It hung in plain sight on Archbishop Nicolet's chest. It would have been seen by the murderer. He did not take it because he was not seeking wealth. He was delivering *death*! And all of us who knew André Nicolet are left to wonder what could be gained by slaying a man known for so many accomplishments and kind deeds? What kind of man would do this? In my heart and soul, I suspect that only a possessed man could perpetrate this monstrous crime. A man possessed by something *evil*. A man compelled by the *devil*! And he walks among us still! *I say beware!*"

The Récollets bishop motioned for Eric Nicolet to kneel before him.

"This blessed artifact is a Nicolet family treasure." He slipped the gold rosary crucifix over the priest's head. "And so we pass it to the family." Then he blessed the priest.

The pain in Philippe's leg vanished instantly. The bishop's words stayed with him for a long time. He had perfectly described the murderer. If the murderer killed the bishop, he might seek his life too.

I hope he tries.

L ouisbourg was an isolated city. The port was indeed frequented by ships and visitors but the fortress city did not grow very much as a result of its commerce. It subsisted mainly on fishing. A lot of fishing. The *faubourg*, as that spread of growth of people and communities around a main city was called, did not burgeon as it did among the larger cities of New France. Governor Augustin de Boschenry de Drucour, when appointed to Île Royale, had been directed by the Naval Minister, Jean-Baptiste de Machault, to increase the population of the island, to develop more agriculture, sustain the fisheries, and promote trade. But the stony lands of Île Royale were not conducive to farming and much less so than the neighboring Acadian lands.

It was near to impossible to get any of those experienced farmers to immigrate. Fishing did indeed flourish, but commercial trade from the visiting ships was not supported by local consumption. There were not that many people. They had little money to spend except for the French government subsidies from the Naval Minister. Nevertheless, the port provided excellent shelter from the harsh seas of the North Atlantic. It was a good place to anchor and conduct cross-deck trading among the foreign ships in the relative safety of the harbor. It was essentially a free-port and smuggling was more or less tolerated. During war between England and France, it was also blockaded, but not all of the time. So a certain amount of hard coin and trade goods did trickle into the city-fortress. It was just enough to leave the people craving for more.

Otherwise, Louisbourg was dull.

The people were friendly. But the women of marrying age did not look kindly on the soldiers and marines garrisoned there. The defending garrison rarely had any money to spend. That these humble men would ever become landed and wealthy was very unlikely. On the scale of desired eligible bachelors, they were at the bottom. For the most part, so were their manners. Younger women married or not, alone or in pairs, were assailed by kissing sounds as they walked by, or low whistles and mumbled compliments. If they turned to scowl at the offenders, the soldiers would look the other way, acting innocent.

The officers of the garrison, on the other hand, were coveted and popular. People recognized that rewards of fame and fortune usually came to such men in wartime. With not many prospects for romance among the bachelor civilians short of scandal, a few of the women took their chances as mistresses of the married officers. And they all eyed the remaining half dozen younger officers shamelessly.

Sensitive to the needs of her citizenry amidst the dreary, endless monotony, Madame Marie de Drucour arranged social gatherings of good food, drink, and dancing for the more polished of Louisbourg citizenry and a few of the garrison, too, if recommended by the officers. These soirées often occurred with the arrival of the larger trade frigates or ship-of-the-line naval vessels. There would be at least one every ten days and sometimes more, except on Sundays.

Kyrielle de Courserac was sixteen years old and hailed from a less wealthy family in Normandy. She grew up in a provincial, sparsely populated farming country. At the urging of her parents, she had been visiting her grand uncle in Louisbourg since April, hoping to improve her chances among the wealthy sea traders towards finding a good husband. She had Celtic ancestry, evident in her black hair and blue eyes. Kyrielle was beautiful and she knew it.

She was eager to trade on her looks for a better life. The men at these Louisbourg soirées, married or not, constantly sought a dance with her, or sat by her hoping to persuade her with veiled propositions to go somewhere more private. She had not been a virgin since the age of thirteen, though she presented herself otherwise. But giving up her *faux* virtue to any of these temporary *visitors* simply did not interest her. Though many of them were handsome and well-spoken, not a single one of them mentioned or even hinted at marriage. And she was not about to become another vulgar tale of conquest for them.

Among the young officers, however, Ensign Henri Gerrard displayed a very appealing presence. He was polite, intelligent, and, to her surprise, modest. He was a marine officer twice decorated for valor and certainly oriented towards women, according to the wagging tongues of other officers. But when they talked, he was oddly aloof. It was very annoying. Nevertheless, she liked him because he was intelligent and knew much about New France. So she would stare at him intently as he talked and explained, watching his excitement over sharing some obscure fact and wondered, *What is the key to unlock your interest in* me, *Henri Gerrard?*

Henri would only attend these soirées if he was *ordered* to go. So he did; two of them. Once ordered by Major Péan and once by order of the governor…*S'il vous plaît, Ensign, be certain you converse with my niece.* He certainly noticed the inviting smiles of the women when he did go, but their appearances always invited comparisons to Madeleine, and they always came up wanting. He would awkwardly try to talk with them, but he felt uncomfortable with shallow conversations. At the second soirée, he did as ordered and conversed with Kyrielle de Courserac, the governor's grandniece. She was definitely *not* vacuous and could converse about many of the books he'd read. And she was also very pleasing to look at, more than any other woman he'd seen in Louisbourg, or even Montréal. But she had this alluring way of staring at him silently…*It's as if she asks if I am hungry too.* Then it occurred to him her expression was exactly the same one Madeleine would exhibit before she smiled and touched him in some powerfully erotic manner.

Kyrielle touched his arm. Henri almost flinched.

"Do you find it noisy in here?"

"Yes…but I have guard responsibilities tonight," he lied. "I must depart this festivity early. But talking with you, Kyrielle," he said truthfully, "has been a most pleasant experience."

He dared not stay longer.

Before he was ordered to attend another event, he was wounded in the shoulder, which gave him a plausible excuse for not going. Then as he healed, he was often sent afield, doing survey work for the governor. Eventually, one day, after working hard on the outlying defensive battlements, another tedious task, he became very restless. It was not just the hard work.

Everyone work hard. He simply wanted to do something else. He convinced the governor to let him stage a spare canoe on the shore of Bras d'Or Lake, the salty inland sea. The journey there and back would take at least a week to do. To him it would be a holiday.

He left immediately.

He carried a two-man canoe over his head while also toting an eighty-pound backpack. Fit as he was, it was strength-sapping work. He made ten miles the first day, starting at sunrise and not stopping until just before full sunset. Sleeping beneath the glittering stars away from the foggy coastline stirred his imagination. He lay on his back and called aloud the names of all the stars in his favorite constellation. Orion, its shoulders and head, *Betelgeuse, Meissa, and Bellatrix*, then the belt, *Alnitak, Alnilam, and Mintaka*, then the legs, *Saiph and Rigel*. He'd learned them all from Captain LaTour. He whispered any others he could recall, *Aldebaran, Dubhe, Merak, Altair, Phad, Megrez, Alioth, Alcor, Mizar, Spica, Deneb, Arcturus*, and *Sirius*, the brightest. Finally *Polaris*, the pole star, and most important to men of the sea, like Captain LaTour. The reddish ones, *Betelgeuse* in Orion's shoulder, *Aldebaran* the eye of Taurus the bull, and *Antares* in Scorpio. And, of course, the wandering stars, Venus, Jupiter, Saturn, Mars, and Mercury. But he could only see Venus and Jupiter that night. They were the brightest of all. And arcing across the entire sky was a strip of stars so numerous they were like powder. He was yawning as he started calling out the constellation names and fell asleep before he got to six of them.

The next day, he crossed at the narrows of Mira Lake. This time, he used another canoe he'd hidden long before and tied off the one he carried to trail behind it. On the other side, he carried it again over his head. Late in the afternoon, he finally reached Bras d'Or Lake. He searched to the left and found the piquet house of Pauloosie and Yakone. He shouted joyfully as he approached the house. The old Inuit couple were as close to grandparents as he had ever experienced. Much of the food he carried with him was a gift for them. *Wait until they taste the sugar*, he thought.

He set down the canoe about thirty paces from the house, turned, and shouted again, when for no reason, it suddenly became hard to see. Everything turned blurry in any direction he looked. He shook his head and rubbed his eyes. He held a hand before his face and could barely make out his fingers. He certainly could not see the piquet house.

What's happening?

"Pauloosie! Yakone!"

No answer. He rubbed his eyes again, thinking them struck by dust from the wind.

No change.

Blindness in the wilderness meant death unless someone was around to help you.

Get to the cabin!

He used the musket as a guide, swinging it slowly back and forth in front of him as he stepped forward. He was facing the piquet house directly before the blindness occurred. He counted his steps as he walked. Suddenly, his musket barrel thumped against wood. It was the piquet house.

"Pauloosie! Yakone!"

No answer.

He felt his way to the door, opened it, and went inside. It was empty. He searched further with his hands and found a small stack of fur skins on the floor, to the right of the door, in the exact same place where he'd slept before. The walls were now bare where they once were covered with a variety of knives, bone tusks, antlers, tools, fishing nets, leather cords, and weapons. He dropped to his knees and touched the sealskin floor. In the opposite corner, he felt the clay and stone hearth. The ashes inside were cold and damp. It had not been used for a long time. There was a tall stack of dried wood next to it.

Henri sat down cross-legged. He rubbed his eyes again, attempting to clear the blurriness. But still found nothing in them that could account for his impaired vision. This could be something worse.

Rub them too much and you might injure them further.

Henri poured a little water from his water skin into each eye. No difference. He recalled his steps of that day. Did he bang his head with the canoe? Did some crawling thing bite him? Had he been stung? Did he get swamp water in his eyes? Did he get scratched by bramble bushes? Were his hands dirty? No, no, no, no, no, and he could not remember.

He recalled soldiers being struck deaf by cannon fire and the next day they were all right. He heard stories that others went blind from being struck in the head by something. Their vision returned in a few instances.

In a few instances.

Henri had journeyed very hard for two days. Maybe he just needed sleep. He was certainly tired. So he slipped off his pack and rested it against the corner. He set his musket, powder horn, pistol, and cutlass in another corner next to the furs. It wasn't too cold yet. He didn't need a fire. The sun had almost set. The blurriness changed into a soft, red opaqueness.

My vision is not totally gone, he reassured himself. *Just very blurry. Go to sleep.*

He spread out the furs to arrange them as a bed, with some rolled up to make a pillow. He pulled out his skinning knife and set it next to the fur rolls. The he lay on his back, clasped his hands together, and prayed. Just before he nodded off, he took hold of the small neck pouch containing Roland's white hairs.

With a lump in his throat, he whispered into the darkness.

"*I need your help, boy.*"

Sleep, he thought. *Blind or not, you need your sleep.*

It was very dark when Henri awakened. His stomach ached and he needed to urinate.

Maybe I ate something poisonous?

But he'd hardly eaten at all. He felt around and found his skinning knife and carefully slipped it back into its scabbard. Touching the wall, he stood, and felt his way outside the door, moving around the outside of the piquet house to a corner from which to urinate. The blackness was now opaque, blurry blackness.

"At least I can pee," he groused as the stream flowed strong and steamy in the cool night air.

He looked up at the sky and started naming the constellations again.

"I can see the stars!" he realized. "Aha! I can see the stars!"

But if he looked straight ahead, nothing, blackness. So he looked at the stars again and slowly dropped his vision towards the ground. At some point, the stars ended and the blurry blackness began. He looked around further and found the moon in a half-moon phase. It was clear too!

He would sleep again. If half his vision returned after sleeping, maybe the rest would by morning. He reentered the piquet and got comfortable under the furs.

Then he prayed.

The next morning brought disappointment. His vision was still blurry. He went outside. There was no difference until he looked at the rising sun. He could see the rising sun! As it climbed higher in the sky and brightened, he could not look at it directly, but he could see it! *Like in the fog. Just head towards the blur*, he reminded himself.

"All right," he told himself. "I'm getting better. Give it time. Eat something."

He went back into the piquet and carefully searched through his backpack with his hands, removing a loaf of hard bread, a block of cheese wrapped in cloth, and a small canteen of wine. Using his razor-sharp boning knife, he very carefully cut some pieces of cheese, guiding the edge with his thumb, and broke his fast with bread, cheese, and sips of wine.

"You survived on less than this, with things that tasted far worse, scraped from the underside of brook rocks!"

As he ate, he posed problems to solve. *What if the blindness does not go away?* He could make the bread and cheese he'd brought with him last for days if necessary. And blind is blind, day or night. So he should travel at night. As long as he could see the stars. *Especially Polaris.* All he had to do was travel east. Keep Polaris on his left. Then if he did not fall into a hole and break a leg, he would eventually reach the Mira narrows.

He finished eating and carefully repacked the food. He decided to wash his hands in Bras d'Or Lake rather than use his fresh water. Just in case his hands were foul with something.

"That was stupid! You should have done that *before* you ate something. You probably just munched down some animal droppings! That's probably why you're fucking blind!"

In the blurriness, Henri walked around the outside of the piquet house. He knew from being there before, the backside of the small cabin faced the lake directly. And it was pretty close. So he positioned himself in the center of the back side and started towards the lake, making holes in the ground with his boots with each step so that he could find his way back to the cabin by touch if it became necessary.

Within twelve paces, his boots splashed in water. He stooped and washed his hands in the salt water of the inland sea. He looked at his right hand and saw nothing beneath its nails. Then balanced himself on his left to inspect the other.

"I can see my hands!"

He stood up. Everything was blurry again. He stooped. Still blurry. He put a hand in the water. His vision cleared instantly. He could see everywhere he looked! But only if he had one hand in the water! So he kept one hand in the water and looked around.

This is not blindness, he realized. *This is caused by something else…*

As Henri looked around, he realized Pauloosie's round fishing boat was nowhere to be seen. They had left this place. That was why the cabin was empty. He was saddened by this, but right now, he needed to focus on surviving. Keeping one hand in the water, he crab-walked to his left and looked back towards the tree line nearby. He saw the canoe where he'd left it. He remembered crossing a shallow stream not too far beyond the tree line. So he could get fresh water there. Eventually, the stream would enter the lake, but he did not know how far away that was. He could not look directly at the sun, but he could use the sun as well to navigate going east.

This cause of the blindness was not natural…if blindness could be called natural. It was not due to a physical injury. It was caused by something *unnatural*. And if it was unnatural, it had to do with the *châsse* and the *wraith*.

Do I wait here and see if the blindness stops…or not?

Something else might happen. He decided to wait one more day, at least. He could now search his pack using his eyes if he brought it close enough to the salty lake water.

*

The Breeding Place

The day was more than half over when the dive occurred. The white eagle began screaming as soon as the *ghost* attempted to dominate her. She stopped flying and dropped directly towards the ground. By now the *ghost* had realized that this passionate animal would allow itself to smash into the ground and die if he did not withdraw his control.

But during the brief dominance, the *ghost* had a chance *to see* for only a few seconds. And then he withdrew. Again. As he'd done so many times before. He had taught her well. Without meaning to teach her anything.

The eagle leveled out and flew back over the lake to hunt again.

For over two moons, the *ghost* had been unable to control the female raptor. Her instinct to care for her chicks was even stronger than her instinct for life.

In the aerie, she had laid two eggs. She sat on them when she wasn't hunting. The eggs finally hatched. Two fuzzy chicks appeared. She then started going from the lake to the chicks, though never satisfying their voracious need for food. A moon earlier, the ghost noticed she was feeding one chick more often than the other. One of the chicks was molting into traditional dark brown feathers. The other one was distinctly white feathered. It was unnatural. Her instincts evidently intended to let the one with the white feathers die.

The *ghost* would not permit that. He could not completely control what was instinctive to the eagle, but he could make her feed both chicks by spurring her instinct to hunt even when she was tired. So he learned to control her by manipulating her natural instincts. The female white eagle felt compelled to hunt from sunrise to sunset because that is what the *ghost* compelled her to do. It was the only thing he could compel her to do.

While never intending to act as a father, the *ghost* ensured the white eaglet lived.

Two moons later, the two fledgling eagles hopped up and down in the aerie, flapping their wings. They had the appetites of fully grown eagles. The raptor was still hunting continuously, but now she was just dropping fish into the nest, allowing the two birds to learn to grasp with their talons and rip into the fish with their sharp beaks. They would both survive if they could feed themselves. And fly!

The *ghost* had surged to interrupt her flight when the white man was killed. For brief seconds, the *ghost* could see the form and face of the demon's servant who killed him. The *ghost* looked quickly at the others and saw no immediate danger.

But with the man's death, the power of the demon increased. It could cause pain in the others. There was nothing the *ghost* could do about this. Not until it could control the female again. And the female raptor was not going to be controlled. She was either going to feed her fledgling eagles until they learned to fly, or she would crash into the ground. This gave *her* control. The raptor's mind was primitive but the *ghost* almost sensed a vindictive satisfaction in the creature.

This will take time, it realized.

*

London

Colonel von Kleinfels was back in London and could walk with a cane. For the last three days, he felt renewed energy, enough to visit the dreams of Carter Trevathan and Alain Marcoux. He would have visited the others too, but he was not strong enough yet. Alain had accomplished the death of the archbishop. Now, his enemies had been physically weakened by this. If he could kill one more, half its power would return. The *vulnax* could now take small sips of life from nearby dreamers and more strongly control the attempts on the lives of the other members of the Great Houses.

He visited Carter Trevathan every night, urging another attempt on the Dutchman since the last one failed. The *vulnax* did not care how many people guarded him.

Use Ritter Monheit. Have the man pose as a courier and when the door opens, kill VanderMeer with a sword. The life of Monheit is meaningless. If Ritter survives, have him leave the city. And the Bristol sisters must poison the magistrate. He suspects you now. It will not be long before you are arrested.

He visited Alain Marcoux the same night and learned another primary descendant of the ancient Great Houses was in Montréal. But the *vulnax* knew this man was of the bloodline of *Adaelric*, the strongest of the great houses and the most dangerous. He must not allow Alain Marcoux to be slain. He had other plans for this servant and instructed him to find passage back to France as soon as possible.

The next morning, the colonel took passage to Antwerp to begin overland coach travel to Berlin to stand before Fredrick II as he'd been ordered. The Prussians were on the march and winning battle after battle. He speculated that Frederick II would want to induce France to stay in its winter quarters until next year and would not attempt an invasion of Hanover or begin open conflict with Prussia. It would be advantageous to both France and Prussia simply to withhold any offensive maneuvers against one another while they achieved their primary goals. France's attention was focused on the Americas, its island territories, and other places globally. Prussia saw Austria and Russia as its main adversaries. The treaty with France had only lapsed four months earlier! They should be secret allies not adversaries.

That would be the argument he would use. But Frederick might have other ideas.

*

Bras d'Or Lake

Henri's vision did not improve the next day. But he did experiment with moving east by using the morning sun as reference. He left his musket behind in the piquet and walked slowly towards the tree line. Once there, he felt the stand of trees until he found a young sapling he could cut down with his skinning knife. He stripped it of its branches, shortening the remaining length to match his own height. He now had a walking stick he could swing back and forth and poke the ground ahead for holes or water.

The morning sun was in the east in front of him. He must keep the blurry spot exactly ahead of him to make his walking line straight. He started counting his steps.

"One, two, three..."

At one hundred and eighty-two paces, his walking stick splashed in water. He knelt and crept forward. Cupping a hand, he lifted some water to his mouth. It tasted cold and sweet. He put his hand back in the water and looked around. Still blurry.

The water has to be salty...seawater, he decided.

He took the water skin he brought with him and drank a lot of it before submerging the skin into the stream. When it stopped bubbling against his fingers he plugged the end again.

Turning around, he started walking, counting down his paces from one hundred eighty-two, with the sun at his back.

"...three, two, one."

Swinging the stick back and forth, he kept going through the trees that interfered with his advance. When he reached a count of twenty-nine, he got clear of the trees. It was the rocky beach. Reaching the water, he stooped and dipped a hand. The blurriness vanished. The piquet cabin was at least a hundred paces off to his right. He started walking that way, stopping at various times to see how much further it was until he finally reached the cabin.

It was a good lesson in his crude navigation. Even using the sun and Polaris as guides, his path would veer, probably to the right, since he favored that leg, usually pushing off with his left.

By as much as thirty paces for every hundred and eighty paces forward, he thought.

Henri wasn't even sure that was right. It would likely be worse if he encountered an obstacle to get around. The thought of being lost as well as blind in a wilderness was not appealing. He decided to stay another day and see what happened.

Suddenly, inspired by a new idea, he felt his way inside the piquet, found his pack, dug to the bottom, and pulled out a small cooking pot. He made his way to the beach and filled the pot with salt water, then dipped his hand in the pot of water. Still blurry.

He put his hand in the lake water and his vision cleared.

It had been worth a try.

Nothing improved on the third day, but he still thought it better to wait. If his blindness had to do with the *châsse*, as he was now convinced, it would have affected Corrinne and Charles too. They would try to do something about it…if they could. He felt the temperature dropping. He would need a fire tonight. That was something else to consider if he tried to go overland. Building a fire in the open? Blind? Feeling around for dry wood? He could die from the cold.

Inside the piquet, he broke and cut kindling with his skinning knife into small pieces and placed them in a pile at the bottom of the small hearth. Then he felt around the wall for his powder horn hanging on a hook. He gave the pile of wood three pressed charges of powder. The flint and striker was in a side pocket of his pack. He positioned himself directly in front of the hearth opening, measured distances with his hands and fingers. He said a prayer and struck the flint stone with the striker in the direction of the hearth. He could see the blurred light from the sparks. But he was not prepared for the enormous flash just short of an explosion that occurred on the fourth strike accompanied by a loud *whooshing* sound.

Henri burned his hands a little and was coughing from all the powder smoke, but the fire was going. He did not try to cook anything and ate more bread, cheese, and a little wine. But that little hearth made the piquet very warm, as he remembered it had from the last time he was here. In fact, he felt around on the walls next to the door and even found the rock Pauloosie used to prop open the door. This set up the cooling draft so the inside temperature would not get too hot.

In the middle of the night, he got up to urinate again. It was really cold that night. The stars were out. The roiling green and yellow auroras were very strong too. He stared at them a while as they twisted and wound up against one another like curtains bunching in the sky. For a few moments, they twisted into a likeness of a wolf's face. Henri's hand went to the pouch immediately. Roland was saying hello to him.

"*I miss you, boy!*" he shouted. The likeness dissolved.

It was a wondrous night. Henri did not feel so alone anymore. And more importantly, he noticed the moon was more than halfway waxing toward fullness. Three more days, and it should be full. If he had to travel at night, he would rather do it when the moon was full. So he decided to wait the extra three days.

But in another three days, Henri didn't need the full moon. The blurry blindness vanished as mysteriously as it occurred when he opened his eyes on the fourth morning. Henri wasted no time. He secreted the canoe and paddles under some dead tree branches and brambles.

He gathered up his things inside the piquet cabin. He looked around and noticed for the first time, the large-eyed leather needle hanging from a red ribbon, high on a wall tied to a bone fish hook. Another ornament hung with it. A large sharp tooth the length of his thumb. He did not recognize the animal. Probably from a sea creature. It was pierced with a hole. And on it had been carved the face of a wolf. Gifts from Pauloosie and Yakone to him, saying good-bye, knowing he would someday come back to the piquet to visit again. They had indeed gone away, probably forever. He pressed the red ribbon and the tooth to his heart. He put them in a tied pocket on his pack.

Then Henri started east, trotting much of the way. He worried the blurriness might strike again.

But it did not.

*

Boston

Charles VanderMeer had made drawings of everything he intended
to create. He purchased new stone-cutting tools, saws, and precision steel
chisels. Four heavy work benches were arranged two to each side of the
room to support his efforts. He purchased bundles of two-by-two, cured
hardwood lumber in eight-foot lengths, plus wood saws, planes, drills,
dowels, and glue.

With temporary guards in attendance, he had the bricks and pieces of
his small jewelry forge brought in on a wagon, to be set up along with a
table and anvil in his artist studio.

The use of temporary guards that day made the issue of his protection
a topic again with Corrinne.

"You should make them permanent. They would not be eating any food
meant for you. They would be there to protect you should someone break
into your office, locked or not, and try to shoot you!"

Charles did not refuse outright as he did the last time. Her logic was
difficult to challenge.

"And I've asked Magistrate Tasker to recommend these men," she
added. "So they are sure to be trustworthy."

"All right, I bow to your judgment. But these men must be told our last
guard was *poisoned* while protecting me."

Jack Tasker, as deputy magistrate, was paid by the city, but his personal
deputies were not. The city paid them for each arrest, but only if the person
arrested was deemed guilty of a crime or misdemeanor by a sitting judge.
Tasker referred to them as Boston's "constable and night watch," though
no one else did. He even had a tailor make them a uniform of sorts; just
a blue coat over a red vest. But since these constables would have to buy
the clothes out of their own pockets, they were never purchased or worn.

Jack Tasker responded to Lady VanderMeer's request by assigning
two of his regular assistant deputies, one for the morning and one for the
afternoon. These men performed this guard duty on their off hours, when
they were not working and would get paid in hard coin, extra money, by
Lord VanderMeer. They were anxious to do it. They were told not to eat or

drink anything while on the premises. Charles brought in books from his library for them to read.

So, once again, there was a guard inside VanderMeer Trading Insurance Company's office. Jack Tasker suggested Lord VanderMeer purchase tailored uniform coats and vests for the guards.

"It will project a more stern impression on any curious visitors coming to the door for a quick peek inside the window."

Lord VanderMeer was happy to do this for the magistrate. In fact, he bought all twelve of Tasker's deputies such coats and vests. Tasker was elated, warning his men these new uniforms were to only be worn on formal occasions, except for the men who would act as Lord VanderMeer's guards. Tasker also insisted on adding a stout cross-bar for more strength on the inside of VanderMeer's office door.

Charles VanderMeer worked with a fervor in the studio at the back of his office. His days were long. Both tasks were artistic. He settled into them with enthusiasm. In the mornings, Charles carefully cut and chiseled the designs into the granite slabs the stone cutters had brought to his studio. There would be larger stone carvings surrounded by the two-by-two pieces of hardwood in rectangular and square picture-frame arrangements. There would be six pieces, four rectangles, and two squares, doweled together to completely enclose the existing *châsse* in something with more heft and strength, both physically and metaphysically.

In addition to the reliquary enclosure, he intended to make much larger rectangular pieces inlaid with granite, chiseled with the eight symbols he'd decided to use. These pieces were to line the tomb vault that Corrinne had designed to be built in Saybrook on the properties they'd purchased from Thomas Hancock. But he would create these after she gave him the dimensions of the vault, its widths and its depth.

In the afternoon, his work shifted to the jewelry forge.

Thomas Hancock had recently introduced Charles to an experienced Boston silversmith named Paul Revere. Lieutenant Revere had just returned from Lake George where he served with the Provincial army in an artillery regiment. After the abortive attempt to capture Crown Point from the French over the summer, Revere came back to Boston to reopen his silversmith business. At Hancock's recommendation, Charles invested money in Revere's business. It would prove to be a shrewd investment. Revere helped him set up a jeweler's forge, bellows, and flue. He also advised Charles on the purchase of the proper gold and silversmith tools. Charles had many of his own tools, but the tools Revere recommended were newer and far superior in quality. Revere was also an artist, just like Charles. They became good friends.

In the afternoon hours, Charles worked on making five more amulets, this time engraved with eight sealing symbols. He used the original four of the cross, the moon, the ax, and the lion. Plus four more: the sun, the moon, the stars, and a symbol for the seas. The silver amulets would be made first and later set with a center jewel. He wanted to use amethysts, but could not find any in the city of Boston to buy. So he settled on emeralds since he had those gems in his personal collection. The other amulet he made also had that gemstone. It worked too. When the first amulet was finished, still without the jewel setting or the symbol engravings, he took it back to the house to show Corrinne. He wanted her opinion and critique of the eight symbols. He brought his sketches.

Entering the house, he could smell Dian's cooking. His mouth watered immediately.

Charles heard a voice from the *cuisine* and opened the kitchen door.

"Your lordship!"

"Mr. Cheever! Your presence is always welcome in our home. You are staying for dinner?"

"I am indeed, sir. Lady VanderMeer invited me." He glanced at Dian with a smile. "But after seeing and smelling what Miss Dian has created, it would be hard for me to leave anyway."

"Well, then I will leave you both and go up and see Lady VanderMeer and the twins."

Upstairs, Corrinne was breastfeeding the twins. She had heard him come through the front door and thanked God silently, as she did every day when Charles came home safely.

"Is your pain still gone?" Corrine asked as soon as she saw him.

Charles nodded. "And yours?"

"Yes. It vanished as quickly as it appeared. And we are left to wonder why."

Charles cooed over Calypso lying in her bed. He tickled her belly gently with a finger.

"Hey, little Callie. Look at that smile!"

Corrinne stood and carefully placed Marcus beside his sister. "Good night, my precious angels." She pulled a thick quilt over them.

She turned down the wicks on all the wall lamps as low as they could go. Checked on them both again. Calypso was still smiling. Marcus had turned close to his sister with an arm over her chest.

"There you go. A little milk and Marcus is out." She caressed the hair on Calypso's head. "Good night, my love."

They backed quietly out of the room.

"How is Molly?"

"She has reached the point of claiming she will never have any more children after this one. And will refuse to share a bed with Captain Martyn. She spends most of the day running to and from the privy. Dr. Angove has said any time now. She sleeps in Mathilde's room."

"You invited Sentry Cheever?"

They were walking down the stairs. "I invited him for dinner and discussions. All the plans for the vault are finished and in the library. I want to construct this before it gets too cold. I need a foreman to watch over the job. I am hoping Sentry can do that for us."

Corrinne went to check on Molly. Charles went into the library, sat in his chair, and pulled the bell cord.

Dian looked in. "Your lordship?"

"Three glasses of brandy, please. And let me steal Mr. Cheever from you. How soon will we eat?"

"Now that you are home, half an hour after Lady Corrinne signals."

"Smells good!"

Sentry soon appeared, carrying a tray with the three glasses.

"Ah, good. Have a seat." Charles poured brandy in all three. He waited for Corrinne and closed the sliding doors to the dining room.

Once Corrinne was settled in the library with them, they toasted one another and took a sip.

Corrinne began. "So here are three rolls of plans. One for each of us. They are all the same. The stone masons will come from New Haven. The depth of the vault is fifteen feet but stoned only to a height of twelve feet. The width is six feet. That provides plenty of room for the enclosed reliquary. There will be three feet of earth covering the top stone. The masons in New

Haven are cutting the stones already. In fact, today they are supposed to be finished. They estimate they can complete their work at the location in ten days. They will bring everything they need. They expect to stay at Winter House. Food and cooks from New Haven will come with them. Once they are gone, we can transport the new sealing sections Charles creates."

The questions began from both men. They would stop to have dinner with Molly, with Dian and Anamosa in attendance. Then they retired back into the library.

"I will cut and finish the granite pieces. They will be enclosed in hard-wood frames. Six of them to enclose the *châsse* on all sides. Now that I have the dimensions of the vault, I will create the larger rectangular sealing sections, one for the bottom, the sides, and the top. I've also added another symbol."

He handed Corrinne the sketches.

"It represents the seas."

"Why?"

"Eight is a more balanced design. The symbol is for water, or the seas, more specifically. To go with the sun, moon, and stars."

Corrinne had been thinking about the words to use in any ritual. Another symbol would only add to the unknowns. Who would do what and using what words? Did they need a priest? All such questions she thought it better to decide in privacy with Charles. She changed the topic.

"There are some other vault designs to do with drainage, expansion, and contraction from the cold. The masons will use rules associated with mortuaries. Essentially, that is what they think they are building. The masons will not be present when we lower the *châsse* into the vault. As far as they are concerned, its intended use is to inter a body."

Overseeing this work did not bother Sentry. But the purpose of this *tomb* made him very nervous.

"So when it is all done, what will prevent robbers from plundering the vault?"

Corrinne shook her head slowly. "Nothing. Only its secrecy, as before. The capstone is extremely heavy. Special rigging is required to lift it. But buried under three feet of earth…after nature reclaims the land with grass, weeds, and other flora, I believe the exact location will be difficult to discern even if someone knows where to search. The isolation of these properties at Winter House creates an advantage."

"So I am to oversee the outside vault construction. And the rest of the inserts will come later?"

Charles answered. "I will bring them as soon as we hear the vault is finished."

"And this...*châsse*?"

"The *châsse* too," Corrinne replied. "But that is our responsibility, Sentry."

*

Two days later, Sentry left on horseback for Old Saybrook. Once there, he stayed at the carriage house hotel on the main road to await the masons. A missive and satchel was couriered to New Haven by relay riders. It was addressed to C. Bernard Conway, Esquire. Corrinne had sent the lawyer a small purse of hard coin with instructions to make payments to the stonecutters. The masons were told where to find Mr. Sentry Cheever in Saybrook.

When Charles came home from the studio that day, he found Corrinne sitting in the backyard near the gravestone, marking the grave she'd made for the white eagle. The stone had been carved with an eagle's image. Charles told Dian to make them both a mug of coffee. He carried a chair and a small wood table from the porch to set between them.

Corrinne had a lap quilt over her knees and a heavy shawl around her shoulders. Her cheeks had a slight rosy glow to them.

"You look cold. Why are you sitting out here?"

"Thinking about things."

Corrinne had never been certain why the white eagle was dropped into the yard. She assumed there was a message for them to discern from that startling event. But she'd not figured one out...not yet. She was also not certain she'd even buried the creature correctly. An Indian she'd asked told her to leave it out in the woods. That was how the eagle died, he had said. She did not like that answer. *Then it should have been dropped in the woods*, she thought. *But it wasn't.*

"Do you want to be alone?"

"No. Stay. Sit with me."

Charles tried to cheer her up. "Are you inspired yet?" He pointed at the grave marker.

"What? From the eagle? No. But it was dropped here for a reason, yes? We've talked about this before. I've also been thinking about the ritual. I'm presuming we would perform the same ceremony we used in Montréal. You and I will say all the words...like before. I assume we will do that again. Only now I presume we need to add the new sealing symbol names. How do we do that? How do we do any of this?" Frustration showed on her face. "Are we doing the right thing?"

Dian came out carrying the coffee mugs. They waited until coffee was poured and they were alone again.

Charles spoke firmly. "Yes, Corrinne. I am *convinced* we are doing the right thing. This is the right thing to do. This is the only thing to do. This is what other civilized people did long ago. And I am convinced they used the right symbols the first time. The sun, moon, and stars. This *thing* only got free because the seals on that tomb were broken. We must bury the *châsse* somewhere secret and secure again. But without tying the seals to us. That is what endangers our lives. Instead, we in the ritual, we will claim the tomb stays sealed until the sun, moon, and stars fall from the sky. And we will add...'and until all the seas boil into vapor.' And we finish burying it and walk away. We cannot keep carrying this *thing* around with us. It draws assassins to us."

Corrinne knew Charles was right. They had talked about this many times.

"I know. I agree. You are right. But I keep thinking we are missing something...something connected to the eagle. The reason why it was dropped right in front of us."

Charles sipped coffee and thought about that too for a few minutes. He had nothing.

"It will come to us," he assured. "Oh, I brought something for you to see." He took a finished amulet from his pocket and handed it to her. It was round, made of silver, and six inches in diameter. It had all eight signs and was set with a large emerald at the center.

Corrinne looked on it with awe. "*Mon Dieu,* Charles, this is beautiful! The engravings are so elegant, so much easier to recognize."

"Well, I had all the right tools this time. And I was not using Fort Niagara's crude forge. I left thicker silver around the top. There is a small hoop on the back to support hanging it from a chain. I can create those later."

"How many?"

"Five more. One for you. Two for the twins. One for Anamosa, perhaps. And one extra."

"And the stone engravings?"

"The stones are all engraved. I am just cutting the wooden frames for them. The measurements will match your design. I trust the masons will not vary from that."

"The masons are artists too. They are practiced at making precise cuts in stone. But I told Sentry he was to measure the final distances in width and depth just to be sure."

"I am only working on the sealing stones and frames, so they will be finished first. The amulets will take an additional two weeks. And I don't think I've told you this before, but these amulets must be joined with the one Anamosa wears and anointed in blood."

"Blood! Whose blood?"

Charles looked grave. "When I made my first amulet, Chittaqua and I cut the palms of our hands and allowed our blood to mingle and drip over the amulets together. He chanted some sort of prayer. I assume that will have to be done again."

"But Chittaqua is dead!"

"I know." Charles was perplexed about that too. "I need to think more about that part. But I am certain this must be done."

CHAPTER 24
MONTRÉAL
SEPTEMBER 1756
"And he walks among us still!"

Philippe was desolate with grief for days afterwards at the thought of never again hearing this wise man's compassionate voice. He spent time walking through the forests north of the city. *Hunting*, he told his scouts. Except he came back empty-handed. Archbishop Nicolet had been like a father to him, he realized too late. And the last words they said to one another? Gone. Lost in a memory burned away by this tragedy. For Corrinne as well as himself, the archbishop had always been there. So common was the presumption of the archbishop's endurance, he had doubted the man's mortality. But he felt his absence now.

The prelate's death had staggered his confidence. The bishop had been murdered, sitting in his library. His blood splattered on his beloved books. Assassinated with Father Tinian and another priest. It had taken only seconds. This purveyor of death thrust once and left. Why would someone do this? For what purpose? To what end?

An act of power, or politics, or high jealousy.

That's what philosophers had written. But when Philippe looked in a mirror and asked those same questions, he had different answers. Because they came from a darker side of his life, one he preferred to deny rather than talk about…except he had discussed it with Archbishop Nicolet. For Philippe, it was the only explanation when other explanations failed.

The wraith. *The* châsse. *Evil.*

Nothing there to chisel on the philosopher's stone.

The Récollets bishop described the murderer accurately. He was an evil, possessed man. *And he walks among us still.* Except suspects alleged with such unnatural attributes seemed farfetched and implausible. They would never be considered viable by anyone in authority in Montréal. As far as they were concerned, this terrible act was perpetrated by a swordsman who was sent specifically by someone in power to assassinate the archbishop. Any person suggesting otherwise would only draw suspicion upon themselves.

The people of Montréal and Quebec City demanded the killer be found and punished. Governor Vaudreuil wanted a name. Intendant Bigôt wanted a name. God help anyone officially accused. But ten days of questioning had elapsed and still the killer's identity was unknown.

Before Philippe left for Fort Carillon, he wanted to speak with Father Eric Nicolet. After the Requiem Mass, he visited Notre-Dame-de-Bon-Secours Chapel the next morning and knelt to pray. But he was really waiting for a Jesuit priest, any Jesuit priest in their distinctive black robes, visiting the chapel for some reason. Many of them were in Montréal for the archbishop's funeral. He spotted one who looked familiar and approached the man. He introduced himself and told the priest he would like to speak with Father Eric Nicolet.

"Father Nicolet asked to talk with me once. I do not want to disturb his grieving, but I am leaving for Fort Carillon soon. Will you tell him that for me? If he still wants to talk, he can reach me through army headquarters."

That afternoon, the same Jesuit priest brought a written request for Captain Gerrard to come to the Terrain des Jésuites to see Father Eric Nicolet.

"I am to be your escort, Captain. The gendarmes are standing guard."

Philippe decided to leave all his weapons behind at headquarters with a sergeant in the scout company. As he approached the front entrance of the Terrain de Jésuites, the gendarmerie guards read the invitation. He was scrutinized for weapons. After waiting a few minutes in the atrium, an unexpected but familiar person greeted him sadly.

"Monsignor Cortois?"

They shared a very long history. Philippe had known Father René Cortois at Saint Ouen's Church in Rouen, France, since he was a boy. The priest had been Philippe's mentor and Henri's as well. Father Cortois had come to New France to become a Jesuit missionary. He departed an Abnaki village mission a week earlier after hearing of the archbishop's death. The life of a missionary had aged the priest dramatically. His hair was totally white.

"It is good to see you again, Father, though the occasion be tragic."

They embraced briefly.

"I have been assigned to act as secretary for the Jesuit Intendant's office until a new intendant is sent to us from France."

"I am here at Father Nicolet's invitation."

"Of course." The monsignor signaled the gendarmes.

Philippe thanked the other priest and followed Father Cortois to the archbishop's office. There were three other Jesuits inside examining books and rolls of papers in the smaller library in and around Father Tinian's desk. Inside the archbishop's office, Father Eric Nicolet was sitting at André's desk, reading through a stack of folios and other papers, things considered the personal property of Archbishop Nicolet. He'd been assigned by Monsignor Cortois to separate the personal papers from those belonging to the Society of Jesus for sequestering. He rose immediately at seeing the marine officer standing in the doorway. Philippe noticed the blood-stained wood on the floor in two places that could not be scrubbed away. He felt a stab of pain in his gut.

"I am so glad you came to see me, Captain." Father Eric Nicolet said, looking relieved. "You were one of my father's closest friends. I have so many questions that I pray you may be able to answer."

Father? Philippe had not known that. Eric had been introduced as the archbishop's younger brother.

"I will help you any way I can. But I leave in two days for Fort Carillon."

"Even an hour may help. Sit. Sit. I don't know where to begin. Well, this one." He held up a written missive. "My father wrote a letter to the Naval Minister on the day he died. What he says sounds very…uncharacteristic for a Jesuit bishop. I do not know what to do with it. It sounds important."

"Seal it with wax, get it to me by tomorrow morning, and I will find a way to place it in a dispatch pouch to the Naval Minister."

"Thank you. And there are dozens of other documents, writings, and things…" His voice dropped to a whisper. "…of an *occult* nature? His personal journal mentions you, Lady Corrinne de Chanaye, a man called Pierre Dunemoore, your son, Henri, a Dutch artist named Charles VanderMeer, strange Indian names, and many other events I find so astounding I am perplexed. I worry about my father's sanity and very much his reputation. I want to burn all of it."

"No, Father. Please do not do that. I can explain all of this. But the story is long and will take hours." Philippe glanced over his shoulder at the other Jesuits reviewing books and documents in Father Tinian's outer office. He spoke very quietly. "You should isolate all these things and safeguard it to yourself. We should meet more privately. My time is short. I also came here to speak with you on a personal matter, for which the archbishop was providing me assistance."

Father Nicolet nodded. He spoke loudly to the other priests. "Monsignor Cortois, please stay with me, and if you please, my brothers, excuse us for a few minutes."

"Monsignor, you should hear this too," Philippe said when the door was closed.

He explained about the English children who were being kept in hiding and the letters that may come addressed to him from the person who cared for them.

"Read the letters for me. I trust your judgment on any actions to take. The Intendant Bigôt and the governor must never learn where they are. I fear they will do them harm. That is another story I can share with you both at another time."

"Do not be concerned. I will give them aid as my father would, even as I am overwhelmed by all of this." He gestured around the room.

Philippe looked at the floor-to-ceiling book shelves. "Your father loved this library. Maybe he left a will?"

Monsignor Cortois nodded. "We are searching for one. But there is so much to search through. This will take us many days. You are leaving?"

"Yes. The day after tomorrow for Fort Carillon."

"I cannot get away from the compound," Father Eric said. "There is too much to do."

"And it may not do you well, Philippe, to be reported spending so much time talking with us," Monsignor Cortois warned. "It might invite more questions…"

"You're right. Let us just say I wanted to personally offer my sympathy to Father Eric. That is the truth anyway. Father Eric, know that I would trust Monsignor Cortois with my life. He protected my son back in France. You can trust him to give you good counsel."

"I already do."

"One more thing. There is a man named Paulus Legate. He is the head clerk at the Dunemoore Company warehouse…or former warehouse. It is outside the west river gate. He is someone you can trust. He safeguards my money. He will assist you with anything regarding the English children within his capability. I will tell him of this conversation. Paulus will also get a message to Pierre Dunemoore at Fort Niagara. He is another man you can trust."

"And Henri?" Monsignor Cortois asked.

"Henri is an ensign in the marines. He was sent to Louisbourg. Many think he is dead. It is better not to disturb that fiction. Governor Vaudreuil invented it. I should go."

"I wish you had more time here," Father Nicolet said when Philippe stood up.

"As do I. Safeguard your father's cross." He pointed at the familiar cross and jewel. "It protects you more than you know. And if either of you are brave enough and don't mind the cold," he said, "come visit me at Fort Carillon and we will talk more. I will certainly come to see you again when I get back."

*

As ordered, two days later, Captain Gerrard left Montréal with his scout company bound for Fort Carillon. He would now report to the fort commander, General François de Lévis, the Marquis de Montcalm's second-in-command.

Philippe soon learned about an American who prowled the forested wilderness surrounding Lake George and Lake Champlain. This man preyed on the French, be they soldiers or not. He rarely showed mercy. He was an exceptional wilderness fighter, or *ranger*, as the colonialists called them. His skills in forest lore, tracking, and ambush were equal to the *coureurs de bois*, and the English would boast even better.

The distance from Fort William-Henry to Fort Carillon was forty to forty-five miles, depending on the wilderness trails followed lying north and south on either side of Lake George. For these wilderness men, not many journeys on such trails were needed to memorize the tortuous steps, a distinctive tree, deep ravines, rugged hilltop climbs, the scalable rock face, warm caves, aeries large enough to sleep in, shallow streams, deep rivers, quicksand swamps, and the best places for ambush. Philippe would travel these distances a dozen times by foot or canoe in any type of weather.

The American and French skirmishers always returned with scalps and prisoners...but never any from the rangers and *coureurs de bois* who followed their respective captains.

They would come to respect one another deeply, even while being brutal enemies.

*

Montréal

Intendant François Bigôt was kept waiting to see Governor Vaudreuil in the company of Captain Trieste. He knew the delay was intentional. The simple act to establish who waited for who in New France suggested who was more important. But Bigôt would not let the governor realize how this recurring snub affected him.

Today's meeting had only one topic. He was not interested in relieving the governor of the responsibility of identifying who assassinated the Jesuit Intendant. François Bigôt looked after official administrative and financial matters concerning all trade, military provisions, food, and management of the cities and outlying posts of New France. These were his responsibilities, and he could stretch them by definition into encompassing just about anything, except for those things he wanted no part of, like the war...or solving unpopular assassinations.

True, the gendarmerie reported to him exclusively, unless the city was under siege, at which time their command reverted to the army. Until then, this meant policing and throwing people into the bastille for questioning and judgment. If one could point out a murderer, the gendarmes were excellent at arrest and incarceration. They could also bayonet bodies when ordered, club people over the head with the butt of a musket, put down the occasional mob, manage drunken voyageurs, and collect taxes from the merchant businesses—their primary function.

But they were not skilled at solving unsolvable murders.

Nevertheless, Intendant Bigôt had been threatening and extorting the citizens of Montréal for any information that might lead to Archbishop Nicolet's murderer. He wanted to know this killer's identity as much, if not more, than anyone else.

This murder meant certain people were making their power felt in New France. This act of villainy was so outrageous it should be apparent to him who they were. But it was *not* apparent. An unacceptable situation. *All right,* maybe he could find a cabal of conspirators, like the Grand Company, as one citizen had suggested and later came to regret. To Bigôt's surprise, the questioning he demanded led nowhere...even when bones were broken and castration threatened. Most people would say anything faced with heavy torture. But they had nothing to say beyond their own invention. And he wanted at least some thread of truth to pull.

Nothing. And if Bigôt had nothing, the governor's nothing was much worse.

Intendant Bigôt gazed out a window. *Let's get on with this. You are wasting my time.* He tapped a foot with impatience. *Actually,* he mused, *an organization like the Grand Company would be a perfect scapegoat.*

Except Bigôt ran that company. And almost every person of importance in New France and a few hundred nobles in the Court of Versailles were shareholders in the profits earned from the inflated prices of everything the company sold...which was *everything* the citizens, the government, or the army of New France wanted to buy. Silver and gold came in chests from the treasury of France to Quebec City, which Intendant Bigôt hand counted himself. A significant portion of the hard coin was sent back, often on the same ship, to be disbursed to his allies in Versailles.

If only the Dunemoore Company had not been dissolved, he brooded. *I could have swooped up Lady de Chanaye, Pierre Dunemoore, and Philippe Gerrard in a single afternoon. Blamed them for the murder of the archbishop and hanged them the next day without trial to the howls, anger, and approval of the citizens of New France.*

A pleasant thought. But even if Bigôt could fashion a scheme to blame someone convenient, it would not solve the problem. He did not know the assassin's identity. And the Récollets bishop's requiem words hung in the air.

And he walks among us still!

It was not a pleasant thought. Caught up in his musings, he realized he was being addressed and spun around. It was Captain Trieste, who repeated himself.

"Excellency, I said Governor Vaudreuil is ready to see you."

Intendant Bigôt followed the captain into the governor's office. Governor Vaudreuil used the very same office and chair of Governor Duquesne. *So this could be worse,* he decided. *At least Vaudreuil is a shareholder. He has a vested interest in not discrediting me.*

François Bigôt bowed formally. "Governor."

Vaudreuil dismissed Captain Trieste with a hand wave.

"Sit." Vaudreuil waited until the Intendant of New France took a chair. The intendant's lips were pursed, his moustache wiggling above them, exhibiting that annoying smug expression he usually proffered.

"We are alone. So give me a name. Or a list of names to choose from."

"Governor?"

"Do not feign ignorance with me! We both know what this is about! Who murdered Archbishop Nicolet? Don't claim you know nothing about this. Men reporting to me and you were tripping over one another the day of the assassination. So set aside all your conceits for once. What names, what suspects, what do you conjure at night about the assassin's identity?"

"Like *you,* I have not been able to identify anyone. And my efforts were tenfold more than yours. I could invent someone to blame, *but,* to quote the Récollets bishop…*he walks among us still!* Except by now, I think the assassin is long departed from the walls of Montréal."

"Then let's start there. Do you have a list of those who departed since the day of the murder?"

"You are jesting? You mean not counting the army, several hundred merchants, and traders…"

"Let's start with those who left by coach or passengers on one of the ships at anchor."

"We've already searched the ships and talked with any of the passengers. There were no viable suspects."

"Coach?"

"The list is small. Most of them are couriers to and from Quebec or officers in the army."

"Eliminate them. Who is left?"

"If I also eliminate the three female mistresses, it leaves two men. And both of these men came to see *you.* Captain Beauregard LaTour, master of the *Falcon Queen,* formerly at anchor in Quebec City. And Monsieur Alain Marcoux, whom I believe spent five days in discussions with you,

Captain Montreuil, and other officers on confidential topics. Which remain confidential, unless one offers large bribes to greedy people and one pieces together what was discussed."

"And that would be?"

"From a rumor...a German mercenary regiment for New France. So I assumed his business with you was legitimate."

"And by this time do you think they have sailed from New France?"

"Captain LaTour certainly has sailed. He had orders to go to Louisbourg next. Monsieur Marcoux went back to Quebec to find the first ship making a crossing. So he may be gone by now too."

"Anyone else?"

"As I said, I found no one to suspect. Much less someone to blame. I detested the archbishop, but he was greatly admired by just about everyone else."

"So it *was* you?"

François Bigôt did not respond or react. He just stared and smirked. *Really?*

"Then Captain LaTour?"

"I have known the captain for ten years. He is a very competent smuggler and was recently promoted to captain in the French navy by Admiral de la Motte for some insane reason. To make use of those smuggling skills no doubt. But other than that, the man is a buffoon. I don't think he has ever held a sword, let alone used one."

"Monsieur Marcoux?"

"I did not interview him. You know more about this man than I do. Something to keep in mind."

Governor Vaudreuil recoiled. "What do you mean by that?"

"Nothing personal, Governor. Except if the Society of Jesus sends over their own inquisitor, a very likely possibility I should add, and the murderer has not been identified, this inquisitor will either select someone convenient, or worse, claim a conspiracy against the church. *Conspiracy*...they love claiming that. That is their usual excuse. Who among us would have cause to conspire against the church, if not the government? The English? The Indians? I thought of that, but no scalps were taken. I submit New France does not need snide inquisitors of the church asking us questions. Who knows what they might discover by *accident*?"

"Then we are back where we started. If the Jesuits can pick a murderer, so can we. And *you* are in this with *me*."

"*Touché*. I am your loyal servant."

"So let's claim it was Captain LaTour."

"I have already tried to blame this on him. It cannot be done."

"Then Alain Marcoux?"

"Potentially. He came to be in Montréal on Captain LaTour's ship. LaTour brought the dispatch pouch to you from France and had it delivered to Captain Trieste by Alain Marcoux."

"All right. Then a conspiracy. You think about this overnight, create a deceit, and come to see me with it tomorrow. We will blame them both. That will be our pronouncement."

"LaTour and Marcoux? For what reason?"

"I don't care. No reason is needed. Just say we know it was them. The accused fled the city after committing this outrageous crime *before* we could question them. It's perfect. Let the Society of Jesus question them back in France. They will confess to whatever the church wants them to say. We will have moved the problem over there and the city will have the names of the assassins to vilify. Let the citizenry speculate as to their guilt and invent the reasons why they did it! Maybe we choose the one we think has the best motive. It will be a competition. Then we tell the church to use this confession. Make sure the pronouncement says the accused have fled from New France, as all accused men do when they are guilty and are going to be arrested. *Voilà*!"

François Bigôt stared.

"What is wrong?"

"Governor, do you believe they did it? Because I do not."

Governor Vaudreuil slapped his hand on the desk. "What difference does that make? The government of New France accuses these two men. If someone has a better man to accuse, say there is a bounty if they come forward and tell us who it is. If he is truthful, he will be rewarded. If he lies, we will hang him. We are at war!"

François Bigôt nodded in agreement. He decided not to say it again.

And he walks among us still!

*

Cape Dauphin
Île Royale

Captain LaTour had completed the fastest transit he'd ever made of the Saint Lawrence River after leaving Quebec City. The "vision" he experienced on the way to Montréal, if that's what it was, still hung heavy in his memory. The stench, the yellow eyes—he could not explain it. He told himself it was a bad dream. But it was the same evil presence he saw personified within Wittmann Bootz. Then out of nowhere, the archbishop was assassinated. Something very evil moved upon this land. The more he thought about it, the more it filled him with dread. He wanted to get away from Montréal. The coach ride from Montréal to Quebec could not go fast enough. And it turned out to be the *same* coach! He did not sleep.

In Quebec City, protocol required he go to the government house and collect any other dispatch pouches that were ready. But he went from the coach directly to a harbor launch for hire and was rowed out to the ship.

Victorio could see the captain was agitated and distressed.

"Captain, thank God you have returned. All of Quebec is burning with the announcement Archbishop Nicolet has been assassinated! What happened?"

"Raise anchor! Prepare to make sail!"

Beauregard LaTour poured over his maps atop the slanted table in his cabin. He had charts lying everywhere. Fully sailed, and moving at sixteen knots by his reckoning, the *Falcon Queen* was now passing east-south-east halfway between the North Cape of Île Royale and Saint Paul Island. Both land areas were deserted most of the time, both miserable places of storms, with drizzly rain and cold. He knew them well. They were smuggling havens full of isolated bays for cross-deck trading of the most illegal kind. Mostly weapons, opiates, slaves, a few pirates looking to sell their wares, or capture the transiting vessel if it did not carry a buyer. He laid out his new courses to hug the coastlines of Île Royale until they passed Scaterie Island, the eastern-most point of Île Royale, and then turn west-southwest to race towards Louisbourg. After that, it all depended on the number and location of any English or American blockade ships to avoid.

He opened his cabin door and shouted for Victorio up the bridge-house ladder. The second mate slid down the ladder, holding onto the rails.

"Here are the courses and the expected times of turn. I am going to try and get a few hours of sleep. Come get me if there are any problems you cannot handle."

"Yes, Captain," Victorio replied in a concerned voice. "Captain…what happened?"

LaTour shook his head. He did not want to talk. "I will tell you later. I need sleep badly."

*

Alain Marcoux fell asleep from exhaustion in his cabin on the French ship *Concorde* sailing back from Quebec City to Brest, France. He was anxious to return to France after four days of discussion with Governor Vaudreuil and his officers. The death of Archbishop Nicolet had destroyed the civil unity of Montréal. Already inflamed by the growing famine, the people were close to rioting and the governor was preoccupied over what to do about it. Marcoux thought the governor might blame him for the assassination. They would have, except Marcoux made certain he was with them all the time. Or so they believed.

Everything had occurred exactly as the night messenger predicted it would.

Fortunately, since the assassination, the night messenger disturbed his sleep only once. He hoped he would not be visited again. He found it hard enough to sleep as it was. But he was successful at convincing Governor Vaudreuil of the need and use of the mercenaries. The colonel would be pleased with that information. Then Alain could rest, drink, and whore, while he did more recruiting over the winter, probably in Baden or Württemburg. The mercenaries in those two southern German states hated Frederick II but loved money.

At least that was Alain Marcoux's plan.

*

Louisbourg

When Henri Gerrard returned to Louisbourg, he reported to the governor and marked on the map the pre-positioned spot of the canoe on Bras d'Or Lake. He learned a fast schooner would be leaving in another day to carry dispatches and citizen mail to Quebec City and Montréal. Henri went straight to the small bunk room in the Grand Bastion he shared with Major Péan and two other officers. He lit the lanterns, sat down at the single table, and started penning letters to Madeleine, his mother, Archbishop Nicolet, and, after some indecision, to Carmen, because he'd promised her to try to stay in touch. That letter he would write last. It would be the hardest. He had finished three of the letters when Major Péan entered. The major was wet with fog from his morning inspection of the guard posts.

"Letters?"

"Yes, there's a dispatch schooner leaving tomorrow."

Major Péan did not want to talk about letters; he never got any. Instead, he would enjoy a few minutes of his favorite pastime, embarrassing Ensign Gerrard. Péan sat on his bunk and rested his head on the wall not two feet from Henri, who sat at a table right next to him.

"So tell me, Henri," he asked, "as a learned student of the sciences, after all your time at Louisbourg, which do you love the most? Your left hand or your right hand?"

"Major, if you please, I need to finish these letters."

The major lifted his head and tried to read what Henri was writing so furiously. Henri frowned and lifted the edge of the page to block his view.

The major resumed his position against the wall and started gesturing with his hands as he talked.

"Personally, I've learned it takes twice as much spit for my left to accomplish its mission, so it follows I favor my right. But my penis does have a formidable length and girth." He started to fumble at the front of his pants. "Maybe I should measure it for you. You want to see it? In fact, let's measure them together."

"*Noo!*"

Péan smiled broadly at Henri's frustration. "Of course, my right hand is my sword hand. And I do need to keep it exercised and strengthened. So if you don't mind, I will just lie here in my bed, watch you write, and exercise it for a while. I will try to be quiet."

Henri set down his quill. "Why do you do this to me?"

"Do what?"

"Taunt me so!"

Péan laughed in a friendly way. "Because I like you, Henri! It takes no effort to embarrass you, even more so when talking of women. Which in Louisbourg is a scarcity, if you haven't noticed. This place is boring. I don't know why the English want it! It only has about three whores. And even their sores have sores. Oh, Christ! Don't look at me like that. Go ahead and write. I will leave you alone. Oh, except the governor asked me to encourage you to go tonight."

"Tonight?"

"Yes, tonight. Madame de Drucour has graciously arranged another revelry for us. Not that they do any good. I will wager young Kyrielle wishes to converse again with the perpetually dull Ensign Gerrard. What is your problem with her?"

"I do not have a problem with her. I try not to talk to her."

Péan sat up. "What? Why not? I am not an expert, but to use a military term, that maiden wants you to *invest* her maidenhead. Do you not see this?"

Henri winced. "Please..."

"Henri, she is dripping when she is close to you. Everyone sees this!"

"*Mon Dieu*! Please stop!"

Péan was laughing so hard he wiped at tears in his eyes.

"All right, all right. I will. But it would help the rest of your fellow officers if you could find a way to convince Mademoiselle Kyrielle that you are not interested in her affections. Give the rest of us a chance. Just give me a signal tonight when you intend to do this, and I will position myself right next to you."

"You are jesting?"

"No, no. I am serious, Henri. That girl is *not* a virgin. I can tell by the way she looks at you. Though she might as well be looking at the sea wall. So, really. I will be right there, close by. Just refuse her in the most gallant way...leaving her overflowing with unrequited desire."

"I never know what to say to her. And I am not good at lying."

"Say something partly true. It makes the best lies. Tell her she is beautiful and that...that you have lice!"

"I do not have lice!"

"Everyone has lice! That is just an example. Make something up."

"All right. But only if you leave me alone and let me finish these letters."

"As you wish." Major Péan stood with alacrity. "But I have your word?"

"*Oui*."

"You gave me your word, Ensign. I am leaving right now. But this soirée starts at sunset. That's about four hours from now. I am going to bathe. You should too. You smell like rotted fish."

Henri continued to write. *Dear Carmen...*

*

Cape Breton Coastline

Captain Conor Martyn of the *Anamosa* changed course again to the northeast. This was his last patrol of the sea approaches to Louisbourg.

He'd just spent six more weeks at sea, first carrying another twenty-eight displaced Acadians from Annapolis Royal in Nova Scotia, this time to Philadelphia. As always, they looked miserable, bewildered, and forsaken as they crossed over his brow to the wharf near the ship-building quays. The only fortunate thing to occur was they were met by the Society of Friends, as they called themselves. These Quakers had majority control over the Pennsylvania legislature and were very resistant to war. They were dedicated to peace and were particularly diplomatic to the Indians. This was not a popular sentiment with the settlers in central Pennsylvania who were being massacred daily by the marauding Delaware.

The Quakers would not serve as soldiers. Captain Martyn had heard the English commanders in Halifax rage about their refusal to join the provincial army. But he did not care about that. All he cared about was that these ten men and women waiting on this pier had arranged a warm warehouse to bed and feed these destitute French-speaking families. It would be the first kindness shown to them in months. Of course, the Quakers also hoped to reform them from their papist ways by this loving, caring welcome. *Join with us!* They had good farmland to offer these experienced farmers as a way to convince them further.

When that trip was done, the *Anamosa* was assigned to patrol up and down the Cape Breton coastline after Commodore de Lisle had broken the English blockade. The English ships-of-the-line had all returned to Halifax harbor for extensive repairs. Now in mid-September, any real naval action was suspended as the winter months approached. The storms in this area of the Atlantic were vicious and unpredictable. They could come from the north just as easily as from the south. His orders were to patrol until the 15th of September. That would be the next day. Then he would set a course to Boston to see Molly and hopefully get there in time for the birth of their first child.

"Maybe we should change course at midnight, Captain," suggested his second-in-command. "That would still be the fifteenth."

"Good thinking, Lieutenant. But we will travel this course until sunrise, and upon seeing nothing again outside Louisbourg harbor, I will make that entry in the logbook and reverse course to Boston. We will raise every sail possible and fly before the wind!"

*

Henri Gerrard finished his sponge bath and dressed in his wrinkled formal uniform. He went first to the government house and placed his four letters in the dispatch pouch bound for Quebec and Montréal. In the back of his mind, he worried constantly the unnatural blindness might return. He'd conceived no intelligent way to talk about this or even explain it to anyone, or if he should even try. There was no one here to talk to anyway. It would only open him to ridicule or worse. *I could see the sun, sky, the moon, and stars at night, but everything else was blurry.* It sounded ridiculous to him even now. People do not become half-blind. Not like that. With each passing day, it seemed more imaginary.

Except it was not. And he knew it.

Henri could hear the violin music as he approached the grand hall. The food smelled good. He knew it would be mostly pastries and sweetbreads wine and cheese. This was the third of these social gatherings he attended. The room was full with the usual attendees. He saw Kyrielle across the room surrounded by two officers and the son of Île Royale's intendant. Henri mingled, and those he knew said hello and welcomed him back. He went to the table where the sweetbreads were and picked up a piece. He noticed Major Péan, leering, not ten paces away. The officer's comical expression almost made him laugh but when he turned away from the food, she was right there, standing before him.

"Henri! You have presumably returned from another one of your adventures. I am pleased to see you unwounded."

Henri finished swallowing the breads in one gulp. To act gallant as the major had requested, he lifted Kyrielle's hand and kissed it.

She looked surprised. "Well, that is a first. What is the occasion? Did you just read a risqué book, perhaps? Something titillating, I trust."

"No…I mean, I was just trying to be gallant." It sounded awkward and he felt awkward saying it.

"Gallant? Very well, I am therefore persuaded by your charm. And you?"

"And me?" Henri was struggling over how to respond to her. She gave him *that* look. "I am persuaded…too?" Out of the corner of his eye, he noticed Major Péan already just a few steps away.

Kyrielle asked him outright. "Henri, do you not find me attractive? Because, I find you very attractive."

"Kyrielle, you are the most attractive woman here…and probably in all of Île Royale."

She had heard these words before, simple clichés. She read his expression. He was indeed sincere.

"Good. Finally. Well said. I am even more persuaded. I know a place we can go. You will have to leave first, because I cannot."

Henri moved to stay her exit.

"What is wrong now?"

"Kyrielle, I love someone else."

"Here?" she replied in disbelief. "In Louisbourg?"

"No. She is in Quebec City."

"Oh, I see. And what does she look like?"

"Well, you remind me of her in many ways," he said.

Kyrielle stepped closer to him and whispered, "Then tell me her name, Henri. And I will pretend for you. Don't look at me so. I am not wanton. I am attracted to you and there is little time for us here."

"I cannot do this, Kyrielle. I love her."

Kyrielle's expression changed to disappointment. "If you love her that much, you should not come to these soirées at all."

"You are right, Kyrielle. I should not be here. But I enjoy talking with you. I apologize if I gave the wrong impression. You are beautiful, and you certainly deserve better than someone like me."

She gazed at him steadily for a few seconds and then lifted her head and kissed his lips lightly.

"*Adieu*, Henri."

She turned and moved across the room.

Major Péan nudged Henri as he passed by to follow her.

Henri slowly moved towards the door and slipped out. He felt guilty for what he said to her and did not understand why. She was right. He should not have come to this soirée. Louisbourg seemed much lonelier now. But he would not go to another one of these.

Chapter 25
Louisbourg
September 1756
Parliament

Captain LaTour came on deck two hours before sunrise in his naval uniform. Victorio soon followed him up. They took up their watch glass scopes and scanned the black horizon, looking for any signs of a shipboard lantern light.

As the sun rose over their left shoulder, they continued to sweep the horizon. Captain LaTour stopped long enough to check the time.

"We are getting close. I am going below to check our position. I will be right back."

He looked at the chart. By dead reckoning, they were much less than an hour from the harbor entrance; maybe less than thirty minutes. The stony shore line of Île Royale was getting closer on their right. He was near the place he was driven upon the rocks in a storm more than a decade ago. He had lost his ship but was hired by Lady de Chanaye soon after. It was fate. What would his fate be today?

"Captain LaTour!"

The muffled voice was Victorio's. He ran up the ladder stairs. *I should not have asked that question*, he thought.

Victorio pointed. "Sails on the horizon. Forty-five degrees to port. They are now on to us. They are changing course to their left as we move across their line of sight. They've seen us."

He checked his watch. "We need to hold this course another eight minutes and then we turn for our run to the harbor." He inspected the set of sails. "We can do better than this. Fly on my *Queen!* Someone is trying to catch you!"

He would keep checking his watch.

Eight minutes had elapsed.

"They are closing fast, Captain."

LaTour scanned them again with his watch glass. He suddenly recognized the arrangement of the sails.

"That is the *Anamosa!*" He looked at the harbor entrance. The light house was passing them on their right. "Close enough."

The crew was waiting on deck and half way up the rigging. They knew the course change was coming.

"Turning!" he shouted at the crew and then spoke to the helmsman. "Come right! Steer west!"

The *Falcon Queen* listed slightly to the left as she cut the water sharply towards the new course. The disciplined crew began adjusting the sails.

Captain Martyn had spotted the trading frigate just after sunrise and came left to intercept. They could take her as a prize!

"Beat to quarters!"

The marines brought up the swivel cannon. Some of his crew stood ready on deck to respond to the sailing commands. Cannon crews manned the guns.

"She looks very sleek," his second remarked.

"We will catch her."

A few minutes later, he saw the ship turning to enter Louisbourg. Its starboard side was completely in view.

As Captain Martyn continued to look through his glass, he had a sick feeling.

Oh, God! That's the Falcon Queen, he thought. *What are you doing here, LaTour?*

Captain Martyn realized with relief, there was no way the *Anamosa* would catch that ship before it entered Louisbourg harbor.

"Secure from quarters! Come right. Steer south. We will not catch her before she enters Louisbourg," he told his lieutenant. "I don't want to get too close to those large shore batteries. They would love to put a twenty-pound ball in us." He lifted his speaking trumpet to his mouth.

"Let's go home to Boston!"

The men cheered.

Captain Martyn went below and made a log entry.

September 15th. Encountered a small French trading frigate entering Louisbourg harbor. Broke off pursuit when we came in range of the harbor shore batteries. Changed course to the south.

*

The saluting cannon began to fire from the island battery as a trading frigate entered Louisbourg harbor. The arrival brought out citizens and soldiers in throngs to the quay. It was a French flag. A trading vessel. That meant more provisions, possibly luxury items. They were waving and cheering.

Henri Gerrard was eating with his platoon in the Dauphin Bastion when he heard the commotion. He hurried up to the wall above the Dauphin gate. He could not believe his eyes.

"It is the *Falcon Queen*! It is the *Falcon Queen*!"

He ran down the stairs and out to the quay wall. Other Troupes de la Marines were already there cheering. This ship was well known to the marines of Quebec and Montréal. Henri wished he had a scope to view the bridge deck. He shaded his eyes against the dim sunlight and grinned at seeing Captain LaTour's familiar figure giving orders on the main deck. He waved and shouted.

"Captain LaTour!"

His voice was drowned out among all the others. He would just have to wait until the captain came ashore with the precious bags of mail.

A flat barge was moved next to the ship after it anchored to make a convenient platform for unloading its cargo to be carried by smaller boats ashore. Captain LaTour wore his spare naval uniform. He was rowed to the Frédéric Gate at the center of the quay wall and stepped ashore, followed by a crewman carrying the bags of mail to the applause and cheers of the people of Louisbourg. He saluted and greeted Governor de Drucour in the traditional embrace and was welcomed also by the governor's wife. They were escorted by the grenadiers to the King's Bastion to formally present the mail to the governor.

Henri followed at a respectable distance so as not to interrupt the delivery of the mail, which was almost a ceremonial requirement by a ship's captain to the governor of Île Royale.

Captain LaTour's head was swiveling left and right, looking for familiar faces in the crowd he might know, Henri's, specifically. Henri stood further apart from the crowd so he would stand alone and be seen. He raised an arm in waving welcome. LaTour finally looked in that direction and smiled broadly. He gestured that he had to go to the governor's house. Henri nodded.

When LaTour entered the King's Bastion, Henri ran back to the quay wall and got some of the happy crewmen of the *Falcon Queen* to take him out to the ship. He ran up the port-side ladder and stopped at the head of the stairs. He saluted the French flag and Victorio standing by the helm.

"Request permission to come aboard!"

Victorio did not recognize the marine officer for several seconds. Henri now stood close to six feet tall. He was in uniform, wearing a sash, a military hat, and a naval cutlass over his shoulder. But the voice was very familiar.

"Henri? Henri Gerrard?! Henri Gerrard!"

They hugged and other members of the crew crowded around him in welcome, making jests and poking fun at his uniform.

Victorio put the crew back to work unloading the cargo to the barge.

"Captain LaTour mentioned you would be here…but you are all grown up…and a marine officer! Have you been in battle?"

"A few. Nothing too serious. Did the captain bring mail for me?"

"Yes! We just came from Montréal and Quebec. He has a lot of mail for you."

"From who?"

Victorio knew but wanted to let the captain tell him. "Oh, I don't know. He is keeping it safe somewhere. You should wait here for him."

"I cannot. See that flag over the King's Bastion? That is officer's call. The governor probably wants to give us mail to distribute to the men. I must go. But I will come back as soon as I can. It is so good to see all of you again."

Henri was rowed back to Frédéric Gate. From there, he trotted to the King's Bastion to the council room. The mail for the troops was still being sorted into piles. A sergeant-major in the grenadiers was calling out names. Color Sergeant Cabrelle was collecting a pile of letters for the Troupes de la Marine. Henri saw Major Péan standing at the back of the room and stood next to him.

"Did you see Captain LaTour?"

The major nodded. "Yes, I did! He is no longer a pirate. I've arrested him, what…maybe six times in the last ten years. And now he wears a French naval officer's uniform! A captain, no less. He is now senior to me! Even with all of his extraordinary luck, there must be an amazing story there."

Seeing the major, Henri had something else on his mind. "So did I keep my word to you?"

Major Péan sighed lustily and grabbed Henri by the shoulders. "Oh, Henri, you are such a fool! You have no idea what you've missed!"

"And I do not want to know! I just wanted to know if I kept my word."

The major smiled broadly and nodded. "Yes. Of all the women I have known—"

"I do not want to know!"

"Well…you are still a fool."

"That's all," the sergeant-major shouted.

Sergeant Cabrelle had two full bags. "I am heading to the Dauphin bastion to hand these out."

"Anything for me?"

"Mail for you, Major…no. But there were three debtors' missives addressed to you."

"You have my permission to burn them."

"Ensign, you have three letters from Montréal and four from Quebec."

It was like Christmas morning. "Can you keep those for me, please? I have to stay here. The governor is addressing us."

*

"In addition to the mail," Governor Drucour declared to the officers and government administrators assembled in the council room, "the *Falcon Queen* brings us a dozen kegs of brandy, bolts of the finest materials in Paris, linen, damask, and *La Gazette* newspapers for the last six months! Plus a hundred bags of wheat flour. Tobacco. Coffee."

A cheer went up as each of the luxury items was declared.

Captain LaTour was standing on the foot-high small stage with the governor at the front of the council. He saw Henri waiting patiently all the way in the back of the room….next to Major Péan!

What is that sea slug doing here?

When the governor finished, he addressed the captain less formally.

"I insist that you join my table at dinner tonight."

"I would be honored, Governor. Is there anything else for the time being?"

"Come back to see me in two hours. I will have read the more important mail by then. I will have more questions, I am sure."

"And Archbishop Nicolet?"

"Not today. Let them all be of good cheer for today. Tomorrow I will announce his death."

"As you wish, Governor. Be warned, my crew may say something to the cargo handlers before then. I see some officers I know. If you will permit, I would like to greet them."

"Of course, of course."

LaTour hugged Henri tightly. "God's balls! Look at the size of you! And a marine officer!"

"I am here too, Captain," said Péan with a smirk, his arms held wide. "Come, embrace and kiss me. You have my permission."

LaTour frowned and declined. "You can no longer arrest me, Major. I was awarded a full pardon by Admiral de la Motte."

"Was I trying to arrest you? I am not even in the gendarmerie anymore. I am part of the garrison here."

The three of them sat down at an empty table and traded questions. LaTour pulled two letters from his inside pocket for Henri: one from his father and another from Archbishop Nicolet. Henri looked upon them like treasures. He slipped them inside of his uniform coat.

"I will read them later."

"I will be going to Boston next. I trust both of you not to tell anyone else."

"Flying a French flag?" Péan scoffed. "You will get shelled and sunk even before you see the city."

"I will fly the Dutch Republic flag under sail as *William's Queen*."

Major Péan's mouth fell open. "You are insane. They will...hang you... for one of several different charges I can think of!"

"I've done it before."

"I did it with him the last time," Henri said.

Ignoring the major's continued sputtering, LaTour addressed Henri. "You may want to send some mail with me. And I will be coming back to Louisbourg before I make the crossing. So I can bring back mail to you as well."

"When do you leave?"

"In three days, counting today."

"I need to write letters." Henri stood up. "If I do not see you again today, Captain, I will come out to the ship tomorrow."

They watched him walk away just short of a run.

"Henri has an obsession with writing letters," Péan said drolly.

"I want to tell you something the governor does not plan to disclose until tomorrow."

"Me? Should I be honored?"

"Henri will want to talk about what I am about to tell you. Archbishop Nicolet was assassinated. Father Tinian, too, along with another Jesuit priest. You noted the archbishop was sending Henri a letter? That may be the last letter the bishop wrote to anyone."

They talked quietly for almost an hour. He told Péan about the attack on Corrinne's life and that Philippe Gerrard did not know of this. By then, word of the tragedy had started to spread from other crew members of the *Falcon Queen*. People began talking about it in the council room.

Major Péan stood up. "Word is spreading. I will tell Henri."

*

The next afternoon, Ensign Henri Gerrard asked to see Governor Drucour.

"Sit down, Ensign. Captain LaTour had many complimentary things to say about you. Of course, none of it was surprising to me," he added. He noticed the very somber look on the ensign's face. "What may I do for you?"

"Governor, I am sure you know that Captain LaTour is leaving tomorrow for Boston. And that he plans to come back to Louisbourg before he crosses back to France. I have a sister living in Boston who was adopted four years ago. If possible, I would like to go with the captain. There may be an opportunity to see her. I know this is a lot to ask, but there may not be another opportunity for me like this again until the war is over."

The request was ridiculous. Governor Drucour regarded him skeptically.

"Ensign, I cannot let you do that. If you are caught, they will hang you as a spy. And then they will hang Captain LaTour and his crew as spies. It's too dangerous. You have duties here."

Henri was not going to challenge those assertions.

"Governor, the same thing can happen even if Captain LaTour goes alone. But he has visited Boston twice before as a ship of the Dutch Republic. They know him. They will not suspect anyone in his crew. And I have crewed with him before. He goes to see Lord Charles VanderMeer, living in Boston, who is the son of the Duke of Brunswick. He has purpose, legitimacy, and precedent for visiting."

"Said the lawyer to the hangman," Drucour replied with mild sarcasm. "Captain LaTour has told me all of this. I have missives from the Naval Minister explaining many more things related to his visit. But your presence? If you were recognized, it would endanger Captain LaTour and his mission. I cannot allow that."

"Governor, I lived in Boston. I schooled in Boston. I know the streets of Boston. I will dress like the people of Boston."

"With your French-accented English, you would not get off the pier. And the tragedy would unfold as I've described."

Henri knew the governor spoke English too, so he impulsively recited a poem he knew in English, but using Boston slang.

Drucour's brow wrinkled. "They talk like that?"

"Down on the docks of Boston they do," he claimed. "It's been only two years and Captain LaTour and his crew did not even recognize me. I will not be recognized by anyone else. I would be very careful."

Governor Drucour saw the fearlessness of youth in his eyes, that natural sense of immortality circulating in the ensign's blood. It was a sensation he had not felt in decades. It made him pause to consider the possibilities of solving a major problem. *Could he do this?* Drucour wondered.

Henri could see the man was deliberating and wisely remained silent.

Governor Drucour had a vital mission given to him by the Naval Minister that currently lay in shambles. The previous June he received a sealed missive from the Naval Minister who ordered Governor Drucour to have intelligence collected on English invasion intentions in New France. Machault's questions were explicit. In addition to the usual troop strength and deployment positions when the fighting season of 1756 came to an end, France needed an assessment of British intentions to attack at some location over the winter. Something the British had never done before. And more importantly, what would be the priorities of any attacks planned for 1757?

The governor had redrafted the original request to make it more legible and had it delivered by the usual chain of fishermen to Boston. The highly placed spy in Boston was a literate, valuable man, well-positioned to collect such information. He was known as *Parliament*. Return information came by the same fishermen chain from Boston to Canceau. Then a Canceau fisherman would rendezvous at sea with an Acadian fisherman out of Port-Toulouse. The Acadian's name was Beau Sarchet.

Any intelligence information was only useful for two months, and given that four months were required for moving the information back and forth across the Atlantic Ocean, the best either side could do was to use such assessments to establish better predictions of future strategy.

Ensign Gerrard's latest survey excursion to Port-Toulouse had brought back the devastating report that Beau Sarchet was dead, lost in a storm at sea, and presumably the information he carried.

But worse, France's most important spy was in Boston; a man who provided information regarding British army movements against New France. They had broken communications with this man too!

The governor gazed at the ensign steadily, evaluating the young officer's courage and conviction. But this mission required more than bravery. It would require unrehearsed inventiveness and determination. *Can he possibly do something like this?* he asked himself again. *LaTour might know.*

"Ensign, my inclination is to say no without further discussion. So take this as a measure of my respect that I will consider your request. I will confer with Captain LaTour before I make any decision. My answer may still be no. And you *will* obey my orders."

Henri stood and saluted. "Yes, sir."

*

After the ensign left, Governor Drucour sent his aide to find Captain LaTour to request his attendance.

The most recent missive from the Naval Minister delivered by Captain LaTour ordered Drucour to send the collected assessment back to France with Captain LaTour. Given the recent victory over Fort Oswego, Governor Drucour was certain the British strategies for New France had changed completely. Coming when it did, this particular collection of intelligence would be the most valuable yet. Maintaining this collection of intelligence was *the reason why* the Naval Minister had chosen Drucour to be governor. He was nothing if not dependable. During wartime, that was an important quality.

Drucour *dreaded* sending the Naval Minister the report that communications with this most valuable spy was broken. He reflected about what Ensign Gerrard wanted to do. If there were only the ensign's personal needs to consider, the answer would be no, for all the reasons he'd mentioned to the ensign. But if Ensign Gerrard could somehow make contact with the French spy in Boston and bring the latest intelligence back with him. *That* would be worth all the danger involved. Even so, he would not sacrifice Ensign Gerrard's life or endanger Captain LaTour's uncontested access to Boston, unnecessarily.

He needed consensus on this.

"Governor? You asked to see me?"

"Yes, Captain. Please sit. I have to tell you something that is known only to Naval Minister Machault and myself. But before I tell you, you should know that Ensign Gerrard has asked to accompany you to Boston to see his sister."

His sister? LaTour thought. But he did not correct that obvious lie.

"But I have a crucial mission for France, which Ensign Gerrard could fulfill."

Drucour explained about the spy and the broken line of communications. The value of this latest intelligence gathered. The great need to reestablish contact with this man.

"Ensign Gerrard is young, but he has proven his resourcefulness to me repeatedly. Or I would not even consider this. But you know him better than I do. This would endanger you too. So I ask your opinion, Captain. Could Ensign Gerrard do this? Before you answer, I have no alternatives for him. If he cannot attempt this successfully, the intelligence will be lost."

When they reached a consensus, Drucour had his aide find Ensign Gerrard. When he arrived, they would talk for another two hours.

"Ensign Gerrard, you will need to think before you act. There can be no failure in this."

"There will not be," Henri stated with confidence. "If what you've told me is accurate, I will find a way to meet with him."

"Captain?"

LaTour was trying to find a way to encapsulate his enthusiasm for what he just agreed to do. *God's balls* no longer seemed a strong enough statement of his reticence.

"If Ensign Gerrard says he can do this…then he can do this. I will get him there and bring him back safely. But Governor, I cannot promise you there will not be other consequences."

Because when you travel with the Gerrards, LaTour did not say aloud, *there are always fucking consequences.*

*

The next morning, Henri Gerrard boarded the *Falcon Queen* bound for Boston. He'd brought no article of uniform or anything else that might identify himself as a marine, except for his cutlass, knives, and bow. Everything Governor Drucour told him about the man they called *Parliament*, he had memorized. He had not been this happy since…well, since the last time he sailed on the *Falcon Queen*.

Henri was bringing certain letters with him but was resigned he might have to destroy them. He'd read and destroyed the three from Carmen. They were painful pleas that he write to her. Which he already had, but only because there was a mail schooner that braved the harbor blockade patrols, which he explained in his letter. He told her he may be going to France soon, and that he'd been recruited to join the French Navy. And left it there. Which was almost true. Two letters from his mother. He would read them one more time before ripping them up and tossing them into the sea. Three from Madeleine. These were so vivid that he assumed they were sinful to read. So he read them all only a dozen more times, memorizing certain parts. He knew he could not read them aboard ship, being surrounded by the crew. Thus, he was undecided what to do with Madeleine's letters. He was certainly not ripping them up. Then the wonderful letter from his father. His father's words of congratulations, about how proud he was, advice about battles, how he hoped to see him again when he returned from Louisbourg, and that he was deploying to Fort Carillon probably for the winter. He asked if Henri knew any more about Corrinne's babies. Henri sent his reply right away; the letter was en route on the mail schooner. And then the wrenching letter from Archbishop Nicolet, telling him more about his father, how proud he was, how the name of Henri Gerrard was sent back to France, by the bishop, of course, to give him more name recognition to important people he knew, asking if he was keeping up his journal, did he read the books, did he have any favorite poems or tales he liked. He answered all these questions in his reply, which was also en route.

Once he learned about the bishop's death he could have retrieved it from the mail, since it would never reach the archbishop. But then he changed his mind. He'd received the bishop's letter after the man was dead and buried, so somehow it seemed appropriate he should put his thoughts into words and mail something back. Maybe the bishop could read his letter from heaven? The bishop's death was a punch to his stomach every time he thought about it. Henri was never going to destroy the archbishop's letter. Not ever. Captain LaTour would have to find a place for him to hide it, along with his journal…oh, and Madeleine's letters too, he finally decided. After all, he was not going to be aboard ship all the time.

With the archbishop's death, Henri had a plausible explanation for his temporary blindness. Though he was uncertain why the archbishop's death would afflict him with such a bizarre type of blindness so that he could still see the sky, moon, and stars, and again, everything else, but only if he stood in seawater. He was sure, however, it had to do with the evilness of the *châsse*. What else could it be? And if it afflicted him, then the bishop's death would definitely afflict his father, Corrinne, Pierre, and probably Charles. He saw what the *châsse* did to them during the sealing ritual in Montréal. But this was his first time to be afflicted. Why? Well, he would think more about that later.

Henri turned his thoughts to Boston. *I should have brought gifts for them. Particularly Anamosa. Maybe I can get something in Boston?*

When the tide changed, to the cheers of many people lining the quay wall, the *Falcon Queen* would follow behind the fast schooner bound for Quebec. When they both left the harbor, the *Queen* headed due east to put some distance between it and Louisbourg before it changed course to the southwest and to Boston. The mail schooner turned northeast to circle around Île Royale to avoid the British patrols out of Canceau or Halifax before entering the Saint Lawrence River.

Governor Drucour said a silent prayer for the safety of the *Falcon Queen*. When he got back to the government house, he found a wax-sealed missive on his desk. He recognized the handwriting.

Uncle,

I will never return to France as you intended me to do. There is nothing for me in France. And there is nothing for me in Louisbourg. I paid the captain of the mail schooner to transport me to Quebec City. I am sorry I did not say good bye. Please do not hate me. I must find my future. I will write to you when I can. Pray for me.

I love you and Aunt Marie with all my heart.

Kyrielle

CHAPTER 26
BOSTON
SEPTEMBER 1756
"Interesting Times, Indeed"

Deputy Magistrate Jack Tasker had been following Carter Trevathan ever since confronting him about the attempted poisoning of Lord VanderMeer.

"I've learned it was a woman. Witnesses claim you know her."

The man flinched. "Know who? Who is she supposed to be to me?"

That physical reaction was all Tasker needed. It took Trevathan several minutes of overlapping lies to dig his way back to a defensive position that he did not have any female friends. That he was too busy with his business to enjoy any romance. Carter Trevathan was indeed involved, Tasker was certain about that now. But this man had not perpetrated the poisoning. The woman had. And Tasker could not figure out who she was. But he would, eventually. For now, he wanted Carter to see him or one of his deputies everywhere he went.

Carter Trevathan was followed constantly.

In the meantime, Tasker went back to work on identifying the woman. Whoever she was, she did not live with Carter Trevathan. But he was able to determine she used to visit Carter several times a week, until recently, according to his neighbors. But none of them could provide an adequate description. She always came and left in the dark. Carter and the woman took great pains to keep her identity a secret. Another confirming behavior. Well, as long as they were avoiding the magistrate and his deputies, they were not trying to kill the VanderMeers. It was a risky presumption.

Tasker also focused on *why* they were trying to kill the VanderMeers. And not just his lordship—but all of them. Of course, there was a war and Charles VanderMeer was indeed the heir to the Duchy of Brunswick, and there was no denying that the royals back on the continent considered murder a legitimate part of the ascension contest. But the arsonist, Felix, came from Philadelphia. Carter from New York. And there was this other man Sentry Cheever claimed to have seen around Boston. But this man was apparently being very careful not to be seen again. Still, Tasker would wager they were all somehow tied to Carter Trevathan. He could not prove this yet…but it was only a matter of time. Time he could not give to solving this as fast as he wanted. If only his everyday thieveries, murders, drunken brawls, and the other usual Boston crimes would stop getting in his way. This potential threat to the VanderMeers was a much more intriguing puzzle. It was a real threat and imminent. These assassins would try again. He was certain of that too.

*

Carter Trevathan awoke nearly every morning with a headache as the night messenger visited him almost every night. The visitations were brief but the physical effects were profound. Every new plan had to be compensated for the magistrate and his men shadowing his every move. So now he was planning two slayings and they were to happen at the same time. He would craft a diversion, kill one of them, and while the shock of that was felt in the city, the other one would be killed. But coordinating this was nearly impossible with Tasker and his deputies following his every movement and even watching his apartment at night.

He must talk with Caroline Bristol. *How?* They must arrange a place to meet. *But where?* Or create a way to pass along discreet messages. *While being watched?* Every idea he pondered had problems. The magistrate was looking for a woman. Mistakes could not be tolerated.

Then Carter learned that Rachel Bristol was no longer working at the Marine Society Hospital. No one had told him this. He learned it by accident. He was leaving his kiosk of business inside Faneuil Hall at midday to get something to eat down by the fishing piers, dutifully followed by one of Tasker's men, when he suddenly saw Rachel Bristol! She was sweeping out a doorway leading into the new Long Wharf medical shelter, formerly the place from which the penny surgeon worked. Except this place was no shack. It occupied half of a small converted warehouse that now had beds and even overnight patients at the corner of Merchant and King Streets. Carter had heard about this as it was being formed because of the pushy women sweeping through Faneuil Hall at least once a week, soliciting donations for charity and the poor. They asked him for money for this new hospital, which he gave to them to keep up appearances. The sailmaker was still at this hospital acting as a "surgeon" for those who were brave enough to endure the pain of his sail-stitching needles, which could qualify as weapons. The old seaman now presented himself as a legitimate doctor. No one cared about the boast. His services were still free! Though he did ask for a charitable donation of money, ostensibly for food, more likely rum. But, in addition, there was a white-haired former army surgeon working there. He could saw off arms and legs and even set broken bones.

Rachel Bristol had elected to act as their nurse.

Carter went into a restaurant across the street from this new hospital and sat by the window to watch Rachel. He wished he had known of this earlier. If he could get a message to Rachel, she would get it to Caroline. But how to do this? He ate some soup and bread and deliberated. Tasker's deputy leaned against a wall in the restaurant and casually watched him eat.

I need someone to use as a go between, he thought. *Someone they will not suspect.*

Just then he saw a young boy, one from a group of a half dozen that usually careened around any location in Boston where crowds would gather. Carter had seen this boy before and admired his ingenuity at thieving inside Faneuil Hall. There wasn't much to steal in Carter's stall, mainly various heavy bolts of cloth. The boy seemed the cleanest of the group and was not the leader. This gang would bounce around Faneuil Hall about every other day, raising a ruckus, picking pockets, and stealing wares from the booths until they were chased out by the hired guards. Most of the Faneuil businessmen tolerated the young thieves as long as they personally were not the target of pilfering that day. They tolerated the boys' presence as many of the businessmen themselves had once been part of a similar bunch of rascals at that age.

The boys would also do minor favors for the Faneuil men, for a fee of course. Fetch them something to eat, deliver packages, often *messages* as well!

This particular boy, that day, was alone, and evidently had cut his hand. Without hesitation, he approached Rachel Bristol. She set aside her broom, retrieved a bottle of alkaline liquid, soap, and water. Tenderly, she cleaned and bandaged the boy's cut right there on the street. She smiled at him when she was finished, caressed his cheek, and ruffled his hair. He hugged her afterwards.

They know each other!

*

Saybrook, Connecticut

The four stonemasons and their apprentices, a group of eight artisans, had arrived in multiple wagons. Three of the wagons were loaded with hard gray granite slabs cut from quarries west of New Haven, plus six large barrels of pebble gravel, pallets of brick, tile, cement, lumber, chains, pulley systems, and all sorts of tools. Another wagon came loaded with food and other provisions. They also brought their own cooks from New Haven. They stabled the horses at the carriage house on the main road and stayed in various rooms of Winter House, which was now fully owned by the VanderMeers.

They had worked diligently on the vault for ten days and planned to be done that day. Sentry Cheever was amazed how smoothly everything went and said so to C. Bernard Conway Esquire, who had come over from New Haven to check on the progress.

"I understand today is the last day?"

"That's what they claim. I found it all interesting to watch. These large quarry stones are cut so perfectly, most of the hard work was digging out the hole, creating the drainage at the bottom, then setting up the winches and rigging necessary to lower the stones into it."

Bernard Conway laughed lightly. "Yes, well, the VanderMeers paid a premium to have this done right. The master mason told me the plans sent down from Boston were created by those who knew what they were doing. They did all the cutting and assembled the finished vault at their workshop and cutting yards in New Haven to check the fit of the pieces before they carted them over here. They came prepared for everything. That was their plan anyway."

"Then it worked," Sentry attested.

"Color-Sergeant Cheever, we are ready for you over here," a mason called.

Sentry walked over to the vault accompanied by Mr. Conway.

"Yes?"

Erected above the hole was an elaborate rigging consisting of chains, pulleys, and support lines connected to a hand-winch associated with a swingable davit. The davit and rigging reminded Sentry of what he'd seen aboard a ship, used to lift heavy cannon or cargo, and just as complicated. From this davit now dangled a flat piece of rectangular, thick stone, held by chains attached to the pulleys. The slab was swung out of the way to one side of the hole.

"All right," said the master mason, "you said you wanted to check these measurements. Here are the design dimensions." He handed Sentry the drawings and pointed at the numbers. "That's your copy to keep and mark. Here's a pencil. We will now call the numbers out to you."

One of the apprentices climbed down the ladder. They started at the bottom of the hole, taking measurements of widths and lengths about every three feet. Checking the corners with a metal right angle for squareness. The final step was to place a long level on the top stones, in multiple places to demonstrate that the top of the vault was indeed level in every direction.

The measurements were as perfect as anything Sentry had ever witnessed, and he said so. Encouraged by his appreciation, the master mason began to describe how the lining stones of the vault were notched and cut in certain ways so they would interlock and support the weight of one another. He pointed this out.

"Very difficult and expensive cuts to make, I should mention. No mistakes allowed. But necessary to permit a slight amount of expansion and contraction that will occur in the rock from the heat and cold. Strong columns of pea gravel mixed around the outside, all the way down. They were thoroughly tamped as they were filled. But porous enough to allow any water to drain to the bottom where the four low-point drain, tile-covered water channels were cemented. This will direct any collected water downhill to the edge of the river. Without this, the vault would eventually fill with water. Cannot have that in a tomb, can we? Don't want any bodies bobbing up."

All the masons laughed so Sentry laughed too.

"We are now at the point of swinging the davit and placing the capstone. Unless you want to inspect anything else. Oh, before I forget, the side stones are all resting atop and supported by a thick foundation stone, four inches wider and longer than this capstone."

Sentry leaned forward a bit and looked down into the dark stone-lined hole. In the dim daylight, he could just barely see the flat foundation stone at the bottom. The vault's deep emptiness seemed to yawn back at him. It was indeed a tomb.

"I expect whoever goes in there has a permanent home," Sentry remarked with a grin.

"Indeed," affirmed the mason. "As it should be. Cannot have any ghosts carousing around here, can we?"

As if on cue, everyone laughed again.

"All right then. If you have no more questions, Color-Sergeant. We will place the capstone. It is three inches larger in length and width than the dimensions of the vault, including the stones on the sides. See these iron straps holding it up? Once this cap is at rest, we will take these out from underneath. You have to save these metal straps someplace safe for when you want to lift the cap again."

There was a deep *THONK!* sound as the final piece dropped the last inch. Of course, the fit was perfect.

"Isn't that a pleasing sound? It's as if the vault says...*was there any doubt*?"

More laughter. The masons all congratulated one another.

The master mason handed Sentry two rolls of documents.

"These drawings are both the same. Two copies just for safety. We will have another copy back at our workshop. They show how all this rigging goes together. Notice how the davit neck slides inside a pipe surrounded by cement. That hole will have a cap cover. Not too complicated once you learn how to do it. Having said that, where do you want us to put all of the rigging components?"

"Um... down in the basement? Do you have an enclosure planned to contain it, so none of the pieces are lost?"

"No," the mason said with a slight frown. "The plans did not call for that. There will be an extra charge. But we'll build something strong out of stone and solid lumber down in the basement for you. It will not take long. Build it to last too, like it was built by stonemasons and not by carpenters."

More laughter.

Remarkably, in a few more hours, the rigging enclosure was finished. The equipment was stowed. The capstone of the tomb was covered in a layer of tamped gravel and another two feet of earth. Near the bottom of the hill, they cut out several lengths of sod and laid it over the top to cover the entrance of the vault, and they also laid lengths of it down the drainage trench line on the side of the hill to repair that view as well.

As directed in the plans.

With that, the masons loaded up the wagons and their belongings. Good-byes were said by all. In a military-like parade they caravanned out the way-in.

"I almost expected a victory song as they rode away in their wagons," Sentry remarked.

"Armies could take lessons in efficiency from these masons," Mr. Conway replied.

Sentry smiled. "I think not, sir. Those men are artists. Builders. Armies are all about destruction."

Conway handed Sentry a wax-sealed envelope. "Here is the final bill, except for the last piece of construction down in the basement. I wrote the figure in pencil on the copy inside. I presume you can validate that to the VanderMeers."

"I will."

"Winter House has been given new locks. Here are a set of keys for you. I will keep a set, and a third set will be given to the daughters of Mistress Barton, if that's acceptable."

"It is, unless the VanderMeers decide otherwise."

"Color-Sergeant, if you don't mind me asking, for whom is the tomb intended?"

Sentry assessed the lawyer.

"I did not ask. And they have never told me. That usually means they prefer it remain confidential."

*

Boston

Captain Conor Martyn of the *Anamosa* weighed anchor once again in the Boston harbor. He established three watch sections and laid out a heavy list of work to do on the ship.

"We will be in port for two weeks, plus a few days, before going back to Halifax. I expect our work to be completed early. If we fall behind on this list at the end of a week, the crew will drop back into two sections. So it is up to the section captains to make sure this does not happen. I will be checking on you daily. As I've said before, do not embarrass my command by carousing in Boston. If you cause problems, your entire watch section will bear the punishment. Other than that, enjoy yourselves. You've earned it."

A cheer went up as shore leave commenced for the off-sections. Captain Martyn was rowed to the center of the Long Wharf. Carrying his bag of dirty laundry, he went to his apartment on Brattle Street and knocked on the door of Mistress Callahan.

"Oh," she said, frowning. "It's you again, and smelling worse than you did the last time."

He took off his hat. "I am here to pay the rent, and I know I am late again."

"Are you now? Well, you will be pleased to hear that your very pregnant wife already paid the rent."

"She did?"

"Her wages from doing home service work, I expect. Her, all miserable, with those swollen ankles, her aching back, wetting herself all the time. And now you plan to ask her to wash your smelly clothes too?"

He spoke humbly, his cheeks burned. "I was hoping…if you have the time…name your price."

"Fifty pence. And a hundred pence for your bath. And I will wash the uniform you are wearing. Aren't you glad now that you left a clean uniform with me?"

"You are much wiser than I will ever be, Mistress. I thought I admitted that to you the last time I was here."

"Well, telling me I am wise is a poor substitute. But I am not pretty anymore, so…"

"Mistress! Don't say that! I can still see your beauty in your eyes. They are green and sparkle…with a delicious gleam of wickedness!"

"Ahhh, go on…" She hit him lightly on the chest. "And more wickedness than you might ever believe! But that's enough. Don't spoil it. And you are carrying the water for your tub. Two full pails are ready now. Use the tub down here, out behind the privy. Better hurry, too, before the sun goes down and it gets cold."

*

The Breeding Grounds

The *ghost* could *see* the demon servants moving again. They were planning to attack. It wanted to surge to dominate the female eagle again. But first, her stronger natural instincts must be overcome.

The aerie nest was now very crowded with three fully grown eagles. The female was making constant trips back and forth from the lake to feed the two males, who hopped up and down and flapped their wings. It was obvious that both of them needed to take flight. The nest was over a hundred feet above the valley floor.

The *ghost* sensed the accumulating exhaustion of the mother. If the eaglets had been left alone, the dark-feathered eaglet would have pushed its white-feathered brother out of the nest over a moon ago. The *ghost* spurred the mother's instincts to keep feeding them both. But the time had come. The mother could not support the three of them any longer.

When she returned with the next wriggling fish, the brown eaglet hopped up to the brim of the nest to be fed first. When she was close, the *ghost* surged. The female moved sideways violently and slammed into the eaglet. It was pushed out of the nest.

"*Skrieee!*"

The young raptor instinctively spread its wings before it slammed into the rocks. It came out of the dive six feet above the rocky floor and swooped upward to a tree across the narrow valley. It landed on a branch two hundred yards away to perch in panic and confusion, crying out for its mother.

"*Skrieee!*"

The mother left the fish with the white eaglet and flew across to her other offspring. She perched on the same branch but further out and screamed loudly. The eaglet began moving towards her hopping clumsily, but she suddenly took flight. The branch began springing up and down. It was less stable than the aerie nest. The eaglet flapped its wings. It lost its balance and fell forward out of the tree, forcing it to fly again. The mother had circled back to fly near him, and he followed her out to the lake. She performed hunting circles, found her prey, glided down, and gripped a small fish in her talons. She flapped hard to regain height, and then suddenly released the fish. The dark brown eaglet followed the dead fish back to the water's surface and clumsily grasped it up with its talons. He regained altitude but did not see the mother anywhere, so it flew to the nearest tree to perch and started eating.

The mother circled, glided, and caught another small fish. She flew back to the aerie. When she neared, the white eaglet hopped to the brim. The *ghost* waited until just the right moment, then surged to dominance as before.

"*Skrieee!*"

The female dropped the fish, which fell clear of the nest, and veered sideways into the white eagle. It squawked and was unbalanced. Its talons ripped out pieces of the aerie's brim as it fell backwards towards the valley floor. Like its brother, it rolled and extended its wings to swoop out of the dive. It flew up the valley towards the lake before picking a high tree at random on which to perch. The female followed and perched between the eaglet and the tree trunk. She made small hops sideways, forcing the eaglet further and further out on the branch, which now dipped precariously from their combined weight. Then she sprung into flight. The branch bobbed up and down vigorously. The white eagle tried to compensate by hopping in unison with the branch, which made the springing worse, until it lost its grip and was forced into flight again.

The female called as she circled back around. The white eagle followed her out to the lake. Using instinctive techniques, she taught her other eaglet how to fish.

She continued the rest of the day flying with both eaglets, gliding, catching smaller fish, releasing the bodies back into the water as her off-spring improved their hunting abilities. When the sun was setting, she left them to find shelter in the trees by the lake. She went back to the aerie to rest for the night.

The next morning, the *ghost* sensed a distinct change in the female's mood and natural urges. She was much calmer than usual. The *ghost* was now impatient. She flew from the aerie to hunt. The *ghost* spurred her direction of flight to an open field where uncounted small, furry rodents lived beneath the ground. The female circled until she spotted her prey and began her deadly glide.

Just a few feet above the ground and on the rodent's blind side, the *ghost* surged to full dominance.

"*Skrieee! Skrieee! Skrieee!*"

The female stopped flying to flop and roll on the ground. Unhurt from the fall she began hopping and flapping her wings in panic. The *ghost* did not withdraw, but exerted its control even stronger than before. It took a long time to calm her down but eventually the female sat still and began to accept the unnatural presence. She saw a rodent nearby and hopped towards it, but the animal instantly dropped back into its burrow. This happened two more times. Finally, the eagle took flight. The *ghost* relaxed its dominance just enough to allow her to hunt, catch prey, and perch on a tree branch. She would feed on six of these creatures while the *ghost* relaxed and surged its dominance to accustom her to it.

The next time she took flight, they turned towards the lake. The *ghost* withdrew just long enough for her to fish, perch, and feed as she naturally would. She would rest at night, and the *ghost* would not disturb her slumber. She awoke and felt the presence. But she could hunt and she could feed. The female eagle now submitted to changes in the direction of flight. It no longer threatened her. The *ghost* repeated the hunting, fishing, and sleeping with her for still another day.

The next morning, the *ghost* started flying south.

*

Boston

Charles had finished all the pieces for lining the vault and the smaller enclosure pieces for the *châsse*. In fact, all of his studio work was complete, including the amulets. He found working with the silver surprisingly easy after some welcome suggestions by Mr. Revere, particularly with the engraving. Four of the amulets would be set with emeralds at their centers, using jewels he carried with him ever since he'd left France. And to his surprise, an amethyst turned up at his office door unexpectedly, brought in by a Boston jeweler who learned Lord VanderMeer was looking for one. It was deep purple, a large stone, already cut with facets and had no discernible flaws. It hailed from one of the Spanish colonies was all the man could tell him. Lord VanderMeer paid twice what he thought it was worth, but he didn't complain or even bargain. The jewel's appearance in Boston almost seemed predestined. That's what he told himself. And that made it special.

He took the amulets home first and put them down in the cellar strong box for security. They would all need to undergo a ritual of blood. He still did not like thinking about what any of that portended. He only knew it worked and accepted that fact for what it signified. The amulets would protect people he loved from evil.

Next came the large pieces intended for the vault. He asked Sentry Cheever to bring the carriage from the hangar behind the house to his office. The color sergeant came into the studio and admired the chiseled symbols in the inlaid granite. They were works of art as far as he was concerned. Certainly better than anything he'd ever seen before.

"These are masterfully cut, your lordship. Wha' are they for?"

This discussion was overdue. "I will answer your questions later, Sentry. Right now, I want to move all these pieces to the carriage hangar behind the house."

With the guards standing by, Charles and Sentry loaded the heavy wood and granite sections into the baggage area at the back of the carriage, along with his saws, wood chisels, hammers, wood resin glue, and dowels. They tied everything in place, covered them all in tarps, and secured three saw horses to the top of the carriage. Moving slowly, they trundled along the Boston streets back to the house.

They opened both doors on the carriage hangar, carefully carried the pieces inside, and leaned them against one wall, covered up by tarps. Charles arranged the saw horses in a line to hold the *châsse*.

"Now wha'?"

"I'm going to surround the original *châsse* with these smaller pieces."

"What will tha' do?"

"You see these symbols carved into the granite inlays?" He pointed. "There is more to explain about these symbols. And Lady Corrinne and I have other things to perform associated with them. But the weight of the *châsse* when I am finished enclosing it will be far too heavy for me alone... maybe too much for both of us. We'll see. I will need your help to bring the *châsse* up from the cellar. I know this thing makes you uneasy. It makes me uneasy too. And I do not want you to suspect Lady Corrinne and I are in league with some type of demon. Or that we practice in the black arts or the occult. But unfortunately, there is a dark history connected to this *châsse*. And there is a legend that comes with it, which began centuries ago. I have collected many old texts and old writings on this to try and understand it. Lady Corrinne and I have studied this history. Like so many ancient legends, a lot of it is very hard for us to read let alone believe. And yet, we have experienced and seen things that perplex us to our very souls."

Cheever felt a chill touch his neck. He did not want to ask, but... "*Things*? What kind of things?"

"We are trying to escape from this...*curse*, for lack of a better word to describe it. I will tell you all about it later today. The vault you supervised to construct is part of that plan."

"The white eagle too?"

Charles nodded. "That creature is also part of this, but only became so in the last few years."

"Bloody hell," Sentry whispered. "I am nah' sure I want to know any of this, your lordship."

"I appreciate the way you feel. At one time, I felt the same way. But the vault you built in Saybrook will be the final resting place for this *châsse*. We intend to take it there once I complete the new enclosure. Which I want to do today. So, if you please, I need your help to bring the *châsse* up from the basement. We'll set it down upon these sawhorses. I will finish the work and cover it with a tarp...until we are ready."

"Ready for wha'?"

Charles rested a hand atop one of Sentry's broad shoulders. "That, my friend, is best explained over a few glasses of brandy."

The *châsse* exuded a repugnant odor and emitted a few low growls from the cellar to the hangar. Sentry had heard and smelled it all before. He did not like any of this. But he assisted Lord VanderMeer. Charles enclosed it among all the new pieces. He glued and pounded home the dowels into the hand-drilled holes. They tried lifting the entire reliquary when it was finished. Sentry could lift one end, but it was now too heavy for Charles.

"Well, that answers that question. We'll need someone your size. So here it stays, until the next time it is moved."

Charles walked out to the front of the house and told the soldiers the carriage hangar was now ready to be guarded. He handed them a slip of paper, which had the address of a carpenter.

"This man has already built a temporary guard shack. Have him bring it over in a wagon. I expect to guard this no more than a few weeks."

"What's in the hangar, your lordship?"

"Come with me. I will show you."

The two redcoats stopped at the doorway and gazed at the coffin-like box.

"So you see? Just some valuable pieces of wood and stone sculpture. Some other wood and stone carvings leaning here against the wall." He lifted the tarps to display them. "They're all very heavy, so they would not be easy to steal. But I do not want them damaged by someone foolish enough to try."

*

Anamosa went into the backyard to the small garden area. Dian had asked her to collect the now ripened corn from the three lines of cornstalks they had planted. It would take several trips to collect it all. She put corn cobs into a small basket until it was full. When she turned to take the basket back into the house, she saw a large white eagle perched atop the carriage hangar, looking down at her.

She set the basket down and stared at the creature without any fear. The amulet around her neck began to feel warm. She slipped it out of her shirt. The purple stone was glowing. She suddenly heard a soundless voice in her head.

Give the amulet to Henri. The words repeated again. The eagle spread its wings wide and flew away.

She watched it fly high into the sky and lazily start circling over the city.

But Henri is not here, Anamosa thought.

The words sounded important. She picked up her basket and carried it in to Dian. She did not tell anyone about what she saw. The words were given to her…not them. She would think about this before she said anything.

*

The day was almost over. Charles invited Sentry to dinner. Captain Martyn had returned to everyone's delight, and most of all to Molly's joy. The baby was due any day. Anamosa was happy to sit next to Sentry. And Dian make a savory beef pot roast, with harvested fall vegetables and berry pies for dessert. The twins in their baby chairs charmed everyone with the expressions and sounds they made.

This dinner would end up having special meaning for them all when they later reflected on it.

After dinner, Lord VanderMeer announced he planned to spend a few hours in the library with Sentry and asked not to be disturbed. Charles had told Corrinne he wanted to explain this to Sentry by himself.

"This should be a man-to-man discussion. Sentry might feel the need to scoff, swear, utter oaths, call me a liar, or give insult. Who knows? I'm not sure I would believe it if our roles were reversed. You not being there will make him less uncomfortable."

When they closed the library doors, Charles stacked up the old books and rolls of even older documents on the small table to use as references. He raised all the lantern lights in the room.

"Before I start, Sentry, know that I am a man of science and mathematics. I was fortunate by birth to be educated by men of genius in my youth. I have an equally strong faith in God and the Bible. But what I am going to tell you conflicts with much of what I believe to be true or accept on faith alone. But you should know that what I *experienced* is absolutely true. Ask any question you want of me. I will not be offended. And I give you my word, I will not lie to you. Then you can be the judge of what I recount."

Sentry declined the offer of brandy.

"I think it's best my mind is nah' clouded by strong spirits. I've long anticipated this explanation."

"Then let's begin." Lord VanderMeer unfolded a roll of paper written in Latin. "This fragile document was written by a Christian archbishop name Brevelaer. It describes the alliance of the Four Great Houses against a Normandie warlord called Vaelblez. I will read parts of it to you and then explain."

"*The Druid priest's name was Daeniel...*"

At the end of the second hour, Lord VanderMeer began describing what transpired during the sealing hex in Montréal, which Lord VanderMeer had personally witnessed. In the middle of that extraordinary recital, Sentry held up a hand.

"If you please, your lordship, I think I will have that glass of brandy you offered."

*

Berlin

The events of the last few months were difficult to recall with any clarity. He recalled bad dreams, followed by delusional periods of wakefulness. The endless nauseating, rocking sensation. Then lying on a stretcher somewhere in London. Crushing exhaustion. Even worse headaches. Weakness to the point of helplessness, unable to even feed himself. Lying in his own waste and urine for hours on end. Then, suddenly, a bursting surge of wellness, good feelings, and optimism. Everything was lucid if only for a week. But long enough to learn of the success of his servants and provide them further direction.

The weakness returned, but the wellness endured as long as he did not try to dominate more than two of the servants across the water. One of them was already returning by ship and needed no further direction. The other needed constant direction. But his new plan was complete. Now the servant only needed to create the opportunity. This left the colonel more time to concentrate on the Kleinfels family's service to its sovereign.

Frederick II had crushed Austria and crippled Russia in less than two weeks. The confident sovereign was surprised and disappointed at seeing the colonel's limp and frowned at the disability when they finally met.

"Colonel, if you can no longer provide service to me, I am sure I can find someone else who can."

"Your Majesty, my affliction is no worse than a temporary injury to my leg. My mental faculties are not affected. I am ready to meet with the Naval Minister and accomplish your intended strategy. Also, the governor of New France has accepted the offer of a mercenary regiment. I have learned that the Naval Minister and Admiral de la Motte will soon make a decision on where to send these men in the spring."

Frederick watched the colonel's physical reactions carefully. He'd seen courageous soldiers attempt to do foolishly brave things out of a rigid sense of duty. But that attitude, while admirable, did not determine success. If the wound was bad enough, it could assure failure at a critical moment in battle. The colonel had proven to be a persuasive man and the Naval Minister had trusted him so far. And Frederick needed the right answer from Naval Minister Machault right away. The colonel must persuade the minister to his cause even if he encountered an adverse opinion.

"Colonel, seeing your frailty suggests I find another man for this vital mission. But that will take a long time and this opportunity will pass. I need an answer now. So I will let you go. You must obtain the answer I want. If you do not succeed, it matters not that you return to tell me you failed. In that event, it may serve you better to seek a commission in the French army for the duration of the war."

*

Paris

Colonel Wilhelm von Kleinfels accepted help descending the steps from the carriage house. But that was the only help he permitted. Using a cane for balance, he marched slowly up the stairs into the building of the French Naval Minister, Jean-Baptiste de Machault. The colonel was not in his uniform as per their agreement. He was directed to wait in a hall filled with other visitors, all of them seeking audience with the Naval Minister. He stayed by a window and looked out over the gardens. The length of the delay in seeing the minister was a measure of the value of the confidential alliance between France and Prussia.

Less than an hour later, an aide came to escort the colonel to a side door leading to a private office. He took a chair and waited an additional hour before the Naval Minister entered the room.

Colonel von Kleinfels rose from his seat, came stiffly to attention, and clicked his heels in salute.

"Sit down, Colonel. I am aware of your infirmity. I do not have much time for you."

"Thank you, Excellency. My debility is temporary and will not diminish the service I hope to provide to you and to my sovereign."

"Very well. You first. Tell me about New France."

The colonel related what was learned from Alain Marcoux's discussion with Governor Vaudreuil.

"Therefore the regiment will be ready in the spring. You only need to pick the location and provide for transport."

"And in return?"

"In return, my sovereign wants agreement that France will not conduct invasive operations to the east before June of next year. That includes Hanover. Accordingly, Prussia will not conduct invasive operations in French territories before June of next year as well. I should add that the

June 1757 date is arbitrary. This delay could be extended by mutual agreement if it is to the advantage of both countries. While my sovereign feels strongly about the German states, he does not covet what has historically been French territory. And until recent events forced the dissolution of the alliance between France and Prussia, he understands France's need for the defensive covenants with Austria."

Machault regarded the colonel with dispassion.

"France is winning its war with England. What is your sovereign's response?"

"Frederick offers his congratulations. And reminds France that England is moving more regiments to America. Twice as many as France intends. He suggests that France needs fight no land battles in Europe while the rule of New France remains in jeopardy. Prussia faces significantly larger armed forces in Austria and Russia. It would seem that both our countries need to conserve their strategic reserves. France for its western territories and Prussia to defend its eastern borders. A confidential truce between us, even until next June gives advantages to both countries."

"Our truce will not last forever. As you say, Hanover is England's weakness."

"But as you say, France is winning without it. And Prussia is required to defend it. Is there any advantage to either country in fighting over it *sooner*?"

The two men stared at each other.

"June is acceptable," Machault announced. "We need to meet again before March."

"I will make plans to return again by the middle of February."

Machault stood. The colonel followed suit.

"Your sovereign acknowledges neither of us can control the offensive actions of our allies."

"Yes, he does, your Excellency. And he finds it ironic that we can influence the offensive actions of our *enemies*, even if it is only temporary."

"Interesting times, indeed." Machault's expression softened. "I hope your observation remains true."

"Excellency." Colonel von Kleinfels clicked his heels and bowed.

CHAPTER 27
BOSTON
SEPTEMBER 1756
The Penny Surgeon

Henri Gerrard manned the helm as *William's Queen* weaved among the chain of islands preceding Boston harbor. They were flying the flag of the Dutch Republic, with the corresponding name plaque in place on the stern. It was overcast, cold, and foggy in some places near the shore. A drizzly rain was falling. Henri was exhilarated at the prospect of seeing Corrinne, Anamosa, and his new brothers and sisters, in spite of the uncertainty they would even be in Boston. At the same time, the enormity of the danger he would place everyone in should his mission to contact *Parliament* be discovered made his heart pound.

The saluting cannon on Deer Island fired a round as the *Queen* sailed by the defensive fort. Other saluting cannons would follow.

"There is no turning back now," Captain LaTour said in a fatalistic tone to Victorio and Henri.

Victorio, now acting as Captain Jaager, tugged at the stiff collar of the Dutch sea soldier uniform he wore. It felt like it had shrunk since the last time he wore it.

Through his watch glass, LaTour could see the pennants at the harbor forts being elevated to alert the port authorities of his arrival. The *Queen* was also flying pennants, ones specified by the British navy to declare the visiting ship was on a diplomatic mission from a neutral country. LaTour had reefed most of his sail so that his approach would be slow and his course easily determined.

"Do we anchor or wait for a pilot?" Victorio asked.

LaTour looked through his telescope. "We will make a starboard side mooring at the head of the Long Wharf like last time. No one is there now. If they want us to move, they can tell us so."

"I see the *Anamosa* anchored over there." Victorio pointed towards the anchorage area to the left of the Long Wharf.

"Oh, shit," LaTour said softly.

"Do you think Captain Martyn recognized us at Louisbourg?" Victorio asked.

"No more than if we were a beautiful maiden at the ball and our gown suddenly fell off."

"What do we do?"

"We continue to moor at the pier."

"The *Anamosa* saw you at Louisbourg?" Henri shot a quick glance at the captain.

"Mind your helm."

Captain LaTour changed course to the right then swung around sharply to the left to parallel the front of the Long Wharf. There were at least thirty redcoats waiting in ranks at the head of the pier. He saw four civilians, a naval officer, and a marine officer.

Henri pulled the sock cap down past his ears with one hand to cover his hair.

"Prepare to handle lines," LaTour shouted in English for the benefit of the observers.

The crew knew what he meant.

"Reef all sail! Put over all lines."

The bow and stern bolos sailed through the air. Longshoremen pulled the bolos and took hold of the lines. Gripping the noose, they slipped it over a bollard. The *Queen* glided slowly alongside the wharf. The deck crew pulled a strain on the lines to stop the ship's movement and laid them in loops around the deck cleats.

"Put over the brow!"

As soon as the brow touched the pier, the three civilians and both officers marched aboard. Captain LaTour had his papers and credentials ready.

The lead civilian talked first. "Welcome back to Boston, Captain. I am Jennings, the customs officer." The customs man reviewed the documents and credentials briefly and nodded with satisfaction. "This is my assistant, Mr. Brown. We will inspect your ship for contraband."

"Of course. Captain Jaager, please escort Mr. Jennings and Mr. Brown below."

The navy lieutenant and army captain saluted. Captain LaTour saluted back. They introduced themselves as the ship liaisons during the time in port. A civilian interrupted.

"Welcome to Boston again, Captain LaTour." They shook hands. "Samuel Grant, from the Selectman Council of Boston, at your service. State your business for the record."

"The business of the Dutch Republic. I carry sealed dispatches from the Duke of Brunswick to his son, Lord Charles VanderMeer."

A man standing next to Samuel Grant was busy scribbling with quill and ink into a log book set atop a portable table propped up by a single leg.

"And your cargo?"

"No cargo at this time. But I intend to cross back as soon as I replenish my food stores and provisions and after my business here is complete. However, in spite of the war, if there is anything I am permitted to purchase in Boston to take back with me to Amsterdam, I would considerate it a courtesy. I can offer hard coin to the merchants."

It was as if he offered water to a dying man in the middle of a dessert. Samuel Grant's brow elevated with interest. He gestured for the scribe to stop writing.

"I am certain something can be arranged. I will also provide guards so you are not trampled by the vendors inside the emporium once they learn you will purchase in hard coin and not on credit. I am speaking of Faneuil Hall, of course."

"I am familiar with that marketplace." Captain LaTour turned to the officers. "Gentlemen, I would appreciate having marines posted on the pier in front of my ship while I am here to offer us security and to check the identity of anyone trying to board us. After what happened here last year, Lord VanderMeer has been under constant threat, as I am sure you are aware. And with the war, this has only gotten worse. My ship may also be in danger. Four marines would be adequate. I am willing to pay for a shelter to be erected for the guards. The ship will offer the men meals plus a gratuity on a daily basis. And my cooks need to go ashore for fresh provisions. Eight weeks in stormy seas has depleted us of fresh foods and water."

The naval officer answered with enthusiasm, now that they knew hard coin gratuities would be coming. "Our marines would be happy to guard you, Captain, and to guide you to the correct locations to purchase whatever you need."

"Splendid. Can we be provided a hand lorry to carry the purchases?"

"Of course." The officers left the ship to arrange for this.

Now that the military was out of earshot, Samuel Grant began speaking in earnest.

"When do you want to visit Faneuil Hall?"

"I must see Lord VanderMeer first and deliver the missives from his father and receive any immediate directives for me. So tomorrow, I think, or certainly by the day after. But it is important I do nothing illegal. I am willing to pay you a fee to ensure that does not happen, say five percent of the total purchase of any cargo I buy…but only after it is safely loaded on board, you understand."

"Of course, of course. In silver and gold?" Grant was already licking his lips.

"In guilders or florins."

"Either denomination will be acceptable. And I am honored to act as your agent."

"I will need a carriage to take me to Lord VanderMeer."

"We can take my carriage. It is waiting on the street at the foot of the pier."

Henri kept working during these discussions, securing the main deck with the rest of the crew, keeping one eye on Captain LaTour, overhearing only bits of the conversation.

It was a long way to the foot of this pier. So the plan was for Henri to go with the cooks to purchase food and provisions. Once Henri got into the city, he would try to locate a man named Robert Butcher.

Governor Drucour had told Captain LaTour and Henri all he knew about the man before they left Louisbourg.

"He is a baker, forty-five years old and well-known for his cakes and pastries. His parents were Acadian and fled to the province of Maine over twenty years ago to escape the Malécites Indian raids. He grew up there. Came to Boston when he was fifteen, in between the wars, and learned the baker's trade. His messages are coded with the word Parliament. His

Acadian name is Robért Boucher. That is all I know, except he has access to valuable military intelligence."

"Are there others in Boston who might help me find him?"

"He is our only *spy in the Massachusetts province. All the others have been captured and killed."*

A baker. Henri pondered the governor's words as he cinched up the rigging lines. There were dozens of bakers in Boston, but somehow this one was able to collect information on English military strategies. That might help in finding him. *Maybe he sold his goods to the English or the provincial government?*

Henri gave Governor Drucour his word that he would complete his mission before he had any contact with Lord VanderMeer. For now, it was Captain LaTour's task to learn the location of Corrinne and if she was still safe.

The customs officers popped up the forward hatch after inspecting the length of the ship with Victorio. No scowls or frowns. So far so good.

The customs officers returned to Captain LaTour.

Mr. Jennings' expression was puzzled. "Your ship is quite empty, Captain LaTour. After coming all this way? I find that surprising. There's no profit in that."

"I am a merchant-trader, Mr. Jennings. You point out a condition of which I am well aware. But my vessel is *owned* by Lord VanderMeer. And because he is the heir to the Duchy of Brunswick, my vessel though family ownership is also at the service of the Dutch Republic. His father, the Duke of Brunswick, has paid me for this crossing to deliver his mail. I do not attest these royal influences to be obnoxious to you. It is simply the truth of how I come to be here. The ship's lack of cargo is of great concern to me. And I am very interested in filling my holds with goods to take back to Amsterdam…if that is permitted. I want to purchase certain goods and sell them again in Amsterdam. That will be the profit of my voyage."

"Yes, yes," interjected Samuel Grant. "All taken care of, Mr. Jennings. I will intercede with the proper authorities and see what can be done to grant Captain LaTour's request in that regard. So is Captain LaTour free to begin his business?"

"I have no reason to delay him further. A pleasure to meet you again, Captain. I am right over there." He pointed at a prominent building on the waterfront. "That is the Boston port authority. It controls all movements in this harbor. If I can be of any further service...you will find me there."

The customs officer handed LaTour a document of clearance.

"Excellent. Thank you, Mr. Jennings, Mr. Brown. If you please, Mr. Grant, come below and enjoy some refreshments while I collect my dispatches and give instructions to my crew."

Victorio walked behind them down to the captain's dining cabin.

"Captain Jaager, entertain Mr. Grant for me. I will not be gone long."

There was coffee and tea available, plus a plate of bread and a small block of very hard yellow cheese, mottled with a whitish-green mold. They took a seat together.

"That cheese looks rather...rancid?" Mr. Grant observed.

"It's not rancid. Simply aged on the surface. We've been at sea for a few months. Allow me," said Captain Jaager. He took his bayonet knife and cut a little off every side of the block. "There. Perfectly fresh. You have to treat cheese like new fruit with a thick skin."

"The bread is stale."

Captain Jaager grinned. "Put sugar in your tea and dip the bread into the brew...Taaa daa! Sailor's sweetbread, if you will allow."

Captain LaTour went aft to find Henri with the cook and three other men. He spoke to them in a hushed voice and explained the arrangements he made for the cook to purchase supplies.

"You have your money?" he asked the cook.

The man patted the purse hanging at his belt.

"Good. Buy the crew something good to eat tonight. Give a gratuity to your guards when you return...five percent at least, but no more than ten, and as you judge their service deserves. Henri, learn what you can but rejoin with the cook to return to the ship. Don't do anything reckless," he said sternly.

"I know. And you should all call me Thom Linden now. T-h-o-m. I am Belgian. Don't forget."

The cook smirked. "We are smugglers, *Thom*. We never forget."

Captain LaTour got the dispatches. The letters meant for Lady Corrinne he tucked inside his coat pockets. He took up another purse filled with guilders and florins and tied it inside his pants and then went back to the dining cabin. He found them having tea.

"Ah! I am all ready," he remarked and patted the dispatch satchel. "But no hurry. Finish your tea. I will have a cup with you."

"So we are cleared to come and go as we like?" Captain Jaager asked the captain.

LaTour nodded and gave Captain Jaager the customs document. "Please take this. You keep it in case anyone else should ask. But…" The captain quickly explained what he had expressed to Samuel Grant.

"If I am safe to ride in your carriage, Samuel, then I will leave Captain Jaager in charge of the ship until I return…just for the first day," he assured at seeing Victorio's disappointment, which was all part of the deceit. "I am ready to depart, sir," LaTour announced. "Captain Jaager, you have command. The cooks will soon be met with a hand lorry and a marine guard, who will escort them somewhere and assist the purchase of fresh stores for the ship. *No one else goes ashore*…not today anyway. Would that be your advice, Mr. Grant?"

"Yes. Once I make my reports to the council and the military, it is probably not safe for them to be walking around the waterfront. Some of your crew speak French, yes?"

"Yes, but I assure you, it stops there. They are common sailors. More at home at sea than on land. Except for when the sirens of drink and women call to them."

They all laughed.

Samuel Grant's carriage was open and uncomfortable in the constant drizzle and windy cold.

"Sorry for this, Captain. I will bring a closed carriage when I retrieve you."

"It's all right. Sea captains are used to being wet. When we reach Lord VanderMeer's home, I may be there for several hours. He will have questions for me after reading his mail. I presume I will wait for you there, and when you return, if I am not delayed, maybe we can go to Faneuil Hall even this afternoon?"

"Yes. Good. The afternoons are always better at Faneuil. Your presence today will give us time to fan some interest. And we can return again in the morning before the hall is open to anyone else. Maybe even hold a bidding caucus? You state what you want to buy and they bid for your business."

The carriage clopped up to the house front. LaTour saw marines guarding the house.

"That guardhouse looks permanent."

"Yes, after what happened before, the marines felt responsible since the killers wore marine uniforms. Lord VanderMeer graciously pays them a gratuity. And since Lady VanderMeer returned, they've doubled the guard."

Returned! LaTour was stunned to hear that. He quickly gathered his thoughts to pretend knowledge of this.

"I knew she was given a fast ship. How long has she been back?"

"About four months now, I think. Of course, there have been other problems…"

"What other problems? We've heard of no other problems!"

"Then I am sorry to be the first to tell you. There was an attempt to burn down their house. That man was killed. Someone also attempted to poison Lord VanderMeer, but ended up killing one of his guards instead."

"*Mon Dieu*! And Lady VanderMeer and her children?"

"They are all fine, Captain."

LaTour spoke with gravity. "Then the assassins are still at work here in the city. The Duke will be very unhappy to hear that."

"We've taken great precautions to protect Lord and Lady VanderMeer," Samuel Grant said quickly. "As a show of our allegiance and their importance to Boston and continued residency, I have introduced a bill in our council to permit four trading ships from the Dutch Republic to visit us and conduct trading. It still needs approval by the crown. No import goods permitted, only export. But American goods are finely made. This trade alliance will show how much the provinces value the friendship of the Dutch Republic. The *William's Queen* is an obvious choice as one of these ships."

Captain LaTour had a practiced ear against deceit. The man was trying to be gracious and opportunistic at the same time. LaTour answered him with a lie.

"The Duke asked me to learn if such an opportunity could be negotiated in the Americas. He thought if not Boston, then maybe New York. There is a large population of Dutch in New York, you see."

"No, no, Captain. We will have the crown's approval for this special trade privilege any day now. Boston is the right seaport for this trade. You will see." Grant looked up at the VanderMeer residence. "And I see someone looking at us from the window."

"I'd better go," LaTour said quickly. "I will await your knock, Mr. Grant. Thank you."

The marine guards stopped the captain's approach and searched the dispatch satchel for weapons. They took LaTour's ceremonial sword, saying he would have it returned when he left.

Captain LaTour stood before the door and moved to knock when it was thrown open. Corrinne's eyes shone with happiness and relief. She dragged him inside so they could shut the door.

"Beauregard! *Beauregard*! God has answered all my prayers. You are here! Your ship is here?"

"Yes, my lady. At the head of the Long Wharf, like before." His eyes, too, were wet. His voice choked a little as he said, "I am so relieved to see you again. And the little ones are well?"

"Oh, yes. They are asleep upstairs. Oh, God, Beauregard! It is so good to see you. You bring us mail?"

"I do, indeed. For you and Lord VanderMeer."

"Oh, Charles is at his office." Corrinne flung open the door and ran out to the guardhouse. She gave one of the marines a silver piece and asked him to fetch Lord VanderMeer. "Tell him Captain LaTour has arrived."

When she came back, she took him into the library where both Dian and Molly had gathered.

"Dian, bring refreshments," Corrinne directed.

"Miss Molly, you look as big as a ship-of-the-line!" La Tour boomed.

Holding a hand to her bulging waist, she smiled. "That's because I have a large cannonball in here, I think. Which may drop at any moment."

"And Captain Martyn?"

"Before you ask, he is the father...and we are married, as we should be. He will be here for dinner later."

Dinner? God's balls! LaTour thought with panic. "That is so wonderful," he lied.

Corrinne tugged impatiently at his coat. "Mail?"

LaTour decided to wait until Lord VanderMeer came to tell them anything about Archbishop Nicolet. He reached into his coat pocket and gave her both of Philippe's letters.

Corrinne's hands trembled as she clasped the letters to her chest. "He is well?" she managed to ask.

"Yes, my lady. I sat and spoke to him at length when I was in Montréal. I will tell you more about that when you are ready."

She made a sound of relief and hugged him tightly. She left the library in a hurry to read the letters in the privacy of her bedroom.

LaTour sat down in a leather chair and sighed, feeling wearied. Dian brought him hot coffee, a glass of brandy, and a plate of sweetbreads.

He stood and bowed to her. "*Bonjour*, Miss Dian. All of these things are luxuries to me."

"Your presence brings us cheer. You deserve the luxury." She kissed his cheeks.

"And Sergeant Cheever?"

"Oh…he will come by soon enough. And he will hurry when he learns of your arrival. Everyone is anxious for news of Philippe. And Henri, in particular." She nodded towards the doorway.

LaTour turned to see Anamosa standing shyly in the doorway to the *cuisine*. He was startled at how tall she was. Nearly a foot taller since he saw her last. Her hair was braided in a long strand hanging to her waist. Her dark blue eyes were wide with hope. She'd just run down the stairs and was breathing heavily, more from excitement than from exertion.

Captain LaTour spread open his arms. She ran to him and they hugged one another tightly.

"*Oh, mon amour petite! Mon amour petite!* Look at how much you have grown!"

"Henri?!"

"Oh…Henri. Yes. I saw him. He said to tell you hello."

"*Hello*! That's all? Hello?"

"No…he said that he loves you too! And he misses you!"

Anamosa was heartbroken. "No…no letter!?"

LaTour would have trouble deceiving her. Her skills in language and nuance had improved too. Simple explanations would not be enough anymore.

"Anna, I have more mail aboard the ship. Sometimes when I see a missive with *Anamosa* written on it, I think it is for Captain Martyn's ship. So I will go back today and search again to see if there is a letter for you. In fact, I remember seeing one with your name on it. So Henri did write to you. Don't worry. I will find it."

"Captain LaTour!"

It was Lord VanderMeer in the open double doors leading to the library.

"My Lord VanderMeer!" He stood and bowed and then they slapped each other's arms and embraced. They did not see Anamosa slip from the library, tears clouding her eyes.

"You've come at a *most* opportune time."

"I have many, many things to tell you, too. But first, I think the mail is appropriate." LaTour pulled out some letters for him. "There is a lot more in the satchel. One of them is a double envelope, I think it may be from your father, but it was sent by Naval Minister Machault. I will leave the dispatch pouch with you. I will visit with Dian in the *cuisine*. I've not eaten anything decent in over a month."

"Where's Corrinne?"

"She is up in her room. I brought letters for her, too, from Philippe."

Lord VanderMeer smiled sadly. Without intending to, Charles had fallen in love with Corrinne. He'd never told her this, of course. He knew her heart would never be his.

"Good. Corrinne needs this long-awaited joy. And forgive me, Captain, for my rudeness as I will excuse myself to read the mail. You are staying for dinner, of course?"

"Of course." He did not want to explain about Samuel Grant. Not yet.

Anamosa heard Corrinne weeping in her bedroom. She wiped away her own tears and went in to see her.

Corrinne was reading Philippe's first letter again. The second letter was intentionally vivid. She stopped reading it after only one paragraph and placed it inside the drawer of the side table to enjoy later after she went to bed.

"Anamosa? What's wrong?" Corrinne held out her arms.

Anamosa rushed to take comfort from her. She started weeping again.

"Ohh, my baby, don't cry." Corrinne kissed her cheeks and forehead. "What is wrong?"

"There was no letter for me...no letter from Henri."

Corrinne felt Anamosa's pain like a stab to the heart, as if Captain LaTour had only brought mail from Archbishop Nicolet to read.

"Ohh, baby. Is that what the captain said?"

"He said there may be a letter he forgot to bring from the ship. One that had my name on it. But I don't believe him. Letters are too important. He would not have forgotten. He only just said that."

Corrinne hugged her even tighter. "Captain LaTour spoke the truth. He would *never* promise such a thing unless it was the truth."

Not if he knows what's good for him, she thought testily. *He better bring her back a letter, even if he has to write it himself.*

Corrinne started humming a nameless lullaby she'd hummed to Anamosa so many times before, knowing it would soothe her. Several seconds went by before Anamosa spoke again.

"I saw the white eagle."

Corrinne stopped humming. "What did you say?"

"I saw the white eagle."

"The white eagle! Where? When?"

Anamosa told her what happened. "Then it just flew away."

"Those were the exact words? *Give the amulet to Henri?*"

Anamosa nodded. "Yes."

*

Henri pushed the hand lorry with another crewman. Two marines were assigned to them along with a sergeant who was pleased that Henri spoke English.

"So you are from Belgium?"

"I am. The ship is not. It's from Amsterdam. And I am not really from Belgium anymore. My life belongs to the sea. I've been aboard one merchant vessels or another since I was ten. My parents were killed by the pox while I was at sea. That was seven years ago. When I came back, all of their possessions had been stolen. I had nothing left there. So I sailed with fishermen out of Amsterdam for a while. That's a hard life. I finally joined Captain LaTour's crew when he visited there from the Antilles Islands. Have been with him ever since."

"How did you learn English?'

"Most people in Amsterdam, Brussels, or Antwerp speak English. Some of us better than others. But we also speak some French, Spanish, and a little German due to all the trading ships that cross the narrow channel. When there is no war, of course. I've spoken English since I was a boy but never very well."

The sergeant snorted. "It's well enough for me. That is the city commissary just ahead. They will have anything you want."

The cook left one man with the lorry so it would not be taken by someone else. There were many market stalls. Henri offered to speak for the cook.

"They might not try to cheat us so much."

They bought seven twenty-pound sacks of flour, a side of beef, green beans, squash, and other vegetables, each time carrying the food back to the lorry. Fresh cream, butter, eggs, chickens, a round of cheese, and bacon.

Henri asked the sergeant if they sold pastries anywhere in the commissary.

"In the commissary? No. The King's Bakery is up the street. They have such things."

"Do you mind if I go and see?"

"No. If you think you won't get lost, go ahead."

"Just wait for me by the commissary door where we came in," Henri told the cook.

Henri knew exactly where the King's Bakery was located. He moved at a fast pace up the street and away from the docks. This bakery had a painted façade, a hanging sign, double doors, and all the markings of a store that sold expensive goods. It was also crowded with customers. There were all sorts of pies and cakes and round sweetbreads. Large muffins of some type with sugary glazes. Chocolate-filled bread rolls. Various cakes decorated for specific celebrations.

Henri hung back to watch and listen to what customers said, what they bought, and how much they paid for it. He spotted two cakes he decided to buy. A simple white cake with a chocolate frosting and another one with pecans on the top with a white, frosted glaze.

Finally, it was his turn. In his best Boston accent he asked for the two cakes. The man behind the counter nodded and placed both of them on the counter.

"Can you give me something to carry them both, so I don't crush one into the other?"

The man nodded again. He pulled out a tall box made of split pine wood slats. It had wooden spacers inside to keep the cakes separated.

"You have to pay for the box, too," he warned.

"All right. How much?"

"Who has your account?"

"No one. I will pay in coin."

"Coin?" The baker was surprised. "What type?"

"Guilders or florins…silver."

The baker held up two fingers. "That includes the box."

Henri discreetly withdrew two pieces from his belt purse and handed them to the baker. The price was probably twenty times more than what he should charge, but Henri wanted to get more out of this transaction.

The man bit the coins for appearances' sake. As he carefully crated the cakes, Henri asked the question.

"Is Robert Butcher here?"

The baker continued what he was doing. "Who wants to know?"

"My name is Thom Linden. I was told he worked here."

"He does, but he's gone for a few days. Why?"

Henri shrugged. "I am looking for work. I'm a baker."

"You? A baker! What do you bake?"

Henri spoke humbly. "Nothing too fancy like this. Mostly round loaves and a few sweetbreads."

"Where did you get all that silver?"

"Earned it. I cook aboard a merchant vessel."

"Which one?"

"*William's Queen*. It's here in port. But cooking at sea is hard work. Thought I might try to work on shore for a while. A marine sergeant recommended this bakery."

The baker was now thinking about that purse of silver and how he might separate more of it from this rather naïve sailor.

"Have you ever baked a cake?"

"A few. But nothing like these."

Then you can be taught, he decided. If he could influence the man's hire, maybe he could earn a private fee?

"Well, Mr. Butcher is in Albany just now. He is expected back day after tomorrow. Come back around then. But he's probably not going to hire you. You won't have the experience for this type of shop. I might be able to influence him to give you a chance."

"I would appreciate your help…um…What's your name?"

"David."

"My thanks, David. I will see you in a couple days."

Henri went back to the commissary and added the cakes to the lorry. They had enough food for several days now. Back at the ship, the cook paid the sergeant and his two men a five percent gratuity. More than they expected. The sergeant said he would help them again. Word of their generosity spread.

Henri spoke to the cook. "I must learn how to bake a cake."

"You just bought two cakes."

"I know, but now I have to learn how to make one on my own."

*

Captain Conor Martyn scanned the Dutch ship moored at the head of the Long Wharf with his watch glass scope. His conscience was in turmoil about what to do. LaTour had taken his ship into Louisbourg harbor and then came to Boston. He should report it to the authorities. But they would seize the ship, jail the crew, and might even hang the captain. Not to forget what this would mean for Lord and Lady VanderMeer. The results were bad for everyone involved or related.

And his own Molly, too.

That thought clinched it. Conor was not reporting anything to anyone! But he was going to find out what Captain LaTour was doing…privately. *Tonight, after dinner.*

*

Brest, France

Alain Marcoux was standing on the deck of the *Concorde* with his baggage in hand as it entered the harbor of Brest, France. The night messenger had told him to find a way to get to Berlin as quickly as possible. But he was not sailing on any more ships. That was about all he had done for the last three months and now he was exhausted from dysentery, spoiled food, and sea sickness. His clothes hung from him from the loss of so much weight.

Once ashore, he purchased overland coach passage to Paris and then hired a series of other coaches as necessary to carry him all the way to Berlin. By the time he arrived two weeks later, he never wanted to ride in another coach either.

About the same time Marcoux reached Berlin, word reached Brest that Archbishop Andre Nicolet, the Jesuit Intendant of New France, was murdered in Montréal by conspirators. The report from Francois Bigôt, the Intendant of New France, named Captain Beauregard LaTour, Master of the *Falcon Queen*, and Alain Marcoux as the conspirators.

The reaction of the French elite to Archbishop Nicolet's death was one of utter disbelief that such a thing could happen. Among the elite of the government and the military were Naval Minister Machault and Admiral de la Motte, the men who had personally sent the accused conspirators to New France on a *mission* sanctioned by them both. Though Paris and Rochefort were three hundred miles apart, their reactions were exactly the same.

Preposterous!

The accused men were ostensibly on their way back to France, claimed the intendant's report. The Catholic Church assigned an inquisitor to question them after they were apprehended.

*

Samuel Grant knocked on Lord VanderMeer's front door and removed his hat when Molly answered.

"Hello, Mr. Grant."

"My goodness, Miss Molly! Should you even be standing up?"

She opened the door wider so he could step inside out of the cold. "The doctors claim it will help the baby come sooner."

"This is your first child?"

She felt a sharp pang at the memory of her first child, who had died while still in her womb. "Yes, this is my first."

"Who's there?" Lord VanderMeer called. "Oh, hello, Mr. Grant. You're here for Captain LaTour?"

"Indeed, your lordship. We are going to visit Faneuil Hall. The captain expressed an interest in buying some of Boston's fine products to take back with him to Amsterdam. Oh, hello, Captain. My compliments, Lady Vander-Meer. You bring warmth and light to this drizzly, cold day. Am I too early?"

LaTour came to the door with Lady Corrinne on his arm.

"No. I plan to come back here at seven for dinner, but I have time to visit your emporium. I must also check on my ship before going ashore for the night."

Dian helped the captain with his overcoat and hat.

Captain LaTour shook Lord VanderMeer's hand and embraced Lady VanderMeer.

"Until tonight then."

After the captain left, Corrinne and Charles went back to the library to discuss what they learned and to talk of things they did not want to say in front of Captain LaTour.

"Philippe is well, I hope?"

Worry marred Corrinne's face. "He is heavily involved with the fighting. He goes next to Fort Carillon on Lake Champlain. When he was held captive by the Oneida, before they would let him go, he was forced to run the gauntlet twice! Twice! Without stopping! He was scarred so horribly before, I can only imagine how he looks now. Philippe did not get a chance to see Henri, missed him by only two weeks, but knows he is in Louisbourg. Captain LaTour will take our letters to him! I can write to Philippe! They send mail from Louisbourg to Quebec City.

"Pierre Dunemoore and Juniata had a baby girl with red hair! Her name is Kateri. Can you imagine Pierre as a father? I've not read Henri's letter yet. And you?"

"I received a thick missive from Naval Minister Machault, which was really covering a missive from my father, the Duke. It's a long letter, but he commanded me to return to Amsterdam to discuss my abdication…and he wants me to bring the children. He wants to meet all of you."

Corrinne was definitely *not* going to Amsterdam or anywhere else in Europe for many different reasons. But she was sensitive of Charles' feelings and was uncertain what to say.

"What do you think?"

"I don't know what to think. I knew this day would come. General Hollenberg warned me it would. But with war declared, I did not think it would be so soon. I do not want to go back."

"Then don't!" Corrinne said too quickly. "I'm sorry."

"No. Don't be sorry. You will not be going back no matter what I decide. Marcus and Calypso will be in danger if they are taken to Amsterdam. They are in danger here too, but at least here we have friends. Over there…we could trust only my father. And he cannot protect us all the time."

A silence ensued as Charles deliberated what to do. Corrinne did not press him to say anymore.

"Well, I have to send a letter back to the Duke with Captain LaTour. But I do not have to write that today." The Duke had actually ordered Charles to sail back with Captain LaTour…*and bring my grandchildren with you.* He did not mention Corrinne's name even once, suggesting he did not care if the mother came at all. Charles changed the subject. "Archbishop Nicolet's letter was very complimentary of Philippe and even more so of Henri. He has grown evidently."

"Henri was decorated for valor…twice," Corrinne said, shaking her head. "That means he puts himself in danger…just like his father. Archbishop Nicolet probably told us both the same things. I miss that man. His intelligence. His wise counsel. I hope to see him again when this war is over."

"Machault's note to me indicated he thought this war would go on for another three years, at least. It all depends on France's ability to win battles. Right now, they are winning all of them. But Machault is not optimistic. He does not think England will ever ask for peace. Not this time. He learned the English are sending more troops to America. And with the addition of the American's provincials, it will be difficult for New France to withstand their combined numbers."

There was a knock at the front door. Charles got up and looked out.

"It's Captain Martyn."

Corrinne clapped her hands. "Good. This will be a happy dinner for all of us, with both our favorite captains here together."

*

Captain LaTour was offered the use of the closed carriage by Samuel Grant after they left Faneuil Hall.

"Don't worry about me, Captain. I can hail several from here. So tomorrow morning, I will meet you right here at ten?"

"Yes. That was a lot of excitement I saw today. And the amount of different goods there is to buy! It's extraordinary. I think there's more here than in England. I had no idea. I am surprised you do not send your ships everywhere."

Samuel Grant laughed. "Ah, yes. That is a topic for another day. A very private topic."

LaTour had the driver take him to the foot of the Long Wharf. He paid the driver and asked that he wait.

"I will be at least an hour, but I will hire you for the rest of the night and probably even further after that."

LaTour walked quickly up the pier, which seemed much longer than the last time he was there. It was full of only English or American ships. Once LaTour reached his ship, he tilted his hat to the four marine guards. They had already erected a sleeping tent for four men, with two men standing guard at all times.

Victorio met him at the top of the brow. "Glad to see your safe return, Captain. Everything is well here. There is good food cooking below. I had no doubt you would come back. But I always have this vexing apprehension our first night in every port, particularly when it is an enemy port, yes? Which seems to be almost every other port we visit these last few years."

"Stop your worry. We are Dutch! The English love the Dutch, and the Americans have agreed to let us buy cargo!"

"At what prices?"

"Does not matter. We just keep tally on what we've bought and what we've paid, and the French government will reimburse us, since the cargo will all be given over to Louisbourg. I will go to Faneuil Hall at ten in the morning to select the goods. You can go with me as my military attaché. Now, where is Henri?"

"Down below, eating with the crew."

"Find him, and send him to my cabin. I don't have much time. I am eating dinner with Lord and Lady VanderMeer tonight. I will be back by midnight I presume."

Henri knocked on the captain's door.

"Come in, Henri. Sit. Speak quietly and tell me what happened today."

Henri did.

"So not tomorrow but the next day you will meet with him."

"Hopefully, that is the plan. I am going to try to work there to learn to make cakes. How are Corrinne and Anamosa?"

"They are both well and very happy to see me. But I did not mention anything about you. Not until your mission is complete. Anamosa has grown almost a foot since I saw her last and is more beautiful than ever. She wept very large tears you did not write to her."

"But I am going to see her!"

"She does not know that yet! Her heart is broken. She thinks you have forgotten all about her. I am going back there for dinner tonight, and I promised to bring Anamosa a letter from you, one that I'd forgotten to bring today. So that is an order. Go write this letter. *Make it a good one.* All you can write in an hour. Write a lot. Make sure to you tell her you love and miss her. Then seal it in wax."

"Of course I love and miss her."

"Really? How would she know? Hurry, please."

*

Carter Trevathan waved Jimmy Cantlin to his stall and gave the boy some coinage to get them both something to eat. Their relationship was two days old, and it was working out better than he had expected. The magistrate's deputy standing nearby usually read a newspaper and hardly took notice of the boy.

Using Jimmy's cheap, fast, and dependable services, Carter had successfully sent a sealed missive to Caroline using Rachel as the go between. And Caroline had responded back through her sister and Jimmy. She was ready to do her part; all he need do was specify a day and a time. A separate note to Rachel directed her to contact Ritter Monheit on her own and deliver a second missive, outlining his role. Ritter responded he was ready.

Carter explained what he was going to do in his dreams to the night messenger. In a rare occurrence, the night messenger invaded the dreams of Caroline, Rachel, and Ritter, though only briefly, to instill fear in them to obey.

Then *William's Queen* arrived unexpectedly. Carter put things on hold until he understood how this might affect the plan. The level and amount of security around the VanderMeers expanded, almost doubling. Deputy Magistrate Jack Tasker was involved in detailing more men. But an extra day of surveillance of Lord VanderMeer's office by Ritter Monheit revealed not much had changed. Lord VanderMeer was in there with a single guard. The stone cutter also ensured that a stave on the back fence of the house was loosened as before. This would be used as a back-up. But the next day, Lord VanderMeer did not go into his office. Nor did he go in the day after that. Lord VanderMeer's location was the key piece to this new plan's success.

Another day would pass. No change. Carter decided to shift the point of messaging to the Penny Surgeon hospital. Caroline would join her sister as a volunteer at this medical shelter for several days. Ritter was told by Rachel to go by VanderMeer's office every morning. The very next time he found Lord VanderMeer in his office, Ritter would come to the Penny Surgeon before thirty minutes past the hour of ten and inform Rachel that VanderMeer was vulnerable. Rachel would send a message through Jimmy.

Carter and twelve-year-old Jimmy Cantlin shared a bowl of hot molasses beans, pork, and buttered bread. He'd learned that Jimmy had no parents. He shared a shack off the waterfront with his sister. She was a prostitute and sometimes brought men home with her at night. He slept in a small closet and covered his head with her old dresses to muffle the noises. *But it's not too bad*, he had offered. *It's my place to sleep and she feeds me at least once a day.*

Jimmy shoveled the hot food into his mouth as if someone lurked nearby, ready to steal it.

"Do you like Miss Rachel, Jimmy?"

"Oh, yes. She is always nice to me. She combs my hair, and even washes my face and hands. I get them dirty sometimes just so she will touch me a lot!" the boy confided.

"Tell you what. Let's do something nice for her. You stop by and see her at the Penny Surgeon at eleven every morning and ask if you might buy her some lunch. But don't tell her it's from me. Let her think it's from you. She will probably refuse at first. But ask her every day. And when she finally says yes, come see me here, and I will give you enough money to buy me something to eat and get her something too."

Jimmy's face brightened. "Oh, that would be great, Mr. Trevathan!"

"All right. But don't tell anybody else or you will ruin the surprise. It's our secret. You want her to believe it was only your idea. And I wager she'll treat you even better after that."

CHAPTER 28
BOSTON
SEPTEMBER 22, 1756
The Head of the Long Wharf

Captain LaTour came back to Lord VanderMeer's house early that evening. He was welcomed by Sentry Cheever at the door. The table in the dining room was already set. As soon as he was announced, Dian urged everyone to sit, that the dinner she prepared was ready. Both Dian and Molly would sit with the family that night. It was a special occasion.

Captain Martyn approached LaTour with a telling expression.

"Captain LaTour!" They shook hands. "You are looking very well. It's been over a year, and yet it seems like only a few weeks since I saw you last."

"I have a lot to tell you, Captain Martyn. But I do not want to bore everyone else. Let's talk later...*in private*."

Anamosa ran up to Captain LaTour and tugged on his coat. He could see hope in her eyes.

"*Bonsoir, mon amour petite.* Is there something you want? Oh, yes... maybe this?" LaTour withdrew a wax-sealed missive from inside his coat.

Anamosa held out her hands, accepting the letter as if it were a precious treasure.

Corrinne's heart was warmed as she watched Anamosa press the letter to her chest just as she had done when she received Philippe's letter. *Henri doesn't realize how deeply this girl loves him*, she thought.

Anamosa glanced at Corrinne and pointed at the ceiling. Corrinne nodded. Anamosa left to go up to her room.

"What is wrong?" LaTour asked, confused. "Is she not happy?"

"Yes. She is very happy. She wants to read the letter now and she wants to read it in private. Can you not tell?" *Men can be so stupid*, she thought.

Corrinne gestured at everyone. "If you please, let us take our seats. Captain LaTour, please sit on my right. Then Molly and Captain Martyn.

558

Leave this chair on my left for Anamosa. Then Dian and Sentry. Marcus in his chair next to me. Calypso next to Dian."

Once everyone was seated, they joined hands. Molly volunteered to say a prayer.

"Heavenly Father, we are grateful for thy bounty and that we share it tonight with Captain LaTour and Captain Martyn who live in danger every day on the seas, and for the generosity of Lord and Lady VanderMeer, and the beautiful innocence of our little children, Marcus and Calypso, and Anamosa…Oh! *Oh*…"

Corrinne spoke. "Anamosa will be down soon. She is—"

"Oh!" Molly's face tightened. "Oh, no! It's now! It's coming now!"

Those around the table erupted with excitement. Chairs were pushed back. Bent over from the pain, Molly was helped by Captain Martyn to Mathilde's room to lie down. Dian and Corrinne went with her. Charles ran outside.

"Miss Molly's baby is coming! Take Captain LaTour's carriage and fetch Dr. Angove."

As the other members of the household were occupied, Sentry sat between the two babies, kissed their foreheads, and then started feeding them mushy foods. He made soft sounds and short words of encouragement.

"Hulloo! My wee bairns! Uncle Sentry is here!"

LaTour took a chair on the other side of Marcus and picked up a spoon to feed the boy. Marcus took the spoon away from LaTour and scooped up some squash from the dish.

"Aha! You've done it, Marcus! Well done! Look Sentry! Who is the better teacher?"

Marcus smiled and threw a spoonful of yellow squash all over the front of LaTour's shirt.

"Ya' must be used tah' tha', Captain. Just pretend your ship is rocking."

Molly's labor would last close to three hours. Four men waited in the library, sipping brandy.

Dian suddenly came into the room.

"Dr. Angove said to tell Captain Martyn that if he wants to see his baby being born, now is the time to come."

"See it born! Is it proper to do such a thing?" Conor Martyn asked, directing his question to Charles.

"Of course it is. She is your wife. To see a baby being born is a miracle. You should go."

Conor looked at Sentry.

"I've seen three bairns born aboard ship. It is something I will never forget. Go on with ya'."

He looked at LaTour.

"I have seen it more times than I can count. I helped deliver two of them."

Conor Martyn drank the rest of his brandy. He stood, took a deep breath, and followed Dian. After he was gone, Charles had to ask.

"Captain LaTour, did you really deliver two babies?"

LaTour shook his head. "Noo. Not once. Never even seen it. You?"

"No, I am ashamed, I lied. But I always wanted to see a baby being born. I wanted to do Captain Martyn a good turn. I hope he doesn't regret this. I will feel awful if he does. Sentry, were you telling the truth?"

"Nooh'! Never did witness it. It was forbidden where I grew up...only women, unless you were a healer."

"Oh, this is not good. This is *not* good. Conor will be angry with us," Charles worried.

LaTour shrugged. "Only if we tell him."

Sentry nodded as he poured himself more brandy. He raised his glass.

"Tha' is right. I say we make a gentleman's toast and agreement. We will swear never to reveal that we all lied." He laughed deeply.

Charles lifted his glass, swaying a little as he did so. "I guess that is the proper course. After all, we do not want to embarrass him. Yes? Here, here."

LaTour followed. They downed the brandy.

LaTour assumed a brooding expression. "I've heard it is all quite messy."

Sentry nodded. "Yes. As bloody as a bayonet charge...so I've been told." He kept one eye on Lord VanderMeer who appeared squeamish. "A lot more screaming though."

LaTour's brow furrowed. "I remember seeing a sheep born once when I was a boy." He gestured with his hands. "This entire little animal started—"

Charles was aghast. "Gentlemen, please! I beg you! Let's talk of something else!"

Dr. Gordon Angove: Medical Journal

Boston, Wednesday, September 22, 1756

Conor Gwyn Martyn II. Born: An hour before midnight. Weight: 8 pounds, 5 ounces. Brown hair and dark eyes. Ten fingers, ten toes. No infirmities noted. The mother's pregnancy was normal. She carried well and labored less than three hours. Father was present for the birth. Vapors of ammonia salts were needed only once.

*

Everyone was exhausted by midnight. The women for certain. Corrinne and Dian, with Sentry's help, moved a small single bed into the room with Molly so Captain Martyn could sleep with her and the baby. There was a bassinette cradle nearby.

Sentry went to sleep in a servant's room across the hall. Dian would later slip under the covers with him.

Captain LaTour went back to the ship.

The dinner was left uneaten and cold on the table. Dian had put Marcus and Calypso to bed during the labor.

Corrinne went up to sleep at midnight. She checked on Marcus and Calypso. Then she took a seat on Anamosa's bed. Anamosa was asleep. One of her hands rested on the letter from Henri, which lay on the pillow by her head. Corrinne tenderly caressed her hair. She was so happy Henri had written Anamosa a letter.

"He loves you," she whispered. "Dream of him. You will see him again. You'll see."

It was what Corrine whispered to herself about Philippe every night before she went to sleep.

"And you have to give him the amulet," she whispered. "As the white eagle said."

*

Two days later, Thom Linden went to the King's Bakery in the afternoon. The crew of the *William's Queen* were now allowed up and down the pier but had been advised to stay near the waterfront. The bakery was a few blocks removed from the foot of the Long Wharf. No one seemed to pay him any attention. He was just another laborer going to work.

As usual, the pastry shop was full of customers. Henri hung back until he caught David's eye, then he raised his hand and mouthed *hello*. David signaled with one finger he should wait. When he finished with that customer he went into the back of the shop.

"The lad I told you about is back again."

Robert Butcher was stirring a pot of thick cake batter; his face and hands were covered in flour.

"I told you, we do not need another baker."

"He seems like a decent boy. Claims he can bake cakes already. Just talk to him for a minute."

Butcher eyed his assistant suspiciously. "All right. What's in this for you?"

"Well, he carries a silver purse. If you hire him, I'll convince him he owes me a fee."

"At least you're an honest thief. I will give him five minutes, no more."

David went to the front and signaled Thom Linden to head to the back of the store.

Henri saw the master baker laboring over a stirring bowl. They were alone. Henri waited patiently until the man poured the bowl's contents into a circular pan, opened up the oven door, and slipped the pan inside. He wiped the flour from his hands and turned.

"Well, go ahead. David says I should listen to you. Talk to me."

"Can we be overheard?"

"What? No."

"*Parliament.*" Henri said the word softly.

The baker frowned and reached slowly for a knife.

"Beau Sarchet and his ship were lost in a storm," Henri said in the same low tone. "We never received your last missive. I was sent to make contact with you."

The baker asked softly in French, "Where are you from?"

"Louisbourg."

They began to speak in French.

"They sent a boy?"

"I am a marine."

"What is my name?"

"Robért Boucher. You are Acadian. From the province of Maine."

"I will have to encode another message," he said. "That will take a couple days."

Henri smiled to put him at ease. "So hire me. I will learn to bake cakes for a few days. Then you can fire me for incompetence."

"If I learn you are lying, I will gut you," he said this in English.

"I am not lying. And New France needs your missive."

"When can you start?"

"Today…right now!"

He pointed. "Hang your coat back there on a hook. Scrub your hands, arms, and face in the basin. And put on one of those aprons."

David was surprised but elated that Robert had taken a chance on the boy. He hit Henri up for two pieces of silver right away.

"I vouched for you, Thom. He only saw you as a favor to me."

As Henri was leaving the shop that evening, he gave David two silver guilders.

"Thank you, lad. You will like working here. We have hundreds of customers. You will learn a lot from Robert. I sure have. He is the best baker I've ever known. And you won't believe some of the sweeties we have coming in those doors every day. A few of them ask for *personal* deliveries…if you know what I mean."

"No, I don't know what you mean."

David frowned. *Idiot*, he thought. "You'll see. Congratulations, you've survived one day. Tomorrow morning then?"

Henri walked down the Long Wharf with his hands in his pockets. The rain had turned to sleet. His nose was dripping as he reached the ship. A guard stopped him but let him pass after a nod from the ship's watch on deck.

In the dining cabin, the cook brought him a tray of beef cooked rare in a marinated sauce of wine and cream with vegetables, fresh bread, butter, and a slice of pecan cake.

"I saved this for you. Can you buy some more of these cakes tomorrow?"

"Of course. Where's the captain?"

"He is dining at the home of a city man. I cannot remember his name. The one he met the first day."

"Are you feeding the guards?"

"Yes. And they love my cooking. Unlike the rest of you *emmanchés*."

"And Victorio?"

"He's asleep. I will get him for you."

Victorio came into the dining cabin shivering and with a blanket wrapped around his shoulders.

"It's cold in the quarters."

"It's sleeting outside."

They shared information about what happened that day.

"So you have permanent work at the bakery after only an afternoon?"

"I am a good baker, evidently."

"All you know about cake is how to eat a slice of it."

"I'm learning. Do we have cargo?"

"Oh, yes. We will be full on our return. It will start arriving tomorrow."

"Sorry I will miss that. I have to be at the bakery at sunrise. Where is the captain?"

"He is eating with Samuel Grant tonight. He said to tell you that Molly had a baby boy. He was too drunk to tell you this last night."

"A baby boy! Good for Molly…I think. Who is the father?"

"Oh, that is the best part. The father is Captain Conor Martyn of the *Anamosa*."

"Oh, shit."

"Yes. A fact better expressed as *God's balls*, I believe."

"Well…if something bad was going to happen here, it would have happened by now."

"Only I get to say that."

*

Henri was awakened by the watch before sunrise. It was freezing. He dressed quickly, drank some hot coffee to warm himself, and left the ship for the long, icy, windy walk to the foot of the Long Wharf. He hurried up the streets to the back door of the bakery and knocked. Seconds later, it opened and Robert Butcher smiled.

"So you do get up early!"

"Am I late? I thought I was early or at least on time."

"No, you are on time. I stayed up half the night coding the new missive. There is new information to add. It will take me another day at least."

"Is David coming in too?"

"I let him sleep in. Told him I would see how you work out in the mornings. So let's get to work. Scrub your arms, hands, and face. Apron. And start pounding and rolling that bread dough. Watch how I do it. We need two loaves as fast as we can and then load them into the oven."

"This warmth feels good."

"It doesn't in the summer."

In about ten minutes, Henri was getting the rhythm of it. It was much harder than he expected. The rhythm was hard to keep when the loaves started coming out of the ovens. He was told to place the hot loaves into towel-lined baskets in the front and to cover them with more towels to hold the heat. He learned there would be a rush for bread three times a day. Robert could tell in the first hour after they opened if they needed to bake more and exactly how many. Most of the customers had standing bread orders, which Robert kept recorded in a book. When the required amount of loaves was either in the baskets or in the ovens, he immediately switched to making cakes and pastries.

"You mix the ingredients like this. These cups are exact measurements. This one is for flour. This one sugar. Two eggs. A bit of yeast. Half cup of butter. A cup of cream. A half cup of water. No more, no less. Then stir the batter. Sometimes we add plums or berries to it. Depends on what is available. Sometimes the customer brings me the fruit. But today just simple white cake. Just keep a bowl of batter whipped until I tell you to stop. Then I pour it in a pan like this…and into the oven like that. Almost in one motion. Leaves little time for settling so the ingredients do not separate. This way the cake bakes evenly and doesn't fall in the middle. Cakes are easier to make than bread, but then I have to decorate them. *That* is an art. The earlier I can start the decorating the more money I make each day. So your speed is important. Just whip up more batter until I say we're done."

Henri concentrated on what he was doing and the baker seemed to be satisfied. Only now and then did the baker ask a question in French.

"Where do you live?"

"I am garrisoned at Louisbourg, but I live in Montréal, mostly."

"Your Boston accent is strong. How's that?"

Henri shrugged. "I've been here before."

"In Boston?"

"It is safer for both of us if I keep to my original story. More importantly, safer for you. I am Thom Linden. I come from Belgium. I've been at sea for ten years. I am looking for a baker's job ashore."

"Yes...of course."

"We also need to work out a new chain of fishermen for delivering missives in the future. Do you have ideas on that?"

"You are certain Sarchet is dead?"

"The fishermen in Port-Toulouse claimed his boat went under in a storm."

"The fisherman I give the missive to here passes it to another fisherman in Canceau. I don't know that man."

"Can we learn where they rendezvous or how? Do they have certain signals? When I go back I can try to meet the man from Canceau by sailing out of Port-Toulouse."

"I will try to find out. Money might help."

"I'm willing to give you my whole belt."

"Not yet. Let me work on this. Learn to work faster as we talk. Mix another bowl of batter."

*

Carter Trevathan had Caroline start following Magistrate Tasker, to learn where he would be on different days at different times, watching for a pattern. She wore various disguises. Ritter Monheit followed him a few times and Rachel did the same, so he would not become suspicious. It seemed everything Tasker did was completely random. He did not even come to work at the same time or place on any given day. But by the third week, they finally determined that every Tuesday at the hour of one, he ate at a Mary's Restaurant on Hutchinson Street.

They had another piece of the plan. But this had a cost. It meant everything would have to be done on a Tuesday. It would be the only time they could count on knowing where the magistrate would be.

Jimmy repeatedly asked Rachel if he could buy her lunch and she kept refusing. He was becoming disappointed and told Carter he did not think she even liked him anymore.

"You cannot give up like that, Jimmy. Try this. Don't bother seeing her for three or four days. Miss Rachel will start missing you. You'll see. I will tell you when to try again."

*

Thomas Hancock called on Lord VanderMeer at his invitation. Captain LaTour was there too, as well as Lady VanderMeer. They sat down together at the dining table for more room. The captain talked about his trip to the Antilles and the ship's prolonged stay at Sint Eustatius.

"I made four copies of the tallies for you."

He passed them around. It was three times more profit than was made the previous year.

Corrine spoke first. "Are these figures correct?"

"They are." LaTour explained how the buying, trading, and selling was organized in the free port of Oranjestad. "I was there four months. I could have stayed longer, but the crew became anxious. I decided to come back before the storm season. I found another French trade ship to work for Vesper Grant and left for Amsterdam. Sold my cargo for an elevated profit after war was declared."

LaTour had changed his story because of Thomas Hancock's presence.

"I received the dispatch pouch from the Duke's agent. I left Amsterdam to make the crossing but was chased into the port of La Rochelle by English privateers. I could have been seized by the French just as easily for entering the port without permission, so I spent two months there getting the ship refitted for sea. Needing repairs was my excuse for entering the port. And the *Queen* needed this work. Those costs have been taken into account, including my shares and the shares of the crew. I arrived here empty of cargo. With Samuel Grant's help, the Boston council just gave special permission to fill my holds with Boston-produced goods."

He explained the special trade privileges for three Dutch ships now offered by Samuel Grant.

"He said it must be approved by the crown. But loading of the *Queen* is underway. I plan to go back to Amsterdam…less profit, but less danger. And continue trading this way unless you direct otherwise."

Corrinne spoke. "Do you know the whereabouts of *Ile Royale*? It's been gone two years."

"I've not seen her. She sails back and forth to the East Indies, according to the agent in Amsterdam. Those are long and dangerous voyages. There are pirates on every line of latitude along the way. If *Ile Royale* has not suffered a piracy fate, eventually it will. I'll not sail those waters, even armed with cannon. I think the years of elevated profit are over until the war ends."

Thomas Hancock shook his head. "Captain LaTour, I am surprised you brought this money back to us. Even I could be tempted by piracy. We cannot bring this quantity of coin ashore. Last time it was difficult. This time…well, does it even make sense to bring it ashore? I mean…in Boston?"

"God forbid, Mr. Hancock, but what if my ship sinks?"

"Would London be better?"

Charles looked at his friend. "Thomas, we may have enough funds in our own strong boxes to cover your share. Let us do that. Transfer by carriage from our house to yours will not be difficult. This does not solve the transfer from the ship, but as you suggest, maybe Boston is not the safest place to keep the VanderMeer fortune. Amsterdam, perhaps? It is neutral. If the proposed trade agreement between Boston and Amsterdam is approved by the crown, then Captain LaTour can bring your share once a year. This could be the best course for all of us. Corrinne?"

The English crown will never *allow such independent trade with the colonies to happen,* Corrinne thought. Samuel Grant's greed created an opportunity this time. But it was not guaranteed to happen again either. Corrinne was not enthusiastic.

"I agree with providing Thomas his share from our own funds. We can do that tomorrow. But I am less certain about having our own funds secured on the continent, be it London or Amsterdam. Using some of it as investment through Amsterdam banks, maybe. But the continent is too far away. An ocean away! Too many months away! Much can happen we cannot control. We need to think about this."

Captain Martyn approached from Mathilde's room down the hall.

Corrinne was immediately concerned. "Is Molly and Conor all right?"

"Yes, my lady. Apologies for interrupting, but Captain LaTour and I have an overdue conversation. I wanted to speak with him before he left today."

"We can do that now, if you like."

It provided an excuse for the meeting to end. Thomas Hancock congratulated Captain Martyn on the birth of his son.

"I will return tomorrow with my carriage as you suggested," he told Lord VanderMeer.

Once Hancock was gone, Captain LaTour faced everyone.

"Your lordship, my lady, what Captain Martyn wants to talk to me about is something you need to hear as well…and privately."

"The library then," Charles directed.

LaTour told them the same story he had related to Thomas Hancock, except for the part where he accepted a commission in the French navy.

"I was offered the choice of delivering stores and mail dispatches to Louisbourg, or having my ship seized. Captain Martyn knows which I chose to do since he chased me into that port."

Charles and Corrinne knew that was not the whole story but did not challenge anything. LaTour's purpose for this confession was to give Captain Martyn a chance to express anger, outrage, and most importantly, what he intended to do...if anything.

Charles spoke, pretending surprise and indignation. "But he was flying the flag of the Dutch Republic. Why would you give chase?"

"He was flying French colors!" Captain Martyn stated tersely. "It was my duty to fire upon you!"

"Please tell me you didn't do that, *did you*?" Corrinne asked.

"No, my lady. I did not do my duty. But if I see the French colors again, I will, the next time," Captain Martyn said firmly.

"You were flying the French flag?!" Charles demanded, pretending indignation.

"Your lordship, I was within the range of the Louisbourg shore batteries. I thought it prudent."

"You are *not* permitted to fly any flag except that of the Dutch Republic. Affirm to me, Captain, you will not do that again."

"Yes, your lordship. I so affirm," LaTour replied humbly.

"Good." Charles nodded. "It was an act of Providence this unfortunate incident did not become a tragedy. We should give thanks for that."

*

Henri Gerrard was rolling and kneading bread dough, keeping pace with Robert Butcher.

"I've brought the coded missive with me," Robert said quietly to Henri. David was in the front tending to the morning customers coming through the doors. "You should plan to leave at the noon hour and take it with you."

"And the man in Canceau?"

"The fisherman here in Boston does not want to do this any longer. Do not worry. He will not give me up, not even for money. New France needs to find another way."

"We should create a chain from the other direction. Have someone contact you?"

"That would be even more dangerous. It would be noticed."

"All right. I will tell the governor. I should do something to permit you to fire me, yes?"

Robert paused and thought about it. "Knock over that stack of cake pans. I will shout at you. I will grumble to David you are too clumsy to work in the confines of the bakery. That this was not your first time. At noon, you can stumble over a crate of eggs. A few of them are certain to break. And I will tell you politely that you have to go."

"Should I put the missive in my coat and do the pans now?"

Robert wiped his hands on a towel and went into the back of the bakery where the supplies were kept. He waved Henri to him and gave him the thick document.

Henri slipped the missive inside the lining of his coat. He walked over to the stack of cake pans and slapped it with a hand. The noise of the tin pans crashing to the floor was very loud.

"That's the third time you've done this, Thom! Wash them up!"

David stuck his head around the corner in surprise.

"What happened?" David whispered to Robert.

"He's done this three times. He's too clumsy. And this kitchen is too small."

"I thought he was working out," David said with disappointment. He liked sleeping until later in the morning.

"We'll see. Maybe he'll learn to be more careful."

*

Early the next morning, Corrinne and Charles worked side by side in the chill of the cellar to audit their funds. They set aside one strongbox with the proper amount for Thomas Hancock. It would amount to two-thirds of their hard coin. The box was heavy.

"We're not strong enough to lift this up the stairway," Charles decided. "I will send for Sentry and ask him to help. I don't want anyone else coming down here."

Corrinne opened the lid on another strong box. The five new silver amulets were inside it. Four with emerald gemstones, one with the slightly larger amethyst. Even in the lantern light, the burnished silver gleamed with beauty.

"What about the amulets?"

Charles looked at them and picked one up. "They are finished. But certain words must be said over them. *Indian words*."

The chill in the cellar seemed to increase.

"To even talk about this again is disturbing." Corrinne shivered and pulled the shawl more tightly around her shoulders.

"The problem is that Chittaqua said the words," Charles continued. "I cannot find that I've written them down anywhere. They are just jewelry without the words. So I am at a loss. And while we are talking about this, we still need to perform another sealing ritual over the *châsse* in the carriage hangar to invoke a hex using the new symbols."

"How are we going to get the *châsse* moved to the vault?"

"Now that Captain LaTour is here maybe we can move it by ship? The large pieces leaning inside the carriage hangar need to be put in place first inside the vault. We could bring them by wagon overland and make it ready."

"There is not enough time," Corrinne said reluctantly. "Captain LaTour is not going to be here long enough."

"Then…we just perform the sealing ritual on the *châsse* to invoke the new hex symbols. That will provide us with better protection. At least I think so."

"You have all the ritual words written out?"

"I do, but I have not decided on who should participate, or who should say what. Part of it is in Latin. You said the sealing words the last time. Do we need a member of the church? That will be difficult in Boston. I need to borrow your genius to think this through."

Corrinne was nervous. "Let's talk about that later today in the library. It's too cold down here."

They left the strongbox with Hancock's money on the floor and went up into the *cuisine*.

At Corrinne's behest, Dian put on her coat and went out to get Sentry.

Since his carriage was unavailable, Charles gave a guard a piece of silver to get a carriage to hire out for the day.

"Can I also use you to accompany me to my office? I need to survey some things to bring to the house."

That was arranged without much trouble.

Charles waited until Sentry arrived.

"Your lordship, my lady, good morning to you. Miss Dian said you need my help."

"Yes, but sit here at the table with us and warm yourself. Enjoy some hot coffee and some of Dian's delicious sweetbreads."

"Ya' nah' have tah' ask me twice. What is my task?"

"I need to bring a strongbox up from the cellar. It is heavy. Too heavy for me, certainly."

"I can do tha'. A heavy strongbox is a happy strongbox, yes?"

"It belongs to Mr. Hancock. I just need to move it up into the mudroom. He will bring his carriage and men today to carry it to his home."

*

Charles unlocked his office door and went inside followed by two redcoat marine guards. They had argued so much among themselves about who should get to go, he ended up bringing them both.

He'd decided it would be better just to move his day-to-day business to the house instead of coming here every day. In the outer office, he pulled out eight volumes of journals and accounting ledgers from under the counters and stacked them for movement to the carriage when he was ready. As far as VanderMeer Trading Insurance Company was concerned, there was little else to do beyond that.

No reason to keep this office, he thought. *Maybe I should sell it.*

In the studio at the back of the office, he studied the small jeweler's forge and changed his mind. *This could still be useful.* He looked over all of his paints, blank canvasses, the easel, plus the sketch pads. This was a lot to bring over to the house. *Should I leave it here?* But the studio was full of granite chips, pieces of hardwood lumber, stone, and wood dust collected against the walls and corners, along with other debris. It needed a thorough cleaning. But who knew what else might be misplaced among the mess. This cleaning was not something he wanted anyone else to do. So he gathered up all of his finished paintings and sketches into a large three-foot-square flat valise and carried it to the front.

"All right, gentlemen. I will have to come back tomorrow and do more cleaning. If one of you can carry that pile of journals for me, we'll head back to the house."

*

"Knock this crate over," Robert told Henri. "These eggs are from yesterday. And only sixteen left out of twenty-four. Let me move it closer to the door so they spill out into the shop. Carry these cakes out the front. Don't drop these. But bang into the egg crate as you go by."

Henri picked up the cakes. "I found bakery work enjoyable," Henri told him quietly. "The work is predictable. The aromas are wonderful. And you've made an art out of cake decoration."

"Thank you. I do like the work. You could be good at it, too, I think."

Henri smiled and shook his head. "If not for the war, I would be a sailor. There is something about the sea and using the stars for navigation. It's like getting a celestial blessing every place you sail."

Robert was amused. "So you're a poet too?"

Henri shook his head emphatically. "I am not that for certain."

"Good luck to you, Henri."

"You too, Robert. Can I buy these two cakes from you?"

"Of course. But ask me out there and I will decide what to charge as a courtesy for letting you go. It will make me more popular with the customers," he said with a wink.

Henri took a breath and walked swiftly to the front of the store, hitting the egg crate so hard, the top crate went flying into the shop, spreading the shell and yoke mess over a large area. The shop was half full of customers who were stunned then murmured among themselves. Henri set the cakes down on a table and started to pick things up.

Robert made a show of storming to the front. "Stop! Look what you've done! I think it would be better for you to find work elsewhere. This was not cake pans. This cost money."

"I'm sorry." He reached into his pocket and pulled out a large silver coin. "Can I pay for what I did?"

"Yes. You can." Robert accepted the coin. "But this is too much. Tell you what. You can have those two cakes. You already stuck your thumbs into the sides of them anyway. You are a good man, Thom, but a bakery is not the right place for you to work."

Henri got his coat from the back of the shop, checked again that the missive was still in the lining, and sheepishly made his way to the front of the shop. He picked up the cakes, nodded once at David in goodbye, and left the store.

When he reached the head of the Long Wharf, the dock area before the *Queen* was filled with goods being loaded aboard the ship. He went over to the marine guards who knew him on sight and gave them one of the cakes, much to their delight.

Captain LaTour was on the main deck supervising the loading.

"So this is what you do all day long. Eat cake?"

"I have the coded missive," Henri replied quietly.

LaTour took hold of Henri's arm and shouted over his shoulder, "Victorio! Take charge of the loading."

`They went below to his cabin. LaTour pulled two obscured wooden levers on his bunk and a small drawer was exposed beneath it with a pop.

"I did not know that was there," Henri said, surprised. He handed the missive to the captain who dropped it into the drawer and slammed it shut again. There was a loud clicking sound.

"Good," LaTour said. "Now you can forget you ever saw it too."

"I want to see Corrinne and Anamosa before we leave."

Captain LaTour sat down in his charting chair and deliberated. "I will go back there and reveal that you are here. There are many guards and strangers around that house. With Miss Molly's new baby, Captain Martyn is there a lot. It would not be good if he saw you. It would cause problems we do not want. We have to plan your visit carefully and do it at the right time. Yes?"

Henri was disappointed. But the risks LaTour described were very real and it would be dangerous to believe otherwise.

"I'll stay here and load cargo."

*

Captain LaTour walked quickly down to the foot of the Long Wharf and hailed an open carriage to take him to the VanderMeer house. He returned the salute of the marine guards in the front with his usual discomfort and knocked on the door.

Dian opened it. "Captain LaTour? Are you expected?" She let him enter.

"No, but I must see them right away."

"Lord VanderMeer is in the library and Lady Corrinne is with the babies. I will tell them you are here."

Charles appeared at the library door. He waved the captain over to him.

"Captain? Is something wrong?"

"Not exactly. There is something I must tell you and Lady Corrinne… but together, at the same time, if you please." He remained standing.

Charles looked quizzically at the captain. "Of course. I hear her steps on the stairs."

"Captain," Corrinne said, "you are always welcome here."

LaTour waited until they were seated. "What I have to tell you is very difficult to say and must remain confidential."

Charles got up and spoke to Dian that they were not to be disturbed. He made sure both doors were closed tightly.

"I have withheld certain information from you. I did so on purpose. I have very good news to share with you. But very bad news as well. Philippe and Henri are both all right, to put you at ease. Unfortunately, Archbishop Nicolet is dead."

Corrinne jerked her head back, her hand covered her mouth. "Nooo!" she groaned.

There was a rapid knock on the *cuisine* door. Charles answered it. It was Dian, a concerned expression on her face.

"I'm sorry, your lordship. I heard Lady Corrinne cry out."

"You did. We will care for Corrinne. Please, bring us some mint tea." He shut the door again. "Go on. Tell us what happened."

LaTour told of his journey to Montréal, but this time added how he'd been forced to take a commission in the French navy and transport Alain Marcoux to Quebec. In the middle of this tale, Dian brought in the tea and left.

"I had no choice, your lordship. The government of France essentially seized my ship. I would have been hung as a smuggler for the charges Intendant Bigôt had brought against me. But France intends to use the *Queen* for smuggling. I report to Admiral de la Motte. Naval Minister Machault was there at Rochefort and witnessed as I was ordered to do these things."

Charles VanderMeer was not happy about this but waited. "Tell us about the bishop."

LaTour disclosed the archbishop's shocking assassination by sword and the death of Father Tinian and another Jesuit in the same way and at the same time.

"It was someone sent to do just that. An assassin. Nothing was stolen. The assassin was not seen entering or leaving the Terrain des Jésuites. As I was leaving Montréal, they were still looking for the man, still questioning people."

Charles looked at Corrinne. "An assassin? The colonel sent someone?"

Corrinne's face was pale, tears streamed down her cheeks. But she focused at the mention of the colonel.

"Of course, the colonel. It makes sense now. The archbishop's death was the reason we felt the pain."

"What colonel?" LaTour asked, perplexed.

"Continue, Captain. We will explain later."

"After completing my mission to Montréal, I sailed to Louisbourg as ordered. And unfortunately was seen by Captain Martyn. I delivered dispatches and a cargo of luxury items to its people and garrison. That's why I arrived here empty."

"Is that all?"

"Naval Minister Machault expected me to come to Boston. He was delivering mail to you at the request of the Duke of Brunswick…at least, that is what I think. But Governor Drucour of Île Royale had another mission he assigned me when visiting Boston. That mission was completed today."

"Is that all?"

Corrinne touched Charles on the arm to interrupt. "You said the admiral and the Naval Minister sent this man…this Alain Marcoux with you to see the governor. Who is Alain Marcoux and what was he to do?"

"I am not certain, but I learned it was something to do with bringing troops to New France…mercenaries I think, from the German states."

"That was an elaborate deceit!" Corrinne replied in earnest. "This man was the assassin. He did this terrible thing. He killed the archbishop."

LaTour was taken aback. "Alain Marcoux never saw the archbishop!"

"So you believe? No one in Montréal had any reason to take the life of such a benevolent and holy man. No one! What was gained by his death? Who profited? No one in Montréal profited. That is why they are still looking for an assassin. But he is already gone. Where did this Alain Marcoux go next?"

"Back to France, on another ship. He may be there already. But after that, I have no idea where he goes. To the German states?"

"Isn't your ship owned by the Dutch Republic, Captain?" Charles asked.

"Yes…but…what?" Captain LaTour replied, uncertain of what Charles was implying.

"You cannot do the bidding of France. To seize your ship is an act of war!"

Corrinne was about to say something, but she saw Captain LaTour bristle and held her tongue.

LaTour spoke in low, even tones. "Your lordship, I hardly know of a port I can visit anymore where I would not be hung for some reason. Hung because I am French. Hung because I smuggle. Hung because France is at war with England and I am a commissioned captain in the French navy. Here in Boston, choose any of those and add the charge of *spying* to it. So you *might* tell me I am not allowed to do this, or not allowed to do that. I will say, yes, my lord. And when I find myself standing in front of the next hangman, I will accede to whatever command he gives me. Because that is my world, the world where I do what I need to do to survive in the middle of a war.

"I have seen you do much the same thing. Remember Halifax? Or here in Boston? I am in no position to press the argument of Dutch ownership to anyone who is pointing a cannon at me, or dangling a hangman's noose. What I do have is loyalty to the two people sitting before me and three keel chests loaded with hard coin, most of it gold, which I brought back to them because of that loyalty. So at least you can be certain I am not a thief! And I can be trusted even when exposed to great temptation. So let's begin with that. You can tell me what you want me to do. I will say, yes, your lordship, but you must leave it up to me as to how I complete my task. And when this war is over, the *Queen* will still be a Dutch ship. That's fair, I think."

An awkward silence fell over the room.

"Captain, I apologize," Charles said humbly. "It was my ego not my common sense that was speaking. Forgive my insufferable rudeness. And you are right. Going forward you have my support without judgment. My only command…if you will permit me to use those words…is for you and your crew to be safe."

"Yes, your lordship. That I can do."

Corrinne spoke to break away from this topic.

"You said you bring us good news too?"

LaTour lifted the cup of lukewarm mint tea and swallowed all of it. Seeing the captain do this, Corrinne and Charles followed his example.

"Now…please…make no outcries," he said. "Please do not repeat aloud what I am about to tell you. Henri Gerrard came with me."

Corrinne gasped, this time with joy, her hands over her mouth. She whispered, "He is here? In Boston?"

"He is aboard the *Queen*." LaTour put a finger to his lips. "Saying his name to anyone would endanger all of us. I had to restrain him from coming to see you. Too many people know him. Too many people know he is a French marine."

Corrinne whispered, "I want to see him! When do I see him?"

"I could bring you both to the ship today to congratulate the crew. Make a show of it for the people standing on the pier. Board the *Queen*, have the reunion, and something to eat out of sight. But before sunset, return to the house. And no one is the wiser. While you visit, we can conspire collectively on how to give you more time together."

"Anamosa must come with us!"

"Um…if you like. But that would be all. I do not think you should bring the babies. This visit will be short. Or we do not try to do this today. And conspire instead how to bring him here."

"No!" Corrinne insisted. "The earth could shake again. I want to see him as soon as possible. Charles?"

"I agree. Let's go there now. Anamosa too."

"Very well, but let's be discreet about our excitement," LaTour warned. "Do not tell Anamosa ahead of time. I will leave now and go back to the ship to make ready for your visit. Come as soon as you are able."

LaTour stood. Corrinne rose and hugged him tightly.

"Thank you, Beauregard!" Her words were choked. "You dear man! Dear friend! Thank you for everything!"

*

Captain LaTour returned to the ship as fast as he could. He arrived in time to see a heavy pallet being winched aboard and lowered down the forward hatch.

"How much longer?" he asked Victorio as soon as he crossed the bow.

"That is the last pallet today. There will be more in the morning."

"Good. Secure the cargo as quickly as you can. Lord and Lady Vander-Meer are coming to visit us."

"Today? Now?"

"Within the hour. You should get into uniform and allow yourself to be noticed by the marine guards. We need to clean up the ship. I will go below and get the cooks started on some refreshments."

"What about Henri?"

"Yes. That is the reason why they are coming. But no one else need know this. I will tell Henri."

LaTour informed Henri about the visit. "I told them about you, but they know nothing about your mission. And they can never know. They are bringing Anamosa with them but not the twins. Anamosa does *not* know you are aboard. This will be a huge surprise for her. You should stay out of sight until they are here and come down below decks. You will have maybe two hours with them today before they have to leave and go back. While they are here, we can contrive to find more time to spend with them. Oh, and you should clean up. You stink."

*

Anamosa was smiling and breathless as she hurried down the Long Wharf. Seeing all the big ships and new sights was exciting to her. Seeing the *Falcon Queen* at the end of the wharf was most exciting of all. She remembered spending time with Henri on this ship. When he would sit on the floor next to her bed and hold her hand while he slept.

The flag of the Dutch Republic, the orange, white, and blue colors, was proudly hanging at the back of the ship. The marine guards formed an honor line, their muskets held at present-arms, at the bottom of the brow as Lord and Lady VanderMeer approached. Corrinne complimented each of the marines by name. Told them how splendid and handsome they looked. Slipped a silver piece in each of their coat pockets. All of these men routinely stood guard at her house as well.

Somehow, two Boston newspapermen had learned they were visiting and were positioned near the brow. They were busy penciling notes. A small crowd of spectators had also gathered to look on.

Captain Jaager saluted the VanderMeers and assisted the women up the brow. The bosun whistled his pipe as they stepped onto the main deck. Corrinne greeted the crewmen on deck, calling them by their first names, which she had memorized many years ago. With caps doffed, they smiled and bowed. Then she waved to the crowd of spectators and went below.

The not unpleasant but pungent odors of the ship brought good memories rushing back to Corrinne as she stepped down the bridge ladder stairs. She knew every inch of this vessel. She'd designed it. When they reached the dining cabin, the door was open, the delicious aroma of French cooking filled the air.

And standing at the far end of the passageway was a tall blond-haired man wearing a big smile on his face.

"Oh, my God! He's become a giant!"

And much as Corrinne wanted to run to embrace Henri, she moved Anamosa in front of her and said.

"Look!"

Henri dropped to his knees and spread open his arms.

Anamosa rushed to Henri, squealing with joy. She rubbed his nose, kissed his cheeks, and started patting his face with her hands, reassuring herself it was him. He picked Anamosa up and went back to Corrinne who was sobbing. She hugged them both.

"Oh, Henri, Henri, Henri! Thank God you are alive and well. Thank God!"

Using his free hand, Henri shook hands with Charles VanderMeer.

Captain LaTour carefully nudged them into the dining cabin. But they remained huddled together at the head of the table. Anamosa, eyes closed, rested her head on Henri's shoulder, her arms hugged one of his possessively. Corrinne moved onto the bench first and Henri slid next to her still holding Anamosa. Charles took a seat at the other end of the table. Captain LaTour sat at the head. Victorio on the other side.

"She's gotten so big," Henri exclaimed.

"*She's* gotten big? How tall are you, Henri? And your voice is so deep! You sound like your father."

Anamosa finally let him go just far enough so they could both eat the savory foods served to them all. For the next few hours, they shared stories and happy laughter. Charles had brought a few recent colored sketches of the twins he'd made for Henri to see.

"They are beautiful, Corrinne. They look just like you! Though Marcus' hair seems redder than Calypso's."

"They are my little angels," Corrinne said tenderly, touching the picture with one finger. "Anamosa is one of my angels too," she added reaching past Henri to caress Ana's face. "Why are you hiding aboard the ship?"

"I am a French officer, someone who should not be here," he said. "You would be in great danger should anyone learn of this."

"Yes, of course, of course," Corrinne replied, shaking her head. "I know that. So what can we do to bring you to the house? You really must see the twins."

"Let Captain LaTour and I discuss this and see what we can plan."

But Henri already sensed this might not be possible. He would not do anything to put them in danger. If he ran into a single person who knew his face, anything might happen and none of it good. He might have to be content with this short visit. Maybe they could arrange another one before they left.

Henri's glance touched on the reddish scar on Corrinne's throat.

She touched the raised skin. "Yes, that was an unfortunate night. Your friend Sentry saved our lives along with the magistrate. Charles was bashed in the head and remained unconscious for days afterwards. Mathilde was stabbed with a sword, but lived. She died a few months ago."

Henri could sense Corrinne's pain. "I'm so sorry."

"But enough of that." Corrinne did not want to talk of sad things. "Tell me what happened to your ear. Tell me about Louisbourg."

They did not talk much longer before Captain LaTour said it was time to go.

"We do not want to be walking the wharf in the dark." He did not wish to mention *assassins*, but his tone was unmistakable as to his meaning.

Corrinne and Charles agreed reluctantly, though Anamosa complained Henri should come to stay with them.

"I will see you again," he promised her.

Anamosa abruptly took off the amulet around her neck and slipped it over Henri's head.

"No, Ana. I want you to keep this."

"The white eagle told me to give this to you," Anamosa said firmly.

"What?"

Corrinne did not wish to discuss any of this in front of Charles, Victorio, and the captain.

"Just wear it for her, Henri. It will make her happy. You can give it back to her later."

Henri was not going to follow them up on deck. Not with reporters standing around.

Corrinne was the last to climb the stairs. She turned and whispered.

"The *white eagle* did visit the house. It did tell Anamosa to give you the amulet to wear," she whispered.

"She saw it? I've not seen the eagle in almost two years."

"It has visited our house several times and saved us when we lived in Connecticut. But that's another story. I think the eagle wants to see you. You need to find a way to get to the house."

"I will try."

"No. You need to promise me."

"All right. I promise."

*

But the incident with the white eagle had been working on Corrinne's mind. Now with Henri's surprise appearance and Anamosa's insistence that Henri receive the amulet, Corrinne now conjured it all to be a warning.

Something is going to happen!

Charles had gone to the office yesterday.

Nothing happened from that. But what if he was noticed?

Corrinne felt a chill. "When will you be finished with that office?" she asked Charles as they walked back down the Long Wharf. There was a discernable tenseness in her voice.

Charles looked at her quizzically. "Tomorrow. I just have to collect a few more things."

"You have a guard?"

"Of course."

Corrinne almost argued the wisdom of him going at all but decided instead to send Jack Tasker a note and request an extra guard be posted at the office tomorrow. She would write it out as soon as she returned to the house and pay one of the marines to hand carry it to the magistrate that night.

"Don't eat anything while you're there."

"Of course I won't."

"And promise to come home early."

"It should not take me too long."

"Promise me."

"*I promise,*" he said indulgently.

CHAPTER 29
BOSTON
SEPTEMBER 28, 1756
A Heavy Iron Long-Hammer

It was Tuesday. Carter Trevathan had gotten a message to Ritter Monheit through Rachel to check Lord VanderMeer's office that morning to see if Lord VanderMeer was there that day. Except for a brief visit on Monday, he'd not been there for over a week.

As usual, twelve-year-old Jimmy showed up at half past the hour of nine with the rest of the gang of small thieves, which was as soon as Faneuil Hall opened for business. He sent Jimmy to see Rachel.

"It's been several days. Now ask Miss Rachel if you can buy her lunch and come back and tell me. Maybe you will get lucky today."

*

Ritter Monheit strolled casually near the VanderMeer Trading office and saw the lanterns lit inside. There was one guard sitting by the inside counter, facing the door. He was reading a book.

Today is the day, he thought. And Ritter was impatient to get this done. Because after this he intended to disappear from Boston and go back to Philadelphia. Ritter walked as fast as he could down to the Penny Surgeon and saw Rachel talking to the boy named Jimmy.

Rachel knew Ritter was going to come and give her one of two messages that morning, so she had found a way to delay Jimmy to stay with her and talk. That was not hard to do. Suddenly, she spotted Ritter on the other side of the street.

Observing that he had Rachel's attention, Ritter raised both arms above his head, then turned and walked away.

"Jimmy, I think you are just too charming for me. So, yes. I will accept lunch from you. Surprise me. Bring enough for both of us, and we will eat it here."

"Really?"

Rachel leaned close and kissed his cheek. "Really."

Jimmy touched his cheek with his fingers and smiled. "I will be back at noon." He ran off.

Rachel took off her nurse's apron and walked fifteen minutes to the Marine Society hospital's back door. She had not worked there in weeks but went in anyway and waited for Caroline to come into the back room. She only had to wait a few minutes before one of the other nurses told Caroline her sister was waiting for her.

When Rachel saw her sister, she spoke briefly in a quiet voice. "He is there today." Then she left and walked to the apartment they shared.

In the apartment, she collected her clothing, her extra pair of shoes, and a few personal toiletries and stuffed them into a large canvas satchel. She also took half the money they kept in a heavy coin pouch below the floorboards and put it in her purse. She rolled open the leather medicine bag and looked at all the vials of poison and smaller pouches full of dried, deadly herbs. She wanted none of it. Rachel rolled up the medicine bag and retied the confining cord. She put the board back in place and looked around the apartment one more time. Other than what she packed, there was *nothing* else she wanted to remind her of the life she'd been forced to live.

Rachel went down the stairs and walked back to the Penny Surgeon, setting the satchel behind the cloak she hung on the wall. When the night messenger had visited recently, she found the effect on her to be little worse than an annoying dream. She could not even recall what it had said to her. The messenger was losing its control. She knew that now. And she planned to escape it forever before it came back. But not with Caroline. She considered Caroline evil and demented, murderously insane, a woman who craved attention from the smarmy Carter Trevathan to the point of obsession. She would be glad to rid her life of Caroline too.

Now all Rachel planned to do before she left Boston was wait for Jimmy and take care of him.

*

Charles knew cleaning up his studio would be dirty work. But once he started, he realized it could take all day. He started with a broom and a shovel, moving all the rock debris, dust, and wood scraps into a large pile in one corner. That took almost two hours. He was not sure what to do with the extra hardwood lumber and several large pieces of smooth, beautiful granite leaning against the wall. Such raw objects of art were filled with beauty waiting to be exposed. They called to his passion. He did not want to throw them away. Maybe he should find another artist and make them a gift? Revere, maybe?

He used a flat-iron stove cover to scoop up the debris pile and dumped it into a large wooden bucket. When full, the bucket was heavy. He pulled the top and bottom bolts and lifted the bar on the seldom-used back door of the office. He emptied the bucket into the deep gutter, which had a flow of foul water in it from all the rain. The air at the back of the building reeked with foulness so he did not stay out there long. The gutter ran into Rill Creek, which emptied into the harbor after flowing a few city blocks. Then he repeated this work carrying the larger broken pieces from the pile that would not fit into the bucket, dropping them directly into the creek.

By noon, his progress was good. He estimated he could be finished before the hour of four if he did not stop to eat. Not exactly early as he'd promised Corrinne, though still not a full day. Another one of Tasker's guards showed up at the office. The man had brought food to share with the other guard. Charles also learned that Corrinne had contacted Tasker and paid for this extra guard to be at the office with him that day.

So as not to be rude, Charles decided to rest for an hour. He shared the basket of food he'd brought with him with the men.

*

Captain Martyn held his son most of the morning, except for when he was being fed. The tide was turning at noon, and he would be sailing to Halifax. He had already stayed two days longer than he planned and could not delay much longer. If he was too late getting back to Halifax, he would anger Commander Rous, who might assign his ship to another long trip of transporting the wretched Acadian families. Then it would be two months before he returned. He explained all this to Molly, so she would understand.

But she didn't. Her eyes were full of tears as he handed little Conor back to her.

"I don't understand. They should let you stay longer or have someone else captain the ship. You have a new son!"

Conor knelt on the floor before the rocking chair and laid his head on her lap. Molly ran her fingers through his hair.

"Conor, we did not even get a chance to lie together…the doctor said next week everything would be healed enough."

He looked up at her wistfully. "I think about lying between your thighs all the time."

"Oh, God! Don't start talking like that now, Conor. You are walking out the door in a few minutes."

"I just want you to know this was hard for me too."

They heard the standing clock in the foyer gong once. Conor knew it meant half-past the hour of ten. There was much to do aboard the *Anamosa*.

Molly wiped at her eyes. "Now?"

"Yes." Conor stood. He bent down to kiss little Conor on the head. Then he kissed Molly tenderly on the lips.

"You'll be back in a month?'

"A month to six weeks. That's what I was told. I will be guarding Louisbourg harbor again."

"I love you, Connor." She said the words as if it were the last time she'd utter them.

"I love you too, Molly. Say goodbye to the others for me."

*

Captain LaTour stood on deck and watched the final load-out of the *Queen*'s cargo holds. He'd purchased things he thought Louisbourg might need, mostly quality furniture for the homes, spinning wheels, five bales of ginned cotton, twenty bolts of woven fabric, dye cakes, metal ware, needles of all shapes and sizes, knives, forks, spoons, pots, pans, kettles, iron tools, axes, shovels, rakes, a few ploughshares with moldboards, scythes, trowels, rakes, leather harnesses, bridles, saddles, a large amount of coffee, fifty sacks of flour, thirty each of beans, squash, and corn, three large sacks of pure white sugar, two of yeast, ten sacks of rock salt, twenty barrels of pork, spices from the East Indies that were barely unloaded in Boston before he purchased them. The merchant for the spices made twice as much profit as usual.

Samuel Grant was standing next to him, slapping his arms to warm himself. When the loading was complete, he did not want his fee for this delayed.

"Unusual mix of cargo."

"Some of the goods you make here are very hard to come by in many of the islands I visit. Not everything will be unloaded in Amsterdam. The Dutch only unload goods where the profits are greatest."

The selectman grunted. "Yes, well you Dutch are not ruled by the English. They are more interested in preserving their empire. That means controlling the way we trade and depriving us of hard coin."

"The American provinces are bigger than England several times over."

"The English consider America just more of England…and intend to add all of New France to it when they win this war."

"You think they will win so easily?"

"You are French, what do you think?"

"A fight to the death is never easy. For countries it is much the same, I think. This war will go on for years."

"Months, years, it makes no difference. England will win in the end. And they know it."

Captain LaTour abruptly trained his watch glass on a ship out in the anchorage.

"See someone you know?" Grant asked.

"The tide's going out. Ships are raising anchor to sail."

And that one is the Anamosa, LaTour did not say.

"When do you expect to leave?"

"That would be up to Lord VanderMeer. But soon I hope. Winter crossings are the worst."

Working on deck, Henri paused long enough to watch the *Anamosa* make sail. That was good fortune. Captain Martyn's presence at the house was a major obstacle to his visiting. Of course, Molly was still there, but she would keep a secret for a few days.

*

Caroline left the Marine Society Hospital around noon. She'd told the doctors she was feeling very sick and thought it better to stay home the rest of the day.

When she reached the apartment, she changed into the disguise she selected. A comely dress of a woman of means and a wig of red hair. She tucked her hair up into the wig and put on a fashionable bonnet that shrouded the sides of her face. The dress hung to the tops of her polished black shoes and it had a lace bib and collar. After studying her image in the mirror, she pulled several tufts of the red hair out the sides of the bonnet so the color was certain to be recognized. Satisfied she was ready, she left and hurried down the stairs, pausing to see if anyone was in the alley before she turned away from the main street. No one saw her emerge. Caroline planned to discard the dress before she returned. The furnishings of the apartment were so sparse she'd not noticed that Rachel's things were gone.

Caroline carried a blue-dyed canvas shopping bag. Her nurse dress and apron were folded neatly at the bottom. She stopped at some farmer stands on the way and purchased a few ears of corn and root vegetables, which, along with the nurse dress, covered the poison knife lying at the bottom of the bag.

The cold in the air was damp and chilling. It did not take long before Caroline's cheeks turned rosy. Her breath puffed vaporously as she walked briskly. She purposely went down Union Street to pass by the VanderMeer Trading office and checked that the lantern lights were on. Through the window she could see a guard sitting in a chair. This confirmed Lord VanderMeer was still there.

Caroline continued down Union Street, crossed through Dock Square, down Cornhill to the corner of Water Street. The other two men were waiting for her. They opened their coats to show her the pistols in their belts.

"Everything is ready," she said. "One of you must linger near this corner for an hour or more until I come back here. I will come from that direction." She pointed down Waters Street towards the harbor. "You know what to do?"

They both nodded.

"Afterwards, you are free to go wherever you please. Just do not stay in Boston. They will be searching for you."

Next, Caroline walked purposefully to Mary's Restaurant. She went into the restaurant, took a seat near a front window by the door, and ordered something to eat, mimicking the typical Boston accent she'd come to know so well as she placed her order. She started with a hot squash soup with bread and butter. She ate very slowly and waited. The magistrate was usually very punctual.

Jack Tasker would not disappoint her.

The deputy magistrate arrived at Mary's Restaurant at exactly one o'clock. The restaurant was full of customers by then, all of them there to partake of the delicious beef pies full of a cream-based savory beef gravy, large chunks of beef, green beans, peas, and root vegetables, all wrapped in a golden, flaky crust. The famous pies were made once every two weeks. Mary Tasker only baked twenty-five of them at a time. She had to save money to buy the beef, and twenty-five was all she could do in one morning. All but six of the famous pies were reserved weekly. The other six were kept for people who came to the restaurant the first time and before two o'clock. At precisely two o'clock, any of the pies left over could be purchased by other willing customers who drew black-and-white agates for them from a bag. All black and a white one for each extra pie. Part of the fun for the customers was this drawing for the white agates.

Mary Tasker had been expecting her brother and rushed out from the kitchen wiping her hands on the apron to embrace him. She was a slightly overweight woman of thirty-eight, light brown hair, a face full of freckles, a big smile, and prone to easy laughter. She had been widowed ten years earlier when her fisherman husband did not come back from sea, leaving behind two sons and a daughter. The daughter now worked with her in the restaurant kitchen.

"How many Tuesdays has it been, Jack?"

The number of Tuesdays in a row that Jack had not missed eating a beef pie.

"Nine by my count."

Jack took his seat near the back of the restaurant by himself and waited for his most favorite food. The restaurant was completely full of customers that day, the colder weather drove people indoors and the aromas of the pies made customers' mouths water immediately.

Mary's daughter, Lisbeth, served him so she could say hello to her favorite uncle, who would always find some compliment to pay. And if a boyfriend broke her heart, and many of them did, as Lisbeth was a little too free with her affections, Uncle Jack would always offer to arrest them for her, or have them shot, hung, or given over to the Indians for torture. Lisbeth would always refuse, but it was a pleasant healing ritual she would go through.

Today, Lisbeth was smiling, so Jack Tasker knew she was being treated well…by someone. He preferred not to know or he *might* arrest the man anyway.

"Right from the oven to the table. Only for you, Uncle." She kissed his cheek.

"You have a graceful walk, Lisbeth. Did I ever tell you that?"

Lisbeth smiled and pecked his cheek again. "No, Uncle Jack, you haven't. And thank you. Just raise your hand if you need anything else."

She left him a cup and a jug of water and tended to the other tables.

Jack cut into the pie and spooned in the first mouthful, closing his eyes to savor the flavor of the first bite. The subsequent ones never tasted as good as the first. He tried to eat slowly but never seemed able to do so. And with the bread and butter, he completely cleaned the eight-inch tin pan of every trace of crust and gravy in about twenty minutes. Then he rested against the wall and belched softly. He would let the meal digest a little before he ventured out into the cold again. He gazed around the room at the customers. He knew nearly everyone. A few people raised a hand to say hello.

Out of the corner of her eye, Caroline Bristol saw that the magistrate had finished his meal. Now she gave the wait her full attention. She had scouted both sides of the streets and had four places selected where she could make her attack. She casually moved the hollow-tip knife to the top of the nurse's dress. It was loaded with a dose of *aqua tofana*.

The proprietress came out from the kitchen and announced that three of the reserved pies were still left. At two o'clock the agates would be drawn for them. This generated a lot of talk in the restaurant. People started ordering other menu items to remain for the drawing.

The deputy stood, went to the kitchen door, and said good-bye to someone.

Caroline could not predict which way he would walk, but she was ready to follow. Without glancing at her, Tasker went out the door and turned to his right. Caroline quickly made up the distance until she was only two steps behind him. The recessed doorway was only four or five more paces away, and she carefully kept walking, intending to try and pass on his left at just the right moment.

The weather had turned windier, the icy breeze streamed directly inshore from the harbor. The few pedestrians moving about were head down as they walked. Magistrate Tasker was no different.

"Excuse me," came a feminine voice on his left, someone obviously in a hurry.

Jack paused half a step to let her go by. She slammed her body into him. He staggered into a recessed doorway and tripped on the step. He barely had time to maintain his balance when he felt an acute pain at the top of his shoulder right next to his neck. The magistrate knew exactly what was happening. He reached out with his hands and scratched both sides of the woman's face before the choking paralysis incapacitated him.

Caroline caught him in her arms and slowly lowered him to the brick-work before the door. Then she rearranged her bonnet and continued walking until she reached the corner of Waters and Cornhill. Her co-conspirators were both standing there waiting.

"Your face is bleeding," one of them said.

She took a handkerchief from her pocket and wiped away the blood.

"It's still bleeding."

"I'll take care of it later. Now follow behind me at ten paces until we see Ritter at the Dock Square. He will raise his arms in the air to indicate he will attack. Then go and wait for him to join you by the cemetery."

Ritter saw Caroline approach but waited until he saw the other two men looking at him too. By that time she was already squinting, wondering why he had not raised his arms, thinking something must have gone wrong.

Ritter raised his arms straight up in the air for a few seconds. He waited to see Caroline and then the two dock workers turn left on Hillers Street. The men would be waiting for him by the Granary cemetery. He turned and started down Union Street.

Inside Ritter's long coat hung a Portuguese blunderbuss. It was a short musket with a two-foot barrel and a sawed-off stock. The barrel diameter was oversized with a flared muzzle two inches in size to allow multiple balls to emerge and spread out when it was fired. Ritter had loaded it with five balls packed in a wad of cotton. Behind that lay a charge of gunpowder large enough to propel the balls with great force. The weapon was powerful, short range, and deadly. He also carried two dragoon pistols in his belt, loaded and primed.

The trading office doors had a bar and bolts top and bottom on the inside. To try and breach this was senseless, but it would not stop him. The weather of the last few days would be an ally. The chilled wind blowing in from the harbor drove most of the pedestrians on the street indoors. He saw two men and one woman going in different directions on the opposite side of the street. He stopped at the head of a walker's alley next to the trading office and retrieved a heavy long hammer at the side of the building, one of two hammers he'd secreted an hour earlier.

After eating a midday meal, Charles VanderMeer paid one of the guards for his help in finishing the work. It went twice as fast. They had just carried the last of the broken debris out the back door, threw the bolts on the top and bottom, and set the cross-bar back in place when the sound of crashing glass issued from the front.

Using the heavy hammer easily, Ritter smashed through the six-pane glass window. Moving speedily, he stepped up to the two-foot window frame, holding the blunderbuss and a pistol. The guard sitting in the office was so startled by the violent entry he was still fumbling with his weapon when Ritter shot him in the chest with the pistol. The guard's body flew backward from the shot and fell dead to the floor.

Dropping the pistol, Ritter elevated the blunderbuss waist high to finish off Lord VanderMeer. He did not expect to see another guard rushing through the door leading from the studio with a pistol drawn. Ritter had no time to think and fired the blunderbuss only an instant before the guard fired his pistol, fouling his aim. The blast from the more powerful weapon at close range blew away half of the guard's torso in a red spray.

Ritter dropped the blunderbuss and pulled out his remaining pistol to finish off Lord VanderMeer. But Charles had picked up the shovel he'd been using and swung it at Ritter's head. Ritter reacted and took a glancing blow. He stumbled but regained his balance. Charles swung the shovel a second time, turning his body sideways as Ritter's pistol fired. The shovel hit Ritter on the side of the head, knocking him momentarily senseless. He fell to his knees.

Charles felt a searing pain in his lower back. He fell to the floor, deafened by the sound of the pistol. His legs had gone numb. He could not move.

Ritter staggered to his feet, confused and uncertain. There was blood everywhere. The guards were dead. Lord VanderMeer was dead. He stumbled into the front office, pulled the bolts, threw over the bar, and went out the front door. The street was deserted. He pulled up the coat collar around his face and started walking quickly to meet the other men at the Granary cemetery. He walked unsteadily and finally made it to his destination ten minutes later.

*

Caroline made it back to her apartment without drawing anyone's notice. She had not planned to come back, but the scratches on her face needed attention before she returned to the Marine Society Hospital. She'd not heard the sounds of any gunfire as she walked. She did not know if that meant something good or bad. In any case, her main concern was to get back to the hospital.

Inside the apartment, she stripped off the dress, wig, and bonnet. She would dispose of her disguise later. For now, she lifted the floorboard, pushed aside the money pouch and stuffed the items beneath the floor. She also placed the poison knife back into the small medical bag containing the vials and other substances. Satisfied that was all she needed to hide, she replaced the floorboard.

The dark blue canvass shopping bag still carried the ears of corn and root vegetables. She would dispose of them somewhere on the way to the hospital. Even a mote of poison on the food was deadly.

Toss it into the harbor?

Next, Caroline looked in the small dressing mirror and saw three long scratch marks on her left cheek. One of the scratches was deep. But the blood was already scabbing. Her right cheek showed four reddish streaks, all of them unmistakable marks of someone's fingernails. She picked away the still forming scabs, daubed liquid from a small bottle of astringent solution onto the tip of a towel and gently stroked the scratch wounds to stop any bleeding before it spread over the surface of the skin.

She opened a small case of cosmetic paints, the kind used by actors, and spread some over the reddish scratch marks until they effectively disappeared, smoothing the paint further until it blended well with her natural skin tone. While she waited for the paint to dry and to see if it concealed the scratches, she dressed again in her nurse's garb and apron.

She drank some water and ate a slice of bread and butter. She pondered what else was important to remember.

I will need to stop at the farmer's market again and pick up more food for supper, she thought. *Rachel needs to tell me what she did with the boy. And with the magistrate's death, Carter will not be followed so closely anymore. We can enjoy one another again.*

*

Rachel let Jimmy carry her bag as they walked all the way to the ship-yards on the north side of the city. They took a seat on a bench at the ferry landing and huddled together against the cold to await a ferry that would take them over to Charlestown on the other side of the harbor. This was the easiest way to leave Boston. Once there, Rachel intended to find work as a nurse or go on to another city. It had taken hardly any convincing at all to get the twelve-year-old boy to accompany her. She had decided not to poison Jimmy. He would help in affirming her new persona. Jimmy could be her brother or even act as her son as part of a future deceit.

"I've decided to take your last name, Cantlin, and pretend I am your older sister. Would you like that, Jimmy?"

"Oh, yes, Miss Rachel."

"Just call me Rachel from now on. Remember, I am your older sister, even though you and I will know better in private that is not what I am," she said in a conspiring tone.

Jimmy could only imagine what that meant.

"We will find a nice place to live. I will work and cook for you. You can go to school."

"School?"

"Oh, yes, Jimmy. School is most important, or you will be living poor and on the streets forever. You will see that I am right."

School? Jimmy was not certain he liked that idea.

Rachel noticed his frown. "Of course, we may have to share a bed together at night until we find a permanent place to live. You won't mind that will you?"

"No Miss Rachel...I mean, no, Rachel. I will not mind that at all."

His eyes were glowing at the memory and images of his real sister, and what she did with those men who shared her bed.

Rachel saw his excited expression.

"Good. You'll see. Soon we will live together in a warm, new apartment and…oh! Look! Here comes the ferry."

*

Ritter's head ached from where he had been whacked with the shovel. He was still dizzy, and he tottered as if drunk. But he staggered along the cold streets and eventually reached the cemetery. The two dock workers were waiting for him patiently.

"Your head is bleeding," one of them said.

"How bad?"

"It's dried now. High up by your right eye."

Ritter pulled a rag from his pocket and spit on it. "Here. Wipe it away for me."

"Is he dead?" the other man asked in German.

"Who? The Dutchman? Yes, he's dead. How many weapons do you carry?"

They opened their coats. Ritter saw two pistols and a knife scabbard on their belts.

"Are your horses ready?"

"Yes. At the stables on Orange Street."

"Let's go over this again. I will stop at the back fence. You go down Winter Street to the corner of Marlborough. You both fire a pistol at the guard house. Don't bother to aim. You are not trying to kill the guards, just alarm them. Then go quickly to your horses and leave the city out the south gate at the neck. Do not gallop! If they stop you and ask, you are just heading to New Brunswick to look for work. Once through the gates, don't stop. Remember, they will come looking for you. They will not arrest you. They will shoot you. Go wherever you want. Just do not come back to Boston."

Ritter waited at the back fence of the VanderMeer house where he had secreted the second long-hammer. When he heard the distinctive pistols shots in the distance, he pushed on the loosened board and stepped into the yard. He presumed the city was already alarmed at finding the magistrate's dead body. By now someone had likely entered the trading office and saw all the dead bodies there. Word of those deaths would also spread quickly.

He entered the back yard and went to the door of the carriage house. There was a heavy lock and hasp on it. He walked further to the edge and glimpsed around the corner. The two guards posted there had responded to the pistol shots and ran to the front.

Ritter's goal was the *châsse*. Once he broke the lock on the door, he intended to smash the *châsse* to pieces, breaking the seals and retrieving the bones if there was time.

*

At the sounds of the first pistol shots, Corrinne sat up straight with a start. She was in the library.

The babies! was her first thought.

"Dian! Go upstairs to the babies' room. There are loaded pistols in the box on the wall by the door. I will help Molly."

Corrinne hurried to Molly who was carefully wrapping Conor in a blanket.

"What happened?"

"I don't know, but we are all safer upstairs."

Corrinne guided Molly to the stairs when she noticed the guards at the front of the house were gone.

"Keep going. I will be along shortly."

Corrinne went into the library and retrieved the two loaded pistols she kept hidden in there. They were smaller in caliber than the ones used by the military, but they both had double barrels.

There was a sudden large crashing sound at the back of the house, which repeated itself. She ran through the *cuisine* and the mudroom and looked out the backdoor.

The guards posted there were gone!

Again she heard the crashing sound coming from the blind side of the carriage hangar. Without hesitating, she went out the door up to the corner of the hangar. She glimpsed carefully.

It's him!

The *ghost* had been circling, watching the servant struggle to enter a place where the *châsse* was kept in hiding. It slowly descended, wary of the other white men carrying muskets. They were not that far away. A single metal ball would be fatal. It must not expose the female eagle to the danger of those powerful weapons.

The servant was about to break down the barrier. The eagle did not have the strength to kill the servant, but it could wound him severely enough to stop him. The *ghost* dived, its long talons extended, intending to claw the servant's eyes, to blind the man, expecting his screams would bring the other white men running with their muskets.

Suddenly, the white woman emerged from the house. She had a weapon! The servant stopped hammering the barrier and advanced on her. The *ghost* pulled out of its dive, back-flapping its wings violently to regain height. The *ghost* circled upward. The *ghost* circled still higher and renewed its watch. This was not the end of the clash. The *ghost* had sensed new preparations being made. A more dangerous encounter with the *demon* itself would happen soon.

The *ghost* must be ready.

The injury to Ritter's head was throbbing, making his movements sluggish. But Ritter had almost broken through the doors. One or two more heavy swings should do it. But his seventh swing was up in mid-air when he saw the blond-haired woman walking towards him. He gawked only for a second. Her death would be a bonus. It was something he had not expected. He raised the hammer and marched towards her.

Something else Ritter did not expect were the two musket balls fired into his gut. Grunting loudly with pain, he dropped the hammer and fell to his knees, gripping the painful, bloody flow issuing from his intestines.

Corrinne walked up and pointed the second pistol at his head.

"This is for Mathilde," she said.

Ritter Monheit's head exploded from the two balls hitting it at close range.

Corrinne heard more footsteps and spun around. It was the two marine guards. They were breathless from running.

"Are you all right, my lady?"

"Yes. The other pistol shots were only a diversion to get you to leave your posts."

The marines had nothing to say to that. They believed the attack was coming from the front. But it had come from the back…which they were supposed to be guarding.

Still carrying the discharged pistols, Corrinne went back into the house. She laid the pistols on the cuisine table and went upstairs. Dian was crouched behind the door with two pistols cocked and ready.

"It's all over," Corrinne said. "The attack was from the back of the house. The man is dead."

Corrinne felt drained. Still trembling, she knelt and threw open her arms. Marcus and Calypso came to her giggling. Anamosa knelt next to Corrinne and hugged her around the waist.

*

Tha magistrate's eight remaining deputies split into two groups. One group was already at Hutchinson Street where the body of Jack Tasker was found dead in a doorway. The purple and black web-like discoloration of his face and neck was hideous to behold. The blood vessels in his eyes had burst. The eyes were completely red, like a demon's, some would later say. A grotesquely swollen purple tongue stuck out of his mouth. His bulging cheeks were full of vomit, some of it already expelled explosively around the tongue and lay all over the clothes and on the walls of the vestibule where he lay. Some people on the street claimed it was a *woman* who did it. *A woman with red hair.*

Many of the deputies were sniffing back tears as they wrapped the dead magistrate in a canvas and put the body in the back of the wagon. Mary Tasker and her daughter Lisbeth were inconsolable, shrieking with anguish, held by neighbors and friends. Jack Tasker was found dead less than a half block from the restaurant where he'd eaten the beef pie he loved so much.

The other group of deputies had responded to civilian calls of a new attack on Lord VanderMeer's trading office. They arrived at a scene of bloody horror. Two magistrate deputies dead from gunfire. One almost cut in half at the waist from the blast of a blunderbuss at close range. But Lord VanderMeer moaned when they touched him.

"He is still alive!"

They temporarily stopped the bleeding from the back wound. The wagon was sent for. Using a litter, they carefully moved Lord VanderMeer into the back of the wagon right next to Jack Tasker's dead body. There was no choice. They drove the wagon to the back of the Marine Society Hospital and unloaded the litter. Two other deputies ran off to the VanderMeer home to see to its safety.

Three doctors at the hospital cut away Lord VanderMeer's shirt and pants. They gave him drugs for the pain. One of them was a former army surgeon. He recognized the wound.

"It was a musket or pistol ball. It shattered the bone of the first lumbar vertebrate." He picked out a few of the largest shards. They cauterized some of the bleeding and turned him over. There was another hole on his right side beneath the ribcage. "The ball came out here. Let's cauterize this bleeding first. Then we can examine inside the wounds to see what else has been damaged."

At Lord VanderMeer's house, the deputies were stopped by the marines posted at the front. There was also an attack at the house, they would learn. But that attacker had been killed.

The deputies ran around to the back and saw the body of a man, though little of him was recognizable. Two marine guards were standing nearby. They saw the carriage hangar door had been hammered to the breaking point. Only the lock and hasp still held the two pieces together.

"What was he trying to do?"

"Get inside the carriage hangar."

"You lads did good work."

"It wasn't us. The attack started in the front. We went to assist. He came in through the fence."

"Then who did this?"

"Lady VanderMeer, using two double-barrel pistols. One to his gut. The other to his head."

"Bloody…! Is everyone else all right?"

"Yes. Why are you here?"

"Lord VanderMeer was attacked and shot. He is still alive. We are here to tell Lady VanderMeer. Worse still, someone also killed Magistrate Tasker," he added grimly.

"The magistrate is dead?!"

Leaving the marines standing in astonishment at the news, the deputies went to the front of the house.

"Lord VanderMeer has been shot. He is still alive at the Marine Society Hospital. Lady VanderMeer will be needing a carriage," they told the other guards. "Can one of you get one for her?"

*

Word finally reached Captain LaTour when a newspaper reporter came to the ship and informed him of what happened in the city.

"Lord VanderMeer is still alive at the Marine Society Hospital. People assert it was another assassination attempt. Do you have anything to say, Captain?"

LaTour was in shock. "Get this garbage off my brow!" he shouted to the marines.

The captain went below and told Victorio and Henri. Henri went into a rage and demanded to leave the ship. LaTour blocked his way.

"Now hold on, boy! Don't go charging off just yet. Let's think this through. Come into my cabin."

Victorio followed them in.

"Whatever happened is over," LaTour said.

"You don't know that! This could just be starting!"

"Henri, if the newspapers are writing stories, the VanderMeer house is already surrounded by the marines and magistrate deputies. I will go and find out what has happened. Don't look at me like that. Now listen to me, Henri. You go charging into all this without a plan, without thinking this through, your identity will be uncovered! You know it will! And you will be arrested at best. Who knows what will happen from there. Don't make this worse than it is. People are searching this city for the killers right now. *Anyone* coming close to the house will be challenged and questioned. So I am going to go. And I am going alone. I want your word you will stay aboard the *Queen*. I'd give you an order to do this, but you would just ignore that. So I want your word you will stay aboard this ship until I say otherwise."

There was a brief stare down. They both knew Henri could slip away from this ship at night without being seen.

"You have my word," Henri said evenly. "But if I hear anyone else has been hurt. I am coming to get them."

Coming to get who? The captain grabbed his hat and long coat. He pointed a finger at Henri.

"You will stay aboard the *Queen* and wait for me to come back," he said sternly.

*

Sentry Cheever arrived at the house. The marine guards had been tripled and were marching guard around the outside.

Lydia Hancock was there. A magistrate deputy was posted in the foyer.

Corrinne wanted Sentry to stay and guard the house. He refused.

"My lady, ya' are nah' going anywhere without me at your side. There could be more of them waiting right now, knowing ya' are going tah' try and see his lordship."

"The marines will be with me," she argued. "I'd feel safer if you were here with the babies."

"My lady, this house is the *only* place in Boston where ya' are safe. If you leave it, I am going with ya'. And tha' is final."

"Let Sentry go with you, my lady," Dian pleaded. "There are plenty of men here to protect us now. He is right."

She looked at Molly holding Conor on her shoulder.

Molly nodded. "Let Sentry go with you. Please!"

Corrinne agreed reluctantly. The sun had set as they went out the front door to the waiting carriage.

She has more marine guards than a fucking admiral, Sentry thought.

A crowd of people across the street were shouting words of love and support. Corrinne held up a hand to acknowledge them before getting into the closed carriage house. It pulled away from the house. Two marines stood at the back. The drivers were both marines. They each had a blunderbuss. Two mounted escorts, one in front and one in back, also travelled the distance with her.

The ride to the hospital did not take long. There were people crowding all of the streets nearby. The crowds would be even larger were it not for the cold. The carriage pulled into the back of the hospital. Marines already there were holding back the crush of the crowd. Sentry used his formidable size to usher her through the crowd and into the hospital.

Two doctors met her as she entered. One of them was Dr. Angove. He held Corrinne in his arms and let her sob. Then she shook her head sharply and regained her composure.

"Lady VanderMeer, this is Dr. Barrie. He is a former army surgeon from the last war. He has seen a lot of gunshot wounds."

She nodded once at Dr. Barrie. "Where is my husband?"

They led her to a private room with a marine guard posted outside the door. Corrinne nodded to him and found Charles lying in a bed on his back. He was sleeping.

"I thought he was shot in the back?"

"He was," replied Dr. Barrie.

Chairs were brought in and they talked quietly for almost an hour. The two doctors explained the extent of the wounds and the anticipated paralysis.

"He will never walk again?"

"No, my lady." Dr. Barrie spoke somberly. "I've seen this type of wound many times. He has lost a lot blood, but no other organs were damaged. If he rests, he will live."

Corrinne pondered the first attempted poisoning on Charles and now the shooting. And Jack Tasker's horrible death.

They will only try again. No matter how many we kill. Unless we find a way to stop it once and for all. But how? It has to be more than the châsse. *This wraith can possess people and make them do these things. How do we stop the wraith? I am missing something.*

"We cannot stay here any longer," she said aloud to herself.

"But he needs constant care, my lady."

Corrinne was talking about Boston. They were talking about the hospital. She decided to answer their presumption.

"I want Charles brought home. We can care for him. Eventually it is up to us anyway. We might as well start now."

"But his body wounds are not healed."

"Then I will hire a doctor to see to him full time…but at my house. Dr. Barrie? Name your price."

The army surgeon knew he would be spending all of his time on this case anyway.

"My price? That will not be the issue, my lady. But let me think this over tonight, and I will give you an answer tomorrow."

"Very well, but I *will* make arrangements to move him tomorrow morning."

"I do not think that is a good idea," Dr. Barrie warned.

"Then help me do it!" She could see their hesitation. "Gentlemen, listen to me carefully. Lord VanderMeer and I suspect the poisoner who killed my maid and probably Jack Tasker too is someone with a detailed knowledge of medicine. The only person I do not suspect is Dr. Angove, and now because you labored so hard to save Charles' life, I do not suspect you, Dr. Barrie. But anyone else working here is a suspect, at least to me. That includes the nurses. You may think that unreasonable, but I do not care. I will come back in the morning to move him to our house. I will have guards posted on this door. I can only ask that one of you be present when any type of medical care is administered. That is my request."

Dr. Angove took her hand. "I will stay with him through the night, my lady. Right here in this room."

Corrinne looked at him with great relief. "Thank you, Gordon. Thank you."

At midnight, Caroline Bristol went by Lord VanderMeer's room and asked a drowsy Dr. Angove, sitting in a chair with his head resting on the wall, if there was anything he needed.

"Thank you, no, Miss Bristol. You are dismissed for the night."

Caroline put on her cape and contemplated what else she might do to cause the man's death without the use of a toxic poison. Something natural and more believable. She was tired after the events of today, so nothing came to mind right away. But the man was paralyzed. His condition might offer opportunities to aggravate the infirmities.

Pour water into his mouth until he drowns or chokes on his vomit?

Well…she would have to study some of the journals in the medical library on this. They usually listed the dangers to life more than the cures. There was time. Lord VanderMeer would not be going anywhere soon.

I will think of something in the morning.

As Captain LaTour traveled to the VanderMeer residence by carriage, he saw the people of Boston moving at a frantic pace on the streets, either going somewhere to check on the well-being of loved ones or trying to get home before darkness blanketed the city. He would later be told... *Because there are people on the prowl, you see, killing other people as they walk down the sidewalk!* He arrived at the house in the late afternoon and was searched and questioned by suspicious marines before he was escorted to the front door. He was admitted only after Lydia Hancock attested to his character.

"Lady VanderMeer is still at the hospital," Lydia told him somberly. "I am certain she wants to see you, Captain, but you will have to wait."

LaTour took a seat in the library, of course. Because of the cold, a fire had been started in the chimney hearth. He stared at it. The firelight glowed with warmth, burning the hardwood with pops and snaps. This was a comfortable room but on cold nights it was even more inviting. It was a place shared willingly by people of intelligence, charitable hearts, and good will. These people did not deserve such violent tragedy in their lives.

Dian entered the room with a tray holding a pot of black coffee, three mugs, cream and sugar, and a plate of sweetbreads. After she set it down, he stood and embraced the stoic cook. His unexpected embrace was all Dian needed to break down into sobs. He held her, rubbed her back, and made soothing sounds until she quieted.

Dian wiped her eyes. "Thank you." Feeling ashamed of her outburst, she left the room with her eyes downcast.

Lydia Hancock joined LaTour in the library and they discussed the day's events. He'd been unaware of the magistrate's death along with two more of his deputies.

"*Mon Dieu!*" he said softly.

LaTour mentioned his notice of the frenetic movement he saw on the streets. She provided the plausible explanation. But learning that at least one of the perpetrators was dead, and at Lady Corrinne's hands no less, brought some solace.

"Two other men escaped the city to the south," Lydia said. "Many soldiers went looking to find them."

"What about the woman who killed the magistrate with poison?"

Lydia shook her head. "She must still be among us."

The front door suddenly opened. A rush of cold air swept into the library through the open door. Lydia and the captain went into the living room as Lady Corrinne came into the foyer followed by Sentry Cheever. Corrinne allowed her old friend to hold her, but she steeled her emotions and did not cry. She'd cried enough. She turned and embraced Lydia.

They sat down while Corrinne talked about Charles' condition. To hear he would be paralyzed for the rest of his life had tears streaming down Lydia's face.

"I am so sorry. What possesses these people to do these terrible things?"

If you only knew, Corrinne thought.

The exhaustion on Corrinne's face was easy to see. To allow Corrinne time to rest, Lydia said she should be going.

"Thank you for staying here for me. Sentry, would you mind escorting Mrs. Hancock to her house?"

"It would be my pleasure, madam."

"I will be all right," Lydia demurred. "My house is not that far."

Corrinne shook her head. "This house may be watched. You cannot leave it alone in the dark. Sentry will go with you. Do this for me?"

After they left, she asked Captain LaTour to wait a while longer. She went up and checked on the babies. They were sleeping. Molly had fed them both.

"They were no trouble. Evidently, I am making a lot of milk."

Anamosa rushed to her next. "Is Henri going to come and see me?"

"I am sure he will. Let me talk to the captain now and learn when."

Corrinne went downstairs and joined LaTour in the library. She collapsed into her favorite chair and exhaled loudly. Seeing the coffee, she poured herself a cup and sipped the invigorating black liquid. LaTour waited until she was ready to talk.

In a toneless voice, she explained what transpired for her, ending with her killing of the man who attempted to smash down the carriage hangar door.

"What did his lordship say?"

"Nothing, as of yet. His lordship was given opiates and is resting. He has no feeling from the waist down. He will be that way for the rest of his life...short of a miracle. But since he is missing a piece of bone from his spine, even a miracle is unlikely."

Corrinne refused to cry. She had no more tears left. She stared at the fire, thinking, making and discarding decisions.

"Is there something I can do?"

"Yes, Captain. There is." She rose and shut the doors into the library first. "We will be leaving Boston. I thought we would be safe here, but we are not. And people are dying all around us because of our presence among them. And that will happen again if we stay."

LaTour was taken aback by the sudden announcement. "And where are you going?" he asked with uncertainty.

"Good question. Where are you sailing?"

"Well, I have been telling everyone who asks me that I sail for Amsterdam next. I might get there eventually, but my first destination is Louisbourg to turn over my cargo and allow Henri to return to the garrison. After that, I sail for Rochefort and report to Admiral de la Motte...my new master."

"I am sure Admiral de la Motte has very important wars to fight, but he will be required to share your captaincy with me."

"Whether he likes it or not," LaTour assured her. "Where do you want to go, my lady? I will take you there."

"Back in time," Corrinne mused. "But someplace where I cannot be attacked so easily. I don't know of such a place, do you? I would go to Quebec or Montréal except for the war...and Francois Bigôt," she added with disgust. "Then I might at least see Philippe again, yes?"

LaTour did not want to say it but he did anyway. "I know a place of safety. But not forever."

"Where?" she asked.

"Louisbourg."

Corrinne frowned. "Louisbourg? Is it not cold and rainy there…all the time?"

"Yes," he said. "But there are some warmer months. The people all speak French. They eat well when they are not starving. Plenty of fresh fish. It is a fortress-port, bristling with cannon. Though the English will lay siege to it someday. But so far they are being defeated by the French navy. It has a full garrison. Over fifteen hundred men. And Henri will be there."

LaTour watched her frown change to great interest at the mention of Henri.

"That's right!"

"And…there is one more reason that may not be that important…but Philippe can take a mail schooner to see you in Louisbourg."

Corrinne needed no further encouragement. "We are going to Louisbourg," she stated with conviction. "For all the reasons you have said. But do not mention Philippe's name as one of the reasons to anyone else."

"The English may try to invade as early as next summer."

"I don't care. I will deal with that problem next spring."

They continued talking until late. LaTour was a great help in asking her the right questions as she decided what she should take with her, because she might not return to America again…not until the war was over…which could be years. *The house?* She would leave it in the joint possession of Molly Martyn and Dianamora. Corrinne would retain ownership but they would be granted lease-rights. *Thomas Hancock will help me with that.* She would give Hancock attorney privileges for the properties. That was a lot to entrust to the man. But she and Charles trusted him a lot.

At that point in the discussion there came a knock on the door. Sentry Cheever stuck in his head from the *cuisine*.

"Apologies for my intrusion, my lady. Can I do anything more for you tonight?"

"Oh! Yes, Sentry. Yes, you can. I want to move Lord VanderMeer to this house in the morning. I would like your help with that."

"I am happy to help you any way I can."

"Good. Dian, can you prepare a room for Sentry tonight? He will be staying over."

"Yes, my lady." Dian tried not to glance at Sentry, but it was easy to see how pleased she was that he would be staying.

"And Sentry, since you are staying here tonight, please join Captain LaTour and me for some discussions."

"As you wish."

"Dian, please bring us brandy too. Sentry, I plan to tell everyone soon, but for now, I need to take you into my confidence."

"Of course."

"I will be leaving Boston. For how long, I cannot say, but it could be a few years."

"When?" was all Sentry could think to ask.

"Soon." She explained the reasons but did not disclose the destination. "Lord VanderMeer and I will have to determine where, but Amsterdam seems likely. The Duke of Brunswick has asked him to return. While I am gone, I need people to care for our properties."

She explained what she intended for the current household. "Molly Martyn and Dianamora will have leasehold-rights to it. Though I still need Thomas Hancock's counsel on this."

Sentry took a large swallow of brandy. He did not want them to go anywhere.

"Forgive me for saying this, but I will be sad to see you go. You've become family...to me."

It was the slight despairing tone in which Sentry said the words that caused another break in Corrinne's composure. She did not reply until she had regained control of her emotions. But the two men saw tears spill down her cheeks.

"Oh, Sentry. God knows we owe you so much. We owe you our lives and more than once. *But we have to do this*...for a while. Despite all the protection, the deputies, and even the marines, they still try to kill us and people around us are dying. We have to leave, if for no other reason than to disrupt their future plans...we know they are making them...even tonight as we talk."

"Then how dah' we make them stop? I will kill them! Just tell me who they are!"

Corrinne admired his strength, his anger, his courage, and most of all his heart.

"Oh, Sentry…I don't know all of them…or even how many there are. But the vault at Winter House is part of our plan to stop them. The vault pieces in the carriage hangar still need to be lowered into place. That is something you can do for us. That is why the man attacked the carriage hangar. He had a long-hammer. He wanted to smash all the vault pieces and break apart the *châsse*. They fear the *châsse* even more than they want to kill us."

Sentry was frustrated. "My lady, ya' have told me all this, but I still dinnah' understand it."

"I know, Sentry. Captain LaTour has the same feelings."

Sentry glanced at LaTour. The captain raised his glass in agreement.

"But if you can set these vault pieces, you will be creating a trap."

"I dinnah' want ta' live at Winter House! You dinnah' want ta' live at Winter House either!"

"You don't have to live there at all. Just finish the vault for us."

Sentry exhaled heavily.

This change was coming too fast for him, she realized.

"I've asked you for too much, Sentry. I apologize. I tend to charge at problems too quickly. Let's speak more of this once Charles is back at home. I am overtired and distraught. You have both been very kind to me today. I will go up to bed. Stay here as long as you wish."

She stood and they both followed suit. She touched them on their shoulders and searched their faces.

"A person could live all their life and be blessed to have one friend like you…let alone two. There is not much I would not do for you. I love you both."

She kissed their cheeks and left the library.

The men sat back down.

"Bloody hell!" Sentry expounded. He took another long swallow of brandy.

"Corrinne is an acquired taste, as the connoisseurs would say. But I am proud she calls me her friend."

They drank and told each other stories. It lifted their moods until the brandy was gone. By then, LaTour was too drunk to go back to the ship. Dian settled him into an empty room on the servants' hallway.

*

October 1, 1756
Berlin

Alain Marcoux sat down with Colonel von Kleinfels at the lavish apartment he'd purchased in Berlin. The city was vibrant with all things martial. Frederick II's sweeping victories over Saxony and Austria further elevated the sovereign's invincible reputation among the German people.

Marcoux related the successful discussions with Governor Vaudreuil for a mercenary regiment.

"They will require this regiment in the spring. We will be told the sailing destination then."

But the colonel did not respond to this. He only wanted to talk about things related to the *châsse*.

"All our efforts produced little. The archbishop's death was not lasting. The man had a son. And he now carries the symbol of a great house around his neck. The artist was injured in the attack but still lives. The seals of the *châsse* were not broken. The people we assembled for all of this are either dead or scattered except for you, Carter, and Caroline Bristol. The white eagle has returned. It damaged me. Boston will become more vigilant. It will be more difficult to attack them. But not impossible. So we will begin."

The colonel withdrew a small bottle of his blood from his coat and poured some of it into a goblet. Then he filled that goblet and another one with a dark red wine.

"A toast to our new plans and future success."

They drank. The blood ritual invigorated Alain Marcoux anew.

"Word has arrived and spread in France that Alain Marcoux is wanted for the assassination of Archbishop André Nicolet in Montréal. Not only you, but also your sea captain."

"Captain LaTour had nothing to do with it! They questioned and dismissed me. I was very careful. Anyone who could be a witness is dead. How would they know it was me?"

The colonel's smile was cold. "They do not know. They picked the two of you because you are no longer there to state otherwise. They probably believe the two of you are innocent. Ironic, yes? They do not care about this bishop. But they also do not want this problem to linger. So someone must be accused."

"What happens now? Changing my identity seems the right solution."

The colonel studied Alain. "I was not aware of your existing prescience. Extraordinary."

The colonel rang a hand-bell. A stern-looking man appeared, dressed in formal service attire. The *servant* clicked his heels in attention next to the table.

"Sir!"

"This man is a former field surgeon in the Hessian army. He is dedicated to me now because of my partial paralysis from the stroke. As you may have noticed, my movements have slowed considerably and I can only move about with the use of a cane. It seems to be getting worse, though time will tell. Consequently, I am no longer fit to lead in the accomplishment of our goals."

He looked at the servant.

"Bring us the standing brazier. The cleaver. The cutting square. The leather cord. Some field bandages. The utensils. And the large metal plate."

While they waited, the colonel untied his shirt and pulled the gold threaded pouch hanging around his neck into view. He opened the top of the pouch and sifted through the desiccated bones inside, finding one that was sufficiently small. It was a quarter of an inch long and black in color. He set the bone on the table in front of Alain.

"Changing your identity is indeed the proper course…the first course, actually." The colonel's expression showed amusement at his own words. "Swallow that with some wine. And you will begin to feel the change."

Alain picked up the bone and looked at it. It seemed harmless, unless it was poison.

"Is it poisonous?"

"No. It is eternal. Swallow it!"

Alain put it on his tongue and drank the wine.

The colonel watched him carefully. Before a minute had passed, Alain Marcoux' eyes widened with understanding as the vulnax began to take full possession.

The *servant* returned with the standing brazier and the other items on a rolling cart.

"Put the brazier here between us and light it. Set the steel plate here on the table with the cutting square in the center."

The servant did as he was ordered.

The colonel took off his uniform coat and rolled up his left shirt sleeve. "Tie the cord right here," he told the servant and pointed at a spot half way between his left elbow and wrist. "Make it as tight as you can."

Alain Marcoux watched intently.

"And now the *main course*," the colonel said, enjoying the allegorical representation.

Wilhelm von Kleinfels picked up the sharpened meat cleaver, laid the palm of his left hand flat atop the two-inch thick cutting square and with one heavy *thwack*, severed his own hand just above the wrist. Blood squirted across the table, but the tourniquet was very tight.

The colonel's face showed no pain. Neither the servant nor Alain expressed any discomfort at what they had just witnessed. The colonel pressed the stump of his arm into the brazier's coals to cauterize the severed veins and arteries. After a short time, he examined the stump and was satisfied the cauterization had stopped most of the major bleeding.

"You may apply the bandages," he told the servant.

While the former army surgeon performed the necessary field bandaging for such a wound, the colonel reached out with his right hand and tilted the wooden block to let the hand slide onto the plate.

"Now you may eat."

Alain Marcoux looked down at the hand, bewildered.

The colonel saw his hesitation and pointed at the brazier. "If you prefer, we can cook it first."

It took another bottle of red wine, but Alain Marcoux consumed the hand, except for the major bones.

"Very good. Now we turn to the dessert course."

The colonel once again opened the pouch of gold threads. He spread it wide with the fingers of his right hand and selected another similarly small black bone. He placed it in his mouth and washed it down with wine. He regarded Alain Marcoux for the last time.

"You need to shave all the hair off your head and keep it shaved. In a few moments, you will put this pouch around your neck. When you do, your identity will become that of Major Karl Dörnberg, formerly of my personal regiment in Hesse. He does not really exist, but I will certify your credentials. I will continue my service to Frederick II as liaison to the Naval

Minister of France and assist you as I am able in pursuit of your primary goals, which will soon become apparent to you. You were the most able of my surviving servants."

Colonel von Kleinfels handed over the pouch to Alain. He watched the other man slip it over his head. At that moment, the vulnax took possession of a new human body. Wilhelm von Kleinfels visibly relaxed as if a great weight had been lifted from of his shoulders. He winced at the pain in his left arm, which was now intense.

"I need an opiate," he said to the servant.

The servant looked at Major Dörnberg for direction. The major made a gesture of approval and the surgeon went to retrieve the medicine.

"We will focus on destroying the *châsse* going forward," Dörnberg stated. "If we can kill the scion of the great houses in conjunction with that objective, so be it. If we had two men instead of one in this last attempt, the *châsse* seals would be broken and the great houses would now be in pain for the rest of their short lives. We will not make that mistake again."

The surgeon returned with a small glass of alcohol with several drops of laudanum added.

Kleinfels drank the solution in one gulp. It would take about five minutes for the opiate to work.

"I have need of a city apartment like this one," said Major Dörnberg. "Use your money to buy one, or move out of this one by tomorrow. You may take this servant with you." He looked at the surgeon. "Find me four new servants. A cook. A valet. And two bodyguards. I want them here tomorrow. Prepare a room for me to sleep."

Carter Trevathan and Caroline Bristol were visited by the night messenger in their dreams that night. The younger and strong physicality of the scarring wraith's new human body permitted it to visit all of its servants over the next week. The message began with a familiar statement.

You will serve me.

*

Boston

Lady VanderMeer got into the closed carriage the next morning accompanied by Sentry Cheever and Captain LaTour. Again, she was guarded by the marines and two mounted cavalrymen. The carriage headed first to the Long Wharf. LaTour dismounted with a promise to return to her house that night.

"Find a way to bring him with you," she told the captain.

Sentry did not need to ask her who she meant as the carriage pulled away.

Corrinne and the captain had a brief, private discussion that morning while breaking their fast about future plans. She wanted to leave Boston as soon as Lord VanderMeer was able to travel, within two weeks. He reminded her the ship was fully loaded and that some of that cargo space would now be emptied to convert it back to cabin space.

"That will make the cargo holds very crowded."

"The *châsse* will be coming with us," she told him. "Unfortunately, I cannot leave it here. Don't look so glum, Captain. I will retain it with us in Louisbourg."

Captain LaTour had his overcoat pulled tight around his body with the collar raised against the stinging rain and wind. Despite the high quality of the brandy he and Sentry had consumed the night before, it made for an equally high-quality headache that morning.

As he approached the ship, he saw that the marine sentries had taken a large empty metal can and started a fire in it for warmth. He went to see them.

"Have you men broken your fast?"

"No, sir," said one of the shivering marines.

"I will have some food and hot drinks brought up to you."

The captain stopped and asked the watch if anything unusual had occurred. Through chattering teeth, he said everything was quiet.

"Stand on the top stair of the bridge house ladder out of the wind. You can see the brow from there. I will send you up a hot drink."

Captain LaTour went below and told his cook to prepare a hot meal for the four marine guards standing watch on the pier. "I want that done every morning. Today, make them hotcakes and use the sugar syrup we purchased. Bring them two pots, one of hot tea and one of hot coffee with mugs."

"Your coffee, Captain?"

"Of course, my coffee. Tomorrow you can serve the standard ship's rations and hot tea. Give me the first cup of coffee when it's ready. And hand a mug up to the watch to drink."

Then he went into his cabin and took out a book with tables on the tides for Boston. He left it out to memorize when the high tides would turn over the next two weeks. Going down the passageway, he went looking for Victorio, who was still asleep.

"Pssst, Victorio! Get up. Find Henri and meet me in the dining cabin."

He was studying his book on tides when they came into the cabin shivering with blankets around their shoulders.

"Lady Corrinne asked me to stay the night for discussions. Your food and drink is being made."

He spent thirty minutes giving them all the news. The food arrived during that time.

"So we will be transporting Lord and Lady VanderMeer, Anamosa, and the twins with us when we leave. That means we need to covert that cargo space back into cabins."

"Captain, we are overloaded. I don't think we have any room to shift the cargo," Victorio said.

"Well, we have at least a week to figure this out. Lord VanderMeer's paralysis requires he be attended to at all times. I will learn more about that today. But find out if there is someone in the crew who might earn a double wage to take care of him. And I mean someone who has actually done this! I am thinking he will stay in a cabin with two bunks, the second bunk will be used by his attendant."

"I will do it if no one else volunteers," Henri said right away.

"Good. The *châsse* will be coming aboard again. My thought is to put it in an empty passenger cabin, tied off securely. I've not seen it, but I've been told Lord VanderMeer surrounded it with a much stronger enclosure."

"When can I visit?"

"Lady Corrinne wants you to come tonight. But you cannot go slinking around the city right now. Soldiers and magistrate deputies are searching for the killers. I've decided the best thing to do is have you dress as a Dutch marine. We have a spare uniform. Victorio has captain insignias on his. He can tailor the other one for you and use lieutenant insignias."

"Did you see Lord VanderMeer?"

"No. He is coming home from the hospital today."

The room became silent as the three seamen strategized privately.

"Sentry is there," LaTour continued. "No one knows about *you* except for Lord and Lady VanderMeer and Anamosa. And other people may show up. Lord VanderMeer is a very popular in Boston. When we get to the house, we will see how to manage this. We certainly need to keep people quiet about who you are. I do not think it is safe for you to sleep even one night at the residence."

"I agree. We need to rehearse my identity story with the crew. And that you gave me permission to work at a bakery to make me a better pastry cook. In case someone asks."

"And who would ask?" LaTour said nervously.

*

Corrinne sat next to Charles as he was waking up. She held his hand and listened to his groans of pain as the opiates wore off. Eventually, he could focus and smiled at seeing her.

"Thank God. You were my last thought as I was shot. That is all I know. Tell me what happened."

In a quiet voice, Corrinne told him what she knew based on what she heard. Charles slumped at hearing about Jack Tasker.

"Oh, God. Not him too."

Then she told him what had happened at the house.

"And he almost succeeded in breaking down the doors. Until I killed him."

"Where were the marines?" Charles was exhausted just hearing about the attack. "Jesus. What are we going to do, Corrinne?"

"We need to leave Boston is what we need to do," she whispered. "Captain LaTour is ready to move us wherever we want to go."

"Move again? And where would that be to this time?" Charles answered in a despondent voice.

"I have an idea we will discuss at the house."

Before she could say more, Dr. Barrie arrived and came into the room having heard a man's voice. He introduced himself and helped Charles drink some water and sat down in another chair.

"So how are you feeling, your lordship?"

"I can...cannot *feel* my legs."

"That's because you were shot."

"Shot?"

With Corrinne holding Charles' hand, Dr. Barrie explained the extent of the injuries and what it meant.

"Paralyzed?!" Charles was lethargic from the opiates, but not enough to shield him from the horror of what he just heard. "You mean…I…cannot walk?!"

The thought was inconceivable. Charles tried to move his legs right away. He found out he couldn't even move his toes. He could not feel them either.

Dr. Barrie had seen this before. The initial shock. This expression of disbelief on the faces of injured soldiers. There was little he could do except explain what the man could expect and emphasize what the man could still do.

"You will need help moving around and other assistance, your toilet for example. But I understand you are an artist. I see no reason why you cannot continue with that pursuit if it is your passion. The flesh and muscle wounds made by the ball will take weeks to heal properly…maybe sooner if you are the type of person who heals more quickly…some people do. Moving you, however, will aggravate this healing. I suggest you stay in a bed until then."

"Where would I run off to?" Charles asked in an angry, sullen voice.

"What is being done here that cannot be done at our house?" Corrinne interjected pointedly.

Dr. Barrie knew her intentions.

"I hear you, madam. The constant examination of his wounds is one thing," the doctor offered. "Watching for signs of infection, which is easily done by doctors and nurses here at the hospital on a rotating basis."

"We can do that at the house. I do not intend to let Charles stay here. Unless you plan to operate or suture him in some way, I came here today to take him home. As I told you I would yesterday."

"While I would like to dissuade you from this action, I completely understand your concern. So this is what Dr. Angove and I propose. We will alternate visits to you. One of us in the morning and the other in the afternoon. We have found two nurses to assist in Lord VanderMeer's care. These are two experienced women Dr. Angove has known for years. We have told them they will earn twice their usual wages. Dr. Angove and I will accept our normal fees. We will only be with you an hour each visit, about as much time as we do here."

Corrinne was greatly relieved. "I cannot express how much I appreciate this."

"The truth is, Lady VanderMeer, I'd rather your husband stay here in the hospital. But too many people I trust in Boston went out of their way since yesterday's events to acquaint me with the constant menace of these attacks. And how much they value you both. I am new to this city. But I am not without sympathy. I, therefore, have come to agree with you that you can protect your husband from the people trying to take his life...at your home. And with a marine platoon as guards, you can do this much better than the nurses at this hospital."

"When can I move him?"

"You are very quick willed." Dr. Barrie paused for a moment. "That depends, my lady, on how you intend to move him. You can see that his lordship cannot even sit up."

I cannot sit up!? Another horrible revelation. With every sentence the description of Charles' condition was getting worse. His head lolled to one side, away from the conversation.

Corrinne had not thought about that. "How would you do this, Doctor?"

"Well, I would use a carriage converted into an ambulance. Before you ask, none of those exist in Boston. But I have used them successfully on battlefields. I could possibly have something created that would temporarily work by noon today."

Corrinne took Charles' hand. "Charles," she spoke softly. "I want to take you home. Are you agreeable to that?"

"It does not appear that I will be able to make choices like that anymore," Charles snapped.

Corrinne could see and feel his pain. "I just think you will be safer at home with me. I want to take you home."

"Who's stopping you?"

Corrinne girded herself against the bitterness in Charles' voice. She looked at Dr. Barrie. The doctor saw the pained realization on Charles' face had now appeared on Lady VanderMeer's face. He'd seen this before too.

"We can be ready by noon, Lady VanderMeer," he said with empathy.

"Thank you, Dr. Barrie. The sooner we can do this, the better."

Through lowered eyes, Caroline Bristol watched the carriage leave with Lord VanderMeer in a cushioned litter and Lady VanderMeer at his side. She had created a small vial of poison made by crushing, boiling, and reducing apricot nuts. She was not certain of its potency, but she planned to give him a lot of it in the meals the hospital would serve him over the next few days.

But that was not going to happen now.

Disappointing.

Still, the night messenger's visit to her dreams the night before was an unexpected surprise. He took control of her emotions in a powerful way no man was capable of doing. She recalled how her hand had slipped beneath her nightgown. Her fingers moved and titillated as it had whispered.

You are the one, it had told her. *You are the vessel of my power. You will serve me. You will feel pleasure.*

Caroline's back arched in a shattering orgasm.

*

By three in the afternoon, Captain LaTour and Victorio had outlined a way to shift the cargo around to allow Lady VanderMeer's quarters to be erected once more, along with three passenger cabins. He inspected Henri as Lieutenant Thom Linden in his sea soldier uniform. In the dark blue pressed colors, he looked very impressive. Much better than he had ever looked.

"Your appearance will do nicely, I think. And you have practiced how you came to be in my service?'

Victorio bridged Henri's purported seamanship of ten years with his joining of the Dutch sea soldiers and assignment to *William's Queen*. That his few days of working at a bakery was permitted by Captain LaTour as Lieutenant Linden was tired of the sea and hoped to find a new life in Boston.

"Which did not work out," Victorio said. "He has four years aboard the *Queen*. When not in uniform, he is a helmsman."

LaTour nodded. "All right. The crew has the same story. Let's go ashore and visit the residence."

The three men stopped by the marine guards to explain what they were doing.

"How was your food this morning?"

"Excellent, Captain. Particularly the coffee. We could do with more of that."

"We'll see. We are off to visit Lord VanderMeer's residence. This is Captain Jaager and Lieutenant Linden of the Dutch sea marines."

"Sea marines? I thought you were trying to be a baker?"

"I was," Henri said in English with a mimicked Dutch accent. "I got let go for being clumsy. Maybe in the next port. My time in the marines has expired. But for now, I like sailing on *William's Queen*."

"Don't forget to tell the next watch we will likely return later tonight."

The carriage arrived at the residence. LaTour, Victorio, and Henri approached the guard house. The marines faced them sternly. The muskets were dressed with bayonets.

"Captain LaTour," the sergeant greeted with a salute.

All three of them saluted back.

"And who are these...officers?"

LaTour introduced them. "My ship belongs to Lord VanderMeer. He is the son of the Duke of Brunswick. It is Lord VanderMeer's flagship. As such, he is allotted two Dutch sea marines. They only get to wear these pretty uniforms in Amsterdam or when they visit Lord VanderMeer."

The sergeant nodded, but was still suspicious. "They will not be carrying those swords any further."

"Of course."

Victorio and Henri gave over their sabers in the scabbards and without being asked held open their long coats for inspection.

"And someone in the household must approve their entry," the sergeant added.

"Of course. Is Lady VanderMeer here?

"Yes, sir. She came back from the hospital an hour ago and brought Lord VanderMeer with her on a litter. He is paralyzed, did you know?"

"Yes, I was told. We came to see him and offer what comfort we are capable of giving."

"Very well, sir. You two have to wait. Captain, you may approach the door and knock."

LaTour knocked. Molly opened it. Henri bowed his head so he would not be recognized while waiting outside. LaTour disappeared for a minute. Then Corrinne came rushing out the door. The marines and Henri and Victorio came to attention.

"Captain Jaager, Lieutenant Linden, you are both welcome in our home."

They bowed respectfully. She embraced and kissed their cheeks as appropriate.

The English sergeant gestured they may pass.

Once the front door closed, a restrained and quiet celebration broke loose with Molly and Dian and Anamosa hugging Henri with enthusiasm all at the same time. Henri took off his long coat and the women cooed over how splendid and tall and muscular he looked in his dark blue uniform.

Victorio nudged Captain LaTour. "I am wearing the same blue uniform, and I outrank him! Yet they are not hugging me."

LaTour leaned in toward Victorio. "You do not have blond hair. He is fifteen years younger than you. And they are all in love with him. Any other questions?"

Victorio smacked his head. "I see. That makes sense. Makes me wonder why *I* do not hug him."

"Ahoy, little lord."

Sentry Cheever had been standing quietly in the dining room watching the welcome in the foyer.

Henri smiled broadly and walked to his friend at a fast step. They slapped their arms around one another in greeting.

Finally, Sentry held him at arm's length. "You stand like a hard oak tree! My God. Look at you. I like your ear. Who did the work?"

"A grenade at Fort Bull," Henri replied modestly.

"Good, lad. Good. Nothing like a grenade to the head to give your brains a proper perspective. What else?"

"What *else* can wait, Sentry," Corrinne said. "Henri should come upstairs to see Lord VanderMeer. He was just given laudanum and will be asleep soon."

Anamosa would not let go of Henri's hand so she went too. Corrinne preceded him and had the nurse wait in the nursery.

When they entered the room, Charles VanderMeer smiled weakly from his bed.

"Oh, my! The boy becomes a man! Henri. Sit. Sit. Before the opiates rob my ability to speak."

Henri took a chair and allowed Anamosa to sit on his lap and rest her head on his shoulder.

"I am so sorry, Charles."

"Yes," Charles agreed in a bitter tone. "The little curse that follows us does not stop attacking. Mathilde was killed a few months ago. This time it was me that was hurt. Did I say hurt? This paralysis makes me wish I were *dead!* But it will likely happen again. So I can always hope."

Henri winced, though he knew Charles did not really mean that.

"I should have been here."

"No, Henri. We are surrounded by marines and magistrate deputies and still they managed to get through and do this to me. Next time it will be Corrinne. *We* should not be here. We need to find somewhere safe. Wherever that is."

"Then come with me," Henri offered right away. "Come to Louisbourg. They will not reach you there."

"Louisbourg?" Charles pondered this. "Louisbourg?" His eyes closed as the opiates softened his consciousness.

"Charles? Charles?"

They waited for him to answer.

"We need to go now, Ana. He is asleep."

CHAPTER 31
BOSTON
OCTOBER 1756
The Cake

Two days later, Captain LaTour and the Dutch marines, Captain Jaager and Lieutenant Linden, came ashore again, this time as part of the escort for Lady Corrinne VanderMeer. She was also accompanied by four English marines. They went to the burial services for Deputy Magistrate Jack Tasker at the Granary Burial Ground. Mary Tasker and her daughter Lisbeth were there along with hundreds of other Boston citizens and elite.

The newspapers wrote stories on this public ceremony. A line of grateful people spoke at the grave site, praising Jack Tasker for his selfless duty and service to the city. He'd solved hundreds of crimes during his tenure. Among the dignitaries present was Governor Charles Hardy, Samuel Grant, and Thomas Hancock.

The eulogy Lady VanderMeer gave was particularly poignant, one newspaper would write.

    Escorting her were two officers in the Dutch
    marines, Captain Victorio Jaager and Lieutenant
    Thom Linden, both crew members of *William's
    Queen*, Lord VanderMeer's flagship currently vis-
    iting Boston and moored at the head of the Long
    Wharf.

After the ceremony, they went back to the residence. A brand new wheeled chair was waiting on the porch, designed by a local carriage maker to aid Lord VanderMeer's mobility. Its four wheels, six inches in diameter on the back and four inches on the front, were supported by steel axles. The spoked wheels were banded with steel hoops made by a local blacksmith.

The chair itself was cushioned on the bottom, the back, and the two arm-rests. Each component was made to be easily replaced if they ever wore out.

Charles's back had not healed enough to try out the chair. But Corrinne was so impressed with the unexpected generosity, she gave three pounds to the carriage maker and two pounds to the blacksmith with the proviso they would make two more of the wheeled chairs and donate them to the city, in Charles VanderMeer's name, care of the Marine Society Hospital.

Captain LaTour, Henri, and Corrinne went as a group to Charles' bedroom to have more discussions on leaving Boston.

"Henri has already mentioned Louisbourg to me. It sounds like a good idea."

Corrinne was encouraged. They went over the reasons again. Philippe's name was never mentioned.

Charles was tired, lethargic, but his mood had improved since the day before. At least a little. He seemed determined to have this discussion. He spoke slowly, carefully enunciating his words to be understood.

"We can *never* mention Louisbourg to anyone in Boston for obvious reasons. I will announce it," Charles said, "probably to the newspapers, that Lady Corrinne and I are returning to Amsterdam for several months, at the request of my father, the Duke of Brunswick. I want to leave the impression we are coming back again."

"Are you planning to come back?" LaTour asked.

"We've not decided," Corrinne answered quickly.

"I think the war may decide for us," Henri said.

"So let's all agree"—Charles gestured with one trembling hand—"that we do not know."

Corrinne spoke. "But as part of our planning to depart, Charles and I decided to lease our two properties. This house to Captain Conor Martyn and Molly and Winter House to Sentry Cheever and his wife, when he gets married."

"Sentry is getting married?" Henri blurted out before Captain LaTour could ask the same question.

"It is a possibility," Corrinne answered. "Do not ask him about this, please."

Charles continued weakly. "They are cherished friends…and will look after these investments for us."

"When are we going?" LaTour asked.

"I think…I hope to be able to journey in another three weeks…whatever date that is. There are other matters we must attend to before we depart," Charles seemed to struggle to say this.

"My lord, I hope you are not offended that I ask so many questions."

"Not at all. I'm given opiates for my pain. So I feel no pain. But not enough to leave me insensate. Corrinne will continue for me."

"There are other matters," Corrinne began, "which have to do with the *châsse*. Charles has constructed a new enclosure. Granite and wood with new symbols. It needs to be sealed again and have words pronounced over the symbols. Charles has written out the ceremonial words we used in Montréal and made substitutions for the new symbols."

Corrinne handed Henri and Captain LaTour the symbol sketches.

"The new symbols are for the sun, moon, stars, and the seas. We all have to touch the top of the *châsse* and recite certain words."

"My lady," LaTour interrupted, there was a halting tone to his words, "with respect, I do not see why this is important to me?"

Corrinne looked at her captain. "Because, the ritual requires a person to represent each of the symbols. I will take the Moon. Lord VanderMeer the Sun. Henri the stars. We need someone to represent the seas. You seemed a good choice…and we have no one else we can ask to do this. Only a few of us have ever been exposed to this *curse*, for lack of a better word. We don't talk about it very much. But it is a persistent menace in our life. The bishop is dead, and Pierre and Philippe are far away. Captain, you've seen evidence of this demon aboard your ship."

"I have. But not by choice," he reminded them…and also reminded *It*…whatever *It* was. *It* was likely invisible and inside the room lurking in some dark shadow, marking a tally sheet with ticks of whom it would torture later and how.

"Captain," Corrinne said loudly upon seeing LaTour's attention wander.

LaTour flinched. "Yes, my lady. Apologies."

Charles took a deep breath and spoke. "This ceremony will permanently seal this *thing*. Then all we have to do is hide the *châsse* in a place where it will not be easily found. *And be done with it!*" He said the last five words as if he wished it was already over.

Beauregard LaTour's heart was pounding. Talking of occult evil beings was not something he wanted to do. And anything to do with this particular growling stink monster in that flimsy wooden box made him want to pee in his boots. LaTour did not want to talk about *It*. At present, *It* was angry at *them*…not him. His gut told him any participation in what they were talking about would change that.

"Not easily found?" LaTour cleared his throat and spoke in a choked voice. "Is there such a place?"

"Yes, Captain. It is a stone vault. But it is still being prepared."

"My Lady Corrinne, you must know…there is nothing I would not do for you—"

"I know this, Captain. That is why I am asking you to do this for me."

"I-I was not finished speaking!" LaTour protested.

Corrinne reached over and touched his face. "You said enough, Beauregard. I know the goodness in your heart better than you."

They waited for Charles to speak. His expression was grave.

"Some of the Celtic writings I've studied say this *scarring wraith,* as it's called, does not like the seas. It has no power over the waters."

"We will all be there," Henri said to the captain.

"The entire ceremony will take no more than twenty minutes," Corrinne added.

LaTour looked queasy but resigned. "I am not as brave as all of you. So do not expect too much of me."

Corrinne went over and hugged him. "Beauregard, you are one of the bravest men I have ever known. You have crossed the seas for decades. You have endured terrible storms. You fight pirates. You outsmart villains."

"I am *not* as brave as *you*…my lady," LaTour protested.

"You are braver than me! But I will be standing right there, right next to you, arm-in-arm."

Then be prepared to see me piss my pants, LaTour thought.

Charles continued but they could all see his weariness growing. He labored to speak.

"After we have sealed the *châsse*…I propose we have it taken aboard *William's Queen* right away."

"Right away!? That *thing* frightens my crew," LaTour said in protest. "I *will not* load it until you are ready to sail, given a few days. Not until just before you go aboard yourself."

The captain was resolved. Charles did not press him further.

"As you wish, Captain…that is what we will do. But I want to finish this sealing as soon as possible."

"Why?" Corrinne had her own reasons for wanting the ceremony over with, but she was curious as to Charles'.

"Because today I possess the will to do this…and I have some physical strength. But tomorrow or the next day…who can tell? You need *me* for this ceremony. So…I say we do this before another week has passed. In the meantime…hire carpenters to build new doors for the hangar. Are the marines in front of the broken doors?"

"Yes."

"So are we agreed? In a week?"

They looked at Captain LaTour. He swallowed a grimace and nodded.

After they were gone, Charles stared at the ceiling. He vowed to keep struggling, at least until they sealed this wraith. He must see Corrinne and the babies safely delivered from Boston and on their way to Louisbourg. After that…he didn't much care. He certainly was not going to sit in a chair for the rest of his life. He still had strength in his arms. He would ask Captain LaTour to allow him to stay on deck when they left port. At some point they would not be looking at him.

*

David was in the kitchen of King's Bakery in the early morning waiting for Robert Butcher to arrive. He prepared some bread dough to knead and roll but they needed to do this together to set two loaves at the same time in the oven. Robert was rarely late, but there was nothing David could do but wait until he got there. He noticed a newspaper from the day before lying on the floor and picked it up to read while he ate some day-old cake.

Most of the columns focused on the recent spate of violence in the city, such as the death of Deputy Magistrate Jack Tasker by poison. Lord VanderMeer being shot and paralyzed by an assassin. Two of his guards killed. Another assassin attempting to break into the VanderMeer residence. Two other men firing pistols at the VanderMeer residence, but then escaping on horseback out the city gate at the Boston neck. Most columns ended with a warning: *The new magistrate believes there are still other assassins at large in Boston.*

"Bloody hell—glad I am not a VanderMeer."

He ate more cake and read a column describing the funeral of Jack Tasker and the names of the elite who attended. He saw a name in the story that made him sit up straight.

"*Lieutenant* Thom Linden?"

Robert Butcher entered the kitchen. "Sorry I'm late. My wife was sick all night. I had to be sure the neighbors were aware she might need help today."

With practiced movements, the baker and his assistant started the bread baking routine they performed daily.

"Hey, did you read the stories in the paper about all those killings?"

"Yeah. Nasty business that. Makes me glad I'm not a nobleman. You never hear of assassins killing bakers."

"At Jack Tasker's funeral yesterday, the story mentioned that some Dutch marines were in attendance. One of them was a *Lieutenant* Thom Linden!"

Robert stopped rolling dough. "Really?"

David handed him the newspaper and pointed at the column.

"Did you know he was a lieutenant in the Dutch marines?" Robert asked.

"No! And why the fuck would he want to be a baker if he was an officer in the Dutch marines?"

Robert speculated. "He told me he had permission from the captain to look for work ashore. That his time in the marines was up. Let's hope he shoots better than he walks, the clumsy fool,"

"It is strange," David said. *Too strange.*

"Enough chat. Let's catch up on the bread. We're an hour behind."

But Robert now had a creeping sense of a growing problem. David tended to have a taste for gossip and he was a curious man. He had to warn Thom Linden about this story to be certain he was aware of it.

But how?

*

Carter Trevathan was amazed at how strongly Caroline Bristol's sexual appetites had been provoked by the night messenger's visit. She begged Carter to say *You will serve me.* And then order her to do things.

"What things?"

"Anything," she said with a gleam in her eyes. "I will do *anything* you ask."

You do anything I want now, he thought. He was not sure what else to demand. Of course, she was never very eager about being buggered, so he asked for that.

"You will serve me," he said in a deep voice. He watched her shiver all over with pleasure. "Turn over."

It was a very tumultuous night. If he did not come up with something more licentious, she did. He did not get much sleep.

The *wraith* visited every three days to find out what Carter had learned. *It* seemed different to him now. Stronger somehow. But the colonel was back in Berlin. Carter presumed another attack would not be planned until the Hessian returned to Boston. In the meantime, he would focus on growing his thriving cotton cloth business and compelling Caroline *to serve him*.

Ritter's death and the escape of the other two men greatly diminished what they could do anyway. And Rachel Bristol had completely disappeared, along with Jimmy Cantlin. Caroline had no idea where she had gone, nor did she seem to care. As long as he serviced her on those nights she came by, she appeared quite content for things to continue the way it was going. The night messenger, however, invaded her dreams much less often than his. That's what she told him. It evidently had nothing to say to her.

Carter had been questioned by a magistrate deputy after all the deaths, but he had been in Faneuil Hall, watched by a magistrate deputy. The very next day, they stopped watching him at all as he had been accounted for during the attacks, and they were short of men.

So now any planning fell to Carter and Caroline, which meant Carter. Two people were not enough. Caroline had a chance to poison Lord VanderMeer at the hospital, but he'd been moved back to the house the next day. And the VanderMeer residence might as well be a fort. It seemed to be guarded by a permanent marine garrison.

The night messenger wanted Carter to focus on finding a way to destroy the *châsse*, which was some kind of wooden coffin box inside the Vander-Meer carriage hangar continuously guarded by three or four marines.

Maybe I can order Caroline to distract the guards with her mouth. She is a master at that! Have them line up to be served? While I smash away with a long hammer, as Ritter tried to do. And failed.

A ridiculous idea. Of course, the newspapers said they were looking for a woman suspected of poisoning Jack Tasker. Caroline was so crazy unpredictable she might even admit to it. No, better to keep her quiet and occupied doing a lot of what she was good at doing.

Carter smiled. *Which is pleasing me.*

*

Robert found the newspaper articles very disquieting. At the end of the day, he had two cakes delivered inside a crate to the captain of *William's Queen* with a note attached, expressing sympathy for the attack on Lord VanderMeer. On the frosting atop one cake, the name Thom Linden was spelled out in a different color. Baked inside that cake was a short missive.

Captain LaTour did not appreciate the name spelled out on the top when he cut into the cake to eat a piece the next morning. But he immediately came across the piece of paper sticking out of the middle.

"What the fuck is this?"

> *Your name was mentioned in the newspaper yesterday as a lieutenant in the Dutch marines. David tends to gossip a lot. And this made him curious. The same newspaper also mentioned the offer of a reward to find the killers. David will likely say something to the magistrate. Be prepared for a visit by someone in authority.*

LaTour choked on the cake. Sputtering and trying to catch his breath, he went looking for Henri and found him up on deck, helping to winch cargo up from the hold. LaTour pulled him back to the helm deck and handed him the slip of paper.

"This was *baked* inside a cake delivered yesterday as a gift of sympathy for the attack on Lord VanderMeer. A cake that has *Thom Linden* written on the frosting as a decoration. I almost shit at the thought that one of the ravenous marine guards could have intercepted this. Who is this David?"

"Someone who worked at the bakery shop," Henri said with dismay. "I better cement my story with Corrinne. If the new magistrate hears of this, he will come to the ship to see me. And he will probably go to see Lord VanderMeer too. That's what I would do."

Captain LaTour could envision the gallows being built right now.

"No. Do not leave the ship. You stay here and keep working. I will go to the residence and talk about this with Lady Corrinne."

"What are you going to tell her?"

"I will…I will discuss *cement* with her, yes?" LaTour replied with exasperation. "But I am not going to lie to her. That is certain. We are all in this together…as you all keep telling me."

Captain LaTour went down the brow and talked with the marine guards. "I am going to the VanderMeer residence in a few hours, should anyone come looking for me. I will not be gone too long."

LaTour walked at a quick pace down the Long Wharf, his mind sorting through the potential problems he may be facing. His head in a noose was at the end of each and every one of his imagined outcomes. Unless fate intervened.

My life ends up in danger every single time I travel with the Gerrards, he brooded.

"God's balls!"

*

Geoffrey Atkins was a merchant trader with deep family roots in Boston going back fifty years. Thirty-four years old, he was educated at Boston Latin but attended Harvard for only a year when an epidemic of smallpox killed most of his family members. His mother survived in a crippled state. Geoffrey and two other siblings somehow escaped the disease. He was, however, forced to stop his education and take work in whatever manner available to support his now infirmed mother and his younger brother and sister, all that was left of this branch of the Atkins family. He was embittered that his family's wealth had been destroyed and more embittered he received little support or empathy from members of the social caste he had previously associated with. These experiences coarsened his nature and his speech. He was given to angry outbursts and vulgarity. But he was a dependable worker, smart, and ambitious. His mother took her own life within six months, heaping disgrace on top of tragedy. Ten years after his mother's suicide, Geoffrey continued to support his brother and sister modestly, finding consistent work as an accountant. He was too smart for just making ledger entries and adding numbers. An accountant's earnings were meager. But after another three years, he managed to save enough money to begin his own import-export trading company. He expected things to get better quickly. They had not. His personal devils were not so easily excised.

Geoffrey was filled with anger that had no outlet. To his surprise, he was not as good a trader as his peers in Faneuil Hall. The other men preferred not to do business with him primarily because of his acerbic nature. Caustic and confrontational, people did not like being around him.

Things did not look good.

When Jack Tasker was poisoned in the middle of a Boston street, Geoffrey saw an opportunity in the subsequent disarray of the magistrate deputies. He asked a distant relative, now a sitting judge, to intervene for him and get him appointed as the acting deputy magistrate.

"Find these killers," the judge advised. "And you will go far."

Geoffrey Atkins was now on a mission to recover the former status his family once enjoyed. Even becoming a selectman in the future was now possible, if this went well. At least, that is what he told himself.

Except there were problems. In the days that followed the attacks in Boston, anyone suspected of involvement was either dead or had escaped the city. Even Crater Trevathan, a man considered a primary suspect by the other deputies, had an unimpeachable alibi. He was in Faneuil Hall being watched by a deputy, the entire day!

Rewards were offered. No one stepped forward to claim it. Every person, accused by an angry neighbor looking to cause trouble, was questioned.

Nothing.

The newspapers wrote that such a broad swath of violence and murders could not be perpetrated without organized planning. That suggested a *leader.*

Geoffrey agreed with that argument. This was not the first time the VanderMeers had been attacked. The perpetrators were alleged to be assassins sent by competing noble families from the European German states who were jealous of Lord VanderMeer's lineage. But based on Jack Tasker's notes outlining his detailed investigation, he had only found links to people from Philadelphia.

Philadelphia?

Geoffrey had the authority to roust anyone he wanted in pursuit of these killers…for a time anyway. He obtained an audience with Lady Corrinne VanderMeer. She was very beautiful, very angry, and very willing to give him ideas on the possible identities of the perpetrators, even accusing a Hessian colonel who was taken back to England months ago after suffering a stroke.

"He was the leader. And Magistrate Tasker was convinced a few of his assassins still remained in the city," Lady VanderMeer told him. "Tasker firmly believed Carter Trevathan was the organizer after the Hessian left. He was close to proving this. That's why they killed him."

"Unfortunately, Mr. Trevathan can firmly account for his whereabouts. He was being watched by a deputy when the attacks took place."

"He was the organizer, not the perpetrator! He is still guilty," Corrinne said undeterred. "Find the woman. The poisoner. She will be linked with Carter Trevathan, you will see. This same woman killed my maidservant, Mathilde. Jack Tasker knew this too. And it was this woman who killed Magistrate Tasker."

"The problem, my lady, is that half of Boston's citizens are women."

"I believe she has a knowledge of medicines. I would question women with this type of knowledge."

Geoffrey wrote that down. "Well, this has been helpful," he said to be polite. It had not been helpful. "Thank you. I will keep looking."

But after another week of talking to random nurses, the only lead he had was a nurse named Rachel, who disappeared from the Penny Surgeon down near the Long Wharf on the day of the murders, inexplicably in the company of a young boy. The lead was thin. Where did she go? Or by what path? No one knew. And she had a week's head start.

People from every social class were now second-guessing the new magistrate and asking about his progress. He needed a break in this from somewhere. *Or he would be blamed.* As he knew someone always had to be blamed. His frustration mounted.

Then into his office at noon walked David, a baker's assistant. A man with an interesting story to tell, but he wanted a reward to share the information.

Magistrate Atkins was tired of citizens asking him for money for information associated with these murders.

"The reward is offered by Lord VanderMeer. You will get no money from me. What you will get if you waste even a *minute* of my time is a day in jail. Do you still have something to tell me?" Geoffrey saw the man's hesitation. "I thought so. Get out."

David abruptly laid a newspaper in front of the magistrate. A name was underlined.

"Lieutenant Thom Linden...a Dutch marine. What about him?"

David took a deep breath. "He serves on the ship mentioned in the story, but he *worked* in the King's Bakery where I work, claiming he was looking for a job as a baker."

Geoffrey squinted at the man.

"It is the truth! You can ask the owner, Robert Butcher. He only worked four days, and then he was let go. I thought it strange that he was from the ship Lord VanderMeer owns...a lieutenant and all. I mean, why would a lieutenant want work as a baker?"

"And what did he tell you?"

"He said his time in the marines was up and he was looking to get work in a new city. But I'm figuring, you know, he must have education to be a lieutenant? So why ask for work as a baker?"

"All right. I will look into it," Geoffrey said, waving his hand in dismissal. David hesitated. "You better not ask me about a fucking reward again." The man slunk out of the magistrate's office.

Geoffrey had heard stranger stories than that, so he went back to concentrating on how to find the woman who had suddenly left the Penny Surgeon, Rachel. *Rachel...what?* No last name was given. Descriptions were not much better. Brown hair and eyes. Short stature. Two tits. Small ass. Nice smile.

A deputy approached Geoffrey's desk. "Magistrate, what now? Are we going to question somebody today?"

"Just...just stop bothering me."

"Well, there is no one else waiting to see you. So I am going to get something to eat," the deputy said. "Do you want to go? We can go back to Mary's Restaurant and see if we missed something."

"Missed something?! We've been there five fucking times already! She is tall, wears a bonnet, and has red hair, didn't say anything, paid for her food, and left. And we have eaten everything on Mary's menu!" He sighed and then glanced at the newspaper. "Tell you what, here's something new. Let's go eat some cake. At least it's sweet."

"Cake?"

*

Captain LaTour handed over his sword to the marines before knocking at the VanderMeers' front door. Molly opened it, holding Conor in her arms.

"Captain? Come in."

"Well, just look at this little man! Big brown eyes! He is beautiful!"

"He sure is. Lord VanderMeer is sleeping and Lady Corrine is upstairs with her babies. Please wait in the library, and I will call her down."

Dian came in from the *cuisine* with a tray of coffee even before the captain sat down.

"*Merci.*"

"*Pas de quoi!*"

Lady Corrinne entered and immediately noticed the sweat on LaTour's brow and his worried expression.

"What's wrong, Captain? What's happened?"

LaTour stood and shut the library's doors.

Corrinne had a sinking feeling.

"Remember that I told you Henri had come with me on a mission ordered by Governor Drucour? Well, that mission may now be in jeopardy."

The captain paused to see how she would react.

Corrinne poured herself some coffee and took a swallow. "Tell me everything, Captain. Leave nothing out."

"That is my intention."

LaTour told her the story of the intelligence collected by the spy in Boston. How the chain of men passing it to Louisbourg had been broken. "Henri volunteered to seek the man out in Boston. The man was a baker. Henri took work with him."

"As a baker?" Corrinne interrupted for the first time since LaTour began.

"Yes, Henri received the coded information. It is safely aboard the *Queen*. That's why I said the mission was complete. Henri was let go, fired for being clumsy as a way to explain his sudden departure. But Thom Linden's name was mentioned in a newspaper story. Other people working for the baker noticed. The fear is one of them may go to the magistrate and report the coincidence. The magistrate may come to the *Queen*, but they may also come here to see you. Henri's—I mean *Thom*'s story was that his time in the marines was over and that his captain, *me*, said he was free to look for work in Boston."

"Why would Thom Linden not seek help from Lord VanderMeer to find work?" Corrinne asked.

"Good question. You may get asked that."

*

Geoffrey Atkins went into the King's Bakery with his deputy, the newspaper tucked under his arm. The crowd of people coming in at the noon hour was already thinning. When it was Geoffrey's turn, he picked the man, instead of the woman, helping customers from behind the counter.

"Are you the owner?"

"Yes. Robert Butcher, at your service."

"Geoffrey Atkins, Deputy Magistrate. Can we sit and talk somewhere quiet?"

"Of course. Come to the kitchen."

The magistrate provided a brief explanation as to why he was there.

"So did you know this Thom Linden was a lieutenant?"

"A lieutenant? No. He never mentioned that. I knew only his name and that he was a member of the crew on *William's Queen*. And that he had the captain's permission to look for work in Boston."

"A marine officer. An educated man? Looking for work as a common baker—no offense."

"None taken. I did not know he was a lieutenant or educated in the four days he worked here. He was a decent sort. But he did not work out. He kept knocking things over, even ruining the cakes. So I let him go. Ask the others. They will tell you the same thing."

Geoffrey pointed to the newspaper. "Your man, David, brought me this story, saying he thought this a strange coincidence."

"Let me guess, he was hoping to collect a reward?"

"Indeed, he was. But it is still a strange coincidence."

Robert smirked. "David took a fee from Thom Linden saying he would convince *me* to talk with him about a job. But David certainly did not give the fee back to Thom when he was fired. Look, this man claimed to be a baker aboard the ship. So I gave him a chance to prove himself. Like I said, he seemed a decent sort, but I had to let him go. Why don't you go question him yourself?"

Geoffrey nodded. "Yes, Maybe I will. This is good cake, by the way."

"Thank you, sir. Baked fresh every day. I decorate them for special occasions. Are we done? My customers are waiting."

Geoffrey left the store licking the frosting from his lips.

"What now?"

"We're near Long Wharf. Let's go to the Penny Surgeon and see what more we might learn about Miss Rachel."

Geoffrey could see immediately why a person only paid pennies to have treatment here. The place was filthy with trash, dirty beds, and foul smells. He was told they had just expanded into half of this small warehouse. Two doctors waited within, one of them an obvious drunk, the other was an old man, a former sailmaker.

"You are the *surgeon* here?" Geoffrey asked, surprised.

"Three-pence a stitch," the man answered. "And I've had no complaints. Are you here to insult me?"

"No, sir, I am not. Geoffrey Atkins, Deputy Magistrate, at your service. I am here to ask you about a woman named Rachel."

"I've already talked to three different magistrate deputies about her."

"And now you will talk to one more. I am new. I replaced Jack Tasker."

"A good man, Jack Tasker. A terrible shame how he died. He was a good man."

"Yes, a good man, indeed. If you please, tell me what you told the other deputies."

Everything the penny surgeon-*nee*-sailmaker said, Geoffrey had already heard or seen in the reports from his men.

"So you never learned her last name? How is that?"

The penny surgeon shrugged. "She was paid every day at the end of the day for her work. Never needed her last name. Lots of people don't give a last name. Afraid of being shamed for coming to see me, I would guess. And I don't know where she lived either, before you ask."

"Did you know the boy?"

"His name was Jimmy. He's one of a hundred rascals that thieve around the city. He seemed to like Miss Rachel. Came to her with his cuts an' bruises."

"And the boy is gone too?"

"Yep. But Rachel was here most of the day when all those killings took place, I can tell you that much. She had a gentle nature about her. You can see that we miss her cleanliness by how our shelter looks now. I've heard the claims the boy went with her when she disappeared, but I don't know. Why would she take the boy?"

"Which way would she have gone?"

"Only a few ways to leave Boston. Use the gate at the neck, or go by boat, unless you are a good swimmer and can tolerate icy cold water."

Geoffrey thanked the man and turned to leave. On impulse, he turned back around and gave him a five pence. People like the penny surgeon might be a good source of information in the future, he'd decided.

"That's for your time. Come see me if you hear anything I might find interesting."

The penny surgeon was genuinely surprised. "Thank you, sir. I will."

"Now what?" the deputy asked.

"*Now what*! Is that all you ever have to say?"

"No. Are we going to the ship now?"

"*William's Queen?*" Geoffrey sighed. "I guess we should. It's all the way at the head of the fucking Long Wharf. Maybe we go back and see Lady VanderMeer instead and ask about this Lieutenant Thom Linden. We will have to go see her anyway. It's just as far and not as cold a walk."

"She has a sister!" the penny surgeon called out.

Geoffrey stopped and turned. "What?"

"Rachel once mentioned a sister. I've never seen her. So I don't know much about her either." The man shrugged. "Only, maybe she's a nurse too?"

*

Corrinne explained to Charles what she had just learned from Captain LaTour.

"I cannot believe they did this," Charles said, suddenly feeling more incapacitated than he was. "This is dangerous for us."

"Possibly, but not likely," Corrinne conceded, hoping not to upset him too much. "If we all have the same story, it will not be a problem." But in truth, she was worried too.

"And our story is?"

"That Lieutenant Linden's time as a marine was over. And he was encouraged to find work in Boston. Nothing wrong with that."

"So why did *we* not help him?"

"Because you got *shot*, Charles, before the lieutenant could ask you."

Charles contemplated this. *This is an omen*, he decided. *Though it could be the opiates talking to me. Still…one brush stroke of bad color can ruin the finest portrait.*

"I want to conduct the sealing ceremony tomorrow," he said. "Let's get this behind us."

Corrinne returned to the library where Captain LaTour was waiting and told him what they would say if asked.

The captain stood. "Thank you, my lady. I will head back to the ship and tell Henri."

"You should have told me about Henri, Captain!" Corrinne said, a note of disappointment in her voice. "What has changed between us? You have always trusted me before. *Never* do this to me again."

"I promise."

"We've decided to do the sealing ceremony tomorrow. What happened today is an example of why we cannot wait. What might come next?"

Other things burgeoned to the forefront of her mind. *Have the nurse dismissed for the evening. Dian and I will take care of Charles. Have the marine guards in the back relieved for the night. That will take some explaining.*

"Sentry will be here to witness this."

"Sentry? He will be in this ceremony?"

"No, but he needs to witness the ceremony. He will be finishing the vault for us."

*

Captain LaTour made the long city journey back to the ship.

"No one has come yet," Victorio said.

"Good." He explained the invented story to Henri and Victorio. "Because Lord VanderMeer was shot. So if we are asked, we all say the same thing.

And you and I will be going to the residence tomorrow afternoon…to assist with the *châsse*. Victorio, you continue the cargo reloading."

"On that topic, I'm not really sure we will have the room," Victorio confided. "We may have to leave some of it."

"No. No. Send some men to buy some tarps and lines. We can lash some of the lighter cargo…like the furniture…on deck and cover them. The furniture is bulky. It takes up a lot of space. We will be unloading it all in Louisbourg, so it's only temporary."

"Was she angry?"

LaTour glanced at Henri. "Worse. She was deeply wounded we did not trust her enough to tell her. And just so you know…I will never do that to her again."

*

Geoffrey Atkins made a list of every single place in Boston that might possibly employ nurses. Of course, the sister was not necessarily a nurse, but he decided to test Lady VanderMeer's theory. And upon recalling the penny surgeon's comments, he was convinced he should start there. But once he started, he wanted to do this in a logical order so that knowledge of his questioning did not precede his arrival.

He lined up his three best deputies, plus the deputy he had started calling "Now What"—he wasn't sure that man could keep any kind of a secret.

"Tomorrow morning we will do a city-wide search for a nurse…at least I hope she is a nurse. What we are doing has to be handled quietly. By that I mean when we leave a place where we do questioning—oh, and *I* will do all the questioning—I do not want word to spread about what we are asking. Many of the other perpetrators have fled the city. There may only be one or two left. We need to catch one of them. I would start this today, but I want to do this all in one day. So be here early tomorrow morning. *Do not* tell anyone else about this…in particular, your wives, your family, or any of your friends. The person we are seeking may flee at hearing a rumor regarding who I suspect. Do you understand what I just said?"

He pointed at them one by one. They repeated his orders.

*

As the furniture was lashed and covered in tarps, the piles on the deck of the *Queen* looked ungainly. A bigger concern was they would interfere with efficient sail handling. But Captain LaTour was not planning to flee a pursuit at the beginning of these winter months. Transporting the Lord and Lady VanderMeer was going to be as comfortable a cruise as possible, if only to ease his lordship's pain.

"Well, the cargo fits, but she has lost her sleek look and smart lines." The captain patted the rail. "Don't worry, my Queen. You will be beautiful again in a few weeks."

"We will have all the cabins slotted into place and fitted out by the end of the day," Victorio added. "We have all the food and water loaded. We are ready to sail."

"Not soon enough." LaTour was impatient. "Henri, or I should say Lieutenant Linden and I have a few more things to do. We will be back later tonight. I have a feeling we will be sailing before another week is up."

*

They were in the small servant's bedroom where they'd spent so many wonderful nights together. Sentry Cheever knelt before Dianamora, holding her hands and asked her for the second time that week. The first time Dian had said she must think on this. That was yesterday. Time enough as far as Sentry was concerned.

"Will ya' marry me, Dianamora? I love you! I've never said those words ta' another woman in my entire life." Sentry paused, considering. "Though I may have said them to my mother…but tha' was long ago! I love you! I want you to be my wife."

Dian's eyes brimmed with tears. "Sentry. I love you too. But I am an island woman. You are a great war hero. My skin is dark. I would dishonor you."

"Dishonor me? Bloody hell…! Never say tha' again! You are my Dianamora! My lady love! Deeya' know tha' I dream of you even as I sleep next to you. Everything I lack in my character, you bring to me. You bring me honor and happiness. I see myself with no other woman but you. Please… please marry me, my love. *Please*."

Dian bent down and kissed the back of each of his huge and scarred hands. She kissed his forehead, then kissed his lips.

"Yes, Sentry," Dian said, nervous excitement causing her voice to tremble. "I will marry you."

"Woo-hooo!" He leaped to his feet and spun her around and around until she giggled with laughter for him to stop.

"Let's do it this week!"

"This week!" Dian protested. "Sentry, that…that is not possible! With everything else happening to the VanderMeers…"

"All right. I will ask Lady VanderMeer first. If she says no, we will wait. But if she says yes, we do it this week. Yes?"

Of course, Sentry already knew what Lady VanderMeer was going to say.

"Sentry, if we marry, where are we going to live? We cannot live here. I am a servant here."

"All right. I will find us a house to live in."

"Then maybe we should wait until you have that house?"

"If I find us a house to live in this week…we get married, this week? Yes?"

He fell to his knees and asked again.

"Yes, my love?"

"If the VanderMeers permit us to marry this week, and if you find us a house…not an apartment above a tavern…a real house. Then yes, we can marry this week. Otherwise we wait."

"As you wish, my queen, my love, so be it! I promise," he answered with a gallant flourish. "Now we can go to bed!"

She put a hand on his chest. "No, Sentry. We are formerly engaged. It would not be proper to lie together in bed. Not until we are married."

"Wha'—"

Dian smiled. "Sentry, this engagement was your fervent request. *Your deepest desire*, so you declared. If you love me, we will wait until the wedding night, as civilized people do."

*

Thomas Hancock took a seat in a chair beside Lord VanderMeer. His heart ached to see the pale complexion of a person who had become his closest friend. Lady VanderMeer sat in another chair. A small table was between them, topped with ledgers and documents, ink and quills. They were meeting to complete the legal and commercial transactions they had discussed over the past ten days. Hancock still felt that for them to return to Amsterdam was to invite greater violence. More than they had seen in Boston. He told them his opinion but could not persuade them. Corrinne showed him the copy of the letter she had given to a newspaper to announce they were leaving and to thank the people of Boston for their kindnesses.

"I still think your decision to leave Boston is precipitous."

"Thank you, Thomas," Corrinne said. "But this is best for all of us."

Corrinne let Charles talk so that Hancock could notarize the agreements and contracts that were to be signed. He must bear witness, claim, and sign that he heard the words quoted himself. Corrinne was witness and the second signature. She was pleased that Charles had been able to sit up straight for the last five days without having to take heavy opiates. He was still depressed but at least something was improving.

Charles explained that Captain Martyn and his wife Molly would have lease-rights to the Boston house, unless and until the VanderMeers announced their return and gave them six months' notice.

"Sentry Cheever will have the same terms for the house and property in Old Saybrook."

"Sentry has no wife," Hancock observed.

Corrinne acknowledged this. "When he takes a wife, her name will be added. I want that in the language. By the way, his real first name is Humphrey."

"Humphrey?"

"Yes, Humphrey. So make it to Humphrey Sentry Cheever and wife. And please keep this confidential. I do not want him made uncomfortable by this disclosure."

"You attest these are to be fully funded leases?"

"Yes," Charles affirmed. "We will leave them funds to cover a two-year period. Part of these funds will be a monthly stipend you and I discussed for household expenses, including food or any repairs. Captain Martyn will receive his wages, paid quarterly in advance, for being Captain of the *Anamosa*. The same terms apply for Sentry. Only his wages will be for safeguarding the properties in Old Saybrook. He will likely gain other employment once there, but those wages will continue regardless."

"This is very generous."

"Thomas," Corrinne replied, "these people are very dear to us."

Charles spoke. "And I attest that at the end of two years, the same terms renew for another two years, unless modified or superseded by instructions from myself or Lady VanderMeer."

"And your personal chest of funds?"

"Lady Corrinne has already counted out the monies needed for a two-year period for both houses. We will give those monies to them to manage. I attest we will leave another two years of monies, with you, Thomas Hancock. You are entrusted as our attorney-in-fact to distribute the monies for us. Your fee will be included in the entrusted monies. If you need more, you only have to write. My thought is I can have funds carried to your agent in London as soon as I receive your request, presuming acceptable reasons are included, of course. Or we can find another way to get them to you. Your choice."

Charles experienced a painful bout of coughing.

Corrinne gave Charles water and said she would speak for him for now.

"Our intention is to provide you with the flexibility you need to take care of our properties and these people for us. If something occurs, such as an emergency, or an act of God, something that requires more monies beyond the allowances provided, we want you to feel comfortable providing those monies and you can trust we will reimburse you."

Thomas Hancock signed papers in duplicate, including the attorney-in-fact. Corrinne read through each document quickly, signed it, and then took a thin wooden signing board over to Charles with ink and quill for his signature. The signing took about fifteen minutes.

Thomas Hancock produced two slender valises, one for his set of papers, the other for the VanderMeers.

"When Captain Martyn and Sentry Cheever have signed these, I hope to hand a full set of documents to you before you leave Boston."

"I hope so too," Corrinne said.

"I have additional counsel for you both. Charles, should anything happen to you, God forbid, current laws in the Massachusetts colony and the Connecticut colony will require your last will and testament to be entered into the court for adjudication before Lady Corrinne is permitted ownership of the properties. Lady Corrinne, I would recommend you create a similar will and testament for the disposition of property and wealth in the event of your death. These are difficult subjects to discuss, but given recent events, I would advise these wills to be filed in the courts before your departure. I am ready to help you and can even give you some examples I think would work for you. But beyond property and wealth, you also have the children to worry about. You should specify who would care for them, even if it's only temporary. But do not leave it up to a court."

It was the first time, Corrinne had *ever* thought about this. Charles' thinking was insulated by the premise that whatever property he owned belonged to the family. But it was clear to him now English law would apply, but after American provincial law was applied.

"This just might be the most valuable counsel you have ever given us. I am amazed we've not thought of this before. Corrinne?"

"I am embarrassed. We need to address this with speed."

"I will bring some examples to you in the morning. You can have a court attorney record the wills after they are drafted."

"Come as early as you like. Break your fast with us. Bring a scribe. After Charles' health, this is on the top of my list."

"Do not be too concerned. It will not be a difficult task. We can do this in less than a day."

Thomas Hancock fell quiet. After a moment, he said, "You are the most generous, honest, and extraordinary people I have ever met. Lydia feels the same way."

"You are honorable and dear to us as well. You can count on us to come to your aid should you ever have a need. And we aren't leaving yet," Corrine said in a buoyant tone.

Thomas responded with a small smile. "Yes, but after this discussion, I am firmly convinced you truly mean to leave Boston. That saddens me."

The *ghost* circled above the city after returning again from deep in the wilderness where it permitted the female to feed and rest. It was flying high to avoid any random musket shots from hunters intending to bring it down. Against the backdrop of the grayish skies the raptor was invisible from the ground. But the *ghost* had observed all the events of the people it protected and the deceits of the servants.

It would happen soon. The *ghost* was ready.

*

As they walked down the Long Wharf, Henri apologized to Captain LaTour.

"I damaged Corrinne's confidence in you, Captain. None of this was your fault."

LaTour grunted. "Yes it was. Lady Corrinne was right. *I* was responsible for telling her the truth. Not you! It's my lapse in judgment that put her and Lord VanderMeer in danger. What if it were not this *David* fellow who made the connection to you? What if it had been one of the marine guards? This situation could have gotten *deadly*! I don't like to think about what could have happened. And it is not over yet! What if a customer in the bakery recalls your name…then reads it in the paper with the same curiosity?"

Henri frowned. "Well, we have a story worked out," he offered.

"Amid all the other dangers now afoot? The magistrates are frantic to find people to blame for the killings? You are involved in *spying*? What if that is discovered somehow? Maybe the bakery owner confesses to it to try and save his own neck? And what do I know about fighting fucking *demons*! Fuck! We need to sail! To get away from here!"

Henri worried about the captain's accelerating angst. "And we will, Captain. I think Lord VanderMeer is as anxious as we are," he encouraged. "We just help them finish this business ashore so they can get aboard."

Captain LaTour did not answer. He bit his lower lip as they reached the foot of the wharf and hailed a carriage.

Upon reaching the house, the marines took their sabers and searched inside their coats for weapons. Molly, carrying baby Conor, welcomed them inside. Dian and Corrinne came down the stairs.

"Oh, I am so glad you both came early. You can help. We need to bring Lord VanderMeer downstairs. Sentry should be here soon. Come sit in the library and get warm first."

They took seats. Corrinne could see the deep worry lines on Captain LaTour's face.

"Is something else wrong, Captain? How is the *Queen*?"

LaTour did not answer. He leaned forward, elbows on his knees, and dropped his face into trembling hands.

"The *Queen* is fine," Henri answered quickly. "The cabins will be slotted into the deck clips and outfitted today. The extra cargo is lashed topside between the masts and covered with heavy tarps. Food and water is loaded. The *Queen* is ready for sea."

Corrinne was only partially listening. She was watching Captain LaTour with concern. Dian pushed open the door from the *cuisine*, holding a tray. Corrinne gestured she should not come in right now.

"Henri, why don't you go up and see Charles. He needs your help with something. I will stay here with the captain and come up and get you when we are ready."

Henri glanced at his captain with anxiousness. He had seen soldiers lose their nerve like this before a battle. He nodded at Corrinne and left the library, shutting the double doors behind him.

Anamosa jumped into his arms as he emerged.

"Oho, Ana!"

Henri hugged her tightly while she rubbed her nose under his chin.

"I have to see Charles. Do you want to go with me?"

"Yes. Carry me!"

Holding Anamosa in his arms, Henri walked carefully up the stairs and into Charles' bedroom. Charles' eyes were closed. He took a seat on a chair at the left side of the bed, still holding Anamosa in his arms. Unintentionally, her body blocked most of Henri's view of a large brass bowl at the side of the bed. It was loaded with objects. Henri saw the bowl, which he presumed was there in case Charles needed to vomit. He did not perceive the glimmering amulets in the bowl.

Henri was not certain if he should wake Charles or wait patiently until the man awoke. But right then, Charles' eyes opened.

"Henri! Ana! How good to see you both. Did Corrinne tell you what I want?"

"No."

Charles rolled his upper body to the right as much as he could and pointed a trembling finger towards the bowl on the floor. Henri eased Anamosa off his lap and now saw the bowl was filled with beautiful silver amulets set with center stone gems, all of them emeralds, except one with an amethyst.

Henri picked one up with care and admired it. "You made all of these?" They were beautifully engraved with eight symbols.

"Yes. Did you forget? I am a jeweler, too. Set the bowl up here next to me on the bed."

Henri did as requested, and when he was done Anamosa leaned against Henri's side and held onto one of his arms.

"Do you have Chittaqua's amulet?"

Henri slipped the talisman from around his neck.

"Good."

Charles told Henri the story of how Chittaqua had made another amulet with him at Fort Niagara, years ago. How they duplicated the original design, except they set it with an emerald.

"It turned out to be just as potent with…*magic*…for lack of a better word to describe it. Chittaqua somehow made the *vulnax* appear to us. The shaman had also drugged my senses with one of his herbs, probably for my own good. The *vulnax* was terrifying, nevertheless. That was the first time I saw it until the ceremony in Montréal. I've decided, with all Corrinne's babies, we needed more of these and with new symbols added. Here they are. Five of them. Now, I want to go through the same ceremony I did with Chittaqua at Fort Niagara. Place his talisman on top of the new ones."

Henri did as he asked.

"As usual, there is blood involved, something I will never understand, but this appears to be the case with anything occult. You and I must cut a finger in a way that our blood mixes and drips onto the amulets. The problem is the shaman said some of his cryptic Indian words when we did this. I do not believe this will work without them. I cannot recall any of the words. I'm hoping you do. Do you?"

Henri nodded slowly. "Chittaqua taught me all the words, what they meant, and what they are for. But is the *vulnax* going to appear when we do this?" He tilted his head at Anamosa. "Can she be here?"

"The *vulnax* only appeared before because its bones were in the room with us at Fort Niagara. It will not appear this time. She can be here if you are not worried about her seeing the blood."

Henri smiled. "Ana has seen more blood than the few drops we will make." Henri noticed a small paring knife lying on the bedside table. "I presume that is why the knife is there."

Charles held out his right hand. "It is a surprisingly simple ceremony. You cut one of my fingers. Then one of yours. You help me to mix the blood together as it drips onto the amulets, making certain the blood runs off the edge of Chittaqua's talisman. Every new amulet must be anointed with the mixed blood. Then you say the appropriate words."

"What happens then?'

"Nothing that I recall, maybe because of the herbs he gave me...until the *vulnax* appeared, of course. I think Chittaqua was testing the potency of the new amulet. Makes me tremble to think what would have happened if it did not work! Here, I think my ring finger is the most appropriate. There is a towel on the table for us to use afterwards."

Anamosa watched calmly as Henri made a small cut on Charles' finger. The he cut his own. He squeezed each of their fingertips in turn, until blood dripped onto Chittaqua's talisman now lying in the bowl with the other amulets. He moved the new amulets around to be sure that blood from Chittaqua's talisman dripped onto each of them.

On impulse, Henri took hold of Anamosa's hand while he said the ancient words of the Andrototekan. Without being asked, Anamosa repeated the words as he recited them.

"Loh cai teem." *Guide to the truth.*

"Loh cai teem," Anamosa repeated after Henri.

"Ha teh ko ha sen kah." *One light, one life.*

"Ha teh ko ha sen kah."

The gemstones in the amulets glowed for several seconds.

They all gazed in wonder.

Charles broke the silence. "I say, that was a most remarkable result! Even magical, I presume! Yes?"

Anamosa smiled. *Henri did this. Henri is magical.*

"We are done." Charles pressed a towel to the small cut on his finger to staunch the blood. "There are enough amulets for Anamosa, the twins, and Corrinne with one extra."

Henri wiped away the blood from the amulet with the amethyst center stone and slipped it around Anamosa's neck.

"Here you go Anna." He kissed her forehead. "Never take it off for very long."

*

It was late in the afternoon when Geoffrey Atkins finally reached the Marine Society Hospital on Sudbury Street. There were two more medical shelters to visit at the northernmost parts of Boston. None of them as sophisticated as this one. He expected if this nurse was to be found, she would be living among one of those poorer districts, not this one.

Geoffrey could see at least a dozen nurses and two doctors at work among the beds. There was also a second floor. This might take a lot of time. He wanted to complete this as quickly as possible so he took a chance and asked one of the doctors in attendance if he could have some of his time.

Speaking to Dr. Angove privately, he explained who he was and what he was there to do.

"You mean to imply one of *our* nurses could be this killer? That is very unlikely, Mr. Atkins," Dr. Angove scoffed.

"I expect you are right, Doctor. But if I may, do any of your nurses have a sister who is a nurse as well?"

Dr. Angove was taken aback. "As a matter of fact, yes. Nurse Caroline Bristol has a sister named Rachel. She used to work here until a couple months ago when she up and walked out one day. I've not seen her since, but I'd heard she took work with the penny surgeon down near the Long Wharf. Do you suspect it might be Rachel? She was very gentle with the patients. A very pleasant person to be around. Certainly no look of a killer, unless she was a master actress."

Geoffrey's temples throbbed, but he remained as calm as he could.

"Based on what you told me, Doctor, it's probably not her," Geoffrey replied agreeably. "But, as an investigator, I should be thorough. Do you mind if I speak to Nurse Caroline for a few moments? She may know the whereabouts of her sister."

"Not at all." He pointed down the ward. "She is the one bent over that patient, the one in a bed at the end of the ward, on the left, furthest to the back."

"Thank you, Doctor. I will try to be subtle."

Geoffrey turned to his deputies, pointed at two of them and whispered. "You and you, go around to the back and guard the door. You other two guard this door. The nurse we are looking for is here. I will approach her. She may try to run. Be ready. Do *not* let her escape!"

Geoffrey Atkins walked slowly by the beds to give his men time to get in position. He nodded at the patients in a friendly manner, even stopping to ask a few how they felt that day, so as not to alarm the nurse. When he was two beds away, he finally looked at Caroline directly, only to find her staring at him intently. Her expression was not friendly, just the opposite, in fact. She was squinting. Her gaze was calculating. Her right hand was tucked deep into a pocket of her apron.

The deputy magistrate took a steadying breath and addressed her in a calm voice. "Are you Caroline Bristol?"

She did not answer.

"Do you have a sister named Rachel Bristol?"

No answer.

Geoffrey was positive he had the right person. On impulse, he tried to provoke her.

"Carter Trevathan told me to talk with you."

Caroline shrieked with anger. "He is a *pig*!"

She charged at Geoffrey while he fumbled to pull a pistol from his belt. Caroline stabbed him in the chest near his shoulder with something pointed. Geoffrey's pistol fired before he could aim. It discharged into the floor. The burning in his shoulder spread rapidly. His mouth began to foam.

Caroline turned and ran out the back door encountering the two deputies posted there. But they had heard a pistol shot and had drawn their weapons.

"Halt!" the first deputy shouted.

She shoved that man aside so violently, his aim was fouled. The pistol discharged harmlessly.

She charged at the other man.

He did not intend to fire his pistol, but when she shrieked and charged his grip tightened in reflex. She was right in front of him. He could not miss. The ball exploded into her heart.

Caroline Bristol died instantly.

*

The afternoon was late. Sentry had arrived and with Henri's help they crossed their handgrips beneath Charles while he laid his arms over their shoulders. They brought him downstairs. He'd taken only half the normal dose of the opiate. He felt pain, but it was tolerable. They set him down amid a heavy quilt laid over the wheeled chair and wrapped the ends of the covering around him.

Corrinne knelt before him. "Are you warm enough?" Charles nodded. "Any pain?"

"A little. But I will manage. Let us proceed."

Corrinne handed him the valise of the documents he'd written out previously. "I've read them all. I have my parts memorized. Actually, I have them all memorized, just in case."

Corrinne looked at Molly and Dian who were wide-eyed, wondering what was about to happen.

"We will be going into the carriage hangar to permit Charles to explain the purpose of the granite sculptures and wooden frames he made. The babies are all in bed, yes?"

"Yes," Molly replied. "And fed."

"Good. Please stay up in the nursery with them until we come back inside. The nurse has been dismissed until tomorrow. I will be taking care of Charles tonight, maybe with a little help from you, Dian?"

"As you wish, my lady."

She knelt before Anamosa who was holding Henri's arm and hugged her. "Anamosa, my *beautiful* girl, will you stay upstairs with Molly and help her for me?"

Anamosa frowned a little. She looked at Henri. He stooped to kiss her forehead. She left the room to go upstairs.

"Henri, wheel Charles to the back of the *cuisine* but stop at the step to the mudroom. There is a small cup of water and a needle waiting on the *cuisine* table. Bring that with you. We will take Charles out the back door from there. Captain LaTour, why don't you wait with Henri in the *cuisine*?"

LaTour did not answer. He jerked his head in reply.

"Sentry, let's go see the marines."

Corrinne went out the front door with Sentry and up to the guards. The three of them came to attention.

"At ease," said Color Sergeant Cheever. He was not in uniform, but they acknowledged the authority of a marine color sergeant.

"Hold out your hands," Corrinne said with a smile. She put two pieces of silver in each one. "My reason for doing this? The newer and stronger doors to the carriage hangar are complete. One is already hung. Color Sergeant Cheever and the other men from Lord VanderMeer's flagship will help to hang the second one in a little while. But first we are going to have a private ceremony inside the hangar. You may hear some noises, but do not be concerned. I am going to dismiss the other guards for the rest of the evening, but I will be giving them only one piece of silver each. You will have two because you will still stand your watch tonight. Does that sound fair?"

"Oh, yes, my lady!" the corporal said.

"Good. Do not tell the other guards you got two pieces from me. You may tell them if you like tomorrow, but not tonight. Understand?"

"Yes, my lady."

"Good. Now I am going to dismiss them. Do not respond to any of their taunts about getting paid and dismissed. Maybe I will dismiss you one night, too. See if you can switch posts to the carriage hangar."

Sentry walked beside her towards the back of the house. "Excuse me, my lady, but isn't this all a little elaborate?"

"You might think so, but now the remaining guards will not intervene no matter what they hear."

Sentry did not like the sound of that. "Wha' are they goin' ta' hear?"

"That's the problem. I don't know."

She paid and dismissed the three guards at the hangar doorway. As they walked happily to the front, she could faintly hear their whistles and taunts. With Sentry's help, she closed the hangar's single heavy door. It was well-balanced and swung easily.

"This bloody thing could be put on a castle," Sentry said with admiration. "I'm not sure we could hang the other one."

"You won't have to. Later, we'll just lean it against the open hole. The workmen will be back in the morning to hang it. We need one door open for the ceremony anyway."

In case the white eagle decides to join us, she thought.

"At least I think we do. The last time we opened a window. When this is over, we can post one guard here tonight. Let's bring Charles into the hangar along with the four lighted lanterns from the mudroom."

Henri spoke. "What do I do with this glass of water?"

"Give to me. I will cradle it in my lap. The needle too," said Charles. He pressed its point through the quilt so he would be able to find it.

Sentry and Henri lifted Charles in his chair, carefully took him down the steps and wheeled him into the hangar. Captain LaTour followed placidly, holding two lanterns by their handles in each hand. He didn't say anything. They set up the lanterns. The hangar interior was already dim as the sun had set. The lantern light was welcome. There was a full moon that night.

The *ghost* was circling high above the small building. It would fly in the open door when the demon appeared.

Corrinne asked Sentry to stand at the side of the door entrance. "In case the guards need more direction," she confided.

Charles spoke. "Thank you, Captain LaTour and Sentry, for agreeing to help us tonight. For Corrinne, Henri, and me, this is something we have to do. We will be repeating words, some of them foreign, words first repeated over a thousand years ago. As we say them, this *châsse* will react in some manner. Maybe with vibrations. Maybe with foul odors. Maybe with growls. It's happened before. But it cannot harm any of us. As we recite the words,

Corrinne, Henri, Captain LaTour, and I will keep one hand on the top of the *châsse*. When we are done, each of us will have to drop something into the *châsse*. It can be almost anything, as long as it is dropped into the *châsse* by your own hand. I plan to do a lock of my hair."

"I will too," said Corrinne.

"As will I," said Henri.

Captain LaTour tore a button off the sleeve of his long coat and gripped it in his hand. His jaw was clenched, and his eyes darted about the hangar.

"After that, this will all be done. However, other things could happen during the ceremony. Just remain calm, hard as that might be. Corrinne, do you have the tool?"

"Yes." Corrinne held up a small tool with a *T*-handle and an *L*-shaped hook.

"There is a small hole at the center of the *châsse* on its top, at two opposite points of a circle of granite four inches in diameter, carved in the granite square. Slip the hook into either one of the small notch-holes and pull to rotate the circle halfway around. Then lift the hook and the circular piece of granite will come up with it. This exposes the hole where we will drop our hair-locks and Captain LaTour's button inside the *châsse*."

At hearing this, Captain LaTour began shaking almost to the point of collapse. Sentry and Henri grabbed hold of him.

"I cannot do this, my lady Corrinne," LaTour said with anguish. "I'm sorry. I just cannot do this!"

Corrinne looked into the captain's eyes. "It's all right. It was a lot to ask of you. It's all right. I do not think any less of you. Sentry, please take him into the library and give him a glass of brandy, then come back."

Sentry nodded. "Come on, old friend." Gripping him around the shoulders, he took the captain indoors.

Charles and Corrinne looked at one another. "We still need a fourth person," he said.

They waited quietly until Sentry returned.

The color sergeant came back into the hangar.

"He's all right. Probably the only time in his life LaTour's ever lost his nerve. It happens to all of us…even the best of us," Sentry said magnanimously. Then he noticed they were all staring at him. *Oh fuck!*

"Does this mean I just volunteered?"

"There has to be four of us in the ceremony," Henri said.

"Well, I've heard it growl and smelled its stink. I can do this. Let's begin."

Charles nodded and was wheeled alongside the *châsse*. Henri and Sentry stood on the opposite side.

Standing next to Charles, Corrinne inserted the hook to open the hole. The stone circle rotated smoothly as she pulled on the hook. She lifted it at the proper point and the circle of granite rose up easily. A noticeable smell permeated the air, something old, rotted, and rancid.

Sentry's eyes widened.

"Your hands please," Charles said. They all touched an edge of the reliquary. "There are three incantations to say. I will begin with the first one. The words are enigmatic. A very old Celtic dialect. You will not understand them, but don't worry."

> *"Who that dares seal a wraith crafts a doorway to hell.*
> *That door must have a lock. That lock a key.*
> *A door thus locked can be unlocked.*
> *And thrice stronger the wraith emerges,*
> *To impart hellish torment on its oppressors.*
> *Those who dare to seal a wraith thus seal their doom.*
> *Beware!"*

From the black abyss, the *vulnax* was drawn instantly into the *châsse*'s interior. A creamy smokiness oozed over the hole at the top of the *châsse*. The candles in the lanterns began to flicker. There was a faint buzzing noise. The foul odor in the air intensified.

Like the smell of death on a battlefield, Sentry thought. *What have I gotten myself into?*

Henri gripped Chittaqua's talisman. Charles wore a newer one. So did Corrinne. The center gemstones in all of them were glowing.

Bloody hell! Sentry thought.

"The next verse is a Frankish dialect," Charles said. "You each have a line to say when urged." He told Sentry the words he would pronounce.

Charles continued reciting the hex. As Charles talked, Henri, Corrine, and Sentry looked at one another. They all sensed the attention of something invisible and pitiless inside the hangar. Inexplicably, the tone of Charles' voice deepened and became more resonant, as if someone else were speaking.

"In the marsh he lay with the crone,
Among the stinkweed and slime.
The crone farrowed there,
And spewed forth the dark one's brood.
From that get rose one,
Vaelblez.
And his house sharked with the moon,
And glut their maw with the flesh of men.
From thence a veil draped the sun,
A tarnish to the moon.

"Now four seals are invoked,
Sun, Moon, Stars, and Seas!"

"*I am the Sun,*" Charles said, then motioned to Corrinne.

"*I am the Moon,*" Corrinne said.

"*I am the Stars, Betelgeuse, Meissa, Bellatrix, Alnitak, Alnilam, Mintaka, Saiph, and Rigel,*" Henri said.

"*I am the Seas,*" Sentry said, responding to their cue.

"And cast into the pit,
He will rot beneath these signs.
Until the Sun, the Moon, and the Stars fall from the skies,
And all the Seas evaporate."

The buzzing noise stopped, replaced by low rumblings that surrounded them from every direction. Sentry felt the air become hot and prickly.

"The last verse is in Roman Latin." Charles nodded at Corrinne. She recited:

"A bane on the house of Vaelblez!
Malus spiritus be condemned to shadow!
Sealed forever beneath the stone symbols!

And until the Sun, Moon, and Stars fall from the heavens,
And the Seas of the world evaporate,
So shall it be!"

The *châsse* was growling. Corrinne took a knife she'd brought with her and cut a lock of hair from her head. She dangled it over the hole and let it drop. Henri took the knife and cut a lock of his hair and did the same. Henri cut a lock of Charles' hair and, with Sentry's help, lifted Charles up so he could drop in his lock of hair. Henri handed the knife to Sentry. He cut some hair and held it over the hole.

"I kinnah' believe I am doin' this," he said softly as he dropped it in.

The *châsse* began to pulsate violently, enough so they had to steady the sides to keep it from slipping off the saw horses underneath it. Sentry held one side, Henri held the other side. Oozing vapor appeared to be bubbling from the hole, as if it were boiling.

They had not seen this in previous sealing ceremonies. Not Charles, not Corrinne, not Henri, and certainly not Sentry, who was silently cursing with every vulgarity he had ever learned. They were all trying to maintain their nerve.

Corrinne was glad LaTour was not there. *He would have never made it this far*, she thought. *I pray the rest of us do!*

Charles decided the last step must be taken before this would all stop. It was the only thing left to do anyway. He took the needle in his lap, pricked the same finger he cut earlier, and oozed a few drops of blood into the glass of water. He handed the glass to Corrinne along with the needle. She pricked one of her fingers and let a few drops of her blood fall into the glass. She went to Henri and to Sentry, who both did the same. The glass now contained drops of all their blood. The *châsse* pulsation and the growling increased and forced Henri and Sentry to lay their arms across the top to steady it.

"If this gets much worse, we may not be able to hold this!" Henri gritted out.

Like a white apparition, the eagle flew in through the open door and landed atop the *châsse* near the hole. The pulsation stopped, the creamy ooze retreated until it was just a bulge above the hole.

They all stared at the great raptor, which perched unmoving. It turned its eyes to look at Corrinne, then turned and looked at the hole.

Corrinne understood immediately. She poured the glass of blood-tainted water into the hole. The ooze disappeared. She lifted the granite stone circle to seal it.

"Symbol side down," Charles urged.

Corrinne noticed for the first time the bottom of the stone circle was divided into eight wedge sections and each section had a symbol carved into it. She set the lid in the hole and rotated it a half circle in the other direction.

The reverberations, the smell, the smoke—everything stopped instantly, as if nothing had happened. The lantern lights steadied.

They stared at the eagle. It seemed to stare at each one of them in turn. Sentry's mouth had sagged open in awe. Then the raptor spread its wings, flew out of the hangar, and disappeared up into the night.

Charles VanderMeer exhaled loudly. "I am glad I took opiates! But that went about as well as we could expect."

"Bloody hell!" Sentry bit out. Then he ran out of the hangar and around to the carriage way to confront what he was certain would be there. Two of the marine sentries, their muskets dressed in bayonets, had already come halfway down the carriage way.

"At ease, men. All is well."

"I need to see Lord and Lady VanderMeer in person," the corporal insisted, still suspicious.

"You are a good marine, Corporal. I would want to see them too. Wait right here. I will bring them to you."

Sentry went back to the hangar and told them what was happening. Corrinne walked quickly to the sentries and Henri wheeled Charles right behind her. Sentry took up one of the lanterns and brought it with him so their faces would be clearly visible.

The marine guards relaxed somewhat when they saw the VanderMeers.

"Apologies, my lord, my lady. We heard noises and were worried."

"Everything is all right. Our little ceremony is complete. The only thing we've left to do is lean the other door over the other half of the doorway. We will finish hanging it tomorrow."

They wheeled Charles around to the front of the house. Henri and Sentry carried him up the steps in the chair and into the foyer. Then the two of them went out the backdoor. They spread a tarp over the *châsse*. They decided to let the remaining lanterns stay lit. They lifted the second hangar door up to cover the hole.

It was heavy and took much strength even to lean it.

Sentry groaned. "It's like a bloody portcullis!"

Henri went back into the house. Sentry went around to the front and told the guards to have one man posted in the back and rotate the guard throughout the night.

Corrinne went up to check on the babies. Charles asked to be taken into the library. They found Captain LaTour there sitting in a chair with an untouched glass of brandy on the table next to him, staring into the fire.

"It's all done, Captain. It's behind us now," Charles said in a sympathetic tone after they were all settled in the library.

LaTour shook his head. "I feel like a coward."

They all spoke at once, protesting loudly that Captain LaTour was not a coward. Henri reminded him of the corsairs and the great storm they endured together when he first came to New France.

"That man was no coward! And you are that man!"

Sentry touched the captain on the shoulder. LaTour turned his eyes to the big marine.

"If I asked, you would carry a sword and fight standing right next to me, facing the same enemy, yes?"

LaTour nodded. "Of course."

"Then, Captain, you are *no* coward. Not in my book."

LaTour smiled weakly and took his first sip of brandy.

Unexpectedly, Anamosa came into the library followed by Corrinne. Henri stood to allow Corrinne to sit. Henri whispered into Anamosa's ear. She went over and crawled up on Captain LaTour's lap. He smiled warmly.

"*Bonsoir, mon amour petite!*"

Anamosa rubbed her nose under the captain's chin.

At Charles' behest, they all raised a glass of brandy in a toast.

"To my greatest friends," Charles said, "who must all be as crazy as I am!"

They touched their glasses together. "Amen!"

*

Henri and the captain walked all the way from the residence to the ship that night. LaTour wanted to inhale the cold air that got saltier in smell the closer he got to the sea. By the time they reached the ship, they were both completely sober, and the captain had recovered from his depression.

"Ahoy, my marine friends! What would you like to eat tomorrow morning?"

"Those hotcakes with syrup would be good again, Captain," one marine said.

"Some more of your coffee!" said another.

"Done!" the captain told them.

They went aboard. Pierrik, the captain's steward-cook, approached him. "You want anything to eat, Captain?"

"No. But make a full pot of coffee and take it up to the marines. If you have any leftover sweetbreads, take that up to them too." He gripped Henri's shoulder. "This has been one hell of a day, Henri. I am going to bed."

*

The next morning, after Charles was clean, propped up with pillows, and ready, Dian brought up a tray of food to them. Corrinne sat in a bedside chair and nibbled at the food from the tray on Charles' lap. Two of the Boston newspapers were on the tray.

"Oh, my God!" Corrinne exclaimed, picking up a newspaper and scanning the front-page headline.

"They killed her!" Charles was reading a similar story in the other paper. "Caroline Bristol, from London."

"*Mon Dieu*! She was working in the Marine Society Hospital! She was right there when you were there! I knew it!"

"She has a sister named Rachel," Charles said, skimming the news, "who has escaped from Boston…no one knows to where. And they arrested Carter Trevathan too!"

"Oh, no," Corrinne whispered. "The new deputy magistrate, Geoffrey Atkins, was killed in the hospital…with a knife…a poison-coated knife!"

Acting Deputy Magistrate Geoffrey Atkins Slain

Geoffrey Atkins, 34, acting Deputy Magistrate was slain during the apprehension of Nurse Caroline Bristol at the Marine Society Hospital. Geoffrey Atkins is credited, after only thirteen

days as acting Deputy Magistrate, with solving the heinous murder by poisoning of former
Deputy Magistrate Jack Tasker. It was determined
Geoffrey Atkins was not killed by the super-
ficial knife wound he received from Caroline
Bristol during her arrest but by the poison
coatings on the blade she wielded. Geoffrey
Atkins is survived by his brother Marshall, 18,
and his sister Helena, 15. Funeral services to
be announced.

Charles was reading another column written by the newspaper editor.

It Is Time for the VanderMeers to Leave Boston

Lord and Lady VanderMeer are charitable,
God-fearing people. We like them. But many of
the families of the Massachusetts colony fled
Europe because of the senseless wars and death
that pervade that continent. Now we are in the
midst of yet another war that permeates this
new American land. To have silent, professional
assassins and killers dwelling among the people
of Boston, all of them intending to kill the
VanderMeers, provokes fear into the hearts and
minds of our families. Certainly this city has
paid with the blood of its citizens to protect
the VanderMeers. And more than once!

This endless war among the noble houses of
old Europe cannot be allowed to infect this city
any longer. Even with the King's brave marines
protecting the VanderMeers, these vicious killers strike with impunity. The VanderMeers are
victims, but no less are Boston's citizens,
some of them poisoned on our streets and inside
our hospitals. This paper is sympathetic to the

VanderMeers. But for the safety of our citizens,
the VanderMeers must leave Boston.

Charles crushed the newspaper in his lap. Corrinne's expression was angry.

"It's hard to argue with them," Charles said. "It was our own conclusion."

"They could have first published the letter I already sent to them! The one announcing our decision to depart and the reasons. They even plagiarized some of what I wrote!"

"It makes no difference."

"It does to me."

"Well, let's not disappoint them," Charles said. "We must pack up the library. Separate our books into what you want to keep with you and what will remain with me."

Corrinne reacted with surprise. "What do you mean by that?"

"I must return to Amsterdam as my father requests. And you must stay in Louisbourg with Marcus and Calypso, along with Henri and Anamosa. Where you will all be safe."

"No! No, Charles! They will kill you if you go there! You will be safe in Louisbourg too! You will be safe with me!"

Charles smiled at her sadly. He reached out and took her hand in his.

"Lady Corrinne VanderMeer…I could not have been happier, pretending to be married to you. But we both know at some point this beautiful, wonderful charade has to end."

Corrinne wanted to reject his words. But he was speaking the truth.

Charles continued. "I have to go back to Amsterdam. My father, the Duke, has ordered me to go, even if I intend to abdicate. The Duke of Brunswick has protected us while we were here. We could not see this, but he did. The killers who sought our lives, we both know that none of them were from the middle kingdoms."

"They may still seek you out," Corrinne argued. "You will be more vulnerable in Amsterdam."

"No. The servants of the *vulnax* will not. I am not important anymore. The seals are of the sun, moon, stars, and seas. They will not fall. That's why these seals were used on the original tomb. That's why I used them on the vault. Now our enemies must break the *châsse* into pieces to break the seals, if they can find it. Slaying any of us does no good."

"I don't want it to end this way," Corrinne said. "We have shared too much."

"It took time and great lengths to create documentation certifying our marriage and to have it registered in a remote church in Europe. After me, only my father knows where this church is. He can destroy this evidence at any time. If he does, you are no longer Lady Corrinne VanderMeer. Why do you think he waits?"

"He wants to see Marcus and Calypso."

"Yes. He asked me to bring them to Amsterdam. But not you."

Corrinne was appalled. "They are *never* going to Amsterdam or even to Europe!"

"I agree," Charles said firmly. "But there is something else for you to think about. Right now Marcus and Calypso carry my last name. There could be benefits for having that surname. There could also be *penalties*. I love them as much as I love you. I care about their happiness. If you tell me to destroy the record of our marriage…I will do as you wish, without acrimony or hesitation. You have my word. Although, my father might do it preemptively," he added, his forehead wrinkling. "But…there is a record of the *birth* of Marcus and Calypso VanderMeer here in Boston that will be more problematic to destroy, independent of what happens to our *faux* marriage documentation. The question is…do you even *want* to destroy their birthing record?"

Corrinne's eyes brimmed with tears. This discussion had turned heartrending.

Charles squeezed her hand affectionately. "Corrinne, my deepest wish, when we depart one another in Louisbourg, is for you to be reunited with Philippe as soon as possible. I was a witness to your marriage, if you recall. The love I saw in your faces…There are no decisions you have to make right now. I just want that brilliant mind of yours to think about it."

A knock sounded.

"I am sorry, my lord, my lady. Thomas Hancock is here," Molly said.

"Show him up. And have more tea and coffee sent up too."

Thomas Hancock had brought wills for both of them to read, sign, and cross witness. Thomas Hancock's would be the certifying signature. Their new attorney-in-fact explained everything in less than an hour. And before another hour followed, everything was signed.

"You just gave Corrinne and me another reason to think about future things, Thomas."

Thomas Hancock knew more related to Philippe Gerrard than he would ever admit to them. Whatever their reasons might be, their secret was safe with him forever.

"All I need now is the signatures of the two married couples," Thomas averred.

Corrinne brightened with that thought. "Oh, yes! Would you and Lydia join Charles and me when Color Sergeant Sentry Cheever and Dian, um, Dian Amora are wedded in our house in two days? I plan to have Rector Hooper perform the service."

Thomas was surprised. "I had no idea…about Sentry and Dian. It would be wonderful. Color Sergeant Sentry Cheever a married man? It will be an event I would not wish to miss. Lydia and I would be pleased to attend. Do the bride and groom know they are getting married?"

Charles chuckled. "Most likely they do not!"

"Stop it. Both of you. They do not know about a wedding. They *do* plan on getting married. And I *certify*—do you like that word Mr. Attorney-in-Fact?—I certify they will be married this week. And it will be their idea, not mine. Events in our lives are moving quickly now. I am just helping them along."

*

Word of the VanderMeers' departure spread through Boston like fire. To Corrinne and Charles' pleasant surprise, the majority of the people in Boston decried the newspaper article calling for the VanderMeers to leave. Many letters protesting the article calling for their departure were written to the competitive papers. But it was easy to tell that it would be happening regardless. Wagons began carrying their belongings to the Dutch ship, *William's Queen*. The first wagon carried crates of books and the *châsse* hidden beneath a tarp. When the *châsse* was winched on board, it was obviously too large to fit into a cabin.

"Books are heavy. They must be stowed low in the ship." Captain LaTour groaned as the front third of the forward hold had to be unloaded again to make room for the books. It was mostly heavy sacks of grains and other foods. Some of it could be loaded into the empty cabins. The *châsse* was lashed and secured so it could be easily plucked out of the hold in Louisbourg. He restacked most of the sacks of grain atop and around the books, and even atop the *châsse*. He no longer cared if the demon minded or not. And to his surprise, strangely enough, as the tarp-covered *châsse* was jostled and banged around, there were no noises, no growls, and no odors.

Whatever they did had worked, he conceded. But he would be glad to be rid of this demon's bed in Louisbourg.

After the books, not much else was brought aboard. Then he received a hand-couriered missive from Lady Corrinne with instructions to buy another bathtub for her to use in Louisbourg. She included the name and address of the place in Boston where it could be bought.

Store it in a protective way. So it will not be damaged on the way to Louisbourg.

"God's balls."

*

Dian had no choice but to happily agree that Lady VanderMeer would plan the wedding. Corrinne moved like a whirlwind. Even so, it would end up taking three more days to get ready, with the ceremony held on the fourth day, but no one cared. She hired restaurant staff to prepare the buffet and six temporary day maids and cooks so that Molly and Dian would not have to worry about anything else, except for the babies, Charles, and the wedding. Tents were set up on the front lawn with tables and chairs. The nuptials would be performed by Reverend William Hooper on the VanderMeer front porch. Corrine had carpenters extend the porch with a temporary platform. She hired her favorite dressmaker, full-time, every day to stitch together Dian's gown in Mathilde's bedroom.

Molly and Sentry sat in the library while Thomas Hancock explained the terms of the lease-right documents. Molly would have to explain all of this to her husband when he returned from sea. They were both bewildered by the generosity of the VanderMeers. Of course, Sentry spoke to Corrinne and privately agreed to some other conditions.

"Finish the vault as soon as possible. Charles has left these drawings for you to follow. Let him discuss with you how they should be arranged. Hire the masons from New Haven again to help. When the vault is complete, have Winter House demolished. Don't forget, we will be entering the vault again someday in the future to deposit the *châsse* in it. Contact this architect in New Haven." She handed him a slip of paper. "He created the designs of the new house for the expanded lot. Review the design with Dian. Make any changes she desires. Add other outbuildings as you prefer, for instance, a barn or a stable or a carriage house. I will still own the property, so don't worry about the cost of the improvements. This house is paid for. I trust your judgment. I would start building the new house in the spring. You and Dian can stay here with Molly and Captain Martyn until then. Take Mathilde's room. Dian and Molly would like that. Thomas Hancock will resolve any financial issues for you."

Corrinne paused. *Have I missed anything?*

Sentry presumed her silence meant he was supposed to say something. "I dinnah know wha' to say."

"Sentry, unless *thank you* is appropriate, where women are concerned you must learn to reply either *Yes, I will* or *I do*. Particularly with Dian," Corrinne teased. "After that, everything will occur as God intended. Dian will sign the lease-rights document as Dian *Amora* Cheever. Having her sign with a maiden surname is important. Never forget this."

At the thought of Corrinne's impending departure, Sentry became glum. "Are ya' really goin' away forever?"

"Of course not, but I expect the war will prolong our absence. Just get used to writing letters. It takes a few months to send one and a few months to receive a reply back. Charles will mail you an address in Amsterdam. Thomas Hancock will have another address that will work in London."

"It will be hard...hard for all of us, my lady...nah' seeing you."

Corrinne embraced Sentry and laid her head on his chest. "It will be hard for me too, Sentry. But I promise, you will see me again."

CHAPTER 33
BOSTON
OCTOBER 1756
Flowers, Tides, and Winds

The wedding was scheduled for the next day. Corrinne had hired plenty of people to worry about the details. *I must try and let them do what I paid them to do.*

She went upstairs and checked on the babies. They were playing in the nursery with two women watching over them. She sat between them both. Marcus was the first to notice she was there and jumped up from his tin soldiers to hug her. Then he growled and charged off to topple the tower of blocks Calypso was building. Calypso's lip trembled, tears close to surfacing. Corrinne held out her arms and let the little girl snuggle close. Mollified, the toddler kissed her mama and went over to the dolls, things that Marcus never touched.

They are safe, Corrinne's conscience assured her. *Go for a walk.* A walk? It would be good to get away from all the activity for an hour or two. She might still be absorbed with the details, but at least she would not be trying to do everything herself at once. She went downstairs to the library. Charles was in his wheeled chair, staring at the fire.

"I am going for a walk," she told him.

Charles turned his head and smiled briefly. "Good. You need it. Take guards with you."

She bent down and kissed him lightly. "When I get back, we will have some hot mint tea together."

Corrinne put on the long gray coat she liked, one with a dark fur collar. It was always warm against the wind that now blew in from the harbor in sudden gusts. She went out the front door and marveled for a moment at how well the flower arrangements were coming together. *So beautiful.* They had covered them partially beneath a tarp for protection and tied them to the columns.

"I would like a bundle of those Joe-Pyes."

The florist in charge of the flower arrangements tied the three-foot stems together with some twine and laid the large pink bouquet across her arms.

"Nothing like a bouquet of pink flowers to warm a cold day." She walked to the guard house. "Good morning. I need two handsome men to escort me on a short walk to Granary cemetery. Here are three silver coins. Flip them. The odd man stays and keeps the coin. The winners come with me. But no muskets."

They had to flip three times before one of them lost.

"We should go right to Winter Street, then up to Common Street. As a diversion to going the shortest way," the corporal explained. "It's what the enemy would least expect."

Corrinne blinked. "A *diversion?* Well, good. That's just what my mind needs."

Once at the cemetery, she asked the guards to wait at the edge. She walked over the wet grasses and soft ground to Mathilde's grave. She laid the Joe-Pyes on it and placed a rock lying nearby atop the stems so they would not blow away. She gazed around the dreary surroundings of lichen-covered gravestones. The gloom was made worse by occasional wind gusts and the tiny drops of rain that came with them.

"Hello, Mathilde. I have to go away for a while," Corrinne began.

She told Mathilde things she never had a chance to say before her beloved friend was so cruelly murdered. She talked about the many times Mathilde had been there to comfort her. How she never complained, even on the days Corrinne was rude to her and demanding. How Marcus and Calypso adored her. She shifted to more current happenings, the wedding, the decision to go to Louisbourg and all the reasons why they were doing this.

Corrinne's tone abruptly turned despondent. "Charles has decided to return to Amsterdam…maybe forever. I may never see him again. I worry so much about him now. The paralysis has robbed him of his joy. Nothing I do seems to cheer him. He still responds to Anamosa and the twins. But what happens when he can no longer do that? Each day he gets weaker. Each day his mood is more morose. He no longer smiles. He seems resigned to some dark fate. I am at a loss what to do for him. If only you were here."

A brief gust of wind lifted the curls in her hair. She shook her head, trying to displace her gloomy feelings.

"Let's talk about Henri! You would not recognize Henri, his size and strength. But that's nonsense. Of course, you would. He is the image of his father, only much younger. Anamosa adores him. Henri still has strong feelings for...*that* girl...in Quebec City. But the devotion I observe between Henri and Ana is so strong. Of course, Anamosa is too young now, but this war is expected to last another five years, at least. Henri will be in the fighting until it is over. Anamosa will be fourteen or fifteen by then..."

Another gust of wind swirled leaves around her.

"This wind! It could blow away all the flowers! I've organized an outdoor wedding for Sentry and Dian tomorrow, but I never considered the weather. I am praying it will not be rainy and cold. But it is October. This is October weather." Corrinne recalled what Mathilde used to say to her, that everything would turn out all right. "Well...if you have any sway in Heaven, maybe you could ask for a little sunshine? Just until the part where Sentry and Dian say *I do*. I realize it is terribly selfish of me to ask that of you. But you spoiled me with your love, I cannot help myself."

A heavier gust of wind blew against the back of Corrinne's coat. She looked at the sky. The clouds were lower than before. She could see them moving faster. A storm?

"Well, I better go back. I will come again and say good-bye before we sail. Rest in peace, Mathilde. I love you."

*

It was to everyone's amazement that Lady Corrinne VanderMeer had assembled this wedding in just four days. "*A tribute to Lady Corrinne's force of will and the persuasion of her purse,*" Lord VanderMeer was quoted as saying. Even the weather cooperated! That morning, the dismal gray skies of October vanished, if only temporarily. Bright cloudless sunshine would prevail for the remainder of the day.

"Thank you, God. Thank you, Mathilde," Corrinne whispered towards the sky as she inspected the flower arrangements the morning of the wedding.

The platform where Rector William Hooper stood was surrounded with large bouquets of arranged flowers; pink and rosy Asters, intermixed with large heads of dusky, whorled blossoms of Joe-Pyes. Accentuated throughout were bundled spires of blue-violet Sage. All of them held in stylish vases that later would be donated to the Marine Society Hospital patient wards. A beautiful wedding arch was set in the middle of the platform, wrapped with multiple vines of white honeysuckle blossoms.

A carpeted six-foot-wide walkway ran across the front of the house from the carriage way-in to the wedding platform, to be used by the bride just before she presented herself to the groom.

Sitting on chairs under the tents erected in the front half of the Vander-Meer yard were the specially invited guests, among them Governor Hardy and Mrs. Hardy, Thomas and Lydia Hancock, Samuel Grant and wife, all the Selectmen and their wives, and Marshall and Helena Atkins, Mary and Lisbeth Tasker and escorts, family members of Lord VanderMeer's fallen guards, and every marine who had stood guard at the VanderMeer house along with a female companion.

Sitting on chairs under the tents in the latter half of the VanderMeers' front lawn closest to the street were the citizens of Boston. Anyone appropriately attired was invited. Chairs were available to those who arrived first.

Three newspapers would report their observations of the wedding.

Red-coated marines in resplendent polished uniforms were arranged to guard the entire service. The guests were given printed ceremonial guides to follow; with ink not yet dry.

At one o'clock precisely, ten musicians playing stringed instruments struck up a tune from where they were set up along the carriage promenade. The bride, Dian Amora, came around from the back of the house. She was stunning, attired in a long-sleeve wedding dress of white silk and white lace, with a hook-and-eye creamy bodice, interwoven with tiny threads of red, gold, and silver. The bodice pushed up her bosom. Her neck was adorned in a web-like necklace of diamonds and opals, loaned to her by Lady VanderMeer. Some guests found this scandalous, but not this reporter. The bride was preceded by a flower girl, Anamosa, in a dress of similar fashion to the bride, her thick black hair adorned with honeysuckle flowers. This beautiful girl with striking blue eyes smiled at the audience and dropped flower petals on the carpet before the bride.

Miss Amora's first appearance in front of the congregation brought gasps of awe from those seated. The bride held a bouquet of white and purple asters, streaming ribbons of matching colors, and the bride's hair was also entwined with honeysuckle flowers. She approached the platform from the carriage way-in on the right escorted on the arm of Lord Charles VanderMeer, who was wheeled in a chair pushed by Captain Victorio Jaager of the Dutch sea marines.

Lord VanderMeer gave away the bride to Marine Color Sergeant Sentry Cheever, dressed in the uniform of the First Carlisle Marine Regiment, a red waist coat with a dark blue vest underneath, and color sergeant stripes on the sleeve. The lapels and cuffs were covered with the Carlisle family tartan of blue-gold-red plaid. He wore an eye patch covered with the same Carlisle tartan. The dress uniform included a ceremonial sash, belt, and a saber at the waist.

With Rector William Hooper of Trinity Church standing on the platform behind them, Lord VanderMeer handed Dian Amora to Sentry Cheever. From that moment, the bride and groom's gazes remained fixed on each other.

Rector Hooper gestured for people to be seated.

"With respect to the other extraordinary preparations and the organization of this wedding, I wish to begin the service with a special prayer. This beautiful and familiar scripture is taken from Ecclesiastes, chapter 3, verses 1 through 4. Most of you know it already. Please pray with me.

"To every thing there is a season, and a time to every purpose, under heaven.

A time to be born, and a time to die; a time to plant, and a time to pluck up that which is planted.

A time to kill, and a time to heal; a time to break down, and a time to build up.

A time to weep, and a time to laugh; a time to mourn, and a time to dance."

The reverend paused and then proclaimed, "There is also a time for *betrothal!* And a time to say *I do!*"

Those in the audience chuckled.

"Dian Amora, do you take Sentry Cheever…"

*

Lady VanderMeer had arranged for food and refreshments in side tents, one for the wedding party and special guests and another long tent with tables full of food was set up along Marlborough Street, which was closed that day for the wedding, tented and roped off. The magistrate deputies hired extra men to keep order during the celebrations.

After the service was complete, the violins were augmented with flutes, horns, and a bagpipe…to commence *a time to dance!*

No alcohol was served except for sparkling wines in the area reserved for the special guests, to permit toasting to the wedding party.

At the request of the city, the wedding festivities ceased by the hour of six o'clock and Marlborough Street was reopened for normal use. There were no fights and no one was arrested. Most of the Scottish attendees thought it was all *a wee bit too civilized.*

"But then again…these people are Dutch. They are not used to raucous excitement."

*

The next day, Corrinne returned to the Granary cemetery, this time with Marcus and Calypso, Dian, and Anamosa. The drizzly rain and wind had returned but she hugged the twins in the folds of her arms against the cold. The twins pointed at random things, dead leaves floating in the air, small birds pecking at the ground, and babbled in happy voices, things Mathilde would enjoy.

Corrinne tearfully said good-bye to her maidservant and long-time friend.

*

Three days after the wedding, the time had come to leave. The final baggage was delivered that morning on a wagon to the head of the Long Wharf. A covered carriage waited behind the house for Lord and Lady VanderMeer, Anamosa, and the twins.

Corrinne finished her arrangements and handed over a small chest of monies to Thomas Hancock with extra coin to cover anything associated with the wedding. She sat down in the privacy of the library with Molly, who was holding Conor, and Dian. They held hands in a circle. Corrinne was overcome by emotion and struggled to retain her composure. Her thoughts were scattered as she bid them farewell.

"This is not forever," Corrinne assured them. "I am overjoyed that you both came into my life as good friends, fell in love with your future husbands in my house and were married here. Molly, I am sorry I missed your wedding. We will make up for that in some future anniversary. Mr. Hancock will provide good counsel to both of you. It is important that you both remain good friends all of your life. Dian, Sentry will be building your house in the spring. I want you to be happy there. He will show you the plans and you can make changes to them before it is built. I trust your judgment. Molly, on my dressing table I left a page of exercises I used after the twins were born. You may find them helpful. Dian, I think that round of cheese in the pantry has gone bad. We will communicate by letters. It takes four to six months to send and receive them crossing the ocean both ways. Molly, this is probably going to be a surprise to Captain Martyn, so make use of Thomas Hancock in helping you explain." She stopped suddenly. "Well, I guess all that is left for me to do is collect my babies."

She stood. Molly and Dian stood too…and then the sobbing began.

Sentry helped Corrinne into the carriage. He handed Calypso up to Anamosa and Dian handed Marcus up to Corrinne. Molly stood by them holding little Conor. The women had said so much and cried so much, there was little more to say and no tears left. Corrinne stretched her hand out the window of the carriage and gripped theirs one more time. Sentry gestured to the marine drivers and the carriage went out the way-in.

As the horses clip-clopped down the streets, to their surprise, many of the people of Boston came out to wave good-bye to them. Corrinne found it heartwarming that after so much tragedy that had followed them here, the gracious people of Boston still wished them farewell. She held Marcus up to the window and helped him wave to the crowds.

Charles spoke. "Does Hancock have the donations?"

"Yes, to all of our charities. I told him not to give over the monies until after the ship has sailed. Did you explain to Sentry how the vault segments were to be arranged?"

"Yes. Did you ask Thomas about Mathilde's grave?"

"Yes. That was the first thing I asked. After what that newspaper had written about us, Thomas said he would take care of it personally. I told him I wanted a larger stone for her grave marker. He asked that I send him what I wanted written. I'm ashamed. I hardly recall what she told me about her earlier life. I don't even know the year of her birth. I remember she lost her children back in France. But not why."

"Just give Mathilde your last name, *de Chanaye*, and the date of her death, as you did before. But add, *Beloved mother to Corrinne. Grandmother to Marcus and Calypso VanderMeer.* Mathilde would like that. She considered herself grandmother to the twins from what I observed."

Corrinne touched Charles' hand. "That is a beautiful sentiment. I should have thought of it."

They both fell silent as the carriage rattled along. Charles seemed reflective. After some time, he said, "Captain LaTour said the tide turns at a quarter past three. I would like to be on deck while we sail from this port. I want to stay on deck until the seas become too rough for me."

"Then that is what you will do," Corrinne affirmed.

"I want to fly the flag of the Dutch Republic the entire way."

"I have already told that to Captain LaTour."

The carriage was permitted to ride out all the way to the head of the Long Wharf. There was a small crowd of people waiting, including reporters. The marine guards pushed them all back except for the customs officers and Samuel Grant.

At least ten of the crew came down to the brow to help them board, among them was Henri. Anamosa called his name loudly when she saw him. He took hold of Calypso and helped Anamosa step down from the carriage. Captain LaTour took Marcus and helped Lady Corrinne. Victorio and other crew members helped Lord VanderMeer out the opposite carriage door. They carried him up the brow and set him upon his wheeled chair that had followed him on board.

The customs officers were accompanied by Victorio as they made a final inspection below decks. Nothing unusual was found. They advised Captain LaTour they considered the ship overloaded. LaTour rolled his eyes and thanked them.

"So how soon can we expect to hear back from the Duke and the Dutch government on the trade ship proposal?" Samuel Grant asked Lord VanderMeer.

"I have all the documents. When the Duke and the government decide on an answer, I will have the response couriered to Thomas Hancock's agent in London, who will courier it back to Boston on the first available ship. I will also include my address in Amsterdam for you."

As the visitors left and the brow was taken aboard, Corrinne wondered if she would ever see Boston again. She loved the city and its people, but the memories she would leave behind were so harsh she didn't know if she could face the reminders of such tragedy again. Except for Mathilde's grave. She would definitely come back just to visit her.

When LaTour marked the outgoing tide had started, he could not wait any longer. "Anyone not going to Amsterdam…it is time to go ashore!" A minute later. "Take in all lines," shouted Captain LaTour. "Make sail!" And in another minute, "Come left!"

Henri expertly turned the ship to pilot through the anchorage.

Corrinne and Charles waved until the turn was complete and they could no longer see anyone's face on the wharf.

"I am taking the twins below," Corrinne said. "It's too cold up on deck." When she was gone, Charles motioned for LaTour to approach.

"Captain, at the top of one of my personal bags down below, you will find the pennant signifying the House of Brunswick is aboard this ship. I want to fly the double-lion of Brunswick at the top of the main mast. This might be the only time I get to sail under it."

Captain LaTour wanted to brush aside those overly pessimistic words. *But I am not paralyzed*, he reminded himself.

"Your lordship, it would be my honor. I will be *proud* to fly that pennant above *William's Queen*."

For over two weeks, before they sailed from Boston, Victorio and the ship's carpenter had worked on a way to move Lord VanderMeer around the ship. They had created an ingenious sliding mechanism to bring him up on the main deck and also to ease the task of taking him below. A ten-foot-long, two-inch-thick, eight-inch-wide hardwood baseboard was constructed to fit into custom footings and was latch bolted onto the cabin deck on one end. The other end could be latched with iron extension rods to similar footings on the main deck, thus making the entire construct stiff and rigid. Any person climbing the steps to the main deck would have to widen their step to either side of the ramp going up and slide their hands on the stair rails while lifting their feet to go down, which is what they did normally. The ramp had a winching device, with handle wheels at both ends. There were notched slide tracks, and the baseboard was augmented with a sliding shelf, mounted on small iron wheels with a fourteen-inch wheel base, and an eight-inch track width. It was a lifting trolley meant to support something larger and carry it up the steps when the winch was rotated.

Down below was the other piece to this invention. A four-foot-long slant board with small four-inch wheels on the bottom. It had a lightly padded seat midway, fourteen inches square, a twenty by fourteen inch padded back equipped with a shoulder harness and support belt. When a person sat in the seat, from the knee to the foot shelf was twenty inches. The bottom of the foot shelf had another set of four-inch wheels. It was a very tall and slender wheeled chair, custom designed for movement up and down the cabin passageway, or for going into and out of the cabin doorways. Special hand grips had been installed inside of the cabin rooms, the privy, and along the passageway itself. A passenger in this chair could pull himself along without any help if he were strong enough. A ratcheting hinge to the back of the seat allowed the passenger to change the slant of the back from vertical, down to a twenty-degree, more restful angle.

Victorio had read the regimen designed by Dr. Barrie. It included exercises intended to increase the strength of the arms, shoulders, and chest of a soldier paralyzed from the waist down. It would be difficult to do such exercises on the *Queen* that had been designed to be done on land. Nevertheless, Victorio had customized the cabin intended for Lord VanderMeer with special grips, handles, and dangling rope loops to permit Charles to perform the strengthening exercises any time he wanted.

He had also fashioned a special set of crutches and leg braces that would lock the knees straight, so that his lordship's arms could indeed become his new legs. But he could not finish these until he took more measurements on Lord VanderMeer's arms and legs.

Charles VanderMeer knew if he was going to do this, he should do it soon. There was no certainty he would be brought up on deck again. The way they'd tied off the chair, it was rigid, strong. All he needed to do was untie the harness, grab the rail, and yank himself over. Even if they saw him they could not turn in time. The hard part would be inhaling the icy cold seawater. But being paralyzed, he would sink like a rock, as they say. It would be over quickly.

Of course, maybe I should wait until Corrinne is safe in Louisbourg?
He pondered that thought for a time.
No. I'm just stalling.
Charles gazed at the water. *Stare at the water long enough and the sea will pull you in.* That's what the sailors had told him.
He untied the harness.

As they sailed among Boston's harbor islands, Victorio asked Captain LaTour if he could approach the man.

Lord VanderMeer's wheeled chair was at the side of the helm deck lashed tightly between the rail and the deck house. His lordship's expression looked stricken from the cold, but LaTour sensed the man might be terrified of going below into the constricted quarters of the ship.

"Might as well. Tell him you've invented something that lets him move around without assistance while he is aboard the ship. It might help."

Victorio took a seat on the deck next to the wheeled chair, leaned his back against the rail, and looked up.

Lord VanderMeer flinched, startled by the man's presence. He looked down at him, puzzled.

"Do you want something?"

Victorio held up the roll of documents and drawings he'd brought with him.

"Yes, your lordship. I have being working with the ship's carpenter to craft some devices that will allow you to move about the ship almost without assistance. I've read the regimen Dr. Barrie gave you. I think you can do those exercises while you are on board. In fact, I see no reason why you cannot move around on your own legs, even when ashore, making use of the devices I have crafted. The movement would be slow, of course, but only limited by your strength and endurance. When you are ready, I would like to show you how these devices work, and I would be happy to assist in your regimen."

Charles had never expected to walk again in his life, let alone learn that he might even do so again aboard a ship.

"Are you serious? That I might walk unaided?"

"Oh, yes, your lordship," Victorio replied with confident optimism. "I have seen many wounded men do this."

"Are those the drawings of the devices of which you speak?"

"Yes, your lordship. But with all this wind, I do not want to show them to you up here as they could blow away. When you are ready, we will have to shift you over to the ramp we created. This wheeled chair will not be useable on the cabin deck. However, we've also crafted a replacement chair that can be used down below. So when you are ready—"

Charles believed in signs. Victorio suddenly sitting here, on deck with him, only moments before he pulled himself over the side, saying he would walk again.

"Indeed a sign," Charles said to the man.

"Your lordship?"

"I am ready now! Get me below and show me everything!"

Victorio waved to the bosun. They untied the wheeled chair and moved Charles close to the deckhouse ladder. The winching board was already in place on the steps.

"Before we begin," he told Lord VanderMeer, "remember, everything we are doing has been tested by us personally. It works. We have to lift you over to this chair. I know it looks slender, but you will see it is quite functional."

With the help of the bosun, Charles was placed into the chair and it was reclined with the ratchet to a comfortable position. Victorio pulled the harness and belt straps around Charles.

"Just for safety," he explained. "Now see these winch wheels. My assistant will turn them for me. I am going to slip by you and wait down below as the chair slowly comes down the ramp."

*

Down below, Corrinne was arranging her bedroom. The two rocking cradles had been secured where she could reach them easily. Anamosa was playing with the twins on the bed. Anamosa would sleep with Corrinne. Charles would be in a bunking cabin, with Henri on the upper bunk to help him. Henri had convinced Charles he could do this.

"We carry and care for our wounded men all of the time. This is nothing new to me, and Victorio has agreed to help too."

Corrinne's biggest concern was Charles' deepening depression. Dr. Barrie said to expect this. *Charles must somehow be able to see a future stretching a long way ahead of him, something other than his infirmity and growing weakness.* Victorio, the ship's doctor for all practical purposes, said he had a plan to help with this. Corrinne hoped so.

*

To Charles' surprise the entire experience was just as Victorio described. In addition to getting to the bottom of the stairs, a latch was released and the chair could be turned. He was wheeled directly into the dining cabin. A few hand pulls on the leveling ratchet, which Charles was encouraged to do himself, and Charles was sitting as he normally would at the dining table.

"That's it," Victorio complimented. "You can also raise and lower your seating height with the left-hand ratchet. Eventually, you will be able to pull yourself into this chair and up and down the passageway on the grips we have installed. I will show you those later. But, you will have to increase the strength of your arms and shoulders. I have a plan to help you with that." Victorio took a seat at the dining table and unfurled the documents he could not show up on deck. "Here are some pictures. We've made some special crutches too. I have to take some measurements of your body before they can be adjusted to make them useable. But these braces, here, will lock your knees and make your legs straight. You will walk with a waddle of a sort using this, but *you will walk unaided,* just as soon as you are strong enough."

Charles' expression was impassive, but within him, an enormous, wonderful sense of relief was washing over his body.

Victorio saw a tear streak down one of Lord VanderMeer's cheeks, and he decided the man needed privacy.

"Your lordship, I need to take down the ramp until you are ready to go up it again. The brakes on your wheels are set. Look through these documents and pictures and we can talk more about it when I come back."

Victorio went into the passageway and shut the door behind him. He went directly to Lady Corrinne's door and knocked. Corrinne answered.

"My lady, his lordship is in the dining cabin. He has experienced a demonstration of the ramp and chair. I've shown him pictures of the new crutches and told him when his strength improves he will walk again... with a waddle, but he will walk. He is looking over those documents now. I think...I think your presence will help him."

"Thank you, Victorio. Anamosa, please stay with the babies for me."

Corrinne went into the dining cabin and found Charles sitting up straight. His cheeks were wet with tears. She slid into a chair next to him.

She caressed his hair. "Are you all right?" she asked tenderly.

"Have you seen these?"

"No. But Victorio told me about them."

"You need to look through these. Your aptitude for such devices is far better than mine. But I believe Victorio. These devices are fairly simple, yet amazing too." He sniffed loudly and then grinned. "I think I will walk again!"

*

A few days later, Charles brought up a new worry to Corrinne, after Henri had made a surprising offer of help to him.

"Once we get to Louisbourg, I will convince Major Péan not to say anything," Henri said.

"Not to say what?" Charles asked.

They were sitting in the dining cabin, just the two of them. Henri had just moved Charles out from the sleeping cabin. Pierrik was cooking something for them.

Henri explained. But before they had much discussion, Henri had to leave to stand watch on the helm.

Corrinne entered only minutes later.

"Good morning, Charles. Did you sleep well?"

"Yes. But today I've just learned about a new problem. Henri told me."

"Told you what?"

"How are we to be introduced to the French governor of the French colony of Île Royale? In particular, who are you? Lady Corrinne Vander-Meer? Or the wife of Captain Philippe Gerrard of the Troupes de la Marine? And what are the children's names?"

They had been acting as husband and wife for so long, the realization this charade might not work much longer was very disconcerting. They never anticipated what might happen when they went back to New France.

Corrinne eyes widened. "Oh...yes? This might be a problem. But we have time to solve this. We've done it before," Corrinne asserted brightly. "Louisbourg is very remote from Quebec society."

"Good. That should help," Charles answered. "Oh, and I should add that Henri graciously offered to speak with Major Péan for us. The major is part of the Louisbourg garrison, you understand, along with a hundred and thirty other marines from Montreal."

Corrinne frowned.

Pierrik entered the dining cabin at that moment. "Coffee, my lady?"

"Yes, Pierrik. And leave the pot on the table."

*

The Atlantic

November 1756

Fifteen Miles Southwest of Louisbourg Harbor

Captain Martyn was halfway along his patrol course of Île Royale, sailing in a southerly direction down towards the Canceau Strait. Once there, he would reverse course and start sailing back up to the northeast. Other than a few fishing vessels, he'd seen no French ships of deeper draft that might be ocean-crossing vessels. He'd been doing this for three weeks and would be doing it for another three weeks before returning to Boston.

The cold and rain had been constant the entire time, a miserable patrol duty. They passed by the entrance to Louisbourg as close as he dared, scanned the harbor through his glass, and saw no activity in the port whatsoever. He could not see far enough to count the warships that he expected would be present. It was near the hour of eleven in the morning.

An hour later, just before twelve, the forward look-out shouted he saw sails on the horizon.

"Where-away?"

"On the bow!"

Captain Martyn ran forward and looked through his scope.

"A trade ship! Fully sailed! Beat to quarters!"

They were closing fast. In a few minutes, he recognized the rigging.

"It's the *William's Queen*," he mumbled to himself. "I don't believe it. After my warning, LaTour is still making another run to Louisbourg."

"Bosun! Fire a warning shot across his bow! But do *not* hit that ship!"

"Aye, sir."

A cannon on the bow of the *Anamosa* belched with flame. Captain Martyn saw a tall splash of water well clear of the *Queen*'s port bow. He saw sails being reefed on the *Queen*.

"That's right, LaTour. You're not getting away. Not this time!"

*

Corrinne had come up on the main deck before noon to see the coastal approach to Louisbourg harbor. LaTour gave her a glass to look upon the shore. It was a barren-looking coastline with huge rocky crags covering the shore. The heavy surf waves crashed over them sending a warning: *No gentle welcome here!* Trees stripped of their leaves by the wind stood starkly further inland. *Visit here and starve naked in the cold!*

"Oh, God!" Corrinne muttered. "Do any of the beaches even have sand to sit upon on that singular day once a year when there is sunlight?"

"I do recall seeing such a beach once—at the bottom of a tall cliff face." LaTour winked at Henri.

Henri was on the helm steering a steady course, easing the ship through the swells. He heard the disappointment in her voice.

"We all speak French here!" Henri reminded her, trying to buoy her spirit. "We have good wine!"

"Mind your helm," Corrinne snapped.

The bow lookout shouted. "Sails ahead."

Henri squinted and could just see a spot on the horizon. Corrinne came up beside Henri.

"Look straight ahead." Henri pointed.

Captain LaTour fixed his glass and looked. He recognized the rigging instantly.

"Oh, my! That would be Captain Conor Martyn and the *Anamosa*," he announced. "To welcome us, I presume."

At that moment, they saw smoke from a bow cannon on the *Anamosa*. Seconds later came the sound of cannon fire. And after that followed a large geyser splash of water off the port bow. Captain LaTour shouted orders to reef certain sails.

Corrinne's mouth sagged. "I cannot believe Captain Martyn just fired a cannon at *my* ship...and from a ship I *own*! Why would he do that?"

"That was a warning shot, my lady. Captain Martyn is advising me in a forceful way to reef sail and prepare to be boarded," LaTour replied drolly. "I believe Captain Martyn intends to lash alongside of us. He will board and inspect our cargo and potentially take us as a prize."

"A *prize*?!"

"My lady, he does possess a letter of marque and reprisal."

Corrinne uttered a series of vulgarities that made the sailors stop and stare.

LaTour looked at Henri and Victorio, who had now joined them on the bridge.

"In addition to the flag of the Dutch Republic"—LaTour pointed at the top of the mainmast—"we are flying the pennant of the House of Brunswick. And Captain Martyn intends to board us!"

"No, he will not!" Corrinne went below to inform Charles.

The *Anamosa* passed them to starboard and came around again to a parallel course. The *Anamosa* reefed some of its sail.

"This will be a very interesting day," the captain told Henri and Victorio. "Reef all sail! Prepare to receive lines from the *Anamosa*!" LaTour shouted through his speaking trumpet to the deck crew. "And a brow...I presume."

Soon, the ships were close aboard and the *Anamosa* did put over a brow.

Captain LaTour raised his speaking trumpet. "Captain Martyn! Before you cross over that brow, be aware"—he pointed up at the pennant—"we are flying the pennant of the House of Brunswick."

"I can see that!" Martyn shouted back. "But I know the Duke of Brunswick is *not* aboard your ship!"

"No. But the Duke's son...Lord Charles VanderMeer...is aboard! So I ask you officially, Captain Martyn. Do you intend to board *William's Queen* under the protest of the Dutch Republic? Or are you inclined to wait until you are *invited* to come aboard? Lady VanderMeer will come back to the bridge at any moment."

Lady VanderMeer! Captain Martyn was confounded. Well, if the VanderMeers were aboard, he would know it soon enough.

"I will await your invitation, Captain LaTour," he said, thinking it was a bluff.

At that moment, Lady Corrinne VanderMeer returned to the bridge. Her expression was not happy.

"Captain Martyn has graciously decided to await an invitation to board," LaTour told her. He was enjoying all of this immensely.

She took his speaking trumpet. "Captain Martyn. His lordship, Charles VanderMeer, invites you, *and only you*, to come aboard, *unarmed*, to explain why we were fired upon. And if you hurry, you may take a midday meal with us."

Corrinne did not wait for a reply.

A scowling Captain Martyn crossed over the brow and saluted. "Request permission to come aboard."

LaTour saluted back with a smile. "Permission granted. The dining cabin is just down that ladder…just there. Yes, that one. The one you are looking at. I think you can find your way."

"What is going on here, LaTour?"

"Oh? You will have to ask them, if you please. I only command the ship. The *House of Brunswick*…makes all the decisions."

Captain Martyn went below. Henri leaned on his helm.

"He did not even notice me."

Victorio spoke. "What will happen now?

"To quote Lady VanderMeer, '*Everything will turn out all right.*' We've only reached Louisbourg and already we've been cannoned by another ship. This is how it is when you travel with the Gerrards."

Two hours later, a chastised Captain Conor Martyn came back on deck.

"*Bonjour, mon capitaine*…what news do you bring me?" LaTour asked in a sanguine voice.

"They gave Molly and me their house in Boston," he said in disbelief.

"Oh? A bribe then! See what happens, Conor, when you treat them with respect? Captain Martyn, will you be good enough to pull back your brow and cast off your lines? I intend to sail directly into the harbor of Louisbourg. Oh, and please do not fire any more cannon at me."

They saluted one another.

Before another hour passed, all the signal cannon in Louisbourg fired salutes of welcome as *William's Queen* entered the harbor. The people along the quay wall cheered.

END OF BOOK 4

Glossary

Captain Conor Martyn, sea
captain and master of the
Anamosa

Wilhelm von Kleinfels, Hessian
colonel, possessed by the
vulnax, secret liaison from
Frederick II to the French
Naval Minister

Victorio; alias Captain Jaager,
first mate to Captain LaTour
on the Falcon Queen

Vaelblez, ancient lord of a Great
House, initial bones of the
vulnax

François Bigôt; Intendant General
of New France, corrupt minister of Governor Vaudreuil,
and enemy of Philippe Gerrard and Corrinne de Chanaye

Juniata; Chittaqua's wife, now
Pierre Dunemoore's wife

Major Michel Péan, head of gendarmerie in Quebec City and
Montréal, decorated
officer in Troupes de la
Marine

Madeleine Louvet, would-be
lover of Henri Gerrard in
Quebec City

Pierre Dunemoore, partner of
Philippe and owner of The
Dunemoore Fur Trading
Company

Archbishop André Nicolet, Jesuit
Intendant of New France,
friend of Philippe and Cor-
rinne, descendant of Bishop
Brevelaer a seal bearer of a
Great House

NEW CHARACTERS, IN ORDER OF APPEARANCE

G. Bernard Conway, Esquire,
New Haven lawyer for
Thomas Hancock

Jenny Barton, housekeeper of
Winter House

Mistress Callahan, landlady of
apartment rented by Captain
Conor Martyn

Ritter Monheit, vulnax servant

Carter Trevathan, vulnax servant

Caroline and Rachel de Propei;
alias Caroline and Rachel
Bristol, assassins

Alain Marcoux, vulnax servant

Dr. Osterhout, chemist and servant of Colonel Von Kleinfels
in Amsterdam

Frederick II of Prussia, or Fredrick the Great, Sovereign of
Prussia

Thomas Pelham-Holles, 1st Duke of Newcastle, Prime Minister for George II of England

Sir Charles Hardy, admiral of the English Navy and New York provincial governor

Lieutenant-Colonel John Bradstreet, logistical officer for William Shirley

Carmen, Henri's lover in Montréal

Paulus Legate; formerly Lady Corrinne's chief clerk, currently clerk for The Grand Company of Traders

Handsome Robert, Delaware war chief and raider of English settlements in Pennsylvania

Joshua and Leah Pouchot, twelve and thirteen, rescued by Philippe from the Delaware

Odara; LaTour's lover in Orangestad

Captain Mistral, French captain of the Lyonesse in Oranjestad, relived Captain LaTour

Denis and Mary; Corrinne's former chamberlain and his wife in Montréal

Lieutenant Gaspard-Joseph Chaussegros de Léry, leader of raid on Fort Bull

Color Sergeant Gosse, of Le Guyenne Grenadier Regiment

Kenneth Randall, English man Henri saved at Fort Bull

Kateri; child of Juniata and Pierre

Captain Marcel Trieste, first aide to Governor Vaudreuil

Augustin de Boschenry de Drucour; Governor of Ile Royale in Louisbourg

Reginald Walters, agent for South Carolina governor for Acadian resettlement

Corporal Luc Chapelle, aide to Ensign Henri Gerrard

Lieutenant Carson, First Officer for Captain Martyn of the Anamosa

Father Eric; André Nicolet son, recipient of the Archbishop Nicolet's cross after his death and new scion of a Great House

Charles Jamison; New Bedford shipping merchant; alias of Charles VanderMeer

Captain Rigaud de Vaudreuil; Troupes de la Marine officer and brother to Governor-General Vaudreuil

Major-General Louis Joseph, Marquis de Montcalm-Gozon de Saint-Véran, forty-four years old, new commanding general of all French forces in New France

Brigadier General François de Lévis, 2nd in Command to General Montcalm

Colonel François-Charles de Bourlamaque, 3rd in Command to General Montcalm

Comte d'Argenson; Minister of War

Lieutenant Michel-Alain Chartier de Lotbinière, engineer/commander of Fort Carillon

Captain Robert Rogers, ranger commander of American Provincial army

Captain Louis Antoine de Bougainville; General Montcalm's aide-de-camp

Rector William Hooper, pastor of Trinity Church ion Boston

Vice-Admiral Emmanuel-Auguste de Cahideuc, Comte Dubois de la Motte, seventy-three year old senior admiral of the French Navy, headquarters in Rochefort, France

Captain Pierre Trémoille; adjutant-aide to Admiral Dubois de la Motte

Colonel David Webb, 3rd in command to Lord Loudoun the commander in chief of British forces in North America

Major General James Ambercrombie, 2nd in command to Lord Loudoun

General John Campbell, 4th Earl of Loudoun, commander in chief of British forces in North America

Felix, vulnax servant

Beau Sarchet, fisherman and spy communications link in Port Toulouse, Ile Royale

Pauloosie and Yakone, old Inuit couple

Commodore Beaussier de Lisle, renowned French Naval Officer, breaks blockade of Louisbourg in 1756

Gunnery Bosun Kerbenard, gunnery bosun of Commodore de Lisle flagship, Le Heros

Commodore Holmes, English opponent and loses engagement to Commodore de Lisle

Lt. Colonel James Francis Mercer, commanding officer of Fort Oswego

Captain Descombles, army engineer for Montcalm in attack on Fort Oswego, killed in action

Lt. Colonel John Littlehales, 2nd in command to Lt. Colonel Mercer at Fort Oswego

Captain Broadly, commander of the single English ship on Lake Ontario

Mervyn Hughes, bodyguard to Lord VanderMeer, poisoned by Rachel Bristol

Lieutenant Culver

Pierrik, steward and cook for Captain LaTour on the *Falcon Queen*

General John Winslow, general in charge of American Provincial army, reports to Lord Loudoun

Father Xavier, door guard at Terrain des Jesuites, assassinated by Alain Marcoux

Vincent Trestle, Alain Marcoux's alias

Kyrielle de Courserac, niece of Governor Drucour, would-be lover of Henri Gerrard

Paul Revere, Boston silversmith and business partner of Charles VanderMeer

Robért Boucher, alias Robert Butcher, alias Parliament, baker of cakes and French spy in Boston

Mr. Jennings; Boston customs officer

Thom Linden, Henri Gerard's Belgian alias

David, works at the bakery of Robert Butcher

Jimmy Cantlin, gang boy, later escapes with Rachel Bristol

Conor Gwyn Martyn II, child of Conor Martyn and Molly

Mary Tasker, Jack Tasker's sister, 38, three children

Lisbeth Tasker, Mary Tasker's daughter

Dr. Barrie, former army surgeon, doctor to Charles VanderMeer

Major Karl Dörnberg; formerly Alain Marcoux, vulnax servant

Geoffrey Atkins; Boston merchant trader, acting magistrate after Jack Tasker's death

Marshall Atkins, 18, younger brother to Geoffrey Atkins

Helena Atkins, 15, younger sister to Geoffrey Atkins

The Andrototekan holy words
All of these words are invented.

An dro to te kan   man of many tribes
Loh cai teem   guide to the truth
The deh roles   cools the burning grief
Bes mi on tig   gives rain to the earth
Soo anlo tamey   unite the weeping hearts
Mah han atakehsey   the ghosts lifting wind
Ha teh ko ha sen kah   one light, one life
Cou ti si mah   my spirit love

References

With the advent of the internet, a huge amount of research for this book was obtained from standard Google searches and the extraordinary trove of information available from Wikipedia queries.

With a respectful nod given to the modern search-engine databases mentioned, I also relied heavily on the list of references below to keep my imagination from getting too far astray from recorded history. Wilderness Empire by Allan W. Eckert (noted historian and seven-time Pulitzer Prize nominee), the second book in a series, is an extraordinary read, and was a primary resource of facts and information. I also relied on several works by René Chartrand who has created a series of books covering various years and aspects of the French and Indian War.

Warden, G.B. *Boston 1689–1776*. NY: Little, Brown, and Company Limited, 1970.

Baxter, W.T. *The House of Hancock, Business in Boston. 1724–1775*. Russell & Russell, Inc., 1965.

Kirby, William. *The Golden Dog (1897)*. Colonial Press, C.H. Simonds & Co. 1911.

Baugh, Daniel. *The Global Seven Years War 1754-1763*. Routledge, Taylor and Francis Group 2014.

McLennan, J.S. *Louisbourg, From its Foundation to it Fall*. The Book Room Limited, 1979.

Chartrand, René. *Montcalm's Crushing Blow*. Oxford: Osprey Publishing, 2014.

Lincoln, Charles Henry, PhD. *Correspondence of William Shirley V2: Governor of Massachusetts and Military Commander in America 1731–1760.* The MacMillan Company, 1912.

Johnson, Michael. *Tribes of the Iroquois Confederacy.* Oxford: Osprey Publishing, 2003.

Eckert, Allan W. *Wilderness Empire.* Ashland, KY: Jesse Stuart Foundation, 2001.

Snow, Dean R. *The Iroquois.* Oxford: Wiley-Blackwell Publisher, 1994.

Graymont, Barbara. *The Iroquois.* New York: Chelsea House Publishers, 1988.

Hutchens, Alma R. *A Handbook of Native American Herbs.* Boston: Shambhala Publications, 1992.

About the Author

Quentin Grady was born in Hartford, Connecticut, and raised in Cleveland, Ohio. Upon receiving a scholarship from the U.S. Navy in 1970, he graduated from the University of Utah in 1972 with degrees in computer science and mathematics. Subsequent to that he completed graduate studies in nuclear engineering. He served as a naval officer on nuclear submarines until 1980. After leaving the service, he held several senior management positions in the software industry for companies like Oracle, specializing in utility applications and engineering solutions. Passionate about fiction writing from an early age, he has devoted the last three years towards getting his first four novels published. Several more are in production.

The Hessian is the fourth book in *Tales of the Ghost Eagle* series. Book 5 is expected to be published in 2016.

He lives in Tacoma, Washington.